WARRIORS OF GOR

WARRIORS OF GOR

GOREAN SAGA * BOOK 37

John Norman

OPEN ROAD

INTEGRATED MEDIA

NEW YORK

978-1-5040-7672-2

This edition published in 2022 by Open Road Integrated Media, Inc.
180 Maiden Lane
New York, NY 10038
www.openroadmedia.com

WARRIORS OF GOR

The point of law is not law, but good. But there are many goods, and what may be good for one may not be good for another. And what is perceived as good may be good but may not be good.

—Saying, from the Codes of Scribes

CHAPTER ONE

"To your cage!" snapped Samos, First Slaver of Port Kar, senior captain of the Council of Captains, that body sovereign in Port Kar.

In a flash of silk and a jangle of bells the dancer, barefoot, scurried away, speeding over the colorful, smooth tiles of the great map floor in the conference hall of Samos.

I thrust back the mug of paga on the low, square, small table behind which I sat, cross-legged.

The musicians, now, following the rising of the czehar player, too, took their departure, two flutists, a kalika player and a drummer, with his double tabor.

I turned, and, with a tiny gesture of my head, dismissed the girl who had been kneeling a few feet behind me and to my left, in attendance, lest I might wish aught. Such as she are unobtrusively present, but clearly present, waiting to serve. She, like the dancer, was barefoot. Her single garment was a slight scarlet camisk. Women such as she, loathed and despised by free women, are dressed, if dressed, for the delectation of men. She looked at me, pressed her lips to the flask of paga, quickly, fervently, and then, head down, rose to her feet, backed away a few feet, and then turned and sped from the large low-ceilinged room, dimly lit by dangling, tharlarion-oil lamps. To one side of the dining area was a scattering of wide, soft cushions.

Samos, with his short-cropped, white hair, sprang angrily to his feet, and spun to face me.

"You are mad!" he said. "Speak no further of the matter!"

"I have said very little," I said.

"So," he said, "a word spoken is a sentence not said, and a sentence not said is a paragraph unexpressed."

"I did not request this meeting," I said. "And time is precious."

"Not so precious as you think," he said. "The matter is likely to be protracted. Justice, policy, theater, demand it."

"And how am I to understand what you are saying?" I asked.

"I am not a fool," said Samos. "And you feign clumsily."

I was silent, looking down.

"You are a poor liar," he said. "You lack deviousness, and subtlety. A draft tharlarion could tread through a crowded bazaar at noon more delicately, less noticed."

"I trust that is not so," I said.

"I asked you here because I could not credit what I have heard hinted," said Samos. "It is too preposterous. It bespeaks unbelievable absurdity."

"Then do not believe it," I suggested.

"I called you here," said Samos, "to convince myself of the emptiness of rumors."

"It is not unusual for a rumor to be empty," I said.

"Sometimes truth wears the cloak of falsity," said Samos.

"You cannot expect me to deny a rumor I have not heard," I said.

"Who speaks rumor to the subject of rumor?" asked Samos.

"And does this rumor go about boldly in the taverns, in the marketplaces, in the arsenal, at the piers?"

"No," he said, "it is far more subtle, more private, more guarded, than that."

"It seems you have keen, well-placed spies," I said.

"In this case," said he, "not spies but friends, your friends and mine."

"And you have heard suspicions, whispers, and fears?" I said.

"Do not do it," he said.

"I must," I said.

"It is bereft of any hope of success," he said. "It courts doom. It is worse than ill-considered. It is no more than a venture into the corridors of madness, an act of blatant insanity. Better to have yourself bound and cast into a foliage of leach plants, better to lock yourself in a pen with starving sleen."

"I intend to leave in the morning," I said.

"Then it is true!" he said.

"What?" I asked.

"Take with you a thousand men," said Samos. "I can furnish them."

"So, too, could I," I said, "but I must go alone."

"Two thousand men!" said Samos.

"Ten times that much and a dozen cities," I said, "could not match the might of Ar."

"You lost your match," he said. "You were outplayed."

"So, too," I said, "upon occasion are Centius of Cos and Scormus of Ar."

"It was a game you should not have begun," said Samos.

"I had no choice," I said.

"She is not worth it," said Samos.

"That," I said, "does not enter into the issue."

"You know she is not worth it," said Samos.

"That," I said, "does not enter into the issue."

"It should," said Samos.

"I leave in the morning," I said.

"Secretly?" he said.

"Of course," I said.

"You are a fool," he said.

"I wish you well," I said.

"Abandon her," said Samos. "She is now, as she should be, long months after her treason, her cruelty and crimes, in custody. Betrayed by her former ally, Lurius of Jad, who deceived her, promising her safety, refuge, and honor, she is currently, doubtless, being conveyed from Cos to Ar, there to face the justice of the city she so unconscionably and grievously outraged. Let her savor the dreadful potion she thoughtlessly prepared for herself. Choices entail consequences. What is done cannot be undone. Belated justice is at last afoot. A polity hungers for retribution. Ar thirsts for blood. The trumpets of vengeance stab the skies."

I rose to my feet.

"Be pleased it is over," said Samos.

"That is my fear," I said, "that it is over."

"It is over," said Samos, "though many do not know it. Indeed, as soon as her capture becomes common knowledge, no longer will bounty hunters, and gangs of bounty hunters, in their hundreds, with swords and flaming brands, scour towns, cities, villages, and camps for the elusive Talena of Ar. No longer then will dozens of innocent women be brought naked and chained to Ar, either on the pretense that, or in the hope that, they were the fugitive Ubara. When it is realized that Talena has been taken, thousands of beautiful women, free or slave, women who might have feared they bore the slightest resemblance to Talena of Ar, or might have even the trace of an accent of Ar, will rest easily."

"She was once my companion," I said.

"The companionship should never have existed," said Samos. "She was unworthy. Put it from your mind. She was a petty, selfish, cruel, vain woman."

"It did exist," I said.

"It was never renewed," said Samos. "It lapsed. It no longer exists. It is as though it had never been."

"That is true," I said. "It is as though it had never been."

"You did not even share the Home Stone she betrayed," he said.

"That is true," I said.

"You owe nothing in this matter," he said. "This is something with which you have nothing to do. There is nothing here in which you are involved. It is all apart from you. In this matter you have no command of honor, no obligation, no duty, no service expected or due."

"I know," I said.

"Do you understand the gravity of betraying a Home Stone?" he asked.

"Yes," I said.

"She betrayed hers," he said. "She conspired with Tyros and Cos, she opened the gates of her city to enemies, she presided over the destruction of its walls, she ruled as a puppet Ubara, with arrogance and cruelty, over looted and occupied Ar, until the surprising return and sudden restoration to power of the rightful Ubar, Marlenus. Now, let her be returned to Ar, and face its justice."

"Would that I had my hands on the throat of Lurius of Jad," I said, suddenly.

"Rather, rejoice," said Samos, "that he apprehended a much-sought fugitive, and thus served the ends of justice."

"The justice of a Marlenus of Ar," I said.

"Naturally," said Samos.

"I fear the justice of a Marlenus of Ar is a dark and terrible thing," I said.

"Commensurate with dark and terrible crimes," said Samos.

"The reward for the capture of Talena," I said, "was enormous, ten thousand tarns of gold, tarn disks of double weight."

"Enough to suborn cities, to build fleets, to recruit armies," said Samos.

"It doubtless constituted something of an inducement to Lurius of Jad," I said.

"That is possible," said Samos.

I had managed to acquire Talena at the World's End, far beyond even the Farther Islands, Thera, Chios, and Daphna, across Thassa, the Sea, herself. I had then returned her, incognito, to the great port of Brundisium, to the south, from which I had had her purchased and transported to Port Kar, where I had had her placed as a lowly tavern slave in the Golden Chain, on Palace Street, an establishment whose proprietor was Ho-Tosk, a friend. Port Kar was far from Ar and the major cities of Gor; it was also a polity which retained something of its former reputation as a dangerous den of pirates and thieves; might not a stranger then, say, a bounty hunter, find himself at risk in such a place; too, surely it would seem an unlikely place in which to seek the proud, regal Talena of Ar; too, who would suspect that a common, even if unusually beautiful, tavern girl, one so publicly displayed to the frank, lustful scrutiny accorded to such properties, might be identical with so desiderated a prize? Beyond such considerations was the fact that few ordinary individuals would be likely to be personally acquainted with the features of the former Ubara, that given the veiling common amongst Gorean free women in public. I had thought that

I had planned well. Surely a mysteriously concealed woman, in a fine house, a keep or castle, might spur unwanted curiosity.

I rose to my feet.

Samos was silent.

But, ela, Talena, even at the World's End, had been recognized by one of the most tenacious of her pursuers, fierce, skilled Seremides, a master of the sword, formerly First Captain in the Taurentian guard, the pledged police of the Central Cylinder in Ar, who had been a colleague in her treason, and an abettor of her crimes, himself now, too, a fugitive from the justice of Ar. The attempt of Seremides to capture Talena later, after her return from the World's End, in Brundisium, had failed, but he had managed to trace her to Port Kar, within the canaled precincts of which it seemed likely he would eventually discover her whereabouts. He was recognized in Port Kar by a slave who had encountered him in Brundisium. At that point, some of my men, in my absence, removed Talena from the Golden Chain, transporting her to my holding for safekeeping. Unbeknownst to my men, or to Seremides at that time, other bounty hunters, including bestial Kurii, were attempting to locate Talena by means of tracking Seremides. Given what later occurred, it seems clear that the efforts of Seremides were being funded and supported by Lurius of Jad, who himself doubtless coveted the reward for the apprehension of Talena. Apparently, when it became likely that Talena was somewhere in Port Kar, Lurius deemed it judicious, lest I somehow manage to confound his plans, to lure me away from Port Kar by the extensive and bloody ruse of sacking and burning villages in the Farther Islands in my name. Given the enmity between Port Kar and Cos, I did not connect the depredations on the Farther Islands, wrought in my name, with the possible fate of Talena, who, as far as I knew when I departed Port Kar, was safe in the Golden Chain. I later realized, to my rage and misery, how completely and successfully I had been tricked. On the other hand, even had I suspected the hoax, I would surely have attempted to put an end to the devastation being inflicted in my name. The kaissa of Lurius of Jad was well played. As Samos had said, I was outplayed. Yet, what else, in honor, could I have done? Some moves, it seems, are forced. I later learned that a massive attack was mounted on my holding in my absence, to obtain Talena, but the attack, by my men, and by the intervention of the irate citizens of Port Kar, was turned back, with great losses to the foe. In the confusion and chaos, however, Seremides, with Talena, was able to flee from the city and keep a rendezvous with a Cosian ship at the nearby Skerry of Lars. All indications are that Talena accompanied him willingly, presumably having been assured of an end to her alarms and terrors as a fugitive, and having been promised not only honor, safety, and comfort, but a cordial state reception, one befitting a visiting Ubara.

"Consider maps," I said, "what they show, and what they do not show."

Samos regarded me, I fear, puzzled.

I turned up one of the dangling lamps, a little, in the dim light, enlarging the flame, to better illuminate the floor, with its variegated shapes and colors, a broad map of known Gor. Shortly before a lovely, belled, barefoot slave, had danced on that surface, on the smooth, colored tiles.

"Even a child must wonder," I said, "what lies beyond the edges of a map."

"The World's End," said Samos. "When we know more, I shall include it."

"We know little of what is east of the Barrens, what is west of the islands of the World's End."

"When we know more, I shall include it," said Samos.

Much of Gor was terra incognita.

"A map is surface," I said.

"It need be no more," he said. "It need not portray the sky, clouds, the moons, stars. It need not portray strata, molten stone, diamonds, then sky again."

"I think," I said, "there are countries on no map, countries of possibility, countries of the heart, countries very real, which we will never understand."

"Seize reality," he said. "That is enough."

"Few," I said, "would grant that that is enough. What point is there in seizing reality unless it be to change it, to remake it, to fashion it closer to your vision, your ambition and desire?"

"The sail," he said, "does not make the wind."

"The sail is cunning," I said. "It surrenders to the wind, and then uses it to go its own way."

"Do not venture forth," he said, "not on a mission so mindlessly mad."

"I must," I said.

"I do not understand you," said Samos.

"I do not understand myself," I said. "Why then should it be easy for you to do so?"

"Abandon her," said Samos. "Leave her to the fate she so richly deserves, that which by treason and perfidy she contrived for herself."

I gazed at the map, in the lamp light.

"You look upon the map," said Samos. "Learn from it. Let it dissuade you. Behold it. A pace here is a hundred pasangs there. Consider distances and dangers, time and space, storms and beasts, guardsmen and brigands. The map itself proclaims the inanity of your intentions."

"You agree," I asked, "that the map is surface?"

"Of course," he said, angrily.

"Men are not," I said.

"Do you think Marlenus is your friend?"

"No," I said.

"As soon as you crossed the pomerium of Ar," said Samos, "did he, or even his most subordinate officer, harbor the least suspicion that you might entertain even a modicum of sympathy for the former treasonous Ubara, you would be seized and placed under arrest."

"I once," I said, "long ago, in the time of the Horde of Pa-Kur, Master Assassin, rendered aid to a beleaguered Ubar."

"I know," said Samos. "Who has not heard the songs, and the tale of the mysterious Tarl of Bristol?"

"Few know he was I," I said.

"True," he said.

"Might that not count for something?" I asked.

"Surely," said Samos. "Thus, were you so fortunate, you might merely be denied bread, fire, and salt, and be banished from Ar, ordered never to return."

"Or slain swiftly, mercifully, at the foot of a throne," I said.

"Possibly," said Samos. "Ubars often fear men such as you, strong, resourceful, powerful men, and it is a dangerous thing to be feared by a Ubar."

"I do not think Talena is now in Ar," I said.

"No," said Samos. "The city, by report, is not now beribboned nor covered with the petals of strewn flowers, to welcome the return of so august a prisoner as a treasonous Ubara."

"Might there not be hope then," I asked, "at least until the gates of Ar have closed behind her?"

"There is no hope," said Samos.

"The way between Cos and Ar is long," I said.

"And dangerous," said Samos.

"True," I said.

"And more dangerous than you might suspect," said Samos.

"How so?" I said.

"You are not alone in this matter," he said. "Consider the reward for the return of Talena. Not all might surrender that guerdon uncontested to Cos."

"The wrath of Cos is much to be feared," I said.

"True," said Samos, "but arguments of gold are seldom examined for cogency. Too, a starving urt will attack a larl for a crumb of cheese."

I reduced the flame in the lamp, and it swung once more, dimly lit, on its short chain.

"Do not go," he said.
"I wish you well," I said.
"I wish you well," he said.
I then withdrew from the chamber.

CHAPTER TWO

"I seek a man," I said, "a cripple, one missing a leg, the left leg, from shortly above the knee, one who may call himself Rutilius of Ar, one who may call himself Bruno of Torcadino. One who would dare not speak his true name."

She, a shapely brunette, moved back, uneasily, on her knees, more back in the shadows, on the furs, in the dim lamp light of the alcove. There was a slight rustle of chain.

"I know of no such man," she said.

"Very well," I said.

"Am I to be beaten?" she asked.

"No," I said, "I have no reason to beat you."

"Masters need no reason to beat a slave," she said.

"True," I said.

"But you will not beat me?"

"No," I said.

"But if I were in the least bit displeasing?"

"Then, of course," I said. "You are a slave."

"I am glad," she said. "I want to obey. I want to have to obey. I want no choice. I want to be owned, to be subject to the whip, to have a master."

"You are a female," I said. "You have been bred for a thousand generations to be owned, to belong to a master."

"At one time," she said, "I did not know that."

"But you have learned it," I said.

"I fear I suspected it—somehow—always," she said.

"I do not think you are Gorean," I said.

"My accent?" she said.

"Of course," I said.

"Do you despise me, as a barbarian, seized and harvested from the Slave World?"

"Not at all," I said. "You might bring as much as a silver tarsk."

"Master flatters a poor slave," she said.

"I gather that you were free," I said.

"Yes," she said, "in my meaninglessness, my ennui, my loneliness, my boredom, my misery, and frustration. I had no identity. I was nothing. I was unfulfilled. I was unhappy. I was no more than a slave without a master."

"On that world," I said, "many slaves lack their masters."

"Doubtless it is called the Slave World because it is a rich source for slaves," she said.

"Quite possibly," I said. "On the other hand, I think some refer to it as the Slave World because many on that world are slaves who do not know they are slaves, slaves who think they are free, slaves who are manipulated by, ruled by, lies."

She was silent.

"But you were free, nominally, legally," I said.

"Yes," she said, "nominally, legally. It is here, on this world, that I am a slave, a beast, a property, goods, a vendible object, something anyone could buy, actually, legally."

"Perhaps this necessitates a readjustment in your self-perception," I said.

"Being a slave is real," she said. "It is an identity. I am now something honest, and, to me, precious. I have my place in society. In my way I am important. Before I was nothing. Now I am something. I know now how to speak, how to act, how to be."

"Or you will know the whip," I said.

"This tavern," she said, "the Mariner's Pleasure, is the largest and most resplendent in Jad. We have more than two hundred paga girls here. Many are far more beautiful than I. Why did Master take me by the hair and pull me to the alcove, why did he tear off my tunic, rather than that of another, and why did he manacle my ankle rather than that of another?"

"I thought it might help you learn what you now are," I said.

"Surely I was in little doubt of that," she said.

"At a table, outside, I thought I heard you use the word 'Master' to a man with less than appropriate deference."

"He was loathsome," she said. "He was drunk."

"He was a man," I said.

"He pawed at me."

"You are a slave," I said. "Be grateful. Rejoice that you are found of interest, any interest, by a free person."

"He did not even notice."

"I noticed," I said.

"You will not beat me?" she said.

"Not for that, not now," I said. "I merely thought it would be well to call it to your attention. Perhaps it will save you a beating later. After all, drunk men, after a time, commonly become sober. I think, to some extent, you may be still learning your collar."

"I think a girl in Master's keeping would soon learn her collar," she said.

"I wish you well," I said.

"Do not go," she said. "Surely Master will enjoy me. It is what I am for."

"I have errands to do," I said, "streets to frequent, piers on which to loiter, markets in which to listen."

"I do not think you are of Jad," she said.

"I am not of Jad," I said. "But, too, many in this tavern are not either."

"I do not know the one-legged man of whom you spoke," she said. "But beware of asking questions. Informants are about. The palace is everywhere. In Jad it is not safe to be too curious, to ask too many questions."

"A tavern," I said, "is much like a crossroads, a market. Paga girls see much and hear much. They are often the best informed of all a city's occupants."

"We often serve unremarked, unnoticed," she said.

I rose to my feet, turned, and reached for the ties that fastened shut the leather curtains.

"Put me to use," she said. "Make use of me! Use me!"

I turned about, looking back to her, in the shadows.

"Stay," she said, "if only for a moment."

A slave may be used, if only for a moment. It helps to remind them that they are slaves, objects, properties, mere worthless beasts. Use them and then cast them aside. But few Goreans are so easily satisfied. How much more pleasant it is, for an Ahn, or two, or a morning or an afternoon, or a day and night, to turn them, in their locked collars, into sobbing, begging, moaning animals, helpless in the heat of their flaming, uncontrollable ecstasies.

"It seems your slave fires burn," I said.

She crawled from the shadows.

She was beautiful in the lamp light, naked and collared.

"I cannot help myself," she said. "Men have done it to me. My fires rage. I am now their prisoner, the captive of their ferocity."

"Excellent," I said.

"Surely you pity me," she said.

"No," I said.

"Is this the way you want a woman before you, naked and collared, on all fours?"

"Or on your knees," I said, "or belly or back."

"Regard me," she said. "I am no longer mine. I am now the belonging of another. I am no longer free. I have been turned into naught but an amorous slave."

"It suits you," I said.

"Yes," she wept, "it suits me!"

"Speak, if you wish," I said.

"I was once proud and free," she said. "Then, in the chains of masters, I was turned into what I always wanted to be, a rightless, needful slave."

"Do not be ashamed of what you are," I said. "Be true to what you are."

I again turned away.

"Do not go," she said. "Do not leave me behind like this!"

I turned back to face her.

The chain fastened to the manacle she wore on her left ankle would not permit her to leave the alcove, but it would permit her to approach me more closely.

I pointed to my feet.

She approached me, head down, on all fours and then lowered her head to kiss my feet, and then lowered herself to her belly before me, and with her soft lips, tenderly, deferentially, continued to render me a slave's grateful, homage.

I then reached down, pulled her to her knees, and threw her back on the furs.

"Yes, Master!" she cried.

"Buy me!" she begged.

"Only a slave begs to be bought," I said.

"Buy me!" she wept. "Buy me!"

"What is your name?" I asked.

"'Iris', if it pleases Master," she said.

I lay on my back, looking up at the curved ceiling of the alcove. The oil in the lamp was now almost gone.

The slave's head was at my waist.

I did not think she was asleep.

On the wall to my right, dangling from rings, were loops of chain. These may be used at the wall, or, if one wishes, employed at floor rings, as well. There are many cunning arrangements of such things. Beside them, on the wall, on hooks, were various disciplinary devices, amongst them switches of various lengths and widths, and the common five-stranded Gorean slave whip, designed to effectively punish but to neither mark nor cut the object to whose attention it might be addressed, lest its market value be diminished. On the opposite wall were slung some coils of rope, hoods, strips of cloth, scarves, blindfolds, and gags. These objects, in their application, are susceptible, too, of many permutations. It is not surprising that paga slaves strive to be pleasing in an alcove. A common permutation,

particularly with new slaves, who are still terrified to find themselves
in a locked collar, and understand what it may mean, is to chain
them naked on their back, in such a way that they know they are
completely vulnerable and absolutely helpless. They are then blindfolded and gagged. The blindfold and gag both enhance the feeling
of helplessness, that they are wholly at the mercy of another. With
respect to the blindfold, the slave does not know what is to be done
to her, say, when or where she will be touched or caressed. Perhaps
the master has a switch or whip in his hand? Will it strike her? With
respect to the gag, she wishes, of course, in her fear and helplessness,
she could assure the master of her total obedience, of her renewed
efforts to be found perfectly pleasing in all respects. But she cannot.
She is gagged. She desires desperately to speak but cannot do so. She
has been denied the use of one of her most delightful and prized assets, her marvelous speech; she is a woman; she loves to speak; she
wants to speak, but cannot now do so. How miserable and helpless
this makes her feel! Incidentally, on Gor, slaves are seldom allowed to
speak without permission, though in many cases they have a 'standing permission' to do so. This standing permission, of course, may be
instantly revoked. Few things so impress her slavery upon a woman
as this requirement, that she may not speak without the master's permission. Yet this arrangement, too, warmly and deliciously reassures
her that she is truly a slave, subject to her master's will.

"Master," whispered the slave.

"Yes?" I said.

"I fear for you," she said.

"Why is that?" I asked.

"Why is Master in Jad?" she asked.

"Curiosity is not becoming in a kajira," I said.

"I fear Master seeks something, in a city where it may not be wise
to do so."

"It has nothing to do with you," I said. "You are a slave. Keep
your neck in your collar."

"I have little choice in that matter," she smiled. "It is locked on
me, closely and securely."

I pulled her higher, from beside me, and kissed her.

"Why would Master seek a one-legged man in the Mariner's Pleasure," she asked, "one of the most expensive taverns in Jad?"

"I seek this one-legged man in lofty domiciles, in affluent districts, on piers where treasures are unloaded, in high places," I said,
"for, though he is one-legged, he is extremely wealthy."

"Perhaps he is not extremely wealthy," she said.

"He must be," I said.

"Why?"

"Curiosity is not becoming in a kajira," I reminded her.

The slave, having assisted me with my tunic and cloak, placed my sandals on my feet, and laced them in place.

She then looked up at me.

"You serve well," I said.

"I am learning," she said.

"It pleases you to serve, does it not?" I asked.

"Yes, Master," she said. "Very much, Master."

"A worthless slave," I said.

"Yes, Master," she said.

"Happiness is where it is found," I said.

"Yes, Master," she said.

"You are crying," I said.

"Master will leave," she said, "and I am left on my chain."

"What was your name, your barbarian name?" I asked.

"Linda Elaine Travis," she said.

"From whence on your former world do you derive?"

"From a place called New York City," she said, "a city larger even than Jad, on the east coast of a large continent, in the northern hemisphere of that world."

She was not the first slave I had heard of, being extracted from that place.

"I congratulate the slavers for picking you out," I said. "I approve their choice."

"I had nothing to say about it," she said.

"You are well curved and extremely sexually desirable," I said.

"Perhaps that was noticed by the slavers," she said.

"And they also picked you," I said, "for high intelligence."

"Oh?" she said, startled.

"Certainly," I said. "That is common. Intelligence is extremely desirable in slaves. It improves their value, considerably."

"But I am still only a slave," she said.

"Of course," I said. "You have had administered to you, I take it, the Stabilization Serums."

"Yes," she said, "but they were not explained to me."

"They protect you against the drying, withering disease," I said.

"I do not understand," she said.

"Aging," I said.

"I am immortal?" she whispered.

"No more than any other young, beautiful woman," I said. "You can easily perish by the thrust of a knife, the bite of an ost. You can be torn to pieces by the fangs of devouring sleen, drained of blood by leech plants."

"Such a gift would be priceless on my former world," she said. "Here I receive it though I am only a slave?"

"Certainly," I said. "Masters do not want you to lose your market value."

"In my taking, my acquiring," she said, "I was not alone."

"Presumably not," I said. "On the Slave World, slavers pick fruit, with little difficulty, from the orchards of beauty."

"There were fifty in my shipment," she said, "from many places."

"And all were destined for the markets," I said.

"Of course," she said.

"Brand!" I snapped.

Instantly, reflexively, without thought, with a snap of her chain, she responded, turning, her left leg extended, facing me. Her hand had even grasped, unguardedly, for a moment, to where might have been the hem of tunic, to draw it up, to her waist, but now, of course, she wore no tunic. This tiny contretemps had embarrassed her, but was to have been expected, given her training. There are several such commands to which a kajira is taught to respond, immediately and without thought. Indeed, sometimes a kajira, hoping to escape in a free woman's clothing, is, by such means, tricked into betraying herself. The girl's left hand was now at her waist, her fingers closed.

"I thought it would be so," I said, "the common brand, the cursive Kef."

"Shortly after arrival on Gor," she said, "I was marked."

"And found yourself in a collar," I said.

"And found myself stripped," she said. "And thus I learned that it would be up to others whether or not I would be clothed."

"And fed," I said.

"Yes, Master," she said.

"It is morning," I said. "I must be on my way."

"Master," she said.

"Yes?" I said.

"As a slave," she said, "I may appropriately beg to be bought. I do so beg."

"As a slave?" I said.

"Yes, Master," she said, "as a slave, the slave I am."

"You juice well," I said, "and you are needful."

"I have been in the arms of Gorean men," she said.

"Doubtless you are now much different from when you were on your former world," I said.

"Not so different," she said, "but on that dismal, polluted, hypocritical world I did my best, as prescribed, to ignore, even to deny, my slave fires, but I can no longer do so. It is not permitted. I am in a collar. In my collar I am freed to be myself."

"Does it trouble you to be kneeling as you now are?" I asked.

"No, Master," she said. "I am now before a free person."

"You are not resentful, ashamed, humiliated?"

"No, Master," she said, "I am now as is right for me. I am now where, and as, I belong. I would be uneasy, even fearful, not to be before you as I am now. I want to be as I am now before you, rightfully submitted, thankful, grateful. It is fitting. I am a slave. I want to be a slave. I love being a slave. It will be hard for Master to understand this, but I have never felt more free, more fulfilled, more me, more happy than I do in a locked collar, owned."

"It is spoken of," I said, "as the paradox of the collar."

"Buy me!" she begged.

I reached to the straps on the leather curtains.

The small lamp glowed for a moment more brightly, and then went out.

Some light could be seen in tiny cracks in the leather curtain.

I reached into my pouch.

I withdrew and unwrapped a small round object.

"I have here," I said, "in the palm of my hand, a hard candy. If you are gentle and patient with it, it will last you a long time. Not using your hands, you may take it from my hand."

"A candy!" she said. "I have served you, abjectly and completely, for Ahn, again and again, for an evening and a night, and you would give me a candy!"

"I see, as I suspected earlier," I said, "you are still learning your collar. I paid for my paga, and you, worthless paga slut, come with the paga. Do you think to bargain? Do you think you are a free woman, to sell favors, to charge for a kiss or caress? You are a slave. One does not pay a slave; if one pays, one pays her master. You are an object, an animal. Nothing is owed to an object, an animal. As a rightless object, a small, nicely curved pleasure beast, you must strive to be pleasing, fully pleasing, and hope to be spared the lash."

She shrank back, frightened.

"Please do not beat me, Master," she said. "Forgive me! Do not beat me! I beg not to be beaten!"

I replaced the candy in its wrapper, in my wallet.

"Do not be afraid," I said.

"In your arms," she said, "it was made clear to me how much a slave I am."

I regarded her.

"Buy me!" she wept. "There are many girls here. We are cheap! Purchase a worthless slave! Teach me my collar! I would learn it at your hands!"

"You will learn it at the hands of any man," I said.

I then undid the leather straps and parted the curtains. It was morning, early morning. Some men were still in the tavern, mostly somnolent, some sprawled across the tiny tables. The paga vat was covered, the lid chained in place. A taverner's man was sitting on a stool, leaning back, near the left side of the wide entrance. For four days I had sought in vain for the one-legged man. He, if anyone, he who had delivered Talena of Ar into the clutches of Lurius of Jad, should know her location and the routes and arrangements by means of which she would be transported to Ar, and the dreadful mercies of its justice.

"Master!" called the slave, from behind me.

I turned back to regard her in the early light.

"Be careful, Master," she said, softly. "This is Jad, and you are not of Jad. The spies of the Ubar are everywhere."

This, as her earlier hintings, or advisements, did little to please my ears. Jad is a large port. I had assumed one could traverse its streets, alleys, piers, and districts relatively inconspicuously. Now it seemed that that might not be true.

"Would you like the sweet?" I asked.

"If Master pleases," she said. "Very much so."

"You would not now scorn it?" I asked.

"No, Master," she said. "I behaved badly. I was ignorant. I knew no better. Please forgive a worthless slave. She begs Master's forgiveness."

"I gather," I said, "that now you might not object to a sweet."

"No, Master," she said.

"It seems now," I said, "you might hope to receive one."

"Yes, Master," she said, "very much so, Master."

"As a slave?" I asked

"Yes, Master," she said. "I desire it, desperately and pathetically—as a slave."

"When did you last have a sweet," I asked.

"Not since my former world," she said.

"I see," I said.

Such things are often precious to slaves. Few girls will let other girls know when they have one. Sometimes they're hidden, and made to last for days, kept to be savored for a few moments now and then. Sometimes they are stolen. Often they are fought over. One cast to the floor may be scrambled for, with cries, scratchings, bitings, pullings of hair, kicks, and blows.

"I trust that you are sure that you would like this tiny sweet, a small hard candy," I said. "Women such as you, when free on your world, I gather, would often be the recipient of large, expensive boxes of sweets, proffered by hopeful, naive, exploited swains, perhaps accompanied by flowers."

"I would be grateful, very grateful, Master," she said. "It is my hope that Master will be kind to a poor slave."

I returned to the interior of the alcove. The slave was at the end of the chain fastened to the manacle on her left ankle. It was not long enough to let her reach the fastenings of closed curtains. I retrieved the candy from my wallet and, bent down, held it in the palm of my hand. Not using her hands, the slave, on all fours, head down, delicately took it from the palm of my hand.

I then departed the alcove, but turned back outside the portal, to look back upon her.

She tried to crawl forward, but was stopped short, her left leg straight behind her.

With her ankle she jerked against the chain in frustration.

"You cannot follow me," I said. "You are chained."

Again she drew futilely, fiercely, against the chain.

"Perhaps now you realize better what it is to be a slave," I said.

Tears sprang into her eyes.

"I wish you well, former Earth woman," I said, "now only a worthless kajira on Gor."

She collapsed then, lying on her left side, her knees drawn up, sobbing on the furs.

I then made my way to the broad doorway of the tavern, the Mariner's Pleasure. The taverner's man posted there seemed half asleep. I wondered if he were. "I wish you well," I said. "I wish you well," he mumbled.

I was then outside, on the street.

I heard the quick flick of a whip, and the then-hastened trundling of a cart, laden with tur-pah. It was drawn by a brace of harnessed female slaves. The peddler stood on a small, narrow platform at the back of the cart.

I think it must then have been something past the Sixth Ahn.

The peddler may have been late.

Gorean markets tend to open early.

I did not understand why the slave in the alcove had been distraught. Had she not been given a candy?

CHAPTER THREE

"I understand, Citizen," I said, casually, "that news flames, that Talena of Ar, the overthrown, treasonous, fugitive Ubara of Ar has at last been captured."

I was in one of Jad's sul markets.

"That is news," said the tunicked seller of brown suls. "Where did this take place, and how did it come about?"

"I know little about it," I said. "I had hoped you might know more."

"There are many rumors," he said. "One does not know what to believe."

"Believe then nothing," said another fellow, a seller of orange suls.

"I had thought, even," I said, "that she might be in Jad."

"Not to my knowledge," said the first.

"Surely we would have heard of it, if that were so," said the second.

"She would have been publicly welcomed in Jad," said the first, "as a former ally, to be accorded honor and afforded security and shelter, refuge and ample sustenance."

"Do not be naive," said the second. "If she were in Jad, she would be expeditiously returned to Ar for the reward, ten thousand tarn disks of Ar, of double weight. Who would be a big enough fool as to deny himself that gain?"

"But she was a reliable and wondrous ally," said the first. "She opened the gates of Ar to our might; she surrendered Ar itself, with all its wealth, its gems, goods, gold, and women, to our steel."

"She is without honor," said the second. "She did treason to her city. She betrayed her Home Stone."

"That is true," said the first.

"So return the worthless she-tarsk to the vengeance of Ar!" said the second. "Get rid of her and bring back wagons laden with gold."

The first shuddered. "The threatened tortures are lengthy and hideous."

"But richly deserved," said the second.

"How long can one stand protracted, excruciating pain and not die?" asked the first.

"If care is taken," said the second, "a long time, perhaps weeks, possibly months."

"I am looking," I said, "for a friend, a wealthy one-legged man, calling himself, possibly, Bruno of Torcadino. Do you know of such a man?"

"No," said the first man.

"Few who are wealthy frequent a sul market," said the second. "They would send their slaves to do that."

I hoped to locate Seremides, if only to kill him. He, if anyone, would be likely to possess information germane to my quest.

"I wish you well, noble citizens," I said, withdrawing.

"I wish you well," they said.

I had grown restless and ever more frustrated over the past several days, fruitlessly, extensively, pursuing my inquiries throughout Jad. Already I was reduced to hazarding my inquiries in common markets, even produce markets. I had begun my labors on the high streets of Jad, well above the harbor, even in the shadow of the citadel itself, on its lofty crag, its walled precincts housing the Ubarial palace, overlooking the city. Desperate, I had risked accosting itinerant tradesmen, gardeners, cooks, grooms, slaves in slippers and golden collars, worth more than the girl herself, and even house masters. None seemed to know anything of the whereabouts, or fate, of the mysterious Talena. Indeed, I knew more than they, for I knew that she had been conducted, or carried, from Port Kar by Seremides, once the high captain of the Taurentian guards in Ar, and embarked from the Skerry of Lars, near Port Kar, on a Cosian ship, presumably bound for Jad, that she be delivered into the grasp of Lurius of Jad, Ubar of Cos, with whom she had conspired to bring about the downfall of Ar. Yet, here in Jad little, if anything, seemed to be known of Talena. Here, as on the continent, one must make do with rumors, some racing about like scampering urts, appearing and disappearing, wild, fanciful, and inconsistent, others hinting soberly, darkly at plausibility, but lacking the granite of fact, the light of evidence. One thing, however, was clear, undeniably, patently, and obviously clear. The presence of Talena in Cos, if she were in Cos, had not been, at least until now, publicly acknowledged. No holiday had been proclaimed celebrating her arrival, no public feasts held to honor her, so august a personage, an esteemed former ally, now rescued, and safe under the aegis of Cos, nor had a quite different holiday been proclaimed, a holiday of justice, in which she had been publicly exhibited as a long-sought, now-captured criminal. Was Talena now in Cos, at all, I wondered, or might she be already on her way, say, secretly, to face the wrath of an outraged city and its Ubar? Might she, even, have escaped, perhaps abetted by former adherents?

CHAPTER FOUR

I stood on the pavement before the canopied slave shelf.

This was the market of Kiris.

The girls, variously chained, usually by left ankle or neck, were mostly reclining on towels spread over the cement.

One, near me, was standing, being examined by a potential buyer who had ascended the shelf. She was in a standard examination position, standing, her legs widely spread, her hands clasped together behind the back of her neck, her head up and back, seeing the sky. The spread-legged position makes it difficult for a girl to change her position and induces a sense of vulnerability. The position of the hands behind the back of the neck or head immobilizes the hands and lifts the breasts nicely. Her head up and back, facing upward, prevents her from anticipating where she might be touched or caressed.

There were some slaver's men about and a handful of bystanders. One seemed familiar, but I could not place him.

The market of Kiris is a secondary market, so to speak. I had already visited some of Jad's more prestigious markets, catering to a more affluent clientele, where girls commonly brought better prices.

"May I help Master?" inquired a slaver's man, beside me on the pavement.

"I am an agent for another," I said, "a man who is interested in bargains."

"Commonly," said the slaver's man, "a customer wishes to select his own merchandise."

"My principal," I said, "is crippled. It would be difficult for him to negotiate the streets. He is a one-legged man, Bruno of Torcadino. Perhaps you know him, or of him."

"Ela," said the man, "I do not."

I shrugged.

"But perhaps, too," said the slaver's man, "he is well fixed, wishes to conceal his station, and is thus reluctant to be seen in the vicinity of the Market of Kiris."

"That speculation," I said, "is yours, not mine."

"Ohh!" cried the startled slave, on the shelf, and collapsed, huddled, shamed, moaning, to the platform.

"I will take her, for the price proposed," said the prospective buyer.

"A silver tarsk, from the mintage of the palace," said the slaver's man, he on the platform.

"Yes," said the prospective buyer.

"Done," said the slaver's man on the platform.

I must have smiled.

"Of what are you thinking?" asked the slaver's man beside me.

"Another woman bought and sold," I said. "Would it not be interesting if the mysterious Talena of Ar, she so elusive, she sought so widely and with such zeal, and so fruitlessly, were somewhere herself bought and sold, unrecognized, as merely another slave."

"Preposterous," said the slaver's man.

And yet it had once occurred, I knew, in an auction in Brundisium.

I glanced about.

Another slaver's man, one on the shelf, with his bootlike sandal, brushed the thigh of a prone slave and pointed to me. She was neck-chained. She went sinuously to her knees and lifted her neck chain toward me, as though offering it to me. "Buy me, Master," she said.

I turned away.

I then, again disappointed, took my way from the Market of Kiris.

Some yards from the shelf I recalled the fellow whom I had seen near the shelf but had been unable to place. He was the fellow whom I had seen some days ago in the early morning, when I had been leaving the Mariner's Pleasure, he who had been posted near the exit, presumably to prevent stragglers from entering the tavern before the Ahn of opening.

CHAPTER FIVE

The Gorean Streets of Coins are sometimes streets, rather literally, but more often a district or area, rather, as one might say, a financial district. In any event, most Gorean banking takes place on the Streets of Coins, loaning money, changing money, borrowing money, investing money, depositing money or goods for safekeeping, buying insurance, and so on.

"This is quite irregular," said the coin merchant. "As I understand it, in Brundisium, a sympathetic benefactor, with whom you did not even share a Home Stone, and whose name you do not even know, gave you, clear of all obligation, twelve golden staters, by means of which you were enabled to free yourself of certain gambling debts, a fate surely preferable to being sentenced to the galleys as a defaulting debtor."

"Yes," I said.

"A rare stroke of good fortune."

"Yes," I said.

"He must have been very rich," said the merchant.

"Undoubtedly," I said.

"And now you wish to repay him?"

"Certainly," I said.

"Why?" asked the merchant.

"What?" I asked.

"If the gift were truly free and bestowed without entailments," said the merchant, "you are under no obligation to repay him."

"I understand," I said, "but I would like to do so."

"He was generous, and you are grateful," he said.

"Yes," I said.

"Interesting," said the merchant.

"I have reason to believe he is of Jad, or somewhere in Jad," I said. "I have contacted several coin establishments, but have been unable to find him. I am sure he is rich and would have dealings on a Street of Coins. I regret I do not know his name, but it should be easy to locate him, given his wealth, and that he is missing a leg, the left leg, from somewhat above the knee."

"We have no clients who answer to that description," said the merchant. "But we would be happy to hold your money on deposit, at a current rate of interest, you having been issued a receipt, of course."

"I thank you," I said, "but I think I shall look further."

"I do not place your accent," said the merchant.

"Doubtless that is frequently the case in a metropolis as large and busy as Jad," I said.

"Other than locating an elusive benefactor," said the merchant, "what is your business in Jad?"

"It is legitimate, I assure you," I said, "but, at the moment, confidential."

"What is your name?" asked the merchant.

"I think that, too, should remain confidential, at least at present, lest my mission, sensitive and subtle, be jeopardized."

"I understand," said the merchant. "There are many such plans best left temporarily undisclosed, not only in the affairs of state but in the high merchantry. A moment of silence is often more valuable than an Ahn of speech."

"How true," I said. "How true."

"I think you carry steel within your cloak," he said.

"It may prove useful in the prosecution of my business," I said.

"From your eyes and hands, your carriage, I feared so," he said.

"My business does not concern you," I said.

"Perhaps you are of the Black Caste?" he said.

"No," I said.

"Of the Scarlet Caste?" he said.

"Think of me as an agent," I said, "intent upon a particular transaction."

"May I inquire, at least," asked the merchant, "your lodging in Jad?"

"I wish you well," I said.

"Hail, Lurius, Glorious Ubar of Cos," said the merchant.

"Hail, Lurius, Glorious Ubar of Cos," I said, and took my leave.

Soon I had the uneasy feeling that I might be watched or followed. But it seemed it was not so. Each of the four individuals I suspected, in one venue or another, had eventually disappeared, presumably going their own way, attending to their business elsewhere.

It is interesting how sometimes an individual may see what he hopes to see, or what he fears to see, or hears what he hopes to hear, or what he fears to hear.

It is not always easy to look dispassionately on the world, and know it as it is.

But, too, sometimes the world is as one hopes to see it, or fears to see it; and sometimes, too, what one hopes to hear, or fears to hear, is what is truly heard.

CHAPTER SIX

"These are the finest odds tables in Jad," said the seated fellow, ensconced behind a long table littered with slips of paper, small scrolls, marking sticks, and heaps of ostraca covered with jotted notations and figures.

"I have heard so," I said. "But I am curious how here in Jad you can record and manage wagers on the rainfall in Thentis, the Tarn races in Ar, the tharlarion races in Venna, the floods of the Vosk, the price of tea in Bazi, the location of the next Fair of the Farther Islands, and such."

"How is there a problem?" asked the fellow.

"How, for example," I asked, "do you know what tarns will race in distant Ar on a given day?"

"We do not, of course," said the fellow, "but it is easy to wager on how many victories will go to what colors in a month, a passage hand, or even a day."

"Granted," I said. "But you must eventually learn the results here in Jad."

"That is easy," said the man. "We are informed of the results within days, on certified slips of coded paper carried by message vulos."

"Clearly all bets must be placed and recorded before the event takes place," I said.

"Certainly," said the man.

"Odds are established as functions of the money wagered, I take it," I said.

"In a sense," said the man, "but, actually, in a deeper sense, they are functions of the wagerers' estimations of probability, which underlie the money wagered."

"Have you recorded wagers on the capture of Talena of Ar?" I asked. "Say, where, or by whom, or by what date, or such?"

"We have taken in many such wagers," said the man, "for several months now."

"What if," I asked, "as a fanciful thought, Talena were already captured?"

"But she has not yet been captured," said the man, suddenly looking at me narrowly.

"But if she had been," I said.

"We must protect ourselves," said the man. "Her capture, for our purposes, would be dated as of the date of its provable and public announcement."

"What if," I said, "one could control that provable and public announcement?"

"That would be a gambler's dream," he said, "a gamble which is no gamble, a wager which is no wager, a bet on something already known, on something already predetermined, on something certain."

I wondered then why Lurius of Jad, presumably through agents, had not yet availed himself, or his party, of so simple a ruse. Was he waiting for better odds? Could it be that he did not have Talena in custody?

"Does Master wish to place a bet?" asked the man.

"I seek a man," I said, "one who reneged on a bet with me, a man who owes me a silver tarn disk of Ar. I come to the tables thinking he, seemingly a gambler, may frequent them. He may be calling himself Rutilius of Ar or Bruno of Torcadino, or any other name but his own true name. He is easy to recognize, for he is missing a leg, the left leg, from a hort or so above the knee."

"I am glad I am not he," said the man. "You carry a sword within your cloak."

"The threat of two-edged war steel can be persuasive," I said.

"I do not doubt it," said the man uneasily.

"Do you know him?" I asked. "Have you heard of him, or seen him?"

"No," said the man. "I am sorry. If you do not wish to bet, please step aside. Others are waiting."

"I am sorry," I said. "I wish you well."

"I wish you well," he said. "Next."

CHAPTER SEVEN

I had barely turned away from the odds table, when, across the small square, lined with shops, some dozen yards away, I saw something remembered, from days ago, from just outside the Mariner's Pleasure. I walked toward the cart, heaped with tur-pah, with its brace of harnessed slaves. The driver, a thin, gaunt man, was standing near the cart. The butt of his long, light, supple switch was resting on the foot platform at the back right side of the cart, held within two rings.

"Master," he said.

It was past the Tenth Ahn, the Gorean noon. The tur-pah, freshly cut, should surely, at least some of it, have been marketed by now or else stored away in some cool, dark shed pending a later sale.

"You wish to speak to me?" I asked, from some few feet away.

"Yes, Master," he said.

The brace of slaves was the same, two fine, well-formed, young animals, but two adjustments had been made to their habiliments, so speak. First, both were now blindfolded, and each now had her hands braceleted behind her back. It is common for a blindfolded slave, particularly a new slave, to have her hands braceleted or tied behind her. In this fashion she cannot tear off the blindfold. A blindfolded slave more familiar with her collar, on the other hand, may have her hands free. She well understands that she is not to remove the blindfold without permission. The blindfold induces in the slave a sense of vulnerability and helplessness, a sense of being in the power of another, which is arousing to her. In a blindfold, whether back braceleted or not, she may kneel and press her lips to her master's feet, begging to be used. To be sure, if a blindfolded slave, even one who has well learned her collar, has her hands free and is sufficiently perturbed or terrified she is likely to tear off the blindfold. This is not practical, on the other hand, if she is back-braceleted or has her hands tied behind her back.

I was then at his side.

He stood a bit behind and to the side of the cart. He looked about, as though assessing the small square, and then, facing away, not looking at me, spoke in a low voice.

"It is my understanding," he said, "that Master seeks information on a one-legged man."

"Yes," I said, "one who may be known as Rutilius of Ar or Bruno of Torcadino."

"For a copper tarsk," said he, "I think I may be of service to Master."

"Speak," I said.

"Forgive me, Master," he said, "but a copper tarsk."

I took a copper tarsk from my wallet and handed it to the fellow. "Now speak," I said.

"Readily," he said, "but not here, not in the open. I think there may be danger in this matter. I fear to be seen talking with you."

"Where then?" I asked.

The fellow pointed to the right. "In the Street of Nicephorus," he said.

"In the Alley of Nicephorus?" I said.

To be sure, many Gorean streets, even in metropolises like Ar and Turia, are narrow and crooked. In some places they are so narrow that one can touch opposite walls with extended arms, so narrow that hands can be clasped between opposite windows.

"Enter the street, seemingly alone," he said, "as though to visit. Some fifty paces on, the street makes a sharp right turn. Take that turn, and proceed twenty paces or so to the end of the street, where it ends in a wall. It is unlikely to be crowded in that area at this time of day."

"It will be deserted," I said.

I assumed that would have been arranged.

"Privacy is important," said the man.

I did not doubt that.

"I shall follow you shortly," he said.

"In this way," I said, "we will not be seen together."

"Precisely," he said.

"Why are your draft slaves blindfolded and back-braceleted?" I asked.

"That they see nothing and understand less," said the man.

"Of course," I said.

"They are a matched pair," he said.

"They are quite attractive," I said. "One would expect to find such women not harnessed to a cart, but rolling helplessly in the furs, in a pleasure harness."

"Let us hurry," urged the man.

A pair of matched slaves is likely to be quite expensive, more so than if they were sold separately. Perhaps tur-pah sold well in Jad.

"Please," said the man, looking about anxiously.

I then, alone, entered the Alley, or Street, if one likes, of Nicephorus.

CHAPTER EIGHT

I soon made the sharp right turn in the street of Nicephorus and followed the street until it ended at a wall. It was, of course, as I had expected, a cul-de-sac. I did not have to wait long for the gaunt fellow to make his appearance. He soon appeared shortly, after the sharp right turn in the street, leading the blindfolded slaves drawing the cart, which was then turned so that, for the most part, sidewise, it blocked the street. Given the turn in the street, what occurred in this portion of the street could not be seen from the other side of the street, that leading back to the small square.

The gaunt fellow seemed in a good humor. With him, carrying clubs, were four men. I recognized them as those whom I had, serially, individually, suspected of following me after my departure from the house of the coin merchant. As each had seemed to go his own way eventually, with no interest in me, I had dismissed my fears at the time that I was followed. I now realized that a relay of trackers had been involved, each discreetly following his predecessor and taking up where the earlier man would turn aside. In this way each seemed independent and unconcerned with me.

I lifted my hand to them, palm facing the side of my head. "Tal," I said pleasantly.

Two of them laughed.

The gaunt man then, who seemed to be first amongst them, and the others, the four with clubs, came about the cart, so that they were between me and the cart.

That, I thought, was excellent. In that way, their exit would be impeded.

The two blindfolded, back-braceleted slaves seemed uneasy.

"I am here," I said. "You may now impart to me the whereabouts of the one-legged man I seek."

"But," said he, "we have no idea as to his whereabouts."

"Return me then the copper tarsk I gave you, and stand aside, for I intend to withdraw."

"Hold!" said the gaunt man.

"You would detain me?" I asked.

Another of his cohorts laughed.

"Are you common brigands?" I asked.

"Hardly," said the gaunt man.

"Am I under arrest?" I asked. "Are you duly authorized officers of Jad?"

"In a sense," he said.

"Secret guardsmen?" I asked.

"We may be deemed so," he said. "We, and others, are charged with the security of the state of Cos."

"With the welfare and prosperity of its Ubar," I said.

"In Jad," he said, "we are wary of strangers."

"And particularly so at this time?" I asked.

"You have been under surveillance," he said.

"Why?" I asked.

"You have acted suspiciously."

"How so?"

"You have made untoward inquiries, pertaining to a one-legged man," he said, "we think a particular one-legged man."

"Perhaps," I said, "he owes me money, or perhaps I wish to find him and repay a debt, or favor. Perhaps we are old friends, and I wish merely to renew his acquaintance."

"Look about yourself," he said. "Did you see the stains on the wall behind you?"

"Yes," I said.

"Look upon the cobblestones at your feet?" he said.

"I see them," I said.

"They are painted with blood," he said.

"It seems this is not your first time on this street," I said.

"It is my favorite place of business," he said.

"I am armed," I said.

"Obviously," he said.

"You would put wood against steel," I asked, "and not even the wood of the great staff of the Peasants?"

"Scarcely," he said. "Emerge, Jurek."

Then, from the midst of the tur-pah on the cart, a tall, dour figure stood, brushing away tur-pah. He then bent down, opened a side panel on the cart, and stepped down, into the street.

"Behold Jurek," said the gaunt man. "He is the finest swordsman in Jad. He has killed more than a hundred men, in arenas, and elsewhere. Behold Jurek, and tremble."

"Perhaps he will approach me," I said.

"Draw your weapon, or die where you stand, like a slaughtered verr," said the gaunt man.

Jurek's weapon left its sheath, suddenly, noisily, brandished. I supposed that was to assist in the intimidation of an opponent. My own sword, the short, double-edged, razor-sharp gladius, was not sheathed. In this way one may gain a fraction of an Ihn.

I wished to separate the swordsman from his cohorts, the gaunt man, and the fellows with clubs.

I backed away, a few feet.

"Stay where you are," said Jurek. "Perhaps I will be merciful."

Three of the four fellows with clubs laughed.

It is sometimes hard to assess opponents. But of the four men with clubs, one was clearly wary, intent and alert. He was the one who had not laughed. He would be the most dangerous. Therefore, in the instant of surprise on which I was counting, he would be the first to grasp the situation and so must then be the first for me to reach.

Jurek, angry, took some steps forward.

I then stepped back another two yards or so.

"There is a wall behind you," called the gaunt man. "Stand, coward, where you are."

I moved back a little.

"Jurek is the finest swordsman in Jad," said the gaunt man. "Perhaps he will be quick."

The three fellows who had laughed laughed again. I again noted the position of the fourth man, he who did not laugh.

I slipped away my cloak, but held it beside me with my left hand loosely. I could then reach my unsheathed weapon and, with one quick motion, free it from its leather sling.

"He fears even to draw his blade," called one of the fellows who had laughed.

The harnessed slaves were clearly agitated.

I backed away a pace, until the wall was a yard or so behind me.

"Go against the wall, coward," called the gaunt man. "Let it be painted afresh with blood!"

This position would bring Jurek, the swordsman, farther forward, separating him more from the men with the clubs, and would still allow me space to move easily to one side or the other.

"Draw your blade at least!" called one of the fellows who had laughed.

"He fears to do so," said another of the fellows who had laughed.

"Beware Jurek, beware, lest he do so!" cried the third in the amused trio.

This mocking warning elicited more amusement.

I was sure that Jurek was no stranger to the sword.

He would set himself.

I wondered what his fee might be for a kill. Perhaps eight or ten copper tarsks?

One does not rush madly upon a skilled antagonist.

But they might expect that of me.

I hoped so.

They had known I was armed, and might possibly be dangerous. Thus, I supposed, they had hired Jurek.

Otherwise, I conjectured that the business in the Street of Nicephorus might have been accomplished, presumably as usual, with no more than clubs and knives.

With a cry I flung my cloak up and across my body like a net and trident fighter and at the same time drew my sword and lunged to the right, forward, past Jurek who, startled and disconcerted, the cloak falling over him, obscuring his vision, stabbed and slashed upward frenziedly. In the moment it took to pass him, I realized I had nothing to fear from him. One does not fight the net, or cloak, but evades it.

In an instant I was in the midst of the four fellows with clubs. I dispatched he whom I had taken to be most formidable first. He, at least, as I had feared, had responded almost instantly to the situation, but my blade reached him even as he raised his arm to strike his blow. The other three, at the moment, had not even seemed to register what was happening, that I had somehow passed the swordsman and was in their midst. I had little time, I knew, to deal with those who were armed with clubs for the swordsman, freeing himself from the cloak, would be at my back almost immediately. I felled one of the three who had been so amused earlier at my putative predicament, as he turned to flee, with a swift cut to the back of the neck. The other two, similarly declining any opportunity to do contest, made for the tur-pah cart. One, stumbling in his flight, struck the cart heavily and, turning wildly to face me, took my blade, in the darting and withdrawing stroke, through the heart. Somewhere I heard women screaming, and, oddly, in the heat of the moment, only a moment later realized it must be the harnessed slaves. To my chagrin the last of the four men who had been armed with clubs had cast down his club, and, slipping between the back of the cart and the wall, had disappeared around the sharp corner in the street, and was running down the street toward the small square at the other end of the street. I turned suddenly, and, with a ringing of steel, and a burst of sparks, blocked the descending blow of the maddened Jurek who had cast aside my rent cloak, surmised the situation, and rushed to follow me. His blow blocked, he stepped back, and we faced one another, each on guard.

The gaunt man, frightened, shaken, his eyes wild, had hurried to place himself in such a way that Jurek was between us.

"Now you will die," he cried. "You face the finest swordsman in all Jad. Kill him, noble Jurek, kill him!"

But then, without so much as a clash of steel, Jurek crumbled.

The gaunt man looked upon this, his face contorted with disbelief and horror.

"Perhaps," I said, "the noble Jurek is not the finest swordsman in Jad."

The gaunt man was shaking with fear.

"The next time you wish an Assassin," I said, "petition a Black Court, solicit the services of one of the Dark Caste."

"Spare me," he said. "Do not kill me! I am unarmed."

"Pick up the sword of Jurek," I said. "He no longer has need of it."

"I would have no chance against you," he said.

"You would have the same chance which you thought to give me," I said.

"I am innocent," he said. "I am a mere hireling, a minion obeying orders."

"Be careful," I said, "from whom, and for what, you take fee."

"I can buy my life!" he said.

"How so?" I asked.

"I am high in the secret circles of Jad," he said.

"What am I offered?" I asked.

"A golden tarn disk, of double weight, from Ar," he said.

"You are indeed rich," I said.

"Yes!" he said, sweating.

"All I need from you," I said, "is a copper tarsk."

"Who are you really?" he asked.

"One," I said, "with whom your business in the Street of Nicephorus did not turn out well."

"Accept my offer," he said, "a tarn disk of gold, of double weight, for my life."

"Where is the one-legged man I seek?" I asked.

His face turned white, and he trembled. "I do not know," he said. "I honestly do not know!"

I was silent.

"But a tarn disk of gold, of double weight, for my life!"

"No," I said.

"Please, noble master," he wept.

"You may go," I said.

"You release me?" he said.

"Yes," I said.

"Why?" he asked.

"Not all blood honors a blade," I said.

He then, keeping as far from me as possible, and not taking his eyes from me, his back against the wall of the street, forced his way between the back of the cart and the wall of the street, and sped away.

I watched him flee.

There would have been little point in killing him. One of the fellows who had had a club had already escaped, and he would presumably summon aid, and, soon, all Jad would be looking for me. I regretted the outcome. My hopes, now, seemed desolate of promise. I would no longer be able to move about in Jad with relative immunity, pursuing my inquiries. I had hoped, through finding the one-legged man, Seremides, once high captain of the Taurentians, to obtain information pertaining to Talena and, ideally, to learn her location. Such information I had learned was neither public in Jad, nor easily secured.

I cleaned my blade on the tunic of Jurek, and returned it to its sling. I then went to where my cloak lay on the stones, where Jurek had slashed it aside. In two places it was rent, and in one place deeply. I placed it about my body. Happily, it still muchly covered the blade I concealed within it. It occurred to me I must have it repaired or replaced.

I went to the blindfolded, back-braceleted slaves. Both, I fear, were still stressed. One was still gasping for air, and the other was whimpering. Both cried out softly as they sensed my approach. I soothed them, stroking their hair gently. "Do not be afraid," I said. "It is over. You are safe. It is done with."

I was weary, and dejected. Surely the success of my enterprise was radically jeopardized, even if all was not lost.

I heard the ringing of the great hollow bar mounted on the wall of the citadel, high on its crag overlooking the harbor.

It was the Eleventh Ahn.

Within the citadel was the Ubarial palace, and within the palace might be Talena of Ar.

I would leave the street of Nicephorus. I did not think it would take long for the two who had fled, the one fellow who had cast away his club and the gaunt man, to summon guardsmen.

I looked about myself.

I had had little choice in the matter. For all I had known, the gaunt man might have had information pertaining to the one-legged man, information he was ready to sell. If that were the case, I must surely pursue the matter.

I then turned the sharp corner on the street, to enter the other part, the longer part, of the street, that which debouched onto the small square where I had recently met and conversed with the gaunt man.

But I stopped, stunned.

I looked about wildly, but I saw nothing, only the two bodies lying in the street.

One was the body of the fellow who had cast away his club and fled, the other was that of the gaunt man. Both bodies were relatively close to the sharp turn in the street. The fellow who had cast away his club had been slain by a single, clean thrust to the heart. The gaunt man had suffered a different fate. The left side of his head was broken open, as if by the heavy, forceful blow of a blunt instrument.

I removed one copper tarsk from the wallet of the gaunt man, and then left the Street of Nicephorus.

CHAPTER NINE

"Of course, I cannot read, Master," she said. "I have not been taught. Why should a kajira not be illiterate?"

"You do not know then what is written on the back of your tunic," I said.

"Of course, I know," she said. "I was told, and, if I had not been told, I think that I could, from the looks of masters, and the instructions issued to me, have surmised its contents rather accurately."

It said "I am Iris. Find me at the Mariner's Pleasure." It is not unusual for a tavern to have recourse to living advertisements. These girls wander about the city, visit bustling markets, frequent busy thoroughfares, meet incoming ships, and so on.

"It must be pleasant," I said, "to be out of the tavern, passing shops, mingling in crowds, going about in the fresh air and sunlight."

"Very much so," she said, "but one must beware of free women."

"Some carry switches," I said.

"Many do," she said. "Often concealed within their robes."

"I did not know that," I said.

"It is no secret to kajirae," she said.

I heard the ringing of the bar.

"That is the Sixteenth Ahn," I said. "Are you not due back at the Mariner's Pleasure?"

"Today I am assigned to the streets," she said. "I need not be back for another Ahn."

"It will be growing dark," I said.

"I will hurry," she said, "if Master wishes."

"Why would I not wish?" I asked.

"I am not unattractive," she said. "I learned that on the slave block."

"As a free woman," I said, "you were priceless."

"But not as a slave," she said.

"Being sold," I said, "can deflate a woman's vanity, but it may also dispel her diffidence."

Gorean men, and, accordingly, Gorean markets, tend to favor the natural woman. Some women, interestingly enough, discover only on the sales block that they are enormously desirable and truly beautiful.

The incident in the Street of Nicephorus had taken place four days ago. The fear I had entertained, that the fellow who had cast aside his club, and, later, the gaunt man, might quickly return, reinforced with guardsmen or cohorts, had proved groundless. The bodies of both had been found shortly about the turn in the street which led to the small square. After a day of unease, and heightened awareness, I determined that, as far as I could tell, I was no longer under surveillance or, if I was, that those who might be following my movements had no immediate intention of revealing their presence. In short, things were, as far as I could tell, much the same as they had been prior to the recent incident in the Street of Nicephorus.

"Is Master still pursuing his quest, to locate a one-legged man?" she asked.

"Curiosity," I said, "is not becoming to a kajira."

"Nonetheless," she said, "as is well known, we tend to be frightfully curious, habitually so, perhaps even incurably so."

"Perhaps you should tell that to the whip," I said.

"We prefer not to," she said.

I thought her legs were superb.

"I have been about," she said, "but it seems that Master has not much noticed me."

"I have been looking for a one-legged man," I said.

"I thought so," she said.

"There are several kajirae about," I said. "Who pays attention? Who notices them?"

"I think Master commonly manages," she said.

"They are not that rare," I said.

"I suppose," she said, "Master thinks we all look alike."

"No," I said, "but you are all dressed much alike."

"Perhaps Master means," she said, "that we are all undressed much alike."

She had a fetching love cradle, a narrow waist, and a lovely bosom, delicate features, dark hair, and dark eyes. Again I congratulated the slavers who had selected her. Did not such women belong on the block, to be sold, and suitably owned.

"How dared you, a slave, accost a free man?" I asked.

"I did so with great politeness," she said, "and I am now before you, on my knees, as is fitting for one such as I, a slave, before one who is free."

"I did not gesture to you and point to my feet," I said. "I did not clap my hands or snap my fingers. I did not summon you."

"Master knows kajirae are needful," she said. "It is not unusual for them to kneel before a free man, press their lips to his feet, and beg to be caressed."

"I am busy," I said. "Go about your business. Wander about, advertise the wares, of which you are one, available at the Mariner's Pleasure."

"So Master is still searching for the one-legged man," she said.

"Yes," I said.

"And is Master still searching in expensive districts, and such?"

"As you can see, looking about," I said, "I have now broadened my search to areas of less affluence."

"But still rather nice areas," she said. "There are areas in Jad which even a drunken mariner would fear to frequent. Even guardsmen avoid them."

"The man I search for," I said, "would not be in such an area."

"Why?" she asked.

"Because," I said, "for reasons I will not deign to make clear to you, he would be extremely wealthy."

"Are you sure," she asked.

"Of course," I said.

Had not Seremides, himself fearfully proscribed in Ar for complicity in treason, with courage, at great risk to himself, with audacity and brilliance, presumably in the fee of Lurius of Jad, managed to do what hundreds of others could not do, apprehend Talena and deliver her into the power of one with resources capable of delivering her to Ar? For such a service would he not have received some fitting fraction of the considerable wealth soon to be obtained by his grateful principal?

"Then," she said, "he is not your man."

"What do you mean?" I asked sharply.

"That the man I am thinking of is not wealthy."

"What man?" I said.

"One who is missing a leg, the left leg," she said, "from a bit above the knee."

"You have found such a man?" I said, eagerly, lifting her up before me by the arms.

"But he is not wealthy," she said.

"But you have found such a man?" I demanded.

"As you, after seemingly extensive and diligent efforts, could not find him in high districts," she said, "it occurred to me, though I am only a simple and lowly slave, that he might not be in a high district."

"Beware," I said.

"Forgive me, Master," she said.

"How did you find him?" I asked.

"By searching where you did not," she said. "It did take days. Slave girls may go places free women do not; they may ask questions free women will not. They may speak to one another, as free women will seldom do. We know much, we see much. Sometimes I reversed my tunic so that passersby and onlookers would not know that *I* was a girl from the Mariner's Pleasure. Sometimes I dirtied my legs, face, and arms. Sometimes I thought it well to feign a limp and affect a dull, broken speech."

"Why did you do this?" I asked. "Why did you look for him?"

"I sensed the matter was important to Master," she said. "I hoped to be of service to him. Master is holding me very tightly."

"Not here, vulgar, tasteless cad," said a passing free woman. "Take her into an alley."

"I wish," said her companion, a younger free woman, both veiled, "he would take me into an alley."

"Be silent, Catia," snapped the older woman. "If you were a slave, I would whip you for that." She then, seizing her companion by the arm, hurried her away.

I returned Iris to her knees, where, as a slave, she would feel more at ease in a free person's presence.

"You may have done well," I said. "Take me to this person."

"I am due back at the Seventeenth Ahn," she said.

"You have been detained by a free person," I said.

"That sometimes happens," she said.

"Do not dally," I said.

"Master is fierce with interest," she said.

"Tread carefully," I said. "My belt, doubled, may decide to speak to you."

"Master may perhaps wish to hire men," she said.

"Why?" I asked.

"The one-legged man is in the district of Porus," she said.

"Lead me to him," I said.

"I know Master is armed," she said. "I learned that while I was pressed to him. But he is but one man."

"Do not concern yourself with that," I said.

"My arms hurt, where Master held me," she said.

"Do you object?" I asked.

"No," she said. "Master is strong. I am a slave. I want Master to be strong. I want to know he is Master."

"Are you sure you can find the one-legged man?" I asked.

"Yes, Master," she said.

"Get up then," I said, "and lead me to him."

"May I remain a moment more on my knees?" she asked.

I nodded assent.

"I have never forgotten Master," she said. "Since Master first put me to his pleasure, as the slave I am, I have remembered him. I have dreamed of him. I have awakened in my chains, sobbing for him. I would that Master were my master."

"You wish to be purchased?" I asked.

"If it pleases Master," she said.

"Do you seek to bargain?" I asked, angrily.

"No, Master," she said, quickly. "It is only that I do not wish to die."

"I do not understand," I said.

"I sense that there is something deep, dark, and terrible in this matter," she said. "I fear more is involved here than is fit for a poor kajira to know. If I bring you two together, in some complicity, I fear I will know far more than I should know, that I will know what I should not know, what might mean my death. Who knows if I might be trusted with such knowledge? Might it not be safer to cut my throat?"

"You suspect that from the nature of the man you found?" I asked.

"I have met him," she said. "I sense that he is loveless and without honor, that he is fierce and dangerous, that he would think little of killing, even a free person. I think he is bitter, and, like iron, single-minded, astute, and implacable."

"His name," I said, "is Seremides."

"I am afraid," she said.

"Direct me," I said. "You need not accompany me."

"I do not know if I could do so," she said. "I know little of Gorean cities, but, surely, in many districts, Jad is a maze of narrow, crooked, unmarked streets."

"That is common," I said, "even in much of Ar and Turia. In certain districts only citizens are to know the streets. Accordingly, they are often unmarked, and maps are not to be drawn. In some cities, it is a capital offense to draw such a map. In this way, defenders may have an advantage over strangers and intruders."

"A slave has been informed," she said.

"It will be enough," I said, "if you lead me to his vicinity. You may then describe what you remember, and leave me to find my own way."

"Master does not understand," she said. "I am already at risk."

"How so?" I asked.

"I have met him," she said. "He has seen me. He knows me."

"What would you have me do?" I asked.

"I think he would feel more secure," she said, "if you owned me, if I were in your collar. I am then at hand, vulnerable and helpless, and much less likely to reveal a secret."

"Lead me to him," I said.

"Master will then buy me?" she asked.

"I promise nothing," I said.

"Of course," she said. "I am a slave."

"Rise now," I said, "and lead me to him."

"Yes, Master," she said. "I trust that Master will follow at a discreet distance, so that we will not seem to be together. I doubt that Master would care being seen, being led by a slave."

"You will heel me," I said, "informing me from behind where to turn, and so on."

"Yes, Master," she said.

Aside from the Gorean convention or propriety involved, this mode of proceeding had another advantage to commend it to my attention. It should make it easier, on the whole, to protect her.

"Begin," I said.

She rose up and placed herself behind me, on my left, some three or four paces back. In crowds, the slave follows more closely.

"Master may proceed, for a time," she said, "in the direction in which he is facing."

CHAPTER TEN

"I have been waiting for you," he said.

It was hard to see in the darkness, down the narrow corridor, or aisle, but he was seated in a heavy-limbed chair, a stout crutch leaning against the arm. I detected no steel.

"This is the place?" I had asked.

She had nodded, frightened.

"It is a bare, crude, displeasing place," I said, "not even a stand for a lamp above the door."

It was what would prove to be a narrow, dismal, unpainted shed, occupying the space between two nearly adjoining buildings. From the outside, it seemed little more than a door fixed in a framework, between two walls of bricks. There was, as I had noted, no mounting over the door for a lamp. I was not clear, from the street, that it was roofed. For all I knew, there might be, in place of a roof, a tarpaulin or canvas strung inside. It was not unlikely that this place, sometime in the past, had been abandoned.

"You are sure this is the place?" I asked.

"Yes, Master," she whispered.

It was hard to think of the proud, arrogant, aristocratic Seremides, once lofty in Ar, once the First Captain of the Taurentians, even condescending to visit such a place, let alone making it his dwelling. And it was in the district of Porus, surely one of the shabbiest in Jad!

Some aspects of the situation did, however, speak to me of Seremides.

Only one person at a time could pass through the portal. And, given the enclosing buildings, there would be no more than a narrow aisle, or corridor, leading inward, perhaps opening later into a wider space behind the immediately enclosing structures. Such aisles, with their narrow passages, are easy to defend.

Given the narrowness of the street, the height of the buildings, some four stories high, and the Ahn, it was nearly dark.

Even had it been totally dark I would, however, have been reluctant to carry light, a torch or lamp, into the cluttered, labyrinthine, urban snarl of the district of Porus. Light marks one's position.

We had been accosted twice.

The first time, a gangling, long-limbed fellow had begged pathetically for a tarsk-bit.

"Certainly," I had said to him, noting meanwhile that he appeared well fed, healthy, and strong. For such fellows there is ample work in Jad, on a hundred piers and quays. Do not let such fellows close with you. A hook knife can be concealed easily in a forearm sheath, that within a long, wide sleeve such as characterized his tunic. "Simply lie prone before me," I said, "with your legs spread and your arms and hands extended beyond your head." At the same time that I issued this invitation, I smiled pleasantly and brushed back my cloak. He would then have no difficulty seeing the gladius in its sling. He did not wait for his tarsk-bit, but turned and fled away.

The second time, we were briefly impeded in our journey was by two heavily bearded men, armed with swords of seemingly poor balance and quality, who, happily, soon left one in little doubt as to their intentions.

"That is a nice slave," said one of them.

Even inferior weapons, of course, may cut and stab with proficiency.

"She is not mine," I said.

"You took her?" said the other.

"Possibly," I said.

Why not let them speculate that I was as much a brigand as they?

"Give her to us," said the first of the two bearded men.

"And your purse," said the second.

"Come and take them," I said.

One of the two stopped short for, suddenly it must have seemed to him, there was a gladius in my hand. Many individuals succumb to the wiles of the magician whose hands may be doing one thing while his attention seems focused elsewhere. The magician directs you where he wants you to look while busying himself elsewhere, somewhere where it might have been more advisable for you to look. Distraction has its place in war as well as in prestidigitation.

"Their price is steel?" asked the first man.

"Yes," I said.

Few carry a gladius who are not prepared to use it.

"We are two and you are one," said the first man.

"No," I said, "you are three. Do not neglect to count the fellow who is approaching me from the rear."

Iris looked about, and gasped.

"Slave," said I, "if he behind you charges, or approaches more closely, fall to the ground. Thus you will clear a path for my weapon, and, if he approaches too hurriedly, or clumsily, he may trip over you, and my blade will be at the back of his neck."

"The slave and half your purse," said the first man.

"There will be little time," I said. "Accordingly, if I attack first, I will have to make a kill." Then I said over my shoulder, "Slave, keep me apprised of the distance, position, and movements of the man behind me."

"Yes, Master," she said, so softly I could scarcely hear her. If a woman's terror does not burst forth in a scream, it is not unusual for it to impede her speech, reducing her voice to little more than a half-paralyzed whisper.

"The slave," said the first man, "and keep your purse."

"No," I said.

"What is your caste?" asked the second man warily.

"One which I suspect is not yours," I said.

"He is clean-shaven," said the second man.

"So are many men of many castes," I said.

The relevance of this small exchange, if any, had to do with the fact that it is extremely rare for a Gorean warrior to have a beard long enough to be grasped by a foe, a beard by means of which a throat might be jerked to a knife. There are, of course, many varieties of facial hair which do not involve courting that particular hazard. Sometimes, of course, in certain units, presumably in the interests of uniformity, discipline, group appearance, group identification, and such, regulations are imposed governing such matters.

"Master," said Iris, "the man who was behind has withdrawn."

"I thought he might," I said. Then I addressed myself anew to the other two, those who had made their appearance first. "Now it is back to two to one," I said.

The two fellows looked at one another and then both sheathed their weapons. "I wish you well," they said.

"I wish you well," I said.

They then left.

"Keep to the center of the street, behind me," I said to Iris, "be attentive to doors and doorways, and look behind yourself frequently."

"Perhaps we should have waited until morning," she said.

"Time is important," I said, "and you might not have been put into the street in the morning."

"Yes, Master," she moaned.

"There is a turn here," I said. "Do we take it?"

"No, Master," she said, "we continue on."

Something like half an Ahn later we had arrived at the unusual door, that which Iris would identify as, and would confirm for me was, the portal to the domicile of Seremides.

"The door is ajar," I said.

"I do not understand that," she said.

"Beware an easy entrance," I said.

"You suspect a trap?" she said.

"If larls had doors on their dens," I said, "they would never lock them."

"Then do not enter," she begged.

I unsheathed the gladius and, with one foot, thrust the door open.

Followed by Iris, I had then entered.

"I have been waiting for you," he said.

It was hard to see in the darkness, down the narrow corridor, or aisle, but he was seated in a heavy-limbed chair, a stout crutch leaning against the arm. I detected no steel.

He lit a small tharlarion-oil lamp.

"Have you come to kill me?" he asked.

"No," I said.

"I thought not," he said. "Let us talk."

CHAPTER ELEVEN

"Is the slave yours?" inquired Seremides.

"No," I said.

"Then you cannot rely on her," said Seremides. "Bind her, hand and foot. We can kill her later."

"Master!" she protested.

"You were not given permission to speak," I told her.

"Forgive me, Master," she whispered.

I crossed her ankles and lashed them together.

"We would not want her to race off, would we?" said Seremides.

When a slave is in your collar, she is yours, wholly. Where can she run, but back to your chains?

"No," said Seremides, "not with her hands before her, but behind her."

I put the slave's wrists, crossed, behind her, and tied them together. This is common in binding a slave. So tied, she is far more aware of her helplessness and vulnerability. Too, in this fashion she cannot fend a blow or impede a caress.

I often tied my slaves in this fashion.

It pleased me to see them so.

"Now, put her aside," said Seremides.

I then placed Iris on her left side, a bit behind me and to my left. She would remain that way, bound and helpless, until men might please to free her.

I retrieved my sword, and returned it to its sling.

"You were a fool," said Seremides, "to leave the lovely Talena at risk in Port Kar, rushing off to inquire into the ruse of the false, marauding Bosk of Port Kar."

"I was outplayed," I said. "But I had no choice."

"Honor is a trap and fetter," said Seremides. "It limits one's options."

"It is the difference between men and urts," I said.

"Would that all my foes were honorable," said Seremides.

"But they are not," I said.

"No," said Seremides, angrily.

My hand moved toward my sword, inadvertently, but then I drew it back.

"How is it," I asked, "that the brilliant Seremides, swift with the blade, formidable in war, marvelous in strategy, captor of the fugitive Ubara, Talena, resides in a hovel, alone, limited in resources, seemingly destitute?"

"Destitute," he said.

"I do not understand this," I said. "It was you, of all the bounty hunters, who were successful. You pursued Talena relentlessly. A sleen, so tenacious in tracking, might have been shamed to compare itself with you. You generously expended time and effort. You courted danger. Yours were the months of seeking, even at the World's End. Yours were the labors, the risks, and perils, and the final triumph, the capture of Talena, and now I find you here, so reduced."

"In squalor, in rags, half starved," he said. "I have fed on garbage, I have begged for a tarsk-bit."

"You should be rich," I said, "rich beyond dreams of richness, resident in a great house, the master of enterprises, served by a thousand slaves."

"I was betrayed," he said.

"Lurius of Jad," I said.

"Yes," he said, "glorious Lurius of Jad, gross Lurius of Jad, the deceitful urt, the lying ost, the hypocritical, deceitful sleen, the pompous, treacherous, bloated tharlarion!"

"Beware your speech," I said. "Such language could bring you to impalement in Cos."

"As it has others," he snarled.

"You had had need of Lurius of Jad?" I asked.

"Of course," he said. "I needed his gold, and support. Look at me! I am a cripple! Men mock me. Who takes a man with one leg seriously? And I am a fugitive myself, wanted for treason, proscribed in Ar. How could I bring Talena to Ar without, at the same time, surrendering myself to its dreadful justice? I even needed a ship to bring Talena to Jad."

"She came with you willingly?" I said.

"Certainly," he said. "I could not carry her off. I had no men, no ships! She viewed me gratefully, seeing in me her savior, her rescuer. She thought herself to be delivered into the sheltering care of a former ally, dear Lurius of Jad. She expected to be received with honor and acclaim. She may still expect it."

"Talena is somewhere in Cos, perhaps here, in Jad?" I asked.

"I think so," said Seremides. "I am no longer privy to the machinations of the glorious Ubar of Cos."

As no word of Talena's leaving Cos or arriving in Ar had been received in Port Kar, I had suspected that she might still be in Jad.

"As the reward for the delivery of Talena to Ar is fabulous," I said, "enough to build fleets and field armies, I had expected you to be rich."

"I had been promised ten percent of the reward," he said, "and refuge in Cos."

"You are living proof of the duplicity of Lurius," I said. "I am surprised that you are still alive."

"Lurius, I think, fears he might still have need of me," he said.

"How so?" I asked.

"There are many subtleties in this matter," he said. "How is Talena to be brought to Ar? Do you think this is simple? The reward stands, regardless of who brings her to Ar. The tarns of acquisition and greed will spread their wings in a hundred places. It might require an army to safeguard her transport to Ar, and armies might meet armies. Borders would have to be crossed, and crossings might be refused or grievously tolled. Men who seek grounds for war seldom fail to find them."

"Transport her secretly," I said, "by unimposing vessels to the continental coast, and from thence by enclosed wagons, or flighted tarns."

"Few secrets can hide from gold," he said.

I was silent.

"Much planning is necessary," said Seremides. "How is the reward, if secured, to be brought back safely to Cos?"

"Let Cos concern herself with that problem," I said.

"Have no doubt she has," said Seremides.

"Much, it seems, is involved in these matters," I said.

"That is why," said Seremides, "I think it likely that Talena is still in Cos."

"But she may be already on her way to Ar," I said.

"That is possible," he said.

I clenched my fists in futility.

"Once I succeeded in bringing Talena from Port Kar to Jad," he said, "of which deed you would doubtless be informed, I expected you to pursue me, to exact vengeance, to hunt me down and kill me."

"A conjecture not without plausibility," I said.

"Do you know a man named Xenon?" he asked.

The bound slave uttered a tiny, inadvertent gasp.

"No," I said.

"The worthless slave does," he said.

"And whom might Xenon be?" I asked.

"He is one of the door guards employed at the Mariner's Pleasure."

"Ah," I said.

"I set him to watch for one such as you," he said.

"I think I know the man," I said.

"In the prosecution of your inquiries, it was almost certain you would visit one of Jad's foremost taverns."

"Assuredly," I said.

"He was an oarsman on the vessel which brought Talena and myself to Jad," he said. "On board he accidentally brushed the tunic of Talena and was to be cast into the sea. He was spared by my intervention. It was thought at that time that I was in high favor with Lurius of Jad. But he could no longer row for Cos. It was easy for me at that time to find him a position at the Mariner's Pleasure. Thus I posted my first, and last, spy."

"I take it he served you well," I said.

"And does so even now," he said.

"Despite the reduction in your fortunes," I said.

"Only an oarsman and a door guard, he remains grateful, attentive, and loyal."

"There are such men," I said. "Debts are involved, and the payment of debts, and honor."

"I find him useful," said Seremides.

"I have long searched for you in Jad," I said.

"Unsuccessfully," he said.

"And it was you," I said, "who hired killers to murder me, their attempt failing in the Street of Nicephorus."

"Not at all," he said. "Your inquiries pertaining to me aroused the curiosity of the secret police, in particular that of Cepheus of Jad, who interpreted his charge to promote the welfare of the state much as he pleased, especially in the case of individuals suspected of possessing a deep purse."

"Cepheus of Jad," I said, "was an angular fellow, narrow of body, and gaunt of feature?"

"Yes," said Seremides.

"After some brief business of the blade," I said, "I found him, and one who had earlier fled, dead on the Street of Nicephorus, where it empties down into a small square, in which one finds several odds tables."

"The Square of Troubled Fortunes," said Seremides.

"One," I said, "he first fled, was slain by a single thrust to the heart. He whom I gather was Cepheus had been slain by a heavy blow. The side of his head was crushed in."

"I know," said Seremides. "I killed them, the first by a single thrust into a terrified, unsuspecting, racing body, the second by a blow of my crutch."

"You labored on my behalf," I said.

"So to speak," said Seremides. "I did not think you were in danger from murderous amateurs. The danger was that one or more might escape, and by nightfall you would be a wanted man in all Jad."

"Would this not have been in your best interest?" I asked.

"No," said Seremides. "Your inquiries pertaining to me, looked into by Xenon, did not suggest a murderous rage, or a ravening thirst for my blood at any cost, so much as an access to information which I might possess."

"You gambled," I said.

"Sometimes one must," he said.

"How did you know of the interest which Cepheus might have had in me?"

"From Xenon," he said, "even from the morning you left the Mariner's Pleasure."

"How is it that you knew of the Street of Nicephorus?" I asked. "How is it that you were in its vicinity?"

"It is where Cepheus made his killings," he said. "Surely you saw the blood stains."

"It seems you may have saved my life," I said.

"At least," he said, "I hope that I saved you the inconvenience and hazards of being hunted like an urt, sought by every guardsman and informer in Jad."

"You seem to have no information of value to me," I said. "Why should I not kill you?"

"You are trammeled by honor," he said.

"Perhaps I know of your sword," I said. "I know you are formidable. Perhaps I would not care to cross blades with you."

"Do not insult me by pitying me," he said. "Even now, crippled as I am, I could best most men with the blade. Once, when whole, I might have presented even you with fine contest. I do not flatter myself I could do so now."

"A knife in the back might do," I said.

"I think we might prove of use to one another," he said.

"How so?" I asked.

"We are both interested in acquiring Talena, are we not?" he said.

"Yes," I said.

"You were holding Talena in Port Kar," he said, "pending her practical, timely delivery to Ar for the reward."

"Possibly," I said.

"You want her for gold," he said. "I want her for gold, and vengeance on Lurius of Jad."

"Does honor enter into this?" I asked.

"Neither for you nor for me," he said. "You do not share a Home Stone with her. You owe her nothing. She is wanted in Ar for treason. One flighted quarrel penetrates two targets. Bring her to justice, a traitress and a sought criminal, and fill a room with gold."

"Your words are weighty," I said, "and your proposition glows."

"Like gold?" he said.

"Yes, like gold," I said.

"Fate enleagues us," said Seremides. "It is your quickness and your sword. It is my cunning, and my knowledge of Cos, of intrigue, and the mind of Lurius of Jad."

"What if I betrayed you?" I asked.

"You would not do so," he said.

"But you might betray me," I said.

"Of course," he said, "and without compunction."

"We do not even know the location of Talena," I said.

"Few do," said Seremides. "But one needs only find one who does."

"You must be clothed and fed," I said, "and brought to better quarters."

"Somewhere near the citadel," he said.

"Excellent," I said.

"You are aware, I trust, that we are not the only ones interested in these matters," he said.

"I would suppose not," I said. "There must be many such. Surely there must remain hopeful, persistent bounty hunters, brigands and bandits unwilling to forget gold, reluctant to admit defeat, men unreconciled to the triumph of Cos, men willing to row swift ships, to swarm upon caravans, to watch the skies for wide-winged tarns."

"Common men?" he said.

"Of course," I said.

"I fear competitors even more fearful," he said. "In the marshes of the Vosk, months ago, I learned of the interest of Pa-Kur, Master of the Assassins, in these matters, and that of a great metal tharlarion from which speech issued."

"The metal tharlarion," I said, "is not a creature. It is the housing of a brain, the brain of a mighty beast, a Kur."

"Are you dissuaded," he asked. "Do such considerations detain you?"

"I shall arrange lodgings in the morning," I said.

"I was contemplating having Xenon contact you on my behalf," he said. "But it proved unnecessary. A slave discovered my abode."

I looked back at Iris, lying a bit behind me, bound hand and foot.

"What of the slave?" I asked.

"Cut her throat," said Seremides.

I stifled her scream, forcibly, with the palm of my hand. Her eyes were wide, and wild, over my hand, like lakes of terror. She squirmed, violently, helplessly.

"She has heard too much, she knows too much," said Seremides.

"One does not kill slaves," I said. "One puts them to use. They are better utilized as work beasts and love beasts, collared, chained beasts at one's feet, from whom one derives enormities of gratification, immensities of inordinate pleasure."

"Kill her," he said.

"No," I said.

"You must either kill her or buy her," he said.

"I will buy her," I said.

I removed my hand from the slave's mouth, and she, helplessly bound, shaking and sobbing, tears in her eyes, thrust her mouth to my hand, licking it and covering it with grateful kisses.

CHAPTER TWELVE

"Can you feign an accent of Ar?" inquired Seremides.

"I need not do so," I said. "I need only be convincing as one whom Ar might plausibly send to effect the confidential mission in question."

Seremides leaned backward in his large chair of stained, polished tur-wood. From such a chair it was easier for him to rise. The massive crutch was resting against the arm of the chair. There was little resemblance between the sleek, rested, barbered, bathed, expensively clad, thoughtful figure before me now and the wretched, starving, unkempt derelict I had encountered six days before in the District of Porus. He pulled a little at his now-trimmed, sharp-edged, dark beard, and adjusted the folds of his golden robe. "You may be right, dear colleague," said he. "Ar might well be reluctant to send a ranking officer or a notable citizen to confirm the identity of Talena."

From the broad porch of the apartment, one could see the double walls of the citadel of Jad on its lofty crag, overlooking the harbor. The day was lovely. The sky was a bright blue and small, fresh white clouds scurried westward, little noting or caring, one supposed, what might lie below. One speaks of the "citadel," but, in this case, this refers not to a particular building, fortress, or such, but to a walled, fortified area containing several buildings, including barracks and warehouses. Indeed, within the walls of the "citadel," as mentioned earlier, one may find the Ubarial palace itself.

"I would think," I said, "given the desire for secrecy, they would prefer to send one unlikely to be suspected of such a mission."

"No," said Seremides, "one would not wish to inform the world of the location of Talena."

"Your ruse was brilliant," I said, "and may bear fruit."

"Let doubt torment Lurius of Jad," smiled Seremides.

"He who betrays," I said, "may well fear betrayal."

We had spread, through the taverns and markets, a contrived rumor, which seemingly had swept the city within three or four Ahn, that Lurius of Jad had thought to acquire the elusive Talena of Ar but had been duped, having been supplied with a false Talena, by his supposed agent, a one-legged man going under the name of Bruno of Torcadino. Interestingly, an emphatic denial of this rumor was issued almost immediately by the palace. It claimed that Talena was not now in Jad, and had never been in Jad, and that the Ubar knew nothing of these matters, that he had never sought to entertain his former, valued ally, and that he had no interest in doing so. This response appeared on the public boards and was also broadcast throughout the city by public criers, for many Goreans, particularly of the lower castes, do not read.

The prompt, forceful, and vast nature of this response to our rumor convinced us, Seremides and myself, first, that it was highly likely that Talena was still in Jad, and that Lurius, who had never met or even seen Talena, must be almost beside himself, torturing himself with the suspicion that he had been tricked, that he, the Ubar himself, was the victim of an excruciatingly humiliating hoax.

"Even before our rumor," said Seremides, "before risking the transportation of Talena to Ar, which may be expensive and difficult, it is likely that Lurius will have sent to Ar for a plenipotentiary to confirm the identity of his prisoner, to confer as to the nature of her delivery to Ar, and to arrange for the payment of, and possible delivery of, the reward."

"Such an agent," I said, "may be already on his way to Cos."

"Thus," said Seremides, "time is short."

"Too," I said, "as Lurius is no common bounty hunter, but the ruler of the most powerful maritime Ubarate on Gor, Ar herself might wish to ascertain the identity of his prisoner before she is brought to Ar, lest a distasteful political incident be precipitated."

"And thus the interests of Ar and Cos coincide."

"You have arranged with uncritical scribes, noble fellows of easy virtue," I said, "to invent plausible documentation to substantiate the identity of such an agent empowered by Ar?"

"The papers and seals should be delivered by nightfall," he said.

"You were extremely courageous," I said, "to have manufactured the rumor of so grievous a hoax. Lurius, racked with doubt, and ready to kill, will be zealous to apprehend you. The secret police must be scouring the city for you."

"I told you Lurius might yet have need of me," he said.

"I went yesterday to your former abode in the District of Porus," I said. "It is gone. It is as though it had never been. Not a plank, latch, knob, stick or nail remains."

The search for Seremides, of course, was being conducted secretly. Lurius, who had publicly disclaimed any shred of plausibility to the rumor, could not address the matter openly.

"If I should see fit," said Seremides, "I can, on any day, at any Ahn, make contact with our glorious, beloved Lurius. In the meantime I think our precautions to conceal my presence are sufficient."

These precautions were various. When Seremides sat in his large chair, his crutch hidden away, his lower body covered with a sheet or blanket, his missing leg was concealed. He could pass easily as an invalid or someone somehow ill or infirm. Itinerant barbers, tradesmen, and merchants would see him so. Outside the apartment he was borne, as many seemingly rich men, in a rented palanquin with its hired bearers. I conducted most business. Our marketing was done primarily by Iris. We gave out to the few who were aware of his presence that he was an affluent recluse, one jealous of his privacy. Another factor accruing to our advantage was the opposite of the premise which had governed my original search for him. I had thought him rich and so had sought him in environments condign to that premise. Now, Lurius and the police, believing him reduced and destitute, were seeking him wholly, or largely, in the poorer, shabbier districts of the city, such as the District of Porus.

I heard an arranged knock on the door, four carefully spaced blows, followed by two quick blows. It was not Xenon, whose life Seremides had saved on the voyage from the Skerry of Lars, near Port Kar, to Jad. Xenon occasionally brought us news, largely picked up in the Mariner's Pleasure, and assisted in diverse tasks. We were particularly interested in the arrival of unfamiliar ships from Brundisium or the departure of state ships for that port. It seemed almost certain that Brundisium would be the likely port of interest if Ar and Cos would wish to communicate with one another. Beyond Brundisium lay the long overland routes to Ar, many of which were dangerous to traverse, even in well-armed caravans. Xenon might also be relied on to deal with sensitive errands. It was he who, for example, had been charged with contacting certain low scribes in connection with preparing forged credentials for a supposed envoy of Ar to Cos, credentials prepared in accordance with the specifications of Seremides. It had been four spaced blows at the door, followed by two swift blows. There are six letters in the Gorean spelling of "kajira."

Passwords, signals, and such, are seldom secure. Such arrangements may be overheard, betrayed, obtained by stealth, by theft, by torture, and so on.

I loosened my sword, and then called, "Enter."

Iris, carrying a canvas sack, entered, smiled, and knelt. Then, seeing that she might rise, she got up and went to a tin at the side, into which she placed four small platelike loaves of bread, a roll of cheese, a cup of olives, and two larmas. After this she returned to kneel again before us. "A slave waits to be commanded," she said.

"Speak," I said.

"I have little to speak of," she said. "As in the last few days, as instructed, I approached various kajirae, hopefully from the citadel."

One advantage of our present location was its nearness to the citadel, and, presumably, thereby, access to various slaves or servants
from within the citadel who might know of, or be capable of sur-
mising intelligently about, items we might find of interest, unusual
visitors, prisoners, guests, or such. As nearly as we could determine
from Iris's reports, there was not even a reluctance, or fear, to be
questioned about such topics. Seremides, who, from his duties in the
Central Cylinder of Ar, during Talena's time on the throne, had been
present at numerous suppers, feasts, state banquets, and such, had
even supplied Iris with a list of delicacies savored by Talena. Were
these being ordered from the citadel or being delivered to the citadel? But it seemed not. At the beginning, before we had generated
the rumor of a false Talena, Seremides, well clad, had even conducted
such inquiries himself, as many in the citadel at the time took it that
he was still in the Ubarial favor.

"But," said Iris, "as before, I received few responses which would
be germane to the interests of masters."

I regarded Iris.

I had paid a silver tarsk for her, the sale arranged discreetly
through Xenon. That price, more than many a Gorean would care
to pay, is a not uncommon price for a paga girl, many of whom are
originally purchased by the tavern, sometimes in lots, for several
copper tarsks. In this way the house usually makes a profit on the
girl and can regularly introduce new girls into its stock, a practice
which appeals to certain customers. The girl commonly rejoices to
be free of the tavern. Most girls hope to be the single slave of a
private master.

"You may speak further, if you wish," I said. It was my impression
that few kajirae savored silence. Few things so impress a girl's slavery
upon her as not being allowed to speak. For my part, I generally
enjoyed listening to women, slave or free. A woman is commonly not
only good at speaking, but enjoys speaking and finds it delightful to
do so. It is no wonder it is a pleasure to listen to them. For example,
what man would not enjoy chatting with a highly intelligent,
animate, half-naked, collared slave kneeling at one's feet, her leash in
your hand, particularly when you may, by a word or glance, to her
frustration, close her lovely lips, silencing her, reminding her that
she is naught but a slave.

"I, for one, however, do not care," said Seremides, "to hear of
Chloe's new tunic, that Tessa's mistress is having an affair with Alessandro of Telnar, that the widths of talmits are increasing or decreas-
ing, that hemlines are going up or down, that Cora may or may not
be given sandals, and so on."

"Kajirae find such things of interest," I said.

"I am aware," said Iris, "that masters may find such things less than noteworthy."

Most men, however, I supposed, did note hemlines. How could one not notice such things?

Iris was in a rather conservative tunic, brown and relatively modest. I do not think she really approved of this, as she was quite attractive, and had learned on Gor not only to be content with her body, but pleased with it, but I did not want her to be overly noticed in the streets. Let our small household be inconspicuous. To be in plain sight but not much noticed is much the same as being invisible.

Similarly she was nicely but not ostentatiously collared. The slave band was typical, flat, light but sturdy, efficient, close-fitting, comfortable, and attractive. Most girls find their collars a lovely accessory, except, of course, that they cannot remove them. Many women do not realize how exciting, how female, and beautiful, they are, until they see themselves in a collar. The lock, as usual, was at the back of the neck. The inscription read, "I am the property of Harold of Skjern," the collar thus providing a name which would not lead one to expect an accent of either Ar or Cos, and making a reference to a town remote enough to be unfamiliar, one about which I was not likely to entertain many questions.

"Did you see anything interesting, or different or unusual, in the streets?" I asked.

"I saw something I did not understand," she said, "two men, strangers one supposes, men in somber garments, in garb bespeaking no caste, each with two yellow cords in his belt, who engaged bystanders, passersby, and even loiterers."

"They are Tharnans," said Seremides. "This can be told by the two yellow cords."

"Do you know of Tharna?" I asked.

"No, Master," she said.

"Did you overhear their inquiries, their conversation?" I asked.

"No, Master," she said. "I feared to approach closely."

"Why?" I asked.

"I am a slave," she said. "I feared the two yellow cords."

"I know their interest," said Seremides. "Long ago an infant male child was stolen from the royal household of Tharna. For several years Tharna has sought for traces of the child, the search becoming more hopeless with each year."

"Pairs of such men are encountered variously," I said, "in towns, villages, and cities, on market islands and along trade routes, as far north as Torvaldsland, as far south as Turia, Bazi, and Schendi."

"For years they have quested," said Seremides, "fruitlessly, always fruitlessly. They are fools."

"Tharna," I said, "was once a typical Gorean city, but, over time, free women, seeking power by various means, the indoctrination of the young, the application of rhetorics, the shaping of values, the utilization of convenient devices such as humiliation, guilt, and shame, induced many men to disarm and deny themselves, to fear and reject masculinity, to divest themselves of manhood, to foreswear and repudiate their blood and very nature. Tharna became a gynocracy. But men, like urts and verr, like tarns and larls, have a nature. They are not malleable clods of formless clay which may be shaped into any eccentric form preferred by those who hold the reins of the state, by the unseen engineers of society. Eventually, men, sickened by self-denial, unwilling to tolerate an outlawed manhood, deciding to discover themselves, deciding to grow and flourish without trammel, revolted. The gynocracy, gradually and subtly wrought, inch by inch, over generations, was suddenly and violently overthrown."

"Today," said Seremides, "there is only one free woman in Tharna, Lara, her Tatrix."

"I think I now understand the meaning of the two short, yellow cords in the belts of the strangers," said Iris, shuddering.

"Did you see or hear anything else which might have been interesting, or different, in the streets?" I asked.

"I heard," she said, "that a cousin of Lurius, Myron, the polemarkos of Temos, is now in Jad."

Seremides and I exchanged sudden, meaningful glances.

Myron, the polemarkos of Temos, in Cos, sometimes spoken of simply as the polemarkos of Cos, was the master general of the land forces of Cos.

"I know him from Ar, and the Occupation," said Seremides. Seremides himself, incidentally, had originally come from Temos, on Cos.

"Events move," I said. "Change is afoot."

"Talena is in Ar," said Seremides.

Presumably the services of Myron and his men would be enlisted in attempting to move Talena from somewhere on the continental coast overland to Ar.

"There is one other thing," said Iris, "but I do not know if it is significant or not."

"Speak," I said.

"One of the central piers in the harbor," she said, "is being festooned with ribbons and banners."

"Then soon with flowers," said Seremides.

"Lurius is preparing a welcome for the agent from Ar," I said.

"Undoubtedly," said Seremides.

"Thus, indeed," I said, "there is little time."

"I fear very little," said Seremides.

At that moment there was a knock on the door.

"That," said Seremides, "will be the papers I ordered, the forged credentials, seemingly bearing the seal of Ar."

"I hope," I said, "the scribes have done well."

"You had best hope so," said Seremides, "for your life depends on it."

CHAPTER THIRTEEN

"These credentials," said the taller scribe, bending over the papers strewn on the desk before him, "seem in order."

"They are in order," I said. "Can you not recognize the high seal of Ar?"

I trusted that he had never seen the high seal of Ar.

"It is only," said a shorter scribe, whose robes were of a darker blue, "we expected the envoy of Ar to be somewhat different."

"How so?" I demanded.

"We do not think you are of Ar," said the shorter scribe.

"I am not of Ar," I said. "I am Harold of Skjern, in the employ of Ar. This matter is delicate. It demands the utmost secrecy. Do you truly think that Marlenus, Ubar of Ar, is such a fool as to dispatch some obvious citizen of Ar, with his accent and rank, on so sensitive a mission? Do you wish to attract the attention of every bounty hunter, thief, and rogue on Gor to the palace of our beloved and glorious Lurius, the wise, compassionate, and noble ruler of Cos? Cry 'No!' to such an absurdity."

I addressed myself primarily to the scribes, but I spoke largely for the benefit of the tall, brush-bearded figure, in a dark cloak, who stood nearby, but somewhat in the shadows, away from the light of the small tharlarion-oil lamp.

"It is late," said the taller scribe.

"Would you have had me appear publicly, at the Tenth Ahn, bearing a standard of Ar, preceded by trumpets and drums?"

"No, no," said the taller scribe.

"But yet you decked a pier with banners and ribbons," I said.

"To welcome you," said the taller scribe, "but your mission was to be given out as one of establishing and securing an overland trade route to Ar. Your true purpose in Jad was to be kept secret."

"Trade routes already exist," I said, "if you have the courage to use them. And does any informed person truly believe Cos will commit dozens of regiments of men to the wilderness, to guard thousands of pasangs of roads through treacherous and inhospitable territories infested with rogues, brigands, and bandits? And would you at the same time lay the cities of Cos open to the depredations of Port Kar and the mercies of the rovers of Torvaldsland?"

"That would be dreadful," said the taller scribe.

"And you would hope to keep secret the true mission of the emissary from Ar by so crude a ruse as a public display and the manufacture of a laughably false explanation for his presence in Jad?"

"What the public is told to believe the public will believe," said the taller scribe.

"Or pretend to believe," I said.

"It seemed that a public welcome, a proclaimed pretext, and a well-kept secret, was less perilous than a clandestine reception which might be discovered, to the embarrassment of the Ubar," said the shorter scribe.

"Do not try to hide a secret in such a way," I said. "Endeavor rather to hide the light of Tor-tu-Gor at the Tenth Ahn."

I had the sense that the tall, brush-bearded, cloaked figure in the shadows might himself have had reservations pertaining to the open welcoming of a diplomat or delegation from the dreaded, hostile polity of Ar.

"Perhaps we were not as judicious as we might have been, in matters of security," said the taller scribe.

"You were not," I said. "You have not even asked me for the password, to ascertain that I am truly the emissary from Ar!" Had such a password been in existence, I trusted that it would have been requested by now.

"Password?" said the taller scribe.

"The one arranged long ago," I said. "'The tarn is absent' responded to by 'The tabuk is pleased.'"

"Yes, that is it!" said the taller scribe. "Forgive us, for omitting it."

I then strode to the table on which lay my supposed credentials and the small tharlarion-oil lamp. "And here," I said, jabbing my finger at the bottom of one of the sheets of parchment, "I suppose you do not recognize the signature of Marlenus, glorious Marlenus, Ubar of Ar!"

"Forgive us," said the taller scribe.

It was surely unlikely that anyone in Jad would know the signature of Marlenus.

I thought the scribe who had prepared the credentials had done a fine job. The signature seemed surely the signature of a Ubar, large, thick, heavy, bold, forceful, proud, commanding, magnificent, decisive, and so on.

"You recognize it, do you not?" I said.

"Yes, yes, of course," said the taller scribe.

"Good," I said, angrily.

"Forgive our hesitation, our surprise, our confusion," said the taller scribe. "We were unprepared for you. We expected a different sort of individual, one who would appear in a different manner, one who would present himself otherwise."

"I was landed secretly, discreetly, south of Jad," I said, "that my presence not be noted. Take me instantly into the presence of Lurius of Jad. I have important business to transact. I do not care to deal with menials."

"There are no menials here," said the figure in the shadows, speaking for the first time. "You deal with high scribes, loyal, trusted servitors. The Ubar does not care to involve himself personally in this matter. I am authorized to represent him, and speak for him."

"I am of the Scarlet Caste," I said.

"I, too," he said.

"May I lift the lamp?" I asked.

"Do so," he said.

I lifted the lamp with my left hand, and then, with the palm of my right hand, struck my left shoulder.

He repeated this gesture sharply.

"You know me?" he asked.

"I have seen you before," I said, "but only at a distance, long ago in Ar, in the time of the liberation of Ar by the forces of Cos, Tyros, and pledged adherents, when many in Ar feared that the city would be sacked and the citizenry put to the sword, that the walls of Ar would soon roar with a cauldron of flame. But then, when all seemed lost, you, in your magnanimity, spared Ar, placing on the throne the noble and beautiful Talena of Ar herself, to rule with kindness, justice, and mercy."

"I do not know you," he said.

"I was then but a lowly guard," I said.

"You can recognize Talena?" he said.

"As if she were once my own companion," I said.

"We shall see," he said. "Follow me."

I then fell into step behind Myron, polemarkos of Temos, high general of the land forces of Cos.

As I left the chamber, I passed the shorter of the two scribes, he of the darker blue robes, that suggesting a certain priority in his caste. He was looking at me, and, about the corners of his mouth, there seemed a small smile.

CHAPTER FOURTEEN

Myron, the polemarkos, and I, in a sense caste brothers, trod a long corridor, two levels below the ground level of the palace where, in a small, private scribal office, I had presented my credentials. Occasionally we encountered gates with doubled guards, through which, after a brief exchange of signs and countersigns, we passed.

"During the Occupation of Ar," I said, "did you not acquire the former Claudia Tentia Hinrabia, the daughter of the former Administrator of Ar, Minus Tentia Hinrabius, as a slave?"

I recalled the slender, dark-haired beauty, so lofty in the society of Ar, who had been a critic of Talena, and something of a rival in beauty to her.

"Talena, as Ubara, had her enslaved," he said, "and at a state supper she had her dance before me, naked in a collar. I found her pleasing and so I threw my sword to the tiles. It muchly pleased the Ubara to see her former critic and rival on her belly licking the sword to which she might easily be put, and then crawling to my feet, terrified, covering my sandals with kisses, begging to be found pleasing."

"Excellent," I said.

"I have her still," he said. "In her belly there is a flaming slave, devoted, loving, and needful."

"Many women find love in the collar," I said.

"Keep them in it," he said. "In the collar they thrive."

We continued on a bit.

"In those days," he said, "it was easy in Ar to take what women one wished for slaves."

"Women of the enemy have always been the booty of the conqueror," I said.

"Needless to say," he said, "we are muchly concerned to identify Talena."

"Particularly, I gather," I said, "in the light of certain rumors."

"To speak frankly," he said, "the Ubar is concerned."

Along the corridor there were a number of barred doors.

"I think we have Talena," said Myron, "but you can clarify the matter."

"I will be pleased to do so," I said, "one way or the other."

"Much more is involved in this matter," he said, "than you perhaps realize."

"Oh?" I said.

"It will not be an easy matter to bring Talena to Ar," he said. "How is one to drag fresh meat through a country of ravening sleen, how convey a tabuk doe safely through a hundred gantlets of starving larls?"

"How do you propose to do so?" I asked.

He looked at me sharply.

"Forgive me," I said.

"Tyros," said he, "is our nominal ally. But Chenbar, the Sea Sleen, no rejector of gold himself, and wary of the ambitions of Lurius, has, in effect, blockaded Cos. Hundreds of his vessels stop our shipping under the pretext of seizing deserters from the navy of Tyros. But they search, doubtless, for Talena."

"I did not know that," I said.

"If we depart in force," he said, "we would risk war with Tyros and, at the least, signal Talena's likely presence and position. Too, one might even risk losing her at sea. Marlenus does not want a dead Talena."

"That would deny him the tortures of legal revenge," I said.

"We stop here," he said. He then withdrew a mask from his wallet. "Mask yourself," he said. "Your identity is to remain secret. Talena is not to identify our informant. We may need him again later."

I donned and adjusted the mask. It covered one's entire face.

He then unlocked and opened a heavy door.

"Enter," he said.

CHAPTER FIFTEEN

The woman had her back to us. Then she spun about to face us.

"Remove your veil," said Myron, polemarkos of Temos.

She did so.

"That is not Talena of Ar," I said. "It seems, indeed, that your noble Lurius has been lamentably, tragically deceived."

"We know she is not Talena," said Myron. "We did not know you would know that."

Then he said, "Forgive us, Lady," and we withdrew from the chamber.

"This woman, too," I said, "is not Talena."

"Let us try another," said Myron.

"No," I said.

"Very well," said Myron.

"No," I said. "Do you mock my mission?"

"Not at all," he said. "But we choose to move carefully in this matter. Please forgive us. Much, as you must understand, is at stake."

"Undoubtedly," I said.

"The next woman resists unveiling," he said. "She is haughty and proud. She is a veritable she-sleen of vanity and arrogance."

"Some, I fear," I said, "have so construed the noble Talena of Ar." I recalled Talena, so impatient, so quick to order the whipping of slaves, so jealous of the beauty of other women, so ready to profit from the spoils of a defeated, prostrate Ar, Talena who had mocked me when I had been crippled, and chairbound, unable to rise to my feet, from the slash of a poisoned sword in Torvaldsland.

"This way," said Myron, polemarkos of Temos.

"Why should I unveil myself in the presence of an anonymous, masked intruder?" inquired the woman fiercely.

"Forgive us, Lady," said Myron, "but we must ascertain your identity, unmistakably, before we can welcome you publicly to Jad, and celebrate your escape from harrowing distress and your late, safe arrival amongst loving friends and loyal allies."

"Have the buffoon with you unmask himself first," she demanded.

"He is a confidential emissary from Ar engaged in a most secret and sensitive mission," said Myron. "His identity, at present, must be as closed to public scrutiny as your own."

"Very well," she said, angrily, and reached to unpin the house veil which obscured her features.

"No," I said, lifting my hand, slightly, "that will not be necessary."

"You recognize her then, even veiled, as the glorious Ubara, Talena?" said Myron.

I faced the woman, and then without warning, suddenly snapped, "Lesha!"

Immediately, reflexively, automatically, without thought, with a tiny cry of misery, she straightened her body, flung her wrists, crossed, behind her, and threw her head up and back. Had she been tunicked it would have been convenient then to bracelet her instantly, helplessly, and snap a slave leash about her neck.

"Forgive me, Master, forgive me, Master," she wept, and, tearing her hood and veils away, she threw herself to her belly, in full prostration, before Myron and, clutching his ankles, pressed her lips to his feet.

"Do not punish her," I said. "She did well."

"Still," said Myron, "she spoke to you in a way unfitting for a slave to a free man."

"For a slave, yes," I said, "but surely not for a free woman, whose role she had undoubtedly been told to assume."

"How did you know she was not Talena of Ar?" asked Myron.

"Instantly, from the voice," I said.

"It seems then," he said, "you are indeed familiar with Talena of Ar."

"Were I not," I said, "I would not have been entrusted with this mission."

"You tested," he said, "to see if she were a slave."

"No," I said, "I knew she was a slave. I merely wished her to show herself as the slave she was."

"How did you know?" he asked.

"The betraying femininity of certain of her movements," I said.

"Of course," said Myron.

The female slave is the most feminine of all women. The collar brings out the softness, and submissiveness, the marvelous femininity, the underlying, precious, fundamental nature of its owned, helpless, vulnerable occupant.

Myron stepped back from the slave. "Remove your clothing, completely," he said, "and crawl to the tiles in the corner of the room, and fasten yourself to the slave ring there by the neck. I will have your keeper, in the morning, herd you to your cage."

"Yes, Master," she whispered.

"Wait," he said. He removed a treat from his wallet and, as she lifted her head to him, placed it in her mouth.

She thrust her cheek against his leg in gratitude.

We then watched her crawl to the corner of the room.

"That is women as they should be," said Myron.

"I doubt that free women would agree with you," I said.

"They are not yet in their collars," he said.

It is a pleasant thing, I thought, for a man to have such a property, to own it, absolutely, completely, such a well-curved, delicious beast. What true man does not desire a slave? What true woman does not desire a master?

"Clearly, noble polemarkos," I said, "you do not have the lovely Talena of Ar in your custody. I must make arrangements to return to Ar immediately."

"There is one more woman to see," he said, "she who was brought from Port Kar to Jad, by a rogue who identified himself as Bruno of Torcadino."

CHAPTER SIXTEEN

Myron, the polemarkos, paused before the next door.

It, like the door to the hitherto entered chambers, was locked. Here, however, he did not simply thrust the key into the lock and turn the bolt. Here he first knocked politely.

There was a pause, perhaps the time needed to adjust a veil.

"You may enter," said a woman's voice.

I must have reacted, for Myron turned to me. "Are you all right?" he asked.

"Yes," I said. How long it had been since I had heard that voice!

Myron unlocked the door and we entered.

The woman, her features concealed by a light but opaque house veil, had risen to her feet, to greet us.

"Lady," said Myron, respectfully.

This chamber was larger and better appointed than the chambers previously visited. On the other hand, it lacked the opulence one might have expected of the chamber of a state guest, indeed, a Ubara, though one deposed.

"Why is the door to my chamber locked?" she asked.

"To protect you," said Myron. "You may have enemies even in Cos."

"I am not a prisoner?" she said.

"Certainly not," he said.

"A guest?" she said.

"Assuredly," he said.

"He with you is masked," she said. "May I inquire why?"

"He is a Cosian spy come from Ar," said Myron. "As you are of Ar, we thought it judicious to mask his features."

"Spy or not," she said, "his role here is to confirm my identity. It seems my word is not enough. It seems I am not trusted."

"Forgive us, Lady," said Myron. "But you must understand that we must have your identity officially ascertained by an envoy from Ar, that before publicly welcoming you to Cos, celebrating your safety, and elevating you to high station in our society."

"It seems," she said, "that the word of my rescuer from Port Kar, the noble Seremides, who was high captain in the Taurentians, is insufficient."

"As a mere, but necessary, formality," said Myron, "Ar deems it not inappropriate to require an independent confirmation in the matter."

"I understand," she said. "And if I am not Talena?" she asked.

"That would be most unfortunate," he said. "You would then be guilty of attempting to defraud the state of Cos and would be cast naked to the eels in the palace pool."

"I shall hope then," she said, "that I am indeed Talena of Ar."

"We shall all hope so," said Myron.

"Where is Seremides?" she asked.

"Doubtless abed," he said, "after feasting, reclining on a Ubarial supper couch, after having engaged in pleasant converse with the Ubar."

"Fortunate Seremides," she said.

"We deemed him in less danger than yourself," he said.

"How can I be in danger, truly, in powerful, allied Cos?" she asked.

"One never knows," he said. "Even a Ubar must be wary of the poisoned goblet, the hidden dagger."

"I see," she said.

"Lady?" he said.

"General?" she said.

"Your veil," he said.

"Of course," she said, and reached for the fastening.

Seremides and I had agreed that I must explicitly identify Talena. It was important to get her out of the palace. Our best chance of acquiring her was somewhere, somehow, on the long journey to Ar. Certainly we could not hope to extricate her from the palace. Too, we were sure, in any event, that the true emissary from Ar would soon appear in Jad, and effect her identification. Despite our plans, so carefully wrought, I was suddenly seized with an irrational untoward reluctance to identify her. As soon as her identity was confirmed to the satisfaction of both Ar and Cos would she not be on her way to the hideous justice of Ar, and an execution which might be prolonged over weeks, or more, of excruciating pain? Then I had learned that if she were not identified as Talena she would be fed to the voracious denizens of the palace pool.

Talena then released her veil and it drifted to the floor.

She stood then before us, straight, proud, insolent, brazen, taunting. Well she knew the effect her beauty had on men!

It was long since I had seen those exquisite features, that olive skin, the green eyes, the sweet lips, that shimmering, glossy torrent of hair as black as the pelt of the black sleen of Anango.

The polemarkos then looked at me.

I nodded.

"Speak," he said.

"Yes," I said. "That is the daughter of Marlenus of Ar, the Ubara of the Occupation, she, Talena, of the High City of Ar."

"He disguises his voice," said Talena scornfully.

"Suitably, Lady," said Myron.

"I am glad the matter is done," she said. "It was prolonged beyond tolerance. Your dalliance was inexcusable. I shall complain to the Ubar. You had the word of Seremides, my rescuer, he, once First Sword of the Taurentians. That should have been more than enough. I am tired of these quarters. Bring me garments befitting my station. Find jewels, necklaces, and bracelets. In the morning, present me to Lurius. It will take time to plan the reception and procession, to plan feasts and games, to organize a proper fete."

"Be at ease, dear lady," said Myron. "Have no fear. All will be attended to. You will be brought a suitable garment, a single garment, a brief gray tunic, such as a state slave might wear. Your jewelry will be shackles and manacles. Your quarters will be a small cell in the deepest dungeon of the palace. Then, as soon as possible, as soon as transportation can be arranged, you will be on your way to the justice of Ar."

"No!" cried Talena. "Your jest is monstrous! I served Lurius of Jad and Chenbar of Kasra. I betrayed my Home Stone! I planned, I conspired! I delivered Ar to your mercies! I am your ally! You cannot betray your ally!"

"We have many reasons for doing so," said Myron.

"There are none!" she cried.

"There are ten thousand," he said, "tarns of gold, tarn disks of double weight."

"Does Seremides know of this?" she asked.

"Of course," said Myron. "It was his charge to deliver you to Cos, so that Lurius can wax great on your reward, a reward in which he, Seremides, was to share."

"No, no!" wept Talena.

"You were a fool," said Myron. "You came willingly to Cos, unsuspecting, like a verr to the slaughter."

Beside herself, Talena sank shuddering to her knees.

I wanted to take her in my arms, to console her, to shelter and comfort her.

But were these not the emotions, I wondered, of a betrayed, effete, ruined, polluted Earth?

"I regret it all," said Myron. "You might have been a beautiful, desirable slave. I have often thought you would look well, in terror, kissing the feet of a master."

Talena, sobbing, reached for her veil, but Myron tore it from her, and cast it aside. She looked up at him, tears in her eyes, and then collapsed to the floor.

As she lay, I could see the lovely curve of her body within her garments.

"Why should such a thing, so exciting, so beautiful, not be owned," I asked myself. Strip it, I thought, completely. Put it on the block. See what it will bring in an open auction. Has not every woman wondered about that? Lead it off in chains, to be owned, to be your property, to be an endless source of inordinate pleasure to you.

These were the emotions, I thought, not of Earth, but of a proud world, fierce and unapologetic, a world terrible in its honesty, its naturalness and power, the world of the tarn and larl, of the master and the slave.

"Cry and sob all you want, traitress," said Myron. "It will avail you nothing."

"Why," I asked myself, "should Talena not be a slave? She is beautiful enough to be a slave. Taught the collar, she might, like any other woman, make an excellent slave."

"Our work here is done," said Myron, polemarkos of Temos. "Will you be soon departing for Ar?"

"Yes," I said. "And you?"

"Possibly," he said.

There is one other item which might be of interest, which took place that evening, an item which I should like, peripheral to our narrative as it may be, to recount.

When I had bidden farewell to Myron, the polemarkos, and, my mask removed, reached the first floor of the palace, I encountered the shorter scribe I had met in the scribal office, he of the darker blue.

"I have been waiting for you," he said.

"Tal," I said.

"Tal," he said.

"Why have you been waiting for me?" I asked.

"I would like to accompany you to the outer gate," he said. "I thought we might have a little talk."

"I know little of scribal matters," I said.

"You know enough," he said.

"Let us walk along," I said. "It is late, and I would like to soon reach my lodging."

"You are in great danger," he said.

"How is that?" I asked.

"You are not an emissary from Ar," he said. "You are a fraud."

My hand went inadvertently to my belt, to the dagger there.

"Stay your hand," he said. "You cannot leave the palace alive without my help. You do not know the signs and countersigns."

"I had no difficulty in entering and being conducted to your office," I said.

"It is one thing to enter the den of the larl," he said, "and another to leave it."

"Speak," I said.

"The Home Stone of Jad is my Home Stone," he said. "I am loyal to Cos."

"But less so to Lurius?" I said.

"He is a tyrant and fat with greed," said the scribe. "Should the reward for Talena's delivery to Ar fall to him, he will embroil Cos in continental and marine wars. He will field armies and bloody the seas. In the end Cos will have lost honor and be the threatened foe of a thousand cities and ports. No matter her wealth Cos cannot occupy, tax, and rule hundreds of thousands of pasangs, cannot indefinitely subdue and hold in check hundreds of resentful, then rebellious, populations."

"What has this to do with me?" I asked.

"You are a bounty hunter, are you not?" he asked.

"I am Harold of Skjern," I said, "emissary from Ar, dispatched on a secret mission."

"You are a liar and cheat," he said.

"How so?" I said.

"Your credentials are forged," he said. "They lack certain features characteristic of the state documents of Ar, some of which are subtle and included to ensure authenticity, features which are predictably absent from your lame fabrication."

"You are mistaken," I said.

"I was in Ar at the time of the Occupation, stationed in the office of diplomatic records," he said. "I accompanied the withdrawal."

"I see," I said.

"Even the seal is false," he said.

"It seems I should kill you now, and be done with the matter," I said.

"It does not matter to me who brings Talena to justice," he said, "as long as it is not Lurius."

"You choose not to speak," I said.

"Yes," he said, "I choose not to speak."

"In any event," I said, "when the true emissary from Ar arrives, the falsity of the credentials I submitted will be clear."

"And you will be a wanted man," said the scribe.

"How soon is the emissary to arrive?" I asked.

"Any day now," said the scribe. "He may have some difficulty, of course, after your appearance, in proving his authenticity."

"Particularly if he does not know the password," I said.

"Yes," said the scribe, "which you probably invented on the spot."

"'The tarn is absent,'" I said.

"'The tabuk is pleased,'" he said.

We came to a guard.

"Hail glorious Lurius," said the guard. "How strong is the larl?"

"As cunning as the sleen," said the scribe. "Hail, glorious Lurius."

"You are free with the password," I said.

"They are changed daily," he said.

"Of course," I said.

Later that night, shaken, I reached the domicile I shared with Seremides and the slave Iris.

"How went matters?" inquired Seremides.

"The credentials were accepted," I said.

"And what of Talena?" he asked.

"Soon," I said, "Talena will be on her way to Ar."

"Good," he said.

"I encountered Myron, polemarkos of Cos," I said.

"I thought you would," he said.

"He knew the woman was Talena," I said, "from Ar, from the Occupation."

"Of course," said Seremides. "But Marlenus would demand an independent confirmation, by one from Ar."

"Then Lurius of Jad did not even trust his cousin, the polemarkos," I said.

"I do not think Lurius of Jad trusts anyone," said Seremides.

CHAPTER SEVENTEEN

"You have had the harbor under surveillance," said Seremides.

"Inconspicuously, I trust," I said.

"And the public boards?" he asked.

"They still proclaim the arrival of an emissary from Ar, here to discuss the establishment, maintenance, and security of overland trade routes on the continent," I said.

Four days ago, with ribbons and banners refreshed, a given pier in the harbor had been strewn with flowers, and by the Tenth Ahn of the same day, amidst the blaze of trumpets and drums, had accommodated the berthing of a festooned round ship from Brundisium.

"By now," said Seremides, "the emissary will have established his authenticity and the credentials you submitted to the palace will be recognized as forgeries."

"Undoubtedly," I said.

Seremides twisted in his chair and regarded Iris, who, kneeling to the side, was mending a tunic which had been torn by a grasping mariner. As I may have mentioned, Iris was quite attractive and her neck, of course, was closely, clearly, encircled by the slave band. Had a similar liberty been taken in the case of a free woman, the mariner might have risked impalement. Free women tend to be jealous of their bodies. This is doubtless one reason why free women, stripped of their veils and robes, may find their reduction to slavery particularly disconcerting. It is one thing to be honored, prized, exalted, and esteemed, to be the jewel of your society, arrayed in fine veils and expensive robes, and another to find yourself cast to a man's feet, naked and collared, owned, subject to his whip. Given the comparative exposure of the typical Earth female, thinking nothing of bared faces, visible ankles, and such, the transition from a nominal, legal freedom to actual slavery is presumably less dismaying than it would be for a Gorean free woman. When a woman so bares herself, her exciting belly, and so on, is she not asking, even begging, to be owned? What woman does not wish, truly, to be owned? In enslaving such a woman, is not one merely making patent what was hitherto implicit?

"Slave," said Seremides, "what is new in the streets?"

"As I am a barbarian, Master," she said, "much is still new to me in the streets, the shops, the stalls, the crowds, the colors, the cooking, the smells, the garments, the robes of free women, so different from the tunics of slaves."

"Yes?" said Seremides.

"Little, I fear," she said, "that would be of interest to Master."

"We shall be the judge of that," said Seremides. "What may be nonsense or meaningless to an ignorant piece of collared girl meat such as yourself may be momentous to a different eye, a different ear."

"Yes, Master," she said.

"From Xenon," he said, "I have word from the taverns; from you, familiar with gossiping, prattling kajirae, I expect word from the streets."

"Surely Master is not interested in the price of tospits, or news pertaining to the recent sul harvest on Thera."

"Perhaps you have forgotten something," I said. "Do you know girls who regularly market for the palace?"

"Two," she said, "Cora and Andrina."

"Perhaps something is new in the palace," I said.

"There is some lingering stir," she said, "about some matter having to do with a false letter of credit."

"You are sure it involves a false letter of credit?" said Seremides.

"That is what I was told," she said.

"Such matters are trivial," said Seremides. "They would not be brought to the palace. There is no false letter of credit. It is a residue of unease, tracing back to the false credentials we submitted to the palace."

"Perhaps there is something else," I suggested, "if not from the palace, then from the citadel, at large."

"I do not think so, Master," she said.

"It seems," I said to Seremides, "we should take in our sail. There is no wind."

"You will continue to watch the harbor," he said.

"Certainly," I said.

"There are two or three things, Master," said Iris, "but they do not really pertain to the streets."

"If they lack import," I said, "nothing is lost. If they have import, something is gained."

"I am not to be beaten, if these things try the patience of masters?"

"No," I said.

"Cora mentioned, in passing, while we idly exchanged views on handsome masters passing by, that Myron, the polemarkos of Temos, had left the palace."

"To where," demanded Seremides, instantly animate, "to what place, to what destination?"

"She did not say," said Iris.

"She would not know," I said. "The important thing is that he has departed from the palace."

"Speculate," said Seremides.

"I think it is clear," I said. "I will be pleased to share my views with you, and my reasons for them, but not at present."

Seremides leaned towards Iris, and she shrank back. "Anything else!"

"It does not have to do with streets," she said.

"Speak," he said.

"Andrina informs me that some new slaves have been brought to the palace, purchased, it seems, locally in Jad."

"Each is a brunette and has the accent of Ar," I said.

Iris looked at me, startled. "How does Master know?" she asked.

"Decoys!" said Seremides.

"It would seem so," I said.

During the Occupation of Ar by the forces of Cos, Tyros, and pledged mercenaries, much of the wealth of Ar was taken from the city, most of which was bound for Cos and Tyros. Prominent amongst the loot, as would be expected on Gor, were hundreds of beautiful women who, collared, would exchange their resplendent robes and veils for a tunic at best. Accordingly, there was no dearth in Jad of brunette kajirae with the accent of Ar.

"Did you hear of the movement of supplies, of food, of water, of naval stores, in, to, or from the citadel?" asked Seremides.

"Andrina told me that the new slaves at the palace had been put to work at the citadel reservoir, filling and sealing small kegs of water."

"But not in composing ample stores of meal, dried, salted meat, crates of larmas, such things?" I asked.

"She said nothing of such things," said Iris.

I sprang to my feet, clapping my hands together, excitedly. "It is as I thought!" I said to Seremides.

"Things will soon move?" he asked.

At that point there was a blare of trumpets, perhaps half a hundred trumpets, from the harbor.

"Things move now," I said.

I, followed by Iris, went to the porch from which we could see the harbor. Seremides flung aside his blanket, seized his crutch from against his chair, and lurched to join us at the railing of the porch.

We watched a succession of knife ships, twenty in all, one after the other, in a serene, stately line, exit the harbor.

"How beautiful they are," breathed Iris, leaning forward, her small hands on the railing.

"Trumpets and daylight!" scoffed Seremides. "Every spy of Tyros in Cos will see this. The air will be filled with the fluttering of their message vulos bound for Kasra."

"It is intended that the spies will see this and that the message vulos will fly," I said. "That is the entire point of this spectacle."

"They hope to bravely shatter the blockade, with pennons streaming, to destroy it by brute force, and then convey Talena to the continent," said Seremides.

"Not at all," I said.

"I do not understand," said Seremides. "You see the very ships before you, setting out to sea."

"Twenty ships," I said. "Tyros could bring a hundred into play. Note the harbor, the mass of the Cosian fleet at Jad rests quietly in their berths."

"Share your thoughts with me," said Seremides.

"When in the palace, posing as an emissary from Ar," I said, "I enjoyed the enlightening privilege of conversing with Myron, pole-markos of Temos."

"Speak," urged Seremides.

"We know," I said, "that Jad has long since probed the block-ade, with single ships. The net of the blockade is tight, its strands closely woven. Interestingly, politically, the blockade does not exist. Individual ships are delayed and searched, supposedly for de-serters from the navy of Tyros, but, actually, of course, to intercept Talena, and use her for obtaining the reward for her capture and delivery to Ar for Chenbar of Kasra, Ubar of Tyros. Cos and Tyros are allies. Neither wishes to precipitate war with the other. Presum-ably that would be the natural outcome of a major sea battle. Thus, we may be confident that a major engagement at sea between two great fleets will be avoided, if at all possible. Too, Talena might well be lost at sea, if such a battle took place. Thus, the ships depart-ing from the harbor constitute some sort of diversion, and Talena would not have been on any of the departing ships. Too, none of the departing ships, as we learned by Iris from the slave, Andrina, was equipped for the long voyage to the continent, say, for Brundi-sium."

"But what of Myron and the decoy slaves?" asked Seremides.

"That is the beauty of the plan," I said, "for, as the departing fleet, a decoy in its own right, distracts Tyros, which could not risk letting it pass, Myron and the decoy slaves have embarked for the Farther Islands, probably to reach Sybaris on Thera, where the power of Cos is greatest. There Myron will doubtless assume command of some ships and a considerable detachment of Cosian land forces already waiting for him, indeed, perhaps most of those stationed out of sight, so to speak, on the Farther Islands."

"The voyage then will be made from the Farther Islands," said Seremides, "thus outflanking the blockade."

"The problem of Cos then," I said, "is to get Talena from the coast across the hundreds of pasangs to Ar."

"What must we do now," asked Seremides, "arrange for transportation to the Farther Islands?"

"No," I said, "for Brundisium."

"Why Brundisium?" asked Seremides.

"For two reasons," I said, "first, given the size of Brundisium, its business and commerce, its richness, its resources, and the hospitality it has always shown to Cos and Tyros, it seems the most likely port to satisfy the needs of Cos. Second, if landfall is made elsewhere, given the size and nature of the landing, it is almost certain that word of it will find its way to the taverns and streets of Brundisium."

"The last of the twenty ships has left the harbor," said Iris.

"What will happen when they encounter the fleet of Tyros, which will be waiting for them?" asked Seremides.

"They will peaceably return to Jad," I said, "their presumed training exercise completed."

"Xenon must accompany us," said Seremides.

My thoughts went to Xenon, he whose life had apparently been saved on the voyage from the Skerry of Lars to Jad by Seremides. He had served Seremides in Jad in various capacities. For example, it was he who, masked, had arranged with a scribe to forge the documents and seal by means of which I had penetrated the security of the palace. He was a short, powerfully built man, with large hands, well adapted to the oar.

"Why?" I asked.

"I trust him," said Seremides.

"You do not trust me?" I said.

"No," he said. "Do you trust me?"

"No," I said.

"Do not fear," he said. "Before we receive the reward for Talena, I will dispose of him."

I did not much care for the sound of that.

He was, of course, Seremides.

"In that way," he said, "there will be more for us."

"Or for you," I said.

"Perhaps," he said.

"Why did you save his life in the first place?" I asked.

"I thought he might prove useful," said Seremides. "It is common for individuals whose life is saved by someone to be grateful to their benefactor."

"I have heard so," I said.

"It is true," he said.

There was little activity then in the harbor. From the porch we could see the sail of the last of the twenty ships in the distance.

The looming citadel on its high crag overlooked the harbor.

"Iris," I said.

"Yes, Master," she said.

"Prepare supper," I said.

"Yes, Master," she said.

CHAPTER EIGHTEEN

"We have been a dozen days in Brundisium," said Seremides, "useless days, wasted days."

"Recall the children's story," I said. "The boy waited a hundred days for the glimpse of a golden tarn. He was scorned, derided, and mocked; yet he was patient. He watched, and waited. On the hundredth day he saw the tarn, shimmering, glorious, glittering, and alive. The moral of the story is that the first ninety-nine days were not wasted."

"There are no golden tarns," said Seremides.

"It is just a story," I said.

"I never heard that story," said Seremides.

"I am not surprised," I said. "I just made it up."

"I think that your projections were awry," said Seremides. "I think an engagement must have taken place at sea, between the fleets of Tyros and Cos, and Cos, outnumbered and defeated, failed to reach the continent with Talena. Possibly Talena was lost at sea or is now a prisoner in Tyros."

"Had such an engagement taken place," I said, "we would have heard of it by now."

"If you wish another round of paga," said Xenon, "I shall signal a girl."

"We have a girl," I said.

Iris was kneeling at hand, possibly comparing herself to the two paga girls waiting on the small, low tables. I did not think she needed be concerned. She had served in the Mariner's Pleasure in Jad.

"This is not an auspicious tavern," said Seremides. "It is a low tavern. It lacks musicians and dancers."

"It's a small tavern, and it's not the busy season," I said.

"Its clientele is shabby," said Seremides. "There is nothing here but riff-raff."

"I trust," I said, "that we fit in."

In circulating about, in visiting various markets, in strolling the streets, in given districts, in patronizing one tavern or another, we made it a point to dress in a manner which, hopefully, would not attract attention. It would not do to attempt to gain entrance to a high tavern in the tattered, soiled garb of a fellow seemingly likely to scrounge his meals from garbage troughs. Presumably one would be stopped at the door. Similarly, it would not be wise to enter a low tavern in, say, the harbor district, in a garmenture more befitting a Silken-Robe Market or a Street of Coins.

In passing, one might note that Brundisium had one of the largest, most formidable, most notorious Black Courts in known Gor, such a court being a facility in which Assassins are recruited and trained, and from which they are hired.

"Paga, Masters?" asked a paga girl, pausing at our table.

"If they desire paga," said Iris, "I shall attend to the matter."

The paga girl then, with a look back at the vat master, near the door on the left as one would enter, turned about, and left.

The Sea Sleen, which tavern we were now patronizing, as Seremides had remarked, was not an auspicious tavern, but it was clean and the paga was not bad.

It was now late and most of the dangling tharlarion-oil lamps, hanging on their three chains from the dark, low-beamed ceiling, had been extinguished. Some four of the alcoves were belted shut from the inside. Sometimes one heard a scream of ecstasy from a ravished slave.

"There is nothing here," said Seremides, reaching for his crutch. "Let us take our leave."

The Sea Sleen was in the vicinity of the southern piers. A sharp slope, some twenty paces or so away, led down to the water.

"Let us wait a moment," I said.

"Why?" asked Seremides.

"I think," I said, "that we are soon to be approached."

Xenon tensed, and his large hand went to the paga goblet, now empty. Both the base of the heavy vessel and its metal rim can deal a serious blow.

"Do not look about," I said to Seremides and Xenon. "I will inform you if a weapon is drawn."

"He is approaching?" asked Seremides, his hand now on the crutch. As it was held, he could now wrench his body around and deal a sweeping, or stabbing, blow to anything within its compass.

"He is considering it," I said. "He is standing. He is looking about, seemingly ill at ease."

"He is armed?" asked Seremides.

"I detect only a dagger," I said.

I myself carried a Tuchuk saddle knife, double-edged and balanced for throwing. Several are commonly sheathed on the side of the saddle. They may be used in close combat, rather as the darts of Anango.

"Do you know him?" asked Seremides.

"In a way," I said. "I have seen him several times, over the past few days, dressed variously, as we have dressed variously, in garments befitting diverse venues."

"He is following us?" asked Seremides.

"Clearly," I said.

Xenon's hand tightened on the stem of the metal goblet.

"He approaches," I said.

In a moment he had come around the table.

"Tal, serene and gentle masters," said the newcomer.

"Tal," we said.

He was a man of medium height with short, dark hair. His dark beard was short and well trimmed, perhaps too well trimmed for the Sea Sleen. He appeared strong, but his carriage suggested neither the ease nor the subtlety of an armsman. I assumed then it was not likely that he was either of the Scarlet Caste, the Warriors, or the Black Caste, the Assassins. He wore a mariner's garb, with the soft, brimless cap, but it showed little evidence of having been exposed to the wind and salt of Thassa.

"I am Kleomenes of Brundisium," he said.

"I am Tisandros of Market of Semris," said Seremides.

"I am Xenon, of Jad," said Xenon.

"I am Geoffrey of Harfax," I said.

"Forgive me for approaching your table uninvited," he said, "but, if I may speak boldly, I have observed you doing much the same recently."

His words were addressed primarily, it seemed, to Seremides.

I wondered if he had been instructed to watch for a one-legged man.

"I am a merchant," said Seremides. "I own wagons, and am in Brundisium to rent them as I can. I, and my colleagues, have inquired assiduously, hoping to take fee for the use of my wagons."

"Why should you think that wagons might now be wanted in Brundisium?" asked he who had introduced himself as Kleomenes of Brundisium.

"For the fields about, for speculators, for the sul harvest," said Seremides.

"It is somewhat late for that," said Kleomenes.

"Why are you speaking to us?" I asked.

"You are not merchants renting wagons, but individuals seeking to learn of the gathering of wagons, wagons being gathered for some overland journey, perhaps for some long journey," he said.

"Perhaps as far as Ar?" I said.

"Perhaps," he said.

"We have seen you before," I said. "You have been following us."

"I hoped I had been more discreet," he said.

"Why did you not approach us sooner?" I asked.

"Courage," he said, "like the wine tree, takes time to grow. I bear knowledge which it is dangerous to bear. I must be careful of its dissemination."

"And what knowledge is this?" inquired Seremides.

"The knowledge you seek," he said, "where the wagons are gathering."

"And where might that be?" asked Seremides.

"Gold loosens tongues," he said.

"So, too," said Seremides, "does torture."

"I offer a tarsk, a copper tarsk," I said.

"You jest," said Kleomenes. "I want a gold piece, a gold tarn, and of double weight! And what I know is worth far more!"

"A copper tarsk," I said.

"Ten silver tarsks," he said, "perhaps."

"One of copper," I said.

"Never!" he said.

"I wish you well," I said.

"Five silver tarsks," he said. "One silver tarsk."

"No," I said.

"I am a poor man," he said.

"You are also," I said, "perhaps a liar."

"You are bounty hunters," he said. "What I know is worth gold, much gold."

"We are simple merchants," I said, "with little interest in the affairs of states."

"I take the tarsk!" he said angrily, snatching the coin. "Two pasangs to the north you will find that for which you search, in the caravanserai of Alessandro of Brundisium." He then whirled away.

"He recognized you," I said to Seremides.

"Clearly," said Seremides.

"He is an informer, a spy?" asked Xenon.

"Obviously," said Seremides.

"We are now far better informed than we were," I said.

"True," said Seremides. "If Cos has planted spies in Brundisium to detect and thwart bounty hunters, Cos has reached the continent, or soon will, and is somewhere in the vicinity of Brundisium, or intends to be, and soon."

"We may also suppose that the gathering of wagons is not likely to be north of Brundisium as he alleged," I said. "Similarly, it seems unlikely that such a gathering would be openly organized and mounted in a public caravanserai, a venue vulnerable to attack. Also,

on general grounds, one would expect the landing, if not in Brundisium itself, within her walls, to be south of Brundisium, to lessen the
distance to Ar."

"It seems," said Seremides, "we have caught sight of the golden
tarn."

"In all likelihood," I said.

"What about the business of the copper tarsk?" asked Xenon.

"If he truly had information to impart as to the gathering of wagons, he would not have accepted a copper tarsk," I said. "By doing so
he revealed his fraudulence."

"He was desperate to have us believe him, and act," said Seremides.

"Cos," I said, "will protect its project at all costs, to the knife and
arrow."

"Then," said Xenon, "it will be dangerous to leave the tavern."

"I suggest, dear Seremides," I said, "that you go first."

"The attack is almost certain to come from behind," he said.

"I shall bring up the rear," I said. "Xenon and the slave will be
between us."

CHAPTER NINETEEN

I was at the water's edge, at the foot of the slope leading down to the harbor. With my foot, I rolled the last of the six bodies into the water.

There was a stirring in the water, possibly the result of the activity of one of the four-foot long, snakelike harbor tharlarions or a small harbor shark, come from between the palings, beneath one of the nearby piers.

"Someone is coming," whispered Seremides.

The area was dark.

In leaving the tavern I had extinguished the small lamp which had hung at eye level at the left side of the tavern's gate, as one would leave the tavern. Within, all was darkness, the tavern having closed.

"Is it finished?" called a voice, softly, from higher on the slope. It was the voice of he who had introduced himself to us as Kleomenes of Brundisium.

"Yes," I said, responding in a hoarse whisper.

"Did it go well?" he asked.

"Yes," I said.

"Have you taken the purses?" he asked.

"Yes," I said.

We had done so. In this way we had seen fit to add substantially to our economic resources. The purses, incidentally, were fat, even heavy, far more amply supplied than we might have expected had the assailants been common miscreants, recruited for an evening's work. We gathered they were Cosian operatives, probably furnished by the secret police of Jad. I wondered if they had been active more than once in Brundisium. Knives, after all, can assure the keeping of secrets.

"Did any escape?" asked the voice.

"No," I said.

"Have you disposed of the bodies?" asked the voice.

"Yes," I said.

"Excellent," he said. "Let us now withdraw."

I did not respond.

"Andros?" he said.

Silence can be deep, as deep as darkness.

"What is that noise?" he asked.

It was the click of the crutch of Seremides on the stones, as he made his way up the slope.

I heard several such clicks.

"Andros?" said the voice. "Phaidon, Kasos?"

By this time I thought that Seremides would be behind Kleomenes.

"Who is there?" Kleomenes called, frightened.

"I," said Seremides, "I, Seremides, he whom you would seek to kill, he who risked much and labored long for Cos, he whom Lurius of Jad betrayed, he whom hundreds have sought vainly, he whom you, to your sorrow, have now met."

"No, no!" cried Kleomenes, who must have turned toward the voice and now, from the sound of movement on the stones, was backing down the slope. I moved to one side, to let him pass.

"Help, help!" cried Kleomenes. "Assistance, assistance!"

I heard the click of the crutch of Seremides on the stones, now approaching.

"Guardsmen, guardsmen!" screamed Kleomenes.

Another click of the crutch.

"Gold!" screamed Kleomenes. "I have gold, gold!"

Again, the tiny noise.

"Approach no nearer!" cried Kleomenes. "There, have it, there!"

I heard the sound of a purse cast on the stones.

Kleomenes backed yet further down the slope.

Twice more I heard the click on the stones.

"Mercy!" cried Kleomenes.

Then he was backing into the water.

Perhaps the water was to his waist when, he screaming, the beasts in the water, come for blood and feeding, drew him beneath the surface.

Seremides was now beside me.

"Xenon," he called. "Kindle the tavern lamp. Let any who might pass by see that all is in order, that all is well."

Xenon pinched the wick of the lamp up, in its shallow pool of oil, and, scratching a Turian fire sliver into its brief brightness, relit the lamp.

The lamp, whose flame by day was almost undetectable, seemed startlingly bright in the darkness.

I could see the purse of Kleomenes a few feet away where it had been hurled to the ground. Here and there, loose on the ground, where they had been spilled free in the shock of their fall, was a scattering of coins, copper, silver and gold.

Iris was kneeling to one side, white-faced, shivering, her arms clutched about herself.

I helped her to her feet, because I was not sure she could stand.

Xenon addressed himself to securing the purse of Kleomenes and those coins which had been spilled about on the stones.

Seremides and I sheathed our swords.

"I suspect," I said to Seremides, "that there are several such kill squads in Brundisium."

"I would think so," he said.

"Perhaps," I said, "we should think about leaving Brundisium, to be about our work."

"Somewhere to the south of Brundisium," he said, "near the coast."

"Was it not worth waiting for," I asked, "the sight of a golden tarn?"

"It was," he said, "very much so."

CHAPTER TWENTY

"A dozen wagons must be burning," I said.

We had seen the smoke from four pasangs away.

I drew back on the reins. "Hold," I called to the small tharlarion which drew our wagon. It grunted, and stopped, dust about its feet. The wagon was laden with bags of sa-tarna meal. By means of this pretense, and our guise as Peasants, we hoped to justify our presence in what might prove to be dangerous, protected terrain. What could be less suspicious and more harmless than some marketing Peasants with a field slave?

I was standing in the wagon.

"What do you see?" asked Seremides from the bench.

"War," I said, "a raid. Tarns in the sky, dozens, darting to the attack. Some landing ropes of infantry. Defenders with spears and crossbows. There must be better than a thousand such, swarming about the wagons, clad in nondescript gray."

"Not the blue of Cos?" said Seremides.

"No," I said.

"But they are Cosians," said Seremides.

"Undoubtedly," I said.

"Gray is common with intercity trail guards," said Seremides.

"It seems," said Xenon, standing beside me, "that the secret of Cos is not well kept."

"It is hard to conceal a hundred wagons," I said. "Too, a single tarnsman can scout countries of pasangs."

"Take our Glass of the Builders," said Seremides. "Look for insignia, for accouterments, for boots."

Xenon rummaged through the long case hidden beneath the sa-tarna, a case which contained numerous articles for which we had speculated we might have need, swords and blades of diverse sorts, a bow of ka-la-na wood, arrows fletched with the feathers of the Vosk gull, a compact crossbow with quarrels, ropes, scarves, slave bracelets, a whip, tassa powder, and such. The only weaponry we kept publicly in the wagon were two Peasant staffs, one for me and one for Xenon. In a moment he had handed me a Glass of the Builders.

"Well?" inquired Seremides.

"Treve," I said. "Treve, the Tarn of the Voltai, an attack in force by Treve. The helmets, the insignia, are unmistakable."

"Such an attack, openly?" asked Seremides.

"Treve seldom deigns to conceal its designs," I said.

Treve was a bandit city, hidden high in the Voltai range.

"How sways the battle?" demanded Seremides.

"As of now, evenly," I said.

The cries of men and the clash of weaponry could be heard, or sensed, dimly, far off, in the distance.

"Cos, glorious Cos, has the numbers," said Xenon. "Soon their weight must be felt."

"Those in gray are now indisputably of Cos," I said. "Their feet are shod in the field boots of the Cosian infantry. The spears have the Cosian taper."

"The women, what of the women!" demanded Seremides.

"There are several about the field," I said, "some confused, some fleeing, all clad in the robes of free women."

"Decoys," said Seremides.

"One may be Talena," I said.

"How fare they?" asked Seremides.

"Some well, others less so," I said.

Through the single lens of the Builder's Glass, I saw a swooping tarnsman's loop encircle a running woman and draw her from her feet in a wide arc into the air, far over the ground. Her scream carried even to the wagon. Another soaring tarn swept down and seized a woman in its talons. On the ground, some of the Trevan infantry, landed by ropes on the field, seized what women they could, some caught in nets cast by passing tarnsmen, binding them, neck-roping them, and whip-herding them from the field. Other women scurried back to the wagons, hiding amongst them, and behind Cosian defenders. Others, doubtless, remained concealed in the wagons which had not yet been fired. As I watched, I saw two wagons set aflame. From each spilled five or six robed women.

Clashes continued, small groups engaging small groups. Tarns continued to swoop, soar, and circle, tarnsmen firing from saddle bows and casting small fire bowls toward the wagons, defenders cutting away burning canvas in an effort to save the wagons.

"How go matters?" demanded Seremides.

"Ho!" I cried. "Several wagons throw back their covers. Bowmen rush forth, forming squares of massed archers."

I gathered that it was only in the press of battle, when the outcome was clearly uncertain, that Cos decided to reveal the pivotal secret of its beleaguered defense, rains of quarrels fired in volleys.

"Tarnsmen do not charge the squares," said Xenon.

"Trevans are cowards and fools," said Seremides. "They do not close with the enemy. They are reluctant to risk their winged monsters against bowmen."

"They are neither cowards nor fools," I said. "They do not wish to fly their mounts into the fangs of certain death."

There was then, coming from the field and sky, several shrieks of piercing whistles.

"What is going on?" asked Seremides.

"The tarnsmen and their cohorts are withdrawing," I said.

Shortly thereafter there was a double blast of a battle horn.

Seremides looked up at me.

"That signifies a cessation of hostilities," I said.

"It is a victory horn," said Xenon.

"In any event," I said, "Treve withdraws."

"But why?" asked Xenon.

"There is little point in seeking a reward," I said, "if, in the seeking of it, one does not live to collect it."

"Talena is safe," said Seremides.

"We do not know that," I said.

"Treve declines engagement," said Seremides. "She abandons the field."

"For all we know, and for all they know, they have taken Talena," I said. "For all we know, and for all they know, she is amongst their prisoners."

"Treve and Ar," said Xenon, "have been at war for generations. How is it then that they would deal with Ar?"

"For ten thousand tarns of gold, coins of double weight," said Seremides.

"Surely Marlenus of Ar would not grant such wealth to Treve, an enemy of Ar," said Xenon.

"He would," said Seremides.

"It has to do with one's word, with honor," I said.

"It could mean the end of Ar," said Xenon.

"Honor is madness," said Seremides.

"Many deem it so," I said.

"It is so," said Seremides.

"I do not think so," I said.

"Then you are a fool," said Seremides.

"Possibly," I said. "But one must be oneself. If one is not oneself, who can one be, what can one be?"

"I suppose," said Xenon, "the women taken are now stripped naked and in flight, bound belly up over the saddle aprons of Trevan raiders."

"One would suppose so," I said.

"How disappointed must the raiders be, to discover they have netted only slaves," said Xenon.

"They can always keep them, or sell them," I said. "Too, some free women might be amongst the catches, and Talena herself might be amongst the catches, possibly branded and collared, being disguised, so to speak."

"And each," said Xenon, "including Talena, would deny hysterically that she is Talena."

"Certainly," I said.

"They may have Talena," said Seremides moodily.

"That is quite possible," I said.

"We will know in the morning," said Seremides.

"How so?" I asked.

"If the wagons move toward Ar," said Seremides.

"Yes!" said Xenon.

"But what," I said, "if Talena is not with the wagons?"

CHAPTER TWENTY-ONE

"I do not think we are the only ones who follow, or parallel, the wagons," I said.

"Presumably not," said Seremides.

"They forsake common routes; they avoid even familiar, established trails," said Xenon.

"They intend to shorten distance, to avoid time on roads," said Seremides.

"They will shorten distance, but they will lose time," said Xenon, "given the irregularity of the terrain."

I thought it interesting that an oarsman of Jad seemed so well informed.

There are various routes, incidentally, from the coast near Brundisium to Ar. A common one is to move south to Harfax, and thence farther south to Samnium, and then move east to Corcyrus, and thence to Ar. Another proceeds to Torcadino, and thence to Ar.

"Pretending to mark out and survey a direct route to Ar from Brundisium comports with the pretense of the caravan," I said, "this dating even from the public announcements in Cos, those supposedly explaining the arrival in Jad of the emissary from Ar."

"Who would believe so foolish an imposture?" said Xenon.

"Perhaps populations," I said. "Many men will believe whatever they are told, whether it is eminently plausible or outrageously absurd."

"In the wilderness," said Seremides, "there are fewer observers, fewer witnesses."

"It is hard to conceal dozens of wagons," said Xenon.

"And supplies and assistance may be more difficult to obtain," I said.

"And soon," said Xenon, "far too difficult to obtain."

"Cos cannot afford to abandon the cloak of its purpose," said Seremides, "the myth of seeking a new passage to Ar."

"Today," I said, "two more wagons were abandoned."

"Broken axles?" asked Seremides.

"Yes," I said.

"Rocks, ledges, crevices, the terrain," said Xenon.

We did not know how many wagons had departed from the coast south of Brundisium before the raid of the Trevans, but we had conjectured something in the neighborhood of a hundred. Given the extent of, and the ferocity of, the Trevan attack, the Cosians must have lost something like forty wagons. Following the attack, the next morning, the caravan had proceeded east in three parallel lines. The center line, consisting of some fifteen wagons, was the shortest of the three lines, this permitting the flanking lines to close and protect it on the front and rear as well as on the sides. As the wagons had continued to move east for the last six days, it seemed likely not only that Talena was still alive and had not fallen to the Trevans, but that she was still with the wagons, and presumably in one of the more protected wagons in the center line, if not in a particular one of them, interestingly, the "golden wagon," namely, a wagon with a golden canvas.

"How many Cosians are with the wagons?" asked Seremides.

"At least a thousand," I said.

"We will have to hire men," he said.

"A thousand?" I asked.

"Do not jest," he said, "but some."

"Where will you hire them?" asked Xenon. "Tarnburg is far away. The nearest mercenaries, free companies, are in Torcadino."

I was surprised that Xenon, a simple oarsman from Jad, could speak with such assurance of the location of mercenary troops. Too, he had seemed more familiar with the local terrain and the obstacles which the Cosian expedition might face than I would have expected.

"Brigands, bandits," said Seremides.

"They are rare, too, in the wilderness," said Xenon.

"Put out a bowl of honey in the woods and the small, thick furred tree sleen will come from afar to find it," said Seremides. "Sharks will follow a ship for hundreds of pasangs through barren waters, for garbage cast overboard."

It was the Eighteenth Ahn, two Ahn before midnight, in our camp. Our fire was small, and sheltered amongst rocks. It would not be visible from the caravan. I would have preferred darkness and a handful of moist meal, but Seremides, for some reason, would have his bowl of hot kal-da. We were a pasang from the encamped caravan, its wagons arranged in three circles, the "golden wagon" in the center of the inner circle. Our small draft tharlarion, unhitched from the wagon, was hobbled nearby. Given the possible dangers of the night, we had our swords and bows at hand. I, though no Thurnock, was reasonably proficient with the Peasant bow, and Xenon, I was sure, though an untutored oarsman, would be fully capable of pulling the trigger of a crossbow, the Assassin's weapon, at point-blank range.

"Should swords be found for hire," I said, "with what will you hire them? Our resources are limited."

"We have the most attractive of resources," said Seremides, "the promise of riches."

"The sword you hire," said Xenon, "may turn against you."

"Let it turn against air," said Seremides. "Before it awakens, before it leaves the sheath, we will have disappeared with Talena."

"You plan ahead," I said.

"It is advisable to do so," he said.

"Let us retire," I said.

"Let us not," said Seremides.

"I am apprehensive," I said, "concerning the fire."

"I have not yet finished my kal-da," he said.

"Ho!" I whispered, suddenly.

"I heard it," said Xenon quietly.

I reached for the Peasant bow and fitted an arrow to the string.

Xenon raised the loaded crossbow.

"Do not kick dirt upon the fire," said Seremides. "I have not yet finished my kal-da."

He leveled his crutch between me and the fire.

The small sound had come from the right. I faced the right. "Cover the left," I whispered to Xenon. It is a common, elementary tactic to call attention to one quarter and then attack from another. I glanced back over my shoulder. Xenon had already been facing the left.

A sound came again, from the direction I was facing, though this time it was different and clearly deliberate, a sound which might have been made by tapping a metal spoon on a metal plate.

"I come in peace," a voice called from the darkness.

There is a Gorean saying, "When a stranger comes in peace, prepare for war." The saying does not translate well into English, as, in Gorean, the same word is used for both "stranger" and "enemy."

"Tal, Bruno of Torcadino," called the voice from the darkness.

"Tal, Aetius of Venna," said Seremides.

"You know him?" I asked.

"Yes," said Seremides. "I have been waiting for him."

I looked into the darkness, and then turned back to regard Seremides.

"Now," said Seremides, "I have finished my kal-da."

CHAPTER TWENTY-TWO

"Permit me to introduce my former associate, Aetius of Venna," said Seremides to myself and Xenon.

The newcomer was apparently alone, and was not, as far as I could tell, armed. Yet his demeanor, and the way he held his body, suggested he would be no stranger to the tools of mortal engagement. He was lithe, dark-haired, tall, and strong. There was one aspect of his features by means of which he might be easily and clearly identified. On the right side of his face, low, to the right of his mouth, there was a small triangular scar, possibly the result of a spent quarrel.

"To be sure," continued Seremides, "our business, long ago in Brundisium, did not turn out too well."

"I was to deliver a particular slave to him," said Aetius, "one I thought of as being of no unusual consequence, but the marked sheet by means of which I was to recognize her had been changed by someone in the House of Anesidemus. In short, I delivered the wrong slave. I did not realize until later he was attempting to acquire Talena, the traitress, the fugitive Ubara of Ar, on whom the bounty was in the thousands of tarn disks, golden tarns, of double weight."

"It is true," said Seremides, "I did not see that noble Aetius needed to be informed of such details."

"I considered killing him," said Aetius, "but instead, later, having come to suspect the actual nature of his quarry, I followed him to Port Kar, trusting that he might lead me to her."

"I was successful in obtaining Talena and having her conveyed to Jad, but I was betrayed by Lurius of Jad," said Seremides.

"Who would trust a Cosian?" asked Aetius.

"I am Cosian," said Xenon.

"He who spoke," said Seremides, "the short, strong, large-handed fellow, is Xenon of Jad, a humble oarsman, to whom I once rendered a service."

"He saved my life," said Xenon.

"Because of a minor infraction, accidentally brushing the robe of Talena of Ar, our prisoner, he was, though not slain, thanks to my intercession, refused an oar in Cos," said Seremides. "While I still stood in favor with the Ubar, I found him a position in the Mariner's

Pleasure, a tavern in Jad. He is a simple, harmless fellow who would, without a thought, give his life for me. He trails me about like a pet sleen. It is sometimes embarrassing."

"And you have another acquaintance," observed Aetius.

"Yes," said Seremides, "Geoffrey of Harfax."

"I assume," said Aetius, "that that is his true name."

"You are free to assume so, of course," said Seremides.

"As I am at liberty to assume that yours is Bruno of Torcadino," said Aetius.

"Precisely," said Seremides.

Aetius and I nodded to one another, much as two territorial larls might eye one another, encountering one another at the perimeter of one's territory.

"That is a lovely slave," said Aetius, eying Iris with the frankness of a Gorean male looking on a female slave. The slave, of course, is an animal and is to be looked on as such. One of the things to which an Earth girl brought to Gor as a slave must accustom herself is being looked upon as no more than what she then is, a pure, raw, collared beast. This tears away hundreds of cultural lies, confusions, and accretions. She then becomes aware, commonly for the first time, of her radical, indisputable femaleness. Men will pay for her, to own her, to have her subject to their whip. And, needless to say, this understanding, enflaming her passions, bringing her into animal heat, liberates her sexually, that bringing her all the more under the control of the male.

"What is your name, pretty tasta?" asked Aetius.

"Iris, if it pleases Master," she said.

"A barbarian," said Aetius.

"Her flanks are exciting," I said.

"She is beautiful enough to be Gorean," said Aetius.

"Barbarians sell much like Goreans," I said.

"They are all women," said Seremides. "Strip, brand, and collar them, and you can't tell them apart."

"I assume," I said, regarding Aetius, "you have not trekked the wilderness and crossed the stones in the darkness to discuss livestock."

"Not at all," said Aetius, forcing his attention away from Iris. She knelt some feet back. She was in the shadows. Her collar did glint in the firelight. In Jad we had given her a rather modest tunic, in order not to attract undue attention to the domicile, that domicile near the harbor which we shared with Seremides. In Brundisium, however, with Seremides openly about with his crutch, we had seen no point in continuing that unnecessary, drab practice. Accordingly, Iris's tunics were now light and suitably "slave short." A slave is clothed, of course, if clothed, as the master pleases. The typical slave tunic makes it clear that its occupant is a property and is designed to leave few of its occupant's charms to the imagination. On Earth, where most individuals are free, or, at least, think they are free, freedom does not mean much. On Gor, however, there is a radical chasm between the slave and the free. Along these lines, consider the contrast between the Gorean free woman, masked in her veiling and bundled in her robes of concealment, and the garmenture, if any, accorded the slave. It would be difficult to conceive of a more startling contrast. How could the distinction between slave and free be marked more clearly? The Gorean free woman, bound by convention, tight in the net of her restrictions, hates the slave for her comparative freedom and exciting appeal to men, but would never dream of letting a mere slave be dressed in such a way that she might be confused with a free woman, nor would she herself, a free woman, dress in such a manner that she might be confused with a slave. Such things would be unthinkable. Therefore, let the free woman have her veils and robes and let the despised, worthless, meaningless slave be clad, if clad, in such a way that her degradation and shame be manifested to all. She is a servile property, a debased beast, so clothe her, if clothing her at all, in such a way that her nature, condition, and status will be clear to all. Let her be suitably seen, displayed, and presented as the object she is, to the disdain and contempt of the free. In her collar, let her, if clothed at all, wear rags, a tunic, or camisk, so that she will know that she is no more than a slave, a purchasable article, a vendible beast. She is a slave; that is fit for her. In the light of such considerations, then, consider the momentous dislocation in self-image should the Gorean free woman find herself enslaved, which is a real possibility given the frequent wars between cities, the vulnerability of ships and caravans, the raids of slavers, and such. The Earth girl, captured, stripped, branded, collared, and marketed quickly learns that she is now a slave, but consider the Gorean woman, so exalted and deferred to in her city, having now become a slave. How different for her that is! Her world has collapsed. Things are different for her now. Now, head down, that she be fed, that she be granted a rag to cover her nakedness, that she not feel the lash, she crawls to her master, and begs to be permitted to lick and kiss his feet.

"Several days ago, in Brundisium," said Seremides, "I encountered the noble Aetius of Venna, and we renewed our acquaintance. My fortunes, given the betrayal of Lurius, had fallen, and his, since Port Kar, had not prospered. Both of us had failed to capitalize on the capture of Talena. Might we not then, in a way, join forces, to our common advantage?"

"We could pool our resources, our men," said Aetius. "Together we might succeed where individually we might fail."

"Our men?" I said.

"Surely sharing fabulous wealth," said Aetius, "is preferable to sharing nothing."

"While I," said Seremides, "and you, dear Geoffrey, and Xenon, remained for days in Brundisium to ascertain the location of a possible landing at Brundisium, or in its vicinity, Aetius would move east, away from the coast, to Torcadino."

"To recruit amongst the free companies?" I asked.

"Scarcely," said Aetius, "free companies are expensive."

"Perhaps," said Seremides, "to recruit amongst fellows who were cast forth from the free companies or who were rejected by them, men who could not win admission to their ranks, fellows not particular as to the uses to which their steel might be put?"

"Precisely," said Aetius, "while the noble Bruno of Torcadino, with his plentiful gold, similarly but surreptitiously, recruited in Brundisium."

"I see," I said.

Xenon, I noted, had not moved his finger away from the trigger of his crossbow.

"We were to rendezvous," said Seremides, "in the vicinity of any large Cosian caravan, should one set forth from the coast. Presumably it would carry Talena of Ar."

"You expected him today?" I asked.

"You were watching the caravan," said Seremides. "I was watching behind us, for three puffs of smoke, a half pasang away."

"I took them for a Peasant's signal," I said, "indicating the presence of strangers, in this case, the presence of the caravan."

"A signal, yes," said Seremides, "but not of the Peasants."

"Talena is with the caravan," said Aetius.

"How do you know?" I asked.

"For three reasons," said Aetius. "First, in Torcadino, rumors are spread that Talena was seized by Trevans near the coast. Thus, Cos wishes, in virtue of this rumor, to deny that Talena is with the caravan. Thus, she is with the caravan. Second, the caravan did not turn back to the coast after the Trevan attack, but continued toward Ar. This makes no sense unless Talena is still with the caravan. Thus, Talena is still with the caravan. Third, protected in the center of the trifold caravan is a 'golden wagon.' That wagon is intended to be taken as the wagon carrying Talena. But it seems that only a fool would thus advertise the location of Talena. Thus, the golden wagon seems to be an absurd trick. But the Cosians are clever. I think that Talena, as few would guess, is actually, in truth, carried in the golden wagon. And, indeed, the very creation of such a supposed deception would make sense only under one supposition, namely, Talena is still with the wagons. And, I am sure, she is within the 'golden wagon' itself."

"Your reasoning is not conclusive," I said, "but, like yourself, I consider it extremely likely that Talena is somewhere in the caravan."

"In the golden wagon," said Aetius.

"Possibly," I said.

"I have planned carefully," said Aetius. "There is a time to move and a time not to move. If we moved too soon after the Trevan attack, vigilance would be high. If we wait too long another may act first."

"And this is the time to move?" I asked.

"In the gray morning," said Aetius, "while the wagons are being hitched."

"There is something like a thousand Cosians with the caravan," said Seremides.

"We have no intention of meeting a thousand Cosians on an open field of battle," said Aetius. "We will apply an overwhelming, irresistible force at a particular, carefully chosen, vulnerable point, say, bringing one hundred men against ten, at a given wagon, and then, seizing our prize, we disappear amongst the rocks, in the morning mists."

"You will be pursued," I said.

"We have bipedalian racing tharlarion waiting," said Aetius.

"Purchased in Venna," I said, "from the racing stables." Venna was famous for its tharlarion races.

"I told you I had planned carefully," said Aetius.

"It is interesting," I said, "that rumors pertaining to the caravan abound even in Torcadino."

"And doubtless, also," said Aetius, "in Corcyrus, Market of Semris, Harfax, Samnium, and elsewhere."

"I wager, then," I said, "that every brigand and bandit between the coast and Ar may know of the caravan."

"Quite likely," said Aetius.

"Secrets are seldom well kept," said Xenon.

"Save by the strangling cord and knife," said Seremides.

"Time is not to be lost," said Aetius. "I have brought forty men. Where camped are your sixty or a hundred, recruited in populous Brundisium?"

"I have three men," said Seremides, "a cripple, that is myself, Geoffrey of Harfax, and Xenon, a simple oarsman."

"I do not understand," said Aetius. "In Brundisium, you, in fine robes, assured me you had the means to hire a hundred swords!"

"Forgive me, my dear Aetius," said Seremides, "but how else could I have arranged a future meeting with you, a meeting which, I hoped, would turn out to our mutual advantage?"

"You tarsk, you abominable urt!" cried Aetius, leaping to his feet, his hand going wildly to his left side, where was suspended, however, no scabbard.

"Notice," said Seremides, "there is a quarrel trained on your heart."

Xenon had lifted the crossbow, a quarrel on the guide. I had not noticed this. I did notice, however, almost instantly, that the quarrel, if discharged, would enter the center of the heart of Aetius, not where most people think the heart is, on the left side, but where it actually is, somewhat more toward the center of the body. I found that interesting.

Aetius's anger subsided, but his face seemed a frozen mask of hatred.

"We are all friends here," said Seremides. "I would not have arranged this meeting if I did not think it would be mutually beneficial."

"You supposed it would be easier to steal Talena from some forty men than a thousand," snarled Aetius.

"I can supply you with something far more valuable than a hundred men," said Seremides.

"What is that?" asked Aetius.

"First," said Seremides, "let me point out that you do not need my sixty men or my hundred men. You have forty men, more than enough to concentrate an overwhelming force on a tiny, given point. Secondly, if I could give you sixty or a hundred men, and you were successful, how would I, and my men, without mounts, in an open, barren country, escape the wrath of pursuing Cosians? I take it, we would be expendable."

"You are a sly sleen, Bruno of Torcadino," said Aetius.

"I have even been compared to Seremides of Ar," said Seremides.

"What is more valuable than a hundred men?" asked Aetius.

"Information," said Seremides.

"'Information'?" said Aetius.

"Have you ever, personally, looked on Talena of Ar?" asked Seremides.

"Few have," said Aetius.

"Cos has arranged many false Talenas," said Seremides, "perhaps dozens, several with suitable accents, and many who might actually resemble the true Talena."

"The problem of identifying the true Talena faces many, perhaps most, bounty hunters," said Aetius.

"How will you know the true Talena?" asked Seremides.

"She will be the one in the golden wagon," said Aetius.

"Perhaps, perhaps not," said Seremides.

"Speak," said Aetius, angrily.

"You may carry the false Talena all the way to Ar, if you wish," said Seremides. "It matters not to me. But then others, in the interim, may seize the true Talena."

"Speak, speak!" demanded Aetius.

"There are two here who know the true Talena," said Seremides. "I am one of them, and Geoffrey of Harfax is the other."

"You would have me bring my capture here," said Aetius.

"Only if you wish to learn whether or not your capture is the true Talena," said Seremides.

"You would think to steal her," said Aetius.

"Are you afraid," asked Seremides, "you, with some forty men, and we being only three, and one a cripple, and another a simple oarsman?"

"I will bring her here," said Aetius, "for a brief moment, before we hurry to our mounts."

"That will prove satisfactory," said Seremides.

CHAPTER TWENTY-THREE

"I hear them," said Seremides, "alarm bars from the Cosian camp."

It was shortly after dawn.

It was cool and damp amongst the rocks. I had already hitched our tharlarion to our wagon, filled with the sacks of sa-tarna. Xenon and I had concealed our weapons in the long, flat case in the bottom of the wagon, under the grain. The only things visible which might serve us as weapons were the two stout Peasant staffs.

"Aetius has made his move," I said.

"I know our friend, Aetius," said Seremides. "He is now either dead or successful."

"He can be no more successful than his men, who must do their part," I said.

"They will do their part," said Seremides. "If one should waver or hesitate, Aetius will cut him down, instantly. Help me to the wagon bench. We may have to move quickly. I do not wish to be an encumbrance. Xenon, fetch me my blanket. It is chilly."

I assisted Seremides to the bench, and Xenon fetched the blanket, which Seremides wrapped about his shoulders. Iris waited at the side of the wagon. She would not enter the wagon without permission. She was white-faced and shivering. "Get a blanket," I told her, "and get in the wagon."

"Thank you, Master," she said.

"Aetius will lead Cosians here," said Xenon.

"No, sweet Xenon," said Seremides. "He will lead them elsewhere, amongst the rocks, and then turn and find his way here."

"As soon as the trail proves barren," said Xenon, "the rocks will swarm with Cosians, in every direction, on all sides."

"By then," said Seremides, "our friend Aetius will have been here and gone."

"Do you think Talena would truly be lodged in the 'golden wagon'?" I asked Seremides.

"I would not think so," said Seremides.

I reached into the cut sack behind the wagon bench and scooped out a double handful of sa-tarna, which I then fed to the tharlarion. Its long tongue went under the backs of my hands and then, curling, went about the sa-tarna, enclosed it, and then slipped back under the backs of my hands and disappeared into the creature's mouth.

"Do not be anxious, Xenon," said Seremides. "Behold the tharlarion. She is calm."

"She is also in no danger of impalement," said Xenon.

"What do you see?" asked Seremides.

I climbed to the wagon bench. "The light is poor," I said. "The air is heavy with water. I see no men. The wagons do not move."

"The wagons may not move," said Seremides, "but amongst them there will be much agitation."

"The alarm bars are still ringing," I said. "Thus, we may suppose that Aetius and his men, or some of them, are still alive."

"A pursuit is doubtless being organized," said Seremides.

This was wise, of course. It costs a few Ehn to bring this about, but it is preferable to a precipitate, reckless chase which would be likely to be both ineffective and costly in terms of men. Few warriors are foolish enough, particularly in small numbers, to pursue a seemingly fleeing foe indiscriminately. Ambush is not unknown in the annals of war. Is he who seems to flee the hunted or the hunter? He may be fleeing pursuers, true; but, too, he may be leading them into a trap. It is not unknown for an old larl to feign decrepitude, thus bringing the throat of its young challenger into the range of his fangs.

Iris uttered a short, startled cry.

"Silence!" said Seremides.

Several men, some bleeding, burst into our camp, from the side, away from the caravan, visible in the distance. One, Aetius, breathing heavily, spattered on the left shoulder with blood, carried a bundled form, wrapped in a dark blanket. He came about the wagon. There, beside the wagon, where we might see it, he flung his burden to the ground. "I give you no more than an Ehn!" he said. He then crouched beside the miserable form of the object he had borne to our small camp. It was whimpering and trembling. He jerked it to a kneeling position and thrust the folds of the blanket down about its shoulders. It was veiled and clad in the robes of concealment, layers of silk, satin, and brocade. He pushed back the hood. It hung behind her and over her back. His fist closed about her veiling. "No," she wept. "No, please!" Then, with a rude, violent motion, he tore aside her veils. She put down her head in misery, face-stripped, her features now as bared as those of a slave. Aetius then, his hand deep in her long, dark hair, jerked her head up, and held it back. "Behold!" he cried, wildly, triumphantly, "Talena of Ar!"

I, standing now beside the wagon, needed not approach her more closely. I could have reached out and touched her, she there, on her knees before us.

"I am not Talena of Ar!" she screamed. "I am not Talena of Ar!"

"She speaks truly," I said, quietly, calmly. "That is not Talena of Ar." And it was not Talena of Ar.

"You lie!" cried Aetius, rising up, fiercely, his hand darting to the hilt of his sword.

"No," I said. "She is not Talena."

"Tell me she is Talena of Ar, or you shall taste my sword!" he cried.

"Your sword, even though my blood be upon it, cannot make her Talena of Ar," I said.

"She was in the golden wagon!" exclaimed Aetius.

"Nonetheless," I said, "she is not Talena."

"You, you, Bruno of Torcadino!" cried Aetius, looking up to the wagon bench. "You know the features of Talena of Ar! This is Talena of Ar! Admit it! Speak the truth."

Seremides leaned forward in the blanket. He looked down on the distraught, pathetic, trembling figure.

"Well?" cried Aetius.

Several of his men crowded more closely about the wagon. Others remained at the edge of our small camp, watchful and wary, looking about.

"Well?" said Aetius. "Is this Talena of Ar?"

"I am not Talena of Ar!" cried the woman, but then recoiled, cuffed back, savagely, by the stinging palm of Aetius, blood then about her lips.

"Speak!" demanded Aetius of Seremides.

Seremides was still, very still, for a moment, and seemed, oddly enough, for that instant, to be thinking of what to say, and then he said, suddenly, as though he had come to a decision, said emphatically, almost with a hysterical force, "No, no! That is not Talena of Ar!"

A wide grin broke across the features of Aetius.

"No," said Seremides. "That is not Talena of Ar! That is not Talena of Ar!"

The features of the captive were suffused with relief and gladness.

"How unfortunate," said Aetius, "that she is not Talena, after the risks we faced, after our expenditure of time, effort, and blood."

"It is unfortunate," said Seremides. "You must be disappointed. But sometimes the tarn flies north and sometimes south."

"What should we do with her?" asked Aetius, smiling. "Perhaps, as she is not Talena, we might leave her behind with you?"

"Do so," said Seremides. "Thusly she will not slow or impede your escape."

"Nonetheless," said Aetius, "I think we will take her with us."

"No, no!" cried the woman.

Aetius turned about, jubilantly, to his men. "To our mounts quickly," he said. "We have Talena of Ar!"

He then, with his men, disappeared amongst the rocks.

"She was not Talena of Ar," I said to Seremides.

"Of course not," said Seremides.

"It seems," I said, "that Aetius of Venna did not believe you, when you said his captive was not Talena of Ar."

"I trusted he would not," said Seremides. "It is sometimes desirable to tell the truth in such a way that it will not be believed."

"And thus one can tell the truth in such a way as to lie," I said.

"It is a skill," said Seremides, "which I commend to your attention."

"What would you have done had the prisoner actually been Talena of Ar?" I asked.

"First, rejoiced," he said, "that our quarry would have been located and within reach, and then, secondly, followed Aetius and his men. Then, sooner or later, on some night, on the way to Ar, we could kill sentries and cut the throats of twenty men in their sleep."

"How could this be accomplished," I asked, "as you are crippled, and Xenon is a simple oarsman?"

Xenon looked away. I could not see his features.

"We have you," said Seremides. "I suspect that you, moving with speed and stealth, could execute such an assignment."

"I do not cut the throats of men in their sleep," I said.

"Ah, yes, honor," said Seremides. "It is an impediment to proficiency. I encourage you to dispense with it as soon as possible."

"Perhaps," I said, "we could subdue guards, seize Talena, and stampede and scatter their mounts, with the exception of, say, three, which we might find useful."

"In any event," said Seremides, "they do not have Talena."

"You hoped they would," I said.

"Certainly," said Seremides. "He had men and we did not. I hoped he would put her within our grasp."

"But he did not," I said.

"I regret that he failed," said Seremides, "but, he having failed, and, thanks to us, being on his way to Ar, we have, at least for now, eliminated a dangerous competitor."

"If he manages to reach Ar, at all, after the long, hazardous journey," I said, "he will not be pleased to discover that he has brought a false Talena to vengeful Marlenus."

"Perhaps Marlenus will nail his skin to one of the smaller gates of Ar," said Seremides.

"The alarm bars no longer ring at the wagons," said Xenon. "Too, I hear the shouts of men apprising one another of their positions, and the beating of drums."

"Cosians," I said.

"Into the wagon!" cried Seremides. "Make haste! Take the reins, Geoffrey, and make away! Make haste! Make haste! Harta! Harta!"

I climbed to the bench, assuming the reins. Xenon, with a surprising lightness, entered the wagon and seized up his staff. Such a weapon, properly handled, can be a formidable implement of war.

"Put down the staff," I said to Xenon, sharply. He did not question my order or ask for an explanation. He put the staff down without the least demur. I saw he knew discipline. If we encountered Cosians, I wanted no appearance which might suggest we intended, or expected, violence.

With one hand, my left, I snapped the reins alerting the tharlarion and, with the other, applied the long, supple wand by means of which the tharlarion would be stirred to move. I had removed the tiny bells which had been sewn on the beast's harness. Might we not, sometimes, wish to move silently, say, at night? As many harnesses are not belled, I did not think this detail would be likely to provoke curiosity.

"What are you doing?" demanded Seremides.

"Going toward the wagons," I said. "We are simple Peasants interested in marketing grain. We know nothing of raids or the doings of war. Flight encourages pursuit. Approach signifies noninvolvement, ignorance, innocence, and peace."

"We will be stopped and questioned," said Seremides.

"That is my hope," I said.

"They will want information as to the raiders," said Seremides.

"And we shall supply it, freely," I said.

"To mislead them," said Seremides.

"Not at all," I said. "That would be dangerous, a deception which might be discovered. We shall tell truths as to men, their number, their condition, and the route they took. This will in no way jeopardize our friend, Aetius of Venna, as he, with his men and prize, will soon be astride their mounts racing toward Ar."

"We might even be allowed amongst the wagons," said Seremides.

"Let us hope so," I said.

Shortly thereafter we heard a gruff cry, "Hold!"

I stopped the wagon, as several men, clad in the gray of intercity trail guards, appeared from amongst the rocks and swarmed about the wagon.

CHAPTER TWENTY-FOUR

"What I do not understand," said Collis, caravan master, "is why we should be attacked. We are simple surveyors and map makers, intent on planning a new overland route between Brundisium, rich in trade, and glorious, high-walled Ar."

"May a humble Peasant speak frankly to the noble master?" I asked.

"You have more than earned that right," said he, "you and your companions, for the aid you have rendered us. Without your help, we might not have been set so swiftly on the trail of the bandits, leading to their abandoned camp."

"You did not apprehend them, I gather," I said.

"Not yet," he said.

Seremides and Xenon had already been questioned. We would be questioned separately, doubtless to see if our stories cohered. We had prepared names and designed a background which might seem plausible, if not looked into too carefully. I would assume the name Bodon, Seremides that of Timus, and Xenon that of Zarm. We would all claim to be of the village of Red Stream, which is the only village we knew to be in the vicinity of this portion of the projected route of the caravan. Iris's collar, which read "I belong to Geoffrey of Harfax" was explained in terms of the well-known stereotype imposed on the Peasants, namely, their unwillingness to part with so much as a tarsk-bit. Keeping a girl in her former collar constituted exactly the sort of saving for which Peasants, at least those of poor villages, were famed.

"Speak," he said. "You may do so frankly."

"I am only a poor Peasant, Master," I said, "but I suspect that the ruffians who molested your wagons were not common bandits."

"How so?" asked he, as though surprised.

"Your caravan is large, and well guarded," I said. "It seems unlikely that a small number of bandits would even approach such a caravan, let alone hope to seize, loot, and burn it."

"Doubtless their project was ill-considered," he said.

"Or their objective was quite specific and limited," I said.

"The golden wagon," he said.

"Forgive me, Master," I said, "but there is a false rumor abroad, one widely spread, abounding even, I have heard, in faraway Argentum, Corcyrus, Samnium, and Torcadino."

"And what is the nature of this rumor?" he asked.

"It is, forgive me," I said, "that your caravan is not what it seems, that its true purpose is not to map a new route to Ar, but to deliver to Ar her long-sought, now-captured, treasonous Ubara, Talena of Ar."

Collis sat back in his curule chair, set on a carpet, on the boot-torn turf, in the center of the wagons.

"Noble and kindly scion of the Peasantry," he said, "clearly you are not simple, but are astute, unlike so many of your caste. I see I could not hope to deceive you, nor will I attempt to do so, though the priorities of intrigue demand that I try. As you have doubtless surmised, or at least suspected, the rumors to which you refer are well founded. The men you see about you are not intercity guards but soldiers of Cos, indeed, some of whom are officers. I myself am not a simple caravan master, but I, Collis, am a general, a high general, one formerly stationed on Thera, of the Farther Islands, in the land forces of Cos. The raiders on whose trail you so helped to put us were hoping to abduct Talena of Ar, our noble prisoner, and carry her to Ar to claim the reward for themselves."

I hoped I looked suitably amazed.

"But they did not so do so?" I asked, scarcely whispering.

"No," said Collis. "They were unsuccessful. They seized, by mistake, the Lady Andrina of Telnar."

"Poor woman," I said.

"Not at all," he said. "She, like many free women, is a taunting, teasing, nasty, vain little she-sleen. She will look well in a collar in Ar, hoping to keep her smooth skin from the whip."

"Lady Talena, then," I said, "is safe."

"Certainly," he said. "She is here, in this very caravan, hidden away, safe, and we will carry her to Ar, and accept the reward for our Glorious Ubar, Lurius of Jad."

"May all Cos rejoice," I said.

"It is interesting that you were in the vicinity of the caravan when the raid occurred," he said.

"A happy coincidence," I said, "enabling us to be of assistance to the noble master."

"You hoped to sell sa-tarna?" he asked.

"This very day," I said.

"It is fortunate that you did not approach the wagons without an escort," he said. "You might have been killed within a hundred yards of the wagons."

"I did not know that," I said.

"Did you truly think that we might have need of sa-tarna?" he asked. "Did you truly think that the army of Cos would be ill-prepared for a long journey overland, a journey such as this? Did you truly think that we would put ourselves at risk by trying to live off the land, so bleak a land, or try to supply ourselves in the midst of possible enemies? Did you truly think that we might buy sa-tarna from a stranger?"

"I am only of the Peasants," I said. "Such things did not occur to me." I internally apologized to my old friend, Thurnock, of the Peasants. Peasants, I had learned, were not simple, and not stupid. They did tend to be shrewd and grasping. Each Peasant village, and each hut, had its own Home Stone.

"Perhaps your sa-tarna is poisoned," he said.

"No, noble master," I said. "I and my companions will eat it, cheerfully."

"Where is the village of Red Stream?" he asked.

"North," I said. At least I knew that much.

"How far?" he asked.

"Fifty pasangs," I said readily. I hoped that the caravan master knew no more than I did about the matter.

"Go to your wagon, and gather your companions, and slave, and leave the caravan," he said. "Do not let us see you in the vicinity of the caravan again."

"I am sorry if we have offended you," I said.

"Do not be concerned," he said. "Times are hard. Days are fraught with peril. As we are not what we seem so, too, you may not be what you seem. Do not ask me to trust you. Do not expect me to trust you. Trust is rare, dangerous, and expensive. What rich man trusts his purse to a bandit; what verr trusts his safety to a sleen, what tabuk to a larl?"

"I understand, noble master," I said.

"I have seen your slave," he said. "She is pretty."

"I think so," I said.

"What is her name?" he asked.

"Iris," I said.

"A Cosian name," he said, approvingly.

"She is a barbarian," I said.

"No matter," he said.

"My party is pleased, if we have been of service," I said. "Now, with the permission of the noble master, we will take our leave."

"Go," he said.

I bowed, and backed away from the presence of Collis, the caravan master, and a high general of Cos.

"Why so despondent?" asked Seremides. "You have had the assurance of the caravan master that Talena of Ar is with the caravan, just as we conjectured."

"It is his assurance," I said, "which convinces me that Talena is not with the caravan."

It was early evening and we were camped some pasangs from the route of the caravan which, in its three lines, had resumed its journey toward Ar, that shortly after we had left the wagons.

"Speak," said Seremides.

"Iris," I said, "did you do what I asked of you, while I, Seremides, and Xenon were enduring our interrogations?"

"Yes, Master," she said.

One commonly pays small attention to the comings and goings of slaves.

"What makes you think that Talena is not with the wagons?" asked Seremides.

"I think we agree," I said, "that Cos would wish, at all costs, to conceal the location of Talena."

"Agreed," said Seremides.

"We also agree, I take it," I said, "that rampant rumors would place the location of Talena with the caravan, and, if she were not in the caravan, it would be in the best interest of Cos to encourage those rumors."

"If she were not in the caravan," said Xenon.

"Yes," I said. "Then note that Collis, the caravan master, engaged in almost no attempt to convince me that the Cosian expedition was confined to a geographical survey, one intending to map a new route to Ar. Almost immediately, he spoke in such a way as to seem to verify the rumor, namely, that the caravan was transporting Talena to Ar. He did not even pretend that Talena had been seized by the raiders. He insisted that she was still safe with the caravan."

"And if she were not," said Xenon, "why else would the caravan continue its approach to Ar?"

"Yes," I said.

"To prolong the deception," said Xenon, "clearly."

"And Collis warned us, supposedly for our own safety, to stay away from the caravan," I said.

"Thus," said Xenon, "we would be likely, in one camp or another, in one village or another, to repeat, even enhance, the rumor of Talena's location in the caravan."

I was surprised at Xenon's contributions to the matter under discussion. This seemed uncharacteristic. I do not think that this pleased Seremides. In this, was he not exceeding his role as a simple servant, helpmeet, and convenience? Might he not, too, have some interest in these matters?

"I regret," said Seremides, "only that we have been warned away from the wagons."

"Our proximity," I said, "would doubtless provoke suspicion, and we might be killed."

"Now it is I who am despondent," said Seremides.

"Be not so," I said, "for I am confident that Talena is not with the wagons, but that the caravan is a diversion, an enormous, expensive ruse."

"Absurd," said Seremides.

"Who owns the highest military office in Cos, under Lurius of Jad?" I asked.

"Obviously Myron, the polemarkos of Temos, he, the polemarkos of Cos, cousin to Lurius of Jad," said Seremides.

"I met him in Jad," I said, "in the Ubarial palace, that night when I was posing as an emissary from Ar, come to identify the prisoner, Talena of Ar. Surely he, one of such stature, would be intimately involved in all dealings with Ar. And on whom else would Lurius rely in matters so important as the delivery of Talena to Ar and the collection of the reward? He even witnessed my identification of Talena."

"And?" said Seremides.

"Myron was not with the caravan," I said.

"Ela!" said Xenon. "We are lost."

"Collis, the caravan master," I said, "was clearly in command. All deferred to him, all men, and all seeming officers, without hesitation or reservation. One notes such things. If Myron was in the camp, given the importance of a raid on the camp and the attempt to abduct Talena, he would have personally presided at our interrogations."

"Perhaps he concealed himself," said Seremides.

"In such a matter," I said, "he would not rely on others."

"Still," protested Seremides.

"I put Iris about the camp," I said, "to absorb and remember any shreds or tatters of talk which might seem of interest. I furnished her, as well, with a description of Myron of Temos, and she, besides her own observations, inquired as to him of slaves, several of whom would know him from the citadel at Jad. The purport of her efforts confirmed my conjecture that Myron of Temos was not in the camp."

"You assume," said Seremides, "that if Talena was amongst the wagons so, too, would be Myron, the polemarkos."

"That is my assumption," I said.

"And if the polemarkos is not amongst the wagons, then neither is Talena."

"True," I said.

"I think I would still follow the wagons," said Seremides.

"Do so, if you wish," I said, "at the risk of discovery and impalement."

"I do not wish to accept what you say," said Seremides, "for, if I do, our journey, all our strivings, are unavailing, fruitless."

"We will have failed," said Xenon, angrily.

"Iris," I said, "have I reported your findings accurately?"

"Yes, Master," she said.

"Have you anything else, even seemingly trivial, to add?" I asked.

"I do not think so," she said, "only camp talk, only road talk."

"Think, recall," I said.

"One girl," she said, "was a source of amusement to others. They were rather unkind to her. She was almost in tears."

"A slave," I said.

"Yes, Master," she said.

"Tell me about it," I said.

"It is nothing," she said.

"Now," I said.

"She had a dream, three nights in a row," she said, "a terrible dream."

"What dream?" I demanded.

"Of tarns," she said. "She is terrified of tarns."

"Well might she be," I said. The gigantic, broad-winged, crested, wickedly taloned, scimitar-beaked tarn was ill-tempered, powerful, aggressive, difficult to control, and often unpredictable. Sometimes they turned on their riders. They could tear the arm from a man's body as easily as one might bend down and tear up a talender by the roots.

"She dreamed she was alone, forlorn, wandering in a great grass-land, and then, looking up, to her terror, she saw tarns, and they saw her, and they swooped toward her, and one, more swift, more fierce, than the others, clutched her in its talons and she, mercifully, awak-ened, screaming the word 'Samnium.'"

"Why Samnium?" I asked. "It is a town on the coast, or near the coast, south of our present position. It is not large. It is not well known."

"It is meaningless," said Seremides.

"Perhaps so, perhaps not," I said. "Dreams are interesting. Often they are woven from disparate materials, things desired, things feared, from past experiences, from present happenings, from a thought remembered, from a remark heard, from things not even much noted during the day."

"What are dreams but the madness of the night?" asked Ser-emides.

"In madness there may be meaning," I said. "It may be reality in disguise."

"Absurd," said Seremides.

"I can understand a girl's fear of tarns, or anyone's fear of tarns," I said, "but what have tarns to do with Samnium? What might the girl have heard? Why should she, in the caravan, in her dreams, link tarns with Samnium?"

"You know little of Samnium," said Xenon.

"That is true," I said.

"There are tarns in Samnium," said Xenon, "but not as you are likely to think of them."

"Go on," I urged him.

"Draft tarns," he said. "In Samnium there are freight companies, companies which specialize in moving wares amongst cities."

"How is it that you, Xenon, a simple oarsman, a simple brother to the oar, know this?" asked Seremides.

"I have often rowed between Jad and Brundisium," he said. "In Brundisium one hears much."

"They move lighter wares," I said, "precious wares, or wares of only a few stone?"

"No," said Xenon. "These are not war tarns nor racing tarns. They are draft tarns. A draft tarn can carry a quarter the load of a common wagon. A string of linked draft tarns is a caravan in the sky. To be sure, such caravans are rare. Draft tarns are expensive, much like a prize war tarn. Tharlarion are much cheaper, easier to care for and manage, and can live off the land. A sky caravan of more than ten tarns is unusual. It can cost as much as a land caravan of forty wagons. Too, a land caravan may have three to four hundred wagons. Given expenses, there is no comparison. It is also more difficult to guard a sky caravan against attacks from rogue tarnsmen."

"But," I said, "if there were sufficient guards, enough tarnsmen aflight?"

"I conjecture then," said Xenon, "there would be no difficulty."

"But who would trust the tarnsmen," asked Seremides, "mercenary tarnsmen?"

"They work for the companies," said Xenon. "Their pay is high, secure, and regular, far more than they would be likely to get from perfidy and thievery."

"Unless," I said, "they were transmitting a cargo of enormous value, a cargo the nature of which they were unaware."

"Yes!" said Xenon.

"Put away thoughts of tarns," said Seremides. "Talena is surely with the wagons, a prisoner in the caravan of Collis."

"Suppose," I said, "two or three ships from the Farther Islands, having been protected on the open sea, broke off from the fleet before its landing south of Brundisium."

"And," said Xenon, swiftly, "disguised as simple merchant ships, made landfall near Samnium."

"They would wait," I said, "for several days, engaging in mercantile activities, thus cloaking their true purpose, while making arrangements and reconnoitering."

"They must wait, too, in any event," said Xenon, "to let the wagons, a marvelous diversion and decoy, mysterious and well armed, move away from the coast, drawing bounty hunters after it like zarlit flies to honey."

"You give undue credit to Cosians," said Seremides. "Such tactics would be worthy of a genius, of a Dietrich of Tarnburg."

"Or a Myron of Temos," I said.

"You are fools to be swayed by the dreams of a frightened, worthless slave," said Seremides.

"Then stay behind," I said, "and attack the caravan."

"That would be madness," said Seremides.

"Our clues are exhausted, our leads are gone," I said. "It is true that a slave's dream is a slender thing, perhaps no more than a puff of wind, a fragment of fog, visible for an instant and then gone, but what else have we?"

Seremides waited for a moment, and then he said, resignedly, bitterly, "I am swayed."

"Then," I said, "we are off to the tarn cots of Samnium."

CHAPTER TWENTY-FIVE

"Read the stone," said Seremides.

"I cannot read, Master," said Iris. Most female slaves cannot read. There tend to be two general exceptions to this. Most Gorean free women of high caste can read; thus, if such a woman finds her neck locked in the collar, one will have a literate slave. Second, the female slaves of scribes are taught to read. I am not sure why this is so. Some say it is to enable the slave to better serve their masters in their work. Others suspect that scribes have the eccentric notion that reading is a wonderful pleasure, in which they wish all rational creatures to share. Beyond that, much depends on the individual master. I can read Gorean but not easily as it is written and printed "as the bosk plows," namely, alternate lines differ, a line written from left to right being followed by one written right to left, and so on. I have been told both lines "go forward," but merely in opposite directions.

"Nor can I," said Xenon.

This was to be expected. One would not expect oarsmen to read. Reading is not required to draw a strong oar. Many Goreans, particularly of the lower castes, do not read. Also, interestingly, they do not see this as a handicap or deprivation. Reading, many say, is for Scribes. Also, if everyone could read and write their own letters, how would Scribes make a living? Some of the Scarlet Caste, the Warriors, who can read, pretend to lack that skill, perhaps lest they be looked down upon as Scribes, perhaps deeming such a skill incompatible with the profession of arms. On the other hand, aristocratic Pani warriors, at the World's End, pride themselves on their literacy, may compose poems on the eve of battles, and so on. In defense of many Goreans, if a defense might seem in order, they do listen to, relish, and often travel far, to see plays, attend song dramas, and hear stories, some of which may take several days to tell, particularly if they are from the lips of famed Singers. The name of this caste does not translate well into English, but it seems to me that "Singers" might be more apt than "bards," "reciters," "story tellers," "poets," and such. Some well-known singers are William of Harfax, Olaf of Kassau, Andreas of Tor, Hakeem of Turia, and Phaidon of Anango.

"It says," I said, "'Samnium—Twenty Pasangs.'"

"Good," said Seremides. "We should reach shelter by nightfall."

"There is little traffic on this road," I said.

"The road is dark and in poor repair," said Seremides. Indeed, in some places it was little more than a narrow, rutted, muddy, winding, leaf-strewn path. Surely there must be better roads to and from Samnium.

Since yesterday and this morning we had seen but two wagons, two peddlers afoot, with their packs, and three carts, two of which were drawn by harnessed female slaves.

"The woods are thick," said Xenon. "This road would well suit brigands."

"I think not," said Seremides. "On such a road, with little traffic, there is little loot, and thus small reward, for brigandage."

Nonetheless, Xenon and I had armed ourselves, I with the long-bow, the Peasant bow, and Xenon with the crossbow. As it was un-likely that Xenon's target, if one presented itself, would be within a pace or so, at point-blank range, I had offered to tender him some instruction in the use of the weapon.

"I am no expert with the short bow," I had said, "but, if you wish, friend Xenon, I would be pleased to assist you, to the extent I can, in its employment."

"You are generous," had said Xenon. "I would be grateful. To me it is an awkward, unfamiliar thing."

"We have no time," had said Seremides, "to make a larl from a tarsk, or an archer from an oarsman. On to Samnium! Each Ahn is important!"

"These woods are gloomy," said Xenon.

"But safe," said Seremides. "One does not look for thieves where there is nothing to steal."

"Perhaps roving brigands, come from afar," said Xenon, "who do not know the country."

"And perhaps sleen wandering in the sands of the Tahari," said Seremides, "and tharlarion cavorting on the ice sheets of Ax Glacier."

"Despise me for my foolishness," said Xenon. "I am but an igno-rant oarsman."

At that moment, from somewhere ahead, out of sight, on that narrow, winding road, we heard a woman's scream, long, shrill, and piercing.

Xenon and I, bows in hand, leaped from the wagon.

"Hold!" called Seremides, pulling our small draft tharlarion to a halt. "Beware!"

"We will move swiftly, cautiously, on opposite sides of the road, concealed in the woods," I said to Xenon.

"Watch," I said to Seremides, who had already unsheathed his sword. "There may be foes anywhere."

"Come back, fools," called Seremides. "Do not involve yourselves."

I looked at Xenon. "Stay back, if you wish," I said.

"I shall take the woods on the other side of the road," said Xenon.

We then proceeded through the woods in the direction from which we had heard the scream.

"He is wounded," I said.

The wagon, much larger than ours, its rectangular roof covered with canvas, was half turned in the road, as though the driver had tried to turn it about and flee.

I turned the brown-clad figure about and half lifted it.

"Caste brothers!" said the man, gratefully.

Xenon and I, and Seremides, back in the wagon, and even Iris, were in the garb of the Peasants.

"His purse strings are cut," said Xenon.

"Do not mind my purse," said the man, hoarsely, intensely, weakly, "save my companion, my beloved Pechia. They seized her." He then pointed in a direction. "That way!" he said.

"How many are there, how armed?" I asked the man.

"That way," he said, again pointing. "That way!"

"The wagon is loaded with suls," said Xenon.

"How many are there, how armed?" I asked the man, again, more insistently.

"Ten, maybe eleven," gasped the man. "Swords, staves, knives."

"Too many?" asked Xenon.

"We shall see," I said.

"Save Pechia, my companion!" said the man.

"Our fellow, and a slave, will soon be here," I said. "They will tend your wound."

"Pechia, Pechia," said the man, and then lapsed from consciousness.

"I have two arrows," I said.

"I have but one bolt," said Xenon, that set in the guide.

"See if there is a weapon in the wagon," I said.

A moment later Xenon said, "No, not even a staff."

I found that strange.

Xenon lifted the lid of the bench box.

"Anything?" I asked, from the ground.

"A sul scraper, a hoe head, some wagon wire, such things," he said.

"You may remain behind," I said. "You can help Seremides and Iris with the Peasant."

"You will continue on?" asked Xenon. "You will stalk?"

"Yes," I said.

He then descended from the wagon.

Our eyes met.

"Shall we proceed?" asked Xenon.

"Are you sure?" I asked.

"Yes," he said. I noticed he had a brought a coil of the wagon wire with him.

"Then let us do so," I said. "The trail will be fresh."

It was clear from their lack of caution that the bandits did not expect to be followed into the woods. The road was little frequented, they had seized the woman, and left the driver for dead. They did, if only as a matter of habit, walk single file. In this way it is necessary only to break a single trail in brush and it makes it more difficult to read the number in the party. The negative aspect of this practice is that it makes it easy to approach the enemy from behind, one man at a time. The wounded man had conjectured ten or eleven foes, but such a figure, given a presumed rush of bodies, and a victim's confusion, dismay, and bewilderment, could easily be in error, by as much as three or four bodies either way.

Amongst the trees, intent on the bandits, I found I was separated from Xenon. As far as I could tell, he was no longer about. I conjectured he might have lost his way in the gloom or thought the better of our business altogether, and, upon reflection, decided to return to Seremides and the wagon. That, of course, would not mean he was out of danger, for some of the bandits, feeling pursuit nonexistent and their escape assured, might have returned to the wagon, to search it more thoroughly or finish off the driver, thus eliminating a witness to their work.

It was, I conjecture, some ten Ehn into my business before one of the bandits turned about, to address some remark to his fellow, he presumably behind him, and discovered, to his consternation that he was alone. I had placed the arrows, from close range, carefully, in such a way as to cause death almost instantly. And I had drawn free, or cut free, the arrow fired four times, so I retained my original two arrows, though one was now thick with drying blood. "Foe, foe!" cried the alerted bandit almost hysterically, turning and fleeing after his unseen fellows. I then seemed alone in the woods, as I cut the arrow free from my last target. I had accounted for five of the bandits, but I did not know how many there were, and those who remained, at least those in the vicinity, would now be alarmed and watchful. I now, an arrow to the string, moved in great stealth. I heard a small bird cry and tensed as I heard a scurrying in the leaves, marking the passage of a startled forest urt. Then I almost cried out, half stumbling over a body. It must be that of one of the bandits. The head was half sliced from the body. The hunter does not move. One casts a stick or pebble to the side. When the target spins about to investigate, the wire is about his throat. I knew then that small, thick-bodied, burly, powerful Xenon had not lost his way or returned to the wagon. He was about somewhere. I looked down at the body. I shuddered. In Ko-ro-ba, the Towers of the Morning, long ago, in my training, I had not been taught to kill in that way. It was not the way of the Warriors.

"Come out and be seen!" called a voice. "Put away your bow. Fair duel! Fair duel!"

Did they know I was of the Warriors! How could they know that? I do not think they knew it. They were gambling. There are the codes, of course, the codes. I wondered if Seremides was right, that codes were for fools. Yet there were codes, the codes.

"Behold, Warrior!" called the voice. "Witness me. I step forward. I present myself. Use your arrow and show yourself a coward, a craven urt, a traitor to your codes, or step forth, weapon to weapon, sword to sword, responding as your codes require, to the challenge of the fair duel."

From the darkness of the wood, I watched him step forth, his sword sheathed. He was a large man. I had no notion of his skill. He might have been of the Warriors. One did not know. He did appeal to the codes.

"Fair duel!" he called. "Fair duel!"

I stepped forth from the shadows.

"Tal, caste brother," he called.

I did not know if he were of the Scarlet Caste or not. It was surely possible.

"Fair duel?" he inquired.

"Fair duel," I said.

"Come closer," he said. "Come within range of my blade, if you dare. Behold, what have you to fear? My steel is still sheathed!"

I bent down and put the bow, and the two arrows, one bloodied, on the leaves. I stood up, and regarded him. "Unsheathe your blade," I said.

"Come closer," he said. "I will unsheathe my blade only when you are within the circle of death."

"You would allow one to that proximity," I asked, "while your blade still sleeps?"

"I trust you will give me time to awaken it," he said.

I then drew my sword and approached him.

"Awaken your blade," I said.

"Behold," he said, half drawing the weapon, "it wakes."

I took another step closer.

"Guard yourself," I said.

He seemed suddenly, decidedly uneasy.

"Draw your weapon," I said. "Let it depart the sheath."

He stepped back a pace, the weapon still half drawn.

I was then closer.

He stepped back another pace, and I followed.

"Draw your weapon," I warned him.

He began to tremble, turned white, began to back away, and called back, over his shoulder, "Fire! Fire! Can you not see him! Shoot! Shoot! What are you waiting for? Do not delay! Shoot! Shoot!"

I crouched down, trying to peer through the gloom of the trees.

He then, letting his blade fall back into the sheath, turned wildly and ran. I followed him, cautiously. He did not run far, only four or five paces, but stopped to regard, with horror, a dangling body, hanging from a low tree limb, its feet some inches from the ground, suspended there by a loop of wire, nooselike, imbedded in its throat. On the ground, near the feet of the dangling body, was a bow, an arrow, and a quiver of arrows, some of which had half spilled from the quiver. It seems there had been a bow amongst the brigands. Apparently it had not been noted by the wounded man, on the road.

The dismayed bandit turned about, whipped his sword from the sheath, and rushed wildly toward me, his blade uplifted. I stepped to the side, entering my blade into the right side of his neck. He ran two or three paces more, and then fell.

"You are not of the Warriors," I said.

A figure emerged from the gloom.

"There is at least one more," said Xenon, "he carrying the woman, Pechia."

"So burdened," I said, "he cannot get far."

"The trail is fresh," said Xenon.

"You saved my life," I said.

"It is thought by some you may prove to be important," said Xenon.

I pondered the oddity of this response.

"Nonetheless," I said, "be thanked."

"It is done," he said. "This way. Follow me."

There was a small but ample clearing in the woods. The bandit, whom I took to be the leader of our foes, may have chosen it with care.

"Hold!" he cried. "Come no closer!"

He held the woman before him. The hood of her robes of concealment had been pulled forward and then down and about her head. It seemed tied in place, by veiling. Too, she may have been gagged. Some ropes had been swathed about her upper body. Her head so covered, and her body so roped, she was as helpless as a hooded slave.

"Stay back!" cried the bandit.

He held the woman to him with his left hand and in his right hand he had a knife, which was at the throat of the woman. A single slash through the garments might have half cut her head from her body.

I stopped, and Xenon, who was somewhere behind me, must have done so, as well. I had recovered my bow, and had appropriated the quiver of the bandit who had been back in the shadows in a former glade, he who was to fire on me when the taunting swordsman had brought me within an easy range of fire. In this quiver I had one of my two arrows, and the arrows of the bandit, including that which was to have been loosed at me. I had one of my arrows, the arrow stained with blood from its several visits to foes, at the string of my bow, but the bow was not bent. Xenon had also retrieved the crossbow with its single quarrel, which instrument to an untrained archer would presumably be little more than useless, unless it could be fired at an extremely close range.

"No closer!" said the bandit.

"Let her go!" I said. "Your life for hers!"

"Put down your bow!" he ordered. I laid it down. I sensed Xenon, who was a short powerful man, moving rather closely behind me. The bandit would know he was there, but my body largely obscured his presence.

"Release the woman," I called. "Let her go free. It will then be safe for you to withdraw."

"I am not a fool!" he shouted.

"Steady!" I cried, for his hand had jerked about with the knife, and I was afraid he might plunge into hysteria, and then I had no idea what might ensue.

"If I let her go," he said, "you will kill me!"

"No," I said. "Trade in lives, yours for hers, hers for yours. Release her unharmed, and you may withdraw in peace."

"I know the trades of such as you," he said. "You gain a woman and I gain an arrow in my back."

"We do not gain the woman," I said. "She is the free companion of the peasant you attacked. We want only to restore her to him."

"I do not believe you!" he said.

"Very well," I said. "We want the woman. What do you want for her? Forty copper tarsks, fifty?"

"I sell her," he said, "and then you kill me and take your fifty copper tarsks back!"

"If you kill her," I said, "you are sure to die."

"I am dead already," he said.

"Then," I asked, "what are you doing?"

"I am buying breath," he said, "the seeing of trees and the sky, for a moment more."

"You may keep the woman," I said. "Do not harm her. You are free to leave. We will not follow."

"I am not a fool!" he screamed. "You are a liar! You will follow and kill me!"

"No!" I said.

"Better two deaths than one!" he cried.

"No!" I said. "No!"

"He is going to kill her," whispered Xenon from behind me.

"I fear so," I said softly, not turning my head.

"Shall we talk further?" asked the bandit.

"As long as you like," I called to him.

"I think I have talked long enough," he called back.

"Down!" cried Xenon, and I, startled, threw myself to the ground, and, at the same time, heard from behind me the heavy, vibrating snap of a cable and the hiss of a flighted quarrel.

I rose to a crouching position, and then rose to my feet, and then walked toward the end of the clearing.

I was trembling.

The guide fins of a quarrel were visible, protruding from the center of the forehead of the bandit. The woman was beside him, inert, bundled in garments and rope, having lost consciousness.

Xenon, with his bootlike sandal, stomped twice on the face of the bandit, forcing tissue and bones down and away from the quarrel, and then, it loosened, jerked it free, put it in his belt, and slung the bow, on its strap, over his shoulder.

"Are you all right?" asked Xenon.

"Yes," I said, "but I want to think."

"I will carry the woman back to the road, to the Peasant's wagon," he said.

"Do so," I said. "I shall be along shortly."

I moved a few feet away from the body of the bandit. I did not care to look upon it.

Many things that I had not really noticed before, I now recalled. These were small things, none seemingly important at the time, which now, considered together, seemed troubling. These were such things as looks, glances, statements, small actions, comments, attitudes, and observations which seemed somehow unlike those which one might expect from a simple, ignorant, illiterate oarsman. Did Xenon not know too much for a simple oarsman? I wondered about the incident on the galley returning from the Skerry of Lars to Jad with Talena. Might not that business have been arranged? Had Seremides truly saved the life of Xenon? Rather, might not some party wish to keep track, somehow, of Seremides of Ar? Did Seremides not relish having individuals beholden to him? Might that penchant not have been cleverly exploited? I was sure now that Xenon was no common oarsman. But what was he? I feared I knew. The garroting in the woods did not speak of the oarsman or of the Warrior. It spoke of another caste. And the shot in the clearing, from some forty paces away, striking between the eyes of the bandit, inches away from the woman, was no result one would expect from one new to, or unfamiliar with, the crossbow. It was a shot worthy of Pa-Kur, Master of the Assassins. And I knew, from Port Kar, that Pa-Kur himself, and, indeed, exiled Kurii on Gor, were interested in the capture of Talena, to access the exorbitant reward being offered, a reward that might assure its recipient of not only enormous wealth, but the influence and power which such wealth bestows.

I rose to my feet, to return to the road.

Xenon was not what he seemed, or wished to seem.

Xenon was an Assassin, and I did not think that he was alone.

I heard the nibbling of forest urts near the body. Swarms of such small creatures, sometimes in their hundreds, can clean the flesh from a tharlarion in a matter of Ahn.

I then began to trek back to the road.

"You have dallied!" said Seremides, leaning on his crutch beside our wagon. "Do you not know we have business in Samnium? Each Ahn may be of importance."

"Where is the wounded man, he of the Peasantry?" I asked.

His wagon was gone and there was no sign of him or the woman.

"His bleeding was stanched and his wound was dressed by Iris," said Seremides.

"He should have returned to Samnium," I said, "to have his wound inspected by one of the Green caste, and then rest and recover."

"He chose not to do so," said Seremides. "When Xenon returned with the woman, he had her placed in the wagon and drove on."

"I trust he was grateful," I said. "We risked much."

"He was very grateful," said Seremides. "He offered to give us half his load of suls for our help in his need."

"Generous for a Peasant," I said.

"I declined his offer," said Seremides.

"Which refusal, I suspect," I said, "he, being of the Peasantry, accepted with good grace."

"They were Rufus and his free companion, Pechia, both of the Village of Two Branches, south of Torcadino," said Seremides.

"That explains their route," I said. "They were going home." I knew nothing of a Village of Two Branches, but I was familiar with Torcadino, the terminus of a noted aqueduct. It was on one of the major routes to Ar.

I prepared to climb into the wagon.

"Hold," said Seremides. "To the right, off the road, there are two bodies, those of bandits who thought to despoil a helpless cripple. You might drag the carrion deeper into the woods. They were heavy for Iris."

"You were once the First Sword of the Taurentian guard in Ar," I said.

"It is dangerous to underestimate a foe," said Xenon.

"And even more dangerous," said Seremides, "not to recognize a foe."

Xenon and I dragged the two bodies several yards more deeply into the woods.

"They had no purses," said Xenon, when we returned to the wagon.

"I have them," said Seremides.

"Add to them, then," said Xenon, "those of nine others." He then, from his tunic, handed a string of purses to Seremides.

"At least," said Seremides, "the morning has not been lost altogether."

We then helped Seremides into the wagon and climbed up after him.

"Hereafter, my friends," said Seremides, "do not go adventuring about without my permission."

"Would you have withheld your permission?" I asked.

"Certainly," he said. "You were both fools. What if one or both of you had fallen to bandits. You put our quest at risk."

"You would have done nothing?" I asked.

"No," said Seremides. "I would have done something. I would have driven on."

"You would have left the man to die and the woman to her fate?" I asked.

"Certainly," said Seremides. "Such things are their concern, not ours."

"I see," I said.

"Now," said Seremides, "we must be on to Samnium. Not an Ahn, not an Ehn, not an Ihn is to be lost."

CHAPTER TWENTY-SIX

Iris screamed, and leaped back.

"Do not be frightened," I said. "The bars separate you from the bird. The bars are strong. You can slip between them, but the bird cannot."

Clearly Iris was unfamiliar with tarns.

The bird had suddenly turned about, looked at her, and snapped its wings. The rush of air, scattering straw through the bars, had whipped our tunics back about our bodies.

"They are big fellows," I said.

I guessed the wingspan would be in the neighborhood of thirty feet. These birds were not the sort which occurred in the wild, but then, for the most part, neither were the tarns with which I was more familiar. Commonly the birds are bred for various purposes, war, raiding, scouting, herding, racing, haulage, and such. Loads in haulage are usually carried in tarn baskets or nets. If tarn baskets are used, the driver commonly controls the bird from the basket. If nets are used, the bird, as with most domestic tarns, will be saddled.

"Forgive me, Master," said Iris, straightening her tunic.

"It is nothing," I said. "Even those familiar with tarns can be terrified."

Eleven birds were in the cot. It could hold several more. There were three such cots, each two stories high, built within a lofty, six-storied, warehouselike building, one cot was reached from the ground level of the building, another from the third level, and the last from the fifth level. We had climbed to the third level. We had been forbidden to climb higher. The cot had two mighty gates, now closed, leading to the open air, each with a perch extending beyond it. Commonly the bird leaves the cot though the left gate and returns by means of the right gate. This was to be expected, given the Gorean practice of keeping to the left side of roads, bridges, stairwells, and such. In this way, typically, one's weapon arm faces oncoming traffic. There were two loading areas where baskets and nets might be loaded or unloaded, one, a smooth, circular expanse outside the building on the ground level and the other on the flat roof of the building. The building itself was cylindrical, unusual in Samnium, but familiar in Gor's high cities, or tower cities, which consist mostly of lofty, cylindrical buildings joined by traceries of narrow, soaring, railless bridges. These cities, in their many colors, are very beautiful, but one supposes, in passing, that one might note, as well, certain other features which might have commended them to Gorean architects, military and civil, such as the maximization of internal space ratios, a round structure's lesser vulnerability to catapult missiles, and the ease with which access bridges can be defended or destroyed, thus transforming each structure, supplied with food and water, into an isolated, defensible keep. A mounted tarn freed of basket or net, of freight, of course, can readily enter or leave such a cot. Tarnsmen who are, in effect, freight guards, or tarnsmen who are bringing the birds to and from the loading areas, for example, would come and go easily.

"I dislike waiting," said Xenon.

"It should be soon now," I said.

"Why will they let us go no higher, Master?" asked Iris.

"I do not know," I said.

"Forgive me, Master," she said. I think she was afraid that I might revoke the standing permission to speak which I had accorded her on the way to Samnium. This permission, like a candy or a bit of meat in her gruel, or a saucer of wine, had been rather in the nature of a reward. The information she had gathered for us from amongst the wagons had put us on the road to Samnium.

Seremides was not with us as he, handicapped as he was, commonly avoided stairs.

The area behind us was mostly flat, dusty, and bare, but, back, toward the wall, stored there, were some miscellaneous paraphernalia not unusual in a commercial tarn keep, harnessing, woven baskets, coiled carrying nets, and such.

"You have selected the birds?" asked Xenon.

"Three," I said, "not the largest, but those I deem likely to be the swiftest."

"The tarnkeepers are not pleased," said Xenon. "They prefer to supply the birds."

"As in buying a woman," I said. "Our coin, our choice."

"There is much pressure on the noble Seremides to rent now, and be about our business. Each day we dally we nourish suspicion."

"We must rent at the proper moment," I said. "Until the target is in place one must not loose the arrow."

At this point two tarnkeepers in short-sleeved leather jackets, who had ascended the nearby stairs, passed us, and then, having went to the stairs leading to the next level, began to climb them, and were soon out of sight. One had muttered something about merchants.

"I trust that your plan may work," said Xenon.

"That is my hope," I said.

"Seremides thinks that Talena of Ar is still with the wagons."

"He may be right," I said.

"Others ascend the stairs," said Xenon.

"I hear them," I said.

"I see your tunics are yellow and white," had said the keep scribe one morning some days ago, looking toward us, away from his standing desk, in the small, first-floor office.

"We are interested in times, schedules, and rates," had said Seremides.

"You are fortunate," said he. "The season is slow."

"Does the House of Iskander," I asked, "have an office in Ar?"

"Certainly," he said. "In season, the traffic is brisk between Ar and Samnium."

"We are interested in Ar," said Seremides.

"So, too, is another party," said the keep scribe.

"Perhaps we might go together," said Seremides.

"I am sorry," said the keep scribe. "The other party wishes privacy."

"Interesting," said Seremides.

"That is often the case," said the keep scribe.

That did not surprise me. Goreans tend to be wary of strangers.

"We do not have much to ship," I said. "I trust you charge by weight."

"Ela," said the scribe, "we charge by trip, and the weight per trip may not exceed a given figure for a given bird."

"How many stages to Ar?" asked Seremides.

"Four," said the keep scribe.

"What do you charge for one basket or net to Ar?" I asked.

"A silver tarsk," he said.

"That is expensive," I said.

"Customarily it is two silver tarsks," he said. "The season is slow."

"Still," I said.

"Wagons, of course, are cheaper," he said a bit shortly.

"We are interested in speed," I said.

"Then you must use tarns," he said.

"We are interested in security, as well," I said.

"Then you must surely use tarns," he said. "Not only are wagons slow, but land routes are perilous. Bandits swarm the roads."

"We will need," said Seremides, "three tarns, one basket, and one net."

"Fees for tarnsmen are included in the price," I conjectured.

"Certainly," said the keep scribe.

"I can handle a tarn from the basket," said Seremides.

"Are you sure?" asked the keep scribe, uneasily. "These beasts are dangerous."

"Do not question me," said Seremides, coldly. It was one of those tones of voice which suggests that steel, somewhere, is eager to leave the sheath.

"Forgive me," said the keep scribe.

"And I," I said, "will handle the bird which carries the net."

"You know the tarn?" asked the scribe.

"A little," I said.

"You have that look," said the scribe. "You will then need a tarnsman for the third tarn, who will, I gather, act as a guard, not that one needs a guard, for few brigands have wings."

"Some do," said Seremides, "those who have at their disposal the wings of tarns."

"The cloud road is safe," said the keep scribe.

"And is the earth where the tarn alights?" asked Seremides.

"Three tarns, one basket, and one net," summarized the scribe.

"You will not need a third tarnsman," said Xenon.

That had been the major weakness in a plan which was bleak to begin with, the enlistment of a stranger.

"The plan requires a third tarnsman," I said, "Seremides for the basket, I for the net, and a third for the purpose I hoped to have made clear."

"That for a guard," said the keep scribe.

"I am the third tarnsman," said Xenon.

"No," I said. "A tarn is not an oar, a weighty object with no mind of its own, waiting to be put to use. It is a living beast, immense, short-tempered, savage, often vicious, sometimes treacherous. Men have been torn to pieces attempting to climb into the saddle."

"I am the third tarnsman," said Xenon.

"You are mad," said Seremides. "Do not be foolish. The saddle of a tarn is not the bench of a galley. Do not risk the blasting, rushing wind. Do not soar, dive, and climb amongst the clouds. Do not face the rain and lightning. Do not brave the sky."

"Perhaps noble benefactor, dearest friend, most worthy mentor," said Xenon, "I have not always been an oarsman."

I attended to this remark.

I was uneasy.

In a way, after the incident on the road, it was unsettling to have Xenon with us, often close, so close, we within the range of a dagger's thrust.

Seremides, however, as far as I could tell, was unaware of my suspicions. Certainly I had not confided them to him. Perhaps he knew more than I suspected. On the other hand, he continued to behave as always with Xenon, treating him as little more than a useful, servile sleen.

"Tarns are not Cosian," said Seremides. "They are not native to the islands. There are few tarnsmen in Cos, and those who serve her thusly are imported men, estranged men, men without Home Stones, mercenaries who will kill for a coin and ask no questions."

"The saddle of a tarn," said Xenon, "is not unknown to me."

"We have our third tarnsman," I told the scribe.

"Then," said the scribe, "three tarns, one basket, one net, three silver tarsks, and payment in advance."

"We expect to leave shortly," I said. "We have some business details to attend to first."

"I understand," said the scribe. "Perhaps Masters might wish to honor the House of Iskander with a small deposit first."

"How much?" I asked.

"Only a silver tarsk," said the scribe.

"That is a third the cost of the entire venture," I said.

"House policy," said the scribe, apologetically.

"One could buy most female slaves for that," I said.

"In some markets," said the scribe.

Iris looked down. Free women know they are priceless. Slaves know they are not.

"Incidentally," said the scribe, "all tarns which are the property of the House of Iskander are banded and marked."

"Where and how marked?" asked Seremides.

"Where and how the House of Iskander wishes," said the scribe politely Then he added, "I trust that you are not tarn thieves, pretending to be Merchants."

"No," I assured him. "But that is more than a female slave, who is usually collared, and marked on the outside of the left thigh, high, under the hip."

"The tarn," he had said, "is far more valuable."

I had then given the scribe a silver tarsk, and then I, Seremides, Xenon, and Iris had taken our leave.

"A party, several," said Xenon, "ascend the stairs."

"Let us continue to observe the birds in the cot," I said. "Turn away."

"They are not stopping on this level," said Xenon, facing the bars of the tarn cot.

"They are then special," I said. We had not been allowed to ascend to the next level.

"They are not to be of interest to us?" said Xenon.

"No," I said, "nor we to them, I trust."

"Were I you," said Xenon, facing the bars. "I would hazard a glance."

"I have done so," I said.

"Was this noticed?" asked Xenon.

"By one or two," I said. "More were interested in perusing Iris." Iris moved a little closer to us.

Women on Gor, both free and slave, have need of the protection of men.

"It might have been more suspect," said Xenon, "if they passed, and we did not note their presence."

"I think so," I said.

"They are gone now," said Xenon.

"We have been long in Samnium?" I said.

"Fifteen days," said Xenon. "Why?"

"You are sure you can manage a tarn?" I asked.

"I have some small knowledge of the straps and saddle," he said.

"You recall my plan?" I asked.

"Certainly," he said.

"Are you familiar with stealth?" I asked.

"I do not understand," he said.

"I had in mind the wire, and the woods about the road to Samnium," I said.

"One must make do with what is at hand," said Xenon. "One must improvise."

"We may need a crossbow," I said.

"I have one, as you know," said Xenon. "You kindly purchased it for me, before we left Brundisium. You thought it less demanding than the longbow."

"You have skill with the device," I said.

"Surely not," he said. "It is a stranger to me."

"In the woods," I said, "you seemed well acquainted with one another."

"The shot was one blessed by fortune," he said. "It is unpredictable upon whom fate will smile. I am only a gentle oarsman. May I ask what purport lies behind your remarks?"

"Soon," I said, "I think we must spend two silver tarsks."

"Things move?" he asked.

"I think so," I said.

"Speak," he said.

"Amongst those ascending the stairs, wearing wind leather and carrying tarn gear, was one whom I recognized, once, long ago, from Ar, during the Occupation, and once, more recently, from the palace at Jad."

"One who was not with the fleet which sailed from Jad," said Xenon, "but was with the ships which embarked from the Farther Islands, and one who was not with the wagons, but one whom you conjectured, if you should find him, you would find Talena of Ar, as well?"

"Yes," I said.

"He was with those who ascended the stairs?" said Xenon.

"Yes," I said, "Myron, polemarkos of Temos, polemarkos of Cos."

CHAPTER TWENTY-SEVEN

From the saddle, in the light of two of Gor's three moons, the white moon and the yellow moon, I looked down and saw the ribbon of a road amidst the darkness of the woods. Samnium was now well behind me.

I drew on the one-strap and the bird began to climb, and then I drew on the two-strap and veered to the right; I then took a deep breath and drew on the four-strap, and the bird dove; with one broad blow of its wings it descended silently, its talons spread like massive hooks; its fierce descent can break the back of tabuk; and then I drew on the six-strap and it wheeled and began to climb to the left. Then I leveled my flight and continued to move east.

The bird was swift and responsive.

I had arranged for a raiding saddle, with its broad leather apron before the rider, across which a woman might be bound, and its saddle rings, two on each side, from each of which a fair captive might be suspended. If one is interested in more than one capture, the early captures are gagged in order that they might not alarm or warn other prey. Commonly, time permitting, the captures are stripped for assessment. One determines whether or not they are beautiful enough to be marked and collared. If they are not, they are released. If they are, they will usually be flown to a temporary camp for processing. Their life as a slave will then have begun. After the camp they are usually transported in slave wagons, or marched across country, under whips, in coffle, to a slaver's house for training and sale.

The swiftest of the three birds I had selected at the House of Iskander was for Xenon. That was important for his role in my plan. The largest, and slowest bird, was for Seremides, who would control its flight from its tarn basket. This, too, figured in my plan.

Across the saddle, in several coils, there reposed a large, light loading net. I wore a long bow, the Peasant bow, over my shoulder. To my left, tied to a saddle ring, was a sheaf of arrows.

As I flew, I thought of many things, and persons, and times and places. I remembered an aunt from long ago who had furnished a child with everything he might want except love. I remembered playmates as a boy, fights over silly things like the outrage of my hair, and the busy streets of Bristol. I remembered the small elite school at which I had briefly taught in the northeastern part of the United States and my friend, Harrison Smith, who became an attorney. And on Gor, this green, fresh, strange, beautiful, and perilous world, I remembered my father, and the warrior, the Older Tarl, and the small scribe, Torm, so impatient of my ignorance of the language, customs, and values of a new and different world. "Put away such thoughts!" I castigated myself. "They are rich, exotic, endless, and often painful. They rise like Tor-tu-Gor, Light-Upon-the-Home-Stone, casting a thousand beams on a thousand realities. How can one live well, if not forward?"

I wondered if I were a coward, and supposed it so. Surely I was afraid. I had often been afraid. Perhaps it is easier to be stupid and unafraid. I did not know. But if one is not afraid, how can one be brave? To see danger, and hold one's place, or advance against it, is to be brave. And bravery so seen is quite compatible with fear. If one is not afraid, how can one be brave? One would not even know what one was doing.

"You are swift, my mighty friend," I said to the tarn. "Do you enjoy the power of flight? I do not know, but I think you do."

I supposed that from the first of mankind, emerging from dens and caves, with rocks and clubs in hand, we had looked into the sky and watched the flight of birds.

Did you pity us, heavy below, walking and crawling things? I thought. Did we shake our fists at the clouds, weeping, amongst which you frolicked? Surely we wondered what it would be to dive and soar, to roll in the wind, to play as you can, and as we could not. Men grew wise and terrible; we invented the knife and the bomb, we learned how to kill one another, ever more widely and easily. But, looking up with bloody hands, did we not, upon occasion, I wonder, envy you again the gift of the sky? We did build machines, heavier and larger than you, machines which can fly higher and faster than you, but it still is not the same, not the same at all. But here, on Gor, some of us, we small and earth-clinging things, share your world, I think as you know it, the world of the sky. We are grateful, we rare few, we who are called tarnsmen.

I flew on.

I was pleased I was on tarnback.

It had been toward dusk when we had seen the flight depart from the roof of the six-story House of Iskander. We had, earlier, counted the tarns flown from the high tarn cot, reached from the fifth level of the building, to the roof. It was on the roof that any baskets or nets would be loaded. There had been fifteen such birds.

"They will fly at night," had said Seremides.

"The tarnsmen will be hirelings from the House of Iskander," said Xenon. "Some may be from Cos, but that is unlikely. In any event, one supposes that few in the flight, of the guards, will have any sense of the value of what is being carried."

"Presumably they will be told the lading is plate, artwork, or semiprecious stones," said Seremides.

"The flight will be expensive," I said.

"Exorbitant," said Seremides. "At least fifteen silver tarsks."

"A small fraction," said Xenon, "of ten thousand tarn disks of gold, of double weight."

"There!" said Seremides, looking up.

I counted six mounted tarns departing the roof.

"One basket!" said Seremides. "And another, and another!"

That was not welcome news.

I had anticipated a single basket.

"Six more mounted tarns," I said.

"Six guards, three baskets, and six guards," said Seremides.

"In flight," I said, "some of the guards will flank the baskets."

"Each basket will have a driver," said Xenon, "presumably furnished by the House of Iskander."

"But each basket will contain at least one Cosian," I said.

"Certainly," said Xenon.

"Eighteen men then," I said, "at least."

"And three baskets," said Seremides, angrily, "and the prize can be in but one. They do not even trust the sky!"

"Look for Myron," I said, "General of Cos."

"It is fortunate that you and sweet Xenon were where you were this afternoon, and noted the presence of the polemarkos," said Seremides. "Otherwise we might have noted not the flight amidst other comings and goings in the House of Iskander."

"Possibly," I said.

We had maintained a close watch.

"The flight, and its departure, such great secrets, would be secrets zealously guarded," said Seremides.

"Great secrets are seldom kept," I said. "They burn like fire in the darkness."

Xenon regarded me.

"Small secrets, unimportant secrets, fare better," I said.

"That is true, dear friend," said Xenon.

"Hold!" said Seremides. "The flight veers north!"

"I made inquiries," I said. "I consulted the board. It is marked for Brundisium."

"Brundisium?" said Seremides. "What has the polemarkos to do in Brundisium?"

"Nothing," I said. "Beyond Samnium, the flight will wheel east, toward Ar."

"Of course," said Seremides.

"Perhaps we should make certain arrangements," said Xenon.

"I have already done so," I said. "Before the bar for the next Ahn, our selected tarns, and a basket and net, will be delivered here, to the ground-level loading dock."

"Can we overtake the flight by the Twentieth Ahn?" asked Xenon.

"Easily," I said, "not only is it a larger flight, which can travel no faster than its slowest tarn, but it is burdened by three baskets, borne by draft tarns, and it must expend time on its diversion north, before turning toward Ar."

"You are sure it will make that turn?" asked Xenon.

"Yes," I said.

"Seremides will have the basket," said Xenon.

"He will lag behind," I said. "When we are ready to begin our operation, he will land and be ready to light a lamp. If all goes well, we can surreptitiously convey our prisoner into his keeping, and lead any pursuit astray."

"There will be at least eighteen men," said Xenon. "We are only two, three, if we count my noble benefactor, Seremides of Ar."

"Recall," I said, "if my plan goes well, we will not engage them."

"But there are three baskets, not one," said Xenon.

"That," I said, "I did not anticipate. It is a most unhappy development."

"So look for Myron, the polemarkos," said Xenon.

"I will," I said.

"Two moons will be full," said Xenon.

"That should make it easier to identify the polemarkos," I said.

"It will also make you a better target," said Xenon.

"That is true," I said.

"Moons bestow their light impartially," said Xenon.

"That is the way of moons," I said.

My tarn sped on, cleaving the night, a swift black cloud amongst others.

My plan was simple. Locating the flight, Xenon, on the swiftest of our tarns, hopefully undetected, would circle about the flight and then approach it from the front, in such a way that he would appear to threaten it, or be ready to threaten it. Perhaps he had expected to find only a single tarn and basket? Then, perhaps he had been dismayed to find a formidable flight, one of three baskets and several guards, and was now fleeing for his life? Knowing that many tarnsmen, particularly undisciplined, mercenary tarnsmen, are eager for combat, and hope to make a kill, one for which they might hope to be rewarded, in prestige, if not in coin, I hoped that the guards would pursue Xenon, leaving the baskets temporarily unguarded. I did not think that Xenon would be in danger, given the swiftness of his tarn and his lead on his pursuers. This form of strategy, in the light of reflection, might seem implausible and transparent, but the history of warfare is replete with examples of its successful execution. The three elements involved are, first, to draw away defensive cover; second, to effect the mission; and third, to escape. I planned one variation on the escape portion of this three-fold action, namely, if possible, in the course of our escape, depositing the prisoner in a secure site, in this case, with Seremides, from which site then, by means of our continued flight, we would divert attention. If all went well, I, Xenon, and Seremides would later rendezvous at a predetermined location, the ten-pasang marker on the small, lonely road we had trekked several days ago on the way to Samnium, when we had encountered Rufus, a Peasant of the Village of Two Branches near Torcadino, and his companion, Pechia.

But there was much more astir in that moonlit night than I knew.

How simple and lovely are plans; how little attention reality pays to them.

I flew on.

CHAPTER TWENTY-EIGHT

It was something past the Nineteenth Ahn when I sighted, far ahead, the flight from Samnium. It exhibited, as yet, no signs of agitation or disarray. By now I supposed that Xenon would be positioning himself for his diversionary sortie. Seremides, somewhere behind me, would not take his tarn down until action was well underway.

I one-strapped to a greater height. This increased the amount of territory I could survey. It also made possible adjustments in a long dive.

Ehn slipped by, and the flight from Samnium continued placidly on its way. I did not see Seremides, with the tarn basket, below and behind me. For most of the flight he was to follow some Ehn behind. There was to have been no obvious relationship between us. But, now, closer to the Twentieth Ahn, it seemed he should be closer. He would have his role to play. Ahead, something seemed different, small perhaps, but different! Was there some reaction to something by the flight from Samnium? Had Xenon approached the flight? Then a cloud obscured the moons, which glowed behind it, like lamps behind a curtain. Then the curtain of the clouds was whipped away. I stood in the stirrups, abruptly. For a moment I thought, wildly, the flight had disappeared. The small dots, swift and lightless, were no longer in formation. They are in pursuit of Xenon, I thought, delightedly. But then, to my consternation, I sensed, and then saw, below me, perhaps twenty tarns, each with a warrior astride. I do not think they were aware of my presence. I sped forward, the newcomers now ahead of me and below me. In an Ehn, perhaps two, at their speed, attack speed, they would be in the vicinity of the flight from Samnium. I could not make out, ahead, for a moment, the guard tarns of the Samnium flight. Certainly they were not in formation. My first thought was that they had been drawn away, perhaps by Xenon, or others, utilizing my own plan of action, to expose the baskets to predation, but, in a moment, I realized, that the matter was quite otherwise. Tarns might not be in a detectible formation, but there were tarns in the vicinity. I was aware of them now. A moment later they seemed to be swarming about the baskets. The Samnium flight was sorely beleaguered. It had been intercepted and attacked, frontally, by a number of tarns, and, shortly, would be struck again, from the rear, by a new wave of assailants, those below and ahead of me. It was a classical, delayed-action pincers attack, attack on one front and then, when the enemy has arranged his forces, attack on another, if possible, unexpectedly, with overwhelming force. Resistance, swept aside, would be futile.

In frustration I maintained my position, above and behind the newcomers. I freed my bow, strung it, and fitted an arrow to the string. I wished that I had the Tuchuk horn bow, the short bow, which easily clears the saddle. Xenon, I knew, wherever he might be, had a crossbow, which easily clears the saddle, but is difficult, on tarnback, to reset.

Then the attackers below me, like a flight of darts, struck the Samnium flight from the rear.

I had, at that moment, little idea of the nature and numbers of those engaging the Samnium flight, front and rear, and no idea of their identity. I supposed them most likely a free company of rogue tarnsmen. Certainly their attack suggested organization, planning, and discipline.

Then I drew back on the straps simultaneously and was hovering over the small war below me. Much was in confusion, tarns were mixed, above, below, and to the sides of the three baskets. Foe met foe, tarn to tarn. There was shouting, and cries of anger, and pain. There was the clash of thrusting spear blades ringing on shields and bucklers. There was the snap of crossbows. In cases, where tarns and riders seemed locked together, where swords met swords, there were sounds of clashing metal and flashes of sparks in the night. Some tarns attacked other tarns, ripping with talons, tearing with massive hooked beaks. I saw some tarns, their breasts masses of blood, or a wing torn away, fall or flutter to the ground, their riders with them. Those of Samnium were outnumbered by at least two to one, perhaps three to one. Most tarn battles, or land battles, do not take place at night. When they do, the battle is referred to as a Moon of Blood. Many of the attackers seemed adept with crossbows, and several, to my surprise, had at least four loaded crossbows within reach. This provided them with a multiplicity of fire and avoided the hazard of struggling to rearm the bow in flight. I did see one thing which dismayed me. More than one of the attackers fired their quarrels into the tarns of the men of Samnium. I knew then that the attackers were not of the Scarlet Caste. To attack a mount is a felon's stroke. It is contrary to the codes. What sort of men could bring themselves to do such a thing? Few of the men of the House of Iskander, whom I could recognize from their livery, were armed with a missile weapon. Their main role was to provide protection for the land camps set up for the stages of flights. I recalled that the keep scribe in the Samnium office of the House of Iskander did not take seriously the possibility of an air attack. I took it that it was so rare as to be discounted. But few flights might be so tempting, or warrant such attention, as the current flight from Samnium. Surely few would transport so rich a prize as Talena of Ar. Below, in the moonlight, I saw one of the tarn baskets forced to earth and, immediately, dismounting attackers rushed to it. If that basket carried Talena of Ar she would be the attackers' prisoner in a nonce. I saw some of the men of Samnium flee the field of the sky. Others remained locked in combat. I had come to seize Talena. I was alarmed. It now seemed that she would fall to others. I must intervene. I must join the fray. I dove into the midst of the tarns and riders below me. I loosed the arrow, from a few feet away, into the heart of an attacker. I fitted another arrow to the string. I think I had fired four times before the attackers realized I was amongst them. I was not in the livery of the House of Iskander. I was armed with the straight bow. Who was I? Was I alone, or was I with others? A quarrel tore at the side of my saddle, sliding against one of the saddle rings. Another, I sensed, sped past. Then another splintered the wood of my bow, rendering it useless. I hurled it from me. I wheeled the tarn away, immersing myself again amongst the whirling men of Samnium and their attackers. The wood of the stout bow, I think, had diverted the quarrel from its likely target, my chest. The attackers wore black wind jackets and black helmets, good for fighting at night. Clouds slipped then between the moons and the fray. Shadows increased. "Beware," called a voice, "an enemy is amongst us!" I deemed myself the object of this cry. Without the bow there was little I could do. To use the sword one must be tarn to tarn and there is seldom an opportunity to trade more than one or two blows. Again then, the clouds torn, scattered, and driven by rushing wind, the moons blazed. I parried a thrust from a spear. The fellow, one of the Samnium flight, probably knew no more, nor cared no more, than the fact that I was not in the livery of the House of Iskander.

Drawing back from the cluster of raging tarns and shouting men, grateful for a moment of tranquility in the storm of combat, I looked, desperately, for the second and third basket. I had scarcely turned about when I saw one of the black-jacketed men fire a quarrel into the side of the large draft tarn which carried the second basket. I was suddenly consumed with rage, improper and dangerous for a Warrior, but such responses can be difficult to control, and brought my tarn up and over he who had fired the bolt, and then drew sharply on the four-strap. My tarn came crashing down on his tarn and my tarn, startled, angry and confused, grasping about, as if it might have fallen upon a running tabuk, seized the rider in his talons. I drew on the one-strap and, at the same time, the rider's tarn reacted. For a moment it seemed both tarns were immobile in the sky. Then the rider's tarn sped away. I saw half of the rider's body still in the saddle, held by the safety strap. My own tarn, its talons bloody, dropped the head and upper torso, it slowly turning, to the ground below. The two male occupants of the basket were both dead. I heard a woman's scream. She may have been prone and bound in the basket. The wounded tarn, bleeding, fluttered downward. "The fool!" cried a black-jacketed fellow. "He risked the Ubara!" "Marlenus will pay not a tarsk-bit for a corpse," cried another. "Who will subject a corpse to a thousand tortures?" The basket had scarcely struck the earth, when seven or eight of the attackers' tarns alighted near it, men leaping from the saddles, clambering about the basket. "We have her!" cried a man, looking upward. "We have Talena of Ar!" Two more of the men of the House of Iskander made their escape. I thought they had fought well. But their cause had been lost. I doubted that they had realized an ally was amongst them. Yet it had made, I was sure, little difference. How strange, I thought, that I, who had hoped to despoil them of their prize, had instead weaponed in their behalf. My hopes were dashed. Talena had been taken! But then, had she been taken? I did not know that. I doubted that he who had cried out so jubilantly upward would be likely to know more of Talena than a description. I soared angrily downward, within a dozen feet of the ground, in the bright moonlight, causing attackers to throw themselves to the ground. In that brief, vivid, flashing moment, I saw the body of a bundled, roped woman and two other bodies, one in the livery of the House of Iskander, the other in Cosian garb, all three having been placed on the ground. I could not tell if the woman was Talena or not. As I drew on the one-strap, gaining height, I sensed two quarrels slip past, like whispers of icy rain, and then, as I sped upward, I saw them seem to pause in the air, spent, and then fall back to Earth. At this time, a wind-swept thickness of dark clouds, heavier and denser than hitherto, brought a darkness into the sky. I felt rain dash upon my face. I took the tarn a few yards higher, isolating myself from the fighting, now desultory, below. It began to rain more heavily. Now I could no longer hear the sounds of war. Darkness had enforced a truce, or perhaps those of the House of Iskander who had not escaped, or had not been able to escape, had made their way to the Cities of Dust. I was disturbed. My plan had come to naught. I had failed. Was all lost? I wiped rain from my eyes with the back of my hand. I feared that the coiled net before me might soon become heavy with water. That might hamper its employment. Thoughts gnawed at the edge of my mind, two thoughts, both on the other side of the door of consciousness. Who were the attackers? I did not take them for common brigands. They were no motley crew. They were uniformed, organized, trained, and disciplined. I was sure they were not of the Warriors. Those of the Scarlet Caste seldom favor the crossbow and would be highly unlikely, given the codes, their pride and honor, to fire on an enemy's mount, be it tharlarion, kaiila, or tarn. Were they then a free company of rogue tarnsmen? They wore black, of course, but that is not surprising when contemplating night action. I then recalled Xenon, whom I suspected of being an Assassin. Then the small hairs on the back of my neck stiffened, and I felt chilled. Had Xenon been planted at the side of Seremides, given Seremides's knowledge of Talena, and his association with Lurius of Jad and the capture of Talena, and even more importantly, now, if Talena was to be stolen from the custody of Cos, who might be better equipped to undertake so hazardous and delicate a mission than the unscrupulous and astute Seremides, he betrayed by Cos and eager for revenge, and the reward for delivering Talena to the courts of Ar? I recalled from Port Kar the interest of Pa-Kur, Master of the Caste of Assassins, as well as that of bestial Kurii, in obtaining Talena, that to exchange her for enormous wealth, wealth sufficient to influence the destiny of a planet or of steel worlds. I was now sure that the attackers, as unlikely as that might seem, here in the remote vicinity of Samnium, were of the Black Caste. Surely there were many things which suggested that. I had not glimpsed Pa-Kur, but I believed his hand was in this. How did they know about Samnium, and the place and time to attack? Might that information not have been supplied by Xenon? Might not Pa-Kur, by means of Xenon, our simple, innocent, devoted, gentle oarsman, be informed of our every move? That seemed coldly possible.

So one thought had broken through that door in my mind, behind which I had sensed something. Assassins flew. And Pa-Kur thrived.

Then the second thought announced itself, darting through that now-opened portal. I had seen what I had seen, but I had not registered it. It was like a sentence heard but only a moment later understood. And only now did I understand what I had seen. At the foot of the second basket, I had, in my close approach, in that vivid, brief instant, seen the roped, bundled figure of a woman, possibly Talena, and the bodies of two men, one in the livery of the house of Iskander, presumably the driver, and the other in Cosian garb. And neither body had been that of Myron of Temos, the polemarkos! In seeing what I had seen, I had not realized the importance of what I had not seen! Perhaps he had been in the first basket forced down. I did not know. But I did know he had not been in the second basket!

Rain drove down. Thick clouds cloaked the sky in darkness. I heard no more sounds of fighting below. Was this still the truce of the night, or merely the silence of a deserted field, where only the dead kept watch? The tarn was becoming difficult to manage. In the wild, tarns do not fly in storms. They seek shelter. Lightning flashed, and the tarn veered away. In that flash of lightning I had seen no war but had seen several tarns, alight on the ground, some dismounted riders, and two baskets. Where was the third basket? It had slipped away in the storm! Thunder cracked the night, and the tarn reacted as if buffeted. I recalled the escape of some of the men of Iskander. Each had sped south, not, as I would have expected, west toward Samnium. In a case of chaos or crisis, a mission disrupted, a good commander, anticipating that possible eventuality, will arrange a rendezvous, a place to regroup. And Myron, the polemarkos of Temos, the polemarkos of Cos, was a fine commander. The men of Iskander who had escaped had been mounted on tarns and had taken their leave well before the third basket, drawn by a slower tarn, a draft tarn, had disappeared in the darkness. I turned my tarn south and urged it to greater speed.

Within five Ehn, ahead of me, in the driving rain, in the flashing of lightning, in the pounding thunder, I saw the third basket.

"Harta!" I urged my tarn. "Faster, faster!"

CHAPTER TWENTY-NINE

I was sure the driver of the third draft tarn, with its basket, had seen me, in the flashes of lightning behind him. Doubtless he had been expecting pursuit. In any event, he increased his speed. But my tarn was swifter than his, and not burdened by a large, square, stoutly woven, dangling basket. It must have been clear that I was gaining and would shortly overtake him, for he ceased to incite his tarn to greater speed, but wrapped the guide straps about the basket's strap post, and turned to regard me.

My heart leaped. It was he, Myron, the polemarkos!

He placed his hands on the edges of the basket. In this way he showed me he held no bow. To be sure, one might be in the basket, perhaps at his feet.

In the pelting rain I drew aside him, some yards away. "Down!" I cried through the storm. "Down! Take the tarn down! Land! Alight! Down!"

"So, pirate," he cried, "you will kill the tarn?"

I did not reply. I preferred to have him think I might well do so. "Alight!" I called. "Down! Down!"

"Where is your black jacket?" he called. "Where is your black helmet? I do not think you are one of them. No. You are an opportunistic fellow, a sprightly knave, an independent rogue."

"Land!" I told him.

"Kill the tarn," he said. "Mayhap you have no spear, no bow, but you might close with it and cut its throat, or, better, wound it a dozen times, weakening it, so that it cannot fly."

"Down!" I said.

"So," he said, "you will not strike the tarn?"

"Take it down," I said.

"I do not choose to do so," he said. "I think you are of the Scarlet Caste, one gone astray doubtless, but yet one still reluctant to scorn the codes."

I was sure he hoped to reach the predetermined rendezvous point, where there might be men waiting, of the House of Iskander, and perhaps even Cosian regulars.

"Bring the tarn down," I said.

"No," he said.

"I can bring it down," I said.

"What is your caste?" he asked.

"I can bring it down," I said.

"Do I know you?" he asked. "I think I know you, from somewhere."

"Descend," I said.

"Do you know who I am?" he asked.

"Myron, of Temos," I said, "polemarkos of Cos."

"No, brigand," he said, "I am Alessandros of Telnar, a merchant."

"Land, polemarkos," I said.

"It seems you know me," he said.

"Your face, your mien, is familiar to many," I said.

"I carry nothing of value," he said. "I will give you a silver tarsk to be on your way."

"Where is your driver?" I asked.

"Killed, pasangs back," he said. "I discarded the body, lightening the load, but it seems not enough."

"I will give you five Ihn," I said, "to begin to descend."

"Let us talk further," he said. "Bargain, negotiate."

"Five Ihn," I said.

He spun about, tore the straps away from the strap post, and snapped the straps viciously, and the tarn, despite its bulk, darted ahead.

I reacted instantly, drawing on the one-strap and then the five-strap, rising above and over the hastening tarn. I then began to uncoil and spread the net, much of which had remained dry, given the coiling. Myron must have grasped my intent, because his tarn then began to beat its way through the rain with abrupt changes of direction and altitude. I knew I could afford but one cast of the net, but given the relative slowness of the draft tarn's responses to the strap commands, I had little fear that my cast would fail of its purpose. Within the Ehn I had spread and dropped the net. It settled gracefully over the speeding bird like a fog of fiber. The bird, happily did not struggle in the net, but, sensing its impedance, half spread its wings and with short strokes, descended rapidly, awkwardly, but safely, to the ground, where it waited, seemingly puzzled and confused.

When I landed my tarn and dismounted, Myron of Temos had already opened the gate of the basket and was waiting for me, his sword drawn.

I unsheathed my blade, as well.

The rain was much lighter now.

"I thought I recognized you," said Myron. "We know one another, do we not? You are Harold of Skjern. We met in the palace at Jad."

"I have been known by that name," I said.

"My offer of a silver tarsk, for your withdrawal," he said, "still stands."

"You carry something of great value," I said. "I will take it."

"Like a thief," he said.

"If you like," I said.

"But I carry little of value," he said.

"You transport Talena of Ar," I said.

"She, a worthless she-tarsk," he said, "save for the price on her head, save for the reward for her delivery to Ar."

"I will take her," I said.

"I have some skill with the blade," he said.

"I am sure of it, polemarkos," I said.

"It seems then," he said, "that either I must kill you, or you must kill me."

"Regrettably," I said.

"That seems a shame," he said.

"Sometimes things are so," I said.

"Before we cross swords, presumably for the first and only time," he said, "you might care to see for whom I, or you, will die?"

He then turned about, reentered the basket, picked up a bundled, roped female figure, and put it on the foot-high, soaked grass between us.

"Here," he said, "is your Talena of Ar."

He backed away a few steps, and I approached the figure, watching him all the time, and then I jerked away the hooding and veiling from the figure.

A lovely, terrified face looked up at me.

It was not Talena!

Instantly it went to its knees, shuddering, putting its head down to the grass.

"I do not understand," I said.

"I told you I carried little of value," he said.

"But it must be Talena," I said.

"Obviously it is not," he said. "Fortunately you can recognize Talena. If you had not been able to do so, presumably, by now, one or both of us would be dead."

"But," I said, "in finding Myron of Temos, one finds Talena."

"We hoped many would deem it so," he said.

"Then," I said, "she was in one of the other baskets."

"No," he said. "But those women are presumably now on their way to Ar."

"I understand little of this," I said.

"The flight from Samnium was a test, a feint," he said. "It would surely be of interest to learn if trying to transport Talena to Ar by tarn was, or was not, promising or feasible. I think we will try it again, by tarn, with certain variations, designed to outwit the curious and predatory. We have profited by this test. Mistakes we made this time, we will not make next time. Our next venture, I assure you, will be better armed, better organized, and better planned. We have learned much. Next time, we will be successful."

"The rain is letting up," I said.

"Yes," he said, "and the moons are coming out."

I struck my left shoulder with the flat of my hand. "Warrior," I said.

"Warrior," he said, returning the salute.

"I will help you disengage the net from the tarn," I said.

CHAPTER THIRTY

"If you cut my throat," said the Cosian mariner, "you will do yourself little good, and me even less good."

"Amidst your cargo," I said, "in your vessel, or in one of your two sister vessels, you brought a free woman here!"

"I trust not," he said. "It is unwise to have a free woman aboard. Who does not know that? They cause dissension."

"Nonsense," I said.

"They raise storms, they bring monsters, tharlarion of the sea, sea serpents."

"And they cause ships to sail off the edge of the world," I said.

"That, too," he said.

"Your home port is Sybaris, on Thera, of the Farther Islands," I said.

"That is true, friend," he said. "Put away your knife."

I sheathed the knife.

"The shippers are merchants," he said. "If all goes well, they cheat the Peasantry, load fine, cheaply bought produce aboard, and sell it on the continent."

"Did all go well?" I asked.

"Less so than in the past," he said. "The Peasantry have acquired the great bow."

"On the continent," I said, "the Peasantry has had the great bow for a thousand years."

"They had not had to deal with Cos," he said.

"You are Cosian," I said.

"Originally from Telnar," he said.

"Here," I said, "near Samnium, you are far from the closest, best continental markets."

"I handle the oar," he said. "I do not chart courses."

"Did your three ships carry any women?" I asked.

"Some slaves," he said, "but they don't count."

"Any free women?"

"Not to my knowledge," he said.

"Were there any sealed cabins, any holds, to which you were denied access?"

"There are always places on a round ship to which common mariners are denied access," he said.

"Have you heard of Talena of Ar?" I asked.

"Of course," he said. "For a time she occupied the throne of Ar. Then, in the time of the restoration of Marlenus, she vanished. Bounty hunters seek her. She is a fugitive. She is still at large."

"She has not been caught?" I said.

"Not as far as I know," he said.

"Are you familiar with the polemarkos, Myron?" I asked.

"Certainly," he said. "We carried him, and some fellow officers, here from Thera, to negotiate some trade agreement with Samnium."

"Does it not seem strange to you," I asked, "that a polemarkos, a general of land forces, should be negotiating trade agreements with a minor city like Samnium?"

"I do the oar," he said. "I row. Others chart courses."

"Where is Myron?" I asked.

"I understand that he is in Samnium," said the mariner.

"Negotiating?" I said.

"That is my understanding," he said.

"You are shipping produce?" I said.

"Yes," he said, "suls."

"Here is a tarsk-bit," I said. There are two taverns in Samnium, the Braided Whip and the Hungry Jard. Buy yourself a drink and some girl use."

"Thank you, noble master," he said, accepting the coin.

"And forget," I said, "that we have had this conversation."

"What conversation?" he said.

I then turned away from the docks at Port of Samnium, and trekked the walled corridor inland to Samnium, whose walls and gate I could see in the distance. The walled corridor allows comings and goings between Samnium and Port of Samnium to be, on the whole, discreet and secure.

After the tarn attack by Assassins, a few days ago, disrupting my plans to acquire Talena, stealing her from the custody of Cos, and my interview with the polemarkos, I had returned to the prearranged rendezvous in the woods, at the ten-pasang stone on the road to Samnium.

Xenon and Seremides were already there.

"I was positioning myself to try to lure the guards from the baskets," said Xenon, "when twenty or more tarnsmen swept by, below me, close to the ground."

"That makes it less easy to detect them, than if they were higher," said Seremides.

"I do not think they even saw me," said Xenon.

"Do you know their nature, their insignia, their garmenture?" I asked.

"No," he said.

"They bore no banners or standards," I said.

"No," he said.

"Who do you think they might have been?" I asked.

"Mercenaries," I suppose," he said. "Some hastily amassed band of brigands. Perhaps some free company."

"What did you see?" I asked.

"I lingered not long in the vicinity of war," said Xenon. "The flight from Samnium was attacked, apparently from both front and rear. The night swarmed with tarns. I saw no service I could do for our cause. I withdrew, coming here."

"I was far away," said Seremides, "on the ground. I lit my lantern, as was the plan, but none responded. After a time, fearing much had went awry, I extinguished the lantern and made my way here, to the point of rendezvous."

"Much had gone awry," I said.

"Are you better apprised than we?" asked Seremides.

"I think so," I said. "I saw two baskets downed, and a third escaping."

"Did the brigands seize Talena, rendering our cause forlorn, our efforts fruitless?" asked Seremides.

"I do not think so," I said. "I pursued the escaping basket, and forced it down. Its driver was none other than Myron, the polemarkos."

"Surely it was he who had Talena in custody," said Seremides.

"But you failed to wrest her away from the polemarkos?" said Xenon.

"He was not carrying Talena," I said. "He permitted me to face strip the woman with him and determine for myself that it was not she."

"Perhaps," said Seremides, "you slew the polemarkos and have hidden Talena away for yourself, to claim the whole reward?"

"I do not think that Talena was with the flight," I said. "Certainly the polemarkos did not seem perturbed on that score. He claimed the flight was a trial, so to speak, a practice flight to test the feasibility of such a mode of delivering Talena to Ar."

"Now he must look for a new mode of delivery," said Xenon.

"Rather," I said, "he seemed sure that such a flight, supplied and altered in some respects, would manage the business quite well."

"He is then preparing another flight," said Xenon.

"It seems he will soon be doing so," I said.

"Where is Talena now?" asked Seremides.

"One does not know," I said. "Presumably either with the ships at Port of Samnium or, as I think more likely, somewhere in Samnium itself, awaiting a new flight."

"You believed the polemarkos?" said Xenon.

"I had little choice," I said.

"She may be back with the caravan, the many wagons," said Seremides, "somewhere east of Brundisium."

"That is possible," I said. "But I do not think so."

"We will return the basket, the tarns, and net to Samnium," had said Seremides, claiming a change in business plans.

"I doubt that we will get much of a refund from the House of Iskander," I had said.

"No," had said Seremides, "not all bandits swarm the roads and prowl the skies."

I was trudging back up the walled corridor between Port of Samnium and Samnium, after my interrogation of the Cosian mariner, when I was accosted by a fellow in the garb of a Metal Worker.

"My captain," he said, "would have a word with you."

"Your captain?" I said.

"Are you Harold of Skjern?" he asked.

"I have been so known," I said.

"Please follow me," he said.

I saw that he wore the sandal boots common in the Cosian infantry.

"Certainly," I said.

After a few Ehn, following the fellow in the garb of a Metal Worker, I entered the now-familiar six-story building owned by the House of Iskander. We ascended the stairwell, noting the first two giant cots and then continued on beyond the third story, at which point Xenon, I, and Iris had been denied passage. We continued past the third cot, which occupied portions of the fifth and sixth stories, and found ourselves on the large, flat, circular roof of the building which, at the moment, was crowded with tarns, and men. I saw no baskets.

"Tal, and welcome," said the polemarkos, beaming, striding toward me. Then he stopped, abruptly, cheerfully, doubtless recalling protocol, and we exchanged sharp salutes. We then clasped wrists, warmly. "How pleased I am to see you, esteemed antagonist, noble opponent. I feared I might not have the opportunity to wish you well."

"You plan to embark," I said. "You will fly?"

"Momentarily," he said.

"I do not understand," I said.

"What do you not understand?" he asked.

"It is day," I said. "Surely you will not risk a flight by day."

"I think it will be safe," he said.

"I see only tarnsmen," I said. "I see no baskets, no basket drivers."

"Some pack tarns will carry more than enough," he said.

"Your flight is local; it is short?" I said.

"No," he said. "It is on to Ar."

"How can that be?" I asked.

"You look for Talena," he said.

"Of course," I said.

"Check the roof," he said. "Examine the saddle aprons, the saddle rings."

"I fear I should find them empty," I said.

"You would, my friend," he said.

"You seem, polemarkos," I said, "in fine spirits."

"Tor-tu-Gor smiles," he said. "The sky is blue, the wind is light, the air is fresh."

"I do not see any women," I said. "I do not see your prisoner. I do not see Talena."

"No," he said. "The business has been long and difficult, but it is now done."

"Your work is done?" I said.

"Yes," he said. "I need stay no longer."

My hand went to the hilt of my sword. "Am I to be slain before Talena is brought to the roof?" I asked.

"No," he said. "But the roof is dangerous. Do not tread too near the edge."

I quickly looked about. No one was immediately near me but the polemarkos himself. Clearly I could free my blade before I was seized, to be cast from the roof.

"Where is Talena?" I demanded.

"Our diversions have been successful," said the polemarkos. "We have given them the time they needed."

"Where is Talena!" I demanded.

"She is elsewhere," he said.

"Is she here?" I asked.

"No," he said. "She is already in Ar."

My body shook. I was stunned.

"How is that possible?" I asked.

"It has been accomplished," he said.

A tarnsman then led a large, fine tarn to us, and steadied it in place. The polemarkos then ascended the leather saddle ladder, with its wooden rungs, tied it up, and fastened his safety strap. He looked back, and down, at me.

"I wish you well," he said.

"I wish you well," I said.

I then watched the tarns, one by one, take to the sky.

I wept.

The gates of Ar had closed behind Talena.

CHAPTER THIRTY-ONE

"Then all is lost," said Seremides.

"Even then," said Xenon, "some fight on."

"Only fools," said Seremides.

"Will you return to Cos?" I asked.

"For what?" he asked. "To beg in the streets?"

"What will you do?" I asked.

"You dare not go to Ar," said Xenon. "You are proscribed. Impalement would follow on arrest."

"And so, too, to all who might shelter or assist me," said Seremides.

"The risk is too great," I said.

"I think," said Seremides, slowly, "you think to cast the marked stones once more."

"One chance in a thousand," I said, "is more than a thousand times more than no chance in a thousand."

"In Ar," said Seremides, "Seremides was proscribed, tall, strong, and fierce, quick with the blade and swift with temper, easy to recognize, not a nondescript, haggard, impoverished, unkempt cripple, the pathetic Bruno of Torcadino."

"Put ambitious, unwary thoughts from you," I said.

"Kindly, sweet, simple, faithful, innocent Xenon, reliable servitor," said Seremides, "are you at my side?"

"As always, noble mentor," said Xenon.

"Would you serve me in Jad?"

"Surely," said Xenon.

"Unquestioningly, like a mindless brute?"

"Yes, mentor," said Xenon.

"And in Ar?" he asked.

"I could serve you even better in Ar," whispered Xenon.

"If nothing else," said Seremides, "we might witness some of the lengthy, hideous tortures by means of which Talena of Ar might, however inadequately, attempt to pay for her treason, perfidy, and greed."

How odd, I thought, is the commerce of punishment. What is it, truly, that the scales of justice weigh, or pretend to weigh?

"Do not return to Ar," I said. "You risk too much."

"Are you going to Ar?" he asked.

"Yes," I said.

"You will wager everything on a last cast of stones?"

"Yes," I said.

"Fool," said Seremides.

"Are you not another?" I asked.

"And I am a third," said Xenon.

"It seems we three are then again together," I said.

"I know men," said Seremides. "You, pleasant Geoffrey of Harfax, hope to cheat me of a mountain of gold."

"Let us postpone such considerations," I said, "until we have a mountain of gold, of which I might then endeavor to cheat you."

"I am not easily cheated," said Seremides.

"I am sure you are not," I said.

"Do not fear, beloved mentor," said Xenon. "Geoffrey of Harfax is a man of honor."

"So, too, once was I," said Seremides.

"Mentor?" asked Xenon.

"Many men who once knew the name of honor," said Seremides, "have, in the presence of power and gold, hastened to forget it."

"How so?" I asked.

"It is simple," said Seremides. "Honor melts in a golden fire."

"I do not think always," I said. "I hope not always."

"I know little of honor," said Xenon. "It is for the upper castes, but I would fear to betray an oath."

"What oath have you uttered, by what have you sworn?" I asked.

"Oh, to draw the oar well, such things," he said.

"You have not sworn by the silent, bloody quarrel, or by the un sheathed knife, blade upward?" I asked.

"Be silent," said Seremides. "Xenon knows nothing of such things."

"I take it we agree," I said. "We are all forth to Ar."

"It will take weeks to reach Ar," said Seremides.

"Not by tarn," I said.

"Have you three silver tarsks?" asked Seremides. "The bandits of the House of Iskander insisted on not only the return of the tarns, the basket, and net, but the return of their entire rental."

"They have their rules," I said. "It is not their fault that we did not, weeks ago, complete the journey to Ar."

"Have you three silver tarsks?" asked Seremides, once more.

"We can sell the wagon and tharlarion," I said. We had already sold most of the sa-tarna from the wagon, to defray our expenses on the road and in Samnium. The coins taken from the bandits on the Samnium road, too, had, by now, been mostly expended.

"That will not gain us even a silver tarsk," said Xenon.

"Iris," said Seremides.

"Master!" protested Iris.

"Not enough," said Xenon.

"We shall have to steal tarns," I said.

"And a basket," said Seremides.

"Or, say, borrow them without permission," I said.

"I do not think that that is practical," said Xenon.

"We must try," I said.

"Even if we were successful," said Xenon, "the House of Iskander would hire riders from the Black Court in Brundisium to pursue us."

"You fear the denizens of the Black Court?" I asked.

"Who would not?" he said. "Once they take fee, they are relentless. They are tenacious, like sleen. They would hunt us down. I, for one, do not care to be hunted by Assassins."

"I shall do what I can alone," I said.

"And leave us in Samnium?" said Seremides.

"If necessary," I said.

"That will not be necessary," said Xenon. "If my mentor, my benefactor, beloved Seremides, wishes to reach Ar, the least I can do is help him to do so."

"I think that you, too, desire to reach Ar," I said.

"Only to serve Seremides," he said.

"How is it that you have such funds?" asked Seremides. "A common oarsman is paid in copper tarsks at best, and only when the voyage is done."

"One saves, over many months," he said.

"I admire your frugality and thrift," I said. "Too, your gift, which we gladly accept, will make our journey not only feasible, but considerably less perilous, given the possibility of an implacable pursuit."

"I am pleased to be of service," he said.

It was highly unlikely that an oarsman would have such funds. In this, I saw the hand of Pa-Kur, Master of the Caste of Assassins. Not only, in my opinion, had he organized the raid on the night flight from Samnium some weeks earlier, but he was hedging his bets, so to speak, in case Seremides and I, both formidable competitors, might somehow be successful in seizing Talena. And, as far I knew, he might have planted spies and agents amongst other bounty hunters. I also expected, from what I had heard in Port Kar, of certain doings in the marshes of the delta, that he might be in league with Kurii.

"This will do very nicely," I said, accepting the coins from Xenon.

I noted that the three coins were, as I had expected, not of the mintage of Jad, or even of another polity on Cos, or of the Farther

Islands, but of Brundisium, home to, after the Caste had been banned from Ar, the largest, richest, and most feared Black Court on Gor.

"I think," I said, "there is little chance we will be successful."

"That is true," said Seremides, "but we will try."

"Gold is persuasive," I said.

"I have often listened to it," said Seremides.

"It whispers," I said. "It need not shout."

"Perhaps you, too, hear it, noble Geoffrey of Harfax," said Xenon.

"Certainly," I said. "Who does not?"

"It is one thing to hear it," said Xenon. "It is another to obey it."

"Precisely," I said.

"Perhaps," he said, "we will learn who will obey the glittering master and who will not."

"That is possible," I said.

CHAPTER THIRTY-TWO

"That is the great gate of Ar," I said.

"Perhaps there is time," said Xenon. "I do not see the skin of Talena nailed to the gate."

"It is too soon," said Seremides. "She would first have to be subjected to weeks of exacting torture."

"I can remember when the gate was burned and the walls were rubble, torn down by those of Ar herself, duped into rejoicing in their own defenselessness, during the Occupation, dismantled stone by stone, to the music of flute girls."

"I, too, remember that," said Seremides. "With glad tears those of Ar were persuaded to celebrate their own ruination."

"One manipulates terminologies, one seizes schools, one controls the public boards, one invents new goods and bads, one praises this and dispraises that," I said. "It is an art, a secret route to power."

"Obviously the walls have been rebuilt," said Xenon.

"And higher and stronger than before," said Seremides.

We had arrived in the vicinity of Ar two days ago. As soon as we had learned that, according to Myron, the polemarkos of Temos, the polemarkos of Cos, that Talena was safely in Ar, we had rented a draft tarn and basket, and two saddle tarns, from the House of Iskander in Samnium, and set out for Ar. Xenon and I had been astride the saddle tarns, and Seremides, from the basket, had controlled the draft tarn. Iris had ridden with Seremides in the basket. Xenon and I thought that this was the best arrangement, as it freed us for maneuverability and weapon use, should we encounter rogue tarnsmen on the flight to Ar. Happily we found the skies clear. For most of the trip, Iris was kept in the bottom of the basket, often bound, hand and foot. Slaves expect to be, and commonly desire to be, secured. Such things, like the locked collar, reassure them that they are property and owned, as they wish to be. When a slave is knelt, collared, with her hands tied behind her back, she well knows herself a slave. In bonds her vulnerability cries out. In chains, her submission needs rage. She knows that she is owned and that she belongs. She is not a free woman; but what she wants to be, a slave who belongs to her master. She does not want freedom; she wants a master who desires her with so fierce and mighty a passion that she need have no fear of being freed. She is desired as what she is—a slave. We did not take the tarns and basket into the city, for we wished to enter as inconspicuously as possible. Accordingly, we arranged, outside the pomerium of Ar, to have them delivered to the office of the House of Iskander in the city. We had then purchased a small wagon, and a small draft tharlarion as we had before, long ago, near Brundisium.

We were in a long line of wagons, carts, hand carts, and fellows afoot, waiting to pass through the gate.

"Do you think the gate will be watched, noble Seremides of Ar, noble Bruno of Torcadino, dear friend?" asked Xenon.

"Certainly," said Seremides. "Gates are always watched. And, I suspect, in times like these, all the more so."

"And who watches?" asked Xenon.

"As many as find a purpose in doing so," said Seremides.

"Should we not then have sought entry by means of a lesser gate?" said Xenon.

"No," said Seremides. "At a lesser gate there is even greater scrutiny. The more obscure the portal, the more likely it is to be accessed by undesirables."

"I trust, beloved mentor," said Xenon, "no one will recognize you."

"Who," asked Seremides, "would recognize the formidable Seremides of Ar in the form of the pathetic cripple, Bruno of Torcadino?"

"And," I said, "those who might recognize him might fear to do so."

"Such terror yet clings to the mere memory of Seremides of Ar?" asked Xenon.

"I think so," I said. "I suspect few would like to point him out if not backed by a dozen, armed guardsmen."

"I see," said Xenon.

"And, who knows, he might have cohorts who would mete out a swift and terrible vengeance to one so unwise as to identify him," I said.

"But he does not," said Xenon.

"Few informers would know that," I said.

Xenon and I were standing near the paused wagon. Seremides was in the wagon, on the bench, reins in hand, and Iris was back in the wagon. Xenon looked over to me. "Do you have friends or enemies in the city?" he asked.

"I suspect," I said, "a few of each."

"Ar is large city," said Seremides. "In it, as in Turia, one will find adherents of many Home Stones."

"Aetius of Venna, the bounty hunter, he of the scar, encountered near the village of Red Stream, by the camp of the great caravan, will have brought the false Talena to Ar," said Xenon. "I do not think he will be well disposed towards us."

"Of what should he complain?" asked Seremides. "We did nothing but tell him the absolute truth."

"But in such a way that he would believe the opposite," said Xenon.

"Let him be on his guard," said Seremides.

"And us, as well," said Xenon.

"Look," I said, "there!"

"What is it?" asked Xenon.

"There, passing," I said, "in betraying garb!"

"It cannot be," said Seremides.

"What?" asked Xenon.

"There, in black," I said, "openly, an Assassin."

"I have heard of them, I have never seen one," said Xenon.

The fellow then passed us.

"He is not hunting," I said. "The dagger is not painted on his forehead."

When the dagger is painted on the forehead, most Goreans will clear the way, standing aside, avoiding the Assassin, letting him be about his business. One often thinks of the Black Caste, the Assassins, as being little more than hired killers; but, in a sense, they are the nearest thing, on Gor, to an international police force. If a crime is committed in one city, say, a murder, and the murderer flees to a different city, the guardsmen of the first city are not going to pursue him, or at least not indefinitely and tenaciously. Their Home Stone is elsewhere. In this way, at least occasionally, the Assassin is a nemesis of the wrongdoer, and an instrument of, if not justice, at least retribution.

"You have never seen an Assassin before?" I asked Xenon.

"No," he said.

"Assassins are not always easily recognized," I said. "They are not always in the habiliments of their caste."

"Interesting," said Xenon.

"I do not understand it," said Seremides. "The Caste of Assassins was outlawed in Ar, after the time of the horde of Pa-Kur."

"Apparently something has changed," I said.

"He has passed through the gate," said Seremides. "He was not challenged."

"Something has changed, indeed," I said.

"The line is moving, let us move up a bit," said Seremides.

We moved somewhat closer to the towering portal.

"Drums," said Xenon.

"Yes," I said.

"Soldiers, a column?" asked Xenon, who turned about, craning to see.

"I do not think so," I said. "It appears to be guardsmen, clients, retainers."

"Make way, make way, to the side, to the side!" called a guardsman.

The pounding of the drums was closer now.

Those in the line, and in the crowds about, began to divide themselves, opening a corridor leading to the gate.

"What is it?" asked Xenon.

"Civilians, and guardsmen, a retinue of some sort," I said, drawing the tharlarion and wagon to one side.

"Who are they?" asked Xenon.

"I do not recognize the livery," I said.

"I do not care to be delayed," stormed Seremides.

"Be patient, gentle benefactor," said Xenon. "I see the flash of sunlight on spear blades."

The drums were now both insistent and close.

"Make way!" called a guardsman. "Make way!"

"What is it, who dares approach a gate with drums, who would press his way before others, who would pass?" I asked a fellow in the garb of the Bakers.

"Stand back," he said. "It is a personage of preeminent importance, the noble Decius Albus, trade advisor to the Ubar."

Several of those about pushed back even further, to better widen the passage for the oncoming entourage.

First came two ranks of five guards each; behind them came two ranks of five drummers each; behind them came four ranks of five spearmen each, and following that came an open palanquin borne by ten massive servitors. Reclining on the palanquin, in lavish robes of white and gold was a large, heavy-faced, closely shaven, saturnine man who stared ahead, not deigning to recognize the throngs through which he was being carried.

"Ai!" gasped Xenon, startled.

"Hold steady," I warned him.

"What is that?" gasped Xenon.

The hirsute, bent, monstrous thing, belted and accoutered, as large as three men, was shambling beside the palanquin, the knuckles of its large paws, like knotted fists, almost touching the ground.

I was startled to see such a thing abroad in daylight, in public.

I also noticed, to my amazement, that its appearance seemed to arouse no dismay or panic in the crowd. Apparently it had seen it, or such things, before.

"It is a form of life," I said, "a Kur."

"I did not know such things existed," said Xenon.

"They exist," I said.

I did not tell him that such things, having ruined their native world, now coveted the fresh, green world of Gor.

I recalled the Assassin earlier seen, bold in his sable habiliments. I looked upon the passing beast. This was not the Ar I knew, not the Ar I remembered.

The beast turned and looked back at me, and curled its lip, revealing fangs.

Does he know me? I wondered. I do not think so. Perhaps it is merely surprised, or displeased, to find that its eyes were met.

Following the palanquin, back-braceleted and chained by the neck, barefoot and in brief livery, were two lines of display slaves, ten in each line. Display slaves are chosen for their grace and beauty. It is not unusual for a rich Gorean's palanquin to be so followed. It is a display of wealth, for the female slave, as an owned object, is a form of wealth. Following the display slaves, bringing up the rear of the retinue, in a single rank, were five shield-bearing, heavily armed guardsman.

"Look upon the slaves, pretty Iris," said Seremides, "see how beautiful slaves can be."

"I may not be so beautiful as they, Master," said Iris, "but I assure you that I am as much a slave as they, and perhaps even more so."

I smiled to myself, pitying the women of my former world, so denied their sex. How they starved in a sexual desert. Few, it seemed, could wear their collars and be handled by masters as the slaves they were save in their dreams.

The sound of the drums then became more faint, and the line was once more formed, and began, bit by bit, to move toward the great gate.

"I fear we have much to learn anew of Ar," I said to Seremides.

"The taverns will be more informative than the public boards," he said.

The Baker, to whom I had spoken earlier, was quite close to us. "We near the gate," he said. "You should have your tarsk-bits ready. The gatesmen do not care for dalliance."

"What tarsk-bits?" I asked.

"You are a stranger," he said.

"It is long since we have been in Ar," I said.

"They will want ten tarsk-bits," said the Baker.

"Absurd," said Seremides.

"Two tarsk-bits for each free person," said the Baker, "two for the wagon, and one each for the two beasts, the tharlarion and the slave."

"Passage to and from the city is free," said Seremides.

"Yes," said the Baker, "officially, but, from some lesser folk, the gatesmen demand a gratuity."

"We will not give it," said Seremides.

"Then you will not enter," said the Baker.

"We will pay it," I said.

"You will have no choice," said the Baker.

"That is corruption, bribery, graft," said Seremides.

"Clearly," I said.

"I do not know," said the Baker. "I am not a Scribe of the Law."

"Next," ordered a gatesman.

I drew the tharlarion forward by its halter.

"Do you carry foreign Home Stones within the gates of Ar?" asked the gatesman.

"No," I said.

"Do you intend harm to the Home Stone of Ar?" he asked.

"No," I said.

"Ten tarsk-bits," he said.

I counted out ten tarsk-bits, slowly.

"Hurry, be quick," said the gatesman. "Others wait."

"How much do you pay, to become a gatesman?" I asked.

"Do you wish to pay twenty?" he asked.

"No," I said. "Ten is more than enough."

The Baker, following us, paid two tarsk-bits.

Inside the gate, and to the side, I spoke to him. "Surely," I said, "the gatesmen do not keep all the money they collect."

It seemed that, if so, they would be fabulously wealthy.

"Certainly not," said the Baker. "It is others who grow rich."

"Assassins," I asked, "administrators, officers, beasts, trade advisors?"

"I do not know," he said.

"And it is not wise to look into the matter?" I said.

"I wish you well," he said, and hurried away.

"I wish you well," I whispered, after him.

It was late afternoon.

"May I speak, Master?" called Iris from the back of the wagon.

"Yes," I said.

"I am hungry," she said.

"We will eat later," I said. "And then, after that, you may feed."

"Yes, Master," she said.

"Cuff her," said Xenon.

"Lash her with your belt," said Seremides. "She should know enough not to speak up in such a manner."

Iris turned white.

"On her former world, she was a free woman," I said. "It is only on Gor that she finds a brand on her thigh and her neck clasped in a locked collar."

"Let her understand her brand," said Seremides. "Let her learn the meaning of the collar on her neck."

"Forgive me, Masters!" wept Iris.

"She is highly intelligent," I said. "She learns quickly."

"Forgive me, Masters," she wept. "I am only a slave!"

"Where is Xenon?" I asked Seremides.

"I do not know," said Seremides.

I was not pleased to hear this for, given my misgivings and suspicions concerning Xenon, I much preferred to keep track of his whereabouts.

"He approaches," said Seremides.

"What is wrong?" I asked.

"I have made inquiries," he said. "I have asked about, pertaining to stables and other matters."

"Try the Metellan district," I said.

I was thinking of boarding in the Metellan district. In that district, it is easy to remain inconspicuous.

"I am uneasy," he said.

"How so?" I asked.

"Do you not think it strange," he asked, "that having arrived in the vicinity of Ar, and having approached, and passed through, the great gate, we have heard nothing of Talena?"

"I had not thought of it," I said.

"Nor I," said Seremides.

"I have made inquiries," he said. "It is strange."

"Speak," said Seremides.

"All to whom I spoke," he said, "believe Talena to be still at large."

"No mention of Cos, or such?" said Seremides.

"No," said Xenon.

"I think she is in the city," I said. "I am sure of it."

"But where? Why have we heard nothing of it?" asked Xenon.

"I do not know," I said.

"I am hungry," said Xenon.

"We will stable the tharlarion and store the wagon," I said. "We will then have Iris prepare something."

CHAPTER THIRTY-THREE

We had now been in Ar for three days.

"Kneel here, to the side," I told Iris. "And do not interfere with the serving."

The Silver Tarsk was in the Metellan district, on the Via Cora, sometimes referred to as Barrier Street, from an instance in the Occupation when some citizens of Ar had barricaded it against Cosian soldiery whilst most other districts, following decrees from the Central Cylinder, were welcoming Occupational forces with wreaths and flowers. This resistance, small and ill fated, had been brief and quickly crushed. Thanks to the indulgence of the Ubara, Talena, these indiscreet patriots were proclaimed to be misguided zealots more in need of pity and instruction than corporal chastisement, such as impalement. Thus Talena, in a notable act of clemency, to the relief and delight of most of Ar's more accommodating citizens, remanded them to the care of selected physicians and scribes, in various facilities, to be cured of improper, unhealthy thoughts. Thus, they became not martyrs but proofs of the kindness and rightfulness of the Occupation. Thus, what might have proved to be an embarrassing, bloody contretemps was turned into a political coup. The prisoners, whose education had apparently not yet been completed, were released from prison at the outset of the brief, savage restoration of Marlenus, in which restoration they then played a fierce, vengeful role. The female prisoners had not been long in prison. They had been branded, collared, and sold out of the city. They would remain slaves. In the Gorean view, if a woman has once been a slave, she is always a slave. Once collared, they are no longer fit for freedom. The collar spoils them for freedom. Once a woman has knelt before a man, what more can she be then, but a slave? What free woman would have anything to do with a woman who was once a slave? They do not consort with slaves. They despise and command them. And the slave, interestingly, having been a slave, and having learned her womanhood, rejoices in service and submission. Many slaves would be terribly uneasy without their collars. They want to be in them, and know they belong in them. Their collars are precious to them. Their collars mean more to them than freedom and gold. They are slaves, and want to be slaves. And do not many women, even free women, long for their collars?

We had now been, as noted, in Ar for three days. Yesterday we had considerably, comparatively, replenished our meager resources by selling the tharlarion and wagon. We had received five silver tarsks. "Observe," I had said to Iris, displaying the coins in my hand, "five silver tarsks. Most female slaves will sell for less than two silver tarsks, and many go for copper, not even a silver tarsk." As Iris was a barbarian, I thought it well to call this to her attention. As a free woman she had been priceless, but now, as a slave, she was worth what men deemed her worth. It is instructive to barbarian slave girls, girls brought from Earth to the collar, and even to recently enslaved Gorean free women, to understand such things. They are commodities and are now valued as such. It is a sobering experience for many of them to learn that in an open market they may sell for less than a domestic tarsk. This can be a chastening experience for many of them, particularly for those who might, from the height of their freedom, have entertained a somewhat inflated view of their value. "That is undoubtedly true, Master," had said Iris, "comparative prices and such, but, still, I suspect most men would prefer a girl, a needful, collared slave, at their feet to a tharlarion."

"In the sul market," I said, "I saw some men of Tharna."

"The same as in Jad?" asked Seremides.

"I do not think so," I said.

"It has been years," said Seremides. "Their cause is hopeless. They will never find the lost child of Tharna."

We heard the bar for the Eighteenth Ahn.

Were men watching us?

But I did not think so.

"I fear for you, noble benefactor," said Xenon to Seremides. "You are wanted in Ar. I fear you may be recognized, even from the great gate."

"That is unlikely," I said. "We have been in Ar unassaulted, and, I suspect, unnoticed, for three days."

"Perhaps they are waiting to strike," said Xenon.

"Why?" asked Seremides.

"For you to first lead them to Talena," said Xenon.

"I do not know where she is," said Seremides.

"Others do not know that," said Xenon.

"You do not know that," I said to Xenon.

"I do not understand," said Xenon.

"It is nothing," I said.

"The tavern is crowded," said Xenon.

"It is the Eighteenth Ahn," said Seremides.

"I would that news was in the air," said Xenon, "as well as the fumes of paga."

"It is," I said. "We must essay the inquiry."

"Do so," said Seremides. "This is an Ahn when men grow loquacious, having drunk enough to regale one another, but not enough to lapse into somnolence."

"Be discreet," said Xenon. "We are strangers here. It is dangerous."

"The hunter who would snare game," I said, "is well advised to leave the house."

"Unless the sleen is abroad or the larl prowls," said Xenon.

"Paga, Masters?" asked the auburn-haired paga slave who had approached the table, and knelt. Auburn hair, other things being equal, is likely to raise a girl's price.

"Yes," I said.

"Master is handsome and strong," she said. "Shall I wind a lace for my wrists about the stem of his paga goblet?"

"Not now," I said, "perhaps eventually, but, first, invite those fellows at the next table to join us. They seem a jolly sort, and I fear their goblets may be little more than damp by now."

"Yes, Master," she said.

The newcomers were four in number, two Peasants, a Wood Worker, and a Tarnkeeper. They all wore the badge of the Blues. In Ar, tarn racing is popular and factions form themselves, based on the riders of different keeps, or companies. The two largest factions are the Blues and the Reds. At some other tables, one fellow or another wore the badge of the Reds. I saw only one fellow wearing the badge of the Yellows. Given the rivalry between these factions, it would be unusual to find individuals publicly adhering to different colors at the same table. Fortunes are won and lost over the tarn races. Requirements, eligibilities, licenses, qualifications, rules, and such, are arranged, set, administered, and enforced by a state authorized agency or commission. Most individuals in the tavern, as nearly as I could tell, were not interested in, nor bore any allegiance, to any of these factions. At least they wore no badges or insignia suggesting they did. It might be noted, in passing, that Seremides, Xenon, and myself were in a rather nondescript garb, which suggested that we might be of the drovers or wagoners, commonly understood as a cousin caste to, if not a subcaste of, the Peasantry. It seemed to us this might make us less conspicuous in the city, certainly in the Metellan district, and would make it easier for us to relate to, and question, members of the lower castes. Men of the lower castes tend to be quieter, and less communicative, more careful in speech, and more subdued in expression, when in the presence of those of the upper castes than otherwise. The stability of Gorean society tends to be the consequence of rank, distance, and hierarchy. There is nothing unusual in this, as an ordered society naturally tends to be more stable than a disordered, chaotic society in which there is a constant warfare of all against all, and each against each, for status, success, wealth, and privilege.

"Tal," we greeted the newcomers, to which greeting they responded affably, the auburn-haired serving slave meanwhile, in answer to my gesture, hastening back to the paga vat, soon to return with a tray of brimming goblets.

"How go the Blues this season?" I asked, to which simple, modest question I received, over the next few Ehn, a great deal more information than I had expected to receive, or cared to have.

"It has been a long time since we were in glorious Ar," said Seremides. "What is new and different?"

"No," I said, "other than in the factions."

"Ar thrives," said the Wood Worker.

"That is because, outside the walls," said the first Peasant, "we plant and harvest in peace."

"We are the ox on which the Home Stone rests," said the second Peasant.

"Merchants buy and sell," said the Tarnkeeper. "Initiates eschew beans and charge for prayers and spells. Scribes ink scrolls, Builders build, Physicians heal, Bakers bake, Metal Workers work metal, Leather Workers work leather, Players battle on the kaissa board, Warriors, in the kaissa of steel, battle on the field and in the sky. Things go on much as usual."

"What do you hear of Cos?" asked Xenon.

"As little as possible, and more than one wishes," said the Tarnkeeper.

"Cos!" said the first Peasant, spitting on the floor.

"You hate Cos," I said.

"Who in Ar would not?" asked the Wood Worker.

"You are not of Cos, I trust," said the second Peasant.

"Certainly not," I said.

"Near the great gate," said Seremides, "I saw an Assassin, openly in the habiliments of that caste, which caste, I thought, was outlawed in Ar."

"No longer," said the Wood Worker.

"The horde of Pa-Kur was disbanded long ago," said the first Peasant.

"It was necessary to restore the legitimacy of the Assassins," said the Tarnkeeper. "Ar had become a refuge city, a shelter city, to which murderers and thieves from all over the world might flock, to be safe and unsought, to go unpunished for far crimes."

"It used to be," said the first Peasant, "that one who murdered and stole in Turia, and fled the laws of Turia, might reside untroubled in Ar and enjoy here the fruits of his unsavory labors."

"Not so easy for them now," said the second Peasant.

"Let them quail for they may be, unbeknownst to themselves, even now hunted by an Assassin," said the Tarnkeeper.

"With the Assassins," said the Wood Worker, "laws have claws, and can scratch in far places."

"I think," said the Tarnkeeper, "Marlenus wished, too, to apply the experiences and skills of the Assassins in the search for the villainous Talena, puppet of Cos, wickedly installed on the throne of Ar."

"Where is Talena?" I asked.

"Who knows?" said the first Peasant.

"She is still at large," said the Wood Worker.

"Some days ago," said Seremides, "as we were preparing to enter the city, we were passed by the procession of the retinue of Decius Albus, the trade advisor to the Ubar."

"He often has duties which take him outside the city," said the first Peasant.

"Beside his palanquin," I said, "there was a fearsomely visaged beast, a pet perhaps."

"It is no pet," said the Tarnkeeper. "Was its chest not crossed with leather? Did not accouterments dangle from its belt?"

"I saw one once," said the first Peasant, "in whose monstrous grasp was a mighty ax."

"It was not a pet then," I said, "but a companion, a confederate, a colleague?"

"I fear so," said the Wood Worker.

"Decius Albus often goes outside the city," said the first Peasant.

"To deal with such creatures?" I asked.

"Perhaps," said the first Peasant.

"We do not know," said the second Peasant.

"He is popular, Decius Albus, the trade advisor, is he not, in the city?" I asked. I had no idea of how the trade advisor was viewed in the city. By this question, I hoped to learn something of the politics of Ar.

Our guests were suddenly silent.

Then the Tarnkeeper said, "He is well regarded when his minions, on either side of his palanquin, scatter copper tarsks in the street."

"He seeks to buy popularity," I said, "with coins rather than deeds?"

"He frequently sponsors games in the arena," said the first Peasant.

"We prefer the races," said the second Peasant.

"So he must be quite popular," I said.

"He is ambitious, and cruel," said the first Peasant.

"He is hated," said the second Peasant.

"Be quiet," said the Tarnkeeper

"It is said," whispered the first Peasant, "he wants to be Ubar."

"Be silent," said the Tarnkeeper. "Your village lies outside the walls. You do not know what is in the city."

"You guard your speech," I said. "Perhaps there are spies about?"

"We do not know you," said the Wood Worker.

"Who are you, really?" asked the Tarnkeeper.

"Simple drovers," I said, "long absent from Ar, inquisitive fellows now seeking to learn what might be new in the city."

"Why did you guest us at your table?" asked the Wood Worker.

"Was it not because paga loosens tongues?" asked the Tarnkeeper.

"We have been long from Ar," said Seremides. "We merely wished, I assure you, as said, to learn what was new in the city."

"And share a bit of paga with friendly fellows," I said.

"We know nothing," said the Tarnkeeper, "and you have learned nothing."

"We are loyal to the Home Stone of Ar," said the Wood Worker. "We are patriots."

"I am sure you are," I said.

"Felicitations to Marlenus, our glorious Ubar," said the Tarnkeeper, "and to his loyal and patriotic friend, a jewel of our city, Decius Albus, the trade advisor."

"We must be elsewhere," said the Wood Worker, rising, as did the others. They then took their leave.

"May the Blues do well," I called after them.

We watched them take their way from the tavern.

I turned to Seremides. "What do you make of that?" I asked.

"They are frightened," said Seremides.

"I think," said Xenon, "that things may not be going on as much as usual in Ar, as was claimed."

"The surface is calm," said Seremides, "but there is stirring in the depths."

"Did you note the hatred of Cos?" I said.

"A heritage from the Occupation," said Seremides.

"When Marlenus posted the reward for Talena," said Seremides, "he could not have anticipated, of the thousands of bounty hunters seeking her, that she might fall into the grasp of Lurius of Jad."

"How would the citizenry of Ar receive the news that the reward, such exorbitant wealth, wealth which might buy cities, build fleets, and recruit armies, will be delivered to Cos?" asked Xenon.

"Not well," I said.

"Chaos would ensue," said Seremides. "The Central Cylinder would be shaken to its foundations. In the streets there would be rage and fire. The throne itself might topple. The brand of revolution would flame."

"I fear so," I said.

"And thus, we know," said Seremides, "that the reward will not be delivered to Cos."

"How do you know that?" I asked.

"Because it would be madness to so deliver it. Only a mad man could risk chaos. Only a mad man could bestow such wealth and power on a mortal enemy."

"Dear Seremides," I said, "you overlook one thing."

"What is that?" he asked.

"Honor," I said. "A promise, a commitment, the pledged word of a Ubar."

"Do not jest," said Seremides. "Honor is absurd. It is a trap, a delusion! Is honor not a sword on which to fling oneself, a dagger to be plunged into one's own breast, a knife with which to cut one's own throat?"

"I trust not," I said.

"Repudiate it," said Seremides.

"I do not think Marlenus will do so," I said.

"Why not?" he asked.

"Because," I said, "he is of the Scarlet Caste."

"May I speak, Masters?" asked Iris, who had been kneeling quietly to the side, evident, but not obtrusive, as befitted a slave.

"Yes," I said.

"I take it," she said, "that Masters believe Talena do be in the city, presumably in the care of a delegation from Cos."

"That is a fair surmise," I said. "Certainly it is my view."

"Whereas it is well known that curiosity is not becoming in a kajira," she said, "it is also well known that kajirae do tend to be inveterately curious."

"I have heard that," I said.

"As I understand it," she said, "it is also common knowledge that what might be common knowledge to one person may not be common knowledge to another."

"I trust this line of discourse is going somewhere," I said.

"Certainly," she said. "It is an unwise kajira who risks the whip."

"Continue," I said.

"This afternoon," she said, "I learned, rather inadvertently, something which is common knowledge in Ar, but was not common knowledge to me."

"Proceed," I said.

"Like many kajirae," she said, "I am fond of beautiful things, like flowers, and I wandered about this morning, to my delight, in the great flower market of Ar, and was struck by the switch only twice."

"You were fortunate," I said. Men tend to tolerate unattended slaves, particularly if they are attractive, but free women are less permissive, particularly if they are attractive."

"I heard," she said, "that soon masses of flowers will be brought into Ar, some by tarn, from as far away as a hundred pasangs."

"For what reason?" I asked.

"A reason," she said, "which was common knowledge to those of Ar, but not to me."

"And what reason was that?" I asked.

"For the holiday," she said, "for the great celebration, the great festival, the anniversary of the Restoration of Marlenus."

Seremides smote the table with his fist. "That is it!" he exclaimed. "On that day, the prisoner, the captive, Talena, the treasonous Ubara, the long sought, hated, now-apprehended criminal, will be presented to the people of Ar!"

"I would not be she," said Xenon.

"When is the anniversary of the Restoration?" I asked Iris.

"Four days from now, Masters," she said.

"That gives us little time to steal her from Cos and present her to Marlenus as our own prisoner!" said Seremides.

"She will be heavily guarded," I said. "We do not even know her location."

"One will know her location," said Seremides.

"Who?" I asked.

"Marlenus, Marlenus of Ar," he said, "who will not wish to bestow the reward for her capture on Cos."

"With information from Marlenus, and the help of guardsmen of Ar, supplied by Marlenus, disguised as mercenaries," said Xenon, "we can seize Talena, and claim the reward."

"Your plan, dear friends," I said, "is brilliant, but flawed. First, we have no access to the Ubar; second, that which occurs so naturally and plausibly to us will occur as naturally and plausibly to numerous others, others who are in a much better position than we to carry it through; and, lastly, Marlenus, if he could prevent it, would not allow so treacherous and dishonorable a scheme to be implemented."

"The Scarlet Caste again!" scoffed Seremides.

"So Marlenus would allow the city to burn and the towers to crumble?" said Xenon.

"Yes," I said, "if he be the Marlenus I once knew."

"Slave," said Seremides. "Have you heard of a delegation from Cos, or any foreign delegation, recently arrived in the city?"

"No, Master," she said.

"All is lost," said Xenon. "There are hundreds of compartments in hundreds of cylinders in Ar, and hundreds of insulae, and common dwellings, too, from hovels and huts to mansions and palaces."

"I am troubled," I said.

"How so, more than we?" said Seremides, angrily.

"Let us assume, as seems plausible, on the word of Myron, the polemarkos, given in Samnium, that Talena is in Ar," I said.

"That seems probable," said Seremides.

"How could she have been brought to Ar," I asked, "with bounty hunters, and brigands, and even Assassins swarming about, with harbors and roads watched, with the very skies scrutinized?"

"What is important," said Seremides, "is that she is in Ar, not how she might have been brought to Ar."

"It seems not to have been by mighty caravans or swift flights of tarns," said Xenon, regarding me closely.

"Two stratagems suggest themselves," I said. "Either she would be delivered by means of massive force, even by regiments or a small army, which might then be challenged by similar forces, possibly precipitating a war, which obviously has not taken place, or subtly, secretly, inconspicuously, unnoticed."

"The polemarkos," said Xenon, "is a master of intrigue."

"And an audacious soldier," I said, "familiar with the screening of movements, one aware of the value of the unexpected, and one who might, in a desperate situation, by subtlety and deceit, boldly seize an opportune risk."

"I am sure we all think highly of the polemarkos," said Seremides. "Let us agree to commend him. Now, what has this to do with anything?"

"I wonder if we know more than we think we do," I said.

"I begin to tremble," said Xenon.

"On what ruse did the three Cosian ships harbor at Port of Samnium?" I asked.

"You told us, to assist the polemarkos on a trade mission," said Seremides, "a lame hoax at best."

"What else?" I asked.

"To cargo suls for continental sale," whispered Xenon.

"It takes time to construct a persona," I said.

"Even now," said Xenon, "we are in the Metellan district, a shabby district, noted for low trade, coarse goods, and staple markets, for suls and sa-tarna, and where one might discreetly hire, or dispose of, a tharlarion and wagon without being subjected to embarrassing questions."

I slapped the palm of my hand down on the table, and, looking about, called "Slave!"

The auburn-haired slave who had brought us paga hurried to the table and knelt. "Paga, Master?" she asked.

"No," I said.

"Shall I bring the lace for the stem of your goblet?" she asked.

"No," I said.

"Master?" she asked.

"You must know friends of ours," I said, "another drover, one who recently returned from the west, perhaps Torcadino, Rufus, Rufus of the Village of Two Branches, near Torcadino, and his free companion, Pechia."

"I know he of whom you speak," she said, "but he has no free companion."

"Where is he?" I asked. "We would sup and drink with him."

"He has not been here in days," she said. "He has changed his name to Ruffio. I think he came on wealth. His fortunes seem to have much changed, and for the better."

"Where is he?" I demanded.

"He moved," she said. "I am not sure where. I think I heard the Tower of Philebus. Yes, that is it. The Tower of Philebus."

"Excellent," I said.

"I am pleased if I have been of service to Master," she said.

"What have you been named?" I asked.

"Cora," she said.

"As in the street?"

"Yes, I was named for the street."

I thought it suitable to keep her name in mind. She, unknowingly, had rendered us a great service.

"You are beautiful," said Seremides.

"Thank you, Master," she said.

I smiled. It was rare for Seremides to pay a compliment.

Perhaps it had to do with the auburn hair.

"Go," I said, gesturing her away.

She rose, frightened, and scurried away, back amongst the tables.

I then called for a coinsman, a taverner's man who collected coins from the tables. Slaves are seldom allowed to touch money, save under particular conditions, as in shopping. Even the money cast to the feet of a dancer is commonly retrieved by a taverner's man.

I paid him the tarsk-bits for the paga we and our guests had consumed.

His hand trembled, fumbling with the coins, and then he had them in his hand, his fist clenched. Sweat beaded on his forehead.

"What is wrong?" I asked.

"Nothing, Master," he said.

"We take our leave," I said. I rose and Xenon rose, and helped Seremides to his feet. Iris rose, too, but kept her head down, that she might not meet the coinsman's eyes directly.

He withdrew, abruptly, stumbling a bit.

"What is wrong with him?" I asked.

"He is afraid," said Seremides. "He draws away, quickly, perhaps to confer with someone, the vat master or proprietor."

"I do not understand," I said.

"The tavern is uneasy," said Seremides. "Look about. We are attended to, but furtively. We are supposedly strangers. We asked questions. They think we are spies, presumably for Decius Albus, the trade advisor."

"Perhaps," I said.

As we made our way from the tavern, the coinsman hurried after us, and spoke. "There are many fine taverns in the Metellan district," he said, "much better than the Silver Tarsk."

"Are we to feel unwelcome here?" I asked.

"Not at all!" he protested. "It is only that the Silver Tarsk is an inauspicious tavern, unworthy of a superior clientele."

"Where better," I said, "than in such a place to hear the rumblings of sedition?"

"We are all patriots here," he said.

"I am sure of it," I said.

"Allow me to return to you the tarsk-bits you paid for paga and service," he said.

I dismissed his offer with a negligent gesture.

"The noble trade advisor is most generous, as always," he said.

Our party then graciously took its leave of the Silver Tarsk.

We paused outside on the street, the Via Cora.

The voice of Seremides shook with emotion. "Do you truly think it possible that we had Talena in our very hands?" he asked.

"I think it possible," I said.

"We never saw the woman's face," said Xenon.

"When we returned her to Rufus, if that be his name, the drover, he offered us half his load of suls in gratitude," I said. "That, in itself, should have made me suspicious. Peasants are narrow traders, eager to drive hard bargains. They are shrewd and thrifty. A Peasant might have offered half his load before his companion's return, but, the return assured, I think his gratitude would be less likely to extend so far."

"I could cry out in rage, I could howl to the clouds in fury!" hissed Seremides. He pounded his crutch savagely on the stones.

"Let us hope few learn of our failure," said Xenon.

I could think of at least one who would not be pleased to learn that Xenon had allowed Talena to slip from his grasp, one whom it would not be well to displease.

"By now," said Seremides, bitterly, "Talena will have been delivered to Marlenus."

"I do not think so," I said. "You must not forget the theater in this. "Politics, in its public image, is largely a form of theater. I am certain that Talena, at long last captured, will be delivered to Marlenus in the course of some carefully planned function, in some public, impressive fashion."

"Ideally on a suitable day," said Xenon, "one marking an important occasion."

"Precisely," I said.

"Such as the anniversary of the Restoration of the Ubar," said Xenon.

"I would think so," I said.

"That is four days from now," said Seremides.

"Time is short," said Xenon.

"It might as well be four years," said Seremides.

"She will, of course, be well guarded," I said.

"One cannot well guard two treasures equally," said Xenon.

"I do not understand," I said.

"Talena is unimportant in herself," said Xenon. "It is gold which is important. Gold is supreme. She is no more than a means to gold."

I did not doubt but what this was true for my colleagues.

For me it was not true.

Were I fortunate enough to somehow seize Talena, would not my two most formidable adversaries then be my present allies?

I did wonder what, were she not Talena, she would bring on the block.

At the time, as indicated, I did not understand the import of Xenon's remark, that about the difficulty of guarding two treasures equally. It did not, at that time, occur to me that he might have information at his disposal lacking to Seremides and myself. He had been separated from us for a time, shortly after our entrance into the city. Or, perhaps, rather, he knew certain others better than we knew them.

"What do we do now?" asked Seremides.

"We seek one who may know the whereabouts of Talena," I said.

"How do we go about that?" asked Xenon.

"We go visiting," I said.

"On whom will we pay a call?" asked Seremides.

"On an old friend," I said, "one met on a road not far from Samnium, Rufus, or Ruffio, whose fortunes seem to have improved as he now resides in a tower, the Tower of Philebus."

"That is one of the most opulent towers in Ar," said Seremides.

"Then it seems," I said, "his fortunes have indeed improved."

"He may not wish to speak," said Seremides, "and we lack gold to tease words from him."

"Sometimes the coinage of steel is even more persuasive," said Xenon, his fingers lightly prowling about the hilt of his dagger.

CHAPTER THIRTY-FOUR

"Approach no closer!" he said. "Armsmen are about, within easy call!"

"They may be close," I said, "and within easy call, but they are currently unresponsive."

"Guards! Guards!" he called.

"In an unkind fashion, they intended to drive a crippled beggar from the portal," I said. "Had they been more generous or more charitably inclined, they might have noticed what was behind them."

The room, one of at least two, was bright, large, colorful, and well appointed. There were two broad windows. In typical Gorean fashion, there was little furniture, but some carpets and cushions. There were no pantries or closets, but storage, as is common in such places, was provided by chests along the walls. There were two cabinets, and there was a low, small table about which one might sit cross-legged. On the table there were two goblets, both on the surface of the table.

"Who are you? What do you want?" he asked.

"Friends," I said, "and what we want you may easily give."

"I will give you a copper tarsk," he said, "a whole copper tarsk! Then be on your way!"

"Perhaps he is indeed of the Peasants," I said.

"He values his life cheaply," said Xenon, his dagger drawn.

"Or a copper tarsk exorbitantly," I said.

"Where are my guards!" he demanded.

"Resting," I told him.

"A silver tarsk!" he said.

"Surely Rufus, dear Rufus of the Village of Two Branches, that within the ambit of Torcadino, you recall us," I said.

"I am Ruffio, Ruffio of Ar!" he said.

"You were pleased enough to see us on a road from Samnium," I said.

"You!" he said.

"How is your companion, Pechia?" I asked.

"I know not whereof you speak," he said.

"Scour your memory," I suggested. "Surely some crumb of recollection will remind you, if nothing else, of her current location."

"A flow of blood," said Xenon, "often loosens the tongue of memory."

"I have no companion," said Ruffio.

"The woman then," I said, "whether she be a Lita, a Renata, or even a Talena."

At the mention of the name Talena, Ruffio turned white.

"How is it that you chose to transport the woman on such a lonely road?" I asked.

"I did not choose to do so," he said. "I was in fee. I obeyed the orders of my principal. The road was chosen because it was gloomy and sheltered, and little known, and commonly carries little or nothing of value."

"You did not anticipate brigands," I said.

"Not on that road," he said.

"It is time for me to use the dagger," said Xenon.

"How did you find me?" asked Ruffio.

"In a tavern," I said, "it seems you boasted of the ascendance in your fortunes, and of a new, projected residence."

"And in the cylinder?" he asked.

"Simple inquiries," I said. "We entered on the bridge at this story."

It was the twentieth story, a story where we would be unlikely to be noticed. Seremides, with his crutch, with a begging pan, stood on the bridge near the entrance to the cylinder. In this way, he kept watch, and guarded the entry by the bridge terminus. Here he could also attend to the two guards, restoring them to unconsciousness should they begin to stir. The bridge was a typical narrow, railless, graceful, soaring, arching bridge, easily defended by one or two men and not difficult to break away and destroy by heavy hammers, if it were militarily advisable.

"He plays for time," said Xenon.

"Who could blame him?" I asked.

"I do not know where the woman is," said Ruffio.

"Liar," said Xenon.

"I think it quite possible he does not know where she is," I said to Xenon.

"Then let us kill him now, and take our departure, undetected," said Xenon.

"And the guards?" I asked.

"Two quick strokes of the knife," said Xenon.

"For a simple oarsman," I said, "you seem unusually complacent with respect to the shedding of blood."

"The stakes are high, the risk is great," he said.

"I doubt that even Bruno of Torcadino," I said, "would be so complacent."

"He is no longer needed," said Xenon.

I shivered, I hoped not noticeably.

"I remember Bruno of Torcadino, the tragic cripple," said Ruffio, "he in the wagon with the comely slave. He seemed both kindly and astute. Doubtless in his suffering he gained much wisdom and his counsel would be one of circumspection and moderation. You should consult him before you do anything rash."

"Do not tempt me," snarled Xenon.

"I really would not tempt him," I said. "He is a splendid fellow, but he has one weakness, killing people whom he regards as difficult or unreasonable."

"You jest," said Ruffio, nervously.

"Of course," I said.

"I am neither difficult nor unreasonable," he said.

"I am glad to hear it," I said.

"Vent no wrath upon me," he said. "I am a simple, ignorant fellow, whose blood would serve no purpose on your friend's blade."

"You fail to do yourself justice," I said. "You are obviously brave, bold, and clever. In selecting you for so delicate and dangerous a mission, your obscure principal exercised a judgment worthy of a high general or even a Ubar. Few of Cos, even high officers, would have had the courage and sagacity even to enter upon that mission which you carried off so brilliantly."

"I was well paid," he said.

"I would hope so," I said.

Following my remark, his demeanor changed. Accepting my words, he no longer assumed the character of an intimidated coward. Is not deception the essence of intrigue, the heart of strategy, even the name of war?

"Kill me," he said, "if you please, or if it should charm your short, zealous, homely friend, but I do not know the whereabouts of Talena."

"I was not certain you would," I said. "I hoped, however, by means of you to make the acquaintance of another, one whom I suspect is near at hand."

"I am alone," he said.

"No, you are not," I said. "Behold the table. On it are two goblets. As each contains wine, we may suppose your guest is still in the domicile. As neither of the goblets are on the floor, we may infer that your guest is a free person."

At that point, a tall, bearded figure appeared in the portal of an adjoining room, a short, military cloak loose over his left arm.

"Tal," I said, and struck my left shoulder sharply.

"Tal," said Myron, polemarkos of Cos, returning my salute, striking his left shoulder with a fist, which was closed about the hilt of a short sword.

"I am armed," he said.

"Clearly," I said.

"Your blade is sheathed," he said.

"Evidently," I said.

"Do you wish time to draw your blade?" he asked.

"I could free it before you could reach me," I said.

"Why is it not free now?" he asked.

"I hoped not to use it," I said.

"Your friend," he said, "carries an unsheathed dagger, now reversed to the throwing position."

"Sheath your dagger," I said to Xenon.

"Surely not," said Xenon. "My dagger, cast, could flash across the room, greeting his heart, paying it deep respects."

"No," I said, "it would be caught in the folds of his opened, interposed cloak."

Xenon angrily thrust his dagger into its sheath.

"Thank you," said Myron. "I am fond of this cloak and would not wish it injured. I wore it even during the Occupation."

"I remember it, or one like it," I said.

"Shall I sheath my sword?" he asked.

"Please, do," I said.

"I could free it before you could unsheathe your blade and reach me," he said.

"Are we not all friends here?" I asked.

"I knew you were in Ar," said Myron. "We arrived first, and I had the gate watched, by Captain Kasos, whom you met in Samnium."

"Just outside Samnium," I said, "he in the guise of a Metal Worker."

"Yes, he," said Myron. "I had hoped, after the delivery of Talena to Marlenus on the anniversary of his Restoration, which is imminent, to see you, and perhaps share a paga or two."

"Where is Talena?" I asked.

"I do not know," he said.

"I find that hard to believe," I said.

"You were counting on it?" he said.

"Certainly," I said. "Who would know the whereabouts of Talena, if not the polemarkos of Cos, he charged with her delivery to Ar?"

"I did have her delivered to Ar," he said. "But within Ar itself she must be hidden. Accordingly, I devised a double masking of her location."

"You entrusted her to a secret confederate," I said, "who then entrusted her to a second secret confederate, one unbeknownst to you, who would then conceal her until her official delivery. In that way, you would not know her location, and the first confederate would not know her location either."

"Precisely," he said.

"But she is somewhere within Ar," I said.

"I would suppose so," he said, "but I do not know."

"Cos has won," said Xenon.

"Wine?" asked Myron. "Ruffio can summon up a tower slave from a lower floor. The cellars of the Tower of Philebus, as I recall, like its kitchens, are amongst the finest in Ar."

At that moment, startling all in the domicile, there was a mighty sound, and the reverberation thereof, the first of a succession of such sounds, issuing from smitten signal bars. Ruffio put his hands over his ears. Sound followed sound. In cities such as Ar there are often several such devices, the tones of any one of which would carry well beyond the walls.

"Alarm bars!" shouted Myron.

The alarm bars are the same bars which are used for signifying time, but there is no comparison between the sounding, often of a single bar, which might signify, say, the Tenth Ahn, the Gorean noon, and the current, repetitious, frenzied storms of sound which, it seemed, might well shake the sky itself.

"The city is under attack!" screamed Ruffio.

"There is no hostile army, or horde, in the vicinity," I said.

"Tarnsmen?" said Myron.

Ruffio ran first to one of the windows, and then to the second. He was followed by Xenon.

"The sky seems clear!" said Ruffio. "I see no municipal tarnsmen taking to the skies, responding to some threat."

"Fire?" I asked. I joined them at the second window. I could see no fire. I could smell no smoke.

Myron, too, joined us.

"There is no sign of fire or war," said Myron, loudly. "I do not understand the bars."

"A revolt, a revolution in the streets?" said Xenon.

"Such seeds take long to germinate," said Ruffio.

"Cos, for one, has sown no such seeds," protested Myron.

"Perhaps they were cast from within the walls themselves," said Xenon.

"If such a plan throve," I said, "the bars would be first silenced, long silenced. They would ring only to announce the victory of insurgency."

"I hear cries in the streets, rising upward," said Ruffio.

"Talena has been discovered, and crowds are tearing her apart," said Xenon.

"Let it not be so!" I said, sickened. "Be it not so!"

"No," said Myron. "They are not cries of vengeance or glee, nor cries of victory or war. They are cries of bewilderment, of consternation."

"For no small thing are the bars so smitten," I said.

Xenon and I rushed to the domicile's entrance, made our way out into the hall, now crowded with residents, and forced our way to the exit, leading onto the bridge, where Seremides, near the portal, was clinging to a stanchion. Some figures were on the bridge, and some were on other bridges, above and below ours, leading to and from other cylinders.

"What is going on?" I shouted to Seremides.

Somewhere a child was crying and a woman was screaming.

"I do not know!" shouted Seremides.

Then, suddenly, the bars, one after another, ceased to sound, and the mighty reverberations which had made the very air tremble, faded from hearing.

"They have silenced the bars," said Xenon.

We saw two birds fly past, between the towers.

Some figures stood still on the bridges, looking about.

"Why did the bars ring?" asked Xenon. "What was it all about?"

"Whatever it was," I said. "It is now over."

CHAPTER THIRTY-FIVE

"The public boards tell us little," said Seremides.

"Intentionally," I said.

We were in a small, rented, basement apartment in the Metellan district.

The attack on the Ubar, Marlenus, was reported in a cursory fashion, possibly because an investigation was ongoing. The official information was merely to the effect that a large, but undisclosed number of unidentified assailants had set upon the Ubar, and a small number of his guardsmen, at the recent session of the Central Cylinder's Court of Complaints and Petitions, which attack had been resisted.

This brief, laconic report, however, was more than amplified, colorfully and extensively, in the streets, markets, and taverns. Rumors rushed about, like hurricanes amongst the towers, many doubtless exaggerated and dubiously evidenced, and certainly frequently inconsistent with one another, but, as nearly as we could determine, from some seemingly recurrent, fundamental congruences, a few basic elements emerged as more than probable, from which elements, and certain matters of general knowledge, we constructed the following rough account.

At the Fourteenth Ahn of the preceding day, between seventy and ninety armed men forced their way into the Court of Complaints and Petitions in the Central Cylinder, where the Ubar, with attending Scribes, was sitting in judgment. The assailants, uttering cries of liberty and freedom, began to cut through the crowded litigants and petitioners to reach the Throne of Justice. The Ubar and some of his guardsmen, Taurentians, managed to withdraw into the court's adjoining vesting room, where court garments might be donned, and barricade themselves therein. At the time of the attack, the assailants had sealed off the Court of Complaints and Petitions itself, this to impede any immediate succor from reaching the Ubar and his handful of cohorts. Recognizing this temporary impasse, and being unclear as to the extent of matters, frantic officials, while summoning and organizing a relieving force, had ordered the ringing of the alarm bars. The door to the vesting room, despite its adornment with symbols of the Tarns of Justice, had not been constructed to resist an onslaught of bodies, benches, and steel. It was soon demolished, its frame, too, broken away, and blades met blades. The crowded petitioners, meanwhile, trapped in the sealed-off Court of Complaints and Petitions, to a man, despite all codes of civility and honor, had been put to the sword by the assailants, presumably either to eliminate witnesses or prevent their participation in the action.

Prior to the attack, fifteen guardsmen, all Taurentians, had been in the room of the court, to guard the Ubar and keep order. Given the unexpected suddenness and force of the attack, six had fallen almost immediately, their weapons scarcely having left the sheath. One junior guardsman, apparently instantly grasping the situation, rushed to interpose his body and sword between the Ubar and the attackers, and, Ihn later, rallied his fellows to form a fighting cordon about the Ubar, which cordon he then ordered, despite his lack of justifying rank, to avail itself of the vesting room. He, and four others, then screened the retreat, and covered their fellows while they withdrew into the vesting chamber. He then ordered his four cohorts to follow the others, and barricade the portal, while he continued to defend the opening. Only the roaring command of Marlenus himself could budge him from his position, which command ordered him, at whatever cost, to join the others. He slipped within the narrowing portal whose protection was, as recounted, brief. Within, they could now hear the sounding of the alarm bars, which sound, while heartening them, must have warned the intrusive force that its time to complete its mission was rapidly diminishing. The attackers' redoubled efforts to force the portal bore fruit, even the frame of the portal being struck away, at which point the defenders issued forth to meet the assailants in a more harrowing but wider field of battle. "Slaughter, slaughter, filthy urts!" screamed Marlenus, upon sight of the confused, reddened, body-cluttered chamber. "Get to the wall!" cried the young guardsman. "Get the wall behind you! Get the wall to your backs!" But Marlenus, enraged at the sight of slain litigants and petitioners, rushed forward against the attackers. "No, Ubar!" wept the young guardsman, hurrying after him. He saw the Ubar fall. "Kill the Ubar!" screamed assailants. But they could not reach him, for the young guardsman, blood flying from his darting blade, must first be displaced. One could then hear pounding, and more pounding, on the outer door of the sealed chamber as reinforcements, Taurentians and regulars, hammered away at the closure. The war in the chamber, to the striking of metal and the cries of men, probably lasted no more than some three or four Ehn, which seemed perhaps to those who fought like an Ahn, but then, soon enough, the outer panel was smitten away and Taurentians and regulars, armed with spears and swords, rushed into the chamber.

"The rumors are unclear as to the condition of Marlenus," I said to Seremides and Xenon. "Some say he merely fell, others that he was struck unconscious, others that he was seriously wounded, others that his wound was light, and some say that he perished altogether."

"The matter will soon become clear," said Seremides. "The laws of Ar do not permit a vacant throne. That is one reason that Talena, in the absence of Marlenus, acceded so easily to the throne."

"Who, if Marlenus is absent, will be Ubar?" I asked.

"As Marlenus was too wise to name a successor," said Seremides, "thus encouraging a particular Assassin, it will be the strongest, the most powerful, the most ruthless."

"Decius Albus?" I said.

"Presumably," said Seremides. "He is close to the throne, of high station, is intimate with the affairs of state, and has a small, private army."

Of the fifteen original Taurentian guardsmen in the Court of Complaints and Petitions, given the first moments of the attack, the withdrawal to the vesting room, and then the issuing forth when the portal and portal's frame were destroyed, only three survived, including the young guardsman. The commanding officer of the guards had been killed early in the issuing forth from the vesting room. Thus, he did not survive to court-martial the young guardsman for his usurpation of authority, an authority which, however, he himself had failed to exercise, presumably because of an initial bewilderment and shock at the sudden concourse of events. Similarly, general charges, carrying penalties, sometimes severe, were not pressed against the young guardsman, possibly because of the success attending his initiative and its consequences. It was later learned that this exoneration was due to the intervention of the Ubar himself, who subsequently, interestingly, named the young guardsman to his personal bodyguard, despite his lack of seniority. Some whispered it about that the Ubar himself, in his own youth, may not have been unduly subservient to the dictates of propriety. Sometimes a young larl has its throat torn out; at other times he ascends to leadership, deferred to by all in the pride. Much depends on the times and the larl. Some say that Ubars are not made, but born.

"It seems," I had said, "there is a new hero in Ar."

"I was once a hero in Ar," said Seremides.

"His origins seem obscure," I said.

"What is his name?" asked Seremides.

"It was not on the boards," had said Xenon.

"Little is," said Seremides.

"In tavern gossip," I said, "he is described, not named."

"In a day or so, the name will be well known," said Xenon.

"I am intrigued," said Seremides, "for reasons I need not make known. Something is in my memory, like a bird, but it nowhere perches."

"There must be several, perhaps hundreds, in certain precincts, and stations, certainly amongst the Taurentians themselves, who know his name," I said.

"What difference does his name make?" asked Xenon.

"Perhaps no difference, perhaps much difference," said Seremides.

"I do not understand, beloved mentor," said Xenon.

"Iris," said Seremides, "attend me."

"I do, Master," said Iris.

"Slaves hear things," said Seremides. "They learn from their masters, and slaves learn from slaves. Go into the streets, and find the name of the guardsman who distinguished himself in the Court of Complaints and Petitions."

"I will try, Master," she said, rising and leaving the room.

"The attack on Marlenus," said Xenon, "was well planned. There was nothing spontaneous in it; it was no act of an inflamed crowd, not the act of a suddenly aroused, outraged citizenry."

"Granted," said Seremides.

"That considerably circumscribes an investigation," I said. "Few would have the resources to organize such an attack."

"Who then might be responsible for such an attack?" said Xenon.

"Any one, or more, of a number of individuals," said Seremides. "There are doubtless several in Ar who might avidly seek the prize of an empty throne."

"Supposedly the assailants rushed in uttering cries of 'Liberty' and 'Freedom,'" I said.

"They may have regarded themselves as patriots," said Xenon, "intent on denying, almost at the last moment, the delivery of great wealth to Cos, a mortal enemy, wealth which might then be used against Ar, reducing her once more to a state of poverty and subservience."

"That is doubtless true," said Seremides, "but, sweet, simple Xenon, whereas you see far, you do not see far enough. Who invents the ideals, and who uses them for what purposes?"

"Who understands these things?" asked Xenon. "Do not ideals grow naturally like flowers? Are they not hatched like tarns, born like tabuks and larls?"

"Let us hope so," I said.

"They are designed to serve purposes," said Seremides.

"Surely not," said Xenon.

"If you want men to serve you, even die for you," said Seremides, "give them ideals, behind which you may conceal yourself."

"I have only heard one speak in such a fashion before," said Xenon.

"Who?" I asked.

"It does not matter," he said.

"Motivations are abundant," I said, "benign or malignant, honorable or self-serving, warranted or askew."

"One thing eludes me still," said Xenon. "It is reported that all the attackers who were not slain in battle, nor massacred in revenge for their perfidy, that all those who were captured after the arrival of the reinforcements, died that same day."

"Perhaps of wounds," I said.

"Some were not wounded," said Xenon.

"It is no anomaly or coincidence," said Seremides. "To those who understand such things, the matter is clear."

Xenon and I looked to Seremides.

"Prisoners might speak, might they not?" said Seremides. "Might they not reveal their principal, or provide information leading to his discovery?"

"Quite possibly," I said.

"It is easy to eliminate that possibility," said Seremides. "It is done with chemicals. Before the engagement the suitable chemicals are administered, for example, in a toast to luck or victory. This poison takes effect within a few hours, and suddenly, once a critical point is reached. The victim is usually unaware of what has been done to him, until it is too late."

"I am revolted," I said.

Even Xenon seemed disturbed.

I had expected him to approve, if only to agree with Seremides.

"Surely, colleagues," said Seremides, "you mark the cleverness, the practical justification, of such a precaution."

"You betray your adherents," I said.

"It is sometimes judicious to do so," said Seremides.

"You are disloyal to your followers?" said Xenon.

"But not to myself," said Seremides.

"I fear to understand this," said Xenon.

"I thought it would be familiar to you," I said.

"I do not understand," said Xenon.

"It is nothing," I said.

"Loyalty is a virtue in followers," said Seremides. "It is a handicap a leader is wise to reject."

"You repudiate not only honor," I said, "but basic rightfulness?"

"Not at all," he said. "I approve of trust, basic rightfulness, and such. Such things are important. Without such, civilization would crumble. Without such, life itself would be imperiled, a horror of risk and danger. I approve of such things, for others. Indeed, one should feign allegiance to such things, while holding oneself apart from and superior to them."

"You hold yourself above such things?" I said.

"They are for others," he said, "not for the elite."

"I see," I said.

"Without them, it would be difficult to understand, predict, manipulate, and exploit others."

"Undoubtedly," I said.

"So, far from repudiating such things, I am the first to acknowledge their usefulness. They are necessary for my success. They serve my purposes with perfection."

"Dear benefactor," said Xenon, "in such matters, how can you exempt yourself?"

"Easily," said Seremides.

"But what entitles you to do so?"

"Your question presupposes that such an entitlement is necessary," said Seremides. "That is to accept the system, not to deny it."

"But there must be some justification," said Xenon.

"If you must have one," said Seremides, "consider benefit."

"You would repudiate the rules," said Xenon.

"Only when it is safe to do so and is to my advantage," he said.

"But you would seem to follow the rules," said Xenon.

"Of course," said Seremides. "That is important, and is to my advantage."

"Prudence and rightfulness, dear Xenon," I said, "do not always recommend the same action."

"Should not Iris be back by now?" asked Seremides.

"Soon perhaps," I said. "But she has not been gone long."

No one gave any thought to the possibility that she might have fled. She was collared, marked, and briefly tunicked. Kajirae are distinctive and conspicuous. They would be terrified, unless they are a free woman's serving slave, even to touch the clothing of a free woman. They would not dare to do such a thing. Severe penalties can pertain to such things. They are not free. They are kajirae. They are helpless, vulnerable joys in the Gorean world. They are a familiar component of Gorean society. On the whole, they are preciously and exquisitely sexually desirable. Otherwise they would not be put in their collars. They are slave beasts and marketable objects. For all practical purposes, there is no escape for the Gorean slave girl. There is nowhere to run. Society wants them in their collars, and will see to it that they stay in them. If, as might happen in some hundreds of times, she might manage to elude one master, she would soon fall into the possession of another, and, as a runaway, would be subjected to a far more onerous bondage than that from which she fled. And, in-

terestingly, they find their true self in the collar. They have an identity and fulfillment denied to the free woman. To know that they are
slaves and will remain slaves unless freed, is for them a reassurance
and comfort. It is said that all women are slaves, only that some are
fortunate enough to be in collars and others not.

"Several traitors, several conspirators, must have been involved
in planning and organizing the attack on the Ubar," said Xenon,
"well beyond those who carried it out."

"Certainly," I said. "And many not even in the plot might approve
it and be unwilling to reveal it. Few in Ar would be pleased to see
Marlenus turn over great quantities of gold to hated Cos."

"In the tavern, recently," said Xenon, "one of the Peasants said
that some thought that Decius Albus wished to be Ubar."

"And, I suspect, so, too, do several others," I said.

"Decius Albus," said Seremides, "might have been able to plan
and organize the attack on Marlenus."

"I am sure of it," I said, "but so, too, might have others."

"Decius Albus," said Xenon, "is reputed to be trustworthy and
loyal."

"And perhaps he is so," I said.

"And perhaps not," said Seremides.

"He sometimes, I gather," said Xenon, "scatters coins in the street,
and organizes free games in the arena."

"A magnanimous fellow," said Seremides.

"One thing disturbs me," I said.

"What is that?" asked Seremides.

"Beside his palanquin," I said, "there prowled a Kur."

At this point a light, particular knock, one prearranged, sounded
on the door of our small, inauspicious apartment.

"Enter, slave," called Seremides.

Iris entered the room and knelt.

How beautiful is a kajira kneeling before masters!

"I have my suspicions, a Kur, an enleaguing," said Seremides.
He then turned to Iris. "Your eyes shine," he said. "Though you are
worthless, and in a collar, you seem pleased with yourself."

"I am, Master," she said, "very much so."

How charming, energetic, lively, and appealing are kajirae, I
thought to myself, particularly in the presence of men, half clad,
owned, collared, and marked, one with their womanhood, so conscious of their extreme, marketable desirability, so aware of their
helplessness, so aware that they are, as they wish to be, at the mercy
of their masters. How different they are from free women! How wonderful are kajirae! But, why not? Are they not subject to the whip,
have they not been marked and collared, do they not belong, fully,

to their masters, are they not owned, completely and helplessly, by their masters, as they wish to be?

"Speak, slave," said Seremides.

"The name of the remarkable young swordsman, he who so distinguished himself in the Court of Complaints and Petitions is Alan," she said, "once of the House of Hesius, a recent recruit of the Taurentian Guard."

"Yes!" exclaimed Seremides.

"You know him?" I asked.

"It was I who discovered him, Alan, of the House of Hesius, an obscure bladesman, at the Gambles of Blades on the Skerry of Lars! It was I who encouraged him, given his redoubtable skills, to seek his fortune in Ar, amongst the fabled, prized Taurentians, whose First Sword I once was."

The Taurentians were the Ubarial guard in Ar. They were recruited from amongst the finest swordsmen on Gor, of whatever Home Stone. Their political fortunes, influence, and power waxed and waned, from time to time, from sometimes being a mere elite appanage of the throne, obedient and subservient, disciplined and loyal, to being a force in their own right, sometimes capable of determining who might occupy the throne itself. Indeed, the support of the Taurentians, under the governance of Seremides, had been instrumental in ending the sequestration of Talena in the Central Cylinder and placing her on the throne during the mysterious absence of Marlenus, who had disappeared in the Voltai mountains while on a hunting trip.

Perhaps a word or two might not be amiss in clarifying and expanding somewhat on certain matters. A "Gambles of Blades" is a commercial enterprise organized by one or more promoters. They occur from time to time in various venues. They are founded on, and profit from, two elements of which many Goreans are fond, contests of weaponry, particularly swords, and wagering. Without going into detail, the contests, on which one may wager, commonly range from relatively innocuous duels in which a touch, no more than a scratch, determines victory to, in some cases, duels to the death. The contests are usually staged in a sand-covered, wooden-floored, walled pit, surrounded by benches, within a large canvas-walled enclosure, striped red and yellow, red for blood and yellow for gold. The participants are commonly, but not always, members of a House, which is a traveling company of licensed swordsmen. Some of these companies are generations old. Indeed, several take in infants or orphaned children, raising and training them for later use in the company. These companies, which are business enterprises, commonly compete with one another. They have various names, but they are not associated per se with given Home Stones or Cities. I did not know the

House of Hesius. Hesius, like Hiseus, and Hersius, is a well-known Gorean name. Hersius, incidentally, most famously, was the name of a legendary hero of Ar. Seremides, we note, claimed to have first encountered the young swordsman on the Skerry of Lars, on which a Gambles of Blades was taking place. The Skerry of Lars is a small, barren island in the Tamber Gulf, some five pasangs from Port Kar. This placed it outside the jurisdiction of the laws of Port Kar, which forbade Gambles of Blades within its pomerium, presumably because of their acceptance of betting on duels to the death. The members of the companies themselves seldom compete in such matches. The members of the companies are analogous to professional athletes, who may compete with one another strenuously but are certainly not interested in killing one another. They have too much self-regard and too much mutual respect for one another for such an activity. The duels to the death usually take place amongst locals who avail themselves of the Gambles, either to enrich themselves or deal with enemies. The "young swordsman," whom we now had learned was Alan, formerly of the House of Hesius, he who had distinguished himself in resisting the attack on Marlenus, was reputed to have killed or wounded nineteen of the assailants. As the assailants had presumably been selected for their proficiency with arms by their principal, this suggested the "young swordsman" possessed blade skills of an unusually high order. Indeed, had not Marlenus selected him to be a member of his personal guard?

"This fellow, Alan," I said, "I take it, is quite good."

"Marvelously so," said Seremides. "And doubtless better now, I am sure, than when I first saw him on the Skerry of Lars. I have no doubt he is now First Sword amongst the Taurentians, as once I was."

"First Sword in skills," I said, "but not in rank."

"No," said Seremides, "not in rank."

"Have you more information about this fellow, Alan," I asked Iris.

"His antecedents seem far from clear," she said. "Some would have him from the Farther Islands, say, Chios or Thera. Others say he is from Telnus, or Jad, on Cos. Some say he is even from far Turia, others that he was a foundling or orphan, left years ago with the House of Hesius at one of its Gambles of Blades."

"In other words, little is known," I said.

"I fear so, Master," she said.

"If he was left with the House as an infant," said Seremides, "he must have been a strong, healthy, sturdy, promising infant. Otherwise such a House would not keep him."

"I have, of course, never seen him," said Iris, "but I have heard he has unusual hair, hair like flame, with a band of blond hair on the left side."

"That is rare," said Xenon.

"Such features are often mocked," I said, "and are often a source of chagrin and grief, particularly in childhood."

I had had my own share of such bitterness, especially in childhood, on a far world.

"But sometimes," said Seremides, "such features are mocked at one's peril, particularly in adulthood."

"The cowardly and cruel often mock the weak," said Xenon, "but seldom the violent and strong."

"I expect, dear Xenon," said Seremides, "given your shortness of stature. the thickness of your body, and your plainness of face, you were, as a child, no stranger to such abuse."

Xenon stared away, to the side, sullenly.

"And might not such a one," I said, "seek training, become formidable, and content oneself with the knowledge that those who mocked him might stand in far more danger than they suspected?"

Xenon said nothing.

"Xenon is strong," said Seremides. "He drew a mighty oar. Many would fear him. His grasp is like the talons of the tarn."

"The anniversary of the Restoration of Marlenus looms," I said.

"It will be followed by days of festival, Masters," said Iris.

"I am sure," said Seremides, "that Marlenus will use the occasion to announce the capture and delivery of Talena to Ar."

"Will her tortures then begin?" asked Xenon.

"I do not think so," said Seremides. "I do not think that would satisfy Marlenus, no, not enough, and not so soon. He would want visibility, and spectacle, something to satisfy and celebrate the triumph of the Tarns of Justice."

I was startled.

"A trial?" asked Xenon.

"I think so," said Seremides.

"But," said Xenon, "the will of the Ubar is law, and law is justice. Thus, it is the will of the Ubar that is justice. Thus a trial would be unnecessary and irrelevant."

"Unless," said Seremides, "the Ubar wishes the citizenry of Ar to share in the doing of justice."

"Preposterous," I said. "Marlenus would never risk a trial."

"There is no risk," said Seremides. "Consider a jury of a thousand outraged, vengeful citizens."

"Still," I said.

"Should the verdict be distasteful to the Ubar," said Seremides, "he may simply reverse it."

"The Ubar is then above the law," I said.

"Certainly, the Ubar is above the law," said Seremides. "He must be; otherwise he could not make the law or change the law."

"A trial then would be a farce," I said.

"But one of splendor, serving the purposes of state," said Seremides.

"I wonder," I said, "if Talena has now been delivered into the custody of Marlenus."

"Probably, secretly," said Seremides.

"But not officially?" said Xenon.

"No," said Seremides, "not officially."

"Doubtless that will require a public ceremony," I said.

"Yes," said Seremides. "And probably in the great plaza, before the Central Cylinder."

"Where Talena, in the robes of the Ubara, so haughtily, backed by the occupational forces, dealt out the justice of Cos," I said.

"Would not that seem appropriate?" asked Seremides.

"The anniversary of the Restoration of Marlenus," I said, "is the day after tomorrow."

CHAPTER THIRTY-SIX

"In the streets, the news roars and flames!" said Xenon.

"It is proclaimed on the public boards," I said.

"I hear shouts, jubilation, Masters," said Iris.

Xenon and I had just returned to our modest, rented dwelling in the Metellan district, where Iris, her left ankle chained to a slave ring, and Seremides, sitting on a chest, his sturdy crutch at hand, were waiting for us.

"Then it is true," said Seremides.

"I fear so," I said.

"We have failed," said Seremides.

"Yet, I do not choose to leave Ar just now," said Xenon.

"Nor I," I said.

"You will see things through to the bitter end?" said Seremides.

"To an end," I said.

There was a wild pounding on our door, below street level, reached by a short flight of steps.

Xenon and I reached for weapons.

"Hold!" warned Seremides.

"Hear, hear, Citizens!" cried a voice. "Come out, come out! Join us! Celebrate! Talena, the loathed she-tarsk, Talena, the traitress, the false Ubara, has been captured!"

Then the pounding stopped.

"Sheathe your weapons," said Seremides. "The fellow has rushed off, to announce the news to another door."

Somewhat chagrined, Xenon and I returned our weapons to their respective housings.

We could sense bodies hurrying past outside.

There was shouting.

"Unchain the slave," said Seremides, struggling to his feet. "I want her beside me, lest I become unsteady, lest I am jostled, lest I fall."

"Crowds swarm, beloved benefactor," said Xenon. "You must remain here, lest you be recognized."

I did not understand Xenon's concern, for he had often accompanied Seremides outside, even on crowded streets, even in busied markets.

Was there something he did not wish Seremides to see?

"To conceal oneself with zealous timidity," had said Seremides, "is to provoke curiosity, to arouse suspicion, to invite discovery. The best concealment is sometimes no concealment. No one would believe that the true Seremides would risk appearing in public. Thus, he who appears in public cannot be the true Seremides."

"I do not advise such an outing, kind mentor," said Xenon.

"Unlatch the door," said Seremides.

I freed Iris's ankle from its shackle.

"Thank you, Master," she said.

Slaves are accustomed to being tethered.

They are slaves.

Xenon and I helped Seremides up the steps to the street. Iris stayed near him.

"Glory to Ar!" said a fellow passing us.

"Glory to Ar," I responded.

"You have heard?" queried a Cloth Worker.

"Yes," I said.

"Glory to Ar!" he said.

"Glory to Ar," I said.

"It is lovely," said Iris. "The very air is fresh and fragrant!"

That was, of course, from the flowers, and perfume, readying the city for the anniversary of the Restoration of Marlenus. Tomorrow, on the holiday itself, there would be parades, performances, and public feasts.

"See the cloths, the banners, the hangings, the draperies, posters, and ribbons," said Iris.

"Even in the Metellan district," I said.

We heard music from somewhere, flutes and drums.

A slave girl sped by. "Glory to Ar!" she cried.

"Glory to Ar," I said.

"The bars are sounding," said Seremides.

"But not in alarm," said Xenon.

"The people are happy, Masters," said Iris.

"Ar congratulates itself," I said.

"One could almost pity Talena," said Xenon.

"Yet," I said, "you would be amongst the first who would surrender her to the implacable justice of Ar."

"Pity is blinded in the blaze of ten thousand tarns of gold, of double weight," said Xenon.

"I always thought," said Seremides, "she lacked the hardness to be Ubara."

"Why then," I asked, "did you, and others, conspirators all, place her on the throne?"

"It was convenient and seemly to do so," he said. "In the absence of Marlenus, opportunity beckoned."

"Cried out, commanded," suggested Xenon.

"And in the shadow of this opportunity," I said, "waiting, there loomed the greed and ambition of enemies of Ar, the maritime Ubarates, Tyros and Cos."

"All fell into place," said Seremides. "She was humiliated by the embarrassment and repudiation of Marlenus, and the shame she had brought on Ar, following her recovery from the north, where she, though the daughter of a Ubar, had begged to be purchased, a slave's act, and was embittered by her subsequent eclipse and sequestration. Her ambition thwarted, her lofty pride grievously stung, she became, though this may not have been clear to her, an enthusiastic and compliant puppet."

"I was in Ar during part of the Occupation," I said. "I witnessed her dealing out what was called justice. I did not find her weak, but petty, arrogant, and vengeful. Many times she used her power to have women who had displeased her, who had mocked or criticized her, or dared to compare themselves with her, particularly her rivals in beauty, prestige, and standing, collared and sent to far markets. Even long ago, before the threat of the Horde of Pa-Kur, it was well known that she was a harsh, feared mistress, even using her female slaves as informants and spies, and, should they fail her or displease her in any way in even the least particular, having them put to the lash."

"That is not unusual for a free woman," said Xenon.

"She was weak," said Seremides. "She refrained from mutilating two slaves, both found less than pleasing, at the Skerry of Lars, before boarding the waiting Cosian ship to speed her to Jad, where she expected to find a wealth, security, and station, furnished to her by her erstwhile ally, Lurius of Jad."

"It is weakness not to scar a slave?" I asked.

"Or not cut away her nose or ears?" said Xenon.

"Mercy is weakness," said Seremides.

"I do not think so," I said.

"Nor I, with apologies, kind mentor," said Xenon.

"Surely the lash is sufficient," I said.

"Mutilating a slave," said Xenon, "considerably reduces her value."

"That is true," granted Seremides.

"Still," said Xenon, "despite what you say, I fear one could almost pity Talena, considering the hideous and lengthy tortures in store for her."

"Think gold," said Seremides.

"One must," said Xenon.

"One need not," I said.

"She betrayed her Home Stone," said Seremides.

"That is true," I said.

"Surely then," said Seremides, "you do not weaken? Surely you do not question our common purpose, that which united us in all our endeavors, to seize Talena and turn her over to Ar for gold?"

I was silent.

"In any event," said Xenon, "it matters little now, as the gates of Ar have closed behind her."

Seremides regarded me, closely.

"What is wrong?" he asked.

"Nothing," I said.

"Wipe your eyes," said Seremides.

I wiped my eyes with the back of my hand.

"The bars continue to sound happily, Masters," said Iris.

"That is because," said Seremides, "it is not yet clear to the citizenry on whom the reward for Talena's capture is to be bestowed."

"When the truth is known," said Xenon, "there could be blood in the streets."

"The gutters could flow," said Seremides.

"May I speak, Masters?" asked Iris.

"Yes," I said.

"It was not easy to bring Mistress Talena to Ar. It demanded much thought, much care, subtlety, and secrecy, and was done at great peril."

"So?" asked Seremides.

"Well," said Iris, "if that is an undertaking so difficult and hazardous, the conveyance of one woman, just one woman, to Ar from Cos, would not the conveyance of ten thousand tarns of gold, of double weight, from Ar to Cos be far more difficult?"

"That is Cos's problem," said Seremides.

"And it is a problem," I said.

"No Street of Coins, nor consortium of Streets of Coins," said Xenon, "would dare underwrite a note for that sum, nor, if they did, risk the loss or destruction of such a note in transit."

"Marlenus is a far thinker," I said. "He made the reward for Talena dependent on her being delivered alive to Ar. In that way he substantially guaranteed that she would, in her own person, face the vengeful justice of Ar. Perhaps that is cruel, but it is also perceptive. Too, he must have realized that, given the resources of Cos, it was possible that they might apprehend Talena, rather than hundreds of others."

"It was a risk, however slight, he was willing to take," said Xenon.

"I see," said Seremides. "He could satisfy his foolish, misguided sense of honor by giving the wealth to Cos, while intending to steal it back from them shortly thereafter."

"I fear, dear Seremides," I said, "your sense of honor is still somewhat askew."

"But he would surely recognize the difficulty of transmitting such a treasure to Cos," said Seremides.

"Certainly," I said, "and honor would not require him to guarantee its safe delivery to Lurius of Jad."

"So the gold would never reach Jad," said Seremides.

"Quite possibly," I said.

"But it might," he said.

"And that," I said, "might be the doom of Ar."

"Let us turn here," said Seremides, "onto the Avenue of the Central Cylinder."

"Let us not, noble friend," said Xenon. "I fear your presence on such a street, so publicly."

"Why just today?" asked Seremides.

"Please, dear benefactor," said Xenon.

"Nonsense," said Seremides.

The great tower of the Central Cylinder loomed in the distance.

"Return to the apartment," urged Xenon.

"Be silent, Oarsman," said Seremides.

We continued on.

"The bars no longer sound," said Iris.

"They need no longer do so," I said. "They have made their announcement. They have conveyed their message of joy."

"Turn back, beloved mentor," said Xenon.

"Desist in your opportuning," growled Seremides. "This day is no more dangerous to me than others, and, given the distraction of the populace, is perhaps less so."

"This walk has a destination?" I asked Seremides.

"I wish to see," said Seremides, "if the great dais has been set up in the Plaza of the Central Cylinder."

"I have heard it would be, Master," said Iris, "that upon which the captured Talena would be exhibited to the crowds and on which her trial would take place."

"We shall see," said Seremides.

It was upon such a dais that Talena had occasionally issued her decrees and pronounced her judgments.

"It may be in place," I said, "but I doubt that it will be used."

"I, too," said Seremides.

"Why is that, Masters?" asked Iris.

"It is too open," I said. "In Ar, Talena is hated. Crowds can be dangerous, irrational and thoughtless, like tidal waves and avalanches. They can become, on a whim, a violent, mindless thing, a ravening beast with many heads."

"Should Talena be torn to pieces," said Seremides, "the Tarns of Justice would be cheated. They could not seize their prey. They would have opened their talons in vain."

"We approach the Central Cylinder," said Xenon. "Let us return to the apartment."

"No," said Seremides.

"I have seen few guardsmen about," I said.

"Even in the Metellan district," said Seremides.

"Clearly they are elsewhere," said Xenon.

"Somewhere I suspect they are massed," said Seremides.

"To protect Talena," I speculated.

"Undoubtedly," said Seremides.

"The Central Cylinder," I said, "would be ill guarded."

"It is safe," said Seremides. "Ar is happy, and at peace."

"Look, Masters," said Iris. "See the great platform!"

"The dais of state," I said.

It was draped with hangings and banners.

We then heard, to our right, a ringing of bells.

"It is a procession of Initiates," I said, stepping back. "Kneel," I whispered to Iris.

She knelt, frightened.

"Be at ease, slave," said Seremides. "You have nothing to fear, at least in public. They shave their heads and garb themselves in white robes. They eschew meat, beans, and women. They purify their minds with meditation and mathematics. They do little and reap much. They accept offerings and solicit donations. They sell prayers and spells. Supposedly they intercede between mortals and Priest-Kings, an enviable skill. They are holy fellows and deal with sacred things, and money. They are monsters of superstition, hypocrisy, and greed."

"They are also," I said, "a high caste, and are taken seriously by many Goreans, particularly of the lower castes."

It was a long line, in single file. There were perhaps sixty or seventy in that line. Usually processions of Initiates are not that long.

Also, interestingly, though commonly Initiates march bareheaded, presumably in order that their shaved heads will be more prominently displayed, this setting them apart from other men, these fellows had each drawn up the hood of his robes, over and about his head.

I would not have expected that.

The bells continued to ring.

I could not see the faces of those in the procession. Most commonly the features of an Initiate are pale and somewhat drawn, perhaps from an overindulgence in perfection, or perhaps because of a lack of sunlight and fresh air, or perhaps from a surfeit of mathematical purification. Too, the bodies of Initiates often seem awkward, spare, linear, and frail, bordering perhaps on a studied, professional emaciation. These fellows, on the other hand, seemed tall enough, strong enough, and coordinated enough to be carrying rocks or loading ships and wagons.

I found that of interest.

"Let us return to the apartment, now," said Xenon. "Now!"

"No," said Seremides.

It was long since I had been in Ar.

It seemed that Initiates had changed somewhat in the interim, and, from my point of view, for the better, perhaps becoming more tolerant of sunlight, fresh air, and such.

That was indeed, I thought, a change for the better.

A wayward thought crossed my mind, the memory of a children's story in which a clever larl, bending over and shuffling, pretends to be a verr, that to gain access to a verr pen.

"Why," I asked myself, "should that story have occurred to me now?"

The hair suddenly rose on the back of my neck and forearms.

I considered the hang of those passing robes. Something seemed different or amiss.

"Those are not Initiates!" I said, and, at the same time, it seemed my head exploded with black night and flying stars, and I was aware, again, as I fell, briefly, of the ringing of the bells, and then I lost consciousness.

CHAPTER THIRTY-SEVEN

I opened my eyes.

Iris took the dampened cloth from my head.

"He is awake, Master," she said.

I was on my back, on a blanket. Looking up, I recognized the ceiling of the small basement apartment in the Metellan district.

"You have been unconscious for several Ahn," said Seremides. "We hired two fellows to bring you here. We have been betrayed by Xenon."

"It was he who struck me," I said.

"Surely," said Seremides.

"Is Master in pain?" asked Iris.

"He lives, what else matters?" said Seremides.

"Those Initiates," I said, "were not Initiates."

"No," said Seremides, "whoever they might have been, they were not Initiates."

"They were Assassins," I said.

"Possibly," said Seremides.

"Xenon," I said, "is an Assassin."

"Surely not," said Seremides.

"He wished to keep you off the streets," I said. "Particularly, he wanted you far from the Plaza of the Central Cylinder. He is informed, independently. He knew what was afoot. He feared your discernment."

"He could have killed you, but he did not," said Seremides.

"Neither you nor the slave," I said, "cried out, concerning the false Initiates?"

"We dared not," said Seremides. "We would have been slain on the street, by Xenon, where we stood."

"He kept us there, seemingly tending you," said Iris. "And then, when the Initiates, or pretenders, were well gone, he vanished."

"His false identity compromised, shattered," I said, "he would rejoin his brothers, his colleagues, in the Black Caste."

"I do not think him an Assassin," said Seremides.

"Surely you do not think him a simple oarsman," I said.

"No," said Seremides, "no longer."

"He was planted amongst us," I said, "to trace our movements and monitor our dealings, on the possibility that through us, and particularly through you, the cunning, experienced Seremides, his principal might be led to Talena."

"And, presumably," said Seremides, "this might have been done with other groups, as well."

"Presumably," I said.

"And who would be his principal?" asked Seremides.

I was silent. One does not lightly speak all names.

"I saved his life aboard the vessel which bore Talena to Jad," said Seremides.

"I think it seemed so," I said, "but I do not think it was so. A captain could be bribed. You are pleased to have individuals beholden to you. You, a cripple, might have much use for a strong assistant and able confederate. I think the whole business was a ruse to place an informer at your side."

"A plot contrived by Lurius of Jad?" said Seremides.

"No," I said.

"Who?" asked Seremides.

"By one," I said, "who, I fear, reports to one far darker and more terrible."

"Who?" demanded Seremides.

I was again silent. Some names are not to be spoken lightly. And other names, perhaps, are best left unspoken altogether. "What," I wondered, "did Seremides know, or need to know, of the conflicts of worlds?"

"I trusted Xenon," said Seremides.

"It was you, you who would betray," I said, "who was betrayed."

"I thought him a simple oarsman, blindly loyal," said Seremides.

"Things are not always what they seem," I said.

"And perhaps," said Seremides, fingering the dagger at his belt, "you, too, are not what you seem."

"That is possible," I said.

"And you, pretty beast," said Seremides, "you, with your lovely neck encircled so closely and nicely with a locked collar, as the beast you are, are you what you seem?"

"Yes, Master," she said. "I have no choice. I am a slave."

"Let us accept," said Seremides, "that we were tricked by Xenon. Let us accept, further, that he is somehow in league with some fellows who may not have been, and most likely were not, authentic Initiates. What then is going on?"

"Consider," I said. "The appearance of being Initiates was a disguise. The purpose of a disguise is to obtain some end by means of deception. There were more than fifty individuals in the procession, at least. This suggests that the end in question is expected to require the action of several men. If so, this suggests no stealthy purloining in the night, no stab in an alley, but some sort of robust enterprise, presumably a surprise attack."

"Then they are fools," said Seremides. "We have noted the paucity of guardsmen in the streets, particularly in the shabby Metellan district. Thus they are massed somewhere, presumably to protect Talena before and during her delivery to Marlenus. Even a hundred men, even skilled mercenaries, could not hope to overcome such a guard, a guard marshaled to conduct Talena safely through vengeful crowds."

"What do you think the purpose of the pretended Initiates was?" I asked.

"What it must have been," said Seremides, "to seize Talena at the last moment and deliver her to Marlenus for the reward."

"But you feel such an effort would have been futile?" I said.

"Certainly," said Seremides.

"And the group in question would not have realized that?"

"Apparently not," he said.

"But what if they had?" I asked.

"I do not understand," said Seremides.

"Supposing they were not uninformed and not stupid," I said, "they would not address themselves to such a task."

"No," said Seremides.

"Then let us suppose, as a possibility," I said, "that they were neither uninformed nor stupid."

"Very well," said Seremides, narrowly.

"Then," I said, "they were not addressing themselves to that task, but to another task."

"What other task?" he asked.

"One far more grievous and important to Ar than the seizure of Talena, one compared to which the seizure of Talena would be negligible," I said.

"What is that?" asked Seremides.

"The theft of the Home Stone of Ar," I said.

Iris lifted her head.

"Masters," she said, "there is shouting in the streets, consternation, running feet, cries of woe!"

"What is wrong?" said Seremides.

"I fear, much," I said.

CHAPTER THIRTY-EIGHT

"You wish to be called Geoffrey of Harfax?" asked Myron, the pole-markos of Cos.

"It will do," I said.

"I sense, even from Jad," he said, "that you are a figure of conse-quence, an officer, or captain, perhaps even from Port Kar, that den of pirates and cutthroats."

"There is now," I said, "a Home Stone in Port Kar, the Jewel of Gleaming Thassa."

"Do you know of that rogue and terror, Bosk of Port Kar?" he asked.

"I have heard of him," I said. "He may not be so bad a fellow as you surmise."

"I think that you are an individual of importance," said Myron, "perhaps even an agent or representative of the notorious Bosk of Port Kar, or perhaps of the Council of Captains of that dreaded port."

The Council of Captains was the body sovereign in Port Kar.

I was once more in that spacious apartment in the opulent Tower of Philebus, that apartment maintained by Ruffio of Ar, whom I had first known as Rufus, of the Village of Two Branches, a village somewhere south of Torcadino. With me was Seremides, and Iris knelt nearby.

"Why, in this crisis in the city, have you invited us to this meeting?" I asked.

"Do you think I do not know the identity of your fellow," asked Myron.

My right hand tensed, moved.

"Do not draw your weapon," counseled Ruffio, standing to one side, flanked by two guards, not uniformed, but doubtless of Cos.

"Bruno of Torcadino," said Myron, "who delivered the traitress, Talena, to Lurius of Jad."

My hand relaxed.

I had feared he knew he who was Seremides of Ar, proscribed traitor to Ar, on whom there was a bounty of a hundred tarns of gold, of double weight. I guessed that even Lurius of Jad had not known with whom he dealt, but had only known Seremides as the promising bounty hunter, Bruno of Torcadino, whose efforts he had agreed to subsidize. Seremides, of course, being himself wanted in Ar and in need of resources, would find such an arrangement acceptable. Had Lurius of Jad realized he was dealing with Seremides of Ar, one supposes he would have had him put into custody, with the ultimate object of collecting the posted reward.

"We attend your words," I said.

"Send the slave from the room," said Myron.

"She assists my friend," I said.

"What I have to say," he said, "should not burden the ears of a slave."

"Leave," said Seremides.

"Master?" asked Iris.

"Await me elsewhere," said Seremides. "I do not know what is to be spoken, but I gather, should you hear it, your life would be worth little."

Silently, Iris rose to her feet, backed away, head down, and then turned and hurried through a nearby portal, one to which she had been directed by a gesture from Ruffio.

"I have contemplated a meeting such as this," said Myron, "either with you, or suitable others, from shortly after having arrived in Ar. In far Jad, so removed from Ar, we did not contemplate the gravity of a certain matter, the lingering, grievous hostility of an impenitent Ar toward fair Cos, a matter of blood, hate, and steel. We learned what perhaps we should have anticipated, that if it should become known that the reward for Talena's delivery to Ar would accrue to Cos, war might break forth in the streets."

"Marlenus will honor his word," I said.

"A word which will mean little," said Myron, "if Marlenus's body, impaled and coated with oil, is set afire."

"You need someone, independent of Cos, to receive the reward," I said.

"Obviously," said Myron.

"One whose accent does not suggest Cos," I said.

"Preferably," said Myron.

"Perhaps a private party from innocent, far Harfax," I suggested.

"That would do very nicely," said Myron.

"Why do you think of me?" I asked.

"I know you from Jad," he said, "I know your familiarity with, and your interest in, these matters, I know you can identify Talena, and, most importantly, I know I can trust you."

"How do you know that?" I asked.

"The codes," he said. "We may be enemies, perhaps even blood enemies, though I would regret that, but we have a bond in common, one stern and adamant, one like stone and iron. We are both of the Scarlet Caste."

"I would be your intermediary, your agent," I said.

"Precisely," he said.

"The gold would be turned over to you, with no mention or hint of Cos."

"Yes," he said.

"How will you convey the gold to Cos?" I asked.

"The transport of the gold, and its disposal, or its fate," he said, "is my concern, not yours."

"Doubtless some remuneration for this possibly hazardous service would be in order," said Seremides.

"Certainly," said Myron.

"I am familiar with the trustworthiness of the word, and the alleged fidelity, of Lurius of Jad," said Seremides.

"I fear you were treated badly by my cousin," said Myron. "But you are not alone. Many in Cos think the throne might be more honorably, more safely, less dangerously occupied."

"You have discussed this matter of concealing the destination of the gold with the Ubar?" I asked.

"Of course," said Myron. "That contingency had to have been taken into consideration. The matter could not have been arranged otherwise."

"Do you know where Talena is?" I asked.

"I do now," he said. "The massing of guards is at the stronghold of Publius. Today, the anniversary of the Restoration of Marlenus, she was to have been trundled in chains on an open cart from the stronghold of Publius to the Plaza of the Central Cylinder.

"That is postponed now, of course," said Ruffio.

"You are familiar, I take it," said Myron, "with recent occurrences."

"One cannot help but be so," I said.

Yesterday, a party of several individuals, disguised as Initiates, unsuspected and secretly armed, soliciting donations, and professing to sell spells and prayers, unchallenged, had ascended to, and crossed, a bridge debouching at the eleventh level of the Central Cylinder, on which level is found the sanctum of the Home Stone. They forced their way into the sanctum and, after a spate of brief, fierce fighting, in which the guards were killed, and several of the attackers, as well, seized the Home Stone, which was then transported to the roof, from which level it was borne away by a lone tarnsman devoid of insignia and garbed in no familiar livery. Four attackers survived of the attacking force who surrendered on the roof without a fight, but were not questioned as they insisted on being removed safely to a predesignated site outside the walls, a demand which, were it not promptly acceded to, would entail the prearranged destruction of the Home Stone. The Ubar, unwilling to risk the destruction of the Home Stone, authorized the conveyance of the prisoners to the site specified. Within an Ahn of the theft of the Home Stone, a ransom demand was received. The Home Stone would be returned unharmed if the gold set aside as the reward for Talena's capture and delivery was to be transported secretly to one or more undisclosed locations. The identity of the attackers remained a matter of conjecture.

"I take it," said Myron, "you know little more of these matters than is available to the public."

"I fear so," I said. "You, on the other hand, given your access to the Ubar, may be more fully informed."

"It seems," he said, "that the object stolen is the genuine Home Stone of Ar. Marlenus's profession to the agent of the attackers, he bringing the ransom demand, was that the stone stolen was inauthentic, a mere substitute for the genuine Home Stone, a substitute kept in readiness for purposes of greater security."

"A lame ruse at best," said Seremides. "Were it not genuine, Marlenus would not have acceded to the demand of the survivors."

"Not necessarily," I said. "He might prolong the deception to uncover more of the plot and its principal, or principals."

"No," said Myron. "Matters must proceed expeditiously. If they did not, he who bore the ransom note assured the Ubar that the stone in the thieves' possession, whether genuine or not, if not redeemed for the gold within two days, would be pounded into dust. The Ubar instantly acquiesced."

"Clearly this bodes ill for Cos," I said.

"For the Ubar, too," said Myron. "Is his first office not the protection of the Home Stone?"

"It could mean the end of Marlenus," I said.

"And perhaps of Ar," he said.

I recalled a time long ago, when I, scarcely understanding what I was doing, in an attempt to undermine the imperialism of an expansionistic Ar, driven by the ambitions of Marlenus, had purloined its Home Stone on the Planting Feast. Chaos had come about in Ar, terror roamed the streets, civility crumbled. Power in the city was seized by Initiates, supposedly unconcerned with worldly things. The horde of Pa-Kur was at the gates. Events had ensued which, colored and exaggerated, were subsequently celebrated about camp fires, at crossroads, and in holdings and halls, by wandering story tellers and chanters, in what came to be called the Songs of Tarl of Bristol.

"I wonder," said Myron, "if you and your fellow, Bruno of Torcadino. might not know more of this than you profess."

"How so?" I asked. "We do not have access to the Ubar."

"You know, do you not," asked Myron, "of a fellow named Xenon of Jad?"

I looked at Myron, puzzled.

"I am sure you know him," said Myron. "He was here before, here with you, in this apartment, in the Tower of Philebus."

"We know him, of course," I said.

"It was he," said Myron, "who brought the ransom demand, he who negotiates on behalf of the thieves."

CHAPTER THIRTY-NINE

"Xenon is of the Assassins," I said.

"But he did not kill you on the street," said Seremides.

"He had not taken fee to do so, even a tarsk-bit," I said.

"If he were an Assassin," asked Seremides, "why did he remain with us, after we reached Ar, and had so obviously failed to seize Talena to deliver her to Marlenus?"

"I do not know," I said. "I suspect it was on orders from his principal."

"And who is his principal?" asked Seremides.

"Pa-Kur, Master of the Assassins," I said.

"You suspect the High Assassin is implicated in the theft of the Home Stone of Ar?"

"Yes," I said, "and behind him, I fear, in the darkness, there lurks another, one far more terrible."

"I do not understand," said Seremides.

"You may not understand all," I said, "but I am sure you know more than you understand."

"How is that possible?" asked Seremides.

"Permit me to explain," I said.

"Do so," he said.

"You have known me as Tarl Cabot," I said, "even from the long voyage on the ship of Tersites to the World's End. And you know me, as well, from Port Kar, as Bosk of Port Kar, a captain in the Council of Captains of Port Kar."

"Of course," said Seremides.

"It was from my holding in Port Kar, in my absence, when I was investigating ravages perpetrated in my name in the Farther Islands, that you, in effect, abducted Talena, eventually to deliver her to Lurius of Jad on Cos."

"All this is well known," he said.

"Hear then something less known," I said.

"Proceed," he said.

"When I returned to Port Kar from the Farther Islands, I learned not only of the theft of Talena, but of mysterious doings in the marshes of the delta near Port Kar."

"I did not know you knew of them," he said.

"I was informed," I said.

"I know your likely informants," said Seremides.

"A young master, Addison Steele," I said, "and a slave, Zia."

"Yes," said Seremides. "I well recall them. Addison Steele was allied, I thought, with a mysterious bounty hunter encountered in the marshes."

"The bounty hunter," I said, "was Pa-Kur, Master of the Assassins."

"And Zia," he said, "was a young, beautiful barbarian slave, who, like others, was helplessly, beggingly responsive in her collar."

There was a tiny, soft, almost inaudible moan from Iris, whom we had placed to the side, facing the wall, kneeling in nadu, a familiar slave position, one often required of pleasure slaves. She could not see us, but she could hear us. That was enough. She was a slave. Slaves, as submissives, are powerfully, even tormentedly, sexually aroused by being subjected to casual, categorical, unqualified dominance. They have sexual experiences of which the free woman can only dream. Iris, like Zia, and many others, had been brought from Earth to the markets of Gor. On Gor, in their collars, at the feet of men, they had found themselves. In their collars, on Gor, they had undergone a liberation into truth and selfhood, into the joy of becoming what they had always hoped to be and feared they might never become, the rightless belonging of a master. On Earth many women are starved of sex; they are alone and unfulfilled; they languish in a sexual desert, yearning for masters they never meet. On Earth, often, they are not permitted their longed-for submissiveness; seldom are they taught, as they wish to be, their femaleness and meaning; on Gor, they are given no choice but to recognize it. Many things are involved here, such as the radical centrality of sex in the human condition, the complementarities of the sexes, and the sexual dimorphism in the human species, both physiologically and psychologically. Even a Kur can easily tell the difference between a human male and a human female. To insist that what is obviously not the same is the same is not a mere mistake; not a simple adventure or journey into falsehood; not a simple affront to reality, but, too often, a claim, an invention, designed to abet an agenda, a tool deigned to serve a contrived, concealed purpose. Those who seek power seek first to shape thought.

Iris moaned, softly, but audibly. "Masters?" she whimpered.

"Be silent," said Seremides.

"Forgive me, Master," she whispered.

"Surely you remember, in the marshes," I said, "an unusual object, emerging from the water."

Seremides, formidable as he was, shuddered.

"Was that not the purpose of that rendezvous in the darkness, to encounter the object?"

"Clearly," said Seremides, "but much which I seem to remember I could not truly remember, because it could not have occurred."

"What do you seem to remember?" I asked.

"It was large, very large; it lifted its head and neck out of the water, as high as a man might stand. It seemed to be some sort of tharlarion, but it could not be a tharlarion, for it seemed like a snake-like thing of rippling, sliding, overlapping plates of metal, and it had fangs like steel hooks, as long as a man's forearm, and eyes that were red, glowing like lanterns. And most strangely—"

"Yes?" I said.

"The thing," he said, "spoke."

"Of course," I said.

"I was dreaming," said Seremides.

"You were not," I said. "Others witnessed all this, as well."

"The voice," he said, "was not human."

"It was mechanically produced," I said.

"It was like listening to noises emerging on cards, cards moved one by one, one after the other."

"There was no emotion detectable from the sounds, no intonations?" I said.

"No," he said.

"But you could understand the sounds," I said.

"Yes," he said.

"So they were words," I said.

"Yes," he said.

"In Gorean," I said.

"Yes," he said.

"There was intellect behind them," I said.

"Yes," he said. "But a tharlarion cannot speak, and pieces of metal, even if bolted into the shape of a monster, cannot speak."

"Do not be uncomfortable," I said.

"These memories frighten me," he said.

"You know of Kurii?" I said.

"Very little," he said, "and that is more than enough."

"Do you remember the large, shambling, ax-bearing beast seen beside the palanquin of Decius Albus?"

"I would that it could be forgotten," he said.

"It was a Kur," I said.

"Yes," he said, shuddering.

"Where there is one," I said, "presumably there are others."

"One fears so," said Seremides.

"What was the purport of the rendezvous in the marshes?" I asked.

"Gold, gold," said Seremides.

"The steel beast, the mechanical tharlarion, you encountered in the marshes," I said, "was animated by a Kur, or the brain of a Kur, most likely one we speak of under the name Agamemnon, the name of a former king on a far world. We could not pronounce his true name. To us, the native language, or languages, of the Kurii sound much like the hisses of sleen, like the growling of larls."

"What has this to do with Talena, with Cos, or gold, or the Home Stone of Ar?" said Seremides.

"Much," I said. "It links Pa-Kur and Xenon with Kurii, and it links Kurii to Talena and gold."

"Speak," said Seremides.

"Lord Agamemnon," I said, "was banished from his world, a steel world."

"There are no steel worlds," said Seremides.

"There are several," I said. "They are artificial worlds. Once the Kurii had a natural world, one perhaps as beautiful as Gor. That world they ruined, century by century, perhaps by war, greed, and exploitation, eventually rendering it uninhabitable. Remnants of the population managed to build, and escape to, a number of steel worlds. Kurii, understandably, want a replacement for their destroyed world. They covet Gor. They are currently held at bay by the technology of Priest-Kings, who, I assure you, do exist. They are not a pure figment of the imagination of Initiates."

"I understand little of this," said Seremides.

"Understand this," I said. "Agamemnon wishes to return to, and reclaim, the steel world of his origins, to use it as a base from which to recruit other steel worlds to join him, to invade, conquer, and possess Gor. To enlist partisans, human and Kur, on this world and others, to abet his scheme, he wanted the enormous treasure offered for Talena's delivery to Ar. Having failed to achieve his aim of capturing Talena, he wants to obtain the gold differently, now as a ransom for returning the Home Stone of Ar. Obviously it is not Talena or the Home Stone in which he is interested, but the gold, however it might be obtained. Indeed, this may have been an alternative plan, a reserve plan, from the very beginning of these matters."

"What are we to do, if anything?" asked Seremides. "What can we do, if anything?"

"Consider the current situation," I said. "Marlenus, and perhaps Decius Albus, are desperate to regain the Home Stone of Ar, and neither, presumably, wants the gold to leave Ar, either as loot for thieves or riches for Lurius of Jad, the tyrant of Cos."

"Marlenus and his adherents, at least, are surely desperate," said Seremides. "Ar is shaken. Anxiety rules. The throne totters."

"I fear so," I said.

"Thousands gather in the streets, at the fountains, and in the plazas, angry and frightened," said Seremides. "Crowds stir and seethe. Throngs call for torches. Men and women, mad with hate and fear, pry up cobblestones to cast."

"And thousands search," I said, "citizens, guardsmen, regulars, all, men and women of both high and low caste, search from street to street, from house to house, from field to field, for the missing Home Stone."

"Ar will burn," said Seremides.

"Unless the Home Stone can be recovered," I said.

"Search for Xenon, our erstwhile colleague, our trusted fellow, the traitor to our cause," said Seremides. "He is implicated in this."

"Even did we know his whereabouts, and could somehow reach him," I said, "I doubt that he would know the Home Stone's location. Few would be permitted access to so great a secret."

"Matters then are hopeless," said Seremides. "Time is short. Marlenus has no choice. He must yield. I suspect that, even now, wagons are being secretly loaded with gold."

"The search for the Home Stone," I said, "is wide and deep."

"And frenzied," said Seremides.

"But the most zealous and resolute of searches will be unsuccessful," I said, "if one looks in the wrong place."

"Obviously," said Seremides.

"Clearly one wishes to look in the right place," I said.

"Few will dispute that," said Seremides.

"And why might one not look in the right place?" I asked.

"Continue," said Seremides.

"One might not look in the right place if it is thought to be the wrong place," I said, "if it is a place where the Home Stone could not be."

"But is?" said Seremides.

"Exactly," I said.

"Kurii," whispered Seremides, hesitantly.

"I think so, very much so," I said. "Those who attacked the Home Stone guard, reduced in number on that day, as many additional guardsmen were wanted to conduct Talena through the streets, were all human, with no suggestion of Kur involvement. Similarly, Kurii, viewed as animals, would not be expected to have any understanding of, or interest in, human things, such as gold, politics, or Home Stones. But we know otherwise, from the marshes outside Port Kar. We further know from the marshes that Pa-Kur, Master of the Assassins, was involved with Kurii. Too, Xenon, I am sure, is an Assassin, and a minion of Pa-Kur. Recall how he kept me from calling out against the procession of false Initiates, how he prevented me from sounding an alarm."

"Kurii are large, dreadful, fearsome beasts," said Seremides.

"Thus, too," I said, "few men would care to question them, to demand access to their haunts, even to be near them."

"I include myself amongst their number," said Seremides. "I would want nothing to do with them."

"Who would?" I asked.

"Where are they?" asked Seremides.

"I do not know," I said.

"Some must know," he said.

"Of course," I said.

"Masters," begged Iris, in nadu, facing the wall, "may I speak?"

"No," said Seremides.

"I think the Home Stone is with Kurii," I said.

"So you would seek Kurii," said Seremides, "to be led to the Home Stone."

"The massive, intense search, otherwise, within and outside the city, has hitherto proven fruitless," I said.

"But you do not know where to find these beasts?" said Seremides.

"No," I said. "But some must be about. One accompanied the palanquin of Decius Albus."

"You will not find the Palace of a Hundred Corridors easily accessed," said Seremides.

The domicile of Decius Albus was often referred to as the Palace of a Hundred Corridors.

"Masters," said Iris.

"Be silent," said Seremides.

"Yes, Master," she said.

"Supposing you should locate the Home Stone," said Seremides, "how do you expect to get it? Do you think the beasts will simply give it to you?"

"Such a gesture would be welcome," I said, "but I do not deem it likely."

"Should you obtain the Home Stone," said Seremides, "you will hold it, I assume, for ransom, for us to obtain the gold."

"Until the Home Stone is in our possession," I said, "we need not concern ourselves with that matter."

"All this is irrelevant," said Seremides, "as you do not know the whereabouts of Kurii."

"May I speak, Masters?" asked Iris.

"Shall I order you to fetch the whip, and crawl to me, with it in your teeth, offering it to me, whimpering for the lashing you so richly deserve?" asked Seremides.

"I hope not, Master," she said.

"You may speak," I said.

"The location of Kurii may not be so secret, or so well concealed, or so unknown as you suspect," she said.

"Speak further," I said.

"We command it," said Seremides.

"Some men seem to know it," she said. "I do not think it is a great secret. To be sure, it is a frightening place, and men commonly avoid it. Some who have ventured there have not returned."

"Tell us what you know, or have heard," I said.

"It is called the Beast Caves," she said.

I recalled instantly many of the Kur domiciles I had seen on a steel world, shadowy, twisting, mazelike, labyrinthine structures apparently congenial to Kur tastes. Such, it seems, were commonly the dens, or lairs, of Kurii.

"You know such a place?" I said.

"I have never been there," she said. "I have heard tell of it."

"In what way?" I asked.

"It figures," she said, "in stories, such as the Reformation of Della."

"I do not know that story," I said.

"I suspect few free persons do," she said. "It seems to figure in the oral lore of slave girls. It is whispered about amongst them. As the story has it, Della was an outspoken, impatient, haughty, critical, lazy slave whose master, presumably because of his fondness for his property, was reluctant to impose discipline on her. Soon Della, despite her tunic and collar, began to assume the airs of a free woman. One night, when Della had neglected to press her lips to her master's thigh and beg to be used, he had had enough. She was, after all, a slave, and not a free woman. He braceleted her hands behind her back and conducted her to the opening of the Beast Caves. "Why have you brought me here?" asked Della. "What are you going to do?" "You have not been fully pleasing," said her master. "I am going to feed you to the beasts." At that point, two of the beasts, growling, their eyes like flaming copper in the light of the moons, emerged from the cave. Della, terrified, instantly threw herself to her knees before her master, begging his mercy and forgiveness, pleading for her life. He said nothing, but turned about and returned to the city, Della hurrying behind him, heeling him. After that, it is said that Della became an obedient, dutiful, and loving slave. She became happy, having learned who was master and who was slave, and that each should be what they are, fully and perfectly."

"It is an interesting story," said Seremides.

"It may be just a story," said Iris, "and I do not know if there was actually a Della or not, but I have met four slaves in Ar who have had such an experience."

"Then there are Beast Caves," I said, "and they have a location near Ar!"

"Yes, Master," said Iris. "But I have never been there."

"Where is this place said to be?" I asked.

"Three pasangs southeast of the city, as the tarn flies," she said.

"There is no road?" I asked.

"There might be cart paths, a wagon trail," she said. "I have not heard of a road. I suspect few care to go there."

"You may turn about, and face us," I said.

"Thank you, Master," she said.

She scrambled about, to face us, still in nadu, which position she had not been permitted to break.

"Keep your hands, palms down, on your thighs," I said.

"Yes, Master," she said.

She had, perhaps inadvertently, opened the softness of her palms to me. There are many ways in which a slave girl can beg for attention.

"I leave tonight," I said to Seremides.

"I would that I were sound," said Seremides, "that I had two strong legs, that I might go with you."

"It is better that you stay," I said.

Seremides pounded the floor with his crutch, once, bitterly, but said nothing.

"I will go with you," said Iris. "Thus, you will have two extra eyes to see, two extra ears to hear."

"You will stay with Bruno of Torcadino, with Seremides of Ar," I said. "He may have need of you."

"No, Master!" she protested.

I anticipated great danger, and suspected that such a mission would have little prospect of success.

How could I tell her that I was loath to risk her?

"No, Master!" she repeated.

"Do you dispute the word, the decision, of a free man?" I asked.

"No, Master," she said, frightened.

"Before you leave," said Seremides, "let us have a cup of ka-la-na together. "We may not see one another again."

"We will have it now," I said. "Then I will sleep. Then I will leave."

"You can sleep, before such a thing, at such a time?" he asked.

"Yes," I said.

At a nod from Seremides, Iris rose to her feet, to fetch the ka-la-na.

CHAPTER FORTY

It was a dark night.

It had rained earlier.

The clouds swept by like barges, again heavy with rain, afloat on the river of wind.

The grass was wet, like knives.

The walls of Ar were behind me. One could see them, now and then, when the clouds broke, seemingly low, in the distance, in the brief light of the yellow moon. How mighty, lofty, and formidable they became as one approached them.

A single tarn beacon, roofed, was lit on the walls.

Tarns seldom fly in storms.

No tarn wire was strung in the city. Ar was at peace. Tonight no enemy fell from the sky.

Such wire can cut the wing from a descending tarn.

It then began, again, to rain.

It was in the vicinity of the Twentieth Ahn, the Gorean midnight.

This area, though not that far from the city, seemed remote.

I supposed, however, that humans were sometimes in this area. A few Ehn ago I had crossed a wagon track. Later I had heard harness bells. I had seen a lantern, too, being carried. Some traffic, I was sure, must take place in this vicinity. Surely men and Kurii must occasionally interact, seeking some mutual advantage.

Since Iris had spoken of "Beast Caves," I supposed that there would be more than one.

I wondered if Kurii posted guards. What had they to fear? If they did not normally post guards, I did not think they would do so now. What had they to hide?

Should I not have brought my suspicions as to Assassins and Kurii, and the Home Stone, to the attention of authorities?

I did not think so.

It seemed to me neither wise nor safe to do so.

Whom might I encounter between myself and the Ubar?

Too, it is not easy to gain access to a Ubar, under any circumstances, for almost anyone, let alone for one such as I, a stranger in Ar, foreign to its Home Stone. This is understandable. Too often the course of history has been diverted by small things, a pinch of poison, the thrust of a knife. Where power resides, power is often sought. And the seeker of power may be a crowd, or a beggar, or a stranger, or may be at one's elbow, the reliable servitor, that loyal ally beside the throne. Authority, success, and glory are not without their risks. He who wears the Medallion of the Ubar must pay its price. Too, oddly, sometimes one who is not the Ubar must also pay its price. It is weighty; it commands; it is to be worn by only one. I myself, I knew, were I to be recognized in Ar, might find myself stopped, detained, and summoned, might find myself publicly denied fire, bread, and salt, might find myself banished from Ar, might find myself ordered never to return. If so, I would understand. I would not object. It was the way of the Medallion. I had once, you see, long ago, done much, perhaps too much, for Ar. I knew the likely penalty for rendering great service to a state. A Ubar is well advised to pay small debts, for such shows his magnanimity; he is less wise to acknowledge larger debts, for it is embarrassing to have owed them; and it is not seemly that a Ubar should acknowledge a great debt, as that is incompatible with the dignity and probity of a Ubar, even to have incurred such a debt. Accordingly, he is well advised to ignore the largest debts. Parity is forbidden. One must not treat as an equal he who must be unequal, or seem to be unequal. For should not he who has saved the throne occupy the throne? But what if the throne is already occupied?

I had, from time to time, returned to Ar, but I had been wise enough to do so secretly, and in disguise.

I did not know, of course, for certain, that Kurii were involved in the theft of the Home Stone, but, given the evidence at my disposal, it seemed overwhelmingly likely.

Too, of course, I did not know that the Home Stone, even if it were in the possession of the Kurii, would be in the Beast Caves. But it was most likely there. Where else could it be hidden, or kept, with such security?

I had with me a dark lantern, now shuttered. I had thought it likely that I might have to look for sign. Kurii, incidentally, though careful of their harnessing and accouterments, were seldom shod, no more than larls or sleen. One can tell much from tracks, their look, their spacing, their depth. Though the Kur commonly stands upright, it will often drop to four limbs when it moves, and always when it runs. Over a short distance a Kur can easily outrun a man, but the beast, despite its strength, unless trained, seldom shows stamina. The common hunting regimen of the Kur in the wild is to stalk a prey and then, when close enough, rush toward it. When stalking, the prints tend to be two-pawed, and closer together, indicating stealth and patience. When charging they are wide, deep, and four-pawed, from the two hindlimbs and the knuckles of the two arms or forelimbs.

I also had with me several strands of rope, wrapped about my waist. I thought it possible such might be useful, or even needed, in negotiating caves.

The rain began to fall more heavily, which did not please me. The drum of falling rain can mask other sounds, such as the movements, even the breathing, of a large animal.

I began to fear that I might have passed the caves.

I began to fear that there might be no caves, but only in stories.

Seremides thought that Marlenus had capitulated, that he had had no choice, that even now wagons might creak under the burden of a golden cargo. Surely wagons would be covered and moved at night. Precautions would be essential. Would not many in Ar, but not of Ar, welcome an opportunity to intercept that ransom prior to its delivery? I thought of one, Aetius, of the small triangular scar, whom Seremides had tricked into delivering a false Talena to Ar. I did not think that Aetius would look kindly on so dubious a benefactor.

Rain pelted down.

I noticed that the grass was becoming thinner. Then I felt mud under the heel of my street sandal.

Could I have attained a traversed area, an area traversed by what?

Crouching down, I unshuttered the dark lantern a tiny bit, then closed it again. I had, momentarily, illuminated a yard or so of ground between patches of grass. I saw nothing that looked like tracks, either of shod feet or paws. How different this terrain was, given the darkness, grass, mud, and weather, from that of a typical forest floor in daylight, where one might hope to notice small meaningful things, a crushed leaf, a dislodged pebble, a broken twig, the imprint of a heel or claw. There seemed neither human or Kur about. But one did not know. I straightened up. I stood there in the rain and darkness, holding the now-shuttered lantern. Perhaps, I thought, the rain, dangerous in masking sound, might in another way prove a boon. Might it not wash scent from the air? One would welcome that. The sleen is Gor's finest, most tenacious tracker, but the senses of the Kur are prodigious, as well. Both can see in a light in which the average human would be helpless. Both can hear sounds which to the ear of the average human would be inaudible.

The wind rose.

I pressed on.

I heard, from behind me, the rumble of distant thunder. The rain continued to pour down. I stopped. I looked back toward Ar. The yellow moon was invisible now, masked by clouds. It was as though it had been taken from the sky. I could see a tiny point of light, intermittently, when the wind whipped apart the curtain of rain, the distant, roofed tarn beacon. Then there was a flash of light behind the city, silhouetting the walls, and, later, the distant, following upheaval of thunder.

The lightning was far behind me, beyond even Ar.

But the wind was at my back, as though it would blast my cloak from my body.

It would move clouds toward me, rapidly.

And were not such clouds the steeds of lighting?

"There is nothing here," I told myself. "Stop. Wait. Go back."

But I continued on.

There was a flash of light and the broad, flat, rude terrain sprang into sight, and then, uncomfortably, too soon, a moment later, the crash of thunder.

Rain persisted, in torrents.

"Clearly," I said to myself, "I have missed the caves, if they exist. I will stay low. I will be safe. I will wait for the storm to pass. Then I will go back. I can try again, tomorrow, in daylight. There is nothing here. It is safe here."

But then there was a blinding flash of light not a dozen yards from me, to the side, to my left and I saw lighting, like a crackling, sizzling fist of fire, seize and illuminate a large, metal, pillarlike, eccentric artifact. And almost at the same time a second, twisting, crooked spear of lighting, like a hammer of fire, struck, and burned on, a similar artifact some yards to my right.

In both cases it was almost as though the lightning, fierce and crackling, had paused at, and clung to, the high metal objects. The ensuing thunder was loud, and proximate, and for better than an Ehn afterward I feared I was deafened. I could hear nothing. In that silence which seemed to fill my world of inaudible, lashing rain, I had glimpsed the summits of the metal pillars, on each of which an eerie fire had paused. Each bore the semblance of a large, double-bladed Kur ax. I was between the two pillars, which seemed like posts marking some sort of passage, hallway, corridor, or gate. In another flash of lighting, silvering torn turf, I saw a low, wide hill, some seven or eight feet high, in which were three or four turned, rounded openings, perfectly formed, like tooled portals. Within those openings I saw receding, metal walls. It was then dark again. But then I saw a dim light within one of those openings, or portals, and sensed, rather than saw, a large shape move within. I had found the Beast Caves. There were no gates, doors, bars, or barriers at those openings, no more than one would expect at the den or lair of a larl. I could still hear nothing, but I had no difficulty in feeling the heavy, furred paw that suddenly covered my mouth.

CHAPTER FORTY-ONE

I did not struggle.

I could sense the force, the strength with which I was held. I did not want to break or sprain my neck.

Whatever held me continued to do so. It neither bit through my neck in the Kur fashion, sucking in the flooding blood, or dragged me toward the Beast Caves.

After a time, the paw was removed from my face, but its claws gripped my shoulder. I could feel the claws through my cloak and tunic. I remained still. I knew the average Kur could tear the shoulder from a man's body.

The dark lantern lay nearby, where it had fallen.

The storm was moving away. The rain fell more softly.

I began to hear again, slightly at first, and then adequately, and, later, normally.

The first thing I could make out was a question. "Why have you not responded to my questions?"

The question was in Gorean, not Kur. Too, it was in a living voice. It was not a placid evenly spaced number of mechanical sounds, the product of a translator. At first I had thought the emission was in pure Kur, but, a moment later, I realized that, despite the beastlike, growling intonation, there was a wrought approximation to Gorean phonemes. Certainly what spoke was not human, or not human as one would ordinarily understand that. It was surely a Kur or something very Kurlike. But it was speaking Gorean, and not by means of a translator.

"I am sorry," I said. "I could not hear."

"The noise, the thunder," it said.

"Yes," I said.

"Rain subsides," it said. "The sky is no longer angry. The second moon sees us."

"I would that my shoulder was freed," I said.

The beast untangled its claws from my clothing and body.

"Thank you," I said.

"It is very dangerous here," it said. "You should return to Ar, immediately."

"You speak Gorean," I said, "without a translator."

"We have been waiting for you, in the city, Tarl Cabot," it said. "We were sure that you would come to the city, sooner or later. You are fortunate I saw you and followed you. What are you doing here? You should go back to the city."

"How do you know my name?" I asked. "Who is waiting for me? Who are you?"

"See my deformity," it said, "and know me."

From behind, he placed his paw before me, and widened the digits. There were five digits, not six.

"Grendel!" I exclaimed, and turned, laughing and crying, in relief and joy, putting my arms, as I could, about that massive body, and thrusting my face against that wide, hirsute chest.

It had been long since I had seen my friend from what had once been the steel world of Agamemnon, the Eleventh Face of the Nameless One, now, given the banishment of Agamemnon to Gor, the steel world of Arcesilaus, the Twelfth Face of the Nameless One. I did not know and could not pronounce the true name of my friend in Kur, nor the names of these others, no more than I could pronounce the names of wolves and tigers in their respective languages, had they languages. As earlier noted, the name of an ancient king on a far world served for the exiled Kur ruler. And Grendel was a name originally ascribed to a fabled monster on that far world. Arcesilaus, too, was a name from that world.

"You are pleased?" said Grendel.

"Yes," I said, "very much so."

Grendel, who was part human, the result of a failed political experiment, designed to mediate between Kurii and humans, was more attuned to human emotion than most Kurii.

"You said some in the city had been waiting for me," I said. "I do not understand."

"It was known that you would seek, however futilely and foolishly, to interfere with the justice of Ar, that you would seek to save the captured Talena, the former treasonous Ubara, the traitress to her Home Stone, from its horrors and ravages. If you failed to do so, it was surmised you would inevitably, vainly, persist in your absurd quest, following her to the very gates of Ar itself."

"I was unsuccessful," I said.

"That was anticipated," said Grendel. "Accordingly, two servitors, known to you, came to Ar, to protect you, to assist you, and, if necessary, to die with you."

"Not servitors," I said, "but friends."

"A Peasant and a fisherman," said Grendel.

"Thurnock and Clitus," I said.

"Yes," said Grendel.

"I ordered them not to follow me," I said.

"Love accepts mutiny," said Grendel.

"And I suspect," I said, "there is a third."

"Yes," said Grendel, "one who hopes to found his own species."

"How is that?" I asked.

"I have a mate," he said, "Eve, who is incredibly beautiful, even more so than the loveliest Kur females."

"She is much like you?" I said.

"Not at all," he said. "I am plain; she is beautiful. You should see the excitement of her fangs, the curves of her claws."

"But she is much like you?" I said.

"She was bred for me," he said, "like myself, a mix of human and Kur."

"That there be things which might serve the purposes of the Kurii," I said, "in their attempt to placate and reassure humans; then to be recruited for the conquest of Gor on behalf of Kurii?"

"Yes," he said, "but the experiment did not work out well. For some reason, humans did not feel at ease with me, or, I suppose, would they with her."

"I see," I said.

"I did not even know of her existence until recently," he said.

"She did not sob and cry, learning her purpose?"

"No," he said. "We decided we would have our own purpose. You would like her. She is sweet and kind. She can bite through the throat of a larl, tear the leg off a sleen. She would love to meet you."

"I would look forward to it," I said, uneasily.

"But now," he said, "let me protect you, and guide you, as you return to the city. You have wandered into the vicinity of the Beast Caves. That is not wise for a human."

By this time the rain no longer fell; the wind, though persisting, no longer tore at one's clothing. The darkness in the sky broke into scudding fragments; the yellow moon reassured a world of its existence.

"I am not here by accident," I said. "I am here to recover the Home Stone of Ar, that I might exchange it for the prisoner, Talena."

I had not seen fit to explain this motivation to Seremides.

"And it is in the Beast Caves?"

"I think so."

"I understand that the Home Stone is of great value," he said.

"Yes," I said.

"Is it a giant diamond or a large object made of gold?" he asked.

"No," I said. "It is hard to explain its meaning, its purport, its value. I think to those who have no Home Stone, no explanation is adequate. To those who have a Home Stone, no explanation is necessary."

"Is it like the preciousness and significance of one's being a legitimate Face of the Nameless One?" he asked.

"I do not know," I said. "Perhaps."

"Let us return to the city," he said.

"You go back, dear friend," I said. "I have work to do here."

"No," he said.

"Go back to your Eve," I said.

"She would despise me, did I do so," he said.

"She is part Kur," I said.

"Of course," he said.

"You are unarmed," I said.

"I am part Kur," he said. "Thus, I am no more unarmed than the sleen or larl."

I recalled, too, that on the steel world where I had first met him, he was no stranger to the sand of the arena.

"Of course," I said.

"You, however," he said, "might be torn to pieces at the very threshold of the caves."

"I must risk it," I said.

"You have rope about your waist," he said.

"In case it is needed, for climbing," I said.

"You will not need it," he said. "These are not natural caves, with cliffs, drops, and wells, unlit and treacherous. However twisting and various in shape and size, these are domicile caves, dwelling caves, whose dangers, if any, would be designed to trap or destroy those who might be menacing or unwelcome."

Grendel then began to unwind the rope from about my waist.

"What are you doing?" I asked.

"Assuring your safety, at least for the moment," he said.

He then removed my weapons, discarded my cloak, and bound my hands behind my back. He then lifted the same strand of rope up from my bound wrists, knotted it about my neck, and threw the remainder forward, where, grasped at the center, it would constitute a leash, and, beyond the center, doubled, might serve as a prisoner or slave lash. All this was done with the same length of rope. Many times I had seen this simple, economical form of tie before, but usually it had been imposed on stripped females of the enemy, arriving at war camps.

Like them, I was helpless.

Grendel gathered up, and secured, my weapons and accouterments.

"What of you?" I asked. "How can you enter the caves?"

"Easily, I trust," he said, "particularly as I am conducting a prisoner. The Kurii are vain, they fear nothing, they will see me as another Kur unless I am examined closely. My Kur is far more fluent

than my Gorean. I may even pretend to need a translator to communicate with my prisoner."

"Are there no passwords, no signs or signals of identification?" I
asked.

"I shall hope not," he said. "I think such would be unlikely. All
Kurii here, or likely to be in the vicinity, I think, will be of the same
party, and no one would confuse a human with a Kur."

Grendel then, my leash in one hand, or paw, conducted me toward the closest, most prominent opening of the Beast Caves.

CHAPTER FORTY-TWO

The cage door was opened and I, then unbound, was thrust within. Then the door was shut behind me.

"I see I have company," said a figure in the cage, sitting with his back against the far wall, which was of metal.

I had found the network of tunnels, and their levels, quite impressive. I expected that each of the outside entrances led, sooner or later, into the complex as a whole. From the steel world I had visited, however unexpectedly and unwillingly, long ago, I was familiar with the general mazelike nature of such structures. Like those on the steel worlds, this complexus was built almost entirely of metal, presumably treated in various ways, though here, of course, unlike those on the steel world, the tunnels ran beneath the surface of a natural world. I had no idea of the actual area of the complexus, but I supposed it might be in the neighborhood of a square half pasang in area, and some number of levels in depth. As I had counted, the cage was five floors down from the surface, and I had seen a broad stairwell leading down to at least one more level.

"I see I am not the only one," said the seated figure, "who was too clever for his own good."

"Tal, Aetius," I said. The cage was well lit, from a bulb in the ceiling outside the cage. Such did not contravene the laws of Priest-Kings, which tended to restrict weapons and means of communication. I knew the Builders had designed such devices, but they were rare on the surface. On the other hand, I supposed that the bulb, like the steel caves, was a product of Kur technology. I had had no difficulty in identifying Aetius of Venna, given the lighting and my earlier encounter with him on the plains not far from the great caravan of Cos, in the vicinity of the Peasant village of Red Stream. I did not need to see the small triangular scar low on his face, to the right side of his mouth.

"It seems," he said, "we think alike. A Home Stone is missing, stolen. A city and its environs are ransacked. A search is widespread, meticulous, prolonged, and thorough. A thousand suspicions and alleged clues are investigated, but all to no avail. Yet, presumably, the missing Home Stone is somewhere in the vicinity, for the convenience of resolving matters quickly, even for its prompt delivery once the ransom is delivered. Where then can it be? Surely with men, for they stole it. Certainly not with beasts, who would have no interest in, or understanding of, Home Stones, no more than tarsks and sleen. But what if beasts were allied with men, and men with beasts? Where better then to conceal the Home Stone but with beasts, with terrible beasts?"

"And perhaps," I said, "you noted at least one beast in the household or entourage of Decius Albus, trade advisor to the Ubar?"

"Of course," said Aetius, "this proving the possible linkage of beasts with men."

"You had men," I said. "Where are they?"

"I could not retain them," he said. "They abandoned me when I could no longer pay them."

"I gather," I said, "that the slave you brought to Ar was not the true Talena."

"Doubtless much to your surprise," he said.

"I had suspected as much," I said.

"She sold for a silver tarsk, two," he said.

This would be a silver tarsk, and two copper tarsks.

"That is not a bad price," I said.

"I had hoped for more," he said.

"It was not enough to hold your men," I said.

"Not for long," he said.

"Perhaps many false Talenas were brought to Ar," I said. "That might bring down prices, particularly for slaves suspected of being false Talenas. Who would want one, not the genuine article?"

"Shall we now attempt to kill one another?" he asked.

"I would recommend a much less wasteful expenditure of energy and time," I said.

"We could always attend to that sort of thing later," he said.

"If you wish," I said. "In the meantime, let us become uneasy, unwelcome allies."

"I have examined the bars," he said. "They could hold a dozen raging beasts."

"Are the jailers or warders human?" I asked.

"Unfortunately not," he said.

I had hoped that the Kurii might have humans about to attend to servile tasks, in particular, female slaves. Such, as I recalled, lovely pets, served Kurii in various lowly ways on the steel world I had visited, in particular, in grooming their masters, biting parasites from their fur, and such.

"Do jailers or wardens enter the cage?" I asked.

"Seldom," he said. "Food is thrust in narrow trays between the bars. Water is available in that depression in the floor to the right.

Perhaps you were thinking of overcoming one or more of the beasts in the cage?"

"Not without weapons," I said. "I thought that, if the cage was open, one person might create a diversion and the other slip away."

"It is a thought," he said, "particularly if I am the one to slip away."

"This place seems large," I said. "Have you seen many beasts about?"

"Oddly, very few," he said.

"Nor I," I said. "And I suspect there are few. This complexus, I am sure, is not of recent origin. I think it might have been built centuries ago, in a different historic time. I am sure its location, near Ar, is not a mistake. There may be a similar complexus near mighty Turia, in the far south. I suspect both structures, if there were two, were abandoned, given the distant fortunes of remote wars, Priest-Kings against Beasts. This one may, for convenience, have been retenanted only recently."

"I know only the place seems large and little occupied. Why?"

"It may be easier then," I said, "to escape to the surface."

"Perhaps you will unlock the cage," he said.

"Another may do that," I said.

"You have a friend, a confederate?" he asked, interested.

"I trust so," I said.

"But a Beast brought you here," he said.

"It seems so," I said.

"It is your friend or confederate?" he asked.

"Yes," I said.

"You are a greater fool than I," he said. "Blood is against you."

"Sometimes there may be more than one blood," I said.

"The heaviness, the sturdiness, of this cage," he said, "suggests it was not made for humans."

"You are wondering why you are confined in it, and were not simply killed?"

"Yes," he said.

"How have you been fed?" I asked.

"Amply," he said, "if not well. Why do you ask?"

"Some of these beasts," I said, "may eat human flesh."

"We are to them, as verr and tarsks are to us?" he asked.

"Something like that," I said.

On the steel world of Agamemnon certain specially bred ignorant and benighted human beings were raised as food animals. That practice had been discontinued after some humans had supported, and participated in, the revolution against Agamemnon, that which had brought Arcesilaus to power.

"I have certainly not been fattened here," he said.

"But you have been fed amply," I said, "perhaps that your agility and strength would be sustained."

"I do not understand," he said.

"Many of the Beasts," I said, "like to do their own killing, stalking and hunting the prey. In that way, sport is involved and appetite whetted. Too, the meat is fresh and the blood hot." I had once observed a feeding with Zarendargar, a Kur general, popularly known as Half-Ear.

"One would not wish to disappoint them," Aetius said.

"Beware the animal who does not wish to be disappointed," I said.

"Where is your friend?" he asked.

"I do not know," I said.

"Should he not have been back by now?" asked Aetius.

"Perhaps," I said.

"He may have been discovered and dealt with by now," said Aetius.

I thought that that was surely possible. Perhaps there might be a pack odor amongst Kurii, as there was with urts, or a nest odor, as there was with Priest-Kings.

"Kur," I whispered suddenly.

"What?" said Aetius.

"Beast," I said. "Beast."

It had come from down the corridor. It was now a yard or so outside the bars.

"Is it the one you know?" asked Aetius.

I looked closely. "No," I said.

"Address it," said Aetius.

"It has no translator," I said.

"'Translator'?" said Aetius.

"It is like a box, and it changes one form of speech into another," I said. Almost all Kurii conversing with another form of rational, speeched life used such a device. There were, however, some Kurii who can produce a semblance of Gorean phonemes. I did not recall that the Kur whom I had seen shambling beside the palanquin of Decius Albus had had a translator. Perhaps then it had not needed one.

"Speak to it," said Aetius. "They may answer you. They did not answer me."

"Tal," I said to the beast on the other side of the bars. "I would converse with one in authority. Take me to such a one, or bring him here."

This overture was met with a quizzical growl.

"They may know of sickness, of diseases, of plagues," said Aetius.

"Undoubtedly," I said. I suspected that any Kur who had lived upon, or had visited, or knew of, a steel world would be well aware of the dangers of disease in so confined or limited an environment. It would be something like the mariner's terror of fire at sea. Should a ship burn, or an earth perish, one is without remedy. "Feign a seizure," I suggested.

"They would then hasten to remove us from their dwelling place," said Aetius.

"Hopefully," I said.

The Kur, who seemed to have been no more than passing, turned away from the bars.

Aetius then uttered an inarticulate cry, threw himself to the steel floor of the cage, and began to roll about, gasping and moaning, as though afflicted with convulsions.

"That is enough," I said. "The Beast has gone."

"He was not interested?" asked Aetius, getting to his feet.

"It seems not," I said. "Incidentally, you did that quite well."

"Next time," said Aetius. "It is your turn."

"No," I said. "I could not hope to equal your performance."

"Have you any other ideas?" he asked.

"No," I said, "not at the moment."

"I have one," he said. "If they wish to use us for sport, for hunting, for eating, for interrogation, for torture, or whatever, they will presumably want us both alive."

"I would think so," I said.

"Excellent," he said. "The next time a Beast passes, we shall attack one another. We shall do so with vigor. Then, lest we kill one another, they will open the cage to separate us."

"As I recall," I said, "you suggested something along these lines earlier."

"One thought leads to another," he said.

"And what if we succeed in killing one another?" I asked.

"That would be a good joke on the Beasts," he said. "It would serve them right. What do you think?"

"Just as long as things work out for the best," I said.

We listened for a time, but the corridor remained silent and empty.

"You know," said Aetius, "they may feed on us."

"It is quite possible," I said.

Then, suddenly, there rang through the tunnels a loud, long, weird, reverberating, howling noise.

"What is that?" said Aetius.

"I do not know," I said.

"It is like a living thing," he said.

"But not living," I said. "It is mechanical, I am sure."

"It is quiet now," he said.

"Surely you do not object," I said.

"Surely your hairy friend should have returned by now," said Aetius.

"I should have hoped so," I said.

"I hear a scratching, on metal," said Aetius. "Perhaps it is your friend."

"I do not think so," I said. "In this unknown place, he would retract his claws, would wish to move silently."

"I see it," said Aetius. "It is a beast. It will pass the cage."

"Yes," I said.

Suddenly, from the side, without warning, Aetius's balled fist struck me heavily on the side of the head, and I staggered to the other side of the cage. "The slave," he said, "was not Talena." "That is not her fault," I said, stumbling back toward him. In a moment then, in a flurry of bodies, seizing, striking, and twisting, wrestling, pulling, pushing, buffeting, and kicking, and grunting and gasping, we were on the floor, off the floor, and back on the floor. "Is it frightened for us? Is it opening the cage?" asked Aetius, who now, like myself, was quite short of breath. There was blood about. I supposed it was partly mine, and partly his. "No," I said. "He is watching. I am not sure if he is enjoying himself, or just puzzled." We then resumed our combat. I was trying to give the impression of an untrammeled, amateur altercation, which, to an untutored observer might seem authentic. For example, I pulled punches, but Aetius, either because he was less skilled in this sort of deception, or was not interested in it, struck me several sound blows. Certainly the fracas had little in it of polish, or grace, and it might have been such as to cause an afficionado of fisticuffs to avert his head in shame, or lead a martial-arts master to close his dojo in dismay. "Is the cage open yet?" whispered Aetius, through a split lip, for I was not always as successful at pulling punches as I had hoped. I rolled over. "No," I said. "He is gone, and perhaps has been for some time." I did not know. Out of the corner of an eye I saw another blow starting toward my face, and I blocked it, and then struck Aetius unconscious. Then, after catching my breath, I pulled him over to the water-filled depression in the cage floor, and, holding him by the hair, thrust his head under the water for a few times after which I desisted, and we, he sputtering, and I beginning to feel considerable pain, rose unsteadily to our feet. I think that neither of us really felt any aches, pain, or misery until we had separated and were trying to recover ourselves. One's mind, one's focus, are on other things. Sometimes warriors are wounded, and even bleeding profusely, and are not, for a time, aware of it. Incidentally, in the course of our performance, I had made, as we grappled, an interesting discovery, which I was soon to look into.

"How," I asked, "given that you supposed the Home Stone of Ar was in the Beast Caves, did you expect to obtain it?"

"How," he asked, "given that you supposed the Home Stone of Ar was in the Beast Caves, did you expect to obtain it?"

"I asked you first," I said.

"I asked you last," he said, "thus most recently."

"I had hoped to penetrate the Caves," I said, "locate the Home Stone, seize it, and fight my way out."

"I would not have given much for your chances," he said.

"Nor I," I said.

"What of your hirsute friend?" he asked.

"Such an ally, unexpectedly encountered, I conjectured," I said, "would much improve my chances."

"From one in ten thousand, to perhaps two in ten thousand?" he said.

"Thus doubling my chances," I said.

"I cannot challenge that mathematically," he said. "But your friend trussed you up like a vulo and then turned you over to his kind, who had you placed in this cage."

"True," I said.

"With such a friend," he said, "you might consider dispensing with enemies."

"I trust him," I said.

"A Beast?"

"More so than with many men I have known," I said.

"More so than with, say, Bruno of Torcadino?" he asked.

"Quite possibly," I said.

"I noticed something while we were grappling," I said.

"My martial skills?"

"No," I said.

"What then?" he asked.

"Within your tunic, up about your chest," I said, "you are carrying a small, solid object."

"Surely you are mistaken," he said.

I balled my fist.

He felt about his chest, high on the left side. "Wait," he said. "You seem to be right."

"Display it," I said.

"It is a common rock," I said.

"I fear so," he said.

"My plan for obtaining the Home Stone," I said, "was by raiding and war, however dubious and impractical that plan might have been, but yours, it seems, was quite different."

"Very much so," he said. "I take it that you are of the Warriors. They tend to think too readily of steel and blood. They are too quick to unsheathe the sword."

"He who first unsheathes the sword is likely to be he who lives long enough to return it to its sheath," I said.

"Not being of so impatient and noble a caste," he said, "I thought first of deception, and then of theft and flight."

"You thought to somehow obtain access to the Home Stone of Ar and then replace it with a substitute?"

"One supposes that one rock looks much like another to a Beast," he said.

"And how did you expect to gain access to the Home Stone and manage the substitution undetected?"

"By pretending to be an emissary of Marlenus, suitably credentialed, sent to determine the safety of the Home Stone and arrange its return."

"Your plan was bold, indeed," I said.

"I deemed the peril of failure was far exceeded by the value of the prize."

"But your plan proved unsuccessful," I said.

"One casts the stones," he said. "Who knows how they will fall?"

"What happened?" I asked.

"I was apprehended almost immediately," he said. "I could not even begin to put my plan into effect. I could not communicate with the Beasts, nor they with me. They could not even speak Gorean, let alone read it, or understand the purport of my forged credentials."

"I see," I said.

"And thus my plan, as it turned out, was as unavailing and foolish as yours."

"Even had things been muchly different," I said, "even did the Beasts understand you, and even had they a human or humans with whom you might deal, your plan was questionable, to an extreme. Who would believe you came from Marlenus? How would Marlenus know where to send such a messenger? If he knew that much, he would have had a thousand armsmen within hail of the Caves, readied to swarm within. Such a man is Marlenus."

"I did not know, of course," he said, "what he knew or did not know. One can only hope. One can only wager. One casts the stones. Who knows how they will fall?"

"You had no ally," I said.

"No," he said.

"And such an inquiry, as to the safety of the Home Stone, and as to arrangements for its delivery," I said, "would not come from

Marlenus, but from another, who would know the location of the Home Stone, an involved conspirator."

"Who?" he asked.

"One," I said, "or maybe two, who would, I believe, be known to the Beasts."

"In any event," he said, "we have both failed."

"Neither, as of yet," I said. "You have a plan, I have knowledge, we have an ally."

"I do not understand," he said.

"Give me the rock," I said.

I placed it in the wallet, slung at my belt.

CHAPTER FORTY-THREE

"Heed me, Foolish Minions," I roared into the translator, grasping the bars, "I am the second emissary to be misused. Are you mindless urts, retarded tarsks? Are you so devoid of probity that you should best be replaced with draft tharlarion? Why were we not welcomed at the entrance to your metal holes? Why were we not met by dignitaries with translators? Are you unworthy of your arena rings and harnessing? How much longer will you strive to inflict shame on your proud, noble species. To what depths do you seek to descend? Patience is not unending. Am I not back in Ar, with my fellow, our mission done, by the Tenth Ahn, limbs will be torn away, and heads will follow! Do you wish your gross, unsightly bodies to be the feasting of swarming, hook-billed jards?"

Four creatures stood outside the bars, three Kurii and Grendel. I am sure Aetius could not distinguish between the Kurii and Grendel. Indeed, it seemed likely that the three Kurii did not even note that Grendel was not one of them, perhaps taking him for one of their own species, though one deformed in certain respects, and somewhat unusually eyed and voiced. One of the Kurii was larger than the others, and closer to the bars. I assumed he was "first," one possessing priority in that small aggregate. Near him, slightly behind him, stood Grendel. Behind Grendel were two Kurii. The first Kur, the largest one, that closest to the bars, had a translator, and a translator was also in the keeping of one of the two Kurii bringing up the rear, the one on the left, as I looked through the bars. The translators were suspended by cords about the neck, this freeing the forelimbs of the beasts. The Kur furthest back, to the right, as I looked through the bars, the one without a translator, carried a large double-bladed ax. The weight of such a weapon makes it difficult to be wielded by a smaller animal, such as a human. The two translators, at first being jointly activated, emitted conflicting successions of sounds, but the one in the rear was quickly turned off, that communication might proceed more expeditiously, more successfully.

It took a few moments for my Gorean to reach the two translators and for the translators to process my emissions and issue something hopefully equivalent in Kur. In the interval, I drew back somewhat from the bars, in case the Kur response to my remarks might not be entirely affable, or affirmative. The lead Kur, you see, he closest to the bars, was initially confused, presumably because of the mutual interference of the two translators, but, after the rearward translator had been shut off and the forward translator's reception reversed to repeat its translation of my remarks, I gathered that the translation of my Gorean into its Kur may have been approximately correct, for he, howling with rage, threw himself bodily against the bars and, extending his right forelimb between the bars, raked the air between us with a mighty six-digited paw, for each digit of which, emerging from the fur, there was a sharp, now-emerged, curved claw.

I was reminded of what was sometimes said of some blades, that they were so sharp they could draw blood from the wind.

I will not dismay the reader, if a reader there may sometimes be, with the Gorean translation of the beast's Kur. Let me merely note that it was not entirely complimentary.

"Shed a drop of my blood, you buffoon," I said, standing well back from the bars, "and you will answer with an ocean of your own!"

"He is going to unlock the cage," said Aetius.

"I hope not now, not just yet," I said.

"Do you think he will tear me to pieces, as well?" asked Aetius.

"I do not know," I said. "You will have to wait and see."

The beast's fury was such, he was so blind with rage, so shaking with venom, he was having difficulty thrusting the key into the cage lock. He had already scratched the plating in several places.

It might help to understand what was going on if it is kept in mind that the average Kur is not only large, impatient, short of temper, fierce, and violent, but proudly regards itself and its species as the glorious pinnacle of nature and civilization, much as many human beings so regard themselves, as well; thus, he does not appreciate having his glory besmirched by what he regards as a pretentious and annoying inferior form of life. The average human being, for example, might not care to be insulted, particularly lengthily, and grievously, by an unpleasant, loud-mouthed, upstart toad or cockroach, particularly if he had seriously negative feelings about toads and cockroaches to begin with.

Then the key was jammed into the lock and spun, freeing the bolt. The door was flung open, banging against the bars.

The giant Kur stood in the opened threshold, fangs glistening.

"Hail Agamemnon," I said, as calmly as I could manage, adding for good measure, though I did not deem it necessary, "Eleventh Face of the Nameless One."

The Kur trembled in the portal, on the brink of rushing forward. He struggled with himself. He tottered; then he righted his large, shaggy frame. And he remained where he was, stopped short.

I heard something like a growl.

An instant later the words "Hail, Agamemnon" were emitted from the translator slung about his wide, hairy neck.

"What is your name," I demanded.

A hesitant, unwilling, almost inaudible rumble came from the beast, and the name Lucilius came from its translator.

"I fear, Lucilius," I said, "that I must report to Lord Agamemnon that you have failed the test. I thought you might."

"I have failed nothing," came from the translator.

As you might surmise, the following dialogue might appear somewhat eccentric, unless you keep in mind that the translator, or at least those in the vicinity, gives no indication of several subtleties in discourse which can be contextually significant, such as intonation contours, spacing, volume, intensity, humor, irony, emotion, and such. For example, the locution "I love you" said tenderly and said sneeringly, insultingly, emerges identically from the translator. Similarly, "I love you" and "I hate you" sound much the same as they emerge from the translator. To be sure, they differ in semantic content.

"Perhaps not," I said, "but my assertion that you failed will put you in a rather bad light."

"If you live to make the report," he said.

"There are three witnesses," I said. "And surely at least one might be either honest or interested in supplanting you in your office."

"You did not tell me that it was a test," said Lucilius.

"Had I imparted that information beforehand," I said, "would that not have rendered the test vacuous?"

"What is the point of so foolish a test?" asked Lucilius.

"It is not unusual for a plan or project of your noble race," I said, "to require the assistance of, the utilization of, the cooperation of, other forms of life, such as, occasionally, say, humans. If that is true, then behaviors such as tearing off the limbs or heads of such allies, perhaps humans, is not likely to advance the fortunes of the plans or projects in question. I take it that that is obviously true. Thus Lord Agamemnon advises his adherents to be patient with, say, pertinent humans, even under conditions of great provocation. Who can hold his temper and who cannot? It is important to know. Who cannot hold his temper may place plans and projects in jeopardy. Thus, the justification and rationale of such tests as I recently conducted. I hope you understand."

"When we no longer need humans," he said, "we will discard them, eat them, exterminate them, keep some in zoos, some as performing animals, some as grooming pets, and so on."

"But until then," I said, "I hope you can see my point."

"I do not think you are a 'pertinent human,'" he said.

"Ask Lord Agamemnon," I said, "if he is not between bodies."

"You know of such things?" said Lucilius.

"Of course," I said. "His last body was that of a gigantic metal tharlarion terrorizing the delta of the Vosk, in and near Port Kar. I do not know his next body, that which is doubtless even now being prepared for him."

"He is not in the Caves," said Lucilius.

"But is nearby?" I said.

"Perhaps," said Lucilius.

I myself thought it quite likely that Agamemnon was actually in the Caves. Where else would he be likely to be? Too, I had heard that long, loud, weird, mechanically produced, howling noise reverberating through the tunnels. Surely its source might have been one of the "bodies" of Agamemnon.

"You seem like a pleasant, sensible fellow," I said. "I think I may have made my test a bit severe, even for one as perceptive as you."

"It was a trifle severe," he said.

"I agree," I said. "Therefore, if you release me, and my colleague, and let us be about our business, we shall consider the entire matter closed and forgotten."

"I think you are a liar," he said.

"Quite possibly," I said. "But you do not know. There are two possibilities, I am a liar or I am not. If I am a liar, and you kill me, the world is little changed. On the other hand, if I am not a liar and you kill me, the world, from your point of view, will be considerably changed, and not at all in your favor."

"What do you want?" said Lucilius.

"What we came for," I said, "to confirm the safety of the Home Stone of Ar and arrange the terms of its delivery to Marlenus, Ubar of Ar."

I then added, thinking it might be helpful, "Hail, Agamemnon."

"Hail, Agamemnon," came from Lucilius's translator.

"You may now step aside," I informed Lucilius.

"Something more obtrudes," he said, a twisted grimace distorting his features, which grimace, I recalled, from the Steel World, was a smile.

"Yes?" I said, interested.

"The names," he said.

"'Names'?" I said.

"Those without which access to the Caves is forbidden to humans," he said.

"Of course," I said.

"What are they?" he asked.

"That of Pa-Kur, Master of the Dark Caste," I said. I was sure that this would be correct. I was sure it had been Assassins, disguised as

Initiates, who had stolen the Home Stone of Ar. Too, did it not seem certain that Xenon was an Assassin, and had he not prevented me from spreading an alarm recently in Ar.

"That is one," said Lucilius.

"Surely one is enough," I said.

"What is the other?" he asked.

"Hail, Agamemnon," I said.

"Hail, Agamemnon," came from Lucilius's translator. Then came from the translator, "What is the other one?"

I noted that Lucilius's smile had broadened, a muscular contracture which did much to enhance the display of his fangs.

Female Kurii, I knew, often regarded their smile as their best feature. I recalled that Grendel regarded his Eve as unusually beautiful.

"The other name?" came from Lucilius's translator.

I was not sure of this second name, but it must be, I thought, that of someone powerful in Ar. I recalled hearing it hinted, or claimed, that Decius Albus, the trade advisor to the Ubar, wanted the throne for himself, doubtless amongst several others nursing a similar ambition. But also, perhaps more tellingly, I recalled seeing a Kur in his entourage.

"The other name," I said, boldly, hoping for the best, "is Decius Albus." Then I added, "He is the trade advisor to the Ubar."

A furious snarl of frustration came from Lucilius. His translator, however, was silent, presumably having failed to detect any succession of intelligible phonemes.

"Now," I said, "please step aside."

Lucilius then, trembling with rage, stepped aside.

CHAPTER FORTY-FOUR

"It is there," said Lucilius, pointing.

A stone, about the size of a clenched fist, lay on a smooth, white, circular table in a domed chamber deep in the Caves, two levels below the level of the cage in which Aetius and I had been confined.

"I must touch it, I must hold it," I said.

"That is not necessary," said Lucilius.

In the domed chamber, aside from Lucilius and myself, were Aetius, Grendel, and the two Kurii who had accompanied Lucilius earlier, one with a translator, now switched off, and one with the large double-bladed ax.

"I am sorry," I said. "It is absolutely necessary."

"I deem it not so," said Lucilius.

"Then I shall return to Ar, now," I said.

"I do not understand," said Lucilius.

"I have my orders," I said. "If you prevent me from carrying out those orders, I must report that to Pa-Kur, Master of the Assassins, and to Decius Albus, the trade advisor. And an account of this interference, I have no doubt, will be relayed immediately to Lord Agamemnon. Be clear, noble friend. The responsibility for the failure of my mission will rest solely with you. I find your obstruction of the will of Lord Agamemnon unconscionable, but I salute your courage in defying his command. Few would dare do so."

"Very well," said Lucilius, "as you have orders."

"I shall replace it promptly," I said.

I reached out and took the stone into my hands. As I did so, I caught my breath, and the hair rose on my forearms and the back of my neck.

"What is wrong?" asked Lucilius.

Many years ago, at the Twentieth Ahn, at midnight, on the Planting Feast of Ar, in a raid on the Central Cylinder of Ar, I had seized the Home Stone of Ar, damp with ceremonial ka-la-na and speckled with clinging grains of sa-tarna. I had leaped to the saddle of my tarn to escape with the prize, the loss of which it was hoped would cost aggressive, imperialistic Marlenus of Ar his medallion of office. I thrust the stone into the saddle pack and drew on the one-strap. The mighty wings of the bird struck the air, and the monster ascended, but its flight was compromised. Its agility and speed were lessened, for Talena, of Ar, the daughter of Marlenus, in a desperate attempt to save the Home Stone, had seized the loosened mounting ladder, and swung below, clinging to it, far above the ground. Rather than cutting away the ladder, I drew her to the saddle before me. In my haste I had not fastened my safety strap. She feigned docility and gratitude, and then, suddenly, seized me about the waist and flung me from the saddle. I fell into one of the huge webs spun by the Spider People, inhabitants of the vast swamp forest north of Ar. Talena could not manage the tarn and it attacked, or was attacked by, one or more wild tarns. In the tarn warring, in the plunging and wheeling, in the sky and sometimes near the ground, amongst the trees, Talena fell into the swamp, and the tarn bearing the Home Stone of Ar sped away. I later encountered the daughter of Marlenus in the swamp and, something like a year later, the saddlebag with the Home Stone was found by a herdsman of verr in the Voltai mountains, together with the rotted shreds of the saddle, reins, and such, perhaps torn away by the tarn against the rocks.

"What is wrong?" asked Lucilius.

"This is not the Home Stone of Ar," I said.

"What?" cried Aetius.

"You lie," came from the translator of Lucilius.

Grendel stiffened.

The two cohorts of Lucilius looked to one another, and to Lucilius.

I had had, long ago, the Home Stone of Ar in my hands, wet with wine, moist with adhering grain. I had forgotten little of that wild, terrible night. The resemblance was close, but the object was subtly wrong, in weight, texture, size, and shape. This was not the stone I had stolen so long ago.

"No," I said. "This is not the Home Stone of Ar."

"Confirm that it is the Home Stone," said Lucilius.

"It is not the Home Stone," I said. "What game do you play? What hoax or joke do you seek to perpetrate?"

"Do you wish to leave the Caves alive?" asked Lucilius.

"If Aetius and I are not back in Ar by the Tenth Ahn," I said, "the adherents of Lord Agamemnon, those who are truly loyal to him, will fill the Caves with fire."

"Show him," came from the translator of Lucilius. He had not spoken, but the Kur with the switched-off translator had said this, and it was picked up and transmitted by Lucilius's translator.

"Wait," said Lucilius. The sound from Lucilius had been an abrupt, vicious, half-snarl, but the phoneme from his translator was, as usual, as simple, unhurried, noncommittal, and emotionless as if it had been inked on a scroll.

Lucilius went to the side of the room and, on a spot on the wall seemingly no different from any other, with one now-emerged nail on his right paw, struck the wall with a short, light, intricate succession of taps.

A panel-like tray came into view, containing a small, gray object.

"Let this not be a trick," I said.

"It was a test," said Lucilius.

"One I passed more successfully than you did yours," I said.

He lifted the object from the tray.

His paw was large, and furred. I hoped it was far less sensitive than the skin, palm, and fingers of a human hand. For example, if I had worn heavy gloves when I had examined the stone removed from the table, I would doubtless have been far less sure of its lack of authenticity.

I had seen the Home Stone of Ar before only in the light of the moons of Gor.

I wanted it in my hands.

I wanted to feel it.

Then I had it in my hands.

It was the Home Stone of Ar, or a marvelous duplicate.

"Yes," I said. "This is the Home Stone of Ar."

At that point, far off, from somewhere in the tunnels, reverberating in the metal, there was a repetition of the long, loud, wailing, mechanical sound which Aetius and I had heard when in the cage.

"What is that?" I asked.

"Nothing," said Lucilius. "It does not concern you."

"It is like the scream of a tarn, but of metal," I said.

"That is the Home Stone of Ar?" asked Lucilius.

"Yes," I said.

"You confirm it so," said Lucilius.

"Yes," I said.

"And how is it to be delivered?" he asked.

"At the Twentieth Ahn of the day the ransom is delivered and secure, presumably two days from now, an Assassin, a member of the dark caste, will come to the Caves and call for the stone."

"How am I to know this human?" asked Lucilius.

"You will ask him three questions," I said, thinking it not amiss to get back at Lucilius, to whom I had taken something of a dislike. "First, what tharlarion balances itself on its tail, second, what tarn has eleven wings and two beaks, and, third, what tarsk is skilled a playing the kalika?"

"Those are strange questions," said Lucilius. "I know of no breed of tharlarion which can balance itself on its tail, nor any tarn with more than two wings and one beak, nor any tarsk skilled at playing a musical instrument, especially a kalika."

"Few do," I admitted. "That makes them excellent questions. Not many, you see, would know the answers."

"And what answers may I expect?"

"Alexander the Great, Julius Caesar, and Napoleon Bonaparte, respectively," I said.

"Those are names?" he asked.

"Yes," I said.

"I trust that they are not familiar to humans," he said.

"Not locally," I admitted. "Do you think you can manage it?"

"Of course," he said. "I am Kur."

"Kurii are marvelous," I said. "They are splendidly uniform, in numerous attributes of excellence."

"That is true," said Lucilius.

I met the eyes of Grendel, hoping he would not be offended, but would cooperate with me. I do not think he understood my intent, but doubtless surmised that I had an intent.

"Is it true," I asked Lucilius, "that your noble race has a base-twelve mathematics, presumably indexed to the six-digited paw?"

"Hand," he said. "But we do have a base-twelve mathematics, presumably not because of a six-digited hand, but because it is far superior to a base-ten mathematics, such as, as I understand it, many humans prefer."

"Yet," I said, "one of you fellows seems to have a five-digited hand, much like humans."

"Surely not," said Lucilius.

"Perhaps I was mistaken," I said.

At this point Grendel shifted guiltily backward, hiding his hands.

"Let us see," said Lucilius.

"He is deformed," said the fellow with the switched-off translator, his comment being relayed by Lucilius's translator.

At this point I slipped the Home Stone of Ar into my tunic, removed the rock I had been given by Aetius from my wallet, placed it on the white, smooth, circular table, and held the false Home Stone, which muchly resembled the actual Home Stone of Ar, in my right hand.

"May I call your attention to business?" I asked. "We must be on our way." I then handed the resembling, but false, Home Stone to Lucilius. "I advise you to lock this away," I said.

An impatient snarl escaped Lucilius, but nothing intelligible was emitted from the translator.

In a moment he had placed the false Home Stone in the panel-tray and closed the panel.

"Aetius, my fellow human, and I, must return to Ar, and swiftly," I said. "Doubtless we are already missed. As we may lose our way amongst the breadth and depth of these metal tunnels, please assign us a guide to bring us to the surface." I then gestured toward Grendel. "That fellow there, who, lacking a translator, mistakenly bound me, will do."

"That is fitting," said Lucilius. "Why should not an imperfect Kur lead lowly humans from our house?"

"You have handled this matter extremely well," I said. "I shall so inform the Master of the Assassins and the trade advisor, who will doubtless relay my commendation and gratitude to Lord Agamemnon."

"Do so," said Lucilius.

"Outside the Caves," I said, "brigands may be about, or, given the Ahn, wild sleen."

The sleen is predominantly nocturnal, particularly in the wild.

"Possibly," said Lucilius.

"Might not our guide then be prevailed upon to conduct us safely at least to the walls of Ar?"

"He may do so if he wishes," said Lucilius. "He is not of our house."

"What if we do not return to Ar safely?" I said.

Lucilius turned to Grendel. "Take them to the walls of Ar," he said.

"Might he not be loaned a weapon, say, an ax, that we be more secure?" I asked.

I did not think it would take the Kurii too long to discover the fraud perpetrated upon them. They need only look closely upon, or examine, the rock reposing on the white, circular table.

"No," said Lucilius. "What has a Kur, or even a Kurlike thing, to fear from men, or a sleen?"

"Of course," I said.

This was a disappointment as I deemed that Grendel, unarmed, quick and powerful as he was, would have little chance against the onslaught of an ax-bearing Kur.

"You may leave," said Lucilius.

"Hail, Agamemnon," I said.

"Hail, Agamemnon," said Lucilius.

"Hail, Agamemnon," said his two cohorts, the one with the switched-off translator and the other with the ax, their words picked up by, and emitted from, Lucilius's translator.

I then turned to Grendel. "Let us proceed apace," I said, "allegedly defective one."

"Defective one," said Lucilius.

"As you wish," I said.

We then left the domed chamber.

CHAPTER FORTY-FIVE

It was not raining.

The air was damp.

A waist-high, soft fog clung about the fields.

Dawn was still some Ahn in the offing, but the now-present, gibbous white moon brightened the fog, the yellow moon having fled the sky. Commonly both moons were visible or not at the same time. In Gorean folklore, the yellow moon is commonly thought of as feminine and the white moon as masculine, possibly because the yellow moon is thought to be more beautiful or because the white moon seems to follow, or pursue, the yellow moon. Sometimes, particularly in the southern hemisphere, the yellow moon is referred to as the Tabuk Moon, possibly from the yellow pelt of the Tabuk, and the white moon as the Sleen Moon, possibly because it seems to trail, or follow, the yellow moon. Gor's third moon, the tiny moon spoken of the Prison Moon, which I had once learned was an artificial satellite, was not visible.

"I no longer regard myself as defective," said Grendel. "I am only different."

"And perhaps better," I said.

"Yes," said Grendel, "perhaps better."

"The second Bar," said Aetius.

This sound drifted to us over the fields. It marked the second Ahn.

"Perhaps," said Grendel, "you should, the both of you, have petitioned for the return of your weapons."

"I did not bring weapons to the Caves," said Aetius. "I did not do so, in order that it might be clear that I came in peace."

"Mine were put away somewhere," I said. "Even had I not entered the Caves as a prisoner, Kurii seldom permit humans to be armed in their presence." This was understandable. Kurii tend to be cautious and suspicious, even paranoid, with other species, and the thrust of a dagger or sword to the heart can kill a Kur as readily as a human.

"You should have asked for their return," said Grendel.

"I do not think so," I said. "Every moment was precious. Any delay would have much increased the chance of their discovering our substitution of stones. Waiting for the fetching of, and the return of, my weapons would have been not only to court disaster, but to do our best to bring it about."

"Sooner or later," said Grendel, "it will occur to our friends that you did not ask for the return of your weapons, and that might pique their curiosity."

"Sooner or later," I said, "but too late for them."

"Doubtless you were right," he said.

"Each moment was precious," I said.

"True," said Grendel.

"One casts the stones," I said. "One hopes they will fall as one wishes."

"Still it would be well if you had your weapons," said Grendel.

"Certainly," I said. "But let us press on. Our fraud will be soon discovered."

"No," said Grendel.

"How so?" I asked.

"It has already been discovered," he said. He had stopped, head lifted, and his large, pointed ears were half turned back toward the Caves, and his wide nostrils were flared, as he faced toward Ar. "Surely you can hear the sounds, the tread, the panting, the growling," he said.

"No," I said.

"Nor I," said Aetius, uneasily.

"Worse," said Grendel. "Consider the wind. It blows back toward the Caves. That carries our scent to our pursuers. And worse, still, it carries the scent of Kurii to us."

"How can that be?" I asked.

"Some Kurii are between us and Ar," he said.

"We are surrounded?" I said.

"I fear so," said Grendel.

Some ten or twelve yards in front of us, two gigantic Kurii, armed with axes, seemed to rise from the fog.

Behind us I could now hear some Kurii, panting. I heard a low growl.

"How many are there?" I asked Grendel.

"What difference does it make?" muttered Aetius, bitterly.

Grendel turned slowly about, ears lifted, nostrils distended. "I take it, six," he said.

"It seems I should have waited for my weapons," I said.

"You behaved rationally," said Grendel. "You cast the stones. They might have fallen more auspiciously."

"Bargain," said Aetius. "The Home Stone for our lives."

"Is the Home Stone, as we, not already in their grasp?" asked Grendel.

"Warn them, if they advance further, we shall cast the Home Stone far away, to be lost in the fog and grass," said Aetius.

"They would see where it falls," said Grendel, "and, if necessary, find it, uprooting grass, one blade at a time."

"I will call to them," said Aetius.

"I see no translators," said Grendel.

"That is informative, in and of itself," I said.

"They have not come to talk, but to kill," said Grendel.

"Speak to them in their own rumbling gibberish," urged Aetius.

"What do you know of the songs of Afrel, the poetry of Himmond, the aphorisms of Darkel?" asked Grendel.

I knew not those names, and suspected that they were surrogates for actual Kur names, as Agamemnon, Arcesilaus, Grendel, Lucilius, and such, were surrogates for actual Kur names.

"There are," said Grendel, "in the languages and dialects of the Kurii, literary traditions that go back thousands of years."

"It is the sounds of beasts," said Aetius.

"Kurii are beasts and are proud of being beasts," said Grendel. "They do not disguise or deny their nature, they do not forswear or regret their quickness, agility, instinct, appetite, blood, and strength."

"Beasts with civilization," said Aetius.

"Yes," said Grendel, "and, in their paws, civilization is fragile and much at risk."

"As it is in the paws of men," I said.

"The noises they make are ugly," said Aetius.

"Young Kurii," said Grendel, "think that the noises of men are like the chirping of birds, the bleating of verr, the grunting of tarsks."

"Speak to them," begged Aetius.

"They have formed themselves about us," said Grendel. "What would you have me say to them?"

"Beg for mercy," he said.

"I would not have them think so little of us," said Grendel.

"Beg," said Aetius.

"I cannot," said Grendel.

"Why not?" asked Aetius.

"I have Kur blood," said Grendel.

One of the Kurii raised his ax and stepped a pace closer to us, uttering a succession of sounds, to which Grendel responded, in Kur. I had always found the sound of Kur fascinating. It is as if sleen or larls were growling and snarling, and yet one could manage to detect, in this seemingly rude churning of sound, a subtle articulation of phonemes, or noises, which one sensed carried semantic content. What a remarkable moment, so momentous and magical, in the history of a species, would have been that transformative moment, that remarkable insight, that a noise could not merely express, but mean. How trivial, compared to the grasp of that possibility, would be the club, the lever, the inclined plane, the stone knife.

"What is going on?" said Aetius.

The mighty frame of Grendel stood out in the river of mist. The low fog came only to his thighs. "They have promised to finish us quickly if we hand over the Home Stone immediately," said Grendel.

"They are generous," I said.

"Surely you do not believe them," said Grendel. "They have been tricked. They have been inconvenienced. Kurii do not forget such things."

I turned to Aetius. "Are you prepared to fight?" I asked.

"With what?" he asked.

"Your hands, your feet, your teeth, your mind," I said.

"Do I have a choice?" he asked.

"Certainly," I said, "to die without fighting."

"I will fight," he said.

"Good," I said. "Make the Home Stone of Venna proud."

"I foreswore it long ago," he said.

"Let then a brave death be your apology, and a fitting end to expunge your disgrace and guilt."

"I doubt that the Home Stone will ever hear of it," he said.

"You will know about it," I said.

"I suppose that will have to do," he said.

"I fear so," I said.

"I take small comfort in that," he said.

"Take comfort in this then," I said, "that you are not dead until you are dead."

"It is difficult to dispute that," he said.

"There is always hope," I said.

At this point there were howls of anger and frustration from the encircling Kurii.

"Ho!" cried Aetius, almost at the same time. "Your monster, your friend, has gone! He has disappeared. He has deserted us!"

Grendel had slipped beneath the fog.

Some Kurii began slashing down, frenziedly, angrily through the fog to the grass and dirt. Others stood poised, with their axes, alert, listening for a small sound, straining to catch a hint of scent, watching for a parting of the fog, a glimpse of pressed grass.

I held the arm of Aetius. "Stay where you are," I said.

"He has fled!" said Aetius. "He has left us to die. We could not even begin to fight. We, too, now, must flee. We, too, now, can slip beneath the fog. Let us do so!"

"They were taken by surprise," I said. "Now they are alerted. If you move, you will be attacked."

"A slim chance is better than no chance," said Aetius. "Let me go."

"Hold," I said. "Now is the time to watch."

"Perhaps your cowardly friend can escape," said Aetius.

"I know him," I said. "He is no coward. He is not leaving us. He is not escaping, or trying to escape. See the foe. They know that. They are now still. They take scent. They watch. Grendel is somewhere about."

"What is he doing?" whispered Aetius.

"I suspect," I said, "he is looking for an ax."

"Does he expect to find one lying about in the grass?" asked Aetius.

"In a way," I said.

At that moment, there was a horrid noise, a startled, abortive, half-choked howl, and a crunching of bone, and we spun about and saw Grendel behind one of the Kurii, behind one who had been between us and the Caves. Grendel's jaws were still locked about the back of the neck of his victim. He then shook his victim, like a sleen, a verr, spattering blood about. He had risen up out of the fog behind his prey, and bitten through its neck, in Kur fashion, through the vertebrae and the lower part of the skull, and he now, his fur covered with blood, reflected in the light of the white moon, cast his victim from him. He then reached down through the fog into the wet grass. Then he stood upright, formidable and snarling, an ax in his hands.

Shock reigned.

Kurii gazed in wild awe.

This had not been anticipated.

How could this have occurred?

But almost instantly they comprehended the shifting in the odds of war.

No longer had they at their simple mercy three defenseless victims.

They were now one fewer, and faced an armed foe of possible skill.

There had been four rather between us and the Caves. Now there were three. Two remained rather between Aetius and myself and the walls of Ar.

One of the Kurii, some yards from Grendel, outraged, in fury, violently, precipitately, foolishly, madly, ax raised, rushed toward Grendel.

Kurii roared, protesting, trying to call him back.

He did not listen.

He died, and the Kurii, those surviving, realized they faced an adversary as terrible as they themselves.

I had not seen Grendel so since an arena, long ago on a Steel World, that which, at that time, was the world of Agamemnon, the Eleventh Face of the Nameless One.

He must recall he was not entirely Kur. Let him recall that. But he raised his head and howled to the white moon. In these moments what human would dare go near him?

One of the Kurii, in a silver harness, perhaps denoting authority, began to roar to the others, to the three left. Instantly, they began to form the box of death, in which Grendel, unable to defend himself from all directions, must die.

This left Aetius and I alone for a moment.

"This," hissed Aetius, "is our chance. Let us escape. Run! Run!"

"No," I said. "We must try to succor our friend."

"You are mad," he said. "Not even a sleen will attack a larl, let alone four such Ubars of the Wild."

"We may distract an attacker," I said, "disrupt their formation."

"Do not be a fool," he said.

"At least one can die well," I said.

"Fool!" he said, and struck me, heavily. I sank to the grass, shaken, trying to recover, and I felt his hand reach within my tunic and seize the Home Stone of Ar. By the time I struggled to my feet, he was fleeing toward Ar.

I heard a bellow of rage from the Kur in the silver harnessing, and he pointed to one of his fellows, and then, savagely, to the fleeing Aetius. Amongst his priorities, doubtless, was the recovery of the Home Stone of Ar, and might not the fleeing human have that very object in his possession? The commanded Kur slung his ax to his back, dropped to all fours, and sped in the wake of Aetius. The Kur in the silver harness and his now two fellows then ranged themselves in such a pattern that they could not well be attacked and Grendel dare not turn his back. Inadvertently the flight of Aetius had delayed the box attack on Grendel. I moved to the side as the pursuing Kur, showing me no heed, on his hind legs and the knuckles of his forelimbs, rushed past me. He would shortly overtake Aetius.

I advanced toward the three Kurii ranged against Grendel, waving my arms, and shouting, and gesturing forward, as though I might be at the vanguard of newly arrived reinforcements.

I was within four yards of the three Kurii when I stopped, short. I felt foolish. Where were my advertised reinforcements? Where were my supposedly newly arriving cohorts, who would lift this small siege? They did not appear, they did not swarm forth, shouting battle cries, brandishing weapons. The field was empty, cool, damp, and quiet. Shreds of fog now parted, and began to dissipate. The Kurii had not been frightened away, or even disconcerted. Doubtless they were better informed than I of the disposition of local soldiery. The ineffectiveness of my unpromising ruse was only too patent.

The Kur in the silver harness glanced at me, and I saw a twisted grimace on his visage, that grimace which commonly indicated amusement amongst his kind.

"Tell him," I said to Grendel, "that I apologize for the inanity of my stratagem."

Grendel apparently did this.

"And ask him," I added, "if he could have come up with anything better in my place."

I supposed that Grendel did this.

Grendel did not translate his response, if any, but the Kur gestured toward me, and one of his fellows facing Grendel, turned about and took a step toward me, and I took a step backward.

"So I gather," I said, "that he could not have come up with something better."

This must have been translated because the lead Kur did not seem pleased.

"Keep moving backward, slowly," said Grendel in Gorean.

This recommendation would presumably be unintelligible to the Kurii for few of them, lacking a translator, can follow Gorean.

I did not understand the point of Grendel's command, or advice, but I complied, being in no hurry to experience an unpleasant encounter with a Kur ax.

Was he aware of something I was not? Did he know something I did not?

I took another step backward, and the Kur took another step forward.

I stepped back, again. I sensed the Kur was enjoying this. Had I turned about and run, I was sure he would have pursued me, and attacked me, immediately. Kurii, incidentally, like to take their prey from behind. I recalled that Grendel had done so. I took a few more steps backward. Then, I sensed that the Kur had had enough of this game. He raised his ax, suddenly, and then stopped, the ax held over his head. I had heard something like a fist striking a chest. He stood so, for an instant, and then, oddly, seemed unsteady, even ready to totter. It was then that I saw the fletching and shaft of a sunken arrow protruding from that broad, hirsute chest. I stepped aside and the beast tottered past me, trying to raise his ax. Four times more I heard the sound of arrows striking their target, and then, some yards from me, the beast collapsed into the wet grass.

"By the Priest-Kings," said a loud, rough voice, "these things are hard to kill!"

"Thurnock!" I cried.

Behind Thurnock stumbled Aetius, a mass of blood, helpless, wrapped in the cords of a net, thrust forward by Clitus, of Port Kar.

"This urt," said Clitus, pushing Aetius forward, "had been caught by a Kur, who, oblivious of me, crouched over him, bloodying him up for the kill, when I dropped the net over both of them, and the thrashing, tangled Kur succumbed finally to a dozen thrusts of the trident.

"Tal," I said.

"Tal," said Clitus. "Here is something the urt carried. You might see if it is of interest."

"It is," I said, taking the object. "It is the Home Stone of Ar."

I slipped it within my tunic.

Thurnock drew another arrow from his quiver.

"Beware!" said Clitus. "Beast!"

Bounding toward us was one of the two remaining Kurii.

"Trident!" I cried, and it was thrust into my hands.

The large, heavy, double-bladed ax raised, the Kur was upon us. I slipped to the side. The descending slash of the blade was poorly chosen. It considerably narrows the width of the kill zone. The blade sank a foot into the soil. I jabbed the trident, twisting, into the Kur's left side. The twisting widens the wound. This also makes it easier to pull back the weapon. The Kur, roaring, wounded, bleeding, jerked the ax free. It stepped back. I fell to one knee and the blade flashed past, over my head, like a horizontal guillotine. I thrust the trident again, this time into the Kur's right side. The ax fell like a beam into the grass, to the beast's left. It then, its eyes not focusing, turned toward me, and reached toward me with those massive hands, nails emerged from the fur. I braced the butt of the trident in the earth before me, and the Kur, continuing to lean toward me, and, slowly falling, began to slowly impale himself on the trident. His paws could not reach me. He scratched at the shaft of the trident. Then the head of the trident disappeared into in the soft tissues of his belly. I feared his weight would snap the shaft of the trident or drive the butt into the ground, but his bulk shifted, and he fell heavily to my left.

I struggled to my feet.

"Where is the last Kur, he in the silver harness?" I asked.

"Gone," said Thurnock.

"Grendel did not detain him," said Clitus.

I twisted and pulled the trident free of the Kur who had charged us. I then surrendered the weapon to Clitus.

Clitus kicked the feet from beneath Aetius who then was on his knees before us, bound in the cords of Clitus's net.

"What are we to do with this thieving urt, who abandoned you in the face of the enemy?" asked Clitus.

"He invited me to flee with him," I said. "I merely declined to do so."

"You would not desert Grendel," said Clitus.

"Grendel is our friend," I said. "The relationship of this fellow, whose name is Aetius, to Grendel was no more than coincidental."

"He ran," said Clitus, "leaving you behind."

"It was not an irrational act," I said.

"He is a coward," said Clitus.

"I do not think so," I said. "And the aperture between the coward and the hero is often small. Who knows how one will behave in battle? One who expects himself to be a hero might leave the field at the mere appearance of the enemy. One who regards himself a coward might find in battle, amidst clashing weapons and spilling blood, that he was hitherto a stranger to himself."

"He was afraid," said Clitus.

"Who is not?" I asked. "He who in the midst of danger knows no fear must be ignorant, stupid, or drunk."

"There is zest in battle," said Clitus.

"At the edge of death," I said, "one feels life keenly."

"You are of the Scarlet Caste," said Clitus. "You know the joy of the sword."

"The wine of war is a heady drink," I said. "Few pleasures compare to those of steel."

"You are a Warrior," said Clitus.

"It is my caste," I said.

"This bloodied urt," said Clitus, jabbing Aetius with the trident, "stole the stone from you."

"The motivation is mighty," I said. "The stone is very precious."

"Let us kill him," said Clitus.

"What do you think your life is worth?" I asked Aetius.

"Very little at present," he said.

"Free him of the net, and bind his wounds," I said.

We were then joined by Grendel, who carried a Kur ax.

"My dear friend," I said. "I hear that you did not detain our enemy, the Kur in the silver harness."

"No," said Grendel. "In his flight, he was already struck three times in the back by the arrows of Thurnock."

"Such beasts are hard to kill," said Thurnock.

"Do you think he could reach the Caves?" I asked Grendel.

"Certainly," said Grendel.

"He is a dangerous enemy," I said.

"Granted," said Grendel.

"But you did not choose to follow him, to kill him," I said.

"That was not necessary," said Grendel. "His fellows in the Caves will kill him."

"Because he did not return with the Home Stone of Ar?" I said.

"No," said Grendel.

"Why then?" I asked.

"You are not of the blood," said Grendel.

"No," I said.

"Because the wounds were in his back," said Grendel.

CHAPTER FORTY-SIX

I awakened.

I had no idea how long I had slept.

I heard, to one side, the clink of chain. "Master?" said Iris, concerned.

I thrust my hand inside my tunic, grasping for the Home Stone. It was gone!

"Where is it?" I demanded.

"What?" she said, startled. She could move about, but was shackled. Such things help a woman keep in mind that she is a slave. We were in the basement apartment in the Metellan district.

"A stone, a rock," I said, "concealed within my clothing!"

"Master Bruno, he of Torcadino, has it," she said.

"No!" I said.

"Is it of value?" she asked.

"It is the Home Stone of Ar!" I said.

"So small, so plain?" she asked.

"Where is Bruno of Torcadino?" I demanded.

"He said it was just a stone," she said, "and if you might think otherwise, you were mistaken or had been tricked."

"Where is he?" I demanded.

"Gone," she said. "I know not where."

"Barbarian slave," I snarled. "What do you know of Home Stones?"

"Little, I am sure, Master," she said.

Last night, Grendel, I, Clitus, Thurnock, and the lacerated Aetius of Venna had reached the walls of Ar. We had delivered Aetius, with coins, to a Physician's Inn on the Viktel Aria, and had then conferred, deciding that we might best scatter our forces. In this way, possible pursuers would not know with which group the Home Stone might be. Grendel housed on Emerald Street, with his Eve, and, as I understood it, the Lady Bina, once a Kur pet on what had been Agamemnon's steel world. Clitus and Thurnock housed in an insula on the Path of Temos, named for the famous paga brewer. And I, at least temporarily, would continue to house in the apartment in the Metellan district which I shared with Seremides and Iris. Our meeting point would be the Silver Tarsk, which was on the Via Cora, also in the Metellan District.

"When did Master Bruno leave?" I asked.

"Yesterday morning," she said.

"What?" I exclaimed.

"Master has slept many Ahn," she said, "more than a full day."

"The wine," I said, "the wine of welcome."

"It must have been strong," she said.

"Tassa powder," I said.

I then lay back on the blanket on the floor to think.

I had not informed Seremides at my arrival at the apartment that I had the Home Stone, so he must have gambled that my expedition to the Beast Caves had been successful. He would, of course, have known nothing of Aetius, Grendel, Thurnock, or Clitus. I was not clear on what Seremides would contemplate doing in the matter of the Home Stone. He, as opposed to the thieves, could not expect to claim the entire reward that had been offered for the return of Talena to Ar. I had planned, secretly, of course, on trying to exchange the Home Stone for Talena herself. Perhaps Seremides would attempt to negotiate some munificent prize for its return. This would leave Talena, of course, as before, at the mercy of Ar, once she was officially delivered by Cos.

I had, as noted, given no indication to Seremides that I had the Home Stone.

But he, with the tassa powder, had gambled and, in this instance, had won.

Who would have suspected so bold an act by a cripple?

How dared he act thusly?

But he was Seremides.

It had seemed unwise to give the stone for keeping to Grendel, for there were few Kurii in Ar, and he was known now to Lucilius and his cohorts.

Perhaps, pending its disposition, I should have left it with Thurnock and Clitus, but they knew little of the intrigues in Ar, and, as the Kur with the silver harness had doubtless reached the Beast Caves and reported, I did not wish to put them at risk.

I wondered if he with the silver harness had long survived his report.

Kurii, I gathered, looked unfavorably on wounds in the back. They are seldom received while facing an enemy. Are they not commonly received in flight?

"May I bring Master food or drink?" asked Iris.

"How goes Ar?" I asked.

"Much the same," she said. "The streets mourn the loss of the

Home Stone. Men weep. Women cut their hair. Children may not shout or play. Gay ribbons and bright banners are no longer in evidence. Balconies and bridges are draped in black. Flowers may no longer be displayed in portals or windows."

"The feast of the Restoration of Marlenus?" I asked.

"Still postponed, of course," she said.

"What of the treasure wagons?" I asked.

"I think they are stopped at the great gate," she said, "there or somewhere nearby."

"What do you make of that?" I asked.

"Clearly that the payment of the ransom is delayed," she said.

"And why might that be?" I asked.

"Clearly," she said, "that the Home Stone has not yet been returned to Ar."

"But if the thieves had the stone," I said, "it should have been returned by now."

"It seems so," she said.

"Thus," I said, "it seems that the thieves no longer have the stone."

"Master Bruno said the stone he took from you was not the Home Stone," she said.

"Perhaps Master Bruno," I said, "is mistaken."

I did not doubt that Seremides, who had been First Sword in the Taurentian Guard, was well acquainted with the Home Stone of Ar. Presumably, at one time, he had held it in his hands, kissed it, and swore to honor and defend it, and all it stood for, to his last breath, to his last drop of blood.

How pleased he would be, cunning, astute, unscrupulous Seremides, to whom honor was a figment and joke, that some men took such things seriously.

"Why are Master's fists clenched?" asked Iris.

"It is nothing," I said.

"Yes, Master," she said.

"I will take some food and drink now," I said. "I am hungry and thirsty."

"Yes, Master," said Iris, happily, turning about, with a soft rustle of the links of her shackling.

"You are a lovely property," I said.

"Thank you, Master," she said.

"Do you like being a property?" I asked.

"Yes, Master," she said, paused, not looking back. "I dreamed of such things on another world. I wanted to belong to a truly fine, strong man, who would understand me as, and treat me as, the slave I am, and want to be. I am thrilled to be owned and collared. I want to kneel before a man, and please him, knowing that I am his and he may do with me as he wishes. I relish my helplessness and vulnerability. I want to be commanded. I want no choice but to obey. I am a slave. It is what I am. I am happy. I am fulfilled. I would not want it any other way."

"You did not know that you would be brought to Gor as no more than cattle," I said.

"No, Master," she said, "but I am wholly and deliciously content."

"But you are subject to the whip," I said.

"I love being subject to the whip," she said. "I respond to my domination. I love being dominated, wholly, helplessly."

"Do you fear the whip?" I asked.

"Very much," she said, "and I hope, very much, that it will not be used on me."

"But if you are not pleasing?"

"Then, of course," she said, "it will be used on me."

"And do you like that?"

"Not at all," she said. "It hurts."

"So you will try to be pleasing," I said.

"Yes, Master," she said, "very much so, Master."

"Proceed," I said. "Bring me food and drink."

"Yes, Master," she said.

CHAPTER FORTY-SEVEN

The wild ringing of the bars shook the sky!

"Glory to Ar! Hail, the Ubar!" cried a man, rushing past.

"Hold, Citizen!" I cried, but he was gone.

I had walked to the Avenue of the Central Cylinder. I had scarcely left the apartment when the bars had begun to sound.

I had thought, through the long morning, that they must soon do so. Then, seeking news, I had departed the apartment, and shortly thereafter, as I had expected, the ringing had begun. The streets, broad and narrow, straight and crooked, were crowded. No longer was garb solemn. The dark ribbons and banners were seized up and carried away. I saw a streamer of yellow fluttering from a high bridge. Song burst forth from a tavern. Flowers reappeared over portals and in windows. I bent down and retrieved a red ball, returning it to the small boy who was evidently in pursuit of it. I doubted that he knew much of Home Stones. He had not yet attained puberty, at which time certain precious secrets would be revealed to him, things that he earlier, as a mere child, would not have understood. Surely he had not yet been permitted to hold the Home Stone, kiss it, and speak certain momentous words.

"Citizen," I called to a fellow, before he raced away.

I was buffeted to the side by another fellow, hurrying past. "Glory to Ar!" he cried, over his shoulder.

"Glory to Ar!" I cried after him.

I knew that the Home Stone of Ar had been recovered, but knew little else.

A thousand rumors raced about, like scampering urts, rumors vague, and rumors improbably specific and clear, jostling about with contrary rumors, similarly specific and clear. It seemed the Home Stone had been won back from emissaries of deceitful, purloining, hated Cos, that it was never stolen but only mislaid, that the Priest-Kings of Gor themselves, in answer to the prayers and sacrifices of Initiates, had caused it to reappear in its chamber, that the very thieves who had stolen it had, in remorse and contrition, at the enormity of their crime, returned it to the city, that a magician mishandling a spell, had rendered it temporarily invisible, that it had been a test contrived by patriots to see if the citizenry of Ar would be devastated by the prospect of its absence, and so on.

A girl, a slim brunette in the gray livery of a state slave, one owned by the city of Ar, her hair clipped in the uniform fashion imposed on such slaves, head down that she not meet the eyes of a free person, was slipping past, and I reached out and knotted my fist in her hair. She stopped, instantly, her head now up and back, tense, frightened, daring not to move. Slaves can be so controlled, perfectly. I then, bending over, slowly, put her to her knees, and held her head down to my sandals. I then released her hair, but she kept her head where I had placed it, at my feet. "Master?" she said.

"Look up, well-shaped kajira," I said. Sometimes one so addresses slaves, say, as "nicely ankled kajira," "sweet-hipped kajira," "pleasantly flanked kajira," "glossy-pelted kajira," and such. It reminds them that they are so looked upon, as openly assessable, vendible objects. The female slave is to be kept fully conscious of her external, physical aspects. Is she not a property? She is never to be in doubt that she has a body. She is, after all, a slave. One would never, of course, address a free woman so. A free woman may be very conscious of her body, unseen, and vulnerable, within her robes, but a societal convention recommends that she, and others, pretend that it does not exist, or is of no interest or consequence. It might be mentioned, in passing, that Goreans, as a whole, lest there be some misunderstanding in the matter, are much interested in the whole woman, including the inner, precious woman. It is, after all, all of her that is owned. For example, Goreans prize high intelligence in a slave. Certainly it commonly raises a girl's price, sometimes considerably. Owners, too, are commonly well aware that a slave is a center of consciousness, has an inner life, has feelings, needs, and so on. Who would wish to own anything less? Just as no one wants a stupid slave, so, too, no one wants a slave who is less than a whole, complete woman. So put her on her knees, put her in a collar, and own her. That is a man's joy, owning a female. And that is a woman's joy, being so wanted that her master will own her, will possess her wholly, fully, categorically, uncompromisingly, as the slave she is and wants to be.

"Thank you, Master," she said, looking up.

"What is your name?" I asked.

"Dora," she said, "if it pleases Master."

"I seek knowledge," I said.

"I know little," she said. "I am a mere slave."

"Slaves," I said, "often know more than the free. They are here and about, they come and go. They listen. They gossip. In discharging their duties, in their errands and shoppings, in their fetchings and deliverings, they see much, and hear much. And you are a state slave. You may be crucially knowledgeable. Do you not, unnoticed, tread the corridors of business and commerce, walk in the halls of administration and justice? Even in your pen, you would be likely to know more than most free persons."

"What does Master wish to know?" she asked.

"Truth," I said. "Rumors fly about like a cloud of startled jards."

"The Home Stone of Ar is back," she said.

"That is well known," I said. "The ringing of the bars announces it. I want to know the details."

"I may not speak," she said.

"Very well," I said. "You may go."

"Master?" she said.

"You may go," I said.

"You would let me go?" she said.

"Yes," I said.

"Not all public boards are posted simultaneously," she said, "nor do they always read the same."

"Speak further, lovely domestic animal," I said.

"Who knows how citizenries will respond to different things?" she said. "Are all truths fit for all citizenries? An angry citizenry, or a frightened citizenry, may burn and loot. Might it not rend itself, or others? Who knows how widely and for how long fires may burn? Guardsmen may be swept aside, thrones may topple. Accordingly truth is best rationed, with an eye for its consequences. But what will be the consequences? One must learn. Truth then should be well guarded, and released a spoonful at a time. In such a way are cities saved. Who knows what, in what tinder, may cause a flame to spring alive?"

"And where is this first, small experiment, that dealing with spoonfuls of truth, being conducted?" I asked.

"I may not say, of course," she said, "but I understand that veminiums now bloom in the Garden of the Hinrabians."

"It is long since I strolled there," I said.

"It is beautiful this time of year," she said.

"May you soon be marketed," I said, "and be purchased by the master of your dreams."

"Thank you, Master," she said, and then, at my gesture, she leaped up and was lost in the crowd.

I arrived at the tall, heavy gate of the Garden of the Hinrabians. To my dismay, I saw several individuals leaving the grounds, and few, if any, entering.

"Hold, noble citizen," I said, detaining a Cloth Worker. "I have come to view veminiums. But men leave. Why? Is something amiss within? Do the veminiums not bloom? Do guardsmen empty the garden? If so, why?"

"The garden is open," he said. "Walk about, as you will. View veminiums as much as you please."

"Something is going on," I said. "I would know what."

"It is nothing," he said.

"Speak," I urged him.

"You know the garden's public board?" he asked.

"I have heard there is one within," I said.

"It is commonly one of the first boards in Ar to be inscribed," he said. "Men often come here to learn the news, before it appears on the larger, more popular boards, those in the plazas and markets, those raised near the juncture of major avenues and boulevards, and so on."

"And what is the news?" I asked.

"Who knows what it is to be," he said.

"I do not understand," I said.

"The board was sponged," he said.

"What was news is no longer news," I said.

"Do not despair," he said. "New news, more appropriate news, more fitting news, will soon appear."

"I see," I said.

"I have seen such things before," he said.

"The responses of citizens to the news were being monitored," I said.

"And recorded by attendant scribes," he said.

"Glory to an objective, free press," I said.

"What?" he said.

"Nothing," I said. "I was thinking of something else, somewhere else."

I wondered if people really wanted an objective, free press. If so, why did they not have it? Perhaps such a press would be boring. Aren't presses more popular which tell you what you want to hear? Perhaps it is not difficult to conjure up alternate realities, each with its own clientele? Does not he who owns the boards decide what will appear on them, or perhaps he who pays the guardsmen, or he who owns the weapons? Is not truth the most praised of all things, and the least sought?

"What do you remember of the news?" I asked.

"Why should one remember what was on a sponged board?" he said. "Is not memory notoriously fallible? Perhaps it is well to forget what was on a sponged board."

"At least the Home Stone is safe," I said.

"The sky rejoices," he said.

"But presumably not the thieves," I said.

"It is to be expected that the same fortune may favor one while not another," he said.

"As the fall of the stones," I said.

"Others now enter the gate," he said. "Perhaps the board will be inscribed anew. Enter with them, if you wish. Question the scribes of the boards, if you dare. Or best, inspect your veminiums, and leave the boards to others. It is sometimes hard to know what you should know, and what you should not know. I must be on my way. This conversation weaves me no cloth."

"I wish you well," I said.

"I wish you well," he said.

I watched him leave, and then turned toward the gate.

CHAPTER FORTY-EIGHT

I looked up at the board, its white, broad surface several feet above the ground. It, like others, was reached by a ladder which led up to a walkway, from which it might be inscribed.

No one was now on the ladder or walkway.

"The board is still wet," I observed.

"It will be dried shortly," said a scribe, with his flat, closed kit, slung from his shoulder, presumably containing scribal paraphernalia, paper, seals, pens, ink, and such. Occasionally they also contain a flask of paga. The lid of the kit, folded back, provides the scribe with a writing surface.

"Some citizens, eager for news," I said, "filter in."

"They will not be kept waiting long," he said.

"I take it that veminiums are in bloom," I said.

"It is that time of year," he said.

"Two scribes at the gate were detaining and questioning some of those who left earlier," I said.

"To ascertain responses to the news," he said. "If you are so detained, be noncommittal. If you are asked your name, caste, and domicile, I recommend that you decline to answer."

"Or answer falsely," I said.

"That will do," he said.

"What news was sponged away?" I asked.

"I forget," he said.

At this point a scribe's boy in a blue tunic climbed the ladder and, moving about on the walkway, wiped the board dry with a large, soft cloth.

"In this way," said the scribe with whom I was conversing, "news may be changed quickly and easily."

"Which may not be so easily accomplished with flyers, posters, circulated papers, parchments, and such," I said.

"Precisely," said he.

When the lad had finished his work, he descended the ladder, and, shortly thereafter, two serious-appearing fellows in scribe's blue, whose mien suggested indubitable reliability and unquestionable gravitas, ascended to the walkway. One, who seemed senior, carried notes, and the other carried a small pot of writing fluid and a wide brushlike pen. The seemingly senior fellow read from the notes he carried, and the other fellow painted the letters on the board.

"We are joined by several noble citizens," I said, "seemingly more than attended the earlier inscriptions on the board."

"That is natural," said the scribe beside me. "Wiser readers often come later, to heed a more official, more evaluated, less dangerous, less experimental version of truth."

"But you were here earlier," I said.

"I like to see the differences," he said. "I find them informative."

"Perhaps you can help me with the board," I said.

"You are illiterate?" he said.

"Not really," I said. "It is just that I may have some difficulty with the alternate lines."

"I do not see why," he said.

"They go backwards," I said.

"No," he said. "They go forwards, only in the opposite direction."

Gorean is written, as it is said, 'as the ox plows'.

"More importantly," I said, "I, too, might be interested in the differences between boards."

"You understand that I cannot recall the first board," he said.

"Of course," I said.

"Truth heeds fact," he said, "but what is said to be truth is under no such obligation."

"I understand," I said.

"For every way there is to be true," he said, "there are a thousand ways to be false."

"I trust that truth does not envy falsity its riches," I said.

"I suspect she is content to be herself," he said.

"Note," I said, examining the board, "the Home Stone of Ar has been recovered."

"That was even on the first board," he said.

"One knows that from the bars," said a fellow nearby.

The bars, incidentally, their loud message joyously and lengthily proclaimed, were now silent. Birds had now, after their first alarm, and after their retreat to the trees, reemerged to be about their business.

"See the board," said the scribe.

"I do," I said.

"There are several differences from the first board," he said.

"Perhaps you could specify some of these, unobtrusively," I suggested.

"As friends?" he asked.

"Of course," I said.

"Perhaps over a mug of kal-da?" he said.

"Not paga?" I asked.

"Kal-da," he said.

I found his insistence interesting. To be sure, it was early afternoon, and many paga taverns would not yet be open. Kal-da shops do tend to open much earlier, many even serving a day's first meal. Still, kal-da shops are patronized largely by the lower castes. Could it be then that he did not wish to be observed by, say, another scribe when conversing with me? Kal-da shops, incidentally, like paga taverns, serve a variety of foods, not just the beverage they are named for. Kal-da itself, a drink usually served uncomfortably hot, at least in my opinion, is made from diluted ka-la-na wine, usually of an inferior grade, mixed with citrus juices, such as those of larmas and tospits, and strong, often fiery, spices. It is a robust, fortifying drink popular with manual laborers. Some individuals of the higher castes, both men and women, keep some on hand, presumably for medicinal purposes.

The nearest kal-da shop to the Garden of the Hinrabians was on South Market Street, the Golden Tospit. It was a small, neat place with, at least at this time of day, few customers. My host, though I was apparently paying for the kal-da, selected a small table toward the back of the shop, about which we sat, cross-legged. The table, I noted, would not be visible from outside, from the street.

I had gone to the interior counter of the shop and placed two tarsk-bits on the yellow, enameled coin plate resting on the worn, brown, stained surface. A bit later the kal-da master, a short, fat fellow who seemed to know my companion, emerged from a side door, perhaps having heard the click of the coins in the plate and dipped his ladle into the simmering pot behind the counter and filled two mugs with the brew.

I now, carefully, placed the mug before me.

It would take time to cool.

"No serving slaves," I said.

"This place is small," he said. "And slaves cost money, and they must be fed and kept, even clothed, if one wishes to do so."

"Still," I said.

"This is a kal-da shop," he said, "not a paga tavern."

"Some kal-da shops have serving slaves," I said.

One of the pleasures of the typical Gorean paga tavern is the serving slaves. It is pleasant to be served by well-collared, attractive, minimally clothed, if clothed, women who know and understand, deeply and fully, that they are slaves, that they are purchasable properties who are owned by men. Also, knowing they are domestic animals not permitted reservations or inhibitions, as is made clear to them by their subjection to the whip and the collars locked on their necks, they are freed to be themselves, vital, natural, needful females.

"This one does not," he said.

"A pity," I said.

Behold, I thought, the helpless, needful slave.

She knows she is choiceless, as she would have it.

She knows she has been uncompromisingly and categorically subdued and subjugated, as she wishes.

Now she has no hope but to be pleasing to her master.

She fears only that she might not be fully pleasing.

She is tormented by her needs.

In her belly burn slave fires.

They are women with masters, the masters of which free women can only dream.

"Further," he said, testing his mug of kal-da delicately with his fingertips, "slaves hear things and say things. If you wish a secret to be rampant throughout a city, from wall to wall, from gate to gate, whisper it into the ear of a kajira."

"Ar rejoices," I said, "that the Home Stone has been recovered."

"But perhaps not everyone in Ar," he said.

"Perhaps not the thieves," I said.

"The theft," he said, "was well planned and executed, apparently by forces well familiar with the ways of Ar."

"I think so," I said.

"In it," he said, "I do not sense the hand of Treve, nor of Cos, nor of Tyros, nor of Port Kar."

"The current board," I said, "does not name thieves nor speculate on their nature or origin."

"Nor did the first," he said.

"Could they be known to Ar?" I asked

"One does not know," he said. "Often one professes not to know what one knows."

"But the thieves must be sought," I said.

"Presumably the matter is under investigation," he said.

Apparently, on neither board, the first nor the current, were Beasts or Assassins mentioned.

"On the first board," he said, "the treasure was halted within the great gate, whereas in the second, it was stopped shortly outside the great gate."

"I remember the second board," I said, "but the difference there seems trivial."

"I agree," he said. "But several other differences are perhaps less trivial."

"Such as?" I said.

"The first board," he said, "was far more generous in its details, true or false. The second board, which you read, was much more bleak, having to do with little other than the effusions of a grateful Ar and the promise of celebratory holidays."

"We are now outside the gate to the Garden of the Hinrabians, and the interrogating scribes," I said. "Perhaps, in the light of this, your recall has proportionately improved."

"Changes were made to the first board," he said, "even in the midst of the inscribing, this seemingly in virtue of certain reactions amongst the viewers."

"And thus," I said, "news itself may hurry about and change."

"On the first board," he said, "the Home Stone was recovered in the vicinity of the Beast Caves."

"There was nothing of that on the second board," I said.

"Presumably for some reason," he said.

"What else?" I asked.

"Two sorts of things primarily," he said, "the first having to do with the brave and noble hero who recovered the Home Stone, and the second with the disposition of the rescued treasure, that to be paid as the reward to the individual or party who delivered Talena, the fugitive, treasonous, false Ubara, to the justice of Ar, her betrayed city."

"I listen," I said.

"The Golden Tospit," he said, "is noted for the quality of its kal-da."

"I am sure it is," I said.

He then took a careful but clear drought of the drink. As he lifted his mug of thick brew to me, pleasantly, I, too, given the seemingly obvious demands of convivial courtesy, tempered with a certain element of circumspection, joined him.

"Excellent," he said.

I supposed there was a time and place for kal-da, but I was not sure that this was either a time or place for it.

"On the first board," he said, "the courageous hero who somehow managed to save the Home Stone was a citizen of Torcadino, a man named Bruno. One could scarcely imagine the dangers he must have undergone in performing so harrowing and perilous a deed, but, interestingly, scarcely was this inscribed when it was revealed that Bruno of Torcadino was actually Seremides of Ar, once the captain of the Taurentian guard, an abettor of, if not the instigator of, the treasons and felonies of Talena of Ar, and doubtless the second most wanted fugitive from the justice of Ar. But he redeemed himself a thousand times over by rescuing the Home Stone of Ar. He was granted a full pardon, a handsome remuneration, and a plaque in the Hall of Heroes."

"I saw nothing of that on the second board," I said.

"It was mysteriously missing," he said.

"Because of some negative reactions on the part of some viewers?" I asked.

"There were calls for his instant seizure, torture, and impalement," he said. "Some suspected him of complicity in the theft of the Home Stone itself."

"I see," I said. "And where is the hero now?"

"Perhaps safe, in honored, protective custody," he said.

"You said something, as I recall," I said, "about the disposition of the reward for the capture of Talena."

"That was interesting, as well," he said. "The first entry there almost resulted in the tearing down and burning of the board itself. It attributed the delivery of Talena to Lurius of Jad, the Ubar of Cos."

"I understand that such a thing might not be well received," I said.

"Can you imagine that, the delivery of such wealth and concomitant power to Ar's most hated enemy, Lurius of Jad, whose brutal and hated troops formed the bulk of the forces that tyrannized and looted Ar during the Occupation?"

"I can see it might not be popular," I said.

"Night would pervade day," he said. "Civility, like helpless guardsmen, would be swept aside; law would be scorned; anarchy would reign; order would become chaos. Crowds would rush about, seeking something, anything, to destroy and burn. The Central Cylinder itself would be torn down, stone by stone. Measure and proportion would flee; ruin would be at large; Ar would collapse; there would be sleen and larls in the streets; society would crumble. All would be lost. The Home Stone would weep."

"That sounds serious," I said.

"Assuredly," he said.

"The board," I said, "was in immediate danger of being forcibly dismantled and burned?"

"Only momentarily," he said. "The inscribing scribes, somewhat desperately, began to laugh, perhaps even more uproariously than seemed necessary under the circumstances."

"The merry scribes had been merely testing the audience?" I speculated.

"And risking their lives in doing so," he said.

"The matter was presented as a large, rich joke," I said.

"Precisely," he said.

"One supposes," I said, "that the scribes, or those instructing them, had anticipated that delivering the reward to Cos might not be well received."

"Doubtless," he said, "for the scribes seem to have been well prepared. In any event, the proffered news, that bestowing the reward on Cos, was instantly removed from the boards, to be replaced by news more congenial."

"There was no mention of Decius Albus on the second board," I said.

"Nor on the first," he said. "Why?"

"Nothing," I said. "It is not important."

"So the reward," he said, "is not to go to Cos, at least not officially, but seemingly to a different party, an individual, one more acceptable, a fellow hitherto little known."

"That makes sense," I said, "particularly if the public recognition of Cos as the recipient of the reward might be ill received."

"It would be," he said.

I recalled that Myron, the polemarkos of Jad, in the Tower of Philebus, had suggested such a ruse. Indeed, he had even attempted to interest me in furthering such a deceit. Needless to say, he who would be so foolish as to accept such a role would be exposed to twin perils, first, that of a solitary, vulnerable individual hoping not only to remove wealth from Ar, an act dangerous enough in itself, but to retain and secure it against bandits and marauders, and second, when his imposture was disclosed, as it would be once the wealth was in Cos, he would be a marked man, viewed as a collaborator in perpetrating a despicable hoax, to be sought throughout Gor. What other than his blood would satisfy thousands of vengeful citizens regarding themselves as vilely tricked and defrauded? Surely I would not care to be he.

"And what?" I asked, "is the name of this fellow who somehow managed to capture Talena of Ar and deliver her to the justice of Ar, he to whom the reward is to go?"

"His name is Geoffrey of Harfax," said the scribe. "Be careful, do not spill your kal-da."

"Geoffrey of Harfax?" I said. "I find that hard to believe."

"The important thing," said the scribe, "is that a large number of citizens believe it, at least for a time."

"To avoid rioting in the city," I said.

"Yes," he said.

I had not authorized Myron, the polemarkos, to use the name Geoffrey of Harfax in connection with the delivery of Talena to Ar. Had he drafted me, in a sense, I wondered, forcing me to participate, willing or not, in his attempt to mislead the citizenry of Ar? That did not seem possible, given the codes we shared. Could there be another person somehow involved, a genuine Geoffrey of Harfax, or, more likely, one who would dare to assume that name? In any case, there must be another person somehow involved. I feared that I might have been placed on a kaissa board, so to speak, to participate in a game I had not chosen and over whose outcome I would have little influence.

"Incidentally, it is interesting that you asked me about Decius Albus, earlier," said the scribe.

"Why is that?" I asked.

"Because," he said, "it was an agent of Decius Albus who pointed you out to me."

"What?" I said.

"Surely you do not think that our meeting this morning was an accident," he said.

My sword and dagger had been removed from me in the Beast Caves. I had not replaced them. I wished I now had such steel about me. Was I in immediate danger?

"And what is the interest of the noble Decius Albus in a poor tradesman?" I asked.

"I am sure I do not know," he said.

"But you have some function in this business, some errand to run, some duty to discharge?" I said.

"I fear so," he said.

"What?" I asked.

"First," he said, "let me tell you one last item which was included on the first board, but not on the second, one item which briefly slipped my mind. I think it may be germane to the charge placed on me."

"Please do so," I said.

"Two days from now," he said, "the public trial of Talena of Ar will begin. It will take place in the great theater of Publius. The jury of a thousand male citizens of Ar, each eager to condemn Talena, has already been selected."

"Male citizens?" I said.

"Certainly," he said. "One would scarcely wish to put the despised and hated Talena at the mercies of free women."

"I see," I said.

"As you doubtless know," he said, "in Ar, the law is the Ubar and the Ubar is the law. But, in this case, the noble Marlenus, Ubar of Glorious Ar, in his graciousness and generosity, will allow the verdict to be delivered by a jury of suitably chosen citizens, subject, of course, to his right to overrule the verdict, should it somehow fail to be in conformity with justice, as he sees it."

"If, somehow, Talena should be acquitted," I said, "the Ubar may void that verdict, and pronounce one of guilt?"

"As is his right," said the scribe. "He is the law, and the law is he."

"It seems," I said, "that Talena has little hope in this matter."

"Further," he said, "the scribe for Talena's defense has been cleverly chosen. They must have looked hard for him. He is a man named Hemartius, an obscure fellow, poorly credentialed and indifferent as to learning, an obsequious urt, a sycophant servile to authority and power, a fellow of small success, a man of tarnished reputation, a joke amongst his peers, and an ineffective mediocrity, one well noted for little other than professional debility, strenuous venality, and an openness to corruption. His career, what there was of it, subsided long ago. He also drinks too heavily."

"It seems Talena is doomed," I said.

"When the Tarns of Justice are hungry," he said, "they feed."

"What was the charge laid on you by the agent of Decius Albus?" I asked.

"It is a simple one," he said. "It is that you should in no way interfere with the trial of Talena of Ar."

"I see," I said.

"There must be no interference with the course of justice," he said.

"I understand," I said. "Is there anything else?"

"Only that you are to leave Ar by nightfall, and never return."

"Do you know who I am?" I asked.

"No," he said. "Who are you?"

"Think of me as Harold of Skjern," I said.

"Very well," he said. "That will do. Now, let us finish our kal-da."

"Very well," I said, "let us do so."

We then emptied our mugs.

"May I ask your name?" I said.

"Hemartius," he said.

CHAPTER FORTY-NINE

"No," I said. "Another. No, another. Another."

"The blades are identical," said the Metal Worker.

"They are not," I said. "Another."

"We have curved blades, from the Tahari," he said, "weighty steel from Torvaldsland, blades from the World's End, so sharp they can part dropped silk, excellent for lifting the veils of captured free women."

"The gladius," I said, "a blade with which I am familiar, another."

The Metal Worker put another sword on the counter.

The Gorean gladius, though double-edged, and capable of cutting on both the forestroke and the backstroke, without turning the wrist, is primarily a thrusting weapon. On the other hand, it is designed with both offense and defense in mind; it is thus suitable for fending as well as delivering blows, being adept in both stabbing and parrying. It is heavy enough to cut through leather and light enough, quick enough and nimble enough, to leap about with thoughtless ease. It is long enough to hold a dagger at bay, and short enough to work its way within the guard of larger, slower, less wieldy blades.

"Ah!" I said.

"It speaks to you?" asked the Metal Worker.

"We speak to one another," I said.

"You should pretend it displeases you," he said.

"I do not lie about steel," I said. "It dishonors it."

"It would not do to put your life in the hands of a blade you had dishonored," he said.

"Would you?" I asked.

"I think I know your caste," he said.

"How much?" I asked.

"Two silver tarsks," he said.

"A fellow could buy two, perhaps three or four, attractive slaves for that," I said.

"I have been accused of being part Merchant," he said. "I acknowledge freely that I am a scoundrel."

"Generally," I said, "bread takes priority over steel."

"But sometimes," he said, "steel takes priority over bread."

"Yes," I said.

"When dark matters, possibly red matters, are afoot," he said.

"Yes," I said.

"I am pleased we are friends," he said.

I drew two silver tarsks, my last two silver tarsks, from my wallet and handed them to the Metal Worker.

"The belt, sheath, and dagger, and sheath, are included in the price, of course," he said.

"I should hope so," I said.

"Wait," he said. He then went to the side and, a moment later, returned, and replaced the dagger by another.

"You know what you are doing?" I asked.

"Yes," he said.

I lifted the blade, hefting it unobtrusively. "It is balanced for throwing," I said.

"I know," he said.

"That post across the room," I said. "Do you mind?"

"You see the small stain of paint on the post?" he said.

"That about the throat level, or that of the back of the neck, of a tall man?" I asked.

"The second," he said.

I faced away from the post, and then turned quickly and released the knife. It struck hard, and vibrated, the point sunk some two inches deep into the post, into the stain of paint.

The Metal Worker went to the post and worked the knife free, and then returned, and gave it to me.

"Now," he said, "I know I know your caste."

"I wish you well," I said.

"I wish you well," he said.

I then left the shop.

CHAPTER FIFTY

"I see you are now armed," said the large fellow, now in the Merchant's yellow and white, stepping forth from a doorway. Clearly there was a sword beneath his robes.

I knew him from the vicinity of Samnium, Captain Kasos, an officer in the Cosian infantry, subordinate to Myron, polemarkos of Temos, polemarkos of Cos, apparently one trusted, surely one occupying a staff position, perhaps even that of adjutant.

"It seems you change caste as easily as your robes," I said.

Near Samnium he had been clad in the garb of a Metal Worker. Too, it had been he who had, in perhaps another disguise, watched at the great gate, to detect the arrival of Seremides and myself.

"I did not think a Cosian uniform would be judicious in Ar," he said.

"Only if you wish to be mobbed and impaled," I said.

"I have followed you," he said.

"I know," I said. "That is why I paused to arm myself."

"I was surprised to see you without weapons," he said.

"Where could one be safer than on the streets of Ar?" I asked.

"Perhaps in the Lands of the Wagon Peoples, in the jungles of the Ua," he said.

"Particularly if you are a Cosian," I said.

"I have been commissioned to speak to you," he said.

"I was thinking of paying a visit to your commander," I said.

"That would be unwise," he said. "There must not be the least hint of any possible connection between Cos and the noble Geoffrey of Harfax, who is slated to be the public recipient of the reward for the capture and delivery of Talena to the justice of Ar."

"I made no such agreement," I said.

"It has been made for you," he said.

"The public boards were changed," I said.

"And changed, again," he said. "The board in the Garden of the Hinrabians is only one of several obscure boards on which candidates for news compete."

"The second inscriptions made no mention of Geoffrey of Harfax," I said.

"That is because the matter was still under consideration," he said. "It was later decided that the item was to be restored."

"Why is that?" I asked.

"When you agreed," he said.

"I never agreed," I said.

"But the item makes it clear you did agree," he said, "and that is all that is required."

"Falsity is fact?" I asked.

"It frequently suffices," he said.

"This travesty is unworthy of the polemarkos," I said.

"Be comforted," he said. "The polemarkos is sorely distraught. He had nothing to do with the matter."

"I am pleased to hear that," I said.

"Indeed, I convey to you his outrage at this imposture."

"Who then is responsible for this?" I asked.

"I think," he said, "Ruffio of Ar."

"Ruffio of Ar may utter words and do deeds," I said, "but I sense a darker, heavier hand behind this."

"Perhaps," he said. "But the kaissa is adamant; the board has been arranged; you are helpless; it is a forced continuation."

"I may simply refuse," I said.

"And be quietly done away with," he said, "while another, one perhaps more innocent and less witting than yourself, would be substituted."

"For anyone the risk is intolerable," I said. "The eventual exposure of such a one would be inevitable. Too, the deceit noted, the tarns of war would once more spread their wings."

"That contingency, given his newly acquired gold and power, would be viewed with equanimity by Lurius of Jad," he said.

"And what fate for the puppet who practiced the deceit?"

"Who would care to be he?" he asked.

"I see little choice here," I said.

"There is none," he said.

"It seems so," I said.

"See this from the point of view of both Ar and Cos," he said. "Cos, in all honor, has earned and deserves the reward. No one more than Marlenus recognizes this. Are the rights of Cos to be spurned? Yet, if Cos dares to publicly claim the reward, Ar will erupt in fury. It would be torn apart, shattered, looted, and burned, rent from within."

"I will play the role," I said.

"Excellent," he said.

"Myron, the polemarkos, knew nothing of this?" I said.

"Not until the matter was done," he said. "Also, I regret that it was I who was designated to inform you of this matter."

"Intrigue abounds," I said.

"It commonly does," he said.

"It is my understanding, from this morning," I said, "that Decius Albus, the trade advisor to the Ubar, Marlenus, has ordered me to leave the city by nightfall."

"Let us trust that the trade advisor will be disappointed," he said.

"I suspect it is dangerous to disappoint the trade advisor," I said.

"We may easily procure another 'Geoffrey of Harfax,'" he said, "so there is little to worry about."

"Splendid," I said. "That sets my mind at ease."

"I hoped it might," he said.

"You need not follow me further," I said, "for I am going home now."

"Very well," he said.

CHAPTER FIFTY-ONE

I walked down the four steps from the street, to the entryway into the basement apartment in the Metellan district.

"Master," said Iris, opening the door, responding to my coded knock.

She seemed nervous. Her eyes were clouded.

"What is wrong?" I asked.

"Master Seremides has returned," she whispered.

I pushed angrily through the door, into the room.

"Welcome, my dear colleague," called Seremides, who was sitting in his usual chair, his crutch resting against the arm. It was easier, of course, for him to gain his feet from such a chair than from the cross-legged sitting position common to most male Goreans south of Torvaldsland. Most female Goreans south of Torvaldsland, slave or free, kneel. Chairs for most Goreans bespeak status. The most common chair is the backless curule chair. Ubars, of course, have their thrones.

"No, dear Cabot," said Seremides, in a gently chiding tone. "Do not upset lovely Iris. Steady. Blades are not to be drawn amongst friends. Ah, that is better. I trust that your head is clear, and that you feel well. Perhaps you are annoyed at my prank. I am the first to acknowledge that I owe you an explanation."

"I can reach your throat," I said, "before you can bring your crutch or sword into play."

"I am not surprised, considering the distance," he said.

I tensed.

Iris drew back, to the side.

"But I do not think you will attack," said Seremides.

"Why not?" I asked.

"Because the first instant of rage, of red, blinding rage, has passed," he said. "I counted on that."

"What of the second instant of rage," I asked, "that of calculated, implacable rage, bleak, cold, white rage, rage like ice?"

"Surely you are aware that your codes do not encourage killing in cold blood. Too, you are trammeled by honor, amongst other things. It is one of your failings."

"Honor," I said, "like other things, is subject to interpretation."

"Not in this case," he said.

"You have great courage, to return here," I said.

"Are you bitter?" he asked, affably.

"Somewhat," I said.

"I am ready to pay handsomely for my lodging," he said.

"And for a sword to protect you from the malcontents of Ar?" I said.

"That, too," he said.

"You drugged me," I said. "You stole from me the Home Stone of Ar."

"May I explain matters?" he asked.

"Please, do," I said.

"First," he said, "you understand something of the value of a Home Stone?"

"I think so," I said.

"It is priceless, like a free woman," he said.

"Very well," I said.

"But far more priceless," he said.

"Very well," I said.

"What were you going to do with it?" he asked.

"Exchange it for Talena of Ar," I said.

"I feared so," he said. "That stratagem was not as well concealed from me as you may have hoped. For example, when Talena was in your power, in Port Kar, you did not rush to deliver her to Ar. You scorned the reward which you later pretended to want. You protected her. You kept her. One would think she was special to you, that you wanted her, and might even care for her. What an odd way to do business. What an economic idiot you were!"

"Gold is less meaningful to some than others," I said.

"Then," said Seremides, "you did not even hide her in your holding, where her presence might have aroused suspicion. You concealed her, brilliantly, openly, as a tavern slave in Port Kar. Who would dream that a lowly paga girl might be the elusive Talena? Who would think to look for her in such a place? And few, of course, even in Ar, had seen the Ubara unveiled, let alone in distant, dangerous Port Kar?"

"These things are known to me," I said.

"And now," he said, "you would use the Home Stone, indeed, grievously insult the Home Stone, by bartering it, like a bag of sa-tarna or a basket of suls, for a mere female?"

"That was my intention," I said.

"What should be done in such a case, which is exactly what I did, was to return the Home Stone to Ar freely, asking nothing in return, and, indeed, in my case, incidentally, at great personal anger as I was proscribed in Ar, having an enormous price on my head."

"But now," I said, "as I understand it, your name has been removed from the proscription lists, you have been accorded a place in

Ar's Hall of Heroes, and you have received a substantial remuneration from a grateful state."

"The least Ar could do for the return of her Home Stone," he said.

"And what was the remuneration, not asked for, but freely given?" I asked.

"Was it not on the boards?" he asked.

"Not to my knowledge," I said.

"Good," he said. "Specification would have been vulgar."

"Undoubtedly," I said. "What was it?"

"A thousand gold tarns, first weight," he said.

The standard gold tarn of Ar is the gold tarn, first weight. It might be recalled that the reward for the capture and delivery of Talena to the justice of Ar was ten thousand tarns of gold, of double weight.

"I will see that you get a half share of one of five shares," I said.

"I do not understand," he said.

"For delivering the Home Stone to Ar," I said, "an action which, incidentally, was not discussed with me and one of which I most strenuously disapprove."

"I do not think I understand," he said.

"Surely you do not think I simply walked into the Beast Caves, picked up the Home Stone, and walked back out. Five individuals were involved, myself, Aetius of Venna, Grendel, a Kurlike creature, and two others, known to me, Thurnock and Clitus, the first a Peasant, the second, a Fisherman. Each is entitled to a full share, two hundred gold pieces each. I will, however, split my share with you, and thus we will each receive a hundred gold pieces, first weight."

"I protest," said Seremides.

"On what grounds?" I asked.

"I should be receiving more," he said.

"You are receiving more," I said.

"What?" he asked.

"Your life," I said.

CHAPTER FIFTY-TWO

"And that," I said, "helps you to understand, somewhat, the public boards."

"You let Seremides live?" said Thurnock.

"I saw little to be accomplished by not doing so," I said.

"So the Home Stone is now back in Ar, and closely guarded," said Thurnock.

"Seremides did himself much good by his sly, foul deed," said Clitus.

"I am sure not as much as he had hoped," I said. "He did, however, by his service, free himself of his debt to Ar."

"And Talena remains at the mercy of the Tarns of Justice," said Clitus.

"As she should," said Thurnock.

"Seremides still has much to fear," I said. "Just this evening, some unknown party, or parties, removed his plaque from the Hall of Heroes and broke it on the steps of the Central Cylinder. There may be hundreds in Ar, private citizens, who, remembering the betrayal of Ar and the miseries of the Occupation, might strive to thrust a dagger into his heart. I think he is in danger, here in Ar, if recognized, of being mobbed on sight and torn to pieces."

"I am pleased that you relieved him of the bulk of the pecuniary Ubar's gift," said Clitus.

"It is meet," I said, "that the Ubar's pecuniary gift be bestowed on those who deserved it."

"You need not have been so generous," said Thurnock.

"It is easy to be generous with the gold of others," I said.

"Why did you allow him even a half share?" asked Clitus.

"It was he who returned the Home Stone to Ar," I said.

"To serve his own interests," said Thurnock.

"At that point his life was most in jeopardy," I said, "for I had hoped to exchange it for Talena of Ar."

"I do not know what I can do with two hundred tarns of gold," said Thurnock.

"Return to Port Kar," I said, "buy ships, hire crews."

"Come back with us," said Thurnock. "You can do nothing for Talena here. Abandon her. The gates of Ar have closed behind her. Leave her here to her well-deserved fate."

"I am not prepared to leave Ar," I said.

"Then neither am I," said Thurnock.

"Nor I," said Clitus.

"Friends," I said, touching a hand of each.

"What of the villain, Aetius?" asked Clitus.

"His share, which he much deserved," I said, "will be sent to the Physician's Inn on the Viktel Aria."

"That should hasten his recovery," said Thurnock.

"Let us hope so," I said.

I suspected that luck and success were sometimes the best of physicians.

"I had thought that this meeting, after the business of the Beast Caves, was to have been to consider our course of action, the Home Stone of Ar in our possession," said Clitus.

"We had not counted on the hand of Seremides," said Thurnock.

"The rush of events," I said, "seldom heeds plans."

We were in the Silver Tarsk, in the Metellan district, on the Via Cora, as we had planned. Grendel was near us, but had remained silent. He was in the shadows, crouched down, largely covered with a dark blanket. We had pinched out the tiny tharlarion-oil lamp near the table. The tavern's men had not been much pleased at his entry onto the premises, but he was with us, and, after a low, rumbling, warning growl and the glimpse of a fang, they had refrained from disputing his passage. Little was to be gained by such an action, and, possibly, much might be lost.

Cora, the slender, auburn-haired paga girl, named for the street, with slave deferentiality, suitable when in the presence of the free, approached the table and knelt. "More drink, Masters?" she inquired.

"Another round," I said.

"Yes, Master," she said, rose to her feet, backed away a step or two, turned, and left.

"Yet no paga?" said Thurnock.

"This is not the night for paga," I said.

I had insisted on a strong Bazi tea, for all of us. The reason for this would become clear presently. Within the Ahn, I would be leaving the tavern and possibly entering into the darkness outside, and I suspected I knew what that darkness might hold. Should I fail to dissuade my friends from accompanying me, as I feared I might, I wanted every nerve and reflex in each of us to be tense, vigilant, aware, and alive.

"I saw on the boards," said Clitus, "that it is some Geoffrey of Harfax who had at last apprehended Talena of Ar."

"She was apprehended by Cos," I said. "Geoffrey of Harfax is to be designated the titular recipient of the reward, that in order that the role of Cos be concealed, for political reasons."

"To avoid rioting and arson," said Thurnock.

"Precisely," I said.

"A monumental fraud," said Thurnock, "an enormity, a gross swindle and sham."

"Presumably better than Ar in flames," I said.

"I do not envy that Geoffrey of Harfax," said Thurnock.

"I would not care to be he," said Clitus.

"I am he," I said. "It is a pseudonym I am using in Ar."

"You agreed to such a hazardous imposture?" asked Clitus.

"No," I said, "it was imposed on me."

"How could it be done?" asked Thurnock.

"By someone in authority," I said, "someone bearing an authority, perhaps temporary and circumscribed, superior even to that of Myron, polemarkos of Cos, someone empowered to act, as he saw it, directly in the best interests of Lurius of Jad."

"Then you cannot flee, you must remain in Ar?" asked Thurnock.

"I understand it so," I said.

"At least, for the time," said Thurnock, "you will be safe in Ar."

"Have you heard of a Scribe of the Law, a man named Hemartius?" I asked.

"No," said Thurnock and Clitus.

"I gather that he is an ineffective and failed Scribe," I said, "assigned to conduct the defense of Talena of Ar."

"She is obviously guilty," said Thurnock. "There is no point in a trial."

"There is a political point, a cathartic point, a theatrical point," I said. "Have you heard of Decius Albus, trade advisor to the Ubar?"

"Of course," said Thurnock. "He is one of the most important and powerful, and dangerous, men in Ar. It is said he wants the throne of the Ubar."

"Hemartius, the scribe," I said, "has informed me that Decius Albus does not want me to interfere in the trial of Talena of Ar and wants me out of Ar today, before dark."

"It is already dark," said Clitus.

"Why does the trade advisor want you out of the city?" asked Thurnock.

"I do not know," I said. "I do not even know how he knows of me."

"I do not see how you could possibly interfere with the trial of Talena," said Thurnock.

"You could not possibly do so," said Clitus. "You are not even a citizen of Ar."

"There is some connection here," I said.

"As I understand it," said Thurnock, "according to Cos you must not leave the city and, according to Decius Albus, you must do so."

"It is like the confluence of two rivers, both of whose origins are obscure," I said. "Where they clash there is chaos."

"Tea, Masters," said Cora, returning to the table.

While she arranged the cups, we were silent.

She rose to her feet.

"Slave," I said.

"Master?" she said.

"While we wait for our tea to cool," I said, "perhaps you might, amongst your various duties, fill a pan with water, and take it outside the tavern, and cast it into the gutter, following which you might return and inform us if you have noted anything unusual in the vicinity."

"Yes, Master," she said, and withdrew.

I sipped my tea.

"I am planning on leaving the tavern shortly," I said.

"You are not leaving alone," said Thurnock.

"The war is mine," I said.

"It is also ours," said Thurnock.

"As you will," I said.

Shortly thereafter we noted Cora leave the tavern with a large pan of water, of the sort in which a mop might be twisted and refreshed. We listened for the splash in the gutter outside. After she had returned to the tavern and disposed of the empty pan she came to kneel by our table.

"Several men loiter outside," she said. "That is unusual."

"How many?" I asked.

"At least ten," she said, "probably more. It was hard to see. They wore dark clothing. They were in the darkness."

"Were they armed?" I asked.

"I think so," she said.

"Withdraw," I said, "and encourage your chain sisters to leave the floor."

Grendel began to peel away the blanket under which, in the shadows, he had been muchly concealed. He began to fold it, and then wrapped it, in its layers, about his left arm.

This was noticed by more than one patron of the Silver Tarsk, several of whom had not even noticed his presence earlier.

At the same time, Clitus loosened his net, and felt for his trident, and Thurnock reached for his quiver and bow which lay beside the table.

"We have two options," I said. "The first is to leave the tavern by the front entrance, as would be expected, after which we will be fallen on in the darkness. The second, which I prefer, is to exit the tavern by the rear entrance, which, when our friends outside investigate, will be understood to mean that we have fled the premises."

"But there is more afoot," said Thurnock.

"After our exit, we will leave Grendel to block the rear exit from the outside, while we circle about. His senses, like those of the Kur, which he so closely resembles, are sharp. He can hear sounds we cannot; he can take scent like the sleen and larl; what is night to us is but dusk to him."

"And one who might plunge from light into darkness, as from the tavern into the night, could be but as penned prey for one such as he, waiting," said Thurnock.

"Soon," I said, "we shall encourage our fellow patrons to exit the tavern, that, as would be expected, by the front entrance. Our foes will fear that I, and any with me, might be amongst those leaving, perhaps concealing ourselves amongst them, so they will close about the entrance, to examine those departing. This will allow us to complete our circling about, behind them. When the foe has determined that we are not amongst those departing, they will presumably wait somewhat longer, still coveting a darkness in which to do their work, but will inevitably grow impatient. Perhaps we have slipped away? When they then, alarmed, suspicious that we may have fled, burst into the tavern to determine what has taken place, we can be behind them."

"And then," said Clitus, "we have them boxed in, in the light."

"You are familiar with the way of nets," I said.

"It is my trade," he said.

"Let us finish our tea," I said.

CHAPTER FIFTY-THREE

"The target and his cohorts have fled," cried the darkly garmented figure, looking wildly about, his sword unsheathed.

He was one of several who had been poised outside the entrance to the Silver Tarsk, and had then rushed in, flinging the double doors inward.

"The cowardly urts!" screamed a man.

"Where are they?" cried another.

"Gone!" cried another.

"Where are the tavern's men, and the slaves?" asked another.

It was my hope that they had temporarily departed the tavern, leaving through the back entrance, as I had advised them to do a moment after I had ordered the customers, at sword's point, to vacate the establishment. None had demurred. It was clear to all that they were in the presence of suddenly transformed, desperate men whose will was not to be brooked. Well then did they sense that the reliable, comfortable world beneath their feet might imminently totter. Wisdom spoke. Prudence lay in departure. We had then followed them out through the back entrance, leaving Grendel to secure that portal. Following that we had hurried through the alley behind the tavern, and circled about so that we could cover, and then penetrate, the front entrance to the tavern.

"Whither the target, whither the sleen, Harold of Skjern?" asked one of the men.

That was the name I had given to the scribe, Hemartius. I supposed I had merely been pointed out to him by some agent of Decius Albus, possibly even in the Garden of the Hinrabians.

"He must have been warned," said another.

"Three entered the tavern with hm," said another, "two men and something large, half shrouded in a blanket."

"A beast," said another.

"Where are they?" asked another.

"Somewhere about," said another.

How true that was, I thought.

"Decius Albus will not be pleased," said another.

I supposed that that was also true.

Standing in the door of the tavern, flanked by Thurnock, an arrow set to the string of his bow, and Clitus, his net eager, almost like a living thing, I counted the dark-clad figures who were now within the tavern, fully illuminated by the lamps. There were sixteen such figures. I supposed that that number had been deemed sufficient by Decius Albus to handle the kill of not only a single individual but of, say, two or three more, if need be.

Thurnock looked at me, and I nodded.

Surprise is a familiar, respected element of warfare. So, too, then, I supposed would be an attack which, though begun, though already underway, was not yet noticed.

The assailants were strung out and not facing us. Their attention was on the seemingly empty, deserted tavern before them.

The half-stifled gasp, followed almost simultaneously by the fall of the second body, attracted the attention of the third closest assailant, who, turning about, grasped the situation instantly and cried out in alarm, and then clutched at the arrow penetrating his throat, and fell.

Dismay and consternation gripped the assailants.

Thurnock had another arrow poised, but did not loose the shaft.

I saw that the assailants were neither Assassins nor Warriors. They were thugs, or so it seemed, hired for a kill. They crowded together, bewildered, as though seeking refuge amongst themselves. They did not instantly break apart and charge. One does not, of course, loose an arrow or fire a sniper's bullet at random into a throng. One chooses a target.

"Rush them!" cried one of the darkly clad figures.

"The bow! The bow!" protested more than one of the figures.

"Who will be first to die?" I called.

This question, I hoped, would keep them some yards away, held in place.

"They are three, we are many!" called the fellow, angrily, who had urged action. "Rush them! Rush them, together!"

"You first!" screamed a man.

Then he who had urged action struck the dissenter across the back of the neck with his sword, and the dissenter fell, his head askew.

"See the fate of he who will not obey!" cried he who had urged action. "Now, together, rush forward!" His eyes were wild. His sword was dripping with the blood of the dissenter. He then raised his blade, as if again to strike. "Who will be the next to die?" he asked.

His question was ironic.

He had identified himself to Thurnock as the current de facto leader of the assailants.

An arrow struck him in the temple and tore through the opposite side of his head.

And another arrow was then at the string of Thurnock.

This was more than enough for the remainder of the assailants. There were cries of misery and terror. "The rear exit!" cried one. "Run!" cried another. "Flee!" cried another, stumbling, and turning. "Escape!" screamed another. "The back entrance!" cried another.

Jostling and buffeting, slipping, impeding, and tripping, one another, they turned away from Thurnock, seeking to flee the floor and gain the rear entrance, which lay through, and beyond, the kitchen.

Another of Thurnock's arrows struck the first man who reached the portal, felling him there.

In this way the aperture was partially blocked.

As they crowded and fought one another to force their way, trampling, through the narrow door to the kitchen, Thurnock's bow spoke again, and he who was last in that scrambling, squirming flight failed even to reach the portal.

I gestured to Clitus that he take up a position to the right of the door to the kitchen, as we faced it, and I took up a similar position to the left of the door, as one would face it.

We stood back from the door on either side. In this way we could not be seen from within the kitchen. I anticipated that our foes, given what they might soon encounter by the rear exit, might rethink their strategy, and, despite their earlier experiences, decide to return by the way they had left.

We waited, tense, ready, on either side of the door leading from the floor to the kitchen.

We did not have to wait long.

There was a howl of terror.

"What is it?" asked a man, perhaps back, in the kitchen, back from the door.

"I do not know!" screamed a man.

"Press through the door," urged a man.

"Force your way through," said another.

"It is in the darkness, a larl, I think, ravenous."

"Not in Ar!" cried a man.

"A war sleen!" gasped another.

Then there was another scream.

"Attack it, kill it!" cried another.

"Together!" cried another.

But the door, unlike the swinging leaves of the front entrance, was narrow. It would not easily accommodate more than one individual at a time.

"Stand aside!" demanded a voice, but, a moment later, there was another scream.

"Back, back up," cried a voice. "Come back from the door."

"There is some sort of animal there in the darkness," said a man.

"Take a kitchen lamp, lift it!" said a man.

There was then a loud, hideous roar, a roar such as I had not heard since the steel world of Agamemnon. It was not unlike the challenge roar of a Kur eager for blood amongst the rings.

"Aii!" cried another.

"It is a beast!" said a man.

"The beasts are our friends," said a man. "Decius Albus has assured us so. They are temperate and harmless."

"Gentle, noble beast," said a man, pleadingly. "We are your friends. Let us pass. Let us pass."

There was then a scream of horror.

I risked a quick glance into the kitchen. All attention was on the rear door.

The huge, monstrous frame of Grendel filled the portal. His massive fanged maw was open, and bloody. The blanket wrapped several times about his left arm was in shreds. In his right hand, he held an arm, torn from a body.

I darted back, blade ready.

There was another roar.

"Run!" cried one of the darkly clad figures. "Back, to the front, out of the tavern!"

Clitus and I exchanged glances.

Sandaled footsteps raced toward us.

A blurred frenzy of bodies, stumbling, partially impeded by the fellow Thurnock had used to block the portal to the kitchen, pushed past us.

I took one in the side and Clitus took another, and then dragged his trident free.

The three remaining darkly clad men then stood, clutching swords, in the center of the floor, wary and ready, between the portal to the kitchen and the front entrance. At the front entrance Thurnock had his bow ready. Behind them, emerging from the kitchen, was Grendel.

"Cast down your weapons," I said.

"Do you think we are fools?" asked one of the men.

"How is it that you would attack us?" I asked.

"We were well paid," said the man.

"But not well enough," said one of the darkly clad men, bitterly.

"Do you know who I am?" I asked.

"No," said the first of the three.

"It does not matter," said another of the assailants.

"Do you know why you were to attack us?" I asked.

"No," said the first of the three.

"It did not matter," snarled Clitus.

"No," said the first of the three. "It did not matter."

"You disgrace the Home Stone of Ar," said Thurnock.

"What is a Home Stone?" asked the second of the three. "No more than a rock, no different from any other lying beside a road or found in a field."

"My Home Stone is a gold tarn," said the third assailant.

"You do not know why you were hired?" I asked.

"No," said the first.

"Who hired you?" I asked.

The three exchanged apprehensive glances. The first then spoke. "We do not know," he said.

"You lie," I said. "You took fee from Decius Albus, the trade advisor to the Ubar, or from an agent of his."

I had gathered that this would be the case from Hemartius, who, I suspected, was well disposed toward me, and wanted to warn me, and encourage me to leave Ar, never to return.

"He is a citizen of great power," said he who now seemed first amongst the darkly clad men.

"I know him not," I said. "How is it that he knows me?"

I recalled that Hemartius, the scribe, had warned me, in that name, in that of Decius Albus, not to interfere in the trial of Talena of Ar, as if it might be possible for me to somehow do so.

"We do not know," said the first of the three.

I did not doubt that.

"Decius Albus, I gather," I said, "is formidable in Ar."

"Second only to the Ubar," said the first of the three.

"And perhaps that not for long," said the second of the darkly clad men.

"Also, I would suppose," I said, "Decius Albus is not a man whom it would be wise to fail."

"We have not yet failed him," said he whom I now took to be the leader of the three.

"Cast down your weapons and leave in peace," I said.

"And stand here defenseless, unarmed?" asked the first of the three.

"To be cut down, weaponless?" sneered the third of the three.

"Do you think we would allow you to leave armed, to wait for us in the darkness?" I asked.

The three men looked at one another.

"Cast down your weapons," I said.

"No," said he whom I now took to be first amongst them.

"There has been enough killing tonight," I said.

"Perhaps not," said the third of the darkly clad men.

I gestured slightly to Clitus with my head and he moved about the darkly clad men to take a position between them and Thurnock. Thurnock had an arrow to the string but the bow was not drawn. I feared one of the assailants might be able to reach him before he could loose another shaft.

"We can see you now," said he whom I took to be first amongst the darkly clad men. "We know your numbers and location. The field is open, and clear. The weapon of surprise has been spent. We are three to two."

"Three to four," I said.

"We discount an unready bow and an unarmed beast," he said.

"Disarm yourselves and go in peace," I said.

"But," said he whom I took to be the first amongst the three, "we have not yet earned our fee."

With the suddenness of a silent but visible explosion, the assailants flung themselves into the aspect of war, one charging Clitus and Thurnock, and two, those closest to me, lunging toward me. I slipped to the side, backing away, fending the clumsy thrust of a single blade. Then, a moment later, I was fending two blades. Some feet away I sensed, as much as saw, the spreading, opening, blossoming swirl of Clitus's net. One of the two who engaged me, he whom I took to be first amongst the darkly clad men, was well skilled. I had not expected that. Twice I refrained from a death thrust because it would have opened me to the thrust of the second man. I contented myself, wisely, I think, given the skills of the one man, to defense. It is difficult for a single foe to strike a skilled swordsman who risks little. On the other hand, a reliance on defense is considerably less feasible when one is confronting more than one foe. The second foe, of course, changes his position, as he can, to move about the solitary antagonist, to deal with him from the side or back. The solitary antagonist then, assuming he is not dealing with inept or clumsy foes, where an exposing death thrust may be practical, must rely on evasive movement, or shift his defense frequently and dangerously. It is also desirable to take advantage of the field, so to speak, narrowing access to his position, for example, by utilizing a portal or staircase. My own solution was to carry the fray into the vicinity of an ally, which maneuver instantly alters the dynamics of the entire situation. In this way I transformed what had been a manageable but unpleasant arrangement of two blades against one into a more modest and familiar arrangement of one against one. The face of the second swordsman was wild with horror as he suddenly realized where he was and felt the jaws and fangs of Grendel close about the back of his neck. My primary antagonist then, he whom I took to be the first amongst the darkly clad men, and I, noted the head rolling to the side. Shortly after that, relieved of the necessity of dealing with a second foe, I finished the last of our assailants. I looked about. Clitus was folding his net and Thurnock had returned his arrows to his quiver and unstrung his bow.

"They should have disarmed themselves," said Thurnock.

"They were afraid to do so," I said.

"They saw others as themselves," said Clitus.

"But surely they saw the odds were well against them," said Thurnock. "There would have been less risk in surrender."

"I think they feared to fail Decius Albus," I said.

"What manner of man can he be?" asked Clitus.

"Apparently one whom even hired Assassins, even hardened killers, would fear to fail," I said.

CHAPTER FIFTY-FOUR

The blast of trumpets shook the stadium. A mighty cheer rose from the tiers.

"Are you ready?" asked Ruffio of Ar, whom I had first met on the road from Samnium to Ar, he then claiming to be the Peasant, Rufus, of the Village of Two Branches, a village south of Torcadino.

"As ready as I am likely to be," I said, "as you have seen to it."

"Courage, Harold of Skjern," said Myron, the polemarkos of Temos, of Cos, now in the robes of a well-to-do Builder. With him, also in the Builders' yellow, was Captain Kasos, who, I took it, stood high on the staff of the polemarkos.

I looked up from the sand in the stadium, at the foot of the stairs, to the raised, temporary, square platform, some twenty feet in height, and twenty feet in width and breadth, in the center of the stadium. At each corner there was a herald, with a large, mounted cone through which he would address the crowd.

"The acoustics are much better in the theater of Publius," said Ruffio.

"Splendid," I said.

It was in the theater of Publius, as I understood it, that the trial of Talena of Ar was scheduled to take place.

Near me, in accompaniment, were Thurnock and Clitus. Also, at hand, was Seremides, now understood to be a hero of Ar, for having returned the stolen Home Stone to the city. His prestige was such that it was thought apt that he be present at an occasion so auspicious as this, the official, public acknowledgement of the return of Talena to Ar and the bestowal of the enormous prize associated with her capture and delivery.

"You are incredibly fortunate," said Ruffio.

"I will hope so," I said.

"You need only graciously accept the reward, and the rest will be managed by others."

"That sounds simple enough," I said.

"Obviously the reward cannot go openly to Cos," he said.

"I understand," I said.

"And you will be substantially compensated for your service," he said.

"As much as a gold tarn?" I asked.

"Possibly," he said.

"And when the fraud is discovered, as it must be, sooner or later, what then would my life be worth?"

"Worry then, not now," he said.

"A tarsk-bit?" I suggested. "Or nothing?"

There was then a second blast of trumpets, and another rousing cheer from the crowd.

"Ascend the stairs," said Ruffio, "lest the crowd grow impatient."

"Am I late?" inquired Hemartius. I smelled kal-da on his breath. His robe was shabby and stained.

"I have been waiting, accompany me," I said.

"A slave," he said, "brought me a silver tarn. I do not understand. I seldom command such a fee. Is there a mistake?"

In many markets, I supposed that Iris might not bring such a price. I had braceleted her hands behind her back, and tied the coin in a small sack about her neck, dangling on its string within her tunic. In this way, she would be helped to keep in mind that she was a mere barbarian garnered from Earth for the markets of Gor, that she was, on this world, no more than a slave. To be sure, Earth girls on Gor quickly learn that fact. Slaves, incidentally, although they are not to touch coins without permission, often handle money, for example, in shopping and arranging services, deliveries, and such. One seldom thinks much of entrusting a coin or coins to a slave. They are tunicked, collared, and marked. There is no escape for them. Coins are often carried in either the hand or the mouth. I did not know the dwelling of Hemartius, but I sent her to South Market Street, near the Garden of the Hinrabians, and had her inquire for the location of the Golden Tospit, where, as I recalled, Hemartius had seemed well known. She was directed to his dwelling, a quite modest one she informed me, which was close by.

"I may need a scribe, a scribe of the law," I said. "You are the only one I know in Ar."

"Please," said Ruffio, "must the trumpet blare again, must the crowd grow even more restless to see the stalwart benefactor of Ar, he who, of all the thousands who tried to apprehend the criminal Ubara, was alone successful, he who alone brought the treasonous fugitive, Talena of Ar to justice?"

Hemartius and the others close behind, I began to ascend the steps. I was in no hurry to do so.

Two soldiers would assist Seremides.

"Will not those of Ar wonder how I, a private citizen, could transport so great a treasure to Harfax?" I asked.

"They will think a thousand mercenaries hired," said Ruffio.

"Who can be depended on," I said.

"They will be Cosian regulars," he said. "It has all been arranged. Keep climbing."

"Who will present the reward?" I asked.

"You will be surprised," said Ruffio.

"The Ubar?" I asked.

"One acting in his name," said Ruffio.

As I left the stairs and stepped onto the platform, trumpets sounded again, and the crowd stood, and hailed me. I lifted my hands to them, turning about, smiling, uneasy, acknowledging the cries and plaudits.

I knew a great deal, perhaps more than it was in my best interest to know. I hoped that I would not experience a knife in my back before nightfall.

The heralds at the corners of the platform cried into their amplifying cones, "Welcome to the noble Geoffrey of Harfax, doer of justice, friend of law, champion of right, benefactor of the state, beloved of the Home Stone of Ar!"

On the platform with the four heralds were two scribes, standing, before a table on which reposed, amongst a miscellany of other objects, some papers, a bottle of ink, and a feathered pen.

Hemartius went immediately to the table and began to confer with the scribes. I had originally given little thought to the possibility that I might stand in need of counsel. I had had Hemartius contacted as little more than an afterthought. But now I was suddenly more than pleased, for some reason, that I had had the forethought, despite some reservations and misgivings, particularly considering the scribe in question, to avail myself of a scribe of the law. I suddenly suspected that things might proceed more subtly and intricately than Ruffio had suggested, and that I had originally anticipated.

I looked about.

"What is wrong?" asked Myron.

"Should not Talena be here," I asked, "that she, perhaps naked and in chains, be solemnly presented to the state of Ar?"

"A free woman, naked?" said Myron, disbelievingly.

"At least in chains," I said.

"Would you have her cry out that you are an impostor, and not her captor, and that the reward will go to Cos?"

"She could be gagged," I said. The thought of the proud Talena, so much the arrogant and outspoken free woman, gagged, and unable to express herself, as helpless as a gagged slave, appealed to me.

"The crowd might rise up and storm the platform," said Ruffio, "and tear her to pieces."

"That would not do," said Myron.

"Certainly not," I said.

There was suddenly a scattering of cheers, mingled with hisses and cries of anger, from the crowd.

I saw Seremides, helped by two soldiers, lifted onto the platform.

"He is viewed variously," said Ruffio, "by some as the savior of the Home Stone, by others as no more than a former accomplice of Talena of Ar."

I went to an edge of the platform, looking down to the sand.

"Those two wagons," said Myron, "contain ten thousand gold tarns, each of double weight, the reward for the capture of Talena and her delivery, safe, alive, and well, that she may be satisfactorily and lengthily tortured, to Ar."

The two wagons were heavily guarded, ringed by several concentric circles of regulars of Ar.

I saw a small group of robed individuals emerge from a door in the stadium wall, far to the side, to the left, and begin to make its way toward the platform.

There was a second set of steps ascending to the platform, on the opposite side from that which I had climbed. The small group which had emerged from the door in the wall far to the side, to the left, would, I gathered, utilize those stairs.

I recalled that I had once fought, long ago, in this stadium.

"All goes well," said Ruffio. "Hail, Lurius of Jad."

"Hail, Cos," said Myron.

"All is in order," said Hemartius, joining me at the side of the platform. "The papers need only the signatures and the Ubarial stamp and seal."

"For a short time, my dear Harold of Skjern, or Geoffrey of Harfax, or whoever you may care to be," said Ruffio, "you will be the richest man on Gor, possessing more wealth than dozens of cities, and hundreds of Ubars."

"Envy me," I said.

"I shall," said Ruffio, "briefly."

The small group which had approached from the side was now ascending the other stairs. It consisted of three robed, hooded, male figures.

They then stood on the platform.

"Tal," I said, greeting them.

They then brushed back their hoods.

"Tal," said their leader, large, heavy, coarse-featured Decius Albus, trade advisor to Marlenus, Ubar of Ar.

"Tal," said Pa-Kur, gray-skinned, with eyes like glass, Master Assassin of the Caste of Assassins.

"Tal," said the third man, shorter and plainer than the others, even ugly, Xenon, he too, I took it, of the Caste of Assassins.

"Ho!" said Seremides, startled, glimpsing Xenon.

"Benefactor," said Xenon, quietly.

"I had not expected to see you here this morning, Harold of Skjern," said Decius Albus.

"That does not surprise me," I said.

"I expected to hear of you last night," he said, "but I heard nothing."

"Sixteen informants," I said, "failed to report to you."

"I should have sent a hundred," he said.

"I was puzzled," I said, "that one of your august stature might have some interest in a humble visitor to Ar, and even associate him somehow with the pending trial of Talena of Ar, but that mystery is dispelled as I see at your side your tall associate, the noble Pa-Kur, Master of the Dark Caste."

"We have met before," said Pa-Kur, "with ready, leveled steel between us."

"Long ago," I said. "Do you care to renew that acquaintance?"

"I have something better in mind," said Pa-Kur.

"I learn from my friend of the Dark Caste," said Decius Albus, "that you have some sort of relationship with the traitress, Talena, and might be expected to attempt some sort of intervention on her behalf."

"How could I do that?" I asked.

"I do not know," said Decius Albus, "but, as I am high in the state of Ar, I do not care to risk it. The processes of the law must proceed apace. Justice must be done."

"The justice of Ar," I said.

"Precisely," he said.

"A justice which enlists a thousand prejudiced jurors clamoring for vengeance, a justice which, should the jurors fail to reach the desiderated verdict, is subject to the arbitrary intrusion of authority," I said.

"Justice is founded on the will of the Ubar," said Decius Albus. "How could it be otherwise? Such is right and law."

"In Ar," I said.

"In Ar," he agreed.

"Where is the Ubar?" I asked. "Should he not be here?"

"This matter, the bestowal of the fortune associated with the capture and delivery of Talena of Ar, is beneath the notice of the Ubar."

I found this hard to believe.

"I stand in his place," said Decius Albus.

"Of course," I said.

"Should we not proceed?" inquired Myron, the polemarkos.

"By all means," said Ruffio.

"You can imagine my astonishment this morning," said Decius Albus, "when I learned that Harold of Skjern and the doughty, celebrated Geoffrey of Harfax, hailed universally in Ar, to whom Ar owes so much, were the same."

"Thus you have less to keep in mind," I said.

"You understand, I trust," said Decius Albus, "that Lurius of Jad is victor here, that the gold is destined, unfortunately, for Cos, that this arrangement, you as a designated recipient, is a monumental fraud to which you are knowingly party."

"He understands," said Ruffio.

"Do not allow yourself or your tall associate, he of the Assassins, to be bitter," I said to Decius Albus. "Your scheme of stealing the Home Stone of Ar, in league with Kurii, and exchanging it for the gold, was brilliant, worthy of the finest of criminal minds."

"I know nothing of what you speak, of course," said Decius Albus.

"Of course," I said.

"I rejoice, of course," he said, "that your associate and colleague, the redoubtable Seremides, despite his handicap, somehow managed to rescue the Home Stone and return it to Ar."

"Naturally," I said.

"The gold is not yet in Cos," said Pa-Kur.

"That is true," said Ruffio.

"Let us not prolong this farce farther," said Decius Albus. "Let it be enacted and promptly forgotten."

"I do not think it will be so soon forgotten," I said.

"What do you mean?" asked Decius Albus.

"Little, or nothing," I said.

Decius Albus then made a sign to the four heralds. Each then, largely in unison, using the giant cones, oriented toward the front, rear, and sides of the stadium, began a series of apparently rehearsed remarks. They began with praises for Ar, synopsizing her history, glory, and prospects. There was then a brief account of Ar's betrayal and degradation by enemies within, an account which concentrated on Talena of Ar and failed almost entirely to allude to other arch conspirators, particularly Seremides. Much was made of treason, tyranny, subversion, suffering, oppression, looting, and corruption, of which Talena was presented as being the predominant architect. The glorious restoration of Marlenus was then rendered in bold, grateful colors, whose restoration we now learned, to my surprise at least, owed much to the secret work and planning of his current trade advisor, Decius Albus. There was then an account of the flight of the false Ubara, Talena, and the long and widely spread search by individuals, organizations, and cities to apprehend her and bring her to justice. Then a hero arrived on the scene who, after many disappointments, hardships, and battles, with men, weathers, animals, monsters, and such, located and captured the fair fugitive, and returned her, a terrified prisoner, to Ar, where the Tarns of Justice were eagerly waiting to grasp her in their talons. This hero was the noble Geoffrey of Harfax. At this point there were more blasts of trumpets, and standing ovations, during which I modestly turned about, to one side and another, rather as before, smiling, and raising my arms humbly and gratefully to the crowds.

"Now," said Hemartius, gesturing toward the Scribes' table, "the signings, and stampings, the affixing of the state seals, and all is done."

"You are certain that this is all legal?" I said.

"Certainly," he said. 'Somewhat unusual or eccentric, perhaps, but all legal."

Decius Albus signed the document for Ar, in a large, vigorous, sharply angled script. I almost feared he might thrust the scratching pen through the rence paper. I hoped that that would not void the document. I then signed where I was told to sign, and the two scribes stamped the document, and affixed seals, and then, as witnesses, added their own signatures in a small, neat hand.

"It is done, noble client," said Hemartius.

"I wish to clarify something," I said.

"Of course," said Hemartius.

But at that moment, there was a cry of astonishment from the stands and thousands, risen to their feet, were looking upward, some shielding their eyes, many of them pointing to the sky.

"Look!" cried Thurnock, pointing upward.

The territorial scream of the tarn is shrill and piercing, carrying in the Voltai or in the mountains of Thentis for pasangs. But this was no cry of a natural tarn, a monster with a mighty beating heart, and vast, thundering wings. It was a hideous, howling, mechanical surrogate of such a cry. I gritted my eyes shut, briefly, painfully, at the flash of light which momentarily blazed off the silver fuselage of the gigantic, birdlike machine overhead. I had seen nothing like this since my time on the steel world of Agamemnon, the Eleventh Face of the Nameless One. I had heard no such sound since shocking, horrifying moments in the steel tunnels when I had sought to purloin the Home Stone of Ar.

"What is that thing?" cried Decius Albus.

"A tarn!" cried one of the scribes.

"Of metal?" cried the other scribe.

"It is a sign, a warning from Priest-Kings!" said a man.

"The Priest-Kings are angry!" said a man. "We must heed the Initiates, and increase our donations to the temples."

"Let us double them!" cried another.

"I saw something like that, but not winged, in the marshes of the delta," said Pa-Kur to Decius Albus.

Suddenly the beak of the birdlike device opened and a torrent of flame briefly spewed forth.

The stands seemed convulsed with terror.

Several occupants of the platform rushed to the stairs, and others leaped bodily to the sand below.

"I do not understand this," said Thurnock. "What is going on? What does this mean, Captain?"

"The meaning is simple," I said. "Agamemnon has acquired a new body."

Long ago, perhaps even before the destruction of the original, natural Kur world, before its disintegration into hundreds, or thousands, of fragments now orbiting between Mars and Jupiter, there was a giant, mighty Kur, a Kur amongst Kurii. He is referred to amongst men, who could not pronounce his name in Kur, by the name of an ancient King on Earth, Agamemnon. The destroyed world, prior to its destruction, had been technologically advanced to the point where it was recognized that it could, and might, perish by means of its own power. Therefore, before it might do so, several lifeboats or escape capsules, the origins of the later steel worlds, had been manufactured in space, and it was in these, following the destruction of their natural world, that the remnants of the surviving Kurii took refuge. Either prior to, or after the destruction of their natural world, Kur science had recognized the dominance of the brain, and its role in sensation and activation. It was recognized, rather early, that a disembodied brain, properly nourished and stimulated, could have experiences indistinguishable from those of an embodied brain. The next step was a natural one, to equip that disembodied brain with one or more bodies, by means of which it could then interact with an actual world. Agamemnon, I knew, had had, upon occasion, different bodies. I had witnessed more than one on his own steel world, before his exile and banishment. The last such body of which I had heard, until today, but had never seen, was that of a huge, mechanical marsh tharlarion in the delta of the Vosk, near Port Kar.

The giant, mechanical tarn circled the stadium three times, and then, descending, hovered, above one of the treasure wagons, and then perched upon it, quietly, regally. The soldiers, the guards, were, as were those in the stands, and on the platform, in consternation. What was to be done? Was anything to be done? Doubtless conflicting orders were being issued. Then several of the soldiers spread out, withdrawing, breaking their surrounding, concentric ranks. I supposed that they had been released from their formation. Certainly they, and their officers, were totally unprepared for this unexpected, formidable, unique challenge, if it were a challenge, from the sky. Might it speak of Priest-Kings? Who would dispute with Priest-Kings? And the thing showed no hostility, no interest in the treasure. Could it be some sort of sign? Some fellows, perhaps not knowing what else to do, cast their spears at the device, from the surface of which they glanced off harmlessly. The head of the giant machine turned about and a cloud of fire rushed toward the intrepid guards who then had more to worry about than possible blasphemy, disrespect, and heresy. Those engulfed rolled screaming in the sand, which promptly extinguished the flames.

This intervention from the sky alarmed me, not for my personal safety, for the thing, the device, was clearly more concerned with the wagons than people, but because I feared it might upset my plans.

I was close enough to overhear Decius Albus and Pa-Kur.

"I do not understand this," said Decius Albus. "Does this have to do with Beasts?"

"Certainly," said Pa-Kur.

"Where is Lucilius, where is a Beast, to inform us?"

"Who would bring a Beast to the platform?" asked Pa-Kur.

"Do you understand what is going on?" asked Decius Albus.

"Yes," said Pa-Kur. "Last night, in the Beast Caves, I was informed."

"I was not," said Decius Albus.

"No," said Pa-Kur.

"Why was I not taken into the confidence of the Beasts?" asked Decius Albus.

"They saw no need to do so," said Pa-Kur.

"I protest," said Decius Albus.

"You do not need to know everything," said Pa-Kur. "I do not need to know everything."

"I am the trade advisor to the Ubar," said Decius Albus.

"In Ar you are large," said Pa-Kur. "This has to do with worlds."

"If you wish my cooperation, and support," said Decius Albus, "you had best keep me informed."

"How so?" asked Pa-Kur.

"Because we are in Ar," said Decius Albus, "and in Ar I am large."

"Beware the impatience or hostility of the Beasts," said Pa-Kur.

"Let them fear me, and my power," said Decius Albus. "Any one of them could perish under a hundred spears."

At this point, its awesome appearance presumably now well noted, the mechanical tarn threw back its head, much like a natural tarn, and, after another scream, another hideous emanation, spread its wings, smote the air, and, shortly thereafter, was lost amongst the clouds.

"I do not understand what has occurred," said Decius Albus.

"Think," said Pa-Kur. "We want the gold. We do not wish it to go to Cos. We have now, supposedly, been given a sign. The sign changes all things. We shall interpret the sign in such a way as to keep the gold in Ar."

"Cos will object," said Decius Albus.

"On what grounds," asked Pa-Kur. "They are not involved. The recipient of the gold is the puppet, Geoffrey of Harfax."

"It will mean war," said Decius Albus.

"No," said Pa-Kur. "None will dare gainsay the sign."

"Excellent," said Decius Albus.

"What more could you want?" asked Pa-Kur.

"The throne of Ar," said Decius Albus.

"You shall have it," said Pa-Kur.

I had heard enough, and I moved away, subtly, through others, and beckoned to Hemartius.

I did not think that my plan, as it seemed to have turned out, had been spoiled by the unexpected and startling appearance of the mechanical tarn, but that it might have been, if anything, enhanced, deepened, strengthened.

"Yes, noble client?" said Hemartius.

A silver tarsk, I supposed, might buy a great deal of kal-da.

"I mentioned to you that I wished to clarify something," I said.

"Of course," said Hemartius. "Just before the arrival of the great tarn. Do you think that it is one of the legendary Tarns of Justice?"

"I doubt it," I said.

I recalled the sounds emitted by the gigantic, formidable, artificial bird.

I had, of course, heard such sounds recently, in the Beast Caves, in the tunnels of steel.

"What may I do for you?" asked Hemartius.

"Am I now the sole and legal owner of the reward?" I asked.

"Yes, for a time," said Hemartius, "until, in another transaction, you transfer the wealth to Cos."

"To Lurius of Jad," I said.

"That seems to be the intent," said Hemartius.

"But," I said, "until then it is mine to do with as I wish?"

"What do you wish to do, what could you do, with two wagons freighted with gold?" he asked. "Do you wish to look upon it? That would be practical. On the other hand, it would take better than a day to weigh and count it. I do not think Cos would be willing to wait that long. The transfer, of course, will be done discreetly, secretly."

"But until then," I said, "the gold is fully, and wholly, mine?"

"Of course," said Hemartius, "for what that is worth."

"I thought so," I said, "but I wanted a legal opinion on the matter."

"Legally, the matter is clear," he said.

"That is all I wanted to know," I said.

I pushed my way to one of the corners of the platform, and thrust the startled herald there from the platform, he then plunging down to the sand. "Thurnock, Clitus," I called over my shoulder, "do me shelter!" They rushed forward, taking a position behind me, facing the others on the platform.

"What is going on?" demanded Decius Albus.

I seized up the cone. "Wise, noble, beloved, long-suffering, muchly wronged citizens of Glorious Ar," I shouted into the cone, the words booming out, "I, Geoffrey of Harfax, your friend, the recipient of your thoughtful, generous reward for the capture and delivery of the despicable, perfidious Talena of Ar to the talons of your gentle justice, I, Geoffrey of Harfax, whom you have muchly honored, address you!"

The stands were suddenly quiet. All eyes were turned to the platform. I sensed a bit of pushing and shoving behind me.

"Ar is mighty," I said, "and Harfax is small. Yet Ar has always looked kindly on small Harfax. While a hundred cities were once crushed under the boot of Ar's benign, liberating imperialism, little Harfax was ignored. This was not because Harfax was remote and poor, protected by a nearly inaccessible terrain and defended by a well-armed, resolute citizenry, but because in Ar's heart there always glowed a warm, loving wealth of affection for tiny Harfax. Then the gates of Ar, betrayed from within by a treasonous Ubara and her wicked cohorts, were opened to heartless strangers, and Ar fell, to be occupied, yes, occupied, by rude, arrogant, greedy, larcenous, tyrannous invaders. Who can recall without horror the long and terrible sufferings which then wracked noble Ar—"

Here there were cries of anger and rage from the stands.

"— until the return of Marlenus to free, with the stalwart aid of his noble friend, Decius Albus, his beloved city of Ar."

"Let him speak," said Decius Albus from somewhere behind me.

"Thus, I asked myself," I said, "how can I show Ar the gratitude of tiny Harfax for the kindly regard in which Ar has long and constantly held her, and how can I, in even a small way, show the grief of Harfax for the oppression Ar has endured and over which she shall prevail. Can Harfax do nothing to assuage that sorrow, to lessen that calamity? While pondering this there came to me, in a dream, the image of a great tarn of silver, or iron, or steel, like the tarn on the silver battle standards of Ar herself, under which she has marched into so many lands, liberating cities with or without their permission, like the mighty tarn you have just seen!"

"A sign, a sign!" cried more than one man in the stands.

"And the great tarn in my dream," I said, "spoke to me and told me what I should do, and what I then fervently wished to do, and now do."

"Beware!" cried Ruffio.

"Accordingly, I now, and herewith," I said, "give the entire treasure awarded to me for the apprehension of Talena of Ar to the people of Ar. Come down from the stands now, noble citizens, take your gold, keep what you wish, and carry the rest into the city, and distribute it as you will, without stint or reservation, to all the citizens of Ar."

"No!" cried Decius Albus.

"Stop, stop!" screamed Ruffio.

"Order the guards to turn back the crowd," screamed Decius Albus.

"The guards are citizens," said a man, looking down to the sand. "They rush to claim their share."

"I, too, am a citizen," cried a man, and turned about, racing for the stairs.

"And I!" cried another. "And I, too," cried another.

In a moment the platform was largely deserted. The three remaining heralds were amongst the first to leave. Several men on the platform had leaped to the sand below, not losing any time in negotiating stairs. I saw the herald whom I had thrust from the platform limping toward the wagons.

I was approached by Myron, the polemarkos of Temos.

I reached for my sword, but he was smiling.

"Well done," he said. "Now there will be no new war, or not soon, between Ar and Cos. Too, Lurius of Jad will now not have the means to do great harm on the continent. Indeed, in Cos herself, many resent the tyranny of his rule, and fear his overweening ambition and his reckless pursuit of vast, dangerous aims. Who then would cheerfully witness the hundred-fold increase of his power? Too, Ar will not now go up in flames when the treasure shows up in Cos, and the stubborn, uncompromising honor of Marlenus of Ar will not lead to the downfall of Ar and his Ubarate."

"Where is Marlenus?" I asked.

"I do not know," said Myron.

"Also," I said, "in this way the gold does not go to Decius Albus, Pa-Kur of the Assassins, or Kurii of the faction of Agamemnon."

"I know nothing of such things," he said.

"It is nothing, do not concern yourself," I said.

"You are today," he said, "the most popular man in Ar."

"Not in all precincts," I said.

"How did you arrange the matter with the large, strange metal bird?" asked Myron.

"I did not," I said. "I never saw it before in my life."

"You then invented much," he said.

"Sometimes," I said, "one makes do with what is at hand. And deception, as well as surprise, is an acceptable element of warfare."

"You spoke harshly of the treasonous Ubara," he said.

"How else could I hope to involve myself in her trial?" I asked.

CHAPTER FIFTY-FIVE

She turned away from me, sharply, haughtily, with a fierce rustle of robes.

"I had forgotten how beautiful you are," I said.

"Return my veil," she demanded.

I tossed it to the side.

"A prisoner under indictment," said Hemartius, "may, at the discretion of the court, be denied the privilege of the veil."

"That is to demean me," she snapped.

"That may be entailed," said Hemartius.

"It will have me as face-stripped as a slave," she said.

"It was so ruled," said Hemartius.

Slaves are denied veiling on Gor. In Gorean law, they are animals, and who would veil an animal?

She spun about to face me, angrily. "Savor your vengeance, despicable, barbarian tarsk," she said.

"He is not here to seek vengeance," said Hemartius.

"You would be even more beautiful," I said, "in the rag and collar of a slave."

"Tarsk, tarsk!" she screamed, and rushed toward me, to strike me, her small fists flailing. I caught her wrists and held her. She was helpless. She sobbed in frustration. I wondered what it might be to be a woman, to know that her strength was less than that of a man. How does this subconsciously affect her? What does it tell her, if anything, of the differences between the sexes? And the sexes in the human race are so radically dimorphic. Even a Kur can tell, at a glance, the differences between a human male and a human female. And women are so soft, beautiful, and sensual! How desirable they are! Do they know how desirable they are? Can they even begin to suspect how precious they are and how they appear to men? Perhaps they have some sense of that when they are put on the auction block, naked, and hear the bidding. I then, by pressure on her captive wrists, forced her down to her knees before me. She looked up at me, furious, eyes blazing. "Release me," she said. "Release me!"

"How does it feel," I asked her, "to be on your knees before a man?"

In such a posture, does a female not know she is in her place?

"Release me!" she screamed.

I did so, and she sprang to her feet, and backed away.

"He is here to help you, to assist in your defense," said Hemartius.

"No," she said, "he is here to spy on you, or to undermine your defense, to control you more than the court itself will do. I have heard how he spoke of me in the stadium, how he referred to me, so maliciously, so venomously."

"Had I not done so," I said, "the court would not have granted my petition to join the noble Hemartius."

"'Noble,' I?" said Hemartius.

"Yes," I said.

"He, the tarsk, the barbarian, should not be placed as he is," she said. "He knows no law. To such a one, courts are alien. He knows only the sword, if that. He knows nothing of scrolls and precedents. He is a verr amongst sleen."

"Given his gift to the people of Ar, and his consequent popularity in the city, and his expressed animus toward you," said Hemartius, "the court saw no difficulty in acceding to his request."

"In accepting this supposed aid, which you might have easily denied, you were duped," she said. "He wishes to be in a position to guarantee that I will be subject to the most grievous of outcomes."

"I do not believe that to have been his intention," said Hemartius.

"What do you know?" she asked. "Do you not know what is said about you, that you are a joke, that you are a court-appointed mediocrity, that you are a worn, spent man, a tattered, failed counselor, perhaps the worst in Ar, a dishonest drunk who would betray a client for a dram of kal-da?"

"I have not had a drink of kal-da in three days," he said.

"He hates me," she said. "Did you not hear his words on the platform of reward and celebration?"

"I do not think he hates you," said Hemartius.

"I hate him!" she cried. "Long ago, absurdly, foolishly, we interlocked our arms, though he was but a barbarian, and I the daughter of a Ubar! How grievously I erred! We drank the wine of companionship. I and a barbarian! Oh, he would carry me on tarnback to Ko-ro-ba, to be accepted and embraced in honor by his father. But after a night of love, I awakened to find myself alone, and abandoned, I, the daughter of Marlenus, the Ubar of Ubars!"

"It was not my doing," I said. "It seems I had served my purpose on Gor. By the might of Priest-Kings, I was returned to Earth. I did not know if ever again I would see the green fields of Gor or take into my lungs its fresh, clean air."

"I, deserted by the tarsk, tried to return to Ar," she said. "But my guards, mercenaries by my choice, I unwilling to accept the protection of men of Ko-ro-ba, robbed me and fled, and I found myself in the wilderness, lost, alone, cold, hungry, and confused, without protection and without possessions. I fell to the capture ropes of the dreaded Rask of Treve. How pleased he was to have the daughter of his enemy, Marlenus of Ar, at his mercy! I found myself well claimed, well owned. My left thigh still bears the mark of Treve, burned there by my captor's iron."

"I had been returned to Earth," I said. "I knew nothing of these things. I am wholly innocent."

"Liar!" she cried.

"No," I said.

"And I," she said, "the daughter of Marlenus, found myself in a Trevan collar!"

"I take it," I said, angrily, "it was well locked on your pretty neck."

"Tarsk!" she cried.

"A collar belongs on it," I said.

"Sleen, vile sleen!" she wept.

"These recriminations, and such, high lady," said Hemartius, "do not much advance the preparations for your trial, which is imminent."

"Be silent, dolt," she said. She then turned again to me. "And Rask of Treve," she said, "did not even keep me! He preferred to me, the daughter of Marlenus of Ar, a worthless, barbarian chit, a blond slave named El-in-or!"

"A man's strong hands," I said, "will reach out to seize his love slave."

"He bestowed me on a woman, Verna, a chieftainess of the northern panther girls. Can you conceive of that? Can it even be imagined? I found myself, the daughter of Marlenus of Ar, taken as the helpless slave of a woman to the northern forests?"

"It was there, as I understand it," I said, "that you were purchased, eventually to be returned to Ar."

"Yes!" she snapped.

"It is said," I said, "that you begged to be purchased."

"Of course," she said. "I was desperate to be purchased, to be returned to Ar, to wealth, honor, position, power, and freedom."

"Legally," said Hemartius, "should a woman pronounce herself to be a slave, she is then a slave, whether she has a master or not. She is then merely a slave without a master, and may be claimed by any free person. And, for example, should a captured free woman beg to be purchased, say, that she may be freed, she acknowledges that she can be purchased, and thus acknowledges herself a slave. And, of course, if she is already a slave, she merely reiterates what is already obvious."

Women often, of course, beg to be purchased, for example, calling to buyers from slave shelves or from within their market cages.

"But, was I to be restored to wealth, honor, power, and position?" she asked. "No! My shame had besmirched the honor of Marlenus! I was sequestered in the Central Cylinder! I was to be shut away, as a reproach to the honor of Ar. I was an embarrassment to the throne and the medallion of office."

"And thus," I said, "when Marlenus disappeared in the Voltai on a hunting trip, and the governance and sovereignty of Ar was in disarray and jeopardy, you became an easy prey to conspirators and dissidents, such as Seremides, who wished to ascend in Ar."

"And needed one of high blood to abet their schemes, an unwitting, easily duped figurehead!" said Hemartius, delightedly.

We were in a barred conference room, in one of the several chambers of the defense in the Cylinder of Justice. I had once, long ago, fought Pa-Kur on the roof of this edifice. Talena had been temporarily released from her cell within a cell to consult with Hemartius and his aide, one still spoken of in Ar as Geoffrey of Harfax.

"Nonsense!" exclaimed Talena. "I was not duped! I was fully aware of what was going on! I seized an opportunity! I would have my vengeance on Marlenus and all of Ar, the entire Ubarate!"

"Perhaps," I said, "you thought that you could ease tensions between Ar and Cos and Tyros, that the maritime Ubarates might somehow improve and redeem Ar, that a healthy, prosperous, harmonious peace might be achieved."

"You were misled in this," said Hemartius, "and dismayed when these dreams, hopes, and ideals proved vacuous and illusory?"

"Not at all!" said Talena. "Do you think I am a fool? Who does not know the cunning and greed, the unbridled dreams and ambitions of Ar's traditional enemies, Cos and Tyros, Lurius of Jad and Chenbar, the Sea Sleen, of Kasra? I knew them well and they would serve me better! I had been mistreated! I would have my revenge on Marlenus and Ar and would use Cos and Tyros as the weapons with which to wreak it!"

"This is not going well," said Hemartius, turning to me.

"Do not let her testify," I said.

"I shall demand to testify," said Talena.

"I sense the court," said Hemartius. "It will be only too pleased to honor her request to testify."

"Do not, high lady," I said, "insist on whetting the torture knives, heating the tongs and irons, sharpening the impaling pole."

"I will be heard," she said.

"All is lost," said Hemartius.

"I am proud of my guilt," said Talena. "I revel in it!"

"The jury will, as well," said Hemartius, "if they do not first rise up and cut you to pieces with small knives."

"I fear your client is headstrong and wayward," I said.

"I am the daughter of Marlenus of Ar," she said.

"I shall struggle to hold my temper," I said.

"You are a weakling and oaf," she said.

"In struggling to hold my temper," I said, "I may be unsuccessful."

"You will be successful," she said. "I am a free woman."

There was a small stool, a prisoner stool, in the corner of the room. Its legs were only a few inches high. It was the sort that is sometimes used to reduce, lower, and humiliate a prisoner who is being interrogated. I, with a sweep of my foot, slid it across the floor to the center of the room. "Sit on it," I said.

"Never," she said. "Oh!"

I had seized her, put her prone to the floor, and knelt across her body.

"Sleen!" she cried.

"Beware!" warned Hemartius. "She is a free woman."

On Gor, a free woman may do and say almost anything without any danger of correction, contradiction, or reprisal.

"A prisoner," I said, "and one under indictment."

"What are you doing?" he asked, apprehensively.

I supposed it was quite clear what I was doing.

I removed two short cords from my wallet. I then crossed her wrists behind her body, tying them together. I then crossed her ankles and bound them together. In a moment, she was helpless. She thrashed a little, futilely. Then she was quiet, fuming, helplessly tied.

"The same knots which secure a naked slave with perfection," I said, "serve as well to tie a fully dressed free woman."

"Tarsk!" she hissed.

I then lifted her up and sat her down, a little precariously, on the tiny, short, three-legged stool.

She could not, of course, rise.

She looked away, not meeting my eyes.

"Speaking of dressing," said Hemartius, "we must consider how to dress her for the trial."

"Let her be naked, confined in a finely meshed chain," I said, "that her beauty be as little concealed as that of a marketed slave."

"Sleen, tarsk!" she said.

"She is a free woman," said Hemartius. "I suggest simple robes, somewhat worn, plain, and shabby, suggesting sorrow, poverty, humility, and contrition. Let the jury be touched. Let tears flow from their eyes, as they contemplate the vagaries of fate and consider the descent and fall of a once-great lady."

"Nonsense," she said. "Rather, robes befitting a Ubar's daughter, bedecked with pearls, glistening with jewels."

"I fear," said Hemartius, "if she insists on that, the court will be only too willing to accommodate her."

"Will the Ubar be present at the trial?" I asked.

"Of course," said Hemartius. "He is the supreme ruling judge."

"He has not been much evident, as of late," I said.

"I know," said Hemartius. "That is puzzling."

"Untie me," demanded Talena, "and let me rise to my feet!"

"Sit still, Prisoner," I said.

"Counselor," she said.

"Yes, Lady," said Hemartius.

"Discharge your untrained, uninformed, clumsy, bumbling, useless colleague," she said.

"The court would be displeased," he said, "for he is popular in Ar, and, given the supposition of his hostility to the defendant in this case, he is deemed an asset of great value to the prosecution."

She squirmed, angrily.

"Consider that," I advised her.

"I was brought from Port Kar by Seremides of Ar, once First Sword in the Taurentian guard, under false pretenses to Cos," she said. "Supposedly I was to be received in honor as a welcome, esteemed ally. Supposedly I was to be guaranteed safety, wealth, position, and station. But, instead, I was incarcerated and then transported to Ar, the reward for my apprehension to be claimed by Lurius of Jad."

"I am familiar with much of that," said Hemartius.

"And wherein in that account," she asked, "does one hear of Tarl of Bristol, Tarl of Ko-ro-ba, Tarl Cabot, Harold of Skjern, or Geoffrey of Harfax?"

"Nowhere, I fear," said Hemartius.

"Do you think it would be judicious to let her testify?" I asked.

"No," said Hemartius.

"I will demand the right to testify," she said.

"If she is so foolish as to do so," said Hemartius, looking at me, "the court will insist on her exercising such a right."

"And," she said, "I will reveal all. I will tell that Cos captured me and brought me to Ar, and that your Geoffrey of Harfax is a but fool and dupe, a fraud and charlatan!"

"And," said Hemartius, "who would believe you?"

"You look foolish," I said, "sitting there on that little stool, so close to the floor, bound hand and foot."

"I hate you, I hate you, I hate you!" she cried.

"It is too bad she is not a slave," said Hemartius. "You could put her under the whip."

"Well, and quickly," I said.

"Sleen!" she cried.

I turned to her, angrily. "Do you remember," I asked, "long ago, when you were brought to Port Kar, from the Northern Forests, and I could have kept you as a slave, but I did not do so. Instead, I had you returned to Ar, as you wished?"

"Of course," she said. "What a man of Earth you were! What a weakling!"

"I had been wounded with poisoned steel," I said, "and could not rise from a chair. I was weak. I was helpless. Do you recall how you demeaned me, and mocked me, ridiculing me for my infirmity?"

"Of course," she said. "How amusingly pathetic you were. You were like a penned verr with a broken back. You could scarcely move. You could not even begin to get up. You were not a man, but a sorry joke. I detest weakness."

"I recovered," I said.

"Obviously," she said. "Then you were only weak in behavior, in will, in manhood, again a meaningless, typical male of Earth."

"All men of Earth are not weaklings," I said.

"Does not their society train them so?" she said.

"Some men are not easily trained," I said. "Biology, even when regretted, feared, and outlawed, exists."

Who, I wondered, is one's most dangerous foe, if not oneself? Why should a man feel guilty for being a man, or a woman feel guilty for being a woman? Why should not a man be true to himself? Why should a woman not be true to herself? Is a self so hard to find? Why should it not speak?

At this point, the barred conference room was entered by a guard. "Your time is up," he said. "It is time to return the prisoner to her cell."

"Surely not yet," said Hemartius. "We have barely begun."

The guard bent down and freed Talena's ankles. He then drew her to her feet beside the stool.

"We have waited three days to see the prisoner," said Hemartius. "One must move with care. The matter is complex. It takes days to prepare a case."

"The prosecution began its work long ago," said the guard, "even before the traitress was taken into custody. It has gathered over a thousand depositions and affidavits."

"I must have time," said Hemartius. "A thousand details must be attended to, a hundred arguments prepared and evaluated. We must consult tirelessly. The defendant must be thoroughly informed, and readied."

Talena's hands were still bound behind her back. The guard did not see fit to relieve her of this impediment. Rather, he put his hand in her hair and thrust her head down to his left hip.

She had thus been placed in a common leading position for a female slave.

"Hold!" I said, angrily, putting my hand on the guard's arm.

"She is a free woman!" said Hemartius, "the daughter of the Ubar!"

"Very well," he said. He then removed his hand from Talena's hair and allowed her to straighten her body. He then freed her wrists, and tossed the cord to the side. He then guided her toward the heavy barred door, and the corridor beyond.

"Wait!" begged Hemartius.

The guard paused at the exit, turning back to face us, his right hand on the left arm of Talena.

"I must be given time to prepare a defense," called Hemartius.

"The court is prepared to proceed," said the guard.

"I am not!" said Hemartius.

"The trial begins tomorrow," said the guard, "at the Tenth Ahn."

"Who is the chief prosecutor?" I asked.

"Decius Albus," said the guard.

"Will the Ubar be in attendance?" I asked.

"Certainly," said the guard.

CHAPTER FIFTY-SIX

"What is this nonsense about being innocent until proven guilty?" asked Hemartius. "Surely you might be guilty before being found guilty, and might be guilty after you had been found not guilty."

"Legally innocent and legally guilty," I said, "which might be quite different from being actually innocent or guilty."

"What seems interesting to me," said Hemartius, "in your barbarian view of law, as you explain it to me, is the presumption of innocence. What sort of legal system would accept that as a presumption? Unless we suppose that judges, attorneys, courts, and such, are incompetent, or corrupt, a defendant would not have been charged and brought to trial in the first place, not unless there was a presumption of guilt. Thus, having been brought to trial is, in itself, evidence that one is presumably guilty. Else why bother with a trial, at all?"

"Systems differ," I said.

"That is true," said Hemartius, "even on Gor."

"Better," I said, "that one hundred guilty individuals go free than that one innocent person be punished."

"It must be dangerous to live in such a society," said Hemartius.

I saw little point in disagreeing with him, and he, I suppose, saw little point in disagreeing with me.

I think we would both agree that, whether or not one is actually innocent or actually guilty, the presumption of innocence favors the defendant. Contrariwise, whether or not one is actually innocent or actually guilty, the presumption of guilt favors the prosecution.

Personally, I favor the presumption of innocence. I have less confidence in the sobriety, diligence, perception, and honesty of the state than Hemartius. The individual has little enough protection against the inertia, weight, and might of the state. Too, in the state is power, and power is a prize commonly sought by the ambitious and unscrupulous. The state is not the individual's benign, trustworthy friend. It is a partisan establishment, infested with the venal and self-seeking, inventing goods and bads as they please, who will exploit it for their own gain and endeavor to remake it in their own image.

In these matters, however, I attempt to console myself, that systems do differ and, as Hemartius granted, even on Gor. Much, it seems, depends on the particular city and even, upon occasion, on the particular judge and court. One of the interesting aspects of Gorean society is the plethora of diverse municipalities, or city-states. In such a situation, one minimizes the dangers which inevitably accompany the rise of an inescapable, crushing tyranny, that of the monster state. Who could approve of such a state except those who wish to create it, guide it, and profit from its power?

CHAPTER FIFTY-SEVEN

"At least they are weary of calling for her blood," said Hemartius.

"Throats grow hoarse, fatigue sets in," I said.

It was the third day of the trial of Talena of Ar. Dozens of hostile witnesses, virulent in attitude and speech, had testified against her. Similarly, hundreds of documents had been entered into the court records, certified as uniformly negative. Indeed, these documents seem to have been selected with negativity in mind, and, apparently, they were the major source from which witnesses had been selected.

"How many death threats have you received today?" I asked.

"Seven," he said.

"That is far less than the sixty-two you received on the first day," I said.

"At this point," said Hemartius, "I may be on the brink of immortality."

The trial was being held in the Theater of Publius, a classic structure noted for its beauty and acoustics, with its orchestra area, currently overcrowded with jurors, not choruses and supporting assemblies of dancers; its deep, generous proscenium, or stage, on which famed artists and popular actors had performed, such as Andreas of Tor and Milo of Ar; and semi-circular banks of high tiers.

I glanced about the theater.

On the deep, broad stage of the theater, above and before the orchestra area housing the jury, were five things, the throne of the high judge, the table of the prosecution, the table of the defense, the dais of questioning, and the dock, a cage, in which the defendant was held. The tables of the prosecution and defense faced the throne of the high judge. The dais of questioning and the dock faced the orchestra area.

On the seat of the high judge, also facing the orchestra area, raised several feet in the air, that one must feel overshadowed, intimidated, and awed before it, so arranged that one must look upward to its lofty precincts as might a child to an adult, reposing in dark-robed splendor, suggesting the might, gravity, and solemnity of the law, was gigantic, bearded Marlenus of Ar himself. Although our eyes met from time to time I did not think, to my surprise, that he recognized me.

Interestingly, Pa-Kur, despite the previous outlawing of Assassins in Ar, was now not only seen publicly in Ar, but was now sitting behind the prosecutor's table, at the very side of Decius Albus. Who could ask for a better evidence of their collegiality? Surely this went far beyond the general amnesty which had been instituted in Ar to open her gates to criminals and exiles who might then bring the fugitive Ubara to Ar without fear for their own lives. But now Talena was in custody. Under these conditions should not the liberties of the amnesty have been promptly revoked? But they had not been. Why not? Why had Marlenus not acted in this matter? And what now, given the loss of two wagons laden with gold, might be the interest of Pa-Kur in the trial of Talena of Ar?

But did Marlenus truly not recognize me? This seemed odd to me. Yesterday evening I had mentioned the matter to Grendel.

Talena, as she had insisted, a demand which had been immediately welcomed by the court, was clad in the colorful, resplendent regalia of an upper-caste free woman, richly enhanced by loops of pearls and ropes of jewels, a flaunting of wealth and position which would have the effect of arousing the envy and hatred of the lower castes, members of which castes constituted the majority of the jurors, as much as if it had been designed to do so. She reclined gracefully, disdainfully, on a silken couch within the cage, exhibiting little interest in the proceedings, seemingly bored.

"She is witless," complained Hemartius. "With luck, were she suitably clothed in modest rags and appeared woefully, demonstrably contrite, shedding tears like fountains, I might have won her a limitation of the days of torture before her impalement."

"She wants to owe Ar nothing," I said.

How proud and splendid she was, I thought, a true upper-caste free woman of Gor. All she needs now is a slave switch.

One concession the court denied her was her demand to shield her features by veiling. To give the court its due, I do not think any bias was involved in this decision. It is common precedent to deny veiling to female defendants. Supposedly this is, first, to make the defendant more vulnerably recognizable, this to make escape, prisoner switches, and such less possible, and, second, to allow the judge and the jury to read what they can from the defendant's features. Is she telling the truth, is she lying, is she mocking the court, is she frightened, is she surly, and so on. One of the reasons, I am sure, that it took so long to apprehend Talena of Ar is that she could be personally identified, face to face, closely, by a relatively small number of individuals, say, some three or four hundred, or so. That also explains, one supposes, the large number of women who had been brought to Ar in chains on the speculation that they might be Talena.

It might be mentioned, in passing, that the principal reason Talena's dock in the trial was a cage was not to prevent her escape, but to protect her in case the jurors or the visitors in the tiers might attack her. Would it not be a grievous matter, even a legal tragedy, should the patient, meticulous barbarity of the justice of Ar be cheated of its victim?

I wondered if Marlenus was well.

I detected the presence of no Kurii in the theater, but I had little doubt that some, at least, were well apprised of the proceedings.

"It is strange that Marlenus of Ar does not seem to recognize you," had said Grendel, the night before, that after the second day of the trial.

"He has forgotten me, or is preoccupied," I had said.

"Perhaps," had said Grendel.

"Decius Albus builds a weighty case against our client," said Hemartius. "With each witness, one following another, each more dreadfully potent than the former, he draws together the cords of his net, ever more tightly."

"Certainly," I said, "he seems well versed in even the subtlest points of the law."

"He has the finest legal minds in Ar behind him," said Hemartius.

"All except one," I said. "Hemartius of Ar."

"Do not mock me, gentle friend," he said.

"I do not mock you," I said.

"Even were I a Centius of Cos or a Scormus of Ar of the law," he said, "I could do little with an impenitent, uncooperative, refractory client whose guilt is overwhelmingly, publicly manifest."

"I can do nothing with her," I said. "She is arrogant and resolute. She listens to no one. She is adamant. She despises me. She despises the jury. She despises Ar."

"She is Talena," said Hemartius.

"She is drunk on pride," I said

"She will be less lofty," he said, "when her flesh, day after day, is cut, burned, and torn, until she begs for the piercing pole yet denied her."

"How can Marlenus contemplate such a prospect?" I asked.

"He is Marlenus," he said.

"I call, as the next witness," intoned Decius Albus, "a noble Cosian, summoned from far Cos at much time, trouble, and expense, solely for the purpose of contributing his valued testimony to this trial, one to be recalled from the horrors of the Occupation, which he, in defiance of the false Ubara's will, strove mightily to mitigate, a secret friend, he who was present during the reign of the heinous traitress, Talena of Ar, Myron, polemarkos of Temos, polemarkos of Cos."

The receipt of this introduction, as might be supposed, was of a mixed nature, mostly an awed silence mingled with scattered hoots and jeers. Many, clearly, had not realized that any Cosians whatsoever were in Ar at present, especially any of note. Many, too, had not realized that any Cosians might have been summoned here to render testimony. Surely that seemed strange. And many, as well, had not realized that Myron, who had been the governor of the military power in Ar during the Occupation, was actually a secret friend endeavoring to reduce and palliate the tyranny of Talena of Ar, the outlaw Ubara.

I am sure that Myron lacked any animus toward Talena of Ar and would have preferred to leave Ar anonymously, quietly and in peace, but he had found himself issued, at the behest of Decius Albus, a summons to appear in court and render testimony. Had it been spurned, or had there been some failure to comply with the summons, I have little doubt that Decius Albus would have made patent the role of Cos in the apprehension of Talena.

As nearly as I could determine, Myron answered each question simply and directly, but carefully avoided providing the negative editorializing which Decius Albus was determined to elicit. To questions such as had Talena betrayed her Home Stone and treasonously surrendered Ar to foreign invaders, he would respond that such questions were beyond his purview. He, as a soldier, did his best to do his duty in a situation in which he found himself, and for which he disclaimed responsibility. His office was not to set policy, but to apply and execute it, to the best of his ability. Policy was the province of states, principally those of Cos and Ar.

"Of Lurius of Jad and Talena of Ar!" roared Decius Albus.

"Of Lurius of Jad and the governance of Ar," said Myron.

"Of Talena of Ar!" insisted Decius Albus.

"That is beyond my purview," said Myron.

"Surely you are aware," said Decius Albus, angrily, "that for months Ar was humiliated, mocked, degraded, and looted?"

"Yes," said Myron, "as would have been Telnus, and Jad, and Kasra, had Ar subdued Cos and Tyros."

It was the Gorean way.

"And were not many of the loveliest women of Ar," said Decius Albus, "collared, and put to the iron, to be taken to the islands or distributed amongst dozens of markets on the continent?"

"Certainly," said Myron, "as would have been those of Cos and Tyros had Ar been comparably victorious."

It is accepted universally on Gor that the women of a conquered enemy are loot, as much as gold, silver, ships, wagons, lands, harvests, other forms of livestock, and such.

"Did not you yourself," snarled Decius Albus, who was clearly displeased at the turn the examination had taken, "lead away the former Claudia Tentia Hinrabia, the daughter of the former Administrator of Ar, Minus Tentia Hinrabius, as a slave?"

"Certainly," said Myron, "and she is amongst the most delicious of my beasts."

Talena's laugh, as of approval and triumph, unrestrained, rang out from the prisoner's cage. It was she who, in vanity and petty spite, had had Claudia, one of her critics, and a supposed rival in beauty, enslaved. Such is well within the power of a Ubar or Ubara. Afterwards she had given Claudia to Myron.

"You are dismissed from the dais of questioning," said Decius Albus, curtly.

Myron, with dignity, if not contempt, withdrew from the dais of questioning. He left the stage amidst cries of hatred and vengeance from the tiers, and many jurors. To the side, he was joined by Captain Kasos, and some others.

"His testimony," said Hemartius, "did the prosecution little good."

"Nor little harm," I said.

"Do you think he will leave Ar alive?" asked Hemartius.

"Certainly," I said. "If nothing else, his sword will purchase his passage."

In looking about, at the low tiers, I saw Thurnock and Clitus. Elsewhere, to my surprise, I saw squat, homely Xenon, of Jad, and face-scarred Aetius, of Venna.

"Noble masters of the jury," said Decius Albus, "what must you gather from the insolent testimony of that arch-enemy of Ar, the Cosian scoundrel, Myron, of Jad, of Cos? You must gather searing memories of the horrors of the Occupation, when no coin was safe in its pot, no woman safe on the streets, no citizen safe in his bed. And to whom do we owe the torment, the tumult, and the insupportable miseries you endured, no, braved, in this terrible time?"

"Talena of Ar!" howled a thousand voices. "Talena of Ar!" came from the tiers.

"Yes, noble masters of the jury, yes, beloved fellow citizens of glorious, outraged Ar—Talena, Talena of Ar!"

Talena, in the prisoner's cage, in her rich raiment, in her jewels and pearls, on her silken couch, appeared to stifle a yawn.

"My client is an idiot," moaned Hemartius.

"Perhaps somewhat unwise," I said.

"Does she want a thousand extra tortures?" asked Hemartius.

"Talena," I said, "is not only a free woman of Gor, but the daughter of a Ubar. She is very proud. She was not raised, like some women on other worlds, in an allegedly democratic society, in which the pretense of equality is honored, even prescribed. She is bred into hierarchy, rank, and distance. It is part of the fiber of her being. She takes herself to be inordinately superior. So she has been taught. So she has been led to believe. She has been accustomed since girlhood, to look down on others, even holding others in contempt."

Well did I recall the Talena I had first met, long ago, on the night of Ar's Planting Feast, when I had seized the Home Stone of Ar, the Talena who boasted of using slaves as informants, the Talena who, as a free woman, thought nothing of putting them under the whip.

"I know the sort," said Hemartius. "They look down on mountains; they look down on stars."

"They come to a better judgment of their worth," I said, "when they find themselves on a slave block, stripped and auctioned."

On Gor, there is a chasm between the upper castes and the lower castes, and a thousand chasms between the free and the slave.

As I have observed occasionally, in a world where all are free, freedom means little. But on a world where some are free and some are slave, freedom means a great deal.

The transition from free to slave is easy for a girl of Earth. She quickly understands the change in her status, from free person to domestic animal. She quickly learns to kneel and kiss the feet of her master. She may learn it from the first stroke of a whip. It is appropriate; she is marked and her neck is in a collar. How quickly she begins, as a female, to revel in her submission! How she longed for that on Earth! How cruelly it had been denied to her! On the other hand, consider the radical, momentous transition from a robed, veiled, free woman of Gor, from the pinnacle of honor, position, status, and station in her society, to a marked, collared slave, a property to be used as her master wishes. Yet she, too, soon enough, rejoicing, learns the slave in the female of her.

"The next witness," announced Decius Albus, "is a hero of Ar, one beloved of all true citizens of our mighty city, he who single-handedly, at great personal risk, against all odds, recovered the Home Stone of Ar, and dared to restore it to us despite knowing himself beneath false charges of sedition and corruption, the noble, astute, and courageous Seremides of Ar!"

The tiers, for the most part, were at first silent. There was a tentative smattering of applause, the striking of the left shoulder with the right hand. Some voices, here and there, called out, "Long live Seremides! Hail, Seremides!" Two armsmen in the livery of the retinue of Decius Albus struck their spear blades on their shields.

But then a lone voice cried out, "No!" and then, after a time, several others, and then, suddenly, hundreds of voices rose up. "No!" they cried. "He is a traitor, a colleague of treasonous Talena. Seize him! Feed him to urts! Cast him to rabid sleen! To the impaling pole with him!"

Seremides, by two clerks of the court, was assisted to the dais of questioning. He seemed, at that time, frail and feeble. Who could not note that? Was he not harmless? Was he not to be pitied? Yet I knew that power, skill, and cunning lurked in that seemingly reduced and worn frame. The blow or jab of that stout crutch, the ost-like strike of his steel, had taught a number of foes the possible consequences of underestimating a foe.

Decius Albus put out his hands and spread them widely to calm, and then silence, the crowd.

Then the crowd was tense, but quiet.

"Noble citizens," he called. "Be patient, be tolerant. Let me call to your attention the true Seremides of Ar! It is not merely that the capital charges against him were cast aside in view of his service in restoring the Home Stone to a grateful Ar. No, upon inquiry, it was discovered that those charges were false to begin with. When the vain, ambitious, greedy Talena, in the tragic, but happily temporary, absence of our beloved Ubar, Marlenus, wrongly, illegally, usurped power in Ar, Seremides had to make a fateful decision. Should he resist the usurpation and be instantly banished or executed, or should he pretend collusion, and secretly fight for right, truth, law, and justice from within? He chose the latter and long labored for these ends. He was ever the archenemy of Talena of Ar, and did his best at all times and opportunities to oppose and frustrate her wicked designs."

I leaned over to Hemartius. "Decius Albus," I said, "was a principal in the scheme of stealing the Home Stone of Ar, in order to collect the ransom for its return, the same gold that was to be awarded for the capture and delivery of Talena to Ar. I suspect he would rather cut the throat of Seremides than praise him."

Hemartius turned pale.

I looked up to the judge's throne. Marlenus seemed distracted, or inattentive. There was little in his passive mien to remind me of the Marlenus with whom I was familiar, alert like a larl, keen-eyed like a tarn, as subtle and dangerous as a prowling sleen, the sort of man for whom scepters are formed. Last night, as mentioned, I had commented on this sort of thing to Grendel. "What are you thinking of?" I had asked him. "Of something once encountered," he said, "long ago, on the steel world of Agamemnon."

"Are you comfortable, noble Seremides?" asked Decius Albus.

"Thank you for the chair furnished by the court," said Seremides, weakly.

This had been provided by one of the attending clerks.

"It is the least one can do," said Decius Albus, "for one who has done so much for Ar."

Most witnesses stood on the dais of questioning, on which the examiner also stood.

"You were at one time, were you not," said Decius Albus, "First Sword in the Taurentian guards?"

"Yes," said Seremides, "long ago when I was whole and strong."

"Many once regarded you as one of the finest swordsmen on Gor," said Decius Albus.

"I was then whole and strong," he said.

"How poignant then," said Decius Albus, "to see you now, so crippled, so reduced and fallen."

Seremides seemed to wipe a tear from his eye.

"Forgive me," said Decius Albus, sympathetically.

I smiled to myself. Seremides was still formidable. It could be death to come within the ambit of his steel.

"Given your handicap and frailty, and in the light of your service to the state," said Decius Albus, "we shall be brief."

Seremides inclined his head, as in a brief moment of gratitude, and then raised it, bravely.

"You stood high in the rogue regime of the traitress, Talena of Ar," said Decius Albus.

"Yes," said Seremides, "in order that I might labor to oppose and overthrow it."

A laugh came from Talena.

"The prisoner will be quiet," said Decius Albus.

"Please, Lady," begged Hemartius.

Again Talena laughed.

"Please, Lady," said Hemartius. "Respect the dignity of the court. You do your case no good by such outbursts."

"It will be easy enough to tie and gag you," said Decius Albus, "or, if you prefer, you may continue to contribute to the proceedings, stripped."

"No, noble counselor!" cried Hemartius. "The defendant is a free woman!"

But women in the tiers cried out in delight, "Away with her clothes! Make her as a slave! Strip her! Give us her robes and adornments! Punish her with exposure and shame, more to be dreaded than needles and hot irons!"

Talena drew back in the cage, terrified. I had not hitherto observed the former Ubara so shaken. I was pleased to see that beneath the commonly proud, insolent, haughty demeanor of the prisoner there was a vulnerable woman, who sensed how fully and easily she might find herself at the complete mercy of men. I thought that

Talena might look well, on her knees, naked, her lovely neck closely encircled with a locked metal collar, mine.

"Noble witness," said Decius Albus, turning back to Seremides, "is it true that Talena of Ar, with unjustified intent and malicious calculation, exploiting her relationship to a missing Ubar, usurped his throne and proclaimed herself Ubara? Is it true that this same Talena of Ar dishonored the medallion of office and, far worse, betrayed her own Home Stone? Is it true that she opened the gates of Ar to foreign enemies, that she presided over the dismantling of the walls of Ar to the music of flute girls, walls now happily rebuilt, that she condoned the ravaging of Ar by alien troops, that she reveled in the humiliation and degradation of her own city by heartless occupying forces? Is it true, as well, that she used her power as Ubara to satisfy a thousand personal grudges and spites, in many cases, consigning women who were allegedly her rivals in beauty or influence, or women whom it was thought might harbor reservations as to her person, reign, or policies, to the collar? And is it true that she, under the name of Ludmilla of Ar, organized brothels in which many former free women of Ar, reduced to slavery, must hope to well and completely satisfy the lusts of any customer with a coin to spare, or know the lash, brothels by means of which she not only satisfied petty grievances but enriched herself? I ask you, noble witness, are not these things true, and a thousand others, comparable or worse?"

"Certainly," said Seremides, "all that you say is true, and more."

"Thus," said Decius Albus, "Talena of Ar is an enemy of the state and an archcriminal, fittingly to be surrendered to the talons of the Tarns of Justice."

"Certainly," said Seremides.

"Is it true," asked Decius Albus, "that you can personally and unerringly identify the culprit, Talena of Ar?"

"Yes," said Seremides.

"Now, noble patriot of Ar, please turn to the dock, to the prisoner cage, and look upon the prisoner, now unveiled," said Decius Albus.

"I do so," said Seremides.

"Is the prisoner Talena of Ar?" asked Decius Albus.

"Yes," said Seremides.

"You are certain?" asked Decius Albus.

"Yes," said Seremides.

There were cheers from the stands, and even, here and there, from amongst the jurors, as well.

"Thank you," said Decius Albus. He then gestured to the two clerks of the court, who were at hand. "Please assist our noble witness from the dais of examination."

Then, arduously, apparently painfully, even with the aid of the two clerks, Seremides descended the dais of examination, and left the stage.

Our eyes met during this exit, and he shrugged.

"I do not think Seremides bears Talena any ill will," I said to Hemartius.

"His testimony is the capstone of the prosecution's case," said Hemartius. "I do not see how it can be overcome."

"It is merely that he wishes to leave Ar alive," I said.

"Now," said Decius Albus, "we wait humbly upon the decision of our beloved Ubar, Marlenus, the voice of law in Ar, to adjourn the court until tomorrow at the Tenth Ahn."

The voice of Marlenus seemed listless, and dull. "The court," he said, "is adjourned until tomorrow at the Tenth Ahn."

The crowd began to find its way to the exits. Jurors filed from the orchestra area. Those involved with the court began gathering their papers and taking their leave. I looked up to the stands. Clitus and Thurnock were withdrawing. I would join them later at the Silver Tarsk. Guards came to return Talena to her cell in the Cylinder of Justice. They put shackles on her slim ankles and braceleted her hands behind her back. She lifted her head, contemptuously, and was conducted from the stage. She was again the Talena I knew, the haughty free woman of Gor. I no longer saw Aetius of Venna or Xenon. Pa-Kur, in exiting, looked back at me, and smiled.

"Tomorrow," said Hemartius, "we will have our say."

"Why did you not examine the witnesses for the prosecution?" I asked.

"Given the nature of the case," said Hemartius, "the court ruled that it was unnecessary."

"And thus it was forbidden?" I said.

"In deference to the jury," he said, "as it was feared some jurors might be confused, this jeopardizing the integrity of the trial."

"We would not want that to happen," I said.

"The court was clear on the matter," he said.

"This is not a trial," I said.

"It is theater," said Hemartius, disconsolately.

"But theater that pretends to be a trial," I said. "Can we not capitalize on that pretense? Is that not our only hope, to rewrite the ending of the play?"

"I see no hope," said Hemartius.

"Fight then all the more desperately, without hope," I said.

"I know my codes," he said.

"Do not let Talena testify," I said. "She will condemn herself a thousand times out of her own mouth."

"I cannot forbid it," he said. "And the court readily obliged her."

"In any event," I said, "tomorrow we present our defense."

"What defense?" said Hemartius.

CHAPTER FIFTY-EIGHT

"Noble jurors, fair-minded, dispassionate, and objective jurors, and citizens of Ar generally, who in a sense are jurors, as well," said Hemartius, "I shall attempt to appeal, in my small, inadequate way, to your legendary common sense and good judgment, renowned on Gor. I trust such things. I know I can rely on you in all such matters."

This preamble was met with a rumble of disapproval and suspicion.

"First, however," he said, "let me commend the prosecution for its diligent and sedulous accumulation of data, prepared carefully over months. Its case is indeed forceful and eloquent. Let us salute, as well, the dozens of witnesses it marshaled, each sober and unbiased, each by their testimony doing their best to fairly and helpfully illuminate the matters at hand. Finally, let me congratulate our valued, skilled friend, yours and mine, and Ar's, the noble Decius Albus, a man with a marvelous legal mind, and the trade advisor to our beloved Ubar, Marlenus, for his brilliant work on behalf of the state. Few, if any, I am sure, could construct so weighty and compelling a case against a client, in this case, unfortunately, mine."

As Hemartius had begun to speak, Decius Albus seemed wary, but was soon beaming with pleasure. The last sentence of Hemartius's remarks elicited a predictable laugh from Decius Albus, the jurors, and crowd, and seemed, in its way, to the satisfaction of all, to concede defeat.

"But," said Hemartius, "even a legal edifice of considerable proportion, one raised by the most powerful and brilliant of legal minds, must be founded on an assumption, and should that assumption prove false, that edifice must be not only irrelevant to the issues involved but must crumble of its own weight."

"Beware!" cried Decius Albus.

"In this case, the false assumption involved is that my client, gentle, innocent, sweet, shy Talena of Ar, was personally responsible for the crimes committed in her name. Guilt here is miserably misplaced."

"No!" cried Decius Albus, springing to his feet.

"My client," said Hemartius, "as I shall prove, is totally innocent."

Here there was laughter and hooting from the jurors and crowd. Decius Albus, contented, resumed his seat.

"Consider, Jurors, with your free and open minds, my client was little more than a simple, naive child, little more than a simple, naive girl, totally ignorant of statecraft, lovingly sheltered and protected within the Central Cylinder, when, in the crisis resulting from the unexplained absence of her loving father, Marlenus, she was unwittingly drawn into political intrigues far beyond her ken. She became a figurehead for plans and polices, even schemes, she could not understand. She was the innocent image, the justifying credential, in the name of which criminality reigned. She was assured that all was well, even as invading forces marched into the streets of Ar. The horrors of the Occupation were concealed from her. Her only error was a natural one, one natural for an innocent waif such as she, to rely on others, others who, in this case, harbored a vile, undisclosed agenda. Ela, she trusted conspirators, acting as they advised."

"Let me understand this," said Decius Albus. "Your point is that Talena was stupid, and duped?"

"That she was naive, innocent, and misguided, through no fault of her own," said Hemartius.

"I call upon the defendant to testify," said Decius Albus.

"No!" said Hemartius.

"The court has ruled on its propriety," said Decius Albus.

Talena came to the front of the prisoner cage, grasping the bars. "I am not naive," she cried, angrily. "I am Talena, daughter of Marlenus! I was Ubara! I am not stupid! How dare you insult me, I, of high blood, who ruled as Ubara! I am not stupid! I was not duped!"

"But, noble jurors, esteemed colleague, Decius Albus, and revered fellow citizens of Ar, all," said Hemartius, "this merely informs us that a darker explanation for the conduct of my client must be sought. Well do we know of the effect of chemicals on the human body and mind, how the will can be paralyzed and the body subdued, and we know, as well, the power some men have over the behavior of others, by means of suggestion or soothing speech. Have we not witnessed performers inducing strange effects in others, convincing one fellow he is a tarn and another that he is a tarsk?"

That is it, I thought, some such effect, chemically or hypnotically, has been wrought upon Marlenus of Ar! How else explain the lethargy, the passivity, afflicting that mighty frame? I now conjectured that Grendel might have suspected that, last night. What had he seen before, long ago, on the steel world of Agamemnon?

"Cease your absurd babbling!" screamed Talena from the cage. "I will not stand for being demeaned. I was subject to no sinister or arcane influence! I knew what I was doing, and I did what I wanted to do. And I did it well, superbly! I had been humiliated and dishonored! When the opportunity arose, in the absence of the Ubar, I did what I did, consciously and rationally, and I would do it again. A thousand times! I wanted vengeance, and, I assure you, I took it! I assure you that I was at all times in the full command of my free and untrammeled senses."

Decius Albus laughed, and I thought I saw, even on the face of Pa-Kur, something like a smile, a cruel smile.

Hemartius threw me a despairing glance.

I clenched my fist and lifted it, slightly, from the table. In this way, in the Gorean way, I encouraged him to be strong and persevere.

"If it pleases the court," said Hemartius, "in view of the uncontrolled outbursts of my client, and her apparent disregard for her own welfare, I must revise my defense. I do so. I now call attention to, and plead, an extenuating circumstance, in the light of which she is absolved from all responsibility for her actions, namely, mental derangement, insanity."

"Very clever, dear colleague," said Decius Albus, "but, I fear, unavailing."

"How unavailing?" asked Hemartius.

"She has shown no signs of mental imbalance or difficulty until the trial, even if now, and her actions in question well precede the trial. She was fully and indisputably in possession of her senses when she committed the crimes for which she is charged. Further, current insanity does not mitigate past guilt, nor should it, nor does it, in Gorean law, modify due punishment."

"But the condition might have existed and affected her behavior long before becoming manifest," said Hemartius.

"Speculations without evidence are legally immaterial," said Decius Albus.

"But she might not even understand for what she is being punished," said Hemartius.

"It is enough that we and the law understand it," said Decius Albus. "Also, in your forlorn attempt to rescue a lost cause, you should, at least, have better tutored your client in the semblance of insanity. Her acting, if acting it is, is surely unconvincing."

"May I speak?" asked Talena quietly, soberly.

"Be silent," said Hemartius, "if only for the sake of the Priest-Kings."

"By all means, face-bared female, speak," said Decius Albus.

"First," said Talena, "my face is not bared by choice. I have been denied the dignity of facial veiling by a ruling of the court. Consider then the shame of a free woman whose stunning facial beauty, a thousand times superior to that of a slave, not just mine, is callously exposed, against her will, to the casual scrutiny of the vulgar, a beauty which may be looked upon then by low-caste scum, such as those here, and on the jury, a beauty which is subject even to the gaze of foreigners, and strangers, which is open to the perusal of coarse, vile, power-mad urts such as Decius Albus, one who is unworthy to even look upon the Home Stone of Ar, let alone touch it, hold it, or kiss it!"

"Lady!" protested Hemartius.

"Let her speak," said Decius Albus, amused. "Meanwhile, let the impaling spear be polished."

"Second," said Talena, "I am not insane, and have never been, now or at any other time, and I have made no effort now, or at any other time, to betray myself, to insult myself, by feigning insanity. I assure the prosecutor, the honorable Decius Albus, the pompous urt, that, if I chose to feign insanity, I would have done so in such a way as to convince not only him but the most skilled diagnosticians and analysts in the green caste. I acknowledge it has been difficult for me, upon occasion, to restrain from what might be termed outbursts. But in such instances I recommend that you blame not me but yourselves for conducting yourselves, and this trial, in so stupid and farcical a fashion that a tharlarion might shake with laughter, a tarn gasp in astonishment, an ost forget to strike."

"That is enough, Lady," said Hemartius.

"Be quiet,Counselor," demanded Decius Albus.

"That all might be clearly understood," said Talena, "understand that I did all that I did by informed choice. I, despite being Talena of Ar and the daughter of Marlenus of Ar, of high lineage and station, had been betrayed and grievously wronged. I yearned for vengeance, a vengeance to which I had a right. Then my stern father, Marlenus, disappeared somewhere in the Voltai Mountains. The throne of Ar was bereft of an occupant. Anarchy must not ensue. The throne must have its occupant. Who had birth and station commensurate with the height of so lofty an office? Who but Talena of Ar? I was freed from an onerous and undeserved sequestration. Who then could be so deaf as not to hear the blaring of the trumpet of opportunity? Elevated to the throne, I spread the wings of my vengeance. I was at last truly Talena of Ar, the Talena of whom, in my long, lonely sequestration, I had dreamed. My enemies lay at my feet, at my mercy. I was supreme in Ar! I was Ubara!"

"The prosecution rests its case," said Decius Albus.

The jury and the tiers were silent.

"Remove the prisoner to her cell in the Central Cylinder," said Decius Albus. Guards then, after shackling and back-braceleting the prisoner, conducted her from the stage.

Finally Hemartius spoke. "I have little to say," he said. "I grieve. I have failed my client. I would only urge the jury to consider an obvious truth. Lady Talena, whatever may have been her motivations and her actions in these dark matters, was only a single person. She, no more than any other Ubar, Ubara, Tatrix, Administrator, or such, rules alone. Always there are others, often unseen. There must be those who advise; those who incite; those who suggest and propose; those who follow; those who accompany and abet; those who transmit orders and those who carry out orders. Talena of Ar could no more alone have wrought tragedy on Ar than she could have moved the Voltai range with a command or uprooted giant Tur trees with her bare hands. Therefore, I beg of you not to visit upon her slender, fair shoulders more than they can justly bear. When honey is available, urts will find it and lap it up. So it is in dark times. The history of the war and the Occupation is rampant with theft, brutality, corruption, and profiteering. Such was wrought by hundreds, both citizens and strangers. Do not ascribe it all to Talena of Ar."

"Thank you, Counselor," said Decius Albus. "Your point is well taken. Many, of course, who consorted with the enemy and exploited the city were, as you know, apprehended and punished, often by impalement. And many who were proscribed fled and are still at large. Indeed, earlier we had thought, mistakenly, that Seremides of Ar was one of those. We need now only for our jury to render its correct and righteous verdict, guilty, namely, that Talena of Ar was implicated in such crimes. That is sufficient. We need not even recognize that she was, as she obviously was, the most heinously guilty of all the traitors and strangers who degraded and looted our beloved Ar."

Hemartius turned about, disconsolately, and rejoined me, seating himself behind the table for the defense.

"I am sorry," he said.

"You did well," I said.

"Noble jurors," said Decius Albus. "You may retire to consider your verdict."

"Guilty! Guilty now!" cried hundreds of the jurors. "Guilty!" cried hundreds in the stands.

"No, dear fellow citizens," said Decius Albus, holding up his hand. "Do not be hasty! Let not the Tarns of Justice descend too eagerly! You must deliberate, carefully, patiently, thoughtfully, and earnestly, before rendering a verdict."

"No!" cried many in the orchestra area and in the tiers. "No need! Guilty! Guilty! Guilty now!"

"But," said Decius Albus, "the fires are not yet lit, the irons are not yet red, let alone white. The knives must be sharpened, the needles and splinters aligned, the vials of dripping acid are not yet filled. After the verdict is rendered, tomorrow, then the weeks, the months, of torture, may begin."

This information seemed to content the jury and the tiers.

"Now," said Decius Albus, "we await the word of our high judge, master of law, paragon of justice, Marlenus, Ubar of Glorious Ar."

"The court," said Marlenus, slowly, carefully, "will reconvene tomorrow, at the Tenth Ahn."

The jurors and the crowd then, apparently looking forward to the morrow, began, in good spirits, to leave the theater.

"Behold the Ubar," whispered Hemartius.

"The session has been long," I said. "He may be tired. Perhaps he is ill, or worse."

I did not confide my suspicion to Hemartius that Marlenus might be under some malign influence, say, a foreign substance or some form of mind control.

"He does not seem so tired," said Hemartius. "It is more as though he were struggling to awaken, to throw off sleep."

"I think you are right," I said.

Marlenus slowly shook his long-haired, bearded head.

I saw Decius Albus gesture to the stands.

Xenon then ascended to the stage from a low tier, climbed to the bench of the Ubar and, from a small medicinal goblet, tendered him a draught of some liquid.

"The Ubar is being drugged," I said.

"Surely being administered medicine," said Hemartius. "He has not seemed well for days. I have seen this twice before."

"It is done naturally, subtly, inconspicuously," I said. "One scarcely sees it being done."

"I saw it twice," said Hemartius. "But I assume it would normally be administered before court, before the Ubar ascends to the bench or after he leaves the court."

I did not doubt but what that was true. This afternoon, however, Marlenus had seemed restless, perhaps unexpectedly so, beneath the influence to which he had been subjected. Decius Albus had then gestured to the stands, a movement to which Xenon had responded.

"Who moves so, visible but invisible?" I said.

"I do not understand," said Hemartius.

"Who is in the room, or crowd, or on the street, but not noticed?" I asked.

"I do not understand," said Hemartius.

"Who is there but, if one is not alert, or not looking for him, or not expecting him, might not be seen, might not be noticed?"

"I do not understand," said Hemartius.

"Who can move in such a way?" I asked.

"I am sure I do not know," said Hemartius.

"An Assassin," I said.

Hemartius gathered together some papers, ordered them, evened the edges, and placed them in his scribe's kit.

"We need not be here on the morrow," he said. "There is no need for us. Everything is done. The destined, foregone conclusion has been reached."

"We will be here," I said.

"I do not care to watch torture," said Hemartius.

"We will be here at the Tenth Ahn," I said.

"If you wish," said Hemartius.

CHAPTER FIFTY-NINE

"What you say," said Grendel, "confirms my suspicions. I shall visit what you call the Beast Caves tonight."

"It is too dangerous," I said.

"I shall take my ax," he said.

"What can you do?" I asked.

"Kurii often take me, uncritically, as one of their own, and the Beast Caves are now denizened, perhaps entirely, by adherents of Lord Agamemnon. Further, Kurii tend to be vain and proud, and, while wary of humans, they think little of speaking freely before their like."

"I know nothing of what your monstrous friend contemplates," said Hemartius, "but if it is dangerous and pertains to the trial, I beg you, succeed in dissuading him, for the trial, for all practical purposes, for all but routine details, is concluded. Things there are done. I confess my failure. Decius Albus has won. We have lost. Talena is lost."

"I am not sure that all is lost," I said.

"I see no hope," said Hemartius.

"What are you doing tonight?" I asked.

"Getting drunk," he said.

"Do not," I said.

"Why not?" he asked.

"You have not drunk for days," I said. "I assure you, kal-da is doing quite well without you."

"It is an old friend," he said.

"One who lies to you and intends you no good," I said.

"A little," he said, "for medicinal purposes."

"He who is well," I said, "does not need medicine."

"There is no harm in kal-da," he said.

"What does not hurt Marcus," I said, "may injure Quintus."

"The case is lost," he said.

"I am not sure of that," I said.

"The quiver is empty," he said. "There are no more arrows."

"Then," I said, "we shall have recourse to a different quiver."

"It is getting late," said Grendel. "I am leaving."

"We wish you well," I said.

I suspected his intention.

"I, too, should leave," said Hemartius.

"Sleep well," I said. "Law is subtle and filled with bluff and ambiguity. I want your mind tomorrow to be unclouded and well rested."

"And devious and inventive?" he asked.

"Quite possibly," I said.

"What are you going to do, and where are you going?" he asked.

"I am going to call on Seremides," I said.

"To kill him?" asked Hemartius.

"No," I said.

"He was the crowning witness for the prosecution," said Hemartius.

"He testified in his own best interest," I said. "I do not think he much cares whether Talena lives or dies. Indeed, I suspect, as a man, given her marvelous beauty, he would prefer for her to live."

"That beauty will not last long, sustaining tortures," said Hemartius.

"Seremides and I, and another," I said, "are not really strangers to one another. We endured time, hardships, and perils together."

"Beware of him," said Hemartius.

"You do not know him as well as I," I said. "Aside from being mendacious, dishonest, ruthless, venal, untrustworthy, and treacherous, he is not a bad fellow."

"I didn't realize that," said Hemartius. "I am pleased to hear it."

"One does not look for perfection in a human being," I said.

"Of course not," he said, "unless one is a free woman."

"When did you begin to overindulge in kal-da?" I asked.

"That is not important," he said.

"Seremides," I said, "as having status as a witness for the prosecution, can go places and do things I cannot."

"But what if he does not care to do so?" asked Hemartius.

"I must then convince him that it is in his best interest to do so." I slapped the scabbard at my side.

"He is also highly intelligent, I trust," said Hemartius.

"That helps," I said.

We then wished one another well, and parted.

This conversation took place near the Garden of the Hinrabians, on South Market Street, not far from the Golden Tospit, a small kal-da shop, past the portal of which I had hurried a rather dispirited Hemartius.

CHAPTER SIXTY

It was not difficult to call on Seremides, for he persisted in sharing the small basement apartment in the Metellan district with Iris and myself. In sketching his attributes to Hemartius, I had forgotten to add in the virtue, or vice, depending on one's view, of thrift.

"I am pleased," he said, "that you did not come back to kill me."

"I thought about it," I said.

"Not seriously, I trust," he said. "It would have been frowned on by your codes."

"You keep track of such things," I said.

"Sometimes it behooves one to do so," he said.

"Where is Iris?" I asked.

"Shopping," he said.

"I do not think you are in regular attendance at the trial," I said. I had not noticed him in the stands.

"No," he said. "I think that the less Decius Albus sees of me the better."

"You served him well enough on the dais of examination," I said.

"And less well," said he, "in the business of the Home Stone."

"Aetius and Xenon, our old friends," I said, "attend."

"I suspect there is little danger in their doing so," he said.

"I wish for you to attend," I said.

"I become apprehensive," he said.

"The trial goes badly," I said. "Talena is in great danger."

"I would suppose so," he said.

"It is expected that the verdict will be officially rendered tomorrow, and the tortures will begin."

"So soon?" he said.

"Yes," I said.

"The Tarns of Justice fly swiftly," he said.

"You and Talena," I said, "were colleagues in crime and treachery."

"As were others," he said.

"You are fortunate not to be the defendant in a similar trial," I said.

"True," he said. "But the charges were dropped. I am no longer proscribed. Recall the matter of the restored Home Stone."

"It is not far from my mind," I said.

"I feared so," he said.

"Do you bear Talena ill will?" I asked.

"Certainly not," he said.

"Yet you testified against her, damagingly, abundantly and severely," I said.

"Decius Albus wished it so," he said. "I thought it judicious to comply."

"I find it ironic," I said, "that Talena's most formidable accuser should be a former associate, whose crimes equaled if not exceeded hers."

"Life," he said, "has its ironies, as well as its opacities, ambiguities, and ambivalences."

"It is expected," I said, "that Talena will be subjected to days, perhaps weeks or months, of torture, followed by a prolonged execution."

"Sometimes," he said, "the Tarns of Justice fly slowly."

"What do you think of Talena?" I asked.

"She is stupid," he said. "She thought she would be safe in the keeping of Lurius of Jad."

"What else?" I asked.

"She is vain, selfish, greedy, haughty, proud, arrogant, impatient, outspoken, critical, and headstrong."

"A typical Gorean free woman, of high caste?" I said.

"No," he said. "She is weak."

"How so?" I asked.

"At the Skerry of Lars, near Port Kar," he said, "we were awaiting the arranged ship which would carry us to Jad in Cos. We had arrived at the skerry in a small, discreet, canopied boat, having recently escaped from the holding of Bosk of Port Kar. Under the canopy, we had two comely slave girls, bound hand and foot, and gagged, completely helpless. These two slave girls were Euphrosyne and Zia, by both of whom Talena had been grievously displeased. Taken to Cos, assuming Talena would be honored and protected, they would have found themselves at her mercy, as her serving slaves, a frightening, miserable fate indeed. Talena asked me for a knife. I gave her my knife. She would show the errant slaves what it might be to displease a free woman! I gathered that some punitive scarring would not satisfy her severe rancor and that she intended to express her displeasure with the two slaves by cutting off their ears and noses. Yet, despite her having been seriously vexed with the two slaves, she used the knife not to cut off their ears and noses but to free them of their gags and bonds, permitting them, when they fled, to escape being shipped to Cos."

"She showed mercy," I said.

"Weakness," said Seremides. "She might as well have been a slave herself. She is unworthy to be a free woman. I despise weakness."

"But other than her weakness and stupidity," I said, "I gather that you bear her no ill will."

"No," he said. "I have seen her in a slave tunic, and she might make a passable kajira."

"Merely passable?" I said.

"Perhaps better than passable," he said.

"If she could be saved," I said, "you would not object?"

"No," he said, "she would look well on a chain."

"If she heard you say that," I said, "she would attack you, physically."

"That does not alter the fact," said Seremides, "that she would still look well on a chain."

"I think," I said, "that there might be a chance of saving Talena."

"You are mad," he said. "Has not the case of Hemartius collapsed? Is the verdict not to be rendered momentarily? Are the irons not being heated, the knives whetted, the needles and splinters arranged, the acids measured? Can you carry away a prisoner cage? Can you melt iron and break through walls? Have you a way to deflect quarrels and arrows? Have you discovered a way to fend the blows of dozens of spears and axes? Do you not realize that Talena, now unveiled, could be recognized by thousands?"

"I have a friend," I said. "You would doubtless see him as a Kur. His name, in Gorean, is Grendel."

"So?" said Seremides.

"Tonight," I said. "He is going to the Beast Caves. I think I know his purpose."

"Excellent," said Seremides. "I am sure I do not."

"Did you notice Marlenus at the trial?" I asked.

"One could not help but do so," he said.

"Did he seem different to you?" I asked.

"I was never well acquainted with Marlenus," said Seremides, "even before he disappeared somewhere in the Voltai."

"Did he seem normal to you?" I asked.

"His mind seemed elsewhere," said Seremides.

"Or trammeled," I said.

"What has all this to do with me, or you, or Talena?" he asked.

"I think Xenon respects you," I said.

"He is a fool," said Seremides.

"You never managed to betray him," I said.

"There was no reason to do so," said Seremides. "And he betrayed us. He is an Assassin."

"He did not betray us," I said. "He just did not inform us."

"He may respect you," said Seremides. "He did not kill you, when you posed a threat to the theft of the Home Stone."

"That, too, I think, is important," I said.

"To what destination, if any, tends all this?" asked Seremides.

"On the voyage from the Skerry of Lars to Jad," I said, "there was an incident."

"When I supposedly intervened to save Xenon's life, after a supposed indiscretion on his part, brushing the sleeve of Talena's robes, or such."

"Yes," I said.

"It later became clear that the incident was arranged, as a trick to induce me to accept Xenon, a spy, as a devoted and trustworthy ally."

"Nonetheless you thought the intervention meaningful at the time," I said, "and I think that Xenon, for some reason, never forgot that. Had the situation been genuine, you would have saved his life. Some men do not forget such a thing."

"I had a use for him," said Seremides.

"Nonetheless," I said.

"Xenon is powerful," said Seremides, "but he is also short and ugly. I do not even think he has been taught the Second Knowledge."

"Yet," I said, "we accepted him. We did not mock him. We treated him as one of us, and he was one with us. With us he endured many hardships and dangers. Some men do not forget such things."

"You want me to contact Xenon, to enlist him in some project?" asked Seremides.

"Listen carefully," I said. I then explained to Seremides what I had in mind.

After a bit, Iris returned from shopping.

"Masters are here," she said, pleasantly, putting down her sack of edibles. "A girl is pleased. What did Masters have to say to one another?"

"Nothing," I said.

CHAPTER SIXTY-ONE

"It is the Ninth Ahn," I said.

"We are early," said Hemartius.

"I am popular in Ar, am I not?" I asked.

"Who could be more popular?" asked Hemartius. "You released wagons laden with gold to a scrambling multitude. Certainly one who is responsible for the distribution, however haphazard, of ten thousand tarn disks of gold, tarn disks of double weight, amongst a population, into a greedy crowd, is not likely to be despised. Had Seremides of Ar done so, I suspect that even he would be regarded more leniently. Even fellows with bloody heads and broken bones sing your praises. You did not even have to organize and sponsor games and races."

"Good," I said.

"Why do you ask?" he asked.

"Some of the jurors are returning," I said.

"They are eager," said Hemartius.

"Why is there a thousand men on the jury?" I asked.

"To reduce bias and eliminate prejudice," said Hemartius. "Too, who could afford to bribe a thousand-man jury?"

"I see," I said.

In a sense, I suspected that I had done my best.

"Too, it is a nice round number," said Hemartius.

"Why are there no women on the jury?" I asked.

"To ensure impartiality," said Hemartius.

"Women might have reservations about Talena?" I said.

"Quite possibly," said Hemartius.

"The men were calling for her blood," I said.

"Yes, but impartially," said Hemartius.

To my unease, I observed clerks of the court mount the stage and begin to ignite braziers and lay out implements and devices of torture.

I saw Thurnock and Clitus arrive, and take their seats in a low tier on the long semicircular stone bench.

We gave no sign that we knew one another.

"The verdict has not yet been officially rendered," I said, "and already the clerks are setting forth the paraphernalia of pain."

"It saves time," said Hemartius.

"What is going on there in the stands," I asked, "with the free women?"

"Each free woman who requests it is being given a numbered ostracon," said Hemartius. "Later a hundred ostraka will be drawn from a bowl."

"For what purpose?" I asked.

"The winners may participate in the torture of the prisoner," said Hemartius.

"That is dreadful," I said.

"Not every winner," said Hemartius, "will choose to exercise that privilege."

"Good," I said.

"They will auction off their winning ostrakon to the highest bidder," said Hemartius.

"Oh," I said.

"Look," said Hemartius. "There is Seremides."

"Yes," I said.

"I did not think he cared to attend," said Hemartius.

"He changed his mind," I said.

Shortly thereafter Xenon appeared, and took a seat some feet from Seremides.

"It is my hope that all went well," I said to Hemartius.

"That what went well?" asked Hemartius.

"Nothing," I said. "Do you think that Marlenus has been administered his medicine?"

"Presumably," said Hemartius.

Given the fine acoustics of the theater of Publius, I could easily hear numbers being called out as ostraka, toward the rear of the orchestra area, were being extracted from a large bowl by a blindfolded little girl. Here and there in the stands, as a number would be called out by a clerk of the court, there was a cry of delight from one or another free woman.

Aetius made his appearance, taking a seat near Thurnock and Clitus. He had, after all, shared the project and adventure of retrieving the Home Stone of Ar from the Beast Caves. Indeed, without his presence, I am sure we would have failed to succeed in that endeavor.

"I hear shouting outside, cries of disappointment, of frustration, of anger," I said.

"People are being turned away," said Hemartius.

"I am not sorry that they might be disappointed," I said.

"Tarn races are more popular," said Hemartius.

A number of women were being guided down from the tiers to take a position rather toward the back of the orchestra area. These

were the winners in the contest of ostraka. The bowl had been removed, and the little girl, her blindfold removed, had been carried
somewhere to the side.

There was a rustle of interest in the tiers and attention was directed toward one of the side entrances to the theater.

"The party of the prosecution arrives," said Hemartius.

"Decius Albus, looks pleased," I said. He was graciously making his way toward the stage, raising his hand upon occasion and
exchanging words here and there. At his side, somber and reticent,
in a sable tunic and long black cloak, was tall, spare Pa-Kur, with
his grayish skin and eyes like glass, Master of the Caste of Assassins.
These two men were accompanied by some scribes of the law and
clerks of the court.

"The Assassin frightens me," said Hemartius.

"Justifiably," I said. "He is one of the most powerful and dangerous men on Gor. His power would be the envy of many Ubars. His
tentacles unite a hundred Black Courts. His word can lift a knife in
Schendi and speed a quarrel in Kassau. In the black dagger, unrestrained by city walls and common codes, resides much power."

"The laws of a city often stop at its pomerium," said Hemartius.
"Were it not for the Black Caste many wrongs could not be righted.
Sometimes gold can buy not only retribution but justice."

"Gold is indifferent as to what it buys," I said.

"The party of the prosecution takes its seats," said Hemartius.

"Pa-Kur is privy to the ambitions and intrigues of Decius Albus
and was instrumental in the theft of the Home Stone," I said, "but I
do not see his role here."

"Perhaps," said Hemartius, "he does not understand yours, and
that explains his."

A shiver passed though me.

"Are you cold?" asked Hemartius.

"Only for a moment," I said.

"Behold," said Hemartius. "Talena."

She was conducted forth by four guards.

Jeers and threats, and some laughter, greeted her appearance. Her
head was high and she ignored the crowd.

"She scorns the tiers," said Hemartius.

"It matters little now," I said.

Her shackles and the bracelets which confined her hands behind
her back were removed and she was placed in the dock, the prisoner
cage. The couch which had been in the dock earlier had been removed.

She had little choice now but to stand.

"The rest of the jury is coming in," said Hemartius.

"It is nearly the Tenth Ahn," I said.

The jury was then assembled, and quiet.

"We now await the Ubar," said Hemartius.

I was muchly eager to see Marlenus.

Then, slowly, responsive to the measured blows which struck them, the great bar, and the many smaller bars, in Ar, began to toll the Tenth Ahn, the Gorean noon.

Marlenus, seemingly unsteady, assisted by two clerks of the court, emerged from a side door.

Hemartius, and I, and those at the table of the prosecution, rose.

Slowly, step by step, Marlenus ascended to the high bench, decorated with the blazoned emblem of two tarns, presumably the Tarns of Justice.

We now, and those at the table of prosecution, resumed our seats.

"What is wrong?" asked Hemartius, concerned.

"He is the same," I said. "He is no different."

"Of course," said Hemartius. "What did you expect. I do not think he has been well, as of late."

Decius Albus rose to his feet.

"Now that our beloved Ubar is present, may the Priest-Kings favor him, this court is once more in sober session. Noble jurors, have you, after considering with care, patiently, and at length, the indisputable facts in this case and the testimony of numerous reliable witnesses, reached a decision?"

"We have! We have!" cried hundreds of voices from the orchestra area.

"Are you prepared to make known that decision?"

"We are! We are!" came from the orchestra area.

"What is your decision?" asked Decius Albus.

"Guilty! Guilty!" cried the jury. "Guilty! Guilty!" rang from the tiers. "Guilty! Guilty!" shrieked the women toward the back of the orchestra area, who had been victorious in the ostracon contest.

I am sure that these cries were audible even beyond the theater. Certainly I heard cheers, faintly, from outside the theater, presumably from those who had failed to obtain a seat inside.

"It is finished," said Hemartius. "Let us go."

In the prisoner cage, Talena had sunk to her knees, head down, shuddering, grasping the bars, presumably overcome, unable to bear her own weight.

"Announce," I said to Hemartius, "that Geoffrey of Harfax will address the jury, the crowd, the citizens of Ar."

"I dare not do so," said Hemartius. "Are you mad?"

"Do so," I said. "Fear nothing."

"I am a failure," he said, "a mediocrity, a spent man, a joke."

"You are the finest legal mind in Ar," I said.

Hemartius looked at me, wonderingly. Then he rose to his feet. He spoke in a loud, firm, clear voice, a voice that commanded attention. "Noble Ubar, noble jurors, noble officers of the court, revered colleagues of the prosecution, noble and beloved citizens of Ar, your friend and benefactor, Geoffrey of Harfax will address the court."

I rose to my feet and made my way to the front of the stage.

CHAPTER SIXTY-TWO

Decius Albus sprang to his feet, addressing himself to the Ubar. "This is unnecessary," he said. "This is irregular. It is time for the disposition of the prisoner. That is the order of events."

I looked back and behind me. It seemed that Marlenus had scarcely understood the words of Decius Albus.

"Let him speak!" cried members of the jury. "Let him speak!" rang from the tiers.

"No!" cried Decius Albus. "No!"

But encouraging roars from the orchestral area and the tiers drowned out his futile protests. Then he subsided. I am sure that Decius Albus realized, as much as anyone, the danger of displeasing a crowd. Have not crowds, like lawless, rushing waters, like stampeding tharlarion, like an irresponsible monster with one body and many heads, swept aside temples and palaces, governments and dynasties? What emperor dares spare the gladiator whose blood is demanded by the crowd?

"Noble jurors, and noble citizens of Ar, all," I said, "I am not, of late, unknown in your glorious city."

Here there was much laughter, and shouts of gratitude, and approval.

"You know my animosity toward the prisoner," I said. "You recall how publicly and virulently I spoke against her. And was it not I who, after surmounting numerous perils and enduring uncountable hardships, captured her and brought her, helpless, to the justice of Ar? Do you think I would do that for mere gold? What gold could be worth such travail and risk? No, her criminality repulsed me! I rebelled at her hatefulness! How distressed I was at what she had done to your beautiful, beloved Ar, a mighty city so understanding and kind to small Harfax! I have despised her, and her pride, dishonesty, and treachery, for years!"

Talena, on her knees in the cage, grasping the bars, looked up, not comprehending, perhaps not even understanding what I was saying.

"Indeed," I said, "I petitioned the court that I be appointed deputy to the noble Hemartius, to distract him, to ply him with kal-da, to sabotage his case at every turn. How harrowing and dreadful was the very thought that somehow the gifted Hemartius might, by some obscure and devious legal artifice, be able to trick the jury and subvert justice! How pleased I was when my petition was granted by the understanding and indulgent court, to find myself in a position where I could ruin the best efforts of his keen legal mind at every turn."

"I am sure the court is grateful to the efforts of the noble Geoffrey of Harfax on its behalf," said Decius Albus, "but let us now proceed to the disposition of the prisoner, before the irons grow cold and the tongs and pincers rust."

"There you have it, noble citizens of Ar," I said. "Mere talk of irons, and tongs and pincers! Does not Talena's guilt far transcend such crude devices, fit perhaps for a mundane villain of little or no consequence, but surely less than suitable for one who betrayed not only her own Home Stone but an entire city, your beloved Ar!"

There were sounds of interest from the orchestra area and the tiers.

"May I ask," said Decius Albus, "what the deputy counselor has in mind?"

"Something other than unimaginative metal and commonplace darting flames," I said, "something other than such brute simplicities."

"I suggest," said Decius Albus, "that the noble deputy counselor submit a list of his suggestions to the court, and they will be given due consideration."

"You do not understand," I said.

"What do I not understand?" asked Decius Albus.

I turned to the theater, the orchestra pit and the tiers.

"Dear friends," I said, "it seems clear that the noble Decius Albus, through no fault of his own, overwrought by the brilliance of his labors for the prosecution, fails to detect the purport of my speech."

A ripple of curiosity coursed through the crowd. Each member of that assembly, I gather, suspected that he might grasp what had apparently proved opaque to the trade advisor.

"Citizens of beloved Ar," I said, "I am told I am popular. Is it true?"

The theater roared with agreement.

"I regret that I had no more than ten thousand gold tarn disks, of double weight, to give to you," I said. "Had I ten thousand more I would be pleased to give them all to you again. I would love to do so. Yet, even those who may have unfortunately missed seizing such a disk will profit handsomely from the presence of such riches which, through the channels of business and commerce, will enliven and stimulate glorious Ar."

There was much assent to this.

"I ask nothing," I said, "but I wonder if you might be disposed to grant me a small favor."

"Yes, yes!" thundered from the orchestra pit and the tiers. "Anything! Speak!"

"Give me the prisoner, Talena of Ar," I said, "to do with her what I wish."

There were a few Ihn of silence in the theater, for those present seemed startled and, for a moment, taken aback.

Then someone cried out, "Yes! Give her to him!" And soon a number of similar cries rang out. "Yes, give her to him!" "The noble Geoffrey of Harfax will know what to do with her!" "The trade advisor is too kind! He is insufficiently severe!" "Far more adequate tortures for the she-sleen!" "Give her to Geoffrey of Harfax." "Yes, consign the traitress to the mercies of the Harfaxian!"

Mixed in with the widespread hearty agreement of most of the crowd there were some protests from some of the free women near the back of the orchestra area who, one supposes, had been looking forward to contributing their bit to the torture of the prisoner.

"No, no!" cried Talena, seemingly now recovered, standing, tightly grasping the bars, dismayed, and wild.

"See!" cried a man, "she fears being given to him! Give her to him! Give her to him!"

Others took up this cry.

"No, no!" cried Talena. "He is a fraud, a charlatan! He did not capture me! He is not even from Harfax. He is a barbarian weakling! I was taken to Jad by Seremides of Ar. Lurius of Jad arranged for my return to Ar!"

"Who would believe you?" cried a man. "Lying she-tarsk!" cried another.

"Good fortune and a full purse to the brave Geoffrey of Harfax!" cried another.

"Dear fellow citizens," said Decius Albus, advancing to the front edge of the stage. "I assure you that no one more esteems the generous, valiant Geoffrey of Harfax than I. No one could be more eager than I to surrender the miserable traitress, a disgrace to free womanhood, to his keeping, but, ela, it cannot be done. The law forbids it. Talena of Ar, a free woman, has been found guilty in a public trial. She cannot thus, as a free woman, be given to a private party. Her fate, as a free woman, is in the hands, as it should be, of the state."

I turned to Hemartius.

He nodded. "It is true," he said.

I had feared this resolution and so had come prepared.

"Be that as it may," I said, "it is irrelevant to the case in point."

"It is the case in point," said Decius Albus. "Regretfully we cannot shatter the reign of law simply in order to accommodate a hero and friend, even one as dear to us as Geoffrey of Harfax."

"I ask not that law be breached," I said, "but, rather, that it be observed."

Even Hemartius gazed upon me with astonishment.

"Talena of Ar," I said, "should I choose to put that name upon her, is not a free woman, but an object, a property, goods, a vendible article, suitable for purchase, a beast, a domestic animal, mine!"

The crowd seemed startled, silent.

"No!" cried Talena!

"I appeal," I said, "to the couching laws of Marlenus of Ar!"

Consternation stormed amongst the tiers.

"Ho!" cried a great voice above and behind me.

I spun about.

No longer did the Ubar, now standing, savage in mien before the bench, seem far away, somnolent, distracted, or dazed. Once again he was the monster of pride and power I knew so well, a Ubar amongst Ubars. I then realized that Grendel had been successful. He had made his way to the Beast Caves. There, he had somehow obtained, by stealth, trickery, or force, the anticipated remedy or antidote for the drug familiar to him from the steel world of Agamemnon, to which Marlenus had been subjected. It had then been given to Seremides who had imparted it to Xenon, who had administered it to the Ubar before his appearance in court. Marlenus then, I realized, as keen-eyed as a tarn, as wary and cunning as a sleen, as shrewd as a larl, had feigned being still under its influence.

"Yes," I cried, "to the couching laws of Marlenus himself!"

Marlenus then, alert, keen-eyed, fierce of visage, resumed his seat.

Decius Albus had turned white. Pa-Kur had half risen from his curule chair but then resumed his place, as though nothing had happened. But I suspected that his entire body, seemingly unconcerned and quiescent, shook with the rushing of blood. Others at the table of prosecution exchanged amazed glances.

"I now ask my learned colleague, the honorable and noble Hemartius of Ar, to sketch out the purport of the couching laws in question."

"Their purport," said Hemartius, seemingly half stunned, "and, indeed, their letter, is well known in Ar, not only to the scribes of the law but to all free persons in the city. Their intent is to discourage wayward free women from shaming themselves, their Home Stone, and their city by forming liaisons with male slaves. Can you imagine the shame and horror of a free woman in the arms of a male slave?"

Gasps of horror, even shrieks of dismay, escaped hundreds of free women in the tiers. Many drew up their hoods and hid their heads in their veils.

But could it be, I wondered, that this possibility, that of such a liaison, say, with a handsome male slave, was truly so remote to the thoughts, and perhaps even to the deeds, of many of the free women present?

"Such a thought is incomprehensible," said Hemartius. "It can scarcely be conceived! Better that they give themselves to tarsks, better that they lie with tharlarion!"

This suggestion was met largely with silence.

I gathered that many of the free women present did not regard the proffered suggestion as truly preferable.

"What should be done with a woman so degraded and shameless," asked Hemartius, "one who so sullies her Home Stone and so mocks and insults the glory, name, and virtue of proud free women everywhere?"

At this point Hemartius paused, letting the crowd contemplate the answer to his question.

"Yes," cried Hemartius, "if she would lie with a slave, let her be a slave! Yes, she should be herself a slave!"

This utterance was met with acclaim by many in the tiers, particularly men.

"And in the couching laws of Marlenus, our beloved Ubar," said Hemartius, "the woman who so reduces herself as to couch with, or prepare to couch with, a male slave becomes herself a slave, and the slave of the male slave's master."

"That is true," said many men.

"But what, dear deputy counselor," asked Decius Albus, "has this to do with the matter at hand? Laws abound. They are not in short supply. Lumber wagons and wagons carrying stone are not permitted on the streets of Ar during daylight hours. The age of wines cannot be falsified. Boundary stones cannot be surreptitiously dislodged."

"I now call to the dais of examination," I said, "Tolnar, he of the second Octavii, a highly respected gens, though, as many of you know, independent of the better known Octavii, the deputy commissioner of the central records office of Ar, and Venlisius, by adoption a scion of the Toratti, his colleague, and corroborating witness, archon of records for the Metellan district."

"This is madness!" cried Decius Albus. "I protest!"

"Proceed," said Marlenus.

"Perhaps some of you recollect Milo, the actor," I said.

There were gasps, and intakes of breath, from several of the free women in the tiers, and even from the back of the orchestra area.

"He was regarded as the most handsome and desirable man in Ar," I said.

"He was not so handsome!" called a man. "No!" agreed another.

"Milo, at the time in question, was a slave, belonging to the successful businessman and impresario, Appanius of Ar, whom he served as a confidante and cup bearer."

"I recall it," said a man.

"The slave in the prisoner cage," I said, "was at that time not only Talena of Ar, a free woman, but the Ubara of Ar. She, as thousands of other women in Ar, could not fail to be aware of the dashing figure of Milo, that paragon of male beauty, on the stage. Unlike most other women, Talena, as Ubara, was in a position to gratify her curiosity. An occasion was arranged, in which, discreetly, Talena, as Ubara, would have him at her mercy. This arrangement, I assure you, was quite independent of the use to which Appanius, in all legality, if not propriety, occasionally put Milo, that of using him as a male lure slave. In such a way Appanius increased the number of female slaves in his pens, and, usually marketing these catches outside the city, augmented his already quite substantial wealth. But that is neither here nor there. To be brief, by means of a comely female slave and Milo's own genuinely aggressive and possessive masculine urges, I constructed a situation which produced a profound breach between Appanius and Milo. Appanius was beside himself with tears and rage, deeming himself betrayed. Thus I managed to buy Milo, actually for a quite nominal price, from the shaken, grieving, furious, distraught Appanius. I then arranged that Talena's sport would turn out rather differently from what she expected. I prepared a net which, when released, would cover the pleasure couch, netting its occupants, and I invited two officers of Ar, the aforementioned Tolnar and Venlisius, to witness the business and provide appropriate documentation, pertinent affidavits, suitable records, and such."

"Say no more!" screamed the prisoner. "You demean me! You humiliate me! Do not disgrace me! Do not shame me! I am not a slave! I am Talena, Talena of Ar, of high blood, daughter of Marlenus!"

"Silence, Slave," I said.

She shuddered in anger and unbridled frustration, shaking the bars.

"Surely you cannot expect the court to believe this wild story," said Decius Albus.

"I now request the witnesses to testify," I said, "and, following, submit records to the court."

Decius Albus glared at Tolnar and Venlisius. "Beware," he growled.

Tolnar and Venlisius looked to me.

I turned about and looked up to Marlenus.

He did not look at me, but at Tolnar and Venlisius. "Do not be afraid," he said. "You are in the presence of your Ubar. You will speak the truth."

Tolnar and Venlisius stepped on the dais of examination.

"It is as the deputy counselor has said," said Tolnar.

"Further," said Venlisius, "I identify the prisoner, now unveiled, as the woman in question, as the former Talena of Ar."

"I, too," said Tolnar.

"Please present your documentation to the court," I said.

The documentation was presented to the clerks of the court, and then submitted to the scrutiny of Hemartius and Decius Albus.

"Everything is in order," said Hemartius. "All the papers are signed. Everything is stamped and sealed."

"Hold," said Decius Albus. "These papers obviously pertain to a slave, but how do we know they are relevant to the prisoner? Time has elapsed. Recollections can soften and fade, even be usurped by unwitting substitutes, each claiming authenticity. Memories are fallible. Identifications can be error. The noble Tolnar and Venlisius may be mistaken."

"This objection was anticipated, long ago," I said. "Examine the records, first, there is a detailed description of the slave, in which each tiny irregularity or imperfection, each tiny scar or blemish, is recorded; second, there are more than a hundred measurements recorded; and, third, fingerprints and toeprints were made."

"Unfortunately," said Decius Albus, "as the prisoner is a free woman, her relationship to a certain slave must remain conjectural."

"Not at all," I said. "In deference to the theoretical possibility that the prisoner is a free woman, let the determination be made by a committee of free women. That is familiar to guardsmen in cases where it is suspected that a robed woman may actually be a slave girl in disguise. This can be easily arranged by clerks of the court. Let a tape measure and calipers be obtained, and let the free women be instructed in the simple procedures of finger and toeprinting, and the results of their endeavors then compared to the original fingerprints and toeprints taken long ago by the noble Tolnar and Venlisius."

"No, no!" cried Decius Albus.

I turned toward the orchestra area. "Noble free women," I said, "I call for volunteers to assist the court in this delicate matter."

The free women who had been successful in the ostraca contest, supplemented by many from the tiers themselves, crying out, pushing and shoving, swarmed toward the stage.

"Hold, hold, noble ladies," I cried, "ten, no more than ten, please!"

After something like an Ahn, all was in readiness.

"No!" screamed Talena. "Do not! Keep them away from me!"

The door to the prisoner cage was opened. "Ladies," I said.

Ten free women, eight selected from the ostraka winners and two from the tiers, crowded into the cage as Talena backed away from them, stopped at last by the bars at the back of the cage. These ten women were amongst the largest, and, I suspected, ugliest women in the theater. They seemed to me the sort which resent and despise femininity, who hate desirability and beauty in a woman, who are enraged to contemplate women of the sort men seek out and hunt, the sort for whom men frenziedly bid, the sort men strip, put on their knees, and collar, the sort for whom men would kill. I had selected them carefully. I did not think they would handle Talena gently.

"Stay away from me!" screamed Talena. "Do not touch me! Do not dare to touch me!"

A large, silken cover was draped about the sides of the prisoner cage.

CHAPTER SIXTY-THREE

Talena knelt, head down, in the empty cage, clutching the shreds of her garments about her.

"The determination has been made," said the chief clerk. "The prisoner and the slave referred to in the documentation are one and the same."

"For the sake of convenience," I said, "I shall refer to the prisoner as Talena, not Talena of Ar, as she, of course, as a slave, being a property and beast, has no Home Stone or city."

The name Talena now, of course, was a slave name, put on her by a free person, much as, on Earth, a pig or dog might be named. Clearly it is useful to give slaves names, to refer to them, to command them, and so on. It amused me that this hitherto lofty and proud name was now no more than a slave name, no different now from, say, Lita, Lana, Tula, and so on. Indeed, given this precedent, it was possible that 'Talena' might become a familiar slave name, one taken for granted as a slave name, one that free women would be scandalized to wear. How that would infuriate Talena. How it would amuse me.

"The prosecution willingly, even gladly, grants that the prisoner is the slave Talena," said Decius Albus, "but that changes little. Aside from the fact that the ownership of the slave is at present unclear, the prisoner, while Talena of Ar, was free and, as a free person, committed numerous crimes such as those listed in the indictment. Accordingly, it is only necessary, once her ownership is established, to restore her to freedom, and then swiftly redraft and expedite one or two details. Then it will be as if this embarrassing hiatus in our procedures did not exist. As of now, the torture fires have burned low and the irons have grown cold, but let me assure the jury and the stands that justice need not despair of receiving its condign satisfaction. Fires may be rekindled and irons reheated. It is as easy to open a cabinet of acids as to close it. Knives and splinters may be wrapped in silk this afternoon, and unwrapped tomorrow."

"I claim the slave," I said. "I do not yield her. Thus, I, her owner, am responsible for her disposition and fate."

"I trust that in dealing with her," said Decius Albus, "should you be found her master, that you will consider the recommendations of the court."

"I am her master," I said.

Talena struggled to her feet, clutching the remnants of her robes about her. Did she release them I thought it likely they would fall to her ankles. The ten examining women had relieved her of the pearls and jewels with which she had been adorned. As these, like her garments, had been furnished by the state, the examining women had turned them over to the chief clerk who had then, interestingly, divided them amongst them, presumably compensating them for their work in establishing the slave's identity. Even one of those pearls or jewels, I was sure, might have been exchanged for a gold piece in the Street of Coins.

"I am free!" screamed Talena. "I am not a slave! He is not my master!"

There were tears in her eyes, not only of frustration, but of pain. I had heard, more than once, from behind the silken cover, after the ripping away of cloth within, the blow of a switch, particularly in the early Ehn of the examination, presumably when Talena had resisted, been less than cooperative, or dared to object, to the examination. After a few Ehn, given the paucity of blows, I gathered that Talena, by then docile, resigned, obedient, and stinging, let the examiners do with her as they wished, scrutinizing her with care, conducting their numerous measurements, and taking finger and toeprints. How she must have smarted with humiliation to be naked, as naked as a slave, in the presence of her fully clothed examiners, to whom, doubtless, she felt inordinately, astronomically superior. Too, despite her background and hauteur, she had found herself switched like a slave, but then, of course, she was a slave. I gathered that she was responsive to the switch. That pleased me. Switches are quite useful in training a girl.

"Bring me clothing!" screamed Talena. "I am free. I am a free woman. I am not a slave! I am not a vendible domestic beast!"

"Have you permission to speak, Girl?" inquired the chief clerk.

"I need no permission to speak!" cried Talena. "I speak when, and as, I wish. I am a free woman!"

"Slaves have no right to clothing," said the chief clerk. "Perhaps you should consider that."

"Strip her!" cried a free woman in the tiers. "Take away her clothing, all of it," cried another. "Do not leave the animal a stitch!" shouted a woman from the back of the orchestra area. "Bring a collar," cried another woman from the orchestra area. "Let that be her wardrobe, and nothing more!"

Talena, holding those pieces of garmenture about her, stifled a protest, presumably fearing that the court might accede to the cries from the crowd.

I noted that the calves and ankles of Talena were exquisite. Such things raise a girl's price.

"What is at issue," said Decius Albus, "is not whether the prisoner is a free person or a marketable beast. That matter is clear. She is kajira, and, as such, can be bought and sold as much as, and as easily as, a lamp or boot, a tarsk or verr. What is at issue is her ownership."

"I own her," I said.

"That is what is at issue," said Decius Albus.

"Tolnar, of the second Octavii, and Venlisius, of the Toratti, can both testify that I obtained her under the couching laws of Marlenus, Ubar of Glorious Ar."

"They need not testify," said Decius Albus, "the most they can confirm is that you, at a certain time, owned her, not that you still own her."

"My title is clear," I said.

"Not as clear as we might desire," whispered Hemartius.

"Perhaps the slave knows her owner," said Decius Albus. He then turned to the dock, the prisoner cage. "We grant you the right to speak, slave," said Decius Albus. "Who owns you?"

"No one owns me!" cried Talena. "I am a free person, a free person!"

"Beware, Slave," said Hemartius. "A free woman may misrepresent, cheat, deceive, and lie. But you are not a free woman. You are a slave. Slaves are forbidden to lie! Severe penalties may be invoked in the case of a kajira caught in even a small lie."

"I am a free woman!" said Talena.

"I fear," said Hemartius, "we must call for the rack."

In Gorean law the testimony of slaves is commonly taken under torture, the theory apparently being that this will encourage veracity.

"Dismiss the wear and tear on the ropes," I said. "My title in the matter is clear."

"I fear it is not clear at all, Deputy Counselor," said Decius Albus. "At the time of the restoration of our beloved Ubar, Marlenus, Talena disappeared from Ar. Much intervened between that time and the present. She might have passed legally from one pair of hands into another. She could have been bought and sold several times. Our search into records and testimony make it clear that Talena, as a slave, was in the Northern Forests, and at a different time than when she was owned by Verna, the Panther Girl, and later, at the World's End. Later, returned to the continent, she was sold from the House of Anesidemus in Brundisium. Subsequently she, with others, was carried to Port Kar, a port on the Tamber Gulf, near Thassa. There she served as a paga girl in a tavern, the Golden Chain, an establishment owned by a man named Ho-Tosk. Later she was carried to the holding of a man named Bosk of Port Kar, a member of the Council of Captains, the body sovereign in the port."

"I arranged for her sale in Brundisium," I said. "Ho-Tosk held her for me. I am known as Bosk of Port Kar."

Some cries of wonder were heard amongst the tiers. But most in Ar, I was sure, knew little of Bosk of Port Kar. Those of Tyros and Cos, however, would know the name well.

"I thought you were Geoffrey of Harfax," said Decius Albus, smiling.

"I am known, too, by that name," I said.

"I note from the documentation, and the corroboration of the noble free women who assisted the court in its inquiries, that her left thigh bears the mark of Treve," said Decius Albus.

"I was abandoned in my companionship, deserted in the wilderness," she said, "and I fell to the capture ropes of Rask of Treve."

"Rask of Treve," I said, "gave her to Verna, the Panther Girl, apparently adjudging her far inferior to a blond barbarian slave named El-in-or."

"Tarsk, sleen!" cried Talena.

"Beware," warned the chief clerk.

"I was brought back from the Northern Forests," said Talena, "and freed, but then sequestered."

"In the Northern Forests," I said, "she begged to be freed."

There were cries of satisfaction from the tiers and orchestra area.

"Thereby acknowledging that she was a slave," said Hemartius.

"I was freed!" exclaimed Talena.

"But later, clearly," said Decius Albus, "you were again enslaved, that in accordance with the couching laws of our beloved Ubar, Marlenus."

"I am a free woman!" she cried.

"Beware," said Hemartius. "It is a serious crime for a slave to pretend to be free. Think of the insult to all free women."

"Strip her!" cried a free woman.

"Whip her!" cried another.

"Teach her what she is," shouted another, "an animal soon to grovel in terror, fearing the whip, and hoping to be found pleasing."

"Throw her bound to leech plants!" cried another.

"Cast her to sleen!" cried another.

"Feed her to eels!" cried yet another.

"Bring a whip," said Decius Albus to the chief clerk.

"No," I said. "That will not be necessary." I then turned to the prisoner cage.

"Get on your knees," I said.

Talena looked at Decius Albus, and those at the table of prosecution. Tears of anger, shame, and frustration sprang into her eyes. How helpless she felt. Then she knelt.

I was pleased that she knelt. In this way, discipline needed not be invoked. Talena did not wish to be whipped. Like any woman, she was afraid of the leather. I found that an auspicious sign.

Slave girls thrill to be subject to the whip, but that does not mean they wish to feel the whip. It hurts. Also, though the slave is subject to the whip, that does not mean that they are whipped, or are often whipped. The normal master would be no more likely to whip a slave than any other animal. And the slave, of course, in being pleasing, makes it very unlikely she will be whipped. Who would whip a pleasing slave or one endeavoring to be pleasing? Occasionally a slave, fearing that her bondage is meaningless, or in jeopardy, may beg for a whipping, to reassure her that she is truly a slave. This is rare, of course, as the Gorean slave girl is seldom in doubt that she is a slave. Masters see to that.

The female slave, as one would suppose, is quite different from a free woman, for example, not only in marking, collaring, and garmenture, but in movement, behavior, carriage, grace, diction, and such. The female slave is the most helplessly, lusciously feminine, and sexual of all women. No wonder she is commonly envied and despised by her free sisters. Some women are less interested in being a man's equal than his treasure. To the free woman, tutored in prescriptions and jailed by convention, the joys of submission are alien. They do not understand, or, scandalized, more likely repudiate in fear commonly suppressed genetic codings. Is the strong, virile, dominant male truly such a terror to them? Why strive to be his imitator? Why not, rather, be yourself, his complement? In any event, free women often fail to understand the liberation of the collar, how bondage can free a woman to be her deepest self. They cannot understand the joy of being owned, of addressing a man as "Master," of kneeling before him, and serving him, in all ways.

"My claim is valid," I said. "I own her."

"She fell into hands other than yours frequently," said Decius Albus, "for example, those of Seremides of Ar, of Lurius of Jad, of Myron of Cos, of Ruffio of Ar, and doubtless those of many others."

"That changes nothing," I said. "One man cannot free the slave of another. If she fled away and was apprehended by guardsmen, that does not make her the slave of guardsmen."

"Beware, dear Geoffrey," said Hemartius. "Things are not so simple."

"Perhaps, esteemed deputy counselor," said Decius Albus, "you might ask your colleague, the noble, learned Hemartius, to quote relevant statutes to you."

"I refrain," said Hemartius.

"Permit me, then, to be of service," said Decius Albus. "The matter is complex and varies from polis to polis, but, happily, it is also covered more generally in Merchant Law, which, as you know, is promulgated at, and revised at, the Sardar Fairs, particularly that of En'kara. For obvious reasons, given the limitations of pomeriums, Merchant Law is commonly, in many matters, accorded a theoretical preeminence. The slave laws tend to be quite similar to those pertaining to chattels in general. Consider some representative cases. An owner disappears or perishes without having made provisions for the disposition of his property. One then considers kin, and closeness of kin. Suppose a slave is a fugitive and her owner is not known or cannot be found. She is then subject to claim. Suppose a slave is lost or has been washed overboard. Then, again, assuming her owner is not known or cannot be found, she is subject to claim. Suppose a woman, of her own free will, has renounced her freedom, declaring herself a slave, perhaps to avoid an undesirable companionship, say, to make herself unworthy of, or ineligible for, companionship, or perhaps to escape a city, or a difficult personal situation, or a simple yearning for a master. She may then be claimed by any free person. A female thief may be given by the state to her victim. A female debtor may be given by the state to her creditor. An unclaimed slave may be auctioned. In some cases, time limits may be imposed, for example, a slave not claimed within twenty days may be sold, and so on. These things are independent, of course, of recognized exceptions, such as attacks, raids, and war. The slave, like the free woman, is loot and loot belongs to the looter. The laws of Ar do not prevail in Treve, nor do those of Treve prevail in Ar. Let masters look after their own slaves, as best they can, as they would their own tarsks, verr, or kailla."

"In short," I said, "laws are complex, tangled, and often obscure."

"And Merchant Law, dealing with this area, is usually ineffective," said Hemartius, "lacking a means of enforcement and being overruled whenever found by cities or individuals distasteful or inconvenient."

"Cities and men do much as they please," I said.

"Not within a city, of course," said Hemartius. "Within a city, laws can be quite stringent."

"Fortunately," said Decius Albus, "the matter here is quite simple and straightforward. Geoffrey of Harfax little or never exercised the imperium of the mastership over the woman in question, over his alleged property. Indeed, she was on the throne of Ar! Did she, I wonder, often ponder that beneath her regalia, beneath her ornate robes of office, there was the naked body of a slave? Then at last, our beloved Marlenus, after his long and tragic absence, returned to our beloved Ar. Ar rose! The invaders were cast out! Talena disappeared. During the time of her disappearance, in one collar after another, she belonged to many masters. The original mastery then, if it existed at all, was superseded and nullified many times over."

"No!" I said.

"But, yes!" said Decius Albus. "The slave herself denies she belongs to Geoffrey of Harfax! Are we to suppose that she does not even know her own master?"

Here and there, there was laughter from the tiers and orchestra area.

I turned to Talena. "Claim me as your master!" I said.

"Never!" she said, from her knees. "Tarsk!"

"Consider your answer," I said.

"You deserted me. You abandoned me!" she said. "Better the most grievous of tortures than accept a favor from you! Better the irons and knives, the flames and acids, than to owe you as much as a tarsk-bit. I hate you. I hate you!"

"Things do not go well," said Hemartius.

I saw little point in disputing this.

"She is mad," said Hemartius.

"Excited, at least," I said.

"It is her foolish pride speaking," said Hemartius. "At the first touch of a hot iron, she would beg to acknowledge you, or any other man, as her master."

"Tarsk! Tarsk!" she cried.

"Do not speak so to a free person!" said Hemartius.

"I am the daughter of Marlenus of Ar!" she screamed.

"It is not in dispute that the prisoner is a slave," said Decius Albus. "Too, it is not in dispute that the slave is the former Talena of Ar. And it is not in dispute that the former Talena of Ar, as the court established, was a traitress, and guilty of numerous crimes. What is in dispute is the ownership of the slave. Considering the obscurities appertaining to that question, a ruling, and one on behalf of the state, is in order."

"No!" I said.

"How else can the matter be resolved?" asked Hemartius.

"And, given the needs of the court," said Decius Albus, "the ruling on behalf of the state, however regretfully, must fall to the hand of the court."

"No!" I said.

"The slave committed crimes as a free woman and she should be punished as a free woman, exposed to the full wrath of the law."

"Find some flaw here!" I demanded of Hemartius.

"I fear there is none, dear friend," said Hemartius.

"Accordingly," said Decius Albus, "the state will claim the slave, free the slave, and then subject Talena of Ar to consequences befitting her crime."

"Stop this," I begged Hemartius.

"Law," said Hemartius, "is majestic and implacable."

"Law," I said, "must succumb to law."

"I do not understand," said Hemartius.

"There are other laws, other codes, other rights, other ways," I said, "other majesties, other implacabilities."

"On behalf of the state," said Decius Albus, "I claim the slave."

"The slave is claimed," said Marlenus.

"I request the court now rule," said Decius Albus, "that my claim on behalf of the state is accepted."

"It is accepted," said Marlenus. "The slave is now the property of the state of Ar."

"She is still a slave, is she not?" I asked Hemartius.

"Certainly," said Hemartius.

"Hold!" I said.

"This is tiresome," said Decius Albus. "Noble, learned Hemartius, please advise your impetuous deputy counselor of his indiscretion. Warn him that further interruptions will not be tolerated."

"I have something to say," I said, "and I say it to Decius Albus, to Marlenus of Ar, to all in this theater, to Ar itself."

"And what do you have to say?" asked Decius Albus.

"Kajira canjellne!" I cried.

There was a great silence in the theater.

This is an ancient cry. I do not know its origins. It might date from the time that Ar was no more than a cluster of villages. It is surely older than the roads of Turia and the aqueducts of Venna and Torcadino. It is in old Gorean, the language from which modern Gorean evolved. The cry does not translate easily or well into English, or modern Gorean, but it is a challenge, commonly followed by the death of one or more individuals. It perhaps dates from a time when slave collars were no more than strips of knotted leather and ropes no more than twisted vines. Women are unutterably desirable. They make superb slaves and men will kill for them. What man does not long for his slave; what woman does not long for her master?

"The motion of the deputy counselor is out of order!" said Decius Albus.

"Such a motion supersedes order," said Hemartius. "It is above and beyond rulings."

"The deputy counselor has no right to make such a motion," said Decius Albus, "no more than any mercenary, no more than any bandit or hired killer."

"That much right I have," I said. "Who dares deny the right of risk and steel?"

"Sword right," whispered one of the scribes at the table of prosecution.

"It is seldom invoked within a pomerium," said another.

"But it has now been so invoked," said another.

"The matter of the ownership of the slave is at issue," said Hemartius.

"No longer!" said Decius Albus. "The claim of the state has been accepted by the state."

"The matter of the future ownership of the slave is at issue," said Hemartius. "The deputy counselor has the only documented proof of a specific, recorded ownership presented to the court. This was shown by the noble Tolnar and Venlisius. This, in itself, enables and legitimizes the deputy counselor's action."

"That is true," said Marlenus of Ar, member of the Scarlet Caste, and knower of codes.

We all looked up to the high bench.

"So let it be so," said Marlenus. "Kajira canjellne."

CHAPTER SIXTY-FOUR

"I do not wish to kill in this fashion," I said.

"So abandon the slave," said Thurnock.

"To so horrible a death?" I asked.

"It is not likely to last more than a month or a few days," said Clitus.

We, with Hemartius, were in the basement apartment in the Metellan district which I shared with Iris and Seremides.

"Do not be so sure of your steel," said Seremides. "This matter is of importance to the state of Ar. They will set a formidable champion against you, to recognize the claim of the state."

"I can do no more than my best," I said.

"The slave is well curved," said Seremides. "There are worse causes in which you might draw your sword."

"Few can match your steel," said Thurnock.

"There need be only one," I said.

"More meat, Master?" asked Iris, serving.

"No," I said.

"More meat, Master?" asked Iris.

"No," said Hemartius.

"I am afraid," said Seremides.

"What do you suspect, or know?" asked Thurnock.

"I think I know who will stand against him," said Seremides.

"Who?" asked Clitus.

"One of the deadliest swords on Gor," said Seremides, "Pa-Kur, Master of the Black Courts."

"I do not fear Pa-Kur," I said.

Had I not, long ago, on the roof of Ar's Cylinder of Justice, out-matched even so skilled and terrible a foe?

"Why must men always do war and kill one another?" asked Iris.

We regarded her.

"Forgive me for not asking permission to speak, Masters," she said.

"To possess tarts and sluts like you," said Seremides. "Continue serving."

"Yes, Master," she said.

Many women, I supposed, regard themselves in the mirror, perhaps naked. How many, I wondered, do so holding their hands behind them, as though braceleted, or hold their hands before them, as if linked with chain? And how many, I wondered, put something about their neck, as though it was a collar. And how many, I wondered, kneel naked before the mirror and whisper, "I am your slave, Master."

I supposed that few women realized how valuable and precious they were, even kettle-and-mat girls. Do they realize how attractive, how desirable, they are? Do they realize how exciting they are? They are females, biologically the property of males. They are women, biologically the property of men. How else explain their responsiveness to masters? So let her lie at the feet of her master, possessed, owned, content on her leash. In her collar she has come home to her genetic codes. In the collar she has found a satisfaction not to be known by the free woman. In the collar the yearnings of her aching heart have at last been satisfied. She now has a master. She is now a property to be possessed and commanded. She has nothing to fear now but the flames in her belly, of which she will soon find herself the helpless, needful, longing, begging, victim.

"What disturbs you?" asked Thurnock.

"I am thinking of Marlenus," I said. "How could he have sequestered Talena, how could he arrange an unimaginable reward for her capture and return to Ar, why is he so zealous to have her prosecuted and punished?"

"Presumably," said Hemartius, "he sequestered her to avenge the slight to his own honor and conceal her dishonor. She did not behave as should have the daughter of a Ubar. That is a serious consideration. The Ubar is vain and mighty. Such a man does not wish to be shamed. As to the prosecution and punishment, surely treason is not to be lightly dismissed."

"Could not the swift blow of an ax or a drop of poisoned syrup be sufficient?" I asked.

"I do not think so," said Hemartius. "Consider the enormity of the crime and the gravity of the insult to the Ubar himself."

"I think that much of this is not about justice but about the wrath of Marlenus," I said.

"Undoubtedly," said Hemartius.

"But his own daughter!" I protested.

"You are a barbarian," said Hemartius. "This is Gor."

"But, still," I said.

"He is Marlenus," said Hemartius.

"And now, I fear," I said, "the Marlenus of old."

"More severe and terrible than ever," said Hemartius.

"Perhaps it would be better if he were still drugged," I said.

"He will understand what was done to him," said Hemartius. "I do not think that this bodes well for Decius Albus, the trade advisor."

"You said, as I recall, dear Cabot," said Seremides, "that you did not fear Pa-Kur."

"I so spoke," I said.

"There is more to be feared than the flash of his steel," said Seremides. "It is not easy to see or weigh all weapons. Beware of touching things he has touched. Do not share with him, the cup of conflict or the wine of war. Do not linger in the presence of unusual odors."

"I know of the cup of conflict or the wine of war," I said. "It occasionally precedes a formal duel, in which each contestant respects the other, though the 'wine' may not be wine, but simple water, supposedly from the melted snow of the Voltai. I do not know, however, about the business of touching objects or detecting unusual odors. How do you know of such things? From where do you hear of them? Who is your informant?"

"The drops of rain on a catapult beam," said Seremides, "the movement of leaves in the clinging tur-pah."

"Forgive me," I said.

"Beware of Pa-Kur," said Seremides.

"I shall," I said.

I turned to Hemartius.

"Dear Hemartius," I said, "I think we know now why Pa-Kur had himself appointed to sit at the table of prosecution. He anticipated the possible emergence of developments with which he, and not Decius Albus, would be uniquely equipped to deal."

"Who knows what he anticipated?" said Seremides.

"You should rest," said Thurnock. "Tomorrow, at noon, in the arena, in the presence of the slave, Talena, the Ubar, Marlenus, the tables of both the prosecution and defense, the clerks and officers of the court, and all Ar, you will meet the champion of the state."

At this point there were three blows on the door of the apartment.

"Iris," said Seremides, "answer the door."

Iris hurried to the door.

She opened the door a crack, and then turned back to face us.

"Who is it?" asked Seremides.

"I am frightened," she said.

"Admit Pa-Kur," I said.

CHAPTER SIXTY-FIVE

The door was thrust open.

Iris backed away, trembling.

The tall, helmeted figure, with a swirl of the long black cloak, entered the room.

Even Seremides struggled to his feet, leaning on his crutch.

The light of the dangling thalarion-oil lamp shone on the right side of the helmet. Then the visitor slowly removed it, and held it in the crook of his left arm.

The skin had a grayish cast; the eyes seemed as if made of glass.

The tunic was a rich and noble sable.

He bore no crossbow. His sword was sheathed.

"We are honored," I said.

"I will speak with you," he said, "alone."

"Be it so," I said.

Hemartius, Thurnock, and Clitus, unwillingly, took their leave. Seremides and Iris withdrew to the back of the apartment.

"It is long since we have conversed, Tarl of Bristol, Tarl Cabot," said Pa-Kur.

"Long, indeed," I said.

"I missed you in Port Kar," I said.

"It was arranged," he said.

"Of course," I said.

"I had been busy with sword work in the Farther Islands, avenging raids and lootings conducted in my name."

"I had once thought I was done with you," I said.

"On the roof of Ar's Cylinder of Justice," he said.

"Yes," I said.

"So thought the world, and Ar," he said.

"The duel," I said, "was lengthy, and well fought."

"Save, perhaps," said he, "for the end."

"I thought you had turned about and leaped to your death," I said.

"Surely you were puzzled that the body was not recovered," he said.

"I thought that it was torn to pieces and disposed of by the crowds below."

"I seized a tarn perch," he said, "and made my way inward to the cot, from which, after dark, I fled."

"By tarn?" I said.

"Of course," he said. "I had one saddled and waiting."

"I gather then," I said, "that it was not a matter of incredible good fortune that, in your leap, you seized the perch."

"No," he said. "I knew it was there."

"I see," I said.

"It is not wise to enter one door without having another by which to leave."

"An Assassin's precaution," I said.

"Surely," he said.

"In that duel," I said, "you expected to kill me."

"Yes," he said, "but what if several others should attack me?"

"It is well to be prepared for contingencies," I said.

"In so far as it is possible," he said.

"You find Talena attractive?" I asked.

"I have known many far more attractive," he said.

"But who were not the daughter of a Ubar," I said.

"Without that what would she be?" he said. "I wonder if she would bring as much as seventy copper tarsks in an open market."

"Far more, surely," I said.

"Perhaps as much as a silver tarsk," he said.

"But as a Ubar's daughter," I said.

"Perhaps then a thousand gold pieces," he said.

"At least," I said.

"It is unfortunate," he said, "that she must be cut and scraped, skinned, strip by strip, burned by flames and chemicals, subjected to numerous tortures, some sharp and brief, and others lengthy, some large and others small, some crude, and some refined."

"Such things are doubtless planned in detail," I said.

"Members of the green caste must intervene frequently," he said, "that she survive to suffer more, and more, until the final longed-for impalement."

"You assume," I said, "that the champion of the state will be victorious."

"Of course," said Pa-Kur.

"Your skills have improved since the roof of the Cylinder of Justice," I said.

"I believe so," he said.

"Mine, too," I said, "may have improved."

"I would not doubt it," he said.

"Your theft of the Home Stone of Ar, was brilliantly done," I said.

"Thank you," he said.

"But you have enleagued yourself not only with Decius Albus, but Kurii," I said.

"Gor will fall to Kurii," he said. "It is better to share victory than defeat."

"You forget Priest-Kings," I said.

"Priest-Kings, if they exist," he said, "are passive, and defensive at best. They see little; they do little. As long as the Sardar is inviolate, they care little about the rest of Gor."

"I do not think that Gor will fall to Kurii," I said.

"It will," he said. "The harsh and ruthless, the adamant and uncaring, the covetous and deceitful always win, until they destroy themselves and their world."

"Kurii need not win," I said.

"If not," he said, "what does it matter? Things will remain then much as they are now. Fields will be sowed and crops harvested. Caravans will trek and ships sail. Wars will be lost and won. Men will love and hate, and live and die."

"Abandon the Black Courts," I said.

"When diamonds cease to sparkle and gold ceases to glow," he said, "when knives cease to cut and quarrels to fly."

"The Ubar," I said, "has shaken off the drug to which he was grievously subject."

"I can withdraw from Decius Albus," he said. "Kurii already grow weary of him."

"I do not think Marlenus will take action until the matter of the trial is concluded," I said.

"I agree with your surmise," he said.

"That leaves little time for Decius Albus to act," I said.

"Granted," he said.

"We meet tomorrow, in the arena," I said.

"I think not," said Pa-Kur.

"I do not understand," I said.

"I am not the champion for the state," he said.

"I do not understand," I said.

"Let me tell you a small story," said Pa-Kur. "Some years ago a prominent Assassin was discomfited on the roof of Ar's Cylinder of Justice. His unfortunate experience was not forgotten by the Assassin. It rankled. Had his pride not been injured? Had it not been dealt an unwelcome blow? In his memory, this misery remained as obdurate and unchanging as stone, as cold as steel. He was patient, an attribute of his caste. He wanted vengeance. Let me now continue the story. Some years ago, in the politics of a small city, following intrigues and clashes, a burning iron was brought to the fair thigh of its lovely, fallen Tatrix. She was subsequently purchased by a barbarian Warrior who, after putting her to appropriate slave use, foolishly freed her. So stupid was he. This warrior, interestingly, was the very

man who had on the roof of Ar's Cylinder of Justice earlier discomfited the Assassin."

"I see," I said.

"To conclude our story, the freed slave eventually returned to the
throne of her city, once more to wear the medallion of the Tatrix. It
seems, however, that the slaver, one of ill repute, a man named Targo,
had either omitted administering slave wine to the slave, perhaps
so soon after her marking, or, more likely, had utilized an inferior
or ineffective potion. After a due interval, the Tatrix gave birth to
a baby boy. The Assassin, by means of confederates, was apprised
of these matters and arranged for the theft of the child. Patience,
as mentioned, is an attribute of his caste. He arranged that the infant, represented as a foundling, be placed in a professional dueling
house, to be raised in, and eventually employed by, that community."

"Your story is strange and far-fetched," I said.

"Strange perhaps," he said, "but not so far-fetched."

"What is the name of this small city and its Tatrix?" I asked.

"Tharna," said Pa-Kur, "and the name of the Tatrix is Lara."

"It is well known," I said, "that designated men of that city have
roved widely, for several years, looking for the missing child of the
Tatrix."

"But unsuccessfully," said Pa-Kur.

"But you have followed the child?" I said.

"Of course," said Pa-Kur.

"And what is the name of the Warrior in your story?" I asked.

"I leave you to speculate on that matter," he said.

"Slave wine seldom fails," I said.

"If administered, and potent," said Pa-Kur.

"This Lara," I said, "after her freeing, may have had several lov-
ers, amongst them perhaps Kron, of Tharna."

"Quite possibly," said Pa-Kur.

"Why do you tell me all this?" I asked.

"I thought you might find it of interest," said Pa-Kur.

"What is the name of the boy?" I asked.

"Now a young man," said Pa-Kur. "He has no Home Stone. But
he is recognized as being of the House of Hesius. He is now a member of the Taurentian Guard, as once was Seremides, who convinced
him, in the light of his sword skills, witnessed on the Skerry of Lars
near Port Kar, to emigrate to Ar. He distinguished himself recently in
doing much to foil an attempt to assassinate Marlenus in a Chamber
of Justice."

"I heard of it," I said.

"He has unusual hair," said Pa-Kar, "rather like yours when you
are not concealing it in a cap or dying it as a disguise, except that it

contains a band of blond hair, the color and texture of which is much like the hair of Lara, the Tatrix of Tharna."

"And what is his name?" I asked.

"Surely you know," said Pa-Kur. "Alan, Alan, of the House of Hesius."

"What has all this to do with me?" I asked.

"Perhaps nothing," said Pa-Kur.

"I do not believe your story," I said.

"That is up to you, surely," said Pa-Kur.

"This has to do less with yesterday," I said, "than tomorrow."

"Certainly," said Pa-Kur. "Alan, of the House of Hesius, has been designated the state's champion."

"Not you?" I said.

"No," said Pa-Kur. "I see no point in risking a repetition of the episode on the roof of Ar's Cylinder of Justice."

"There might not be a perch to which to leap," I said. "There might not be a door through which to slip away."

"Precisely," he said.

I was silent.

"So tomorrow," said Pa-Kur, "you will meet the champion of the state, Alan of the House of Hesius."

"I see," I said.

"He is your son," said Pa-Kur.

CHAPTER SIXTY-SIX

"It is near the Ninth Ahn," said Thurnock.

"Already the stands are filled," said Seremides.

He, now blinking, trying to adjust to the darkness, leaning on his crutch, had hobbled in from the bright sand, having assessed the crowds.

"Few wish to risk being turned away," said Clitus.

"Are the heralds in place?" I asked.

"Not yet," said Seremides.

"There will be trumpets," said Hemartius. "The first notes will signal the entrance of the heralds, the second that of the disputed object and her guards, the third the parties of the prosecution and defense, the fourth the Ubar, the fifth, and last, the entrance of the contestants, from opposite sides of the arena."

It was half dark in the chamber of the challenger. Doubtless it was the same in the chamber of the state's champion.

"You do not seem yourself, Captain," said Thurnock. "Are you all right?"

"Yes," I said.

"If you are ill," said Clitus, "you may withdraw."

"That would forfeit the object to the state," said Hemartius.

"I am all right," I said.

"Did you sleep well?" asked Thurnock.

"No," I said. "I did not sleep well."

"I have known you to sleep well before many engagements, many battles," said Thurnock.

"This is the Stadium of Blades in Ar," said Hemartius. "Such a venue would be enough to shake a larl, to awe a war tharlarion."

"You are popular in Ar," said Thurnock. "Many will favor you in the challenge."

There was a blast of trumpets.

"Those are the first trumpets," said Seremides.

"The heralds will measure the war square," said Hemartius.

"The dais of the Ubar is already in place," said Seremides.

"I am sure something is wrong," said Thurnock.

"No," I said.

"Pa-Kur," I said to Seremides, "is brilliant, and leaves little to chance."

"Fear not," said Thurnock. "Long ago you defeated him, and you can do so again."

"Pa-Kur," I said, "is not the state's champion. It is a young swordsman, First Sword in the Taurentians, Alan, of the House of Hesius."

"He will know nothing of your style and skills," said Thurnock.

"Nor I of his," I said.

"Beware of him," said Seremides. "I have seen him, on the Skerry of Lars. Indeed, it was I who urged him to emigrate to Ar, where his steel could bring him name, power, fame, and wealth. I think he could have beaten me even when I was whole. I have never seen one so young so formidable with steel. It is like the sword is in his blood."

"He is your protégé," I said.

"In a sense, yes," said Seremides.

"So you wish him well?"

"Yes," said Seremides, "but, too, I wish another well."

"Thank you," I said.

"The second trumpets," said Clitus.

"The conducting forth of the object," said Hemartius.

There was much hooting and jeering from the stands.

"How will she be led forth?" I asked.

"I trust," said Thurnock, "as the worthless slut she is, naked, on a chain leash, her hands braceleted behind her back."

"No," said Hemartius. "They wish her, though a slave, to appear more as a free woman, because they expect her to be freed immediately after the combat, freed for the first few inches of a prolonged execution, one which might last weeks or months. Accordingly, she will be clad in a single garment, a modest gray tunic, such as are placed on female criminals. Somewhere under the stands, even now, the implements, flames, and chemicals of her torture are being readied."

"The hundred women who won in the ostracon contest in the theater of Publius have a special seating section in the stands," said Seremides.

"The third trumpets," said Clitus.

"I must go out now to take my place on the sand, as chief counselor for the defense," said Hemartius, "along with our adversaries, Decius Albus, Pa-Kur, and the others of the prosecution."

"I wish you well," I said.

"I wish you well," he said.

We grasped wrists, and then he, shielding his eyes, made his way through the gate, out onto the sand.

"I am sure there is something wrong," said Thurnock.

"No," I said.

What if, last night, Pa-Kur had spoken the truth?

I feared that he may have spoken the truth.

Suppose he had spoken the truth.

Then either I withdraw from the contest and Talena is forfeit to the state, to be freed and then punished, or I kill my own son, or I, myself, die at the hands of my own son.

Pa-Kur had been patient.

He had planned well.

Now, he had placed his piece, one long held in reserve, on the board.

"The trumpets, again," said Clitus. He went to the door, and opened it a few inches. "It is Marlenus," he said. "I see the purple cloak against the sand. There are guards, too, and some functionaries. Marlenus now ascends the dais of the Ubar. He now takes his place on the wooden throne. The others stand."

The purple of Marlenus's cloak was the Ubarial purple. That is a special color. Only Ubars may wear that color.

"We will accompany you," said Thurnock.

"No matter what you see, or hear, or seem to see, or hear," I said, "dear friends, do not think ill of me."

"There is the bar for the Tenth Ahn," said Thurnock.

Shortly thereafter the notes of the trumpets again sounded, and we advanced, single-file, across the bright, warm sand.

CHAPTER SIXTY-SEVEN

"Go to that corner of the square," said the herald, "that corner opposite your opponent."

The sides of the square were some forty feet in length.

"When the trumpets sound again," said the herald, "you will advance to the center of the square, to greet one another, and honor one another, sharing the cup of conflict, the wine of war. Then you will return to your respective places. At the next sounding of the trumpets, meet again at the center, blades unsheathed."

"I understand," I said.

I looked to the opposite corner. Alan, of the House of Hesius, was watching me. I was sure he respected me as an opponent, if not as a man. He exhibited no sign of feigned assurance or arrogance. I did not think he needed to. He made no attempt to intimidate me by swelling his body, stamping the ground with his bootlike sandals, or by sneering or laughing, or glaring and frowning, trying to stare down an adversary. There are many psychological artifices which may attend and complicate altercations. These can sometimes be quite effective, using an opponent's vanity, insecurity, doubts, or fear against him. I was pleased to note the apparent absence of these artifices in my opponent. I felt somehow proud that he was as he was. Might not Lara, too, were she indeed his mother, despite her fears, considering his possible jeopardy, given the profession of steel, think well of him? Might she not justifiably be proud of him? Did not such a man well honor the sword he bore and the Home Stone of Tharna? But perhaps women did not think in such ways.

"Noble Cabot," said Pa-Kur, approaching me across the sand, "the time is nigh and the Ehn is apt. I honor you as an able and worthy scion of the Scarlet Caste, which has so much in common with my own caste."

"Less perhaps than you might suppose," I said.

"Worthy foe," he said, "I bare a gift."

He bore an object wrapped in silk.

"You are generous," I said.

"I well know," said he, "the feel of weapons, the weight and balance, the grip and heft, and how one grows accustomed to their nature and character. Recently you left in the tunnels of steel, in the Beast Caves, your sword. You are now rearmed, of course, but with a less familiar weapon, one perhaps less to be trusted. Accordingly, in deference to our long and noble enmity, which means much to me, each respecting the other, allow me to return to you your sword. You may find it a valuable friend."

"I think not," I said.

"Warrior?" he said.

"Remove your glove and seize its hilt in your bare hand," I said.

"Sleen!" he hissed, and, turning, hurled the sword, spinning, outside the square of battle.

I am sure few in the stadium understood this, but I suspected Seremides did.

Almost at the same time I felt something splash against my left shoulder and the air swirled with an unfamiliar, unpleasant odor. Instantly I tore away the upper left side of my tunic and cast it behind me, outside the square of battle. Then I changed my position, rapidly striding yards away to the corner of the square to my right.

"Return to your place," said a herald.

"This is my place," I said.

"No!" said the herald.

"Do you wish to keep your blood inside your body?" I asked.

"Barbarian," sneered the herald.

The herald, perhaps despairing of dealing with a stubborn barbarian, or concerned to keep his blood in its usual place, waved Alan, of the house of Hesius, to the corner opposite mine.

Again did sound the trumpets.

My opponent and I crossed the sand, stopping some feet from one another.

"Stranger," said young Alan, politely.

I wondered if he who addressed me as 'stranger' were my son. I did not know. I did know that Pa-Kur, Master of the Black Caste, was cunning. Was his protestation true or brilliantly contrived? How did I know, even, if this Alan were truly a foundling, or even long of the House of Hesius? Might not the protestation of the Master of the Assassins be no more than a hoax to unsettle an enemy, a way of affecting the cast stones of chance?

"Stranger," I said.

How odd, I thought, were Alan of the House of Hesius my son, that I should address him as "stranger."

Two heralds then approached us, each bearing a goblet.

One of the heralds said, "The cup of conflict, the wine of war." One then handed a goblet to Alan and the other to me.

Alan lifted his goblet to me and then drank.

I remembered Pa-Kur. I did not drink.

Alan seemed surprised, and disappointed.

"It is only water," said the herald to me, he who had handed me my goblet, "water from the spring thaw of the mountains of the Voltai."

I handed him back the goblet.

"You will not drink?" asked Alan.

"No," I said.

Alan then handed his goblet back to the herald from whom he had received it.

"I honored you," said Alan, "but you do not honor me."

"Forgive me," I said.

"Drink," he said.

"No," I said.

"You do me insult," he said.

"Such is not my intention," I said.

"I am insulted," he said.

"I am sorry," I said.

"I understand you are skilled with the blade," said Alan.

"I understand that of you, as well," I said.

"Then why do you resort to games, why do you attempt to rouse my anger? Do you think it will make me more precipitate and less careful, that it will lock or tighten my grasp, that it will affect my timing?"

"No," I said.

"Perhaps," said Alan, "you might comment on my unusual hair. I have been the butt of such sport since childhood. But seldom more than once from any single person."

"I would not subject you to such criticism," I said. "I have endured similar things."

"Your hair is dark," said Alan.

"I have kept it so for months," I said.

I had kept my hair dyed since taking ship to Jad.

"To be less conspicuous, less noted, less recognized?" said Alan.

"Yes," I said.

"Why?" he asked.

"Why does the yellow-pelted tabuk frequent groves of ka-la-na trees?" I asked. "Why is the black sleen nocturnal?"

"Are you ready to return to your places?" asked one of the heralds. "The trumpets will then sound."

"I am," said Alan.

"Hold," I said.

"What is it?" asked one of the heralds.

I ignored him. Rather I spoke to my opponent.

"Consider what you are doing," I said. "Consider whom you serve. Consider for what you fight."

"I am a sword of Ar," he said. "I am a Taurentian. I serve Marlenus of Ar. I am appointed champion of the state. I act on behalf of a court of Ar. I am in fee. All that I do is legitimate and lawful."

"And do you approve of everything that is legitimate and lawful?" I asked.

"I am in fee," he said. "Such considerations are beyond my purview."

"Look about you," I said. "See the dais of office, and Marlenus, robed in purple, on his temporary throne; see the party of the prosecution, Decius Albus, Pa-Kur, the Assassin, and others; see Hemartius, chief counsel for the prisoner; see crippled Seremides, returner of the Home Stone of Ar, and others."

"I see them," said Alan, "and thousands in the stands, as well, who will soon grow impatient."

"Now look," I said, "at the prisoner at the pole, pathetic and helpless, in her thin, gray gown, her only garment, her hands braceleted high and back, over her head, her sleeves falling down her arms, to the elbows, a belly chain pulling her back against the pole, her shackled ankles, visible below the gown, the chain run behind the pole."

"I chose not to regard her," said Alan.

Interestingly, Talena seemed different now from before. She was pale, and seemed distraught. She pulled a little, futilely, at the cuffs on her wrists. She was well held. Where now was her arrogance and scornful demeanor? She cast me, I whom she hated, an agonized look. I thought her lips framed the name Tarl. Despised as I was, might I not yet serve her purposes? What other hope had she? Her eyes were wild, pleading. I wondered if, perhaps, last night, she had overheard the raucous jargon of guards, discussing what was to be done with her. Or perhaps she had dreamed what it might be to pay the penalty for her crimes. Had she awakened screaming, to which outburst the guards responded by laughter? Perhaps, alone in her cell, late at night or early in the morning, she had sensed the merciless tongs of reality opening and reaching for her. I had the sense she was, at last, truly afraid. Talena did not want to die.

I was confident that Alan would not turn to look upon the prisoner, perhaps fearing he might feel pity.

But then might he not, instead, a Gorean, feel scorn?

I would appeal to his manhood, to a man's regret at the spoiling or loss of splendid girl meat.

"Is she not slender and soft, and stunningly beautiful?" I asked. "Can you not sense the enticements of her figure beneath her thin gown?"

"Desist in your games," said Alan.

"Surely you know the fate that will befall her should you be successful in this match."

"So I should arrange to be unsuccessful?" he said.

"Even now, within the stadium, in ill-lit chambers, fires are kindled, irons are heating, instruments and means of torture are being readied. Do you truly want that fair form and body to be lacerated and burned, twisted and torn?"

"You are clever," said Alan, "and, as you obviously wish to accrue undeserved advantage to yourself, I think, a coward."

"Be careful of your speech, noble swordsman," said one of the heralds. "Geoffrey of Harfax is popular in Ar."

"He is a tarsk," said Alan. "He seeks to sway me from my duty, to blind my eyes with tears, to slow my blade, to blunt its edges."

"I ask you only to consider what you do," I said.

"The woman is a traitress," said Alan, "duly tried and found guilty in a court of law, and is thus subject to suffering the consequences of her crimes. Your transparent machinations, I assure you, will neither slow nor quicken my blade."

"Return to your places," said one of the heralds.

"Noble Geoffrey of Harfax," said Alan, "when first I came upon the sand, I thought you worthier than I find you. No matter how this match may enfold, know that I despise you and denounce you as both a villain and coward."

"Your places," urged the second herald.

"Do not drink," I said to him, for he held my goblet.

"It is just water," he said.

"Do not drink," I said.

He poured the contents of the goblet into the sand.

Alan and I then went to our places.

Shortly thereafter, the heralds withdrawn and the sand cleared, there was a blare of trumpets, and a cry of anticipation from the stands, following which Alan and I advanced toward one another.

CHAPTER SIXTY-EIGHT

The two blades inquired of one another.

There were two or three flashes of steel.

Neither of us were willing to extend ourselves. Sometimes what seems an opening is not an opening, but a trap.

Alan was a fine swordsman. If he were truly a foundling, raised in the House of Hesius, he would have been familiar with bladework from early childhood. I knew that Seremides had been much impressed with him on the Skerry of Lars, and Seremides was not a fellow easily impressed. Certainly he had regarded him as worthy of the Taurentians. I knew it was not impossible that Alan had been a foundling given to, sold to, or discovered by, a sword house. Such houses, like establishments of many other sorts, farms, factories, shipyards, and such, muchly replenish their stock thusly. Female foundlings, on the other hand, are usually picked up for the slave houses. The girls, usually after their first bleeding, are marked and collared. They seldom object because for years they know what will be done with them and have been eagerly looking forward to their first master. Few children thusly, at least on Gor, perish of neglect or exposure.

There were four guards about Talena.

For the moment, Alan and I backed away from one another. In a formal duel this is not that unusual. Sometimes thoughts come at such a time. One looks at the duel, briefly, as if from the point of view of a spectator. What did we note about one another? What had we learned of one another?

One of the guards standing near Talena made a gesture as if he, with a knife, were opening her belly to the neck, and she screamed in fear, and he laughed. Then she cried out, wildly, "Fight! Fight! Kill him! Kill the state's champion! Kill him! Kill him!"

"Let us re-engage," said Alan.

"Of course," I said.

Again our blades met, quickly, sharply, but tentatively.

I had the impression that even if Alan did not honor or respect his opponent, he respected the blade which faced him.

After some two Ehn I was confident I could kill my opponent. I wondered if he felt a similar confidence in his own skills. It is hard to say about such things. Was I correct? Could I kill him, or had he, in some intentional way, meant to convince me of that?

Was he my son?

I did not think it likely. Surely it was some scheme of Pa-Kur to slow my arm, to weaken my blade, to cause me to inadvertently hesitate, hesitate at a moment when hesitation might be the difference between victory and defeat, between life and death.

I stepped back and placed my blade on the sand.

The stands were quiet, stunned.

"No! No!" screamed Talena. "I do not want to die!"

"Pick up your sword," said Alan.

"I decline," I said.

"The prisoner will be forfeit to the state," said Alan.

There was much hooting and jeering from the stands.

"Strike," I said.

"I am not a butcher," said Alan. "You have your life, your worthless life. I, in contempt, give it to you."

"Coward! Coward!" screamed the crowd.

I had adjudged Alan's response accurately. I was still alive.

Many about the square of battle seemed stunned, or dismayed. Seremides, leaning on his crutch, regarded me with disbelief. Thurnock and Clitus appeared stricken. Hemartius appeared relieved. Decius Albus was smiling. I sensed that Pa-Kur's mind was racing, trying to fit this development into some significant pattern, and was unable to do so. Even the faces of the heralds were covered with scorn.

"You cowardly urt!" screamed Talena, shaking her chains, tears streaming down her face. "Urt! Urt!"

Her four guards seemed pleased.

Alan placed his sword atop mine in the sand, and, turning, approached the dais of office on which was seated Marlenus of Ar.

I then lost not a moment but quickly drew my sword from beneath that of my previous opponent, and sped toward him. There was shouting, and, as he turned, startled, I struck him with my shoulder, sprawling him half in the sand and half on the dais, and I had the point of my sword at his throat.

His hands were clenched, he was half on his back.

"Strike, strike, sleen!" he cried, tears in his eyes.

I drew back my blade, as though to plunge it into his throat.

"No!" said Marlenus. "Do not strike!"

I lowered my sword, sweating with fear. Happily, I had adjudged the response of Marlenus correctly.

Alan scrambled to his feet.

He raced to the sword, thrust the hilt into the sand, and prepared to throw himself on the point.

"Do not!" commanded Marlenus, as I had expected. I knew Marlenus better than Alan. Alan, tears in his eyes, stood up, straightening his body.

"Pick up your sword," commanded Marlenus.

"I am no longer worthy to do so," said Alan.

"That is my judgment," said Marlenus. "Not yours. Pick it up."

Alan did so, looking at me with hatred, his face stained with tears of rage and frustration.

"You are young, you will learn from this," said Marlenus. "The duel is done." The Ubar then turned to me. "The slave is yours," he said. "Once again, deceit, cunning, dishonor, and cowardice reign victorious." He then said to the guards of Talena, "Release the slave."

The stands, like spreading fire, burning through dry grass, began to grow enflamed, as they began to understand what was happening.

I thought it would be wise not to remain long in Ar.

Stadium keepers had arrived, with rakes, to smooth the sand.

One, bending down, retrieved the sword Pa-Kur had offered me, which I had refused to accept and which he had cast angrily out of the square. Another reached down and picked up the part of the tunic I had torn away after being splashed with the strange-smelling fluid.

Talena, freed, rubbing her wrists, turned and spat upon the pole to which she had been secured.

"You had no permission to do that," snarled a guard.

She then angrily, furiously, spat upon the guard. The guard was startled and I was horrified. In an instant he, recovered, had his hand in her hair, had flung her to his feet and ripped his sword free of the sheath. His eyes were wild.

"Hold, hold!" I cried, rushing forward.

I placed my body between the blade and Talena. It trembled in the air, wavering, and then he thrust it angrily in his sheath, and turned away.

I lifted Talena to her feet. "You are mad," I said. "Do you not know what you do?"

"I do what I wish!" she cried. "I am Talena of Ar, the daughter of Marlenus of Ar!"

Seremides then, with Hemartius, Thurnock, and Clitus were about me. Thurnock's and Clitus's faces betrayed grief. This hurt me. Then they faced away, eyeing those about, prepared, no matter what I had done, to defend me. True friendship, even under the most terrible of stresses, does not alter.

"Excellent, friend Cabot," said Seremides. "I myself could scarcely have managed so clever a victory."

"The stands grow restless, dark, unsettled, and ugly," said Hemartius. "You are no longer favored by the crowd."

"We must leave Ar, as soon as possible," said Seremides. "There will not be enough guardsmen to protect us, even should they wish to do so."

At that moment there was a scream of pain.

One of the stadium keepers, he who had retrieved the sword offered to me by Pa-Kur, was down on his knees, frenziedly thrusting his right hand into the sand.

"What is that?" said Hemartius. "Has he been bitten by an ost?"

"There are no osts in arena sand," said Seremides. "But one may be burned by another venom, a different venom, one which lies in wait on a surface, perhaps the hilt of a sword."

"Let us leave," said Talena.

"We are going," I said.

"I am a free woman," she said. "You must protect me."

"You are not free," I said.

"Do not joke," she said. "I could put guardsmen on you."

"A moment ago, you could have died under the blade of one," I said.

"We are in danger," said Hemartius. "See Decius Albus, Pa-Kur, and others of the prosecution. They observe; they confer; they do not wish us well."

"As I am free," said Talena, "I must be guarded with your very lives. Nothing must happen to me. I fear the crowd, the rabble. Let us hasten away. I do not wish to risk torture again."

"You were never in danger of torture," I said. "It was arranged. Thurnock had an arrow for your heart."

Talena turned white.

"I do not think the crowd will stay long in the stands," said Hemartius. "They will pour forth; they will leap to the sand at any moment. Hear the cries, the threats!"

"Guard me," said Talena. "Conduct me to safety. Do it. I demand it! Now!"

"Beat her," said Seremides.

"Sleen," said Talena.

She took an angry step, toward one of the exits.

"Do not go that way," said Hemartius. "Something is wrong there. See the stadium keepers. One of their number totters. He can scarcely stand."

"It is he," said Seremides, "who, raking and dressing the sand, picked up the cloth which friend Cabot tore from his tunic."

"I do not understand," said Hemartius.

"Like the sword hilt," said Seremides, "the lair of a hidden enemy, an engineered impairment designed to weaken or temporarily disable its victim."

"But not to kill its victim?" said Hemartius.

"Certainly not," said Seremides. "The victim, by plan, given the challenge, was to die by the sword."

"And," I said, "doubtless the fluid in the cup of conflict, that in the wine of war, was similarly seasoned."

"Undoubtedly," said Seremides.

"Did Alan, he of the House of Hesius, the state's champion, know?" asked Hemartius.

"I do not know," said Seremides.

"I do not think so," I said.

"Hurry, fools," said Talena. "I must be sped from here, to be suitably veiled and gowned, and carried to safety."

"You are clothed now, far more than the law decrees," said Seremides, "for what you are."

"For what I am?" she said.

"Kajira," he said.

"Insulting tarsk!" she said.

"She is too stupid to understand her condition," said Hemartius, "let alone to rejoice in it."

"I am not stupid," said Talena. "Rather it is you who are stupid. My body, my priceless beauty, mine own and no one else's, may be muchly covered, but the garment is thin, of poor material, and drab, and it is my only garment. It is unworthy of me. It is insulting! And I have no veil! Even the lower castes may look upon my features boldly."

"What a tragedy, what a feast," said Seremides.

"Urt!" said Talena.

"This way," I said, earnestly, "the side entrance though which we trod out upon the sand."

Talena spun about and ran toward the foot of the dais. On it, still on the temporary throne of wood, was Marlenus.

Beside him was Alan, apparently having been permitted the honor of standing at the side of the throne.

"Come back!" I called to her.

She stood before the dais. "See, Father," she cried. "I am here! I stand before you, impenitent and defiant! You did not have your way! Be chagrined! Be shamed! You do not have my blood! I live! I am alive! You did not have your way!"

Marlenus was impassive.

"Come away," said Seremides. "What do you know of the way of a Ubar?"

"Hurry!" I said, seizing Talena by the arm.

My eyes met those of Alan, the young swordsman of the House of Hesius. In his eyes I saw only hatred. My eyes met, too, those of Marlenus. In his eyes I saw only contempt.

Then, half dragging Talena across the sand, I, followed by the others, rushed toward the side entrance though which we had, not so long ago, first entered upon the sand.

In a few Ehn, we were making our way through the labyrinth of dark, clammy tunnels which lay below the Stadium of Blades.

"We can reach the streets though a shaft," I said. "Exits may be watched."

"They will be," said Seremides.

"Carry me," said Talena. "The tunnel is damp. I am uncomfortable. I may soil my feet."

I lifted her into my arms.

So we continued, for some time, to make our way through the tunnels, sometimes narrow and low.

"Wait," whispered Seremides. "We are being followed."

We could see the dim light of a tharlarion-oil lamp flickering behind us.

CHAPTER SIXTY-NINE

I lowered Talena gently to the floor of the tunnel in the darkness.

I put her behind me. Hemartius went to stand beside her. I quietly eased my sword from its sheath. So, too, so quietly, was drawn the sword of Seremides. Thurnock fitted an arrow to his bow. The arrow was trained on the darkness below and to the left of the lamp. Clitus shook out his net.

"Attack them!" whispered Talena, urgently. Then there was a stifled sound as Hemartius apparently placed his hand over her mouth and held her to him. Hemartius was not a large or strong man, but his strength was more than enough to subdue a woman. I wondered if women ever gave much thought to such things.

"They have stopped," said Seremides.

"Because we have stopped," I said.

"I would expect them to extinguish the lamp," said Clitus.

"They do not do so," whispered Thurnock.

"I take that," said Seremides, "to be a good sign."

"Or one of stupidity," said Thurnock.

"Hold," I called down the tunnel. "Identify yourselves."

"Friends," came the response.

"Beware," whispered Thurnock, "the larl and sleen may proclaim friendship to the tabuk and verr."

"Beloved mentor," said a voice.

"It is Xenon," said Seremides.

"The Assassin," I said.

"You are alive now," said Seremides, "because Xenon warned me of the devices of Pa-Kur."

"Approach slowly," I said, "and hold the lamp so we may see your features."

"It is Xenon," said Seremides.

"Who is with you?" I asked.

"I am Aetius of Venna," said the other voice.

"It is he," said Thurnock.

I sensed Talena squirming in the arms of Hemartius.

"Let her speak," I said.

"Uncover the slave's mouth," said Seremides.

"They are enemies," whispered Talena. "Kill them now, quickly, before their ruse of friendship proves successful, before it secures them victory."

"Cover the slave's mouth," said Seremides.

There was sudden sound of stifled protest. I sensed, once again, Talena's futile attempt to free herself from the grip of Hemartius.

"I thank you for my life," I said to Xenon.

"We have shared food, we have shared drink," said Xenon.

"Your allegiance," I said, "is to Pa-Kur, to the Black Caste."

"I am strong," he said, "but short and homely. Few oarsmen even cared to share a bench with me, but I pulled more than my weight, plying those mighty levers. Who cares to be looked down upon, who cares to be despised? Who admires a draft beast of a man? But the Assassins were feared. If I shared their cloak I, too, could be feared. Let those then who had laughed at me shudder instead at the sight of my sable garb. But the Assassin has his work and his place in society and I did not care for the work or the place. Too, many of the Assassins are handsome, and tall. One cannot expect them, any more than the handsome and tall elsewhere, to seek my company. It is a hard thing to bear, being a monster, misshapen and ugly."

"You are not a monster, nor are you misshapen and ugly," I said.

"Free women scorn me," he said.

"So little do some know, so little can some think," I said. "And many of the most beautiful women, well collared, respond a hundred times more to intelligence, strength, and power in a man than to symmetrical features and a fair frame. In need of a master, they often dream of being at the feet of such a man. Men seek beauty, but beauty seeks man."

"With you and Master Seremides," he said, "I was respected and accepted. How could it be? But it was. Master Seremides, even, on the voyage from the Skerry of Lars to Jad, would have saved my life, whatever might have been his purpose or motive. One does not forget such things. I served Pa-Kur loyally and well until it seemed I should no longer do so. Perhaps somewhere between Jad and Ar, or even in Ar itself, I realized that the black dagger was not congenial to the grip of my hand. I do not know. It did not fit. I have left the caste."

"Beware," said Seremides, "one does not lightly put aside the sable cloak."

"That is well known to me," said Xenon. "When one wearing the black dagger seeks me, I, too, might then, for the last time, put that terrible stain upon my forehead."

A desperate whimper came from Talena.

"Why do you cover the mouth of the slave?" asked Xenon. "Why not just silence her with a word, silence her by the master's will?"

"Let her speak," I said.

Hemartius removed his hand from Talena's mouth.

"The other one," she said, "is Aetius, of Venna! He is a bounty hunter! Guard me! Protect me! Kill him!"

"You seem to be eager to have others do your killing for you," I said.

"And what bounty is on you now?" asked Seremides.

"And to whom should I turn you over, and for what reward?" asked Aetius.

"You are no longer a fabulous prize," said Seremides. "You are no longer worth more than any other comely slave."

"You beast," she said.

"You might be subject, of course, to common slave theft," said Hemartius.

Slaves, of course, as other properties, might be stolen.

"I am the daughter of a Ubar!" she said.

"One who has disinherited and disowned you," said Seremides.

"I carry the blood of a Ubar!" said Talena.

"That is true," acknowledged Hemartius.

I wondered if it were so, recalling a speculation which I had entertained long ago, even from the World's End.

"Why have you joined us?" I asked Aetius.

"I received two hundred gold pieces for my part in the recovery of the Home Stone of Ar," he said. "I did not expect to receive a tarsk-bit. Might I not follow you, hoping more coins might fall from your purse?"

"We walk with danger," I said.

"To walk so is not unfamiliar to me," he said.

"Decius Albus is not pleased with the outcome of the challenge," said Xenon. "He will act against you."

"Robe me in splendor," said Talena, "and flee from the city."

"He will expect flight," I said. "The gates will be watched. It will be safer to remain in the city, unseen."

"Pa-Kur knows of our domicile in the Metellan district," said Seremides.

"Surely he would not be foolish enough to think you would return there," said Hemartius.

"On the contrary, I think he might think us exactly foolish enough to do so," I said. "He will at least place the domicile under surveillance."

"Why would you return?" asked Talena.

"Iris," I said.

"Who is Iris?" asked Talena, not pleased.

"A barbarian slave," said Seremides.

"Only a slave, and a barbarian yet," said Talena. "Let her go. Forget her. Get me safely out of Ar."

"You still think of yourself as a free woman," I said.

"I am free!" she said.

I gathered that she did not understand how Iris might be viewed.

I gathered that she did not know the possible meaning of a slave to a man, one who holds her chain.

"Discard her," said Talena. "Slaves are worthless."

Did she not know that men would risk their lives for them?

"Who would drop a silver tarsk and not bend down and pick it up?" asked Seremides.

"Get me out of Ar!" demanded Talena.

"Clitus and I have a room in an insula, near the public tharlarion stables," said Thurnock. "I do not think it is known."

"It will not do," said Talena. "The odor is offensive, unacceptable."

"You were seen with me in the stadium," I said, "a Peasant with a bow, a fisherman with a net and trident. Inquiries will be made. Sooner or later men will be referred to that building."

"Something further might well be considered," said Seremides. "Decius Albus may be in greater jeopardy than we."

"That is true," I said. "Marlenus, no longer drugged and the challenge done, is likely to seek a reckoning with the trade advisor."

"Which means," said Seremides, "that the trade advisor, in desperation, frightened, may seek to strike first."

"There must be a grating nearby, overhead," I said. "We have passed several. As soon as it is dark outside, we shall lift it and slide it aside, and then venture upon the streets."

CHAPTER SEVENTY

"There are three, and they are not Assassins," said Thurnock, "one on the balcony below, with a bow, two on the street, with swords, in the shadows, one on each side of the door."

"I count the same," I said.

Seremides was not with us, as the stairs and ladders of the dismal insula opposite that other which contained our basement apartment, one of several, could not be well managed by one with his handicap. With him, in the vestibule of the insula on whose roof we stood, which they had entered from the rear, were Xenon, who did not wish to leave his side, and Aetius.

"There may be others nearby, who will issue forth, responding to a signal," said Thurnock.

"That is likely," I said. "Decius Albus leaves little to chance."

"But he may need his men more urgently elsewhere," said Clitus.

"Let us hope so," I said.

"I fear this will be a night to remember in Ar," said Hemartius.

"I hope not," I said. "I wish merely to retrieve Iris and make away."

"You are a fool," said Talena. "Leave now. Do not waste time. It will be light soon."

"No," said Hemartius, "we have not even heard the bar for the Twentieth Ahn."

"Still, light will come too soon!" she said. "We need every Ihn. Leave the slave. Forget her. Slaves are cheap, and meaningless. Buy another, if you wish. We must seek a hiding place, find me regalia, preferably that of a rich merchant woman, a splendid disguise, and await our chance to slip from the city."

"No," I said.

"If you will not listen to reason," she said, "there is a simple way to bring you swiftly to your senses. I need only scream and the enemy, if there is one, will be alerted, and the neighborhood will be aroused."

"Do not!" said Hemartius.

Clitus seized Talena from behind, pulling her to him, his right hand clapped firmly over her mouth. She could scarcely move.

"What shall we do with her, Captain?" he asked.

"Cut her throat," said Thurnock.

"Gag and bind her, hand and foot," I said.

"As a slave?" asked Hemartius.

"Yes," I said.

Talena struggled furiously, futilely.

Hemartius then, as Clitus held her, served her as I had suggested. He did this swiftly, and with efficiency. Gorean boys, as part of their growing up, are taught to gag and bind female slaves, rendering them utterly helpless, even to speak. Talena thrashed angrily, helplessly, at my feet.

"Wrists to ankles?" asked Hemartius, looking up.

Talena shook her head wildly, desperately, negatively.

"Yes," I said.

I then thrust her to her right shoulder, on the roof on which we stood. She twisted to look up at me. She struggled a bit, but quickly realized that she was totally helpless. She then, quickly, looked away. There was a frightened, wild, strange look in her eyes. She could not have her way. It would be done with her as others pleased. I considered asking her forgiveness, but thought the better of it. Her relatively long, modest, if drab and flimsy, gown, was high on her thighs. I considered adjusting it, but I did not do so. She had excellent legs. It was pleasant to look on them. Why should they not be seen? I looked down on her, not dissatisfied. Then I turned away. She could stay there on the insula roof, gagged and helpless, until we decided what to do with her.

"The fellow on the balcony below, with the bow," I said, "is a lookout. He watches. He signals the foes who lie in wait."

"And perhaps others," said Clitus.

"Quite possibly," I said.

Thurnock fitted an arrow to his bow.

"Should he lift his bow, or reach for a whistle, or such," said Thurnock, "it will be the last time he will do so."

"Clitus, Hemartius, and I," I said, "will descend within the insula to the vestibule. Clitus and Xenon will then exit through the back of the insula and circle about, Clitus to take the foe on the left, by the door, and Xenon to take the foe on the right, on the other side of the door. Wait until I emerge abruptly from the vestibule and walk hurriedly across the street toward the door of the basement apartment. This will startle the foes, and engage their attention. Then as they, their attention on me, hasten to close with me, you will be behind them. If they turn to face you, I will be behind them."

"And Aetius and Seremides might then emerge, as well, to assist us," said Clitus.

"Yes," I said. "It is unlikely that the foes know that we are now two more, Xenon and Aetius."

"What of me?" asked Hemartius.

"Should a legal matter arise," I said, "we shall summon you."

"It seems they should have more in reserve," said Clitus. "Three seems not so many."

"They may depend on the bowman, ensconced in his supposedly unassailable position," I said.

"I suspect others are concealed, waiting to rush forth," said Thurnock.

"Yes," I said, "if Decius Albus does not wish to apply them elsewhere."

"I feel this is a night of terrors in Ar," said Hemartius. "Ar may change hands before dawn."

"Those are terrors," I said, "in which we need not participate."

"They may be terrors in which we cannot help but participate," said Thurnock.

"How so?" I asked.

"Imagine the resources of Ar in the hands of Decius Albus," said Thurnock, "conjoined with the forces of Kurii, and the naval might of Cos and Tyros."

"It could be the end of the small cities, the capture of Torcadino and Brundisium, the end of Port Kar," said Clitus.

"Perhaps of Gor," said Thurnock, "as we know it."

"The hurricanes of war will rage as they will," I said. "We can do little about it."

"Sometimes," said Thurnock, "swords must be lifted, even if only against the wind."

"That is futile," I said.

"There is a saying," said Clitus, "that if the sword is sharp enough, it can draw blood from the wind."

"Such things are the concerns of states," I said, "not ours."

"When the scales are balanced," said Thurnock, "a pebble may decide the fate of mountains."

"Let us put our immediate plan into action," I said.

We then, Clitus, Hemartius, and I, descended from the roof of the insula, by means of ladders and then stairs, through levels and shafts, hallways and corridors smelling of garbage and urine, to the floor from which the street might be directly accessed, leaving behind us Thurnock with his readied arrow, and a gagged, well-trussed slave.

CHAPTER SEVENTY-ONE

I kicked open the door.

"Master!" wept Iris.

I hurried to her side and thrust the key into the manacle clasping her left ankle, opened it, and slid it, and the chain, away from the ring.

"There were men outside," she said. "Beware! I heard them."

"They are no longer outside," I said. "Others, however, may appear at any moment. Fetch what food and drink you can and heel me."

Swiftly she thrust some bread, cheese, and dried coils of verr meat into a sack.

We then departed the apartment.

A frightened gasp escaped her as she saw two bodies sprawled in the street. In the darkness she did not discern that one had been cut at the back of the neck with a single, clean stroke suggesting the skill of an Assassin and the other had three puncture wounds in the back, apparently delivered with one thrust of a single weapon.

I made my way across the street to the vestibule of the insula from which I had emerged shortly before.

"Oh!" said Iris, moving to the side to avoid a body lying on the pavement, near the door, a snapped arrow in its back.

Apparently the cohort of Decius Albus, struck by the arrow, had plunged forward, breaking through the railing on the balcony, and plunged to the pavement below. The body must have twisted in its flight or rolled after the impact as the arrow was broken some horts below the fletching.

I entered the insula through the heavy, narrow, now-opened door, followed by Iris. Most Gorean dwellings are constructed with the possibility of defense in mind. This accounted for the narrowness of the portal and the weight of the door. The door also consisted of two horizontal parts, each of which could be individually barred. If the top portion of the door is opened, one gains some protection but, more importantly, one can see who is at the door, can look about and reconnoiter the vicinity, and so on. If the bottom of the door only is opened then anyone who enters is much at the mercy of the defenders.

Within were Thurnock, Xenon, Clitus, Seremides, Aetius, Hemartius, and, on the floor, a gagged, bound slave.

"There was no signal given," I said to Thurnock.

"Much happened quickly," said Thurnock. "I think no opportunity presented itself."

"Decius Albus, tonight, I suspect," said Seremides, "is concerned to conserve men, but it seems unlikely he would have had only three employed here."

"Others will doubtless appear, sooner or later, to check with their fellows," said Clitus.

"Then we should make away as quickly as possible," I said.

"It may be too late," said Thurnock, peering through a rectangular, sliding panel in the upper portion of the door.

I stood beside him and he stepped to the side.

"Perhaps they were waiting for a signal which never came," said Thurnock.

"It is near the Twentieth Ahn," said Hemartius.

"I count only eight," I said.

"So few?" said Clitus.

"Something else is afoot," said Hemartius, "more of concern than we."

"They have discovered the two bodies by the door," I said. "One now enters the apartment across the way, through the door hanging awry."

"He emerges," I said. "He has discovered that Iris is missing. They confer. One sees the body of the fallen bowman. They look this way."

"They suspect we have taken refuge here?" said Aetius.

"I do not know," I said. "They may well suspect we have left the vicinity."

"I do not think they will attempt the insula," said Seremides.

"Not with so few," I said.

In the field, advantage commonly accrues to the offense. Within walls, the advantage commonly accrues to the defense. A hundred men can defend a holding against a thousand. Statistically, few sieges are successful. There are three major reasons for this, it is difficult to maintain and supply the large number of men necessary to invest a holding, town, or city in the field, the disproportionate risk to attackers facing a sheltered foe, and the risk of unexpected sorties by the defenders, the nature and timing of which is at the election of the besieged.

"I suspect," said Hemartius, "their appearance is less motivated by curiosity, given the absence of a signal, as it is by some independent consideration."

"What?" I asked.

"Participation in a coup," said Hemartius. "After the recovery of Marlenus and the surprising outcome in the Stadium of Blades, Decius Albus must act."

"Much is thus explained," said Thurnock. "Else he would have had a hundred men in the street."

"When he owns Ar," said Hemartius, "he can always attend to the rectification of small grievances, settling temporarily neglected accounts."

"How can Decius Albus own Ar?" asked Aetius, skeptically.

"It is not as difficult as you might think," said Hemartius. "His private army has some fifteen hundred men. There is presumably something like a thousand guardsmen in Ar, including the Taurentians."

"What of the citizenry of Ar?" asked Aetius.

"They will awaken, confused, to shouting and the clash of arms," said Hemartius. "They will not understand what is going on. They will believe what they are told. Assuming that Marlenus is quickly done away with, Decius Albus may claim he has intervened to protect the Ubar, his intervention unfortunately too late, against a usurpation by guardsmen and Taurentians, perhaps disgruntled by, even outraged by, this afternoon's developments in the Stadium of Blades, the escape of Talena from the Tarns of Justice."

Talena, bound, whimpered in her bonds.

"Who could believe that?" asked Aetius.

"Many," said Hemartius. "You know little of Ar. For years, Decius Albus has courted the favor of the people of Ar. Is he not a noble benefactor and philanthropist seeking selflessly only the welfare and happiness of his fellow citizens? Has he not sponsored games and races, paid for song dramas and plays, organized parades and spectacles, provided lavish public feasts? Who would not be pleased with a Ubar who asks nothing of his subjects but to entertain, feed, and please them?"

"I have seen his statues about the city," said Aetius.

"You can also buy figurines in local markets," said Hemartius.

"Our friends are leaving," I said, moving back a bit from the panel in the heavy door. "We will reconnoiter and withdraw through the rear exit of the insula."

"The Twentieth Ahn looms," said Hemartius.

"You think that our friends wish to be in place by the Twentieth Ahn?" I asked.

"I would not be surprised," said he.

Thurnock regarded me. "Do you think a coup is planned?" he asked.

"I do not know," I said. "Hemartius thinks so. He may be right."

"Then our plans must change," said Thurnock.

"Not at all," I said. "We will find a hiding place, robe Talena suitably, as she wishes, and wait, later to try to escape from the city."

"All to protect Talena?" asked Thurnock.

"Each may go his own way," I said.

"I do not understand," said Thurnock, "how one who can handle a sword as you do can be such a fool."

"What would you do with Talena?" I asked.

"Throw her to sleen," said Thurnock.

"Dear Hemartius," I said. "We soon leave. Free Talena, that she may accompany us."

Iris was regarding Talena uneasily.

"What is wrong?" I asked her.

"She is not collared," whispered, Iris. "Is she a free woman?"

"No," I said. "Do not be afraid."

Still Iris moved away from Talena.

Shortly thereafter Talena's ankles were freed and she struggled angrily to her feet. Her hands were still tied behind her, and a long length of rope fell behind her from her bound wrists.

"The gag?" asked Hemartius.

"Remove it," I said. "She may be uncomfortable."

As soon as the gag was pulled away, Talena looked angrily at me. "Beast!" she said. "Never treat me again as you did! Do you understand?"

"Leech plants might do, too," suggested Thurnock.

I turned away from Talena.

"What is that?" I heard her say. Then she said, "Is that what you risked us for, a mere slave, a collared she-tarsk?" Then she snapped, "Down, slave, on your knees! You are in the presence of a free woman!"

I spun about.

Iris was on her knees, trembling, head down, terrified.

"Were my hands free!" said Talena. "Would I had a switch! I would teach your legs and arms what it is to stand in the presence of a free woman!"

"Get up," I said to Iris. "She is as much a slave as you."

Iris rose to her feet, shaking.

"Skinny she-tarsk," said Talena. "What did you sell for, a tarsk-bit? A crumb of bread, a rind of larma to flavor tea, or did they give you away?"

"Do not mind her, Iris," I said.

"I am afraid, Master," she said.

"Do not be," I said.

"Give her to me," said Thurnock, "that black-haired, green-eyed, olive-skinned, curvaceous slab of collar-meat! I'll have her begging to lick and kiss your feet in five Ehn."

"She is overwrought," I said.

"She must be taught that she is no more now than any other worthless slave," said Thurnock.

"Please," I said. "She has endured much. Do not offend her sensibilities."

"Barbarian!" said Talena. Then she turned to Iris. "Get out of my sight!" she said.

Iris scurried to the side.

"Look," I said to Talena, "I can name a first-girl here, and, if I do, it will not be you."

"No, Master," exclaimed Iris, shaking her head wildly. "I do not want to be first-girl. I am afraid of her. She is a free woman, or too much like a free woman!"

"You would not dare!" said Talena. "Free my hands!"

"I hear the babble of two slaves," said Seremides, "one of whom does not know she is a slave. Let us be on our way. If Decius Albus is concerned to accomplish a coup and is successful, it would be best not to be easily noted."

"Quite," I said.

"I must be removed safely from Ar," said Talena, "as soon as is practical. Many in Ar, particularly in the lower castes, do not understand me, and do not approve of me, and might wish to do me injury. But, first, I must be well housed and well disguised. The raiment and veils of a woman of the high Merchants will do nicely."

"But many," said Aetius, "do not recognize the Merchants as a high caste."

"Exactly," said Talena. "Thus, all the better, as a disguise. Who would expect that Talena of Ar might conceal herself in the robes of a low caste?"

"It might not be easy to conceal ourselves," said Clitus, "particularly if calls go out for us, if a search is made."

"I refuse to be ill housed," said Talena.

"Perhaps we could keep her in a tharlarion stable," said Thurnock. "Several are near where Clitus and I were lodging."

"Peasant," said Talena, "why do you not go somewhere and shovel dung or pull a plow?"

"I would like to hitch you to a plow and use the whip on you," said Thurnock.

It is not unusual, in the fields, to yoke slave girls and use them to plow. To be sure, most such girls would be considerably larger and stronger than Talena.

"Peasant tarsk!" said Talena.

"The Peasantry is the ox on which the Home Stone rests," I said.

"Obviously," said Seremides, "we cannot return to the apartment."

"We have coin," I said, "and coin can buy many things, even silence."

"Speak," said Seremides. Xenon was at his side.

"They will search for us, if they do," I said, "in dingy, crooked streets, in crowded hovels, in dismal precincts, in foul insulae, in houses where a tarsk-bit buys you a bowl of porridge and a bed for the night, but why not buy our way into safety and luxury? Why not rent where we could not rent. Why not rent where gold can buy us comfort, privacy, and security? That option is not likely to occur to men who search for frightened, desperate, penurious fugitives. Who moves from the Metellan district to, say, the tower of Philebus?"

"That will do," said Talena. "Certainly the Metellan district will not."

"Your plan meets with the slave's approval," said Thurnock.

"Fortunate," said Clitus.

"I think we should soon take our leave," said Seremides.

"Free my hands," said Talena.

"A problem presents itself," said Seremides. "The green-eyed slave is not collared. Thus she might be taken for a free woman."

"I am a free woman!" snapped Talena.

"But," said Seremides, "she is not veiled, and her garment is not only her only covering, but it suggests, if not abject destitution, the raiment accorded a female criminal. Thus, I think, it would not do for her to simply accompany us as if she were a free woman. I think she would attract less attention if she were regarded as a prisoner, perhaps an apprehended thief, a catch of guardsmen, citizens, or such."

"Never!" said Talena. "Free my hands, now!"

"I think you are right," I said.

"No!" said Talena.

"The rope," said Hemartius, "may serve as a leash, as well."

"Use the wrists-to-collar-to-leash tie," I said.

"No!" said Talena.

But the rope was taken up from her bound wrists, behind her back, to encircle her neck a few times, where it was knotted. The remainder of the rope then, dangling from the rope collar, lifted, could serve as a leash. There was also, in his case, enough rope left over to serve not only as a leash, but as a whip, should the leash holder wish to so employ it.

"I am not an animal!" said Talena.

"You are an animal, fully and legally," said Thurnock, "a slave."

"No!" said Talena. "I will scream!"

Behind her Hemartius lifted the gag, questioningly.

I nodded.

Then the gag was put in place, and secured.

Talena regarded me. From her eyes darted knives of fury.

Why do I put up with her? I thought. Why does she not regard me with fear, and then tremble, and hope to please me? Why should she not scurry to her knees, head down, when I enter a room? Why should she not crawl to me on her belly and kiss my feet? Why is she different from any other slave? Why is she different from any other woman? Why should she not be put in a collar, and taught its meaning? Why should she not be stripped and fastened to a slave ring at the foot of my couch? Would she not look well there? And would she not look well crawling to me, on all fours, as the beast she is, the whip in her teeth, to be lifted to me, then waiting to see if it would be used upon her?

No, I thought to myself. No! Such thoughts are inappropriate for a man of Earth. Men of Earth are to renounce biology and foreswear their ancient blood, put aside ambition, possessiveness, passion, aggressiveness, power, and command; they must be weak, diffident, pleasant, kind, and accommodating, subservient to conventions extolling self-denial, deceit, and hypocrisy. How unacceptable to think otherwise!

"The Twentieth Ahn!" said Hemartius. "The great bar sounds! I fear Decius Albus will act. I fear the coup."

Thurnock looked at me.

"We must take our leave," I said.

"There may be no coup," said Seremides.

"The eight enemies outside have taken their leave," said Thurnock.

"Then soon, soon!" said Hemartius.

"Who knows?" said Thurnock.

"Dear Hemartius," I said, "be calm. Do not trouble yourself."

I picked up Talena's rope leash and thrust it into the reluctant hands of an unwilling Iris.

"No, Master," she whispered. "Please!"

I turned to an angry, disbelieving Talena. "You are in the keeping of Iris," I said. "You are to give her not the least trouble. You will be led like the tethered, speechless beast you are. At the least sign of resistance or recalcitrance, I will transfer the leash to Thurnock. Do you understand?"

After a moment a single muffled sound escaped Talena's gag.

"Good," I said.

In such a situation, by convention, one sound, one grunt or whimper, means "Yes," and two mean "No."

Talena then raised her head proudly, contemptuously, and turned away.

"If you are not pleased with her," I said to Iris, "double up the long end of the leash, and whip her."

"Yes, Master," said Iris.

Talena turned back and looked at me, disbelievingly.

Iris, of course, had received her instructions. Talena, Gorean, understood that.

I thought that Talena's figure would be fetching in a slave tunic, and that her ensemble would be much enhanced if her lovely throat were encircled closely by a locked collar.

Then I tried to put such thoughts from me.

I wondered what she might bring, if I decided to sell her.

Then again I thrust the thought away.

But it was an intriguing thought, selling Talena. As she was a slave, it could be easily done, as with any other vendible property.

The great bar continued to sound out the Ahn.

"I am afraid," said Hemartius.

"How so?" I asked.

"What of Decius Albus, and what of Ar?" he asked.

"We must avoid Decius Albus," I said, "and Ar is not our concern."

CHAPTER SEVENTY-TWO

"It is expensive, but imminently suitable," I said to my party. "We will have a suite on the eleventh floor, and there is access on that floor to two high bridges. From time to time, we can send out one of our number to reconnoiter, to gather news, and check gates. It would be well to stay together, but, if necessary, one or two of us can try a gate at a time, and, eventually, given an agreeable fortune, we can gather outside the walls."

"I wish to remain in Ar," said Hemartius.

"Given the politics of the Theater of Publius and the Stadium of Blades, that might not be wise," I said.

"Ar is the city of my Home Stone," he said.

"Your Home Stone," said Seremides, "can fare happily without you. It stands in no need of your protection."

"Have you not held and kissed the Home Stone of Ar?" asked Hemartius.

"It was expected," said Seremides. "But I am originally, long ago, from Jad."

"What then of the Home Stone of Jad?" asked Hemartius.

"Jad is faraway," said Seremides.

"Do you not understand what a Home Stone can mean?" asked Hemartius.

"I understand what it can mean to others," said Seremides. "That is often useful."

"We had best leave the street," I said.

"I will carry you up the stairs, Mentor," said Xenon to Seremides.

"If it pleases you," said Seremides.

"Scribe," said Thurnock, "the Twentieth Ahn has come and all is quiet."

"I do not understand how Decius Albus can be quiescent," said Hemartius. "Surely Marlenus will act as soon as Tor-tu-Gor peers over the horizon."

"If Decius Albus is wise," said Clitus, "he will have fled the city."

"That is not his way," said Hemartius.

Iris was kneeling to the side, still holding to the rope leash which looped up to the neck of Talena. Talena herself was standing, gagged, with her hands tied behind her.

"You are in the presence of free persons," said Thurnock.

Talena did not grant him her attention, but looked away, annoyed.

"Give her to me for only one Ehn," said Thurnock.

"I will do so," I said, "if she does not kneel immediately."

"I wish she had dallied," said Thurnock.

Talena was on her knees.

She, as other women, looked well so. I wondered if women, as a whole, realized how lovely they were, how beautiful they were, how right they were, on their knees. Slaves, after having learned they are slaves, having learned their collars, love the rituals, attitudes, and postures of submission. They find them natural, appropriate, exciting, reassuring, and profoundly fulfilling. A slave would be acutely anxious and miserably uncomfortable if not permitted to kneel in a situation in which kneeling would normally be expected. The Gorean slave has her particular and special identity, culturally sanctioned and societally expected. She knows how she is to speak, act, and move, how she is to be. She is content, fulfilled, pleased, and happy in what she is. She does not want to be other than she is. Her collar is precious to her; it makes it clear to all, including herself, that she is worth owning, and is owned, that she belongs to a master.

At that moment a single sound, loud and reverberating, rang out over Ar.

"Of course, that is it!" cried Hemartius.

"What?" we asked.

"The First Ahn!" cried Hemartius. "The First Ahn! When better, how better, could the Revolution begin?"

"It is quiet now," said Thurnock.

An Ehn passed, and then two Ehn.

"Let us leave the street," I said.

"Wait, wait!" said Hemartius. "Do not go into the building!"

"The street is too open," I said.

"Wait!" begged Hemartius. "Listen! Hear it!"

"I hear it!" said Thurnock. "It begins!"

"I, too," exclaimed Aetius.

Gradually increasing in sound were the alarm bars of Ar and then, suddenly, they ceased their insistent message.

"The alarm bars have been silenced," said Seremides, his head lifted, listening.

"The coup has begun!" said Hemartius. "I must hurry to the Central Cylinder. I must protect Marlenus! I must protect Ar!"

"Hold, dear friend," I said. "You are not even armed."

"I shall find a club, a stick, anything!" said Hemartius. He then turned about and began to run down the street.

"Who here loves Ar?" I asked.

There was no response from my party.

"Who then," I said, "loves the scribe Hemartius?"

There were cries of assent.

I drew my sword. "Follow me who will," I said, "to the Central Cylinder!"

I ran from before the Tower of Philebus down dark streets toward the Central Cylinder. As I ran, I heard hurried footsteps behind me.

A few Ehn, later I saw a shaking red sky and the bursting ascent of spumes of sparks.

And shortly after that, I heard the clash of metal.

As I sped toward the sound, I recalled a saying of my caste: "If you would wear my scarlet cloak, run to the clash of metal, ride to the clash of metal; if you would wear my cloak, seek the clash of metal."

CHAPTER SEVENTY-THREE

I slid the attacking blade to my right, and the attacker's thrust, unbalanced, carried him beyond me, where he was caught on the trident of Clitus. Hundreds of men were engaged in the broad Plaza of the Central Cylinder. Smoke emerged from some of the narrow apertures in the towering cylinder. I gathered, from shouts and cries, warnings, and such, that the balance of Decius Albus's private army had slipped into the city through the great gate whose guards had been suborned. Hemartius had conjectured that the armed followers of Decius Albus would number some fifteen hundred men. Most were now, presumably, in the city, either here near the Central Cylinder, intent on apprehending Marlenus, or seizing major intersections, fountains, and public boards. The forces of Decius Albus would be met by local guardsmen, some seven or eight hundred in number, and, one supposed, the two hundred or so men in the Taurentians.

"Stay behind me!" I ordered Hemartius.

"Never!" he said, jabbing at a now-turned-about fellow in the livery of Decius Albus with a spear he had apparently discovered from somewhere amongst the debris of battle. His stroke was turned aside by the foe's buckler. Before the foe could rush forward, I stepped between the two, and the foe reconsidered his options and drew back.

Several buildings about the plaza were aflame.

The flames were red and dancing on the unsheathed steel. Local guardsmen, and, I suppose, some Taurentians, were trying to hold the plaza. When we had first come upon the scene our work had been easy for the two fronts had been formed, and we had come up unexpectedly on the rear of the men of Decius Albus. Our attack was initially disconcerting to the men of Decius Albus, for they were at first unclear as to the nature and size of the force which was now attacking them from the rear. Some broke and ran and others literally threw down their weapons, terrified that they had been trapped. We did our best, hurrying and shouting, looking back, gesturing, waving, and such, to encourage this delusion, that we were part of a much larger, more dangerous force which had suddenly come upon them. But the disproportionate damage we had wrought on the present forces of Decius Albus was soon nullified as they came to under-

stand we were less than ten men gnawing at their last line. Foes now
began to sweep about us.

"Circle!" I shouted. "Bow to the center!" We then, six of us, as if
by instinct, formed a small defensive circle, dangerous to approach,
not unlike that of the snow bosk of Ax Glacier, defending themselves from the attack of predatory sleen. In the center of our circle,
however, were no females and young, but our seventh man, massive
Thurnock calmly, methodically, discharging flighted death. We had
left Iris and Talena, the latter, to her outrage, still gagged, bound,
and leashed, at the far edge of the plaza. Even Seremides held his
place in the ring and those who thought to break our linked chain
at that point discovered that they faced a sword that had once been
the most feared blade amongst the Taurentians. I kept Hemartius to
my right where I could, to some extent, shelter him under the metal
wing of my sword. A heavy spear charge, even of fifteen or twenty
men, could have crushed our small, gallant circle, but the spears of
Decius Albus were mostly employed, as one would expect, in his
front line. The Gorean spear, lengthy and heavy, thrusting and battering, is seldom thrown. What infantryman cares to risk the loss
of his primary weapon? Casting weapons are the javelin and pilum,
with its detachable head.

A battle horn sounded from the side and forward, and several of
the men testing and threatening our small formation, backed away.

We did not know whether it was a signal to the men of Decius
Albus or to the engaged defenders of Ar.

It did grant us a surprising, welcome respite.

Battles, large and small, often contain their ambiguities. The warrior's war is often narrow, confusing, disconcerting, and brief, sometimes no wider than a handful of feet or yards, surveyable with a turn
of the head, sometimes as short as the passage of a rushing body. If a
battleline extends over pasangs it is often unclear to the individual
combatant what is going on. Is the battle being won or lost? Here it
is being won; there it is being lost. It consists of a thousand particles
whose fates and destinies may differ. Was the battle won or lost? Perhaps tomorrow one will learn. Sometimes results are unclear. In such
a case, it is not unusual for both sides, licking their wounds, to draw
away from one another, and for each to claim victory. Certainly few
commanders will claim defeat. And some victories, authentic victories, are more costly than a hundred defeats.

"Citizen!" called a voice from out of the half-darkness.

"Yes?" I said.

I saw a pale, bearded face. The man was unarmed, save for a belt
knife. He carried a now-shuttered dark lantern which had probably
served him well in the dark streets. We could here, however, well

enough make out one another, given the flames about the plaza. I took him for a worker in wood or a cloth worker.

"You are not in uniform!" he said.

"One does not need a uniform to fight," I said.

The man looked about. "Do the citizens rise?" he asked.

"I do not think so," I said.

"Then leave the plaza," he said. "Go home. It is dangerous here. Guardsmen of Ar and Taurentians have risen! They intend to betray and depose Marlenus! Decius Albus, beloved servitor of the Ubar, is trying to stop them!"

"Who told you that?" I asked.

"It is common knowledge," he said. "Everyone knows it."

"I do not!" cried Hemartius. "Decius Albus covets the medallion of the Ubar. He wants to kill Marlenus and seize the throne!"

"No!" said the man.

"Decius Albus is a thief," said Hemartius. "He would steal the city!"

"No," said the man. "Decius Albus is a benefactor and patriot! Who has not attended his games and eaten at his tables of public feasting? He is trying to save Marlenus. Decius Albus loves Ar!"

"Yes, he loves Ar," said Hemartius. "He loves every tarsk-bit of it!"

The fellow with the lantern, perhaps confused, turned about and sped away.

"The fighting will resume," said Seremides.

Thurnock left the circle and began to extract his arrows from several bodies near the periphery of the circle. This was not easy as they had been fired from almost point-blank range. Indeed, I suspected that Thurnock had contributed markedly to our defense, and the reluctance of more men to attack us. Few men will, so to speak, walk into the muzzle of a gun.

I was not clear as to why the fighting stopped.

Then I heard a cry that seized and shook me as a sleen might an urt. It was carried from voice to voice. "Marlenus is dead! The Ubar is dead!" From a hundred yards or so before our ragged, panting line, no longer a circle, I heard sounds of woe. But then the closer troops, the swarms of Decius Albus, uttered cheers, and clashed weapons on shields. And moments later their lines rushed forward once again, heartened and assured of victory.

"All is lost!" cried Hemartius. He leaned upon his spear, head down, weeping. And the rest of our small line, stunned, shaken, tried to peer forward amongst the shadows and flames.

"It may not be true!" I cried. "Few could strike down Marlenus, Ubar of Ubars!"

Hemartius turned about, hope flaming on his countenance.

The value of a false announcement of the death or capture of a champion or leader, assuming it is not obviously false, is twofold. First, it heartens one side, quickening its resolve and suggesting the likelihood of its victory, and dispirits the other, shaking its resolve and suggesting the likelihood of defeat. Sometimes a battle may turn on such a psychological device, such an announcement, even if it is wholly false, the champion or leader not even endangered or wounded. Secondly, it is likely to bring the champion or leader into a particular and prominent location, namely, one where he can visibly, and perhaps at great peril, reassure his troops of his well-being. In theory then, the champion or leader is more exposed and vulnerable to attack. The risk of such a device, of course, becomes obvious if the leader reappears, as he is almost obliged to do, is not particularly imperiled, shows himself well, active, and dangerous, puts the lie to the enemy, rallies his troops, and supplies them with a fresh incentive to fight.

What of the citizens of Ar?

Surely the citizens of Ar were no longer asleep. The alarm bar had sounded, however briefly. Fire was in the sky; words must pass from domicile to domicile; in the vicinity of the Central Cylinder, the sound of combat would be audible. But what would they know, what could they do? The agents of Decius Albus had already supplied a ready interpretation to dispel the mystery. But what would be believed? Surely, in the city, the image of Decius Albus was not entirely untarnished. For every one who lauded him for his benefactions might there not be two who feared his power and suspected his ambition?

I suspected that word of our earlier attack on the rear of the forces of Decius Albus had not much penetrated, if at all, to the interlocked front lines of battle. We were too few and our molestation had been too brief. Accordingly our intervention, on the whole, seemed to have done little to either hearten the defenders or discomfit the foe. We had then found ourselves surrounded and fighting for our lives. But then the battle horn had sounded, whatever might have been its source, and we found ourselves neglected, abandoned, and isolated. It had been then that the cries of the demise of Marlenus, welcomed diversely with utterances of anguish and cheers, had wracked the plaza.

"Marlenus lives!" came a cry. "The Ubar lives!"

"Glory to Marlenus, glory to the Ubar!" cried Hemartius. "Long live Marlenus, Ubar of Ubars!"

This report, true or false, I was sure, would have its effect on the lines of battle. Such things, true or false, can sway delicate balances, may turn armed tides.

For a moment it was like the sway of wrestlers, neither giving ground.

Then Seremides cried, "Ar advances! The flood of war rises! It flows once more!"

It was not that the men of Decius Albus were routed. It was rather that, along the lines, blow upon answered blow, they were being beaten back.

"Long live Marlenus!" cried Hemartius.

"Draw back," I said. "We may soon again be engaged!" I had no desire that my small group should be again surrounded.

There were two obvious dangers. The first was that if the forces of Decius Albus continued a slow, fighting retreat, we would find ourselves enmeshed in their lines. The second was that if the nerve of the retreating force, sensing one yard lost after another, sensing impending defeat, should snap, panic would crack like thunder, and a rout would ensue, transforming a formation of disciplined troops into a disorderly, fleeing, terrified rabble. I was not interested in having that wash about us or over us, nor was I eager to be at risk from pursuing men of Ar eager to strike at anything they might encounter in the plaza.

But then I heard behind us a blare of battle horns and a great bellowing. Too, I could see torches in the distance, on the far side of the plaza.

"What is it?" cried Hemartius, turning about.

It was indeed a sight which might terrify anyone unfamiliar with Gorean field war.

It was a horror scarcely to be dealt with by infantry.

And here there was no forest of inclined stakes which might hope, even splintering and shattering, groaning, bending and snapping, to deter the advance of such a monster!

It was like an advancing mountain, a mighty engine of iron, enormous and implacable. What could stand against it?

And it was alive.

"It is an armored war tharlarion!" I said.

Again there was a blaring of battle horns, and a bellow that might have shaken the Central Cylinder itself.

It was massive, even for its kind.

On its back there was an armored castle.

The men of Decius Albus, crying out gladly, in a maneuver which had doubtless been much practiced, opened their ranks that the vast quadrupedalian beast, ringed with plates of steel, might pass unimpeded, and that the defenders might see and tremble before the apparition advancing upon them.

"Who is in the castle?" asked Aetius.

"Surely Decius Albus," said Seremides.

"It is armored," said Thurnock. "Arrows will leap from its surface."

"Spears, too," said Clitus.

"It cannot be stopped!" said Seremides.

"It will crush the men of Ar! It will trample them!" said Aetius.

"Behold!" said Xenon. "Marlenus will face it boldly!"

"He will be crushed, he will be trampled!" said Hemartius.

"Men will swarm about it," I said. "It will tread men like mud and straw. But its motion will be slowed, arrested. There will be a great press about it, both of the men of Ar and those of Decius Albus."

"See the metal casing on its head," said Hemartius, "and the sicklelike blades attached to that casing!"

"It is trained to swing its head and thresh men like sa-tarna," I said.

"It is a fearsome, invincible killing thing, impervious to all attacks," said Aetius.

"No," I said. "The head blades cannot fully protect its eyes. Armor, which is heavy and slows movement, even if with overlapping plates, must have openings, to make motion possible. Axes can attack legs. Its underbelly is open. It is vulnerable, particularly when slowed or still."

"Guardsmen are not field infantry," said Aetius. "You cannot expect them to set stakes and dig pits. You cannot expect them to brace massed spears."

"Stakes must be heavy, sunk deep, and sharpened," I said. "Braced spears may be used against charging infantry. Against an armored tharlarion spears would be snapped like straws."

"Ar is lost," said Hemartius.

"No," I said. "Such beasts have blood and breathe. They are vulnerable, with or without armor, and can be stopped. Their major military value is to disrupt formations and terrify an enemy."

"We can do nothing," moaned Hemartius.

"Would that we could reach it," said Thurnock.

"We cannot," said Seremides. "The men of Decius Albus are between us and the monster."

We heard a short scream and saw the half-severed body of a man of Ar lofted through the air, flung from one of the sicklelike blades attached to the head casing of the tharlarion. A rain of blood fell to the ground, reflected in the light of the flames.

"Even if one could reach it," said Clitus, "it is surrounded by embroiled, battling men. Hundreds of blades encircle it, both of Ar and of Decius Albus."

"And we, lacking uniforms, are alien to both forces," said Seremides.

"That is it!" I said. "Good Seremides! Wise Seremides. Astute Seremides!"

"Where are you going? What are you doing?" called Hemartius after me, for I was making my way back to where the rear ranks of the men of Decius Albus had closed again, after the passage of the giant armored tharlarion.

In few battles, particularly those of hundreds, or more, of men, are all combatants engaged.

I looked back at my party, and behind them, at the far edge of the plaza, I saw a large number of torches, seemingly arrested, still, not moving, perhaps curious, or indecisive.

Those are brandished by citizens, I thought. The awakened, the curious, gather.

Then I hurried forward.

I approached one of the men of Decius Albus from behind, one rather apart from the others, whose attention, like that of the others, was focused on the fighting.

I yanked away his helmet by the crest, spun him half about and struck him heavily on the side of the head with my fist, in the grasp of which was my sword, thus making my blow more formidable than it would have been otherwise.

He collapsed senseless at my feet and I tore away his cloak, with its black background and two white stripes, and began to force my way toward the center of the fighting, in the midst of which was the tharlarion.

It took only a few thrusting, pressing moments, shoving and cursing, to get to the point where few combatants cared to be, so close I could almost place my hands on the shaking, moving armor of the huge, grunting, snorting, hissing tharlarion. I fended blows, and struck away some of the swords of Ar from my path. I do not doubt but what I saved the life of more than one of the men of Decius Albus. Certainly I received more than one glance of relief and gratitude from a beleaguered cohort of Decius Albus. Wildly, briefly, I caught sight of Marlenus of Ar who, helmeted, with shield and spear, was embattled only feet from me. He did not seem surprised to see me in the cloak of one of the fellows from Decius Albus's private army. He threw me a look of hatred and contempt, and tried to force his way toward me but, in the swirl of battle, was unable to close the gap between us. Alan of the House of Hesius, helmeted and sweating, was at his side. I then threw myself down and rolled under the tharlarion. Once under the tharlarion, I reached up and fastened my hand in one of the cinch straps that held the armor and the armored castle in place. I was then, grasping the strap, back to the ground, half dragged, half lifted. I did not think the beast would lie down, even if it sensed me, as they seldom lie down, and, like the kaiila, commonly sleep standing. This, and brief sleep periods, are not unusual with animals subject to predation. Too, I hoped that feeling the stress on the strap, if it managed to do so in the midst of the alarms and clashing metal ringing it about, would not disturb it. It must be accustomed to the slackening and tightening, the removal and placement, of the straps, from the placement and adjustment of the armor and castle. From where I was, I could not well reach either the neck or heart of the beast, nor did I wish to do so. Both were shielded, the neck by a wide collar, and the heart by a sort of breast plate. I did not so much wish to kill the beast as to enable others to do so, if it had to be done. Indeed, I was muchly impressed with that gigantic lifeform, and I wished it no harm. Indeed, it was, like others of its kin, a herbivore, and, in nature, generally a peaceable, browsing beast. It was not, like several of the two-legged tharlarion, an aggressive, territorial, dangerous carnivore. Too, in any event, a beast of that size, with its thick hide, is not easy to kill.

Under the beast, clinging to the strap, I was, in effect, housed in its armor. It was odd to hear blows striking on the plates within which I was shielded. Those who might have seen me disappear beneath the dangling plating, perhaps slipping and falling, knowing nothing of the strap to which I clung, might well suppose I had lost my footing and had been trampled. The reality, of course, was far otherwise. I released the cinch strap, and, on my feet, half bent over, slashed it apart. There were several such buckled straps, broad and heavy. Once I lost my footing and was nearly crushed by one of the beast's wide, heavy, nailed feet. Suddenly a wide swath of plating fell from the beast's side. The tharlarion then began to shake itself with a rustle, and then a clanging, of metal. It reared up, suddenly, briefly with its forefeet, a dozen feet from the ground, and I was lifted from my feet by the strap I was trying to clutch and sever. And then its ponderous weight came plunging down, its trunklike forefeet thundering down on the pavement of the plaza. And another swath of plating came tumbling free! I heard shouts of alarm and screams of fear. Again the beast shook itself as though to rid itself of its encasing encumbrances. I did not know for a moment what was happening, but then I gathered that the armored castle on its back had slid from its back, and come crashing to the pavement. Much of its armor gone, the beast was now exposed to spear thrusts and sword cuts. Stung and bleeding, confused and maddened by pain, it spun about and fled from the scene of the battle, dragging the half-tethered armored castle after it, scraping across the paved plaza. As soon as the beast had turned about I had torn away the black, white-striped cloak I had used to penetrate the ranks of the men of Decius Albus. Let all see now only a stranger in their midst, one whose allegiance, if any, was unclear. I looked about, ready to defend myself. I saw Marlenus, who regarded me, astonished, wonderingly. Then, as politely as possible, I worked my way through the ranks of the men of Decius Albus, in the wake of the departing tharlarion.

"Forward, to war!" cried Marlenus, from somewhere behind me.

Shortly afterward I found the remains of the broken armored castle which, with more plating, caught in the stones of the plaza, had come loose in the tharlarion's flight. About it were the men of my party, Thurnock, Clitus, Seremides, Aetius, Xenon, and Hemartius.

"Decius Albus?" I asked.

"No," said Seremides. "A Kur, its neck broken."

I looked into the remains of the castle.

"It is not Lucilius, the fellow of Decius Albus," said Aetius.

"No," I said. "Where is Decius Albus?"

"We do not know," said Thurnock.

"I did not note him in the battle," I said.

"He is doubtless safe," said Seremides, "abiding the outcome."

A civilian, with a shuttered dark lantern, approached.

It was he who had earlier sung the praises of Decius Albus.

"What ensues?" he asked.

"War," I said. "Mercenaries strive to slay Marlenus, your Ubar, and seize Ar for the traitor, Decius Albus."

"Some think so," he said. "Can it be?"

"It is," I said, pointing back. "Even now Marlenus fights for his life, for you, and Ar."

"It is said," said the man, "that Decius Albus has been seen at the great gate."

"Then," said Seremides, "he is not at the Central Cylinder, attempting to succor Marlenus."

"His forces must control the great gate," I said. "Most of his private army entered the city by means of the great gate."

"Controlling the great gate," said Thurnock, "he is in no danger, if things proceed awry, of being trapped in the city."

The fellow seemed in consternation.

"Inquire," said Seremides. "Truth here, often so subtle and obscure, sheds its robe of mystery. It blazes like Tor-tu-Gor at the Tenth Ahn."

"I do not know," moaned the man.

"As yet," I said, "victory has not bestowed its favors."

"Hundreds of torches burn at the far edge of the plaza," said Clitus.

"You come as an envoy, or scout, do you not?" I asked.

"Yes," said the man.

"What is your code?" I asked.

"One for Decius Albus," he said, "two for Marlenus."

I glanced at Thurnock, and nodded.

"Stop!" cried the man.

Thurnock had the lantern now in hand, raised it high, and un-shuttered it twice. The hundreds of torches then began to move over the plaza, approaching us.

"I do not know if that is the right signal!" wailed the man.

"We do," said Seremides.

"Rejoice," I said. "You are a hero."

In about an Ehn, men, variously armed, even with clubs and tools, many with torches, began to stream past us. "For Marlenus, for Ar!" they cried. "Death to Decius Albus!"

"The people rise," said Seremides.

"For Marlenus," I said.

"Had there been a single flash of the unshuttered lantern," said Aetius, "they would have as easily risen for Decius Albus."

"It is that way with storms," said Seremides.

"Master!" called Iris, emerging from out of the darkness, from amongst the streaming, armed, determined men, leading a very un-willing, angry Talena.

"You are safe," I said, with relief.

"I do not know," said Iris, looking about, frightened.

"Nor, truly, do we," I said.

CHAPTER SEVENTY-FOUR

"There is no way I can stay in Ar," said Talena, seated in an ornate curule chair, brushing back the jeweled veil now that Thurnock had exited the chamber, one of five, on the eleventh floor of the Tower of Philebus. "There are many reasons for this. I no longer have position here. I no longer occupy the throne. I have been humiliated during my trial, my features bared to multitudes, even to those of low caste, my body insulted by a prisoner's gown, thin and drab, little more than a lengthy rag. I am now, in a sense, a fugitive. I dare not risk the streets. Many, however irrationally, think ill of me. I could be in personal danger."

"I am cognizant of these discomforts, and perils," I said. "We will leave the city as soon as it is practical."

"You have gold," she said, "enough to settle and sustain me in honor and comfort. That gold, all or most of it, properly invested on some Street of Coins, should suffice nicely. I shall select a city neither too large nor too small, one suitable in climate, beauty, and cultural advantages. There I shall establish my new identity, and Ar will be far behind me."

"I am to handle such things?" I said.

"You owe me much," she said.

"How so?" I asked.

"Your vile and cowardly abandoning of me," she said.

"I bear no fault there," I said. "It was the doing of Priest-Kings."

"If their laws are unbroken," she said, "Priest-Kings do not intrude into the affairs of men."

"They sometimes do," I said.

"You are not only a barbarian," she said, "but a liar."

"And what is to become of me once I have ensconced you in security and comfort, if not luxury?" I asked.

"Go off somewhere," she said. "It does not matter to me. I do not wish to see you again."

"I and others risked our lives for you," I said. "Are you not grateful?"

"Free women," she said, "are entitled to such considerations. You accorded me no more than was my due. I am not a slave!" She then clapped her hands together, sharply, and Iris, from the next room, hurried into the chamber and knelt before her. "Wine, a golden ka-la-na, slave!" commanded Talena.

Iris cast me a frightened look, and then whispered, "Yes, Mistress."

"Chilled," said Talena.

"Yes, Mistress," said Iris.

In Ar there were certain emporiums, and cylinders, of which the Tower of Philebus was one, to which snow from the peaks of the Voltai were flown in by tarn.

At this point there was a coded pounding on the primary door, the receiving door, of the suite.

Xenon, a knife in its sheath behind his back, would attend to it.

Talena, uneasy, in house robes, resumed her veil.

"Are you afraid?" I asked.

"No," she said.

"I do not think your enemies are all in Ar," I said.

"Oh?" she said.

"Lurius of Jad," I said. "He hoped to accrue a great fortune from your return to Ar. Doubtless he is muchly disappointed with the way things turned out."

I supposed that Myron, the polemarkos of Jad, and his party, were now well on their way to Cos.

"The island Ubarates will not do, of course, for my refuge," she said, "perhaps Market of Semris, or even Harfax."

"I fear you are in greater danger than even you may realize," I said.

"Out of Ar, I think not," she said.

Xenon then ushered Aetius into the room.

Talena did not acknowledge his presence, nor did he hers.

"How goes the city?" I asked

"Sedition is crushed," he said. "Between irate citizens and the spears of Marlenus, few of the men of Decius Albus lived to exit the gates. Decius Albus fled earlier, when informed that the tide of battle had turned. He is searched for outside the walls."

"Unsuccessfully?" I said.

"Yes," he said, "unsuccessfully."

"What of Kurii?" I asked.

"None within the city," said Aetius. "The House of a Hundred Corridors is empty. Beyond that little is known."

"The Beast Caves?" I asked.

"I do not think they are abandoned," said Aetius. "Doubtless some Kurii lurk within."

"So, too, might Decius Albus," I said.

"I do not think so," said Aetius. "He is no longer prominent in Ar, and the Beasts choose their allies with care."

"What of Pa-Kur?" I asked.

"The amnesty accorded the Black Caste has been rescinded," said Aetius. "Once again the dark caste is forbidden within the walls of Ar."

"Once again," I said, "Marlenus is secure upon the throne of Ar."

"As much so as any Ubar," said Aetius.

At this point Iris reentered the chamber and, kneeling before Talena, proffered a goblet. Talena took it, and took a sip behind her veil. Then her eyes flashed. "This wine," she said, glaring at Iris, "is insufficiently chilled!"

"Forgive me, Mistress," said Iris, frightened.

"Do not address her as Mistress," I said.

"Yes, Master," said Iris, relieved.

Talena turned her gaze to me. "I want a switch to deal with this displeasing barbarian slave," she said.

"No," I said.

"Little snow and ice is left, gracious one, and it melts," said Iris.

Talena, with an annoyed, impatient gesture, cast the goblet and wine from her, to the floor. "Clean that up," she told Iris.

"Yes, beautiful one," said Iris, rising and hurrying from the room.

"Did you actually pay money for her?" asked Talena.

"Yes," I said. "And more snow and ice will be delivered tonight." Such deliveries were usually made after dark, to take advantage of lower temperatures. Surely Talena knew that the supply of these expensive cooling materials was either exhausted or in short supply, and that their next delivery was not due at the cylinder until the Nineteenth Ahn. Why then had she insisted on chilled wine? I did not think that Talena cared for Iris. Could she be jealous of her? I knew this was not impossible for free women often resented and envied kajirae, but was not Talena herself, in full legality, kajira herself? I recalled, long ago, Talena boasting to me how she used her female slaves as spies and agents to further her intrigues, often ordering them to couch with men not their masters in order to garner information. Such gave her power, the means of intimidation, blackmail, and such. I also recalled how she had had her girls severely punished if they failed to manage such matters to her full satisfaction.

There was much, I thought, in the maddeningly desirable, incredibly beautiful Talena which was in need of correction.

And I recalled that I owned her.

Then I put that unworthy, disturbing, troublesome thought from my mind.

"How go the gates?" I asked Aetius.

"Well, and ill," he said. "Well that charges are no long imposed for entering and leaving the city. That ceased with the downfall of Decius Albus. But ill that guardsmen are vigilant, seeking to detain certain individuals."

"What individuals?" I asked.

"Ela," he said. "I do not know their orders."

"Are there free women at the gates, possibly to provide assistance to the guards?" I asked.

He thought for a moment. "Yes," he said.

"Then," I said, "I think we know at least one person they may wish to detain."

"They are dissatisfied with the outcome of the trial," said Talena. "They wish me harm!"

"Who?" I asked.

"Many," said Talena.

"Quite possibly," I said.

"The people," she said. "I could be killed on the street, torn to pieces!"

"The memory of Ar is long," I said.

I believed Talena's fears of being attacked in the street were justified. On the other hand, that would be the spontaneous action of a mob. The action of guardsmen checking those who entered and left the city hinted at a higher or more official interest.

"It seems," I said, "that this is not the time to try to remove our party from the city."

"I must escape Ar!" said Talena.

"Others may be in danger, as well," I said. I knew that Marlenus now recognized me as Tarl of Bristol, or Tarl Cabot, and I supposed that I should now, at least after the trial of Talena, not be in Ar. The truce, so to speak, which had tolerated myself, Assassins, and perhaps other undesirables, exiles, objects of banishment, and such within the walls may well have expired. Aetius had referred to the expulsion of Assassins.

"The city festoons itself," said Aetius. "In the streets there is perfume, flowers, banners. and ribbons. The five-day feast celebrating the Restoration of Marlenus begins today."

This feast had been postponed for days due to the delivery of Talena to Ar, the business of the bestowal of the reward for her capture and delivery, her trial, and the kajira challenge.

"Five days of festival will be welcomed by the people," I said.

In such feasts there would be parades, processions, dancing, street music, feasting, concerts, plays, song dramas, public kaissa matches, tarn races, and open contests with prizes, athletic, literary, and artistic.

"But," said Aetius, "apart from jubilation, crowds, and rowdy pomp, dark movements, scarcely noted, may take place in shadows and curtained rooms."

This seemed to me plausible. Might there not be lingering adherents of Decius Albus yet in Ar, or, indeed, perhaps others, dangerous and lurking, of whom I knew nothing. I did not envy the state of a Ubar. The urt is cunning and the ost venomous.

"Wealth and power always attract the jards of greed and envy," I said. "It is not uncommon for malcontents to seek to turn society to their advantage."

"In the festival, I fear Marlenus will be too visible, too accessible," said Aetius. "He is too bold and hearty. I fear the drawn knife, the flighted arrow, the dram of poison."

"He has men who are loyal to him," I said, "men who have fought at his side and would defend him with their very lives."

I thought of one, a young Taurentian, a fine swordsman, Alan, of the House of Hesius.

How absurd was the very thought that he might be my son.

"When do we depart?" asked Talena. "When will you take me from Ar?"

"The gates are not easily passed, Slave," said Aetius.

"Do not use that word to me!" she snapped.

"Has she permission to speak?" asked Aetius.

"I have permitted it," I said.

"I see," said Aetius, less than pleased.

"Have you answered me?" asked Talena, sharply.

"I have been thinking," I said.

"When do we depart?" she asked. "When will you take me from Ar?"

"Perhaps tonight," I said.

CHAPTER SEVENTY-FIVE

"You will not leave me in this place," said Talena.

"There is an alternative," I said.

"What is that?" she asked.

"That you are stripped and chained by the left ankle to one of the tubs in the inn's bathing chamber," I said, annoyed.

Comely bath girls, serving guests, is one of the pleasures of a well-appointed establishment. The girls, adept in the use of strigils, oils, sponges, towels, and such, are trained to bathe guests. A relaxing bath is commonly welcome after a long, hot, dusty trip. The bathing, in itself, is included in the price of the stay, but if the bath girl is put to slave use, it is a common courtesy to leave a tarsk-bit in the slotted, metal bowl near the door when one takes one's leave.

"You would not dare," she said.

"Probably not," I said. "Your clumsiness might lead the astute to suspect your identity."

"This is an inferior inn," said Talena. "It is unworthy of me."

"Consider it part of your disguise," I said, "like the sandals, robes, and veils of a free woman of the Merchants."

"I do not care for this inn," she said.

"Actually," I said, "this is a fine inn, reputable and secure. Certainly it is costly enough."

"What inn is it?" she asked, "or may I know?"

"It is the Inn of Livius Major, on the Torcadino spur from the Viktel Aria," I said.

"I do not know it," she said.

"And yet," I said, "it is muchly frequented and prospers."

"Do you plan on leaving me here?" she asked.

"Temporarily," I said. "Have no fear. The inn is strong. Your identity is not known. You will be safe. I cannot stay long. I must be back to Ar. There are others to get through the gates. The tarnsman, the driver, he who delivers ice, he whose tarn and identity banner I borrowed, though well paid, will be anxious. He will have his schedule to keep. If he is missing too long, inquiries will be made."

"It was not necessary to gag and tie me, hand and foot, in the tarn basket, under a blanket," she said.

"Not necessary, but wise," I said. "Would you have preferred to have been stripped and tied on your back over the saddle apron before me, where I might wile away the time in flight caressing you, until you begged in tears for a surcease of your needs?"

"I do not care for this room," she said. "It is too small."

"It is one of the best rooms in the inn," I said.

"I assume you devised some pretext for my being here," she said.

"You are a free woman of the Merchants," I said, "fleeing an unwanted companionship, one which your family wished to impose on you."

"Excellent," she said.

"Your suitor was interested only in your wealth," I said.

"Why is that?" she asked.

"Because," I said, "you are as ugly as a she-tharlarion."

"Was that necessary?" she asked.

"I thought it would add an element of piquancy to your disguise," I said.

"Perhaps," she said, but I do not think she was convinced.

"I have no money," she said. "You have been unduly parsimonious."

"So you can bribe someone to help you make away?" I asked.

"No," she said, "rather for incidentals."

"Those will be supplied by the inn," I said.

"You are cheap," she said.

"Parsimonious," I said.

"What are you doing?" she asked.

"Preparing to chain your left ankle to the slave ring," I said.

"I forbid it," she said.

"I do not see that you are in a position to do so," I said. I opened the shackle and prepared to clap it about her left ankle.

"Do not do so," she said.

"I want you here when I come back, if I can, and do," I said. "I do not want you to wander off somewhere."

"You need not fear," she said. "I am no fool. Why should I risk losing a tower or villa, and a generous fixed income? One needs means to fit into, and later command, a society."

"Can I trust you?" I asked.

"Yes," she said.

"Do I have your word that you will remain here until I return?" I asked.

"Certainly," she said. "I give you my word."

"I accept your word," I said. "Now I must return in haste to Ar. Without your presence, I think I can get those members of my party who wish to leave Ar through one gate or another, one or two at a time."

As I left the Inn of Livius Major, I recalled another time I had trusted Talena. It had been the night of the Planting Feast in Ar, long ago, when I had purloined the Home Stone of Ar. She had been with me on the tarn, fleeing through the night under the moons of Gor. She had seemed so helpless, and fearful. I had pitied her. I had reassured her. Then she had flung me from the saddle, down through the darkness to the Swamp Forest far below. I had heard her triumphant laughter, fading as I fell. My fall had been broken as I had landed in the web of Nar, of the Spider People.

CHAPTER SEVENTY-SIX

I had scarcely brought the tarn, with its basket, down on the roof of the Tower of Philebus, given the waiting driver his second gold piece, bade him well, and watched him depart, when Thurnock appeared on the roof.

"We think, Captain," he said, "that Aetius has been recognized."

"By Ruffio?" I asked.

"No," said Thurnock. "I think Ruffio knows little or nothing of Aetius. Aetius was not with us, not near us, not even on the same tier, at the trial."

In the cylinder itself, I had not feared Ruffio. Gold goes far in assuring discretion and silence. And even had we not been concerned to protect and nourish our privacy, a casual encounter with him, given the size of the cylinder, would have been unlikely. Indeed, if he was still housed in the cylinder, which I doubted, given the shift of fortunes of Cos in Ar, his residence there would have been another recommendation for its choice. Who would search for fugitives in places and situations where their presence would be deemed to border on the unthinkable? Too, it was not likely that Ruffio, should he prove uncooperative or dangerous, could escape Clitus's net or outrun one of Thurnock's arrows.

"How then, who then?" I asked.

"A Taurentian," said Thurnock, "who recognized him, as one of us, from the fighting yesterday night."

"This recognition took place earlier this evening," I said, "at dusk?"

"Or late afternoon," said Thurnock.

"Are you sure he was recognized?" I asked.

"We do not know," said Thurnock. "He fears so."

"Why does he think he might have been recognized?" I asked.

"He noted this Taurentian, more than once, in the crowds in the streets, during the Restoration festivities."

"It could be a coincidence," I said.

"Surely," said Thurnock.

"He sensed he was being followed?" I asked.

"He feared it," said Thurnock.

"Then we, too, shall fear it," I said.

"I think that is wise," said Thurnock. "Only the stupid fail to note shadows and ignore small sounds."

"In a situation like this," I said, "a Taurentian or guardsman is unlikely to initiate action without authorization. He will report, and the report will be considered, and then, if it is deemed appropriate, an action will be taken, all of which takes time."

"Perhaps that time has elapsed," said Thurnock.

"Why do you say that?" I asked.

"Come to the edge of the roof," said Thurnock. "Look down to the street."

"What do you see?" I asked.

"Guardsmen and Taurentians," he said. "There may be fifty of them. They are entering the cylinder."

CHAPTER SEVENTY-SEVEN

"How is it possible?" I demanded.

"I do not understand your question, noble master," said the deputy innkeeper. "Free persons may come and go as they please. The house of Livius Major has no authority to restrain the decisions or movements of free persons. It is not a prison. It is not in league with captors or slavers."

"She gave me her word to wait for me," I said.

"She was a free woman," said the deputy innkeeper. "As such, she is entitled to lie, to break her word, to do as she pleases, without penalty. What might be a grievous offense in a slave is entirely permissible, even expected, upon occasion, in the case of a free woman."

"How could she leave, where could she go?" I asked. "She had no means, no money?"

"How could it be," asked the deputy innkeeper, "that she, a free woman, and of the Merchants, lacked either means or money?"

"Do not concern yourself," I said. "Perhaps she had been robbed."

"It seems unfortunate then, noble master," he said, "that it slipped your mind to remedy that lack before you left the inn."

"She could not just leave the inn and wander about alone on the roads," I said. "Without protection any bandit or rogue might pick her up for the collar."

"Perhaps there was little danger of that," he said.

"How so?" I asked.

"Was she not as ugly as a tharlarion?" he asked.

"She had every motivation to remain at the inn," I said, "to receive, despite otherwise looming hardships and threatening destitution, the promise of economic and personal security, the prospect of eventually receiving an attractive domicile and a comfortable living in the venue of her choice."

"Perhaps she received a better offer," said the deputy innkeeper.

"She did not go off alone?" I said.

"If she lacked coin, how could she do so, rationally or wisely?" asked the deputy innkeeper.

"Was she carried off?" I asked.

"Certainly not," said the deputy innkeeper. "The Inn of Livius Major is not one of those cheap, remote inns where a woman arrives in the robes of concealment and departs in a sack, tied and naked. She went fully of her own accord."

"With whom did she go?" I asked.

"With a party of Merchants," he said. "They arrived the night after you left."

"They traveled in darkness?" I said.

"As it happens," he said.

"Merchants from what city?" I asked.

"We do not inquire into such matters," he said.

"Where were they bound?" I asked.

"We do not inquire into such matters," he said.

"How many wagons?" I asked.

"Four," he said.

If there were ten to a wagon, that would be forty men. To be sure, there might be more than one such group.

"Perhaps you noted something of their route," I said.

"They were proceeding northwest," he said.

"On the road to Torcadino?" I said.

"Yes, noble master," he said. "I am sorry that I cannot be of more service, but it is a policy of the inn not to intrude on the privacy of its guests."

"I understand," I said.

"May I inquire," he asked, "on your relationship to the lady in question?"

"Would that not be an inquiry into the privacy of your guests?" I asked.

"Forgive me," he said.

"She is an acquaintance," I said.

"We found her a most unpleasant and demanding guest," he said.

"I am not surprised," I said.

"I did not think you would be," he said.

"I wish you well," I said.

"As I wish you," he said, politely, and turned away.

I turned back to Thurnock, who was near.

"You heard?" I said.

"Yes," he said.

With us were Clitus, Seremides, Xenon, near Seremides, and Aetius, of the small scar. Hemartius had elected to remain in Ar. It was the city of his Home Stone. Iris remained in the second of the two tharlarion wagons we had purchased in the wagon yards outside the walls of Ar.

* * *

"Come to the edge of the roof," had said Thurnock. "Look down to
the street."

"What do you see?" I had asked.

"Guardsmen and Taurentians," he had said. "There may be fifty
of them. They are entering the cylinder."

"You have seen them," I said. "Thus, they have, unbeknownst to
themselves, lost the element of surprise."

"May we find some profit in that," said Thurnock.

"We will," I said. "There is much profit in it."

"How so?" asked Thurnock.

"He who does not know the game is begun is already defeated,"
I said. "He who knows the game is soon to begin can prepare his
pieces."

"Time is short," said Thurnock.

"Less short than you think," I said. "Presumably they know little
more of Aetius than the fact that he fought with us at the Central
Cylinder, and, today, was seen entering the Tower of Philebus. Thus,
they will not know our exact location. This will give us time."

"As I am one of your pieces," said Thurnock, "I am curious as to
how we are going to be moved."

"That is one of the beauties of kaissa," I said. "The pieces do not
ask for explanations, nor do they quibble, or object."

"Men," said Thurnock, "are not wooden figures on a board of a
hundred red and yellow squares."

"We will descend to the suite, immediately," I said. "We will bar
the door, heavily. This will suggest to our friends that we plan on
holding the suite. We will then exit through the suite's rear entrance."

"Soon?" asked Thurnock.

"Very soon," I said.

"The bridges adjacent to the cylinder will have been closed off or
will be under surveillance," said Thurnock.

"Only," I said, "as our friends make their way from floor to floor.
Too large an investment of men and time would be required otherwise."

"I hope you are right," said Thurnock.

"Do not forget," I said. "Our friends think they possess the element of surprise."

"But they do not," said Thurnock.

"Thanks to you," I said.

"How do you wish to proceed?" he asked.

"Following our exit from the suite," I said, "we will ascend the
cylinder several floors, and then exit, one or two at a time, via one
or more of the higher bridges, those less likely to be under surveillance, reach one or another cylinder, and then descend to the streets,
to try various gates, again one or two at a time, and, if all goes well,

rendezvous outside the walls at the public tharlarion yards. We can secure transportation there to make our way to the Inn of Livius Major, where I left Talena, on the nearest road to Torcadino. With fortune we will have the start of much of an Ahn and be through the gates before our friends reach and manage to break open the receiving door of the suite."

"What if we meet opposition on the bridges?" had asked Thurnock.

"If all goes well, we will not," I had said.

"But if we do?" had asked Thurnock.

"Then," I had said, "we will cut our way through it."

"The innkeeper's deputy," I said, "knows little, or pretends to know little, as to those in whose company Talena took her leave."

"Given the she-urt's mercenary nature, which comports well with her assumed Merchant's robes," said Thurnock, "I would have expected her to wait for you at the inn."

"The innkeeper's deputy," I said, "speculated that she might have received a better offer."

"Forget her," said Seremides, leaning on his crutch. "She is worthless, or worth no more than she would bring on the sales block. Her pretensions are arrant and hollow. She is worth no more than a thousand other slaves. You have gold. You can buy a hundred better than her."

"I fear my noble benefactor is right," said Xenon.

"Where is Aetius?" asked Seremides.

"He was here a moment ago," I said.

"We are now clear of Ar," said Thurnock. "Perhaps he has taken his leave."

"He would not do so without informing us," I said.

"What are we going to do?" asked Thurnock.

"I know what I must do," I said. "I must search for Talena. I know not what others will do."

"My captain is a fool," said Thurnock. "But he is my captain."

"And mine," said Clitus.

"The roads are dangerous," said Seremides. "I am reluctant to forgo the shelter of the sword of Tarl Cabot."

"I have found myself accepted and respected in this company," said Xenon. "No more need be said."

"Surely," said Thurnock, "we need not harness the tharlarion and rush off immediately."

"No," I said.

"I am one for sampling the fare of this inn," said Thurnock.

"Let us do so," I said.

"Aetius is missing," said Clitus.

"I am sure he is about," I said. "I will take the liberty of ordering for him."

"If he does not show up," said Thurnock, "I will not let his share go to waste."

The fare served in the spacious, well-appointed dining hall of the Inn of Livius Major in no way diminished its fine reputation. The portions were ample and delicious, and I am sure, despite the fact that I was somewhat preoccupied, that the beauty of the briefly tunicked slaves who served the meal did not detract from the pleasures of the occasion.

Partly through the meal, and perhaps to the possible disappointment of Thurnock, Aetius appeared and joined us. After the meal he invited us outside, and to the side of the Inn. "I have something to show you," he said.

A naked slave girl was chained by the neck to a heavy stake sunk deeply into the ground. When we appeared from about the corner of the inn and she glimpsed Aetius, she, trembling, went immediately to first obeisance position, kneeling, her head down between her extended arms, the palms of her hands on the ground. Her neck was encircled with the inn collar. An inn tunic, presumably removed from her, had been cast to the side where she could not reach it.

Removing clothing from a woman convinces her, as few other things, of her softness, her difference, and her vulnerability. This is particularly the case when the woman is naked and the others in the vicinity are fully clothed. For example, it is common that victors will see themselves served at their victory feasts by the stripped women of the enemy. I did not know what Aetius had done to this slave but her demeanor left no doubt that she knew herself to be a slave in the presence of a master.

"Kneel up!" he said.

Instantly she obeyed.

"Get your knees apart, she-tarsk," he said.

Her knees were then spread, broadly. I did not think that Aetius's epithet was warranted. The slave was quite attractive.

He then, with his boot sandal, thrust her to her left side in the grass.

"Speak," he said, "as I told you."

"Master inquired at the desk the room slave who had attended to the needs of the Merchants who had recently left the inn, those whom the woman of the Merchants had accompanied. He learned it was I. He then dealt with me as he wished, and subjected me to a lengthy and close interrogation. Despite my intention and my hope to be fully pleasing, I could little satisfy his curiosity for I knew little. One thing I said seemed to him important. That was when, in serving the room, I found unusual cloaks, several of the same sort, hidden amongst their belongings."

"Describe the cloaks," said Aetius.

"They were black," she said, "save that each bore two white stripes."

"Men of Decius Albus!" said Clitus.

"And perhaps Decius Albus himself," I said.

"Or men intending to join him," said Thurnock.

"These are dangerous men," I said. "Rethink your allegiance."

"We need not do so," said Thurnock. "We are with you."

"Sometimes it is not wise to follow a wounded larl," I said.

"And beware the wild bosk," said Thurnock. "It can double back and attack suddenly from the brush."

"Leave me," I said.

"No," said Thurnock.

"No," said the others.

"As you wish," I said, gratefully.

"Wipe your eyes," said Thurnock.

I was ashamed, but they did not berate me. They were Gorean, and they knew that warriors could shed tears, tears of rage, tears of grief, tears of gladness, tears of gratitude. Strong men are subject to strong, deep, violent emotions. But should one acknowledge them? Should one reveal them? One supposes that there is a cultural component in such things.

Aetius then freed the slave of her metal tether, and threw her the torn tunic.

"Clothe yourself," he said. "Return to your duties."

"Yes, Master," she said. "Thank you, Master."

"How was she?" asked Thurnock.

"Excellent," said Aetius.

"I am not surprised," said Seremides. "The Inn of Livius Major has a fine reputation."

"I have something else to show you," said Aetius.

He led us to a patch of open ground some yards away.

"There," he said, pointing.

"We may not be the only ones who seek Decius Albus," I said.

It was the tracks of a Kur.

"And what of Marlenus?" said Seremides. "He, too, might seek Decius Albus. Had the slave heard aught of him?"

"She said nothing of the Ubar," said Aetius.

"Doubtless then," said Seremides, "he is still in Ar, presiding over the festival of his Restoration."

"I did not see him at the festival of the Restoration," said Aetius. "He must have concealed himself."

"Or was not there," said Seremides.

CHAPTER SEVENTY-EIGHT

"We do not know the location of Talena," I said. "It seems she was taken by Decius Albus or his men."

"Be patient, Captain," said Thurnock.

"Should they not be here, somewhere along the road to Torcadino?" I asked.

The light of our small campfire was reflected in Thurnock's heavy, unkempt beard.

"They could have turned away, overland, in a hundred places," said Seremides.

Iris, kneeling, turned the wild vulo on its spit. The odor of its roasting carried well back to the road and into the surrounding woods.

"We have done our best," said Aetius. "We have made many inquiries, at inns and villages, and both of travelers bound for Torcadino and of those coming from Torcadino. We have even, here and there, left word of coin available to those who might assist us in our quest."

We were within a hundred paces of the road, and had deliberately made no effort to conceal our location. We wished to be available to any who might wish to profit from furnishing us with useful information, information which they might deem it best to deliver under the cover of darkness. Those who keep unconcealed camps, particularly in desolate places are usually either fools or such as have little to fear. Indeed, such camps are sometimes trap camps, lit largely to invite predators who would too late discover their error. Bandits sometimes use this ruse to rid their territories of unwanted competitors. We, however, were not in a desolate place; rather we were within easy walking distance of the wide, deeply rutted wall road referred to on most maps as the Leccian Way, but locally called the North Road, by those who look toward Torcadino, and the South Road by those who look toward Ar; we were now, given the last pasang stone, less than a hundred pasangs from Torcadino. Most roads are not wall roads, but several are, in particular those which link larger cities. Wall roads last indefinitely without repair, save for clearing leech plants from about their edges. Those I was familiar with had surely been in existence more than a thousand years. The most famous is the Viktel Aria. They are called "wall roads" because they are built like walls. One is, in effect, walking or riding on the top of a wide wall sunken into the earth. Eventually the wheels of thousands of wagons and carts over hundreds of years wear ruts in the surface. Sometimes disputes arise between north and south, or east and west, traffic, as the wagons tend to follow the ruts.

We were camped beneath the great aqueduct, that which conveys water from the melting snows of the Voltai to Torcadino. Long ago, a captain of one of the larger free companies, Dietrich of Tarnburg, had seized Torcadino by smuggling men into the city, over the walls, wading in the aqueduct.

From our camp we could see two of the moons of Gor, the white moon and the yellow moon. The white moon was full and the yellow moon gibbous. Gor's third moon, the tiny "Prison Moon" was not in the sky.

Our two draft tharlarion, unhitched, grazed nearby.

"Someone approaches, two men," said Clitus, not looking up.

"They do so openly," said Aetius.

"That is sometimes the best concealment," said Thurnock.

"Perhaps they have information for sale," said Seremides.

I hoped that this would be the case, certainly if the information was not irrelevant or invented.

Though there was gold in the camp, we had had the judgment to limit our inducements to supply information to tarsk-bits or copper tarsks. One could always go higher if the climb seemed promising. Few travelers on Gorean roads hint that their purse is weighty.

Weapons were loosened in sheaths.

"Tal," I said, pleasantly, rising to my feet.

One glance told me that these two men had not come to exchange information for copper.

Their garments were nondescript. I placed them in no caste. The first was of medium height with a touch of gray hair at the temples. The other was taller, blond, handsome in a cruel way, with thin lips and, as nearly as I could make out in the light, with cold blue eyes.

"May we be of service?" I asked.

Neither of our visitors had responded to my greeting.

"Is one named Xenon of Jad in your party?" asked the shorter man, who seemed senior in office, he with some gray at the temples.

"No," I said.

"We have reason to believe he is of your party," said the shorter man, he whom I deemed senior of the two men.

"We do not know him," I said.

"We are not to be deterred, or misled," said the shorter man.

"Do not divert us from our path," said the taller man. "Do not interfere in any way."

"We know of no Xenon of Jad," I said. "There is no Xenon of Jad here."

"I am Xenon of Jad," said Xenon, stepping forth from the shadows.

"We will be calling upon you," said the shorter man.

"I am ready," said Xenon.

"Do not interfere," said the taller man, the blond man, to me.

The two men then went toward the road, but, at the edge of the firelight, turned about, to face Xenon.

They did not speak.

"I will be waiting," said Xenon.

They then went on their way.

"We will break camp," I said, "and in ten Ehn we will have disappeared in the darkness."

"No," said Xenon. "Do not interfere."

He then went to his things, and drew forth a small mirror, a vial of fluid, and a marking stick or brush. I could not tell in the light. He then armed himself with his crossbow, two quarrels, and a loop of strangling wire.

"I wish you well," he said to us.

"You expected them?" I said.

"Yes," he said.

We wished him well.

"This is the last time," he said. "I will never do this again."

Then he slipped into the woods, outside the light of the fire.

A few Ehn later, the two men who had inquired after Xenon of Jad arrived in our camp. They were clothed in black. Both were armed with a crossbow, a quiver containing several quarrels, a belt knife, and a sword.

On the forehead of each, as had been on Xenon's forehead, there was drawn, clearly and precisely, a small black dagger.

It is a sign not so much that the Assassin is hunting as that he is near the kill.

"We are calling on Xenon of Jad," said the shorter man, he whom I took to be the senior of the two.

"Perhaps," I said, "he will be calling on you."

"Where is he?" asked the shorter man.

I gestured toward the darkness of the woods.

"The roast vulo is done, Master," said Iris. "Shall I serve?"

"No, lovely, naive barbarian," I said. "We will eat later, if we choose to eat."

"Xenon!" I cried, rushing forth to embrace him. The rest of us greeted him, as well. Even Seremides, pulling himself up by his crutch, hobbled to Xenon, and clutched his sleeve.

"It was the last time," said Xenon. "I will never do it again."

"You have wiped away that dreadful sigil," said Thurnock. "Therefore, be Xenon, our fellow, our friend, once more."

"May I serve supper, Masters," asked Iris. "The vulo will grow cold."

"Vulos should never grow cold," said Seremides, pinching Iris sharply on the fundament. She cried out with surprise and pain, leaped away, and hurried, laughing, to her work. A kajira, it is said, need be concerned only when such attentions become infrequent.

We had nearly finished the vulo when Xenon spoke. "It is strange, dear friends," he said, "how precious to some men can be but an Ehn or two of life."

"It seems it would make little difference," said Thurnock.

"To some it seems so," said Xenon. "To others not. The light was poor. The quarrel had lodged near his heart, that of the blond visitor. I approached and drew my belt knife. It is the Assassin's way. The task is to be discharged. 'Stay your hand,' he begged. 'Give me another Ehn to live.' 'What have you to sell?' I inquired."

"And had he anything to sell?" asked Seremides.

"Decius Albus and several of his men have joined forces in the woods near Samnium," said Xenon. "They may, altogether, some four or five parties, number some two hundred men. They are desperate, vigilant, wary, and frightened. They now intend to remain together, charter coast ships and reach Brundisium. With them are Pa-Kur, and Lucilius, the Kur."

"And Talena?" I asked. "What of Talena?"

"She is with them," said Xenon.

"And then you plunged your knife into his throat," said Clitus.

"I sheathed the blade, and waited," said Xenon. "I stayed with him until he died."

"That is unusual for one of the black cloak," said Thurnock. "Are you not to make your kill and vanish?"

"I wiped the dagger from my brow," said Xenon. "I was no longer of the Black Caste."

We finished the vulo, licking our fingers, and then wiping them on our tunics, thighs, grass, firewood, or what might serve.

Some men have their slaves kneel nearby, and put their heads down, and then they wipe their hands on the hair of their slaves, but this is rare and generally disparaged. It is stupid to soil a lovely property. A slave is much more attractive when she is clean and well groomed. Also, there is much that can be done with hair in the furs.

"We are six men," said Thurnock. "Decius Albus, as we learn, may have something like two hundred."

"I seek Talena," I said.

"Forget her," said Thurnock. "Buy a hundred others."

"I choose not to do so," I said.

I saw a tear in the eye of Iris.

"How will you waft Talena from the midst of armed men?" asked Seremides.

"Particularly if she does not wish to be wafted?" said Clitus.

"I do not understand why she left the Inn of Livius Major with strangers," said Xenon.

"She would not have known them to be adherents of Decius Albus," I said. "They must have posed as sympathizers with her former cause."

"Many Merchants prospered during that time," said Seremides.

"As did you," I said.

"To be sure," said Seremides. "Who does not pick up gold when it lies within reach?"

"What could they have promised her?" asked Xenon.

"As much as she demanded from the captain, and then more," said Clitus.

"But why would they want her?" asked Xenon. "What would they do with her?"

"Dear Xenon," said Seremides, "you draw a strong oar and you are well practiced in the craft of the Black Caste, and I am extremely fond of you and respect you highly, but I fear you have devoted less time than judicious to the subtleties of economics and politics."

"There is no longer a great reward posted for the apprehension of Talena," said Xenon.

"Why would Decius Albus approach Brundisium?" asked Seremides.

"Presumably for its access to Cos, to Jad," said Xenon.

"Precisely," said Seremides. "The fortune which was to bring continental Gor under the spears of Cos was lost. That loss does not endear its object, troublesome, lovely Talena, to its Ubar."

"Surely," said Xenon, "you cannot impute motives as petty as spite and vengeance to Lurius of Jad, glorious Lurius of Jad, Ubar of mighty Cos?"

"Easily," said Seremides. "I have dealt with him, and I know him personally, and far better than you, dear, loyal Cosian. Sometimes things which look large and splendid from afar, are revealed to be less large and less splendid when seen more closely."

"How could great Lurius blame Talena for his loss, a loss of what he never had in the first place?" asked Xenon. "It is not the fault of Talena that he failed to receive a vast, anticipated fortune."

"He might be pleased to vent his frustration on her," said Seremides.

"That would be irrational on his part," said Xenon.

"Wearing a medallion of office need not confer rationality," said Seremides. "Too, conclusions follow from an irrational supposition as easily as from a rational supposition. Indeed, the irrational has its own rationality. If one thinks all men are his foes, it is rational to suppose that the next fellow who shows up is a foe."

"Thanks to Xenon," I said, "we have a location for Talena. Seize rest. We shall start at dawn. There may still be time to reach the encampment of Decius Albus before they can hire coasters for Brundisium."

"Dear Cabot," said Seremides. "We are six, and I am crippled. How do you propose to deal with some two hundred men?"

"We shall cross that bridge when we come to it," I said.

"It is commonly advisable to think about crossing bridges before you come to them," said Seremides.

"I am curious," I said, "to know the whereabouts of Marlenus."

"I was in Ar," said Aetius. "The festival days of the Restoration were in progress. I visited several sites. I saw nothing of Marlenus."

"The days of the Restoration can be dangerous," I said. "Crowds abound. Marlenus might be wise to avoid too accessible a presence."

"Marlenus," said Aetius, "is a larl amongst men. He is not one to shrink from sight."

"What is then to be inferred?" I asked.

"I would suppose," said Seremides, "that he is not in the city."

"Where then is he?" asked Thurnock.

"I suspect," said Seremides, "that he, as we, is on the trail of Decius Albus."

"That," I said, "does not bode well for us." I recalled the outcome of the trial of Talena.

"Excellent," said Seremides. "We could be crushed between two hostile forces, either one of which could annihilate us."

"We leave at dawn," I said.

CHAPTER SEVENTY-NINE

Far behind us and to our right, we saw the walls of Torcadino.

We regretted abandoning the Leccian Way, because our wagons made much better time on its stone surface, but our goal was not Torcadino, but the environs of Samnium. Therefore, this morning, south of Torcadino, near the Village of Two Branches, we had turned overland to locate a field road or a forest road which would give us a more direct route to our destination.

"Behold the golden sa-tarna," said Thurnock, walking beside me, leading the first tharlarion. "Is it not beautiful?"

"Sa-tarna", in Gorean, means "life-daughter." It is the major grain crop of continental Gor.

"Yes," I said, viewing the large circle of tillage. "But I would prefer that it was not in our way."

Whereas there are certainly rectangular and square fields of sa-tarna, these are commonly found away from villages. Village fields tend to radiate out from the villages, rather like triangles. In this way, the holdings are not isolated and vulnerable. The village, which is usually palisaded, has its Home Stone, and the individual dwellings within the palisade are likely to have their own Home Stones, as well. There is a Gorean saying to the effect that in the holding of his Home Stone even the least of men is a Ubar. Goreans tend to be individualistic but each village usually keeps one or two fields which are seeded and tilled in common. Villagers who might find themselves, through no fault of their own, truly needy, have first call on the produce of such fields. Generally, however, the produce is shared amongst all the villagers.

"I would we had a tarn," I said.

"We do not," said Thurnock, unhelpfully.

"Shall we circle south and west or north and west," I said. Both routes, of course, would take us wide of the most direct route to Samnium.

"I do not know," said Thurnock.

Neither Thurnock nor myself, despite our sense of urgency, considered taking the wagons through the burgeoning fields. One does not trample sa-tarna. Too, we had no wish to be hunted down by an

offended, irate, righteous, vengeful mob of Peasants, intent on collecting either our blood or a confiscatory compensation for damages.

"North and west," I said.

"Why?" he asked.

"Because a decision must be made," I said.

It is doubtless desirable to make the best decision. But what is the
best decision? Sometimes no decision is the best decision. Sometimes
any decision is better than no decision. In this instance, it seemed to
me that a decision was needed, so I made one. Who knows whether
or not it was the best decision? It was better than no decision. It is
interesting how many people look up to individuals who make decisions. It is apparently difficult for some people to make decisions. In
many cases, then, they look up to individuals who make decisions,
individuals who may not really know any more than they do. But
it is nice to have a decision. Too, in many cases, one can make any
decision do. Leaders need not trouble followers with such thoughts.

After an Ahn or so, we had circled the great field.

"Wait!" called Aetius.

We paused the wagons.

He descended from the first wagon, and went to the edge of the
field.

"What are you doing?" I asked.

"See," he said, "some of the sa-tarna has been broken, trampled."

"By careless Peasants, working the field," said Seremides, from
the second wagon, Xenon at his side, on the wagon bench.

"Some damage is inevitable," said Thurnock. "But not like this."

"What do you make of it?" I asked.

"Someone, a large man," said Thurnock, "clumsy, uncaring,
surely not of the Peasants, came through the field and emerged here."

"A gross, unthinking man," said Clitus.

"Not a man," said Aetius. "See?"

He was crouching down, pointing.

I went to his side.

"Yes," I said.

There were prints, those of a Kur.

"It may be the same as that whose prints were found near the Inn
of Livius Major," said Aetius.

"Quite possibly," I said.

"Bound for Samnium?" said Aetius.

"I fear so," I said.

"Then we may be on the right trail," said Seremides.

"There is still time to turn back," I said.

"We have already lost time avoiding the field," said Thurnock.
"Let us press on."

A bit later we were crossing a small creek.

The wheels were scarcely out of the water when Aetius, who had waded beside the wagon, stopped. "Here are more prints," he said.

We gathered at the edge of the creek.

"Those of two Kurii," he said.

"Or a Kur and something like a Kur," I said.

"Are they together?" asked Seremides.

"No," said Aetius, "one set of tracks is older, the other is fresher."

"It seems that only one Kur made its way through the sa-tarna," said Thurnock.

"And you suggest that the other avoided it, that it respected it?" asked Seremides.

"It is possible," said Thurnock.

"Absurd," said Seremides.

"Perhaps not," I said. One set of prints was clearly Kur. One could tell that by the impression of six digits which had left their mark in the ground. That was the older set. The other set of prints, those formed more recently, was formed by paws which had only five digits.

What is a Kur?

How could I explain to my friends or to others without certain experiences, that two entities which might seem indistinguishable might be radically unlike? It is clear that two indistinguishable boxes may contain quite different contents. Who does not recognize that? It is obvious. But how to explain, or get people to understand and accept, that two quite similar appearances or shapes might not house similar values, dispositions, wants, or responses? But is not one larl the guide to the next, one sleen the key to another? And Grendel, my friend, I knew, had in his veins Kur blood.

But what now of Kurii?

Where were they?

They were seemingly vanished from Ar. Would they accept, with good grace, the reversal of the fortunes they had shared with Decius Albus? I did not think so. Would they attempt to salvage his fortunes and turn him back to Ar? Perhaps. Or would they visit upon him the wrath of a disappointed ally?

In any event, I conjectured that Grendel, suspicious, curious, watchful, like a motionless sleen in tall grass, like a shadow in the night, had lurked in the vicinity of the Beast Caves. I conjectured further that something had left the Beast Caves, something which, for some reason, was now following Decius Albus, something which Grendel was himself determined to follow, to trail and watch.

It was late in the same afternoon that we encountered a field road which, while not a wall road, consisting of layered stone blocks, enabled us to leave the grass of the open country and considerably increase our rate of travel. Indeed, as we could tell from the woods lying ahead, this same road would soon be denominable a forest road. The distinction between a field road and a forest road is not always one simply of location, one of open country as opposed to wooded country, but also one of nature, upkeep, and responsibility. The field road is commonly maintained by local Peasantry and is usually little more than a wide, cleared path. If one encounters an obstacle on such a road, say, a washed-out ditch or deep mire, one simply leaves the road and returns to it as soon as it is practical. A forest road, on the other hand, is usually maintained by local woodsmen, or foresters, and, as it is not easily left and rejoined, is likely to have its bridges and, in certain areas, its paving of planks or logs. As a result of this arrangement, having to do with upkeep and responsibility, one sometimes encountered anomalies such as stretches of forest road in open country, and stretches of field road in the woods. The forest road which was ahead of us now was the same road which we had utilized earlier in leaving Samnium, the same road on which we had encountered Rufus and Pechia, supposedly a couple of the Village of Two Branches, south of Torcadino.

"Hold," I said, lifting my hand.

The tharlarion were checked and the wagons stopped.

I turned about and faced my fellows.

"The woods are before us," I said. "They are deep and dark. Bandits sometimes frequent them. In them are forest panthers and forest sleen, perhaps even the black larl. We are components in no ample, well-guarded caravan. Too, somewhere in these woods, if our intelligence is accurate, though doubtless far from the road, is the encampment of Decius Albus."

"The picture you paint," said Seremides, "is dismal, indeed. You have chosen your colors well to impress upon us possible dangers. Let us tremble. Yet you might, in all fairness, recognize that this road, by all accounts, is familiar and well traveled. Peddlers, minor merchants, Peasants, and others make use of it on a near-daily basis."

"Very well," I said, somewhat annoyed. "I have done my best to warn you. It seemed to me that I should do so. So I did so. I rejoice if you are not deterred."

"The time to have been deterred," said Aetius, "were we open to the matter, was just after we left Ar."

"Doubtless," I said.

"Let us be realistic," said Seremides. "We do not even know if the dying Assassin spoke the truth. Why should he not lie? We could be on a false trail. This may all be a mistake."

"It seems likely, in any event," said Thurnock, "that the two beasts whose prints we found are somewhere in the woods."

"Presumably," I said.

"I am afraid," he said.

"We all are," I said.

"I am not," said Aetius. "A quick thrust of steel to the heart and such a thing, however ugly and massive, is dead."

"Have you delivered such a thrust, ever?" asked Thurnock.

"No," said Aetius.

"Such things are hard to stop," said Thurnock. "Twenty Ihn after its heart no longer beats, it can still tear away your throat."

"Then I will cut to the back of the neck," said Aetius.

"You are not afraid?" I asked.

"No," said Aetius.

"One thing you have still failed to make clear, dear Cabot," said Seremides, "is how you plan to remove Talena from the midst of the men of Decius Albus, perhaps two hundred of them, quite possibly without her consent."

"One enters the enemy encampment surreptitiously," I said. "One is a shadow amongst other shadows. A knife can open a portal in the back of a tent. One can then gag and bind a sleeping woman. Slavers are adept at such things."

"And then," said Thurnock, "you bind her on her back before you, on the saddle apron of a tarn, and make away, to strip her in flight, at your leisure, with your knife."

"All you need is a tarn," said Seremides.

"A brief turning, a restless awakening, a single cry can defeat such a plan," said Clitus.

"Forget her," said Thurnock. "Buy others, even more beautiful."

The late afternoon sun was bright on the field road, at the edge of the woods.

"Look!" cried Xenon, near Seremides, turning, rising to his feet in the second wagon, pointing upward.

"What is it?" cried Iris.

"A tarn!" said Thurnock.

It flashed in the sky.

"Like a tarn!" I said.

"It is approaching!" said Clitus.

"I do not think it sees us," said Seremides, looking up, shading his eyes.

Then it passed overhead, over the edge of the woods, toward Samnium.

Against the clouds, high, perhaps two hundred yards in the air, there had been a gigantic, winged form. The wings had moved, slowly, in a deliberate, stately fashion, but I did not think that they either lifted the body or propelled it. They were part of the seemingness of a tarn. We had seen it at the Stadium of Blades, days before.

"Surely a tarn!" said Thurnock.

"No," I said, "like a tarn, meant to be thought a tarn. It is a machine. It is metal. It is a housing of the brain of Agamemnon, the Eleventh Face of the Nameless One, another of his bodies."

"It seems we are on the right trail, after all," said Seremides.

"Now," said Aetius. "I am afraid."

We then entered the woods.

CHAPTER EIGHTY

I inserted the point of the knife into the canvas, and slowly moved it downward.

The night was cloudy and the white moon, the only moon in the sky, was no more than a slim crescent. The joke was that it was a "slaver's moon." On such nights, guardsmen are especially alert.

The lonely forest road to and from Samnium was narrow and encroached on by overhanging branches and dangling leaves. In this way, it and its margins, particularly in the stirrings of wind, were beset by shifting patches of light and shadow. In those who are concerned with such things, this produces uneasiness. Who knows who, or what, may be watching?

We were now sure that the account given by the dying Assassin to Xenon was substantially correct. Independent pieces fit well into such a pattern. It seemed plausible that the fugitive Decius Albus and the remnants of his small private army would wish cover, such as a forest would provide. Surely they would do their best to conceal their location, as Marlenus and soldiers of Ar might be in pursuit. In this respect, having smaller contingents of followers rendezvousing at a predetermined site, such as a location in this forest, would seem tactically advisable. Beyond these considerations, it seemed likely that the Kur whose prints we had found might be concerned to find Decius Albus, for one reason or another. Then we had seen the metal tarn.

"The forest is long and wide," had said Thurnock. "Decius Albus could be anywhere within its dense precincts."

"I do not think so," I said. "He is likely to position his camp on the left, or south, side of the road, not on the right, or north, side of the road. In that way he will not have to cross it. Secondly, assuming he is interested in chartering a small fleet to convey himself and his men safely to Brundisium, he will want to be relatively close to the edge of the forest, so they can move quickly, and be less exposed, as he hurries to embark on the chartered ships."

"Then we are almost certain of his location," said Thurnock.

"I would think so," I said. "We shall, in any event, hope so. Certainly we do not have weeks to spend combing the forest."

"This is muchly predicated," said Seremides, "on the expectation that Decius Albus wishes to reach Brundisium with a substantial force of men at his disposal."

"Certainly," I said.

"And intends to deliver Talena to the vengeful mercies of Lurius of Jad?"

"That seems likely," I said. "Presumably Lurius of Jad would pay well to obtain her."

"And Decius Albus will be in desperate need of coin," said Aetius.

"Yes," I said.

"What of Talena in all this?" asked Clitus.

"She is probably thinking only of reaching Brundisium, or the Farther Islands, or even the World's End, where she might expect to begin a new, comfortable life, presumably under an assumed name."

"She is naive," said Seremides.

"Trusting, desperate," I suggested.

"I wonder if we are right about the likely location of Decius Albus?" said Thurnock.

"I think we are," I said. "One thing is beyond conjecture."

"What is that?" asked Thurnock.

"That if he is where we think he is, he knows our location," I said.

"How is that?" asked Thurnock.

"He will have had the road watched," I said.

"We are in danger," said Aetius.

"I think no more so than other travelers," I said. "Presumably we are what we appear to be, Merchants or Peasants, with two wagons, two draft tharlarion, a single slave, and so on. If Decius Albus interfered with the traffic on this road, it would soon become evident. Individuals would be missed, deliveries would fail to be made, and so on. The last thing he wants to do is to bring about an investigation."

"Presumably he will soon manage to find ships which can convey him and his men to Brundisium," said Thurnock.

"I suspect that fishing fleets come and go every few days," said Clitus. "A fishing fleet could make it easily from Port of Samnium to Brundisium. Perhaps Decius Albus is waiting for the return of such a fleet."

"Quite possibly," I said. "When it reembarked no one might know it was now bound not for fishing banks or the open sea, but for Brundisium."

"Such ships might also provide good cover for his departure," said Clitus.

"True," said Aetius.

"Such fleets come and go every few days?" I said.

"Yes," said Clitus.

"Such a fleet might then be due any day," I said.

"Yes," said Clitus.

"I fear then," I said, "we may have little time in which to act."

The canvas of the tent parted easily.

There were only two tents in the camp which had private guards. The larger of the two had six guards and the smaller of the two had two guards. I assumed that the larger of the two would be the tent of Decius Albus and the smaller would be the prison tent for Talena. I wondered if she knew it was a prison tent. Perhaps she believed the guards were posted not to prevent her escape but for her safety. I conjectured that if she were later to embark from Brundisium, she would not realize the devious plan of Decius Albus until her ship reached the twin pylons marking the harbor of Jad.

I crawled on my belly through the rent canvas.

A tiny tharlarion-oil lamp dimly lit the interior of the tent.

Talena was lying on a wide sleeping cushion, under a silken coverlet. I stood in the tent. I heard one of the guards outside say something, indistinctly, to the other. There was a small laugh and then silence. I tested the draw, for a hort, of the sword. Then I eased it back into the scabbard. I looked down on the sleeping figure and then, gently, lifted away the coverlet. Talena stirred, and turned a little, but then subsided. She wore an ankle-length, silken sleeping gown, but it had risen to her calves. I found her very beautiful. Women are so beautiful. I supposed that many did not even know how beautiful they were. Talena, however, was not one such. She was not ignorant in that particular. She was well aware of her appearance, and its likely effect on men. Beauty is a coin with which a clever woman can buy much.

There are many ways in which a woman can turn and pause even in the robes of concealment, many ways in which a veil can be adjusted or arranged, many ways in which a hem can be lifted lest a garment be soiled in crossing a damp street. And what of shy, inviting, darting glances, soft, seemingly inadvertent sounds, mock scoldings, pretty supposed confusions, tones that can hint, words that seem the name of ambivalence, and laughter that suggests dangling keys and portals somehow left ajar?

Clearly Decius Albus, for whatever reason, whether for his own amusement, as a cruel joke, or to turn his men away from her, that they be less tempted to put her to their use, or to temporarily ease his custody of her until they arrived in Jad, was treating her as a free woman. Presumably that charade well comported with his plans for her. Certainly there was no chain on her ankle, no collar on her neck, no rag on her body, no thin cloth between her and the ground.

How precious, how wonderful, and how dangerous, is the beauty of a woman!

And few women I had ever known had been as skillful as Talena in wielding the weaponry of her beauty.

Such beauty has opened the gates of cities, despoiled fortunes, and undone Ubars.

It is no wonder men put them in collars.

I crouched near the sleeping form, the soft cloth in my hand, and about my wrist a wide strip of cloth.

I placed the palm of my left hand behind the back of her head and, quickly, lifted and turned her head toward me. Her eyes opened wide, suddenly, startled, and, as I expected, she opened her mouth to scream, upon which action I thrust the wadded cloth into her mouth and, a moment later, had secured it in place. I then drew her off the sleeping cushion and put her to her stomach on the tent carpet. I quickly crossed her wrists and fastened them together with a strip of binding fiber. I then crossed her ankles, and tied them together.

I then stood up and regarded her.

I let her squirm helplessly for a bit, that she would better understand that she had been tied by a Gorean warrior. We are trained in the swift imposition of capture knots. In the sacking of cities, amidst fires and carnage, there is commonly little time to waste in such pursuits. One competes with one's fellows and there may be more women to acquire. At such times, too, warriors commonly tag their captures, inserting a wire and tag through an ear lobe or septum. Females, like gold and silver, are a form of wealth.

I then drew her by the upper left arm to the tiny tharlarion-oil lamp, and placed her on her knees.

Women so positioned are well reminded of their biological reality, of their sex. Well then they understand that they are not men, that they are something quite different, something infinitely desirable and ownable.

I looked down on my prize. It is one thing of course, to have a prize, and quite another to have the time, opportunity, and security to put it satisfactorily to the purpose of a prize.

I crouched down before Talena and spoke very quietly.

"You are in great danger," I told her. "Decius Albus intends to convey you to Cos and sell you to Lurius of Jad."

I had, of course, considered the likely difficulties of removing Talena safely from the camp of Decius Albus. It is one thing to slip about like the nocturnal black ost in darkness, strike, and draw away, and quite another to convey a second person out of an armed camp, particularly if the second person is difficult or uncooperative.

As Thurnock had pointed out, I had no tarn.

Talena's eyes flashed angrily over the gag.

"That is the intention of Decius Albus," I said. "It is true."

I saw that she did not believe me.

I hoped that the second portion of my plan would prove successful. Much depended on timing. Even if the second portion of my plan should proceed as I hoped, our departure from the camp would be extremely hazardous, and this was especially the case if Talena should prove unwilling or recalcitrant. If at all possible, I hoped I would not have to carry her. Better to have her afoot, muchly concealed behind me in the darkness. In that fashion I would be free to move and unsheathe my weapon.

"What I tell you is true," I said. "You are in great danger. Decius Albus is not your friend, not your ally or benefactor. Why should he be? Do you think he pities you, that he wishes to repay you for some favor he may have received from you from the days of your glory? He intends to sell you to Lurius of Jad for coin, or power, or shelter. His coup failed in Ar. He is conniving, and desperate."

A look, as of seeming fear, came into Talena's eyes.

"Yes," I said. "It is true. I speak the truth!"

I was sure then, from her demeanor, that she was attentive, convinced, enlightened, and was now wracked with terror. I had not expected to be so successful so quickly. Now, I thought, she grasps that what is at stake is her own life as well as mine.

"Will you be silent," I asked, "if I remove the gag?"

She made a small noise. In common Gorean gag signals, one such noise means "Yes," and two means "No."

"You give your word?" I asked.

She nodded, affirmatively.

I removed the gag, casting it aside.

I then removed her bonds, and she rose to her feet, watching me, rubbing her wrists, and backing toward the portal of the tent.

"We must leave through the back of the tent," I said, softly, "through the opening I made."

"I am Talena of Ar," she said, "daughter of Marlenus of Ar, Ubar of Ar, Ubar of Ubars. I do not exit tents like a thief."

"There are guards," I said.

"For your information, unwise, clumsy intruder," she said, "I am not in danger. There is nothing of Decius Albus in this camp. It is the camp of Tramio, a Merchant of Ti, who, it seems, profited indirectly but considerably, from my glorious occupancy of the throne of Ar. As he is profoundly indebted to me, he wishes to conduct me in honor to a place of comfort, station, and security."

"To a dungeon in Jad," I said.

"How insulting," she said. "You must think me a fool."

"This is the camp of Decius Albus," I said. "His coup failed in Ar. He is a fugitive. He is waiting on transport to Brundisium, and from hence to Cos. He hopes to secure safety and gold in Jad, following your delivery to Lurius of Jad."

"Liar!" she said.

"We must try to escape, together," I said. "There is much danger. Our chances are slim."

"Your chances are less than slim," she said.

"I do not understand," I said.

"You are a barbarian weakling," she said, "confused and conflicted, without direction or power, a scion of your faltering, tottering world, frail of will and lacking in resolve. Are all men of your world as weak and feeble as you?"

"The men of my former world," I said, "bear the same genetic heritage as those of Gor. Their hearts beat and their blood flows as does that of the men of Gor. If there is a difference, it is cultural. The stoutest of trees, the finest of animals, can be clipped, reduced, stunted, and poisoned. Were those of Gor tricked from childhood into abandoning nature and betraying their blood, taught to prize demasculinization and strive for mediocrity, they would be as pathetically inept as many of the unwitting males of Earth."

"The women of Earth sell well in Gorean markets," she said, scornfully. "They make superb slaves."

"On Gor," I said, "they are rescued from their sexual desert. On Gor they find themselves in the world of which they have dreamed, and in which they have longed to find themselves. At last things are meaningful to them, and they find their home and identity. They undergo the liberation of the collar. In their collars they are freed to be themselves."

"They are as dust beneath the sandals of the proud free women of Gor!"

"What are the proud free women of Gor," I asked, "but slaves as yet uncollared."

"Tarsk!" she hissed.

"The women of Gor and those of Earth," I said, "share the same genetic heritage."

"We are infinitely superior to them," said Talena.

"Do you think I have not seen the women of Gor writhe on the auction block," I said, "dance naked in bells tied on their wrists and ankles, squirm on their knees, begging the least caress from an indifferent master?"

"Tarsk, sleen!" she said.

"All are women," I said, "slaves, with or without masters."

"Why should I listen to you?" she asked. "You are a weakling, a feckless barbarian. You had me at your mercy, and, like the fool you are, you removed my gag and relieved my limbs of bonds."

"I trust you," I said. "I have your word."

"You did not tear away my gown," she said. "You did not put me to your pleasure."

"I want to save you," I said. "You may not understand it, but you are in great danger."

"Not so much as you," she laughed. Then she cried out, "Guards! Guards! Intruder! Guards! Guards!"

CHAPTER EIGHTY-ONE

I spun about and threw myself, rolling, to the carpeted floor of the tent, thrust up the rent canvas, and forced myself outside.

"Lady?" I heard, a man's voice, presumably from within the tent or at its portal.

"There!" cried Talena, presumably indicating the point of my abrupt exit.

I sprang to my feet.

I hoped the guards would have enough common sense not to crawl after me, as that would place them at the mercy of a waiting assailant.

I resisted the impulse to run.

If the guards had any sense of their own, and their prisoner's, best interests, as soon as they recognized that the intruder was not inside the tent, they would exit the tent through the main portal, on their feet, weapons drawn, provide for the security of the prisoner, and summon light and help. A massive search of the camp would then ensue.

I hoped they were wise enough, or experienced enough, or trained enough, to proceed in that fashion.

When a sleen is about, one does not rush foolishly into the darkness. The sleen might not slip away. It might be tenaciously, compulsively, on a scent. You might be in its path. You might rush into its jaws. Similarly, if an intruder is about, an intruder who may well be armed, you might rush into his sword.

I must not run.

I must be calm, I must be part of the camp.

Two men rushed up to me.

"What is going on?" one asked.

There was shouting toward the front of the tent.

"An intruder, I think," I said.

I hoped the second part of my plan, that which, hopefully, would have allowed me to escape with Talena, would unfold promptly.

Things were not going as I had hoped.

I moved away from the back of the tent with the two fellows who had arrived beside me. Then I let them precede me and I slipped back a bit, toward the farther side of the camp. Some other fellows ran past me. I could see torches and lamps being borne toward the front of the tent. As it was dark, and there must have been two hundred or more men in the camp, I did not expect to be immediately recognized as a stranger of sorts. As one would expect, given the priorities of Decius Albus, stealth and anonymity, his men were in no particular uniform, certainly nothing which might have suggested the habiliments of the small private army of Marlenus's erstwhile trade advisor. If there were passwords or signs, of course, I did not know them. I hoped that Talena would have been conducted by now to a place of putative safety. It would not do at all for her to see me and instantly point me out as the sought intruder. Two fellows, swords drawn, detained a figure not three yards from me. "What says the yellow tabuk?" one of them hissed to the fellow detained. "Do not enter the den of the black larl," he responded. "Pass," I heard. I moved a bit closer to the far side of the camp. I could not, forever, of course, if I remained in the camp, avoid detection and apprehension. There would be many things, names, places, stories, anecdotes, details of the camp, and of Ar, which the men of Decius Albus would know and I would not. I sensed now that groups of men, bearing light, were starting to move about the camp. I trusted that Thurnock and the others would soon act. Surely it was time to do so. Perhaps it was past time to do so. In an Ahn, daylight would be imminent. I suddenly found myself surrounded by some five of six presumably armed men. "What says the yellow tabuk?" said one of them. "What he would be well advised to say," I said. "Do not enter the den of the black larl." "Pass," I heard. "Do not be clever, Tarl," I said to myself. "Passwords are not to be belittled or mocked. They are serious business. Not every sword is patient. Not every sentry can be expected, confronting a stranger in the darkness, to share a merry jest. He is more likely to dislodge a quarrel or sound an alarm. Still, some temptations are difficult to resist."

To those hurrying past me toward the lights in the distance, I would seem something like a bystander, waiting, puzzled, to find out what might be occurring. I was, however, making my way, as I could, when I could, toward the far side of the camp. Then, to my relief, I heard shouting from the opposite side of the camp. I saw a large flame in that quarter, and then another, probably from burning tents. Thurnock and my fellows were feigning their attack on the opposite side of the camp. There would, if all went well, seem to be a quick, violent sortie by forces whose numbers would be difficult to judge in the darkness and then a swift withdrawal into the woods. That would have been the time, if any, as men rushed to that point, to convey Talena, willing or not, from the camp. I certainly could not have managed to carry or lead her to safety through the camp in its present state. From the point of view of the camp, the search for an intruder was now in abeyance. A more serious problem had seemingly presented itself. I wondered if Decius Albus had emerged from the commander's tent to organize the search for the intruder. I wondered if he were now hurrying to the scene of the apparent attack, to organize a defense or a pursuit. "What is going on?" cried a man. "There is an attack on the camp," I cried, pointing back. Then I began to shout in the midst of the tents. "Awake! Awake! An attack! An attack! To arms! To arms!" Then I stood aside, while men, in various states of dress and weaponry, began to race past me.

Then I turned about and continued on my way, to leave the camp. My sword was drawn.

Two sentries emerged before me.

Obviously I had come, somehow, from the camp.

I pointed back.

"To the fighting!" I said. "Every man is needed. It is the order of the noble Decius Albus. Hurry! Hurry!"

They looked at one another, and then, as if by an unspoken agreement, they ran toward the distant fighting and flames.

I stood there at the far edge of the camp.

I thought of Talena.

I was angry, very angry.

Dark thoughts welled up within me.

I had risked my life to rescue her. My effort had failed. What had I received in return? I had received nothing in return. I had trusted her. She had given me her word. I had freed her of her gag and bonds. Then she had belied her word. Then she had betrayed me. Then she had called for the guards.

I was fortunate to be alive.

Thurnock had told me to forget her.

But it seemed to me that I would remember her, that I would remember her well. I did not think I would forget her.

Then these dark thoughts burst to the side, like an awakened, startled bird, for I realized, shaken and astonished, suddenly, that much more was going on at the far edge of the camp than could be attributed to the small diversion I had planned. Several tents were afire. There was much shouting and clashing of weapons. There was a blasting of battle horns and the thunder of drums. A frantic tabuk bounded past me, come somehow from amongst the tents. Then a rush of forest urts scrambled past. Something, obviously, had been moving through the forest toward the edge of the camp, frightening animals. I backed away from the close edge of the camp into the darkness. I hoped that my fellows were safe, that they had not been overrun, that they had managed to reach the prearranged rendezvous point, at a nearby bridge, which we called the bridge of Clearchus, at which I had hoped to join them, with a freed, grateful Talena at my side. Far off I heard the roar of a larl. A moment later, I stopped, abruptly, perfectly still, and I felt my left leg brushed by the coat of a running sleen. Even in the slim light of the white moon there was no mistaking the swift, low, serpentine gait of the animal. Seek the stealth of your burrow, friend, I thought, the night is loud and unpleasant.

I would circle about and attempt to reach what we called the bridge of Clearchus. That was, at least, the name carved into the railing. One does not know if the carving had any significance beyond, perhaps, the vanity of a particular fellow, or if it designated the fellow who was responsible for the bridge, keeping it in repair, and so on. I favored the vanity hypothesis as most of the small bridges we encountered on the forest road to Samnium bore no nomenclature. It was important to us, of course, that we be able to identify a particular meeting point, even in the dark. As this bridge had already identified itself, so to speak, we needed not mark it further, which change might be noted by a perceptive stranger. This bridge had the additional advantage of its proximity to the camp of Decius Albus.

As I made my way through the darkness, I considered with whom I might share the forest. Certainly there was Decius Albus and his men, and, I hoped, my fellows. Too, somewhere, would be lovely, meretricious, scornful Talena, whom I had hoped to save, she who had betrayed her word and set guards on me. Too, there was clearly a force in the forest which was capable of assaulting the camp of Decius Albus. I did not think that there was any local force capable of doing that. Thus, I suspected that I shared the forest with yet another individual who might have business with Decius Albus. Thus, I suspected that I shared the forest with an old acquaintance, with a vengeful Marlenus of Ar, doubtless backed by picked swordsmen of Ar.

CHAPTER EIGHTY-TWO

I ran my fingers over the railing of the short bridge.

I heard the tiny sounds of water flowing under the wood.

I then spoke softly to the darkness. "With what do the laws of Cos march?" I asked.

"As ever," came from the darkness, "with the spears of Cos."

This was a variation on a maxim familiar in the more western latitudes of the Vosk Basin. We had chosen it because it suggested an affinity with Cos, the eventual shelter of which was doubtless of great interest to the camp of Decius Albus.

"Captain," said Thurnock, his voice soft from amongst the trees.

In a moment I was again amongst my fellows.

"Where is Talena?" asked Thurnock. "I expected her to be with you, beaten and stripped, as the worthless slave she is."

"I trusted her," I said. "I was betrayed."

"Of course," said Thurnock. "My captain is a fool."

"Less so now," I said, "than before."

"We began our diversion," said Thurnock. "But we had scarcely shouted and cast a torch amongst the tents, when many men were swarming about us, intent on bringing swords and fire to the encampment of Decius Albus. It was dark. They may have thought us part of their own group. The work of the diversion more than done, we withdrew to the bridge, hoping we would hear from you."

"Tell me of the assailants," I said.

"We detected no special uniform or livery," said Clitus.

"But," said Seremides, "their accents were those of Ar."

"How many do you estimate?" I said.

"Perhaps five hundred," said Aetius.

"Too few to invest the camp," I said, "but more than enough to deal with the men of Decius Albus." Certainly I had encountered no encircling soldiers when I had left the camp. "Was Marlenus of Ar with the assailants?" I asked.

"We do not know," said Clitus.

"If the assailants were of Ar, as seems likely," said Aetius, "I think he must have been. I do not think he would have left so delicious a task as dealing with Decius Albus to another."

"You detected no uniforms, or such?" I asked.

"No," said Seremides.

"Did you sense standards, or did you hear wars cries of Ar?" I asked.

"No," said Seremides.

"Marlenus is wise," I said. "He would not risk his expedition being construed in such a way as to constitute a provocation, an incident, a raid, an invasion, of sorts. His forces might even be thought to be that of a free company."

"By now," said Thurnock, "the men of Decius Albus will have been put to rout."

"One can see the flames of the burning camp through the trees," said Aetius.

"Smell the smoke," said Clitus.

I glanced to the side. Iris, in her brief tunic, was gagged, and bound, her back to a small tree, her hands fastened behind her, about the trunk. She would have been left behind when the men had set out on their diversion. She was not to interfere with the work of men, either inadvertently or deliberately, no more than a penned tarsk or a tethered kaiila. She squirmed a little, pathetically, but we paid her no attention. She was a female, and a slave.

"What of Talena?" I asked.

"Who knows, who cares?" said Thurnock.

"What of Decius Albus?" said Clitus.

"I do not think he could be taken alive," I said. "More likely he will have thrown himself on his own sword, or ordered a subordinate to dispatch him."

"You underestimate him," said Aetius. "If only a handful of men escape the onslaught of the assailants, Decius Albus will be amongst them."

"And, if possible," said Seremides, "he will have Talena with him. She is his hope of security and bounty, of protection and wealth, in the palace of Lurius of Jad."

"How is it," asked Clitus, "that Marlenus of Ar, assuming he is with the assailants, discovered the camp of Decius Albus?"

"He may, as we," said Seremides, "have conjectured that Decius Albus would seek refuge in Cos, and would thus try to make his way to the coast, and eventually to Brundisium."

"But that covers much territory," said Thurnock.

"It is likely," I said, "that Marlenus has advantages we did not. He may have had the services of tarn scouts, say, four or five, who can reconnoiter hundreds of square pasangs in a day. I do not think such a small number would attract too much unwelcome attention."

"He may," said Xenon, "have been following the two Kurii whose tracks we noted, or the flashing silver tarn in the sky, or even us."

I shivered. I supposed that that was possible. It might have been we who had led Marlenus to the camp of Decius Albus.

At that point there was a frantic crashing through the brush, near us. The sky was lit in the distance with burning tents. One could smell smoke. There were no sounds of battle, no shoutings of men, no ringings of steel, no rolls of drums, no blasts of battle horns.

"Hold!" I said. "What says the yellow tabuk?"

"Do not enter the den of the black larl," came from the brush.

"Approach," I said.

A disheveled figure approached.

"Rope him," I said.

A cry of dismay and alarm escaped the figure. Then his body was swathed with ropes.

"Are you of Ar?" he cried.

"No," I said.

"You know the password!" he said.

"Of course," I said.

"Do you not know me?" he cried.

"It is dark," I said.

"I am Tramio, of the men of Decius Albus, pretended Merchant of Ti," he said.

"One so high in the favor of Decius Albus must know much," I said.

"The camp is overrun," said Tramio. "You are fortunate to have escaped. Blood flows. Men scatter. Each hopes to save himself. Release me! We must flee."

At that moment, from somewhere to the east, say, two or three hundred yards away, there was the roar of a larl, quite possibly the same animal I had heard earlier, when several animals, driven from the woods, were fleeing through the camp of Decius Albus. The beast, I supposed, understandably, I granted it, was not happy with the disquiet of a forest, much of which he might well regard as his own domain. Whereas larls, panthers, and sleen can be quite dangerous, they seldom attack humans. Exceptions most often occur when they are startled, are unusually hungry, feel they are confronted and challenged, or sense an objectionable territorial intrusion.

"Its lair is nearby," said Thurnock. "I discovered it earlier. The tracks and odor are unmistakable."

"Release me!" said Tramio.

"The proximity of the beast must be familiar to the camp," I said. "It doubtless suggested the password."

"We must flee," said Tramio. "The woods will be searched."

"Not until daylight," I said. "Your enemy is not stupid."

"Time is short," said Tramio.

"Yours may be even shorter," I said.

"I do not understand," said Tramio.

"Were Decius Albus and the female prisoner taken?" I asked.

"I do not think so," said Tramio.

"If they cleared the camp," I said, "where would they go, what would they do?"

"I do not know," he said.

We heard again the roar of the disturbed larl. This time the sound was unmistakably closer.

Inadvertently we shuddered.

"Plans are always made for such contingencies," I said. "Surely one such as you, high in the favor of Decius Albus, would have some cognizance of such things."

"I know nothing," said Tramio.

"Very well," I said. "Take him to the lair of the larl, bind his feet together, and throw him within."

"No!" he cried.

"And ungag and free the slave," I said. "Thus, she will have an opportunity to try to save herself if the larl objects to our presence. It would be unfortunate if so comely a property perished like a tethered verr."

Tramio, crying out, was dragged through the brush by Thurnock and Clitus, the rest of us following. In the dim light of the slim white moon, we soon arrived at a large, vine-beset, descending, cavelike opening in the side of a nearby hillock. There Tramio's ankles were bound together and he was rolled to the opening, and then downward through it.

"I wish you well," I called to him.

About the same time, we heard another roar in the darkness. Its source could be no more than some fifty paces away.

"Do not leave me!" screamed Tramio. "I will speak! I will speak!"

"Extricate him," I said.

"That will not be easy," said Thurnock. "The lair is dark and deep, inside, he may have rolled down an incline."

"I will speak!" screamed Tramio.

"Try," I said.

A little later Thurnock and Clitus had dragged Tramio out of the lair, and I, and the others, began to shout and pound our weapons together, creating a small din in the vicinity of the lair. The larl could easily have torn his way amongst us, scattering us, bleeding and dismembered, from its path, but larls, like some other forms of life, have genetic codings in the light of which some behaviors are likely to occur and others not. For example, evolution has selected for the tendency to avoid strong and unexpected stimuli, presumably because such stimuli are likely to be associated with danger, for example, with the strike of a predator. Life-forms which did not find strong stimuli aversive presumably, statistically, were less likely to replicate their genes. Too, certain behaviors and responses seem coded. For example, to advert to experiments on my former world, a chicken raised in laboratory conditions, who has never seen a chicken hawk before, will panic and flee at the first sight of one, or something which resembles one. I am sure that our noise confused and annoyed and larl but, as I expected, and hoped, he did not charge forth and attack us. Indeed, societies have known for centuries that many animals will retreat before lines of women and children shouting and beating on pots and pans, women and children who may be herding the animals, such as the giant, tawny northern tabuk toward waiting hunters.

We withdrew, thankfully, from the vicinity of the larl's den.

Once again there was relative silence in the forest.

To be sure, we had made a great deal of noise to discourage the approach of the larl. That was doubtless to be regretted, but I had thought it preferable to possibly being torn to pieces.

"It will soon be light," said Thurnock, "and the assailants will be combing the forest for survivors from the camp of Decius Albus."

"With our two wagons and a slave," I said, "I do not think we will be mistaken for fleeing mercenaries."

I then turned to Tramio.

"You may now speak," I said.

"Release me, if I speak," he said.

"Your speech will be examined and tested," I said, "and, if it turns out to be true, you will be released. If it does not turn out to be true, we will cut your throat, instantly."

"What if my words should prove to be mistaken?" he asked.

"Then your throat will be cut," I said, "instantly."

"If Decius Albus escapes those who have stormed his camp," said Tramio, "it is almost certain he will make his way to his contrived place of refuge, that prepared in case such an emergency should arise, a protection house, a secret house, in Port of Samnium, near the docks."

"Is it within the double walls leading from Samnium to Port of Samnium?" I asked.

"Yes," said Tramio.

"Samnium may be closed to us," said Thurnock. "The walls could be hard to scale."

"What is the name of this house of refuge," I asked.

"The House of the Sea Hith," said Tramio.

"There are no such things," said Aetius.

"The house is in the keeping of a man called Ruffio," said Tramio, "who is also the agent of Decius Albus in Port of Samnium, charged with chartering ships for conveying Decius Albus and his men to Brundisium."

"I think I know the man," I said. "He is a tool for Lurius of Jad."

"What allies are within the high circle of Decius Albus?" asked Seremides.

"I do not understand," said Tramio.

"Are there beasts?" asked Seremides.

"There is a guard beast, a Kur," said Tramio.

"It is not a guard beast," said Seremides. "It is a colleague, and one who, in a subversive, minacious faction, may have higher standing than Decius Albus himself."

"What of Assassins?" asked Xenon.

"There were two," said Tramio, "but they disappeared somewhere on the march."

"There was no sinister figure with grayish skin and eyes like glass?" I asked.

"No," said Tramio.

"What of a tarn, large, silverish, metallic, and stately?" asked Aetius.

"There were no tarns in the camp of Decius Albus," said Tramio.

"It is not a living tarn, no more than a catapult, or wagon," I said, "though there is a life within it."

"Is the refuge house easily taken?" asked Thurnock.

"No," said Tramio. "It is less a house than a small fortress."

"How close is it to the docks of Port of Samnium?" I asked.

"Perhaps five hundred paces," said Tramio.

"Then it could easily be cut off from the docks," said Thurnock.

"It would seem so," I said. I was surprised. It seemed to me that this would be a serious flaw in the escape strategy of one as astute as Decius Albus.

"How many men escaped the camp with Decius Albus?" asked Thurnock.

"I do not even know if Decius Albus escaped," said Tramio. "Nor would I know anything of accompanying men, perhaps ten, perhaps fifty, I do not know."

"Samnium will be dangerous," said Seremides. "There are sure to be men of Decius Albus there, or men in sympathy with him. Too, Ar will not be popular on the coast. The sympathies of Samnium, if any, are likely to be aligned with Tyros and Cos."

"We could be in danger, too, from Marlenus, and his men," said Aetius. "We could be crushed between two stones."

"It is nearly daylight," said Clitus. "I think it would not be well to encounter either desperate refugees from the camp of Decius Albus or merciless soldiers of Ar who are hunting them."

"Our pose is that of harmless travelers bound for Samnium," I said.

"Many a harmless urt has been trampled by some passing tharlarion," said Aetius.

"We could try for Brundisium," said Seremides. "We could turn back to Torcadino. We might try Harfax, Market of Semris, any of a thousand cities, towns, and villages, even Venna or Ar itself."

"I favor Samnium," I said.

"Are you still interested in the miserable slave, Talena," asked Thurnock, "worthless collar meat, after she betrayed you in the prison tent?"

"If anything," I said, grimly, "more so now than before."

"Then," said Thurnock, resignedly, "it is on to Samnium."

"Not necessarily," said Aetius. "The woods are doubtless filled with soldiers. Decius Albus, if alive, is now informed and wary. The slave is unwilling and uncooperative. Things have changed."

"We are only six, and a slave," said Seremides. "Let us take a vote."

Just then Iris screamed and we were aware of motion amongst the trees and amidst the brush about us.

"Hold!" said a commanding voice. "Hold!"

We found ourselves ringed with leveled spears.

"Tal," I said. "We are travelers, bound for Samnium."

"Who is that fellow tied amongst you?" asked the voice.

"A local thief," I said, "caught stealing suls. We are taking him to Samnium, for an archon to put him beneath the snake."

The snake is a heavy whip. Sometimes glass and bits of metal are worked into its leather. Men have died beneath its blows. It is never used on women.

"You may be travelers, you may not be travelers," said the voice. "You will come with us."

"We have two wagons," I said.

"Hitch them up," he said.

"May I ask where you are taking us?" I asked.

"Samnium," he said.

"Well," said Thurnock. "That solves that problem."

CHAPTER EIGHTY-THREE

Shield on his left arm, spear grasped in his right hand, huge, bearded Marlenus, looking up, addressed himself to the figures on the low parapet. He was backed by better than four hundred men. Amongst them, refusing to meet my eyes, was the Taurentian swordsman, Alan, of the House of Hesius. I was sure that discipline, and nothing else, kept him in his place, in his line. There were several figures peering down from the low parapet. Centrally there was large, coarse Decius Albus. Flanking him, on either side, were several of his men. Amongst those on his right, muchly cloaked, was a mountainous, hirsute figure, that of an unusually large Kur, whom I supposed was Lucilius, Agamemnon's liaison with his allies in Ar. On the left of Decius Albus was his agent, he whom I had first known as Rufus, of the Village of Two Branches, south of Torcadino, Ruffio of Ar.

"You neglect your duties as my trade advisor," called Marlenus up to Decius Albus.

"I resign the post," called down Decius Albus.

"In favor of the throne of Ar?" asked Marlenus.

"Would that it were better occupied," said Decius Albus.

"I offer it to you," said Marlenus.

"Doubtless subject to a condition," said Decius Albus.

"Come down and do battle, one upon one," said Marlenus. "If you slay me, the throne is yours. I say it so. Should I slay you, you need not fear the humiliation of public impalement."

"I fear your offer is not as generous as it seems," said Decius Albus. "My skills with the blade do not equal yours. I am not one of the fastest, mightiest swords on Gor."

"Choose then a champion," said Marlenus.

"I choose Alan, of the House of Hesius," said Decius Albus.

"I decline to accept the appointment," said Alan.

"You will stand high in Ar, and be rich with gold and women, if you win the throne for Decius Albus," said Marlenus.

"I decline to accept the appointment," said Alan.

"Then," said Decius Albus, "I choose one to whom even Pa-Kur, Master of the Assassins, would defer, one who is incognito amongst you now, he whom you once knew as Tarl of Bristol!"

"Stand forth, Tarl of Bristol," said Marlenus.

I stepped forward.

"Be the champion of Decius Albus," said Marlenus.

"Let me fight him, Ubar!" cried Alan.

"I prefer not to lift my sword in the cause of the former trade advisor of Ar," I said.

"Do you scorn riches?" asked Marlenus.

"No," I said. "I prefer other things more."

"Such as your skin!" cried Alan.

"Be silent," roared Marlenus.

"Forgive me, my Ubar," whispered Alan.

"Come down and fight!" called Marlenus to Decius Albus.

"A wise man lets others do his fighting," said Decius Albus. "The risk is less, the gain the same."

"Then, send down a champion!" said Marlenus.

"Perhaps a hundred champions, at once, together," said Decius Albus.

There was laughter amongst those on the parapet.

"Then you turn your back on the throne of Ar?" asked Marlenus.

"Not at all," said Decius Albus.

"I do not understand," said Marlenus.

"Ar is faraway," said Decius Albus.

"How many men have you left?" asked Marlenus.

"Enough," said Decius Albus.

Given what I had gathered of the raid on the encampment of Decius Albus and the ensuing combing of the nearby woods for fugitives, I suspected that no more than fifty men had accompanied Decius Albus in his withdrawal to the house at Port of Samnium.

"Your situation is hopeless," said Marlenus. "You are cut off from the sea. You can be stormed, you can be starved."

"The fishing fleet is due any day," said Decius Albus. "We have enough stores and water to last for months."

I looked to the docks. They were almost empty. There were two small ships moored there.

"Forget succor," said Marlenus. "We are between you and ships, those of a fishing fleet or others."

"You are far from Ar," said Decius Albus. "You are not popular here. On the coast, sympathies favor Tyros and Cos. Beware Samnium!"

"In a single raid a thousand tarnsmen could reduce Samnium to ashes. Who dares to brook the fury of Ar?"

"May fortune be with you," said Decius Albus, "trying to feed your men off a hostile countryside for months, while conditions in a volatile Ar take what direction and shape they will."

"I think," said Marlenus, "your patience, your resolve, your desperation, your valor, your stores, your water, may not stand you in as good a stead as you believe."

"We are content!" called down Decius Albus.

This declaration seemed to receive assent amongst his men.

Strange, I thought, how Decius Albus had elected a holding so far from the kiss of Thassa. Did he really expect to cut his way through superior numbers to reach the docks?

Yesterday morning I, and my fellows, and Iris, with other civilians, so to speak, had been conducted to Samnium under guard. We had been interrogated, treated well, fed, and released. My party may have been particularly favored for it contained Seremides, who, it will be recalled, had managed to return a purloined Home Stone to the safety of Ar. Now, we, and some others, doubtless variously motivated, some perhaps by mere curiosity, lingered on within the double walls which linked Samnium and Port of Samnium. Many had never seen, of course, Marlenus of Ar, or armed men of Ar. Away from the holding of Decius Albus, but within the double walls, were five saddle tarns. These were a component of the pursuing force of Marlenus and had doubtless played some role in his pursuit of Decius Albus. Shortly after we had been released from the custody of our guards, we had unroped Tramio and observed him speeding relievedly away, doubtless determined to avoid larls, and other such predators, if at all possible.

"I have word for you, dear Decius Albus, beloved friend," called Marlenus, up to the parapet, "word which may leave you less content."

"Then speak it, glorious Ubar," said Decius Albus.

"We do not intend to mount a siege," said Marlenus.

"Then I am more content than ever," said Decius Albus.

"It will not be necessary," said Marlenus, "nor do we intend to waste the time."

"Depart promptly then," said Decius Albus, "and be wished well."

There was laughter from the parapet. Even the cloaked Kur, presumably Lucilius, his mighty torso shaking, seemed amused.

"In five days or less your holding will fall," said Marlenus.

"Our walls are ample and their height sufficient," said Decius Albus. "We fear neither attack nor fire."

"My weapon is more fierce than either," said Marlenus. "It is gold! I have a sack of gold for he, or those, who first open your gates."

Several on the parapet stirred, uneasily regarding one another.

Decius Albus blanched.

"It is a weapon with which you are well familiar," said Marlenus. "Let it now be turned against you. What steel can match its edge?"

"You will not let a man of yours enter the gate," screamed Decius Albus, "for, if you do so, your daughter, who is my prisoner, will be instantly killed."

"I have no daughter," said Marlenus. "When she shamed me, I disowned her."

"She is of your blood!" cried Decius Albus. "That no law, no decree, can change! Bring the woman forth!"

I tensed, behind the distributed men of Marlenus.

"Be steady, Captain," whispered Thurnock.

In a moment, a bundled female figure, swathed in the voluminous, colorful Robes of Concealment, was forced forward, and held beside Decius Albus. Decius Albus reached to her veils and tore them away.

It was Talena!

Doubtless now, I thought, vain, beautiful, meretricious Talena understands in whose charge she is, not in that of a Tramio, a concerned, benevolent Merchant of Ti, but in that of Decius Albus, who despises her, who sought her destruction in Ar.

"Behold, glorious Ubar," cried Decius Albus, "the daughter of your own blood and flesh!"

Marlenus, to my astonishment, threw back his large, bearded head and a mighty, roaring laugh escaped his lips.

"If it pleases you," cried Marlenus, "kill her now, for she is no blood of mine."

"Beware," cried Decius Albus, "I will not be tricked!"

"She was adopted in infancy," said Marlenus, "on the contingency that her companioning might one day further the designs of Ar. Politics can draw much profit from the value of such assets. Might not her companioning someday weld a significant alliance, say, with far Turia, or even with Tyros or Cos? The daughters of Ubars are prizes, do you not know, as valuable as steel and coin. They are useful in the subtlest of enterprises. They are precious counters in the weightiness of negotiations."

"But there is only one such!" said Decius Albus, half hysterically, his voice shaking.

"Deliberately," said Marlenus, "that her value be increased a thousand times."

"I could have told you this," said Thurnock to me, "but I did not care to crush you. I did not care to disillusion you. Anyone who has bred beasts would see that the woman is not the blood daughter of Marlenus. Consider the skin, the eyes, the hair. What have they to do with the monstrous size, the tawny, burly might of Marlenus? You might be fooled, and Ubars, fools that they are, might be fooled, but few would be fooled in even the simplest and most remote of Peasant villages."

I had suspected this sort of thing from as long ago as the World's End.

"Forgive me, Captain," said Thurnock, "if I have dismayed you. The edges of truth are sometimes jagged."

"I am not dismayed," I said. "Indeed, I am somehow relieved, even pleased."

As a free woman, Talena would be priceless, and thus without value. Thus, a free woman is worth less than a slave, who has her actual market value, large or small. As Talena was a slave, I wondered what might be her market value. Certainly she was quite beautiful, but then so, too, were many slaves. Most would not be granted collars were they not desirable enough to be put in them.

"You are lying! You are lying!" cried Decius Albus.

"She dishonored me, and she betrayed Ar," said Marlenus. "She is nothing to me. Cut her throat now, if you wish."

Thurnock seized my arm. "Do not move," he said. "Decius Albus will not harm her. He needs her. How else will he buy comfort and security in Cos?"

"If she is not your blood daughter," said Decius Albus, "swear it so, in the name of the Home Stone of Ar!"

"I swear that she is not my blood daughter," said Marlenus, loudly and clearly, and amused, "nor, now, even my adopted daughter, having been set aside, having been repudiated, having been disowned, and I swear all this in the name of the Home Stone of Ar!"

"No!" screamed Talena, and then collapsed, unconscious, in the arms of the man who held her.

"My offer stands," called Marlenus, up to the men on the parapet. "A sack of gold for he, or those, who first open the gate!"

"Clear the parapet, dear friends, trusted brothers, loyal followers," said Decius Albus. "Do not even pause to scorn his wretched proposal, that which insults your honor so grievously. Let only the watch remain."

Ruffio shook his fist at Marlenus. The Kur thrust back his cloaking. It was indeed, as I had anticipated, Lucilius, whom I had known from Ar, and from the Beast Caves. It interested me that the Kur did not seem troubled by the offer of Marlenus. These two then, Ruffio and the Kur, like most of the others, withdrew from the parapet.

"I expect the gate will be open by morning," said Seremides.

There was then some screeching and screaming from the five tarns inside the double wall leading from Samnium down to Port of Samnium, to the docks.

"The birds are afraid," said Iris.

"Or angry," I said.

I looked up. I saw what I expected to see.

"They are disturbed," said Seremides.

"Rightly so, Benefactor" said Xenon. "Look!"

"Yes!" said Aetius.

A large shadow swept past.

"It is our friend," said Seremides. "The giant silver tarn."

The device now hovered some hundred or so feet in the air, over the men of Marlenus, who, holding their position, looked up, in fear and awe. Its talons opened and closed twice. Then it turned about, and disappeared over the double wall, in the direction of the woods.

"I have never seen such a tarn," said Xenon.

"It is not a tarn," I said. "It is a machine, one of the bodies of Agamemnon, Eleventh Face of the Nameless One."

"If it is a machine," said Seremides, "it is clearly in violation of the laws of Priest-Kings."

"It is a machine," I said.

I looked down, toward the docks. They were almost empty. As mentioned, two small ships were moored there.

One could, of course, see little because of the double wall.

"If the gate is not immediately surrendered," said Thurnock, "Decius Albus, fearing imminent betrayal, will try to have his men cut their way to the docks."

"I do not think so," I said.

"Why is that?" asked Thurnock.

"For two reasons," I said. "First, Decius Albus is astute and cunning; second, because his holding seems too easily cut off; it is not adjacent to the sea."

"With loyal cohorts, he could withstand a siege indefinitely," said Thurnock.

"I do not think he has any intention of doing so," I said. "That remark was for the purchase of Marlenus. He is as anxious to get to Brundisium, and Cos, as Marlenus is to keep him from doing so."

"Where is Iris?" asked Seremides.

"Near the men of the Ubar," said Aetius.

"You had better call her back," said Seremides, "before she threatens discipline, distracting men from their duties, and finds herself tonight giving pleasure to dozens of aroused armsmen."

"She is a slave," said Thurnock. "Perhaps that is what she wants."

"No," said Aetius. "I have been watching her. Her little movements, her subtle twistings, and glances, and smiles, are more focused."

"Call her back," I said. "We have too much to contend with, as it is."

Aetius slapped his hands together, sharply, and called out, "Iris, here!"

Instantly, commanded, she spun about and hurried to our side, where she knelt, head down, trembling, fearing she might have been found in some way less than fully pleasing.

The armsman, a young Taurentian in whose vicinity she had been lingering, looked after her, and then looked away.

"There was a Kur on the parapet," said Seremides.

"Lucilius," I said. I had no idea what his name might be in Kur. Whatever it was, I doubted that I could have pronounced it. How could a human, had they languages, say a name in Larl or Sleen, or in Urt or Tabuk?

"If it intended to kill Decius Albus for his failure in Ar, would it not have already done so?" asked Seremides.

"It seems so," I said.

"Perhaps it is biding its time," said Thurnock.

"Or waiting for something to occur, a signal, or such," said Clitus.

"It seems unlikely that Decius Albus can recoup his fortunes in such a way as to once more approach the throne of Ar," said Seremides.

"Even if Marlenus was removed," said Aetius.

"Perhaps," I said, "the presence of Lucilius is then to be accounted for otherwise." To be sure, I was aware that an action might well be motivated by more than one consideration. What capable commander does not have plans within plans?

"There was another Kur," said Seremides, "one who followed the first."

"Not a Kur," I said, "like a Kur."

"Where is it?" asked Seremides.

"I do not know," I said.

"Perhaps," said Aetius, "it turned back, toward Ar."

"I would not think so," I said.

"Why did it follow the first?" asked Aetius.

"I suspect," I said, "to protect us. Few things can stand against a Kur. The Kur is a beast whose strength and ferocity are akin to those of the larl, a beast whose sharpness of senses, resolution, cunning, and tenacity are akin to those of the sleen, one whose subtlety, foresightedness, and probity are equivalent to, or superior to, those of a human. To stand against a Kur, must not one be as wise and terrible as the Kur itself?"

"I see no sign of the Kur, or of a Kurlike thing," said Aetius.

"Nor I," I said.

"It is gone," said Aetius.

"Possibly," I said.

"What do we do now?" asked Thurnock.

"Very little," I said.

"That is easily managed," said Thurnock.

"I, however," I said, "will crave an audience with the Ubar, and the assistance of some fifty or sixty of his men."

"Why is that?" asked Thurnock.

"For two reasons," I said. "First, I cannot see through walls, and, second, I think that Decius Albus is not to be underestimated."

"I do not understand," said Thurnock.

"Look to the docks," I said. "Granted that a fishing fleet, or fleets, are still at sea, does it not seem strange to you that only two vessels would now be wharfed at Port of Samnium?"

"The others are at sea," said Thurnock.

"Perhaps," I said.

CHAPTER EIGHTY-FOUR

"There!" said Thurnock.

"Yes!" I said.

Samnium, as perhaps has been made clear, is linked with Port of Samnium, and the sea, by a long, narrow corridor of land which lies between two walls. The point of this is to make it possible to supply Samnium by sea should it find itself beleaguered. It also serves to conceal troops and individuals who might wish to approach or exit Samnium unbeknownst to observers in the surrounding countryside. Similarly, troops may be safely and surreptitiously moved between Samnium and Port of Samnium as the need might arise. In a sense then, Samnium and Port of Samnium are like two keeps, each at the opposite end of a long, narrow, single fortress. The gold of Marlenus, not surprisingly, as easily as that of Decius Albus, had purchased passage between the walls. Samnium and Port of Samnium, whatever might be their covert sympathies, are declaredly, professedly, even belligerently, neutral with respect to the differences separating Ar and the major island Ubarates, Tyros and Cos, as behooves municipalities which are relatively vulnerable by both sea and land. Samnium and Port of Samnium, like many municipalities, would rather profit from wars than participate in them.

"You expected this?" said Thurnock.

"I thought it likely," I said.

Thurnock and I, followed by Clitus, Aetius, and Seremides, who was aided by Xenon, had, water to our chests, just waded about the corner of one of the two walls joining Samnium and Port of Samnium, the wall to the right, as one would look from Samnium to Port of Samnium. There, before us, but well offshore, were five ships, masts and sails down. They, like many Gorean galleys, being shallow-drafted, were low in the water. Had we not been looking for them, we might not have noticed them.

In a short bit, soaked, and shivering, we had waded onto the beach, outside the right wall.

"Unfortunately," said Thurnock, "your audience with the Ubar did not turn out well."

"It was not a total loss," I said. "To be sure, it could have been better."

There were, behind us, ten soldiers of Ar, under the command of the young Taurentian, Alan, of the House of Hesius.

"I asked to lead this detail," he had said to me.

"I am uneasy," I said.

"Well you should be," he said.

"Am I to expect a sword thrust in the back?" I asked.

"If nothing else," he said, "I am here to protect you, lest you fall to a blade other than my own."

"Did I not know better," I said, "I would suspect you had a score to settle."

"In the Stadium of Blades," he said, "you, fearing to fight me, tricked me. You cheated in an affair that should have been honorably adjudicated. You humiliated me, shaming me before the Ubar and all Ar. You made me seem not a man, not a warrior, but a child, a naive, witless child, a gullible fool."

"I had a reason for doing so," I said.

"Cowardice, and cunning," he said.

"If you wish," I said.

"We are not done with that affair," he said.

"Be done with it," I had said. "Let it pass."

"When the Voltai crumbles to dust," he had said. "When Thassa abandons her shores."

"There are ships there," said Thurnock, looking out to sea, "enough to easily carry two hundred men."

"His forces before the attack of Marlenus," I said. "I conjecture he now has less than a hundred men at his disposal, perhaps only forty or fifty."

"The ships must have arrived only recently," said Clitus, "else Decius Albus would have left his camp earlier."

"Perhaps yesterday," said Seremides.

"I think," I said, "they must be one of the fishing fleets, or a part of one of the fishing fleets."

"Last night, or early this morning," said Thurnock, "Ruffio, or someone, must have had them leave the wharves and take their present position."

"More likely," said Seremides, "Ruffio arranged some days ago to dispatch a ship to contact them at sea, and arrange for them to hasten back to Port of Samnium, and take their present position."

That seemed to me a plausible conjecture.

"In any event," said Thurnock, "they are well offshore."

"A strong swimmer could reach them," said Aetius.

"They have launched no longboats," said Clitus.

"Presumably they are awaiting a signal to approach more closely," I said.

"Apparently no signal has been received," said Thurnock.

"Then Marlenus has taken the fortress," said Alan, he of the House of Hesius.

"Unlikely," I said. I expected the signal to be delivered from the beach itself. Any alternative would immediately generate suspicion.

"I look for longboats," said Aetius.

"Do not," I said. "Consider the beach, its long, gentle slope; consider the ships, so shallow-drafted. They can approach quite closely. Many men can wade out to them and clamber aboard, utilizing ropes and oars. There is no need here for longboats, and successive trips. Fifty men, wading out, could be boarded in two or three Ehn."

I looked back, to our left, far now, toward the docks jutting out from the shore between the two walls. There were two figures there, seemingly small, Iris, and an armsman of Ar. The role of the armsman was clear. If anything untoward should occur in the vicinity of our party, particularly if we needed assistance, he was to signal back to the main force of Marlenus, which was now investing the House of the Sea Hith, now serving as the stronghold of Decius Albus.

"Look back," I said to Alan. "With your fellow, there is a slave."

"I know her," he said. "She is a nuisance."

"Most men," I said, "would not consider her a nuisance. I suspect that few men would object to being bothered by such a one. Indeed, many might hope for such a pleasure."

"She is concerned for you," he said. "It is appropriate that a slave be concerned for her master, as a kaiila or sleen for its owner."

"I think she may be concerned, as well," I said, "for another."

"Perhaps for the handicapped fellow, Seremides," he said.

"Possibly," I granted him.

"Who would not esteem Seremides?" asked Alan. "He is a great hero. It was he, crippled as he was, who boldly and bravely, at great risk to his own life, recaptured the Home Stone of Ar from dangerous thieves and returned it safely to Ar."

"Such would be an awesome achievement, indeed," I granted him.

"Historically, too," said Alan, "he stood high in Ar. And it was he who, while commander of the Taurentian guard, strove secretly to mitigate and undermine the illegitimate Ubarship of the treasonous, hateful Talena."

"So I have heard," I said.

"And personally," said Alan, "I owe much to Seremides. It was he who, on the Skerry of Lars, near Port Kar, encouraged me to bring my sword to Ar."

"I had hoped for fifty men from Marlenus of Ar," I said, "not ten."

"Do not seek to delude me," said Alan. "I am no longer the trusting fool I was in the Stadium of Blades. In that afternoon I grew much.

You knew the Ubar would not give you fifty men for some absurd project, observing some desolate beach, so weakening his investing forces. Therefore you hoped, unhindered, to escape the double walls to which you and your party had been brought from your capture in the woods. But you will not escape, for I and my men will see to it that you, shamed and foiled, are returned to the double walls."

"Marlenus," I said, "is Ubar. He has mighty aims and heavy responsibilities. I am nothing to him. He would not much care if I wandered away, unnoticed, unmissed."

"But I would care," said Alan.

"You have business with me," I said.

"The business of blood and steel," he said.

"I regret that," I said.

"Well you might," he said. "I shall challenge you, when permissible and opportune. You will have two choices, either to meet me and be cut to pieces, stroke by stroke, at my pleasure, or, openly and publicly, to acknowledge yourself a worthless cheat and arrant coward."

"The morning is still," said Thurnock. "The weather is cool. Gulls fly about. The beach is empty."

"This place is far from the House of the Sea Hith," said Aetius. "War is elsewhere. Why did you wish to come here?"

"See the ships," I said, "those to sea."

"Five vessels," said Aetius. "But they cannot abet Decius Albus. The former trade advisor has missed his chance, perhaps by only a day. He has been cut off from the shore."

"I do not think so," I said.

"Surely Decius Albus cannot fight his way to the shore through the men of Marlenus," said Aetius. "He would be considerably outnumbered."

"As I read Decius Albus," I said, "he would not risk so desperate a measure unless there was no other choice."

"There is no other choice," said Thurnock.

"That," I said, "is what is at issue."

"Decius Albus," said Aetius, "will attempt to outstarve the besiegers."

"Not with a sack of gold nailed to his outer gate," said Seremides.

"One traitor is enough to undo him," said Clitus.

"He must issue forth and make for the shore by tomorrow, or the next day," said Thurnock. "The stress of anticipating betrayal will become unbearable."

"Let us return to the camp of the Ubar," said Alan, addressing me. "You cannot escape. Your pathetic ruse has failed. I have seen to it."

"Cease to be annoying," I said. "Take the matter up with the Ubar. Otherwise, content yourself with continuing to prevent my escape."

Our clothing was now muchly dried, from our wading up to the beach. The wind, however, was still chill, so near the water.

I watched some gulls circling about.

"It must be well past the Ninth Ahn," said Clitus, looking up.

To be sure, Tor-tu-Gor, Light-Upon-the-Home-Stone, was near meridian.

"The beach is empty," said Thurnock.

"No!" I said, suddenly, pointing. "Look!"

"Where did he come from?" asked Thurnock, astonished.

"He did not pass us!" said Clitus.

Some seventy yards away from us, a lone figure had appeared, as if by magic, on the beach. I did not think he saw us, as he, somehow, wherever he had come from, was between us and the water. He carried a large, scarlet cloak, which he spread, and then began to lift and lower.

"It is Ruffio," said Seremides.

"Emerged from nowhere," said Xenon.

"Look to the sea," I said. "The ships stir."

"No masts are raised, no sails take the wind," said Clitus.

"Oars move," said Thurnock.

I turned to Alan. "Taurentian," I said, "signal your man on the dock. We cannot close the tunnel and defend the beach at the same time. Act quickly, or all is lost."

"This is another trick," said Alan.

"Not one of mine," I said.

"I see no tunnel," said Alan.

"It must be there," I said. "We do not know its width. We do not know how many men it can spill onto the beach at one time."

I hoped it was narrow. Presumably it would be, to have saved time in its digging.

"The fellow with the cloak slipped past us," said Alan.

"A poor commander lets hatred cloud his judgment," I said. "Your Ubar deserves better of you. Act quickly. The men of Decius Albus can be evacuated in a matter of Ehn."

"The ships are approaching," said Thurnock, half closing his eyes against the glare on the water.

With a cry of rage, Alan turned away and raised his buckler.

His fellow, the distant armsman on the dock, Iris small beside him, acknowledged this signal, raising his own buckler.

I turned to the armsmen with Alan. "Get to the shore," I said. "Warn the ships away. They are not naval ships, not warships, not transports for troops. They will be common ships of Port of Samnium, for fishing or coastal hauling."

"Hold!" said Alan.

The men looked to one another.

"I command these men, not you!" he said.

"Then do so," I said. "You are too young to command. You are not yet ready to command."

"Draw your weapon!" cried Alan.

"When I wish," I said.

"Where is Ruffio?" asked Aetius. We saw no sign of him on the beach.

"He has gone," said Thurnock.

"He has withdrawn into the tunnel," I said.

"I see no tunnel," said Alan.

"He will have looked about, he will have scanned the beach, he will have seen us," said Seremides.

"Get to the beach!" I ordered Alan's ten men.

As Alan did not restrain them, they hurried to the beach.

I regretted usurping the command of the young swordsman, which usurpation he could view as only another humiliation, but he seemed so consumed with his hatred and suspicion of me that he was blinded to the tactical situation confronting us. Better his humiliation than his dying beside us, from inaction. I had wanted fifty men from Marlenus; I had received only ten, and a commander not yet seasoned to command. I was grateful that his men, presumably uncertain of his leadership, had seen the necessity of taking action. "Command voice" is often obeyed, even when the value of doing so is unclear. I supposed it was another instance of the readiness of men to respond to either leadership, or its semblance. Had he been more experienced or even had his men been more familiar with him, I doubted that my arrogation of authority would have been practical. It also helped, I was sure, that I was clearly the leader of our little expedition to the beach and thus, in a sense, stood higher in a presumed chain of command.

Chagrined, Alan descended the beach to join his men by the shore.

"Follow me," I cried, and sped toward the point where we had first noticed Ruffio. Then I stopped, distraught, suddenly.

"Too late!" cried Thurnock, as a broad blockage of thin sand seemed suddenly to rise in the air, and then fall back, sliding, down a roof of wood. Almost at the same time fifteen or twenty men of Decius Albus, in a broad front, rushed up from beneath the ground and fanned out on the beach, forming a line behind which others could safely emerge. The tunnel may well have been long and narrow from the House of the Sea Hith to the beach, but, at the beach end, it had been widened so that several men, massed together, could leave it simultaneously.

The opportunity to close the tunnel and seal off the escape of Decius Albus was gone. At this point there were two obvious possibilities, first, for I and my fellows, well outnumbered, to abandon the beach and withdraw to the cover of Marlenus's main force by the House of the Sea Hith, or, second, to join the young Taurentian and his men at the shore before they were overwhelmed, slaughtered as they were driven back into the water.

"Those who will," I cried, "to the shore!"

Even Seremides, assisted by Xenon, hobbled to the water's edge.

"What are you doing here?" cried Alan.

"Postponing my escape," I said.

"Ela," said Thurnock. "We underestimated the forces of Decius Albus. There must be more than fifty men on the beach."

"Closer to a hundred," said Clitus, gloomily.

I thought then that the original camp must have held more than the surmised two hundred or so we had anticipated. Again I gave Decius Albus credit for generalship. The housing of troops can be a tactic. One can put fewer in a tent, or even have empty tents, and it may be supposed you have many men, given the large number of tents. What Decius Albus, had done, apparently, was to put more men in a tent than would be expected.

"The ships, behind us," said Thurnock, "move closer."

"Soon," said Clitus, "it will be feasible to wade to them."

"Worse," said Thurnock, "in each of those ships I see some men, four or five, in the livery of Decius Albus, doubtless put there to guide the ships in and manage the crews."

"Decius Albus leaves little to chance," I said.

"We will be attacked from front and rear," said Seremides.

"I hear battle horns," said Aetius.

"Marlenus marches," said Alan. "He comes to our relief."

"He will be too late," said Aetius.

We had seventeen men at the shore, myself, Thurnock and Clitus, Aetius, Seremides and Xenon, Alan, of the House of Hesius, and his ten men.

I surveyed the beach. The men of Decius Albus formed four extended ranks of something like twenty or twenty-five men each.

"The House of the Sea Hith has been abandoned," said Thurnock.

"Marlenus has no assurance of that," I said. "He will leave at least a token force to keep it under surveillance."

"He will still far outnumber the men of Decius Albus," said Aetius.

"That means nothing if he cannot close with them," I said.

Once again we heard battle horns.

"Decius Albus will evacuate every man he can," said Clitus. "He wants every man he can keep."

"We can be easily outflanked," said Alan, the young Taurentian. "If the enemy chooses to do so," I said. "He would prefer to ignore us and be on his way."

"Then," said Alan, "you risked little by coming to our aid."

"If you wish to prevent the escape of Decius Albus," I said, "I have risked a great deal."

"The Kur!" said Thurnock, pointing. Behind the four lines of the men of Decius Albus, we saw Lucilius, with a great shield he carried easily and a large double-bladed ax.

"See, behind him," said Seremides, "Decius Albus!"

"And at his side," said Aetius, "is Ruffio."

They did not speak it, but a bit back, in the custody of two men-at-arms, bundled in the Robes of Concealment, but without facial veiling, was a woman.

It was Talena.

I gathered she had not been permitted veiling since her abrupt face-stripping on the parapet of the House of the Sea Hith yesterday afternoon. She would feel the shame of that keenly. If she should come into my keeping, I would similarly, of course, deny her, a slave, facial veiling. One does not veil animals. And I would, too, consider the more general question, independently, of permitting her clothing, except, of course, a comfortable, close-fitting, locked, metal collar. I conjectured that Decius Albus had kept her face-stripped, in case he needed a human shield, one which few human males would be likely to fire on. Comely slaves are seldom put to that employment. Even free women, so used, despite their modesty, are likely to tear off their own facial veiling, to dissuade wary marksmen from risking the loss of, let us say, potential, desirable, marketable collar meat.

"Keep between Decius Albus and the ships," I said.

"Keep between Decius Albus and the ships!" said the young Taurentian, to his men.

"Good command," I said. "You learn quickly."

"Wait!" he snarled. "We may survive this."

"I intend to," I said.

"I, too," he said, his voice hoarse with menace.

I did not think it would do, to confide to the young Taurentian that I had little interest in Decius Albus. I did expect that he and Talena would continue to be in proximity to one another, particularly as he would want her for presentation, as his prisoner, to Lurius of Jad. But, if they should be separated, I would pursue not Decius Albus but, surprisingly perhaps, a mere slave, one, however, in which I had some interest.

"Thurnock, Xenon," I said. "Watch the ships. They may have bowmen aboard, or try to approach us from the rear."

By now, several men of Marlenus, in lines, had rounded the nearest of the two aligned walls and, weapons and shields held over their head, were wading, as we had, through the chest-high waters toward our beach.

There was a cry, close at hand, and one of Alan's men spun about and dropped to one knee in the water, an arrow embedded in his shoulder. Another arrow sped past us and sank deeply into the sand.

"I see one," said Thurnock, and loosed an arrow.

"I, too," said Xenon, and there was the sudden, heavy vibration of the fired crossbow.

I suspected that there were now two on the ships who would release no further arrows.

"Some wade toward us," said Aetius.

"Decius Albus moves," I said. "Quick. To the left, the left. Keep between him and the water!"

We moved swiftly to the left.

"He will mass his men shortly," said Alan, "and sweep us into the sea."

"His men are mercenaries," I said, "variously hired. They may kill for their pay, but they do not wish to die for their pay. Marlenus is near."

"Some, even now," said Seremides, "are wading out to the ships."

"The men of Decius Albus will not permit them to board," I said.

Thurnock loosed another arrow. "One will not prevent them," he said.

We were now squarely before Decius Albus, he some forty yards higher on the beach. With him were Lucilius, Ruffio, and the two fellows who had Talena by the arms.

I looked back, to the right. The men of Marlenus were now emerging from the water, a large figure in their fore.

Decius Albus, facing us, sword in hand, cast a wild glance to his left, noting the troops of Marlenus. Clearly his time was limited. Then he pointed to us, screaming. "They are few," he cried. "You are many! Ten lines! Locked shields! Prepare to rush forward! Kill them all! Be, my brave fellows, the very avalanche of the Voltai! Force them into the sea! Redden Thassa! Turn the sea scarlet! Wipe them out!"

"Wedge," I cried.

I tore away the buckler and spear of the nearest of the young Taurentian's ten men, ordered him back, and then ordered two of the ten to take their position behind me, and then ordered four more to stand behind them. We braced our spears.

"Charge!" cried Decius Albus.

There was a clatter of metal, the clashing of shields and bucklers. The impact was fierce. It was hard to hold the point, hardest, too, for the two men behind me. But the charge of the men of Decius Albus was divided, some men plunging into the water, to the side, unopposed, and others, exposed and vulnerable, found antagonists at their side, not before them. Bodies were kicked aside, floating in the water. Some of the men of Decius Albus continued on, making for the ships. Some turned about, to attack us from behind, waist deep in the water, but an arrow from Thurnock and a quarrel from Xenon left two lost in the water, and four others turned about, to flee toward the ships.

"Back!" called Decius Albus. "Form again. Charge!"

"Cup!" I called. This tactic has several names in Gorean infantry tactics. I have heard it referred to as the Bowl, the Goblet, the Crater, the Vessel, the Vase, and such. It is the tactic of the "Yielding Center." It was originally used to sacrifice one's weaker troops to provide one's superior troops with an advantage. One puts one's weakest troops in the center of the line, and, as they are beaten back by the enemy, one's stronger troops, on the edges, outflank and decimate an essentially surrounded enemy. In this instance, our center, drawing back, defending itself, would appear to be on the verge of defeat, at which point the enemy, ideally, would find foes on three sides.

It worked well.

Then we heard battle horns, now close. I looked about, and saw, before the advancing soldiers, leading them, helmed, with shield and spear, the mighty figure of Marlenus of Ar.

There had originally been five ships waiting offshore to evacuate the men of Decius Albus, but there were now only two. Three apparently, presumably given the disturbances and fighting ashore, had thought the better of the business. They had taken fee to load and transport troops, not to lose their ships and risk their lives. The men of Decius Albus who had been aboard those ships, had apparently been killed, had been thrown overboard, or had decided, all in all, to accompany the recalcitrant crews to relative safety. Mercenaries, as is well known, are paid to fight, not to die.

One of the men of Decius Albus advanced on Seremides, who was seemingly unsteady and tottering. I supposed that the man of Decius Albus sensed an easy kill. He was mistaken. Seremides blinded him with a handful of sand, and then, as the man struggled to clear his vision, dispatched him with an almost casual cut to the back of the neck.

Several of the men of Decius Albus appeared to have lost their taste for battle, comprehensibly enough, given the proximity of Marlenus and his men of Ar. Some were trying to wade, or swim, out to the two ships remaining near the shore. Others were fleeing down the beach, to our left.

Decius Albus, with Lucilius, Ruffio, Talena, in the keeping of her guards, and some twenty men, were moving away, to our left.

"Hurry," I said to those with me, standing amongst bodies on the sand. "We must prevent Decius Albus from escaping."

I and the others, Alan at my side, sped down the shore. Already two of the men of Decius Albus had swum to the nearest ship and clambered aboard. Four others were wading to the ship, now in water to their waist. It neared the shore a little, oars moving softly, water falling from the blades, and swung about, the double rudders now parallel to the beach. "Hurry!" I said. "Hurry!"

"No need," said Thurnock and loosed an arrow. One of the fellows wading to the ship disappeared under the water and then the body surfaced, rolling about, the arrow with its soaked fletching upright like a marker in his chest.

Xenon, with his set quarrel, gestured to the other three men in the water that they should return to the shore.

They did so, and thus lived.

Decius Albus, standing on the beach, looked angrily at us, and then at the two ships. Had his look been an ax, both ships would have been demolished before our eyes. The nearest now swung about and, oars gently dipping and drawing, drew further offshore, beyond convenient arrow range. The other had maintained its position, a little further out, with little change all morning and early afternoon.

A few Ehn later, we had made our way to the other side of Decius Albus and his men, and he, and his party, including Talena, and her guards, were situated between my group and Alan and his men, and the advancing Marlenus and his men.

"You did well," I told Alan.

"We have an appointment," he said.

"If you wish," I said.

"Note," said Thurnock, "only one amongst our foes seems little discomfited."

"What has a guard beast to fear?" asked Alan.

"It is an unusual guard beast who carries a shield and ax," I said.

"Doubtless they can be trained," said Alan.

"Undoubtedly," I said.

"Such a beast is too ignorant to be afraid," said Alan.

"Or," I said, "it sees no reason to be afraid."

"I do not understand," said Alan, angrily.

"Decius Albus has lost," said Thurnock, grimly, facing me. "His end is nigh. Soon Marlenus will see to his reckoning with the treasonous trade advisor, and you, should you wish, will have a lovely but worthless, wretched slave in your arms."

"Let her serve our victory feast, collared and naked," said Aetius.

"Such a thing helps a new slave to understand her collar," said Seremides.

"Should we now dispute, coward, cheat, and fool?" asked Alan of me.

"By the affection I bear you and our memories of the Skerry of Lars," said Seremides to the young Taurentian, "do not be rash. You do not know what you are doing. You do not know he whom you would challenge."

"I fear no man who pretends to abandon his sword and then seizes it up again when an opponent's back is turned," said Alan.

"It is seldom wise, young Taurentian," I said, "to draw your blade against an unknown foe."

"Proclaim yourself tarsk and urt, and beg your life," said Alan, "and I may choose to spare you."

"I beg you," said Seremides to the young Taurentian, "do not press him. Resolution might seize him. It would be a fearsome thing to see. It would be a Warrior's resolution, nothing reckless or primitive, but an unswerving resolution, cold, calculating, swift, merciless and terrible, like a mathematics of blood. I know you both. Friends are precious and rare. I do not wish to lose one, let alone two. Reconcile."

"Never," said Alan.

At that point, there was a cry of fear and awe both from the men of Marlenus and those of Decius Albus.

Soldiers of each were looking up, frightened, and pointing.

For a moment the bright rays of Tor-tu-Gor flashed on that large, silver, winged frame, and then it dove toward the beach, screeching, huge metal talons widened and extended. It seized a soldier in the retinue of Marlenus, as a living tarn might have seized a tabuk, and ascended to the zenith, and then it released the man and he fell, arms flailing and screaming, hundreds of feet down to the beach. "It is coming again!" screamed a bodyguard of Marlenus, and again the machine was amongst the guard and it seized another fellow, but this time it ascended little more than a hundred feet. The talons, like mighty pincers, closed on the man and blood fell like rain to the beach, and then the two parts of a divided body.

"It seeks Marlenus!" I said. Then I called out, over the heads of the men of Decius Albus. "Discard the helm of command! Put aside your shield with the Ubar's insignia." But Marlenus, if he heard me, amidst the shouting and confusion, neglected to do so. "Hide amongst your fellows," I cried. "Beware, Ubar! Beware!"

A cheer arose from the men with Decius Albus, who had now grasped that they were not in danger, but that the fearsome thing ruling the beach and sky was intent on dealing out its destruction and terror amongst their foes from Ar.

I looked to the men of Decius Albus. They were clustered together, about Decius Albus. Ruffio was beside him, and nearby were Talena and her two guards. But Lucilius was not to be seen. His shield and ax had been discarded.

I realized then that the appearance of the mechanical tarn had either been planned, or anticipated.

Lucilius, unburdened by arms, was doubtless on his way to some rendezvous.

The machine now soared over the sand like a winged scythe and seized another man, gained some altitude, tore him apart with its talons, and scattered the parts below. In its next dive it seized an armsman with its beak, shook him savagely in its ascent, as a jard might a tiny urt, loosed the sundered parts, spattering blood about, and then dived again, seeking another victim. Spears struck the metal body, sometimes with a flash of sparks. Arrows snapped against the metal. Quarrels caromed away. Many men of Ar now began to scatter. Marlenus was much alone. The blade of his great spear had been struck away; his shield was spattered with blood, fallen from the sky. Near him, in the sand, was a severed arm and a head. Then there was a ragged cheer from some of his soldiers scattered about, no longer in formation, still on the beach, for the five tarns which had been a component of his force were now visible, come from between the walls, darting toward the beach, armed tarnsmen astride. But how could a flesh and blood tarn compete with, or rationally fight, an unfeeling, impervious, winged metal monster? Certainly I, Tarl Cabot, once of another world, Earth, did not share the relief and cheer of the men of Marlenus. I recalled, rather, a war from my former world, one in which I, as a child, had not participated. I recalled stories of valorous, saber-wielding cavalry men attacking tanks. How brief, futile, and noble were the efforts of those heroic anachronisms, charging out of a past into a future with no place for them.

The metal tarn turned about, hovering, facing the oncoming tarns. It aligned itself five times, moving about, like a rifle. And five times a stream of fire burned though the scalding air. Three times one could even feel the heat on the beach. Four tarns and riders, incinerated, tumbled, smoking and aflame, from the sky. The fifth tarn, its rider limp, black with burned flesh, awkwardly, a wing seared, disappeared back, away, between the two walls from which, a bit ago, it had risen.

Marlenus, mighty, belligerent, defiant, stood alone on the beach, watching the metal tarn which was now turning back toward him.

Why, I wondered, in its brief career of carnage, had the metal tarn not employed its fiercest and deadliest of weapons, the stream of fire, against the troops on the beach?

I suddenly realized, shuddering, with a plummeting wrenching of fear, what must be the answer.

And I, so egregious a fool, had urged Marlenus to discard his helm of command, and the shield which bore the Ubar's insignia!

That might have been his end.

Agamemnon did not wish to risk killing Marlenus. Decius Albus had failed him. Decius Albus had lost. He had been repudiated by Ar. If Agamemnon were to have at his disposal the resources and prestige of the greatest and most populous city in Gor's northern hemisphere, how better to achieve that end but by means of its accepted, familiar Ubar?

Marlenus, sword drawn, looked up at the machine hovering above him. Then the metal tarn's talons reached down, closed about him, firmly, and the tarn rose, almost vertically, into the air, and took flight, leaving behind him the beach, the wondering, and the fallen.

I turned toward the double wall.

I would attempt to follow the flight of the metal tarn.

CHAPTER EIGHTY-FIVE

I ran down the beach, through confused soldiery, toward the double wall. I plunged into the water and swam to the half-emptied docks of Port of Samnium, emerged from the water, and climbed the corridor to the portion of the interior wall opposite the House of the Sea Hith. It was to that point that the tarn, as I had expected, had returned. Its left foot had been roped to a heavy block of stone, and a net had been cast over its wings. It was shuddering as though cold. I could smell burned feathers. Its rider, who had apparently lost consciousness, perhaps as a result of the pain of burned flesh or shock, had been removed from the saddle and safety strap, and was being tended by two members of the green caste, doubtless summoned from Samnium. A hundred men or so, soldiers of Ar, were still monitoring the House of the Sea Hith, which, unbeknownst to them, was presumably abandoned by now.

"How goes battle?" inquired an officer.

"You will receive a full report shortly," I assured him.

"What happened?" asked one of the physicians. "Men speak of terrible things in the sky."

"They speak truthfully," I said.

I then pulled the net away from the shaken, trembling tarn.

"What are you doing?" cried a tarnkeeper.

"Freeing the wings of a tarn for flight," I said.

"Do not," he said. "The bird is crazed."

Tarns are commonly secured either by containment in a cot or by a chained ankle. The net was presumably to keep the tarn still, to prevent it from injuring itself or whatever might be in the vicinity.

"Beware," cried a second tarnkeeper. "It is a tarn! It does not know you. Keep from it! You could lose an arm! Your life! Do not approach it!"

I could not dispute his warning.

Tarns are large and dangerous. They can be aggressive and impatient. They are high-strung. They are easily disturbed. They tend to be skittish of strangers. He who displeases a tarn can be subject to a fierce rebuke, administered with a slashing beak and grasping talons. Too, they can sense fear, and this, unfortunately, perhaps suggesting prey, can precipitate an attack.

Few who aspire to the leather of a tarnsman ascend to the saddle.
I rolled the net and cast it up, over the saddle apron.

"Stop!" said the first tarnkeeper.

I slashed the rope apart which bound the beast's ankle.

"What occurs here?" demanded an officer, hurrying to the wall.

"I commandeer this mount," I said.

"On what authorization?" he demanded.

"Forgive me," I said.

"For what?" he asked.

"For this," I said, striking him from my path.

I climbed to the saddle.

"There will be an inquiry," said the first tarnkeeper, looking up.
"Who are you?"

"One who is unknown to you," I said.

I buckled the safety strap.

"Who shall we say did this?" asked the second tarnkeeper.

"One who is a tarnsman," I said, and drew on the one-strap.

The mighty wings opened, and spread, and then, as the bird
threw back its head and screamed, the wings snapped, scattering
dust, staggering the tarnkeepers who, half-blinded, stumbled backwards, and then the wings smote the air again, and again, and the
bird ascended, and I could see the double wall, the corridor, Samnium, and the woods beyond Samnium.

To be one with the bird, to share its power, its swiftness, its freedom, its flight, is a wondrous, precious thing.

It is to know the joy, the rapture, of the clouds and skies. It is to
be a tarnsman.

I was gentle with the bird.

It had earlier had an extreme, terrifying experience to which it
might easily have succumbed. Its flight was awkward; it was troubled,
if not erratic. It favored its left wing, compensating with adjustments.
Yet I sensed it no long trembled; it was reassured; it had returned to its
element. It was well that it had returned to the air, I thought, before
some dark trepidation could sink into the depths of its brain and make
it fear to enter upon its country, the sky where it had encountered sudden, unexpected, incomprehensible, hissing fire.

As Lucilius had deserted the beach upon the appearance of the silver tarn, I was confident that he was on his way to some predetermined
rendezvous point, one prepared in advance should the situation in the
field merit such a junction. As Lucilius was afoot, I was sure that the
rendezvous point would be quite close. If that was the case, the flight
of the silver tarn would be relatively short. I would have much preferred to follow Lucilius rather than the metal tarn, but I had no hope
of being able to track him once he was beyond Samnium.

I took the tarn no more than a short time, no more than few Ihn, over the woods beyond the outskirts of Samnium. Then in my mind, I outlined a large grid over the forest, one of some five square pasangs, and began to guide the tarn over the horizontal lines of this grid, rather as Gorean is commonly written, left to right, and then back, right to left, and so on. If I failed to detect the metal tarn and its rendezvous point, perhaps having overlooked it, I could then make a new, perhaps more careful search, back and forth, tracing the vertical lines of this imaginary grid. If this failed, I could dismount and try to do something similar, though more tortuously, afoot. All this, of course, was predicated on the hypothesis of a rendezvous, and a close one. If Agamemnon was bound, say, back to the Beast Caves near Ar, or some other distant point, all was, for the time at least, lost. I was confident of my hypothesis, however, for I was sure that Agamemnon would need the aid of a confederate in dealing with Marlenus, presumably Lucilius.

As I flew my pattern, I sometimes found it difficult to keep my mind on the woods. What puzzled me was that Agamemnon, perhaps in desperation, had dared to utilize a body so conspicuous and so obviously incompatible with the technology laws of the Priest-Kings. Did he not know the danger of such a venture? Men had been subjected to the dreaded flame death for so little as an attempt to design an experimental musket. It is one thing to utilize a body resembling an aquatic tharlarion, usually submerged, as was done, I was told, near Port Kar, and quite another to produce one capable of flight, powered by some unusual and sophisticated propulsion system, which he had dared to demonstrate in various venues, from the stadium of Blades in Ar to the beaches near Port of Samnium.

I was deep in my pattern and had begun to be torn with doubt, when the tarn, unexpectedly, began to fight the straps, and fight its way back toward Samnium. "Steady, steady!" I said, soothingly. Clearly the bird was disturbed, and on the verge of being uncontrollable. I loosened my sword in the scabbard, fearing it might turn on me. The flight became abrupt and jagged, almost as if it were the victim of some eccentric compass whose needle would seize on one or another direction, as if hoping it might find that which it sought. I was flung against the safety strap a thousand ways. One might have thought it a captured wild tarn harnessed for the first time in a training cot in Thentis. It dove down amidst trees, tearing its way amongst branches. I lowered my body, fearing to be torn from the saddle. Then, rather than kill the tarn or be swept from its back, I drew on the four-strap and brought the mount down amidst the trees. "What is wrong?" I asked it, as if it might reply, expressing my own dismay and confusion. I released the safety strap and slid from the saddle. My sword was ready. But it did not attack me. It was not angry. It was not enraged. I was now in no danger. It was trembling. I recalled the first moments when I had recently seen it, near the House of the Sea Hith. What, I wondered, could produce so violent an agitation in the bird? Normally, when a tarn is disturbed, it is vocal, so to speak. It hisses, it screams, it screeches. At such a time it is well to vacate its vicinity. How much warning does one need? But this tarn, though clearly in distress, was silent. "When," I asked myself, "is an animal most likely to be silent?" The answer was clear and the hair on the back of my neck and on my forearms rose. It is silent because it does not wish to be heard, as the prowling sleen, or it is silent because it fears to be heard, as the frightened, stalked tabuk or wild verr. I tied the guide straps of the bird's harnessing to a nearby sapling. I knew then I was in the vicinity of Agamemnon, that ambitious, mighty, savage brain ensconced in another sophisticated, powerful, electronic body.

At that moment, senses keenly heightened, I heard, behind me, and to the side, a tiny movement of brush. My sword was in my hand. I had not needed it to defend myself from the tarn. I crouched down. Something large and Kurlike, almost as if on all fours, widened nostrils flared, was within yards of me. An ax was strapped to its back. It was not Lucilius then. It did not notice me, which I found unusual for such a beast. It clearly had something different on its mind. It, like a sleen, oblivious of its surroundings, its attention narrowly focused, was intent on a scent, perhaps one thin and fading.

"Grendel," I whispered.

Instantly, like a sudden electric shock, the demeanor of the large, shambling figure in the brush was transformed. It rose to a crouching position, its eyes blazed, the claws of its forepaws emerged, and its large, pointed ears lifted and oriented their haired hollows toward me.

Then the claws retracted.

"Tarl," it said.

I knew it would take a moment or so for my hearing to adjust to the version of Gorean phonemes which emanated from that large form, and they were closer to Gorean than those commonly heard from Kurii trying to form such sounds. Usually, a translation device is used by Kurii who would converse with humans or humans who would wish to converse with Kurii. Similarly a translation device is commonly used between humans and Priest-Kings or between Kurii and Priest-Kings. The latter devices are far more sophisticated than the former devices because Priest-Kings commonly communicate with one another by a syllabary of some four hundred odor signals.

"Did you see the metal tarn over the beaches of Port of Samnium?" I asked.

"Of course," he said. "It carried a human in its talons."

"Marlenus," I said.

"I feared it might be you," he said.

"Lucilius left the beach," I said. "I think he intends to rendezvous with Agamemnon."

"Undoubtedly," said Grendel. "I know the place. It is well sheltered, well camouflaged. I picked up his trail days ago, and am following it now, again."

"The trail then is not fresh?" I said.

"Not this trail," said Grendel. "But I assume, by now, he is again on his way to the lair of the metal beast."

"We are deeply into the woods," I said. "He has not yet had time to reach this point."

"The rendezvous point is well chosen," said Grendel. "It is obscure, and far from the road. It is not easily accessible from Samnium. It is unlikely to be discovered by the stray traveler or a local woodsman."

"Lord Agamemnon will be waiting for him," I said.

"Certainly," said Grendel. "But how is it that you are so close to the rendezvous point? Little time has elapsed since the business at the beaches. It is well concealed from the air. How did you find it?"

"I did not find it," I said. "I have not found it. I do not know where it is. The tarn, who earlier this afternoon survived a blast of fire, must have somehow seen or sensed the device. It became excited and hard to control. I brought it down. Then we encountered you."

"The bird seems calm enough now," he said.

"Were it released," I said, "I am sure it would lose little time in returning to Samnium."

"Why is there a folded net on the saddle apron?" he asked.

"I removed it from the tarn," I said. "I thought it might prove useful."

"As well oppose a charging larl with a wisp of straw," said Grendel. "You might tangle the wings of the metal tarn but the wings are part of the hoax. They have nothing to do with the movements of the device."

"Might not Lucilius be along presently?" I asked, uneasily.

"I think so," said Grendel. "I will show you the rendezvous point."

"Let me take the tarn a bit away from the trail," I said.

"Do not do so," he said.

"It might be detected," I said.

"Let us hope so," said Grendel. "Let Lucilius be alarmed that the rendezvous point may have been discovered, or might shortly be discovered, and that Lord Agamemnon may be in danger. If that does not disrupt their plans, it should hurry them, and hurried plans are imperiled plans. He who moves too quickly in kaissa is in danger of losing his Home Stone."

"The rendezvous point is close?" I asked.

"Very close," said Grendel.

CHAPTER EIGHTY-SIX

In the forest glade, under a framework of branches, ropes, and shreds of irregularly placed green cloth, half withdrawn into the side of a small hill, was the metal tarn, its grasping, pincerlike talons still closed about the figure of Marlenus. In a hundred places the talons had been marred or scratched by the futile blows of the sword of Marlenus, most such blows presumably having been struck shortly after he had been seized by the talons, before it had become clear to him that they would have little or no effect on the heavy curvatures within he was imprisoned. Marlenus, a native Gorean, unlike men of Earth, Kurii of the Steel Worlds, or the Priest-Kings of the Sardar, knew little or nothing of machines which might race along roads or speed amongst clouds. So, too, might a Hannibal or Caesar wonder at a tank or airplane. Many Goreans, particularly those of the lower castes, who have not ascended to the Second Knowledge, believe that nature is alive and filled with living things. A woodsman often requests the pardon of the tree he will fell. A traveler may pay his respects to the stream for allowing him to safely wade its waters. The average Gorean does not see himself as some sort of exile or stranger inhabiting an incomprehensibly vast, inert, indifferent, lifeless, alien environment. He sees himself as a living thing in a living world. Most Goreans would then, at least initially, and surely at a distance, take the metal tarn to be alive. It is not a wagon or cart, to be pushed or hauled about. It moves itself, and what moves itself must be alive, in some way, somehow. Consider the ponderous tharlarion, the majestic tarn, the regal larl, ten hands at the shoulder. Each moves; each lives.

Grendel motioned me to be silent.

He had placed us downwind of the small enclave in the woods.

I regarded the patchwork of branches, rope, and irregular scraps of green cloth stretched over the rendezvous point. From below, on the ground, one could easily look up through that porous canopy and see the sky. On the other hand, from above, from the likely height of a soaring tarn, those scraps of green cloth would appear to be a solid roof of foliage.

From our cover we could see the held, distraught, angry Ubar.

"Release me, hideous beast, contrived, winged artifice, strange wagon that forsakes the ground, that rolls without wheels amongst clouds, product of sorcery, mystery of Priest-Kings, defier of Priest-Kings, or whatever you might be," demanded Marlenus.

No sound came from the machine.

The pincers moved slightly, pressing a tiny bit more closely about the Ubar's body. He then, grimacing, held his tongue.

For the better part of an Ahn, Grendel and I crouched to the side. Grendel touched my arm.

A moment later, Lucilius, wary, looking about, nostrils flared, emerged from the trees. Then, in Kur, he addressed the machine. In response, sound emerged from the machine, mechanically reproduced, but in recognizable Kur. I could make nothing of this, but, happily, it would be intelligible to Grendel.

Lucilius now fixed his eyes on the helpless, prostrate Ubar. He spoke to him, swiftly and harshly, in what, after a moment, I recognized as an approximation to Gorean. Clearly, Marlenus made little or nothing of this, either because it was so strange to him, or he did not even comprehend that it was intended to be Gorean. Few Kurii can speak Gorean, and, as far as I know, no human can communicate in Kur, unless it be with a syllable or two. I had never seen a translation device present when Lucilius and Decius Albus were together, so I reasoned that the Gorean of Lucilius must have been comprehensible to Decius Albus, or, at least, sufficiently so. On the other hand, as so few Kurii can even begin to approximate Gorean, I expected that Lucilius, given the ambition and vanity common to his kind, would be quite proud of his Gorean, and would not be pleased, at all, if Marlenus would find it, from his point of view, nonexistent. "Go grunt, snarl and hiss elsewhere," said Marlenus, angrily. Lucilius roared with anger and the claws on his forepaws, long, curved, and white, sprang into view. I conjecture that Lucilius thought that Marlenus was lying, that he was merely feigning an inability to understand a Gorean which, from the point of view of Lucilius, was doubtless fluent and superb. I do not know what might have transpired a moment later, had not Agamemnon saw fit to intervene, in Gorean. "Do not kill him, yet," came from the metal tarn. Lucilius responded in Kur, and, happily, almost simultaneously, we heard, "Very well. I refrain, Eleventh Face of the Nameless One." Clearly, fortunately, there was a means of translation embedded in the body of the metal tarn which had at least a modest range and had now been activated. Lucilius retracted his claws. I wondered if Marlenus knew how close he might have just come to having his throat torn open. In the heart of the Kur, as in the heart of some human beings, ignitable violence lurks. There is a flash point which, when touched, may precipitate a mindless, uncontrollable, unwelcome explosion. This is possibly a response which was selected for in the course of evolution, statistically facilitating survival in certain situations in remote epochs, but which, today, would seem to be an unfortunate anachronism. But it is hard to tell about such things. We may not be as far from the flint knife and the stone ax as we suppose. In any event, it is dangerous to anger a Kur, even unintentionally, even inadvertently. An attentive, placid, civilized animal may, in a moment, seemingly inexplicably, be transformed into a ferocious beast.

In what follows I shall omit references to Kur, and submit for your attention, some of the ensuing exchanges as though they were directly uttered and responded to in English.

"Disarm the prisoner," said Agamemnon.

"Surrender your sword," said Lucilius to Marlenus.

"Come and take it," he invited the Kur.

"Noble lord," said Lucilius to Agamemnon, "his blade is sharp, his arm strong, his hand quick. May I get a branch or stone, and break his head or body, or arm."

"That would be inhospitable to our guest, the noble Ubar of Ar," came from the fuselage of the tarn, in evenly spaced, mechanical noises. "I shall attend to the matter."

At that point the talons of the tarn began to close and Marlenus, with a cry of rage and pain, cast down the sword.

"Thank you," said Agamemnon, through the embedded translator.

"What of the tarn and the prowling foe, or foes?" asked Lucilius.

From this I gathered that Lucilius, in his approach to the rendezvous point, had discovered the tarn. Presumably this had been communicated to Agamemnon, instantly, upon his arrival at the rendezvous point, in the exchange which I could not understand, but which Grendel, doubtless, heard and understood.

"Shall I kill the tarn?" asked Lucilius.

"No," said Agamemnon. "Do not kill it, that will alert the enemy that we know of his presence."

"I sense nothing," said Lucilius, lifting his head and turning about, scanning with distended nostrils.

"They have no sleen," said Agamemnon. "They are doubtless stumbling about somewhere in the woods."

"It may be a tarn thief," said Lucilius, "and have nothing to do with us."

"Quite possibly," said Agamemnon, "but we must be vigilant. In sensitive matters, risk is intolerable. If possible, it must be removed altogether. Let us transact our business with dispatch."

"Torture takes time," said Lucilius.

"We shall therefore replace torture with prompt negotiation," said Agamemnon. The large metal head with crest and beak inclined downward, toward Marlenus. I noticed, within the half-opened beak a blackened nozzle, that through which, doubtless the stream of fire had issued.

"My dear Ubar," came from the device, "I, the Eleventh Face of the Nameless One, greet you as one potentate to another. Your domain is distant, mine is more distant, and, regrettably, under the current usurpation of a fraudulent adventurer who dares proclaim himself a Face of the Nameless One. I desire to reclaim my world or have another in lieu of it. To support this project, I require land, wealth, and power. With such means I can recruit adherents, undermine governments, and suborn foes. I have access to knowledge which can form engines of war and span the dimensions of space. I can make you the mightiest of humans on this world, second only to myself, and my seed brothers. Swear to me by the Home Stone of Ar that you will be my human, obeying me in all things, and your ascendency and fortune begins this afternoon."

"I swear it not," said Marlenus. "Go, roll in a nest of osts."

"Perhaps I have not made myself clear," said Agamemnon. "Would you prefer to be torn to pieces, eaten alive, or dropped from a great height to the beach at Port of Samnium, a warning to any who might dare to displease me?"

"Swim with carnivorous eels," said Marlenus. "Take fresh meat from a starving sleen. Steal the first cub of the she-larl."

"You dissent?" asked Agamemnon.

"He dissents, exalted one," said Lucilius.

"Very well," said Agamemnon. "Time is short. We do not know who roams the woods. Enemies may be near. Bite off his feet, his hands, and then his head."

Lucilius snarled, and then opened his maw, eagerly, lined with glistening fangs.

I attempted to leap up but I was forcibly restrained by Grendel, his left arm about my chest, his right paw capped tightly over my mouth.

"Desist, bind him," said Agamemnon.

I then felt foolish. Perhaps we dealt with beasts but Agamemnon was no common Kur, nor was he in the grasp of some unleashed storming rage. Of course, Marlenus was more valuable alive than dead. Might he not be exchanged for some exorbitant ransom or delivered to his enemy, Lurius of Jad, for a galley, sluggish with gold?

With his paw, with a blow that I feared might break a neck, Lucilius snapped Marlenus's head to the side, and the talons of the metal tarn relinquished their hold.

What then ensued between Agamemnon and Lucilius I more sensed, than understood, for the translation device had apparently been deactivated. The unconscious body of Marlenus was swathed with ropes. The metal tarn made its stalking way to one side, to a hillock, where it could ascend or descend beyond the canopy of the camouflage net. Lucilius broke off a stout branch and then, half crouching, nostrils distended, drawing in air, left the rendezvous point. Shortly after that, with no motion yet of wings, their deception apparently not being deemed necessary at the moment, the body of Agamemnon rose silently, gracefully, into the air, over the trees. I hurried to Marlenus, determined that he was alive, and then cut away his bonds. I did not think he would soon regain consciousness. "Lucilius," said Grendel, "searches for the scent of intruders. He intends to clear the immediate vicinity of the camp. He will soon return to guard Marlenus. Agamemnon is apprehensive. Where there is one tarn, there might be others. There are tarncots in Samnium, as you may know. Should there be tarnsmen aflight, Agamemnon intends to burn them from the sky. He then intends, the skies clear, to make his way back to the Beast Caves outside Ar, with Marlenus as his prisoner."

"Care for Marlenus," I said. "Return him to his men as soon as possible."

"I shall," said Grendel. "I expect a patrol or more will be met on the road to Samnium."

"Beware of Lucilius," I said. "He has a fearsome club."

"I have stood in the rings," said Grendel. "I have an ax."

I began to tear large swatches of cloth from the camouflage net.

"What are you doing?" asked Grendel, lifting the large body of Marlenus lightly in his powerful arms.

"Plotting to restore the confidence and self-esteem of a tarn," I said. "I wish you well."

"I wish you well," said Grendel, and hurried from the rendezvous point.

CHAPTER EIGHTY-SEVEN

I took the tarn higher and higher.

It was important to be above the silver tarn.

I would seek the "tarn's ambush," so to speak, to strike from above, the descent masked by Tor-tu-Gor, Light-Upon-the-Home Stone, the blazing sun at my back.

I assumed that Agamemnon would maintain a low altitude, to facilitate observation and display the mechanical tarn in all its full and terrifying detail.

I had seen no evidence that the silver tarn's firepower emanated otherwise than from its beak. I would therefore attack from the rear or flanks, and, as far as possible, avoid meeting the device head-on. This would be possible, at least initially, given the element of surprise. Too, I suspected that the tarn, the living monster, which can stop, wheel, hover, and change direction almost instantly, would be more maneuverable than a large, bulky, weighty machine. I did suppose, naturally enough, that the silver tarn could fly faster and farther than the living tarn. Thus, it could outdistance the living tarn, turn about, and bring its firepower into play. If this seemed imminent, I would hastily surrender the field, so to speak, before the device could turn about and locate us, taking refuge in the nearby woods.

As I knew little of the silver tarn, I had no clear idea how to attack it, let alone disable it, or take it down. I was confident I could harass it, at least briefly. Perhaps then, somehow, Agamemnon might err in its control, perhaps bringing about the device's damage or destruction. My weaponry was sparse and likely to be ineffective. I had the net which had originally been flung over the tarn to control and calm it in its earlier agitation, but I did not expect it would be of any use at present. A well-thrown net can bring down a living tarn but the wings of the silver tarn, as noted earlier, functioned independently of the silver tarn's propulsion system. They were merely part of the machine's disguise, suggesting that it was an actual tarn. Similarly, I knew of nothing analogous on the machine to rotor blades or propellers which might, in theory, be susceptible to a flung net. The net would be useless. I had not understood that, of course, when I had fastened it across the saddle apron when appropriating the tarn. It had become clear at the rendezvous point when I had been able to see the machine at close range. One might as well try to net a flying tank. I considered casting the net aside. My other weaponry consisted of four heavy stones. When one is within a machine, say, a vehicle, an impact is often alarmingly loud, even though the actual damage to the machine is negligible. I supposed that Agamemnon would have little understanding, at least at first, as to the extent of possible damage. I had, of course, my sword, but I had already seen, in the case of Marlenus, how futile and ineffective would be the application of such a weapon to the steel of Agamemnon's current body.

I suddenly tensed in the saddle. Far beneath me, I saw the silver tarn.

Before ascending, I had wrapped large swathes of the green cloth from Agamemnon's camouflage net about the head and eyes of the tarn. Accordingly, he was, in effect, flying blind, his actions responsive to the six straps that guided his flight. A similar arrangement, though more formal and sophisticated, a hood, is used to train a tarn for flight at night, or, if its vision should be impaired, due, say, to whipped, wind-blown sand or spattered or flowing blood.

I feared that the tarn, if brought wittingly into the vicinity of the silver tarn, might be traumatized and reduced to its former condition of shivering trepidation.

I did not think that Agamemnon would be expecting an attack from above.

I adjusted the bird's flight and drew sharply on the four-strap. We soared downward and I drew on the one-strap, swinging up, and cast the first of the four stones onto the fuselage of the machine. There was a loud noise and a jagged scratch in the body of the device. This noise would be unexpected, startling, alarming, and incredibly loud within the machine, much more so than outside of it. I then wheeled the bird about and struck the machine to starboard, port, and aft. The machine then, erratically, crookedly, began to pitch and turn. Agamemnon, within, would presumably be startled and confused, and would have no immediate sense of what damage, if any, might have been sustained. I then took the tarn higher and again higher. And then, again, the sun, blazing Tor-tu-Gor, was at my back and the silver tarn was far below, hovering, turning.

There seemed nothing more I could do now.

I would give the tarn its chance to deal with its pain and its memories.

I drew my sword and cut away the bandages that covered the eyes of the tarn, and the cloth fluttered away.

The tarn began to circle, and then it must have seen the silver tarn below, as I had anticipated it would. What would be its response?

"Become yourself," I said to it, soothingly. "Become yourself, if you wish. I effect nothing critical, either way." I left the straps loose.

Sometimes, in war, the mount, as well as the rider, is injured. In the code of the tarnsman, it is regarded as dishonorable to strike a tarn. On the other hand, such beasts are sometimes injured unintentionally, and sometimes, regrettably, intentionally.

It is dangerous, of course, to mount a battle-shy tarn. It may turn on its rider, or it may become difficult or impossible to control, thus jeopardizing both itself and its rider. Normally, tarns, like war sleen, both mighty beasts, recover, returning eventually to their nature, habits, and training. Indeed, some become even more belligerent and dangerous, almost as if, somehow, having tasted shame or pusillanimity, perhaps sensing they have disappointed themselves, or their keepers or riders, they are eager to redeem themselves. Others do not recover, and are either killed or trained as draft tarns.

The tarn was high, and behind, the metal tarn, far below.

I had no more stones to hurl at the machine.

Return to Samnium, brave, noble creature, I thought. You have recovered your vision and equanimity. You have looked upon the machine and have not quavered. You have returned to yourself, a stabler, stronger self. Return to Samnium.

Suddenly it began to descend, throwing me back violently against the broad safety strap. I had nothing to do with this as the reins were slack. I had not even called "tabuk," which notifies, and frees, the tarn to feed. The tarn, clearly, was internally motivated. Swifter and swifter it descended. Wind tore at my tunic. The strike of a tarn can break the back of a tabuk or kaiila, which can then be fed on in the grass or borne away to a nest. I began to regret that I had unbandaged the eyes of the tarn. I had not counted on so violent a response. The tarn's talons were spread. Swifter and swifter it knifed through the air toward, I first assumed, its supposed prey. I should not have unbandaged its eyes. This was madness. But it was not seeking prey I suddenly realized. That strange machine could not be mistaken for a tabuk or kaiila. The tarn was not seeking prey, or feeding; it was maddened; it was seeking to destroy an enemy.

There was a horrendous ring, and impact, as the tarn struck the machine with its plummeting speed, buffeting it yards to the side and down, and then, as the tarn pursued it, and grasped it, there was a hideous scratching and striking as talons and beak raked and struck the fuselage to which it now clung. Added into this tumult the tarn's screams of hate and rage rent the air.

It is one thing to strike a giant, or an overwhelmingly fearsome foe, and make away as quickly, and safely, as possible, and quite another to make yourself evident to such a foe and grapple with it.

I had hoped the tarn might manage to view the silver tarn without paralysis or trauma; I had not expected it to seek revenge.

I tried to regain control of the mount, but failed to do so. Then, abruptly, suddenly, the silver tarn, with a rush of acceleration, sped away, perhaps a pasang, and then, having eluded and outdistanced its troublesome attacker, it slowly swung back, and began to approach. I was unsure of the range of fire which might emerge from the metal nozzle concealed within the metal beak, but, from the displays of its power over the beach at Port of Samnium, I knew it could be effective within at least a hundred yards or so. To my dismay the tarn began to beat its way toward the machine. I had carefully avoided facing the head of the machine. It was there that the flame cannon was mounted. It was from that section of the device that the torrent of fire would storm forth. The tarn, obviously, was giving no thought to the possibility of being incinerated, but that possibility, I assure you, was very much on my mind. I had no wish to perish in a burst of flame and feathers, or, possibly, if struck at point-blank range, to be swept from the saddle in a blazing wind of hot ashes.

The woods were below, thick with trees, broken here and there with a small hillock or a low outcropping of stone.

The silver tarn, doubtless aware of the tarn streaking naively toward it, was now content to hover, and wait for its feast to deliver itself to the waiting furnace.

I seized and shook free the net which had been folded across the saddle apron, that net which I had originally removed from the tarn before flight, the net designed to settle and calm the bird, the net which, I now understood, would be useless against the silver tarn, the net which I had considered jettisoning but moments before.

I hurled it over the sounder of the two wings of the bird, the right wing, that which had not been injured earlier in the afternoon, and it struggled, shrieking in frustration, to dislodge the encumbrance. It also began, handicapped as it was, to descend amongst the trees. As it neared the tree tops, I saw that the silver tarn was now in motion, hastening to approach, doubtless intent on bringing the tarn and its rider into range before they disappeared amongst the trees.

Then I was on the ground and out of the saddle, and was leading the confused, frustrated, flight-impeded tarn amongst the trees.

We are safe! I thought.

But then the silver tarn, hovering, inclined downward, was at the tree tops. I had the odd sense of a sleen scanning for scent. Then a ripping blast of fire tore downward amongst the trees. It was some yards from us. Then, several yards away, on the other side, there was another torrent of fire. This continued, again and again, as Agamemnon, by now perhaps disturbed and irrational, discharged flame into the woods. We could feel the roaring heat; trunks and branches were aflame; leaves burst into fire; sparks showered about us. I drew away the net from the tarn. We would separate. I did not wish to risk both of us being caught in the same blast of fire. Perhaps Agamemnon would follow one of us, that permitting the other to escape. I did not know which of us would be his preferred target, the monstrous tarn, most obvious and forward, or the rider, presumably inciting and guiding its movements.

"Go," I said to the tarn. "Return to Samnium! Seek your keepers! Seek the men of Marlenus! Fly, be off, be away!"

The Gorean, of course, would be unintelligible to the tarn, but I hoped that my tone, mien, my gestures, and such, would make it clear enough that I was urging a parting of company. A tree, flaming, crashed near us, and the tarn beat its way up through fire and smoke and took flight toward Samnium.

I waited in the woods, eyes stinging, half choking.

The silver tarn had apparently followed the escaping tarn.

I was safe.

Then another torrent of fire flashed down through the woods.

Agamemnon had apparently elected to pursue the rider.

His pattern of fire made it clear that he was not sure of my location. On the other hand, it does not make much difference in which room a fugitive might be hiding if the entire house is burned down.

Agamemnon, like the sleen, was tenacious.

He was but feet above the tree tops.

Another torrent of fire ripped downward.

I wondered if I might not be able to turn his zeal into his undoing.

I supposed that Agamemnon, having been aflight, would not know that Marlenus of Ar had been rescued and might, even now, be back amongst his men. Lucilius, of course, would know, having returned to the rendezvous point and having found Marlenus missing. I did not know where Grendel might be. I supposed it was possible that both he and Lucilius had seen the silver tarn in the sky. And both, now, would be much aware of fire in the woods. That would be evident even in Samnium.

Fire was still crackling about me but now better than an Ehn had passed and no more streams of fire had been launched into the woods. I thought it possible that Agamemnon had at last exhausted whatever fluid or substance he might use to produce his linear hurricanes of fire. Might he not be out of ammunition, so to speak? To be sure, it is a common strategy to pretend to be out of ammunition, to lure an indiscreet or careless foe within range.

I no longer saw Agamemnon hovering above the tree tops.

Where was he?

Perhaps he had returned to the rendezvous point to meet with Lucilius, perhaps to utilize a supply depot of sorts. Might not such a body, from time to time, have to replenish its resources? Might not the living brain ensconced in the machine require its own nutriments of some sort? Then I shuddered.

Not fifteen yards away I saw the silver tarn, on the ground, amongst the trees. It moved, silently, stalking a few feet, with a stiff, regal gait. Then it was still again. Its head swiveled about on its shoulders, and it stared at me. I had no doubt that those large, round, glowing eyes were transmitting information to the brain of Agamemnon. The beak opened and I saw the nozzle. The stream of fire is swift, but not like a bullet. I thought I could leap behind the blackened tree trunk beside me, before the stream could reach me. I awaited the torrent of fire, but it did not come. Rather the tarn, wings folded, lurched toward me. The large, hooked, heavy, tarnlike beak opened, and snapped shut. I had no doubt it could, in one motion, sever an arm or cut a head from a body. I was reasonably sure that the silver tarn was still capable of flight, and that its appearance on the ground was merely to facilitate stalking ground prey. I was also sure that it, abetted by its propulsion system, could, given clear ground, be upon me almost instantly. I had no thought that I could outrun it. My only chance, as I saw it, was to make an ally of the woods, and perhaps one of Agamemnon himself.

"Turn on your translator," I invited the silver tarn.

I then hoped he had done so.

"Your body is unsightly and clumsy," I said. "No one would take it for the handsome, majestic tarn. A tabuk would scorn it. A verr would laugh. Perhaps it could frighten a tiny urt, one fearing to be stepped on."

That engine was, however, powerful. It thrust its way between two trees, half uprooting one, and I backed away.

It approached more closely. A thick branch blocked its way. It snapped it in two with one opening and closing of that heavy, hooklike beak.

"I did not know a metal tarn could be such a weakling," I said. "A true tarn would not waste his beak on such a twig. With a robust exhalation, he would just blow it from his path."

The right leg of the silver tarn lifted, and reached out, and its talons extended about, and grasped, a burned tree trunk, and then it slowly, shedding ash and carbon, tore at the tree. The curved furrows in the trunk were clearly some inches deep.

I admitted to myself that I was impressed.

As this brief but remarkable demonstration did not close the gap between myself and the tarn, nor it did it seem to further its likely projects in any significant manner, I suspected that what I had witnessed was mere displacement activity.

It is well known that kings, emperors, warlords, chieftains, and such, seldom respond well to criticism, however worthwhile and benignly intended it might be. Therefore, I speculated that my observations, however far off the mark they might have been, might have succeeded in annoying the Eleventh Face of the Nameless One.

As I moved, it moved, sometimes seemingly eccentrically. After some three or four Ehn, I became aware, not to my reassurance, that I was being denied, bit by bit, access to the more thickly wooded ground about me. I was being cut off from better shelter. Trees were becoming more sparse. I continued to back away from the machine. Behind me, on a relatively flat, stony upgrade, there was a semicircular clearing, a surface of a sort in which trees would find it difficult to take root. In shape it was much like one of the low, round bluffs that occasionally broke up the density of the woods. I was being driven to this clearing. I backed up the slope. The machine emerged from the woods. It was now only a few yards from me.

I picked up a stone, and then another. I cast these at the machine, and they bounded harmlessly away from the fuselage.

They surely did not damage anything, unless it might be Agamemnon's sense of propriety. Such behavior on my part, a mere human, would at least be regarded by the average Kur as an unfortunate and regrettable lapse of respect or courtesy.

The silver tarn was now clearly between me and the woods. Behind me there was a ledge where the upgrade abruptly terminated. I guessed, from the apparent height of my current position, that there would be a drop of some twenty or thirty feet. I could, glancing over my shoulder, see the tops of trees, where the woods had reasserted itself. There was smoke in the air and the smell of smoke and burned wood.

Agamemnon had, with intent, in his effort to kill me, set fire to a thriving, living woods. Far lesser infringements on nature's well-being were regarded by many Goreans as a capital offense, requiring a capital retaliation.

I was sure I could not reach the ledge behind me and fling myself over it, hoping to survive in adjacent branches or clinging shrubbery, before the machine could overtake me.

I picked up another rock.

I hoped this would seem amusing to Agamemnon, reinforcing his presumed sense of superiority to a seemingly foolish, doomed member of an inferior species.

Let your enemy underestimate you. Few things are more to your advantage.

I also hoped that, even in his metal ensconcement, he would be subject to the instinctual withdrawal from strong stimuli likely to be selected for in the course of natural evolution, subject to it if only for a fleeting instant.

The great hooked beak opened and I regarded the concealed nozzle. I tensed. There was a sudden rush of air, jerking my tunic back, and almost causing me to lose my balance, but no flame issued from that hidden barrel.

I clutched the rock.

Then, with a whir of sound, the two large metal wings of the machine carefully, slowly, unfolded and extended themselves, so that they were parallel to the ground. The forward edges were tapered in such a way, I suddenly realized, that they constituted blades. Thus, even if one might elude the grasping of talons and the slashing and tearing of the metal beak, one might, in the machine's charge, be cut apart by the bladelike wings.

I hoped that Agamemnon, before charging, would provide me with an instant in which I might admire the formidableness and beauty of the powerful machine in which he was a temporary component.

I suddenly screamed and pretended to hurl the rock at the machine while at the same time racing toward it.

Since when does the verr charge the sleen? How long has it been since the tiny, graceful tabuk last attacked the larl?

I was at the machine clambering on its extended left wing, pounding on the nearest round, glowing eyelike sensor in the head of the tarn. But, ela, the blows of the stone, hammering on the lens-like protuberance, barely scratched its surface. The apparatus by means of which the active brain of Agamemnon was informed of the world outside the machine was neither fragile nor easily injured. I supposed I should have realized that so sophisticated a device of conquest and war would not be easily subject to attack and damage.

I discarded the rock and began to search for some aspect of, or part of, the machine on which I might gain some purchase. Surely the machine must be constructed in such a way that it can be opened and closed, that the living brain of Agamemnon could be inserted into it or withdrawn from it, that it could be serviced or repaired, that it might be resupplied with flammable materials, with nutriments to nourish the controlling brain, and so on.

"Where have you gone?" inquired the machine, in its evenly spaced, quiet, mechanically constituted phonemes. I suspected that this audio tranquility did not do justice to what must be the agitation, rage, frustration, and roiling emotions seething now in the ensconced, unseen brain somewhere within that large, metal body.

"Where have you gone?" came again from the machine. This time the volume was increased, but there was no sign beyond that of possible interest, concern, stress, or urgency.

"Speculate," I said, looking for something to which I might cling.

"You are close," it said.

"Not far," I granted it. Then, to be helpful, I pounded on the fuselage a few times with my fist.

"Depart," said the translator.

I did not respond.

The head of the machine rotated. The metal talons trembled but, as the machine was constructed, I did not think they could reach me. Similarly, the large beak opened, and then snapped shut, hideously. But, pretty obviously, the machine had not been constructed in such a way that it might easily remove an unwanted guest from its exterior, at least as it was presently oriented and situated.

"Begone, leech," said the machine.

I was pleased that the machine was not built closer to the anatomy and musculature of an actual tarn, or it would have allowed for preening, in which case I would be well advised to leave my post promptly.

"I can be rid of you easily and quickly," said the machine.

"I am then in serious trouble," I said.

I found some small, recessed depressions on the fuselage where, I supposed, it might be opened with a key or tool, but, to my annoyance, I could locate no rings or handles to which I might cling, should the machine leave the ground.

"For a human," said the machine, "I find you a brave and noble fellow. I like you. Let us be friends."

"Few things would please me more," I said. I was not sure that this was true, but some things seemed called for in the name of civility. Rudeness is seldom deemed a social virtue.

"You are not as sophisticated, learned, well groomed, nicely polished, smoothly spoken, or as affable as Decius Albus," said the machine, "but then you are a barbarian, as I understand it."

"From the Gorean point of view," I said, "I believe you, too, would be considered a barbarian."

"Ela," said the machine, "that is doubtless true. Goreans can be insufferably vain. They often do not even realize that they, lacking the civilized graces of Kurii, are, like you, a barbarian."

"I had not thought of it that way," I said.

"Despite his manners," said the machine, "I have occasionally thought that Decius Albus was something of a lout."

"I do not know him very well, personally," I said.

"Now that we are friends," said the machine, "you may dismount and be on your way."

"It is not polite to desert a friend," I said.

"I can use a brave, enterprising fellow like you," said the machine. "Enlist in my service and you will become rich. When Gor is a

Kur world, and I am its sole Ubar, as must inevitably come about, you will stand high, be given cities, ships, gold, power, women, whatever you like."

"I am willing to wait," I said.

"I am not," said the machine.

"You set fire to the woods," I said. "It still burns. That displeases Goreans."

"I am the Eleventh Face of the Nameless One," came from the machine.

"You tried to kill me," I said.

"That was before we were friends," came from the machine.

"If I dismount," I said, "have I your guarantee that I will not be harmed?"

"Certainly," came from the machine.

"How do I know I can trust you?" I asked.

"You have my word," it said.

"Upon a Steel World," I said, "you once promised amnesty to rebels, but you betrayed your word, and did much slaughter upon them."

"That was long ago and faraway," he said. "Such things are now irrelevant. I have changed."

"You were exiled," I said. "You were banished."

"I have adherents, Kurii, and humans, on Gor," came from the machine. "Too, I have secret adherents on the Steel World of which you dared to speak. I will have my world, either my former world, or another."

"Gor?" I said.

"Yes," came from the machine.

"How do you propose to achieve such an aim?" I asked.

"By bribery, subversion, division, and recruitment," came from the machine. "Even today I have made a fine start, for Marlenus of Ar is my prisoner. His ransom will fund several projects."

"Marlenus of Ar," I said, "is now safe amongst his troops."

"You jest," it said.

"Not at all," I said.

"You lie," it said.

"Marlenus was freed," I said, "while his warder, Lucilius, sought to apprehend a possible intruder."

"The falsity of your words is easily determined," it said. "I need only look into the matter. I can do so within Ehn. Dismount. Do not fear. You will be quite safe."

"I am not sure that leaving my present position is in my best interest," I said.

"I must insist," it said. "Dismount."

"Do you not fear Priest-Kings?" I asked. "Your aerial device would seem to incorporate capacities and components clearly proscribed by their technology laws."

"Much occurs on Gor of which Priest-Kings are ignorant," it said. "A few cubic feet of apparatus somewhere on an entire world is unlikely to be noticed by the Sardar, or, if noticed, would provoke interest. Too, Priest-Kings are weak, or passive. Dozens of Steel Worlds, lusting for their world, threaten them, and they remain inert. They see little; they care little."

"You have appeared publicly in Ar, in the Stadium of Blades," I said. "You have warred at the beaches of Port of Samnium. You have streamed fire into the woods of Samnium. It seems such things might be noticed."

"They are inattentive," it said. "One can steal their world while they do not even notice."

"Beware of Priest-Kings," I said.

"Priest-Kings care only for the Sardar," it said. "I may let them keep it. I have no great interest in it. Dismount."

"At the moment," I said, "I am content to be where I am, as I am."

"Very well," it said.

I faced a rather obvious dilemma. If I were to descend from the machine, I would be at its mercy. If I did not descend from the machine, I would be not much less at its mercy, for, if it took flight, it would be very difficult to cling to its surface.

I did not have much time to ponder this dilemma because, suddenly, the machine rose into the air, some forty feet or so, hovered, and then began a sharp ascent. The metal wings began to move, their beating simulating the motion of a tarn's wings, but one could tell, certainly from my position, clinging to the crest of the head, that the lifting power of the machine was independent of the wings. I was reminded of the transportation disks of the Sardar Nest, a drive which was somehow accessing and exploiting the ambient environment itself, possibly utilizing and manipulating local gravitational forces.

The device reared up from its sharp ascent and for some three or four Ihn sped vertically into the clouds, whose moisture coated my face and the fuselage of the machine. Then the machine leveled its flight, and inverted, and I was dangling, my arms about the head and beak. The machine then began a succession of rolls, and I, hands and arms now bloody against the metal, fought to keep conscious. Originally I feared the machine might ascend to a height where the air would be insufficient or the cold intolerable, but it did not do so. I did not know its ceiling, but I now reasoned that the machine would have been engineered for needs far short of high-altitude flight and pressurization. There would be no need for, or justification for, such properties, properties far beyond those of an actual living tarn.

Then the machine descended to perhaps three or four hundred feet. It then hovered, paused in the air. The wings even stopped moving.

There was a silence.

It must have lasted twenty or thirty Ihn.

I supposed that Agamemnon would suppose that I had been dislodged from my position long ago, but that he would not be sure.

Below us, the woods were still smoking.

"Are you there?" came from the machine.

I supposed that he expected no answer to that question, either because I was not there, or because I would have the common sense to remain quiet. I suspected that he was really talking more to himself than to me, and the translation device had not yet been deactivated. Who but an idiot would respond to that question? Certainly the supposition of the question was less than flattering.

On the other hand, if I remained quiet and slipped away, or tried to slip away, from the machine after it landed, things would not be much advanced. Agamemnon would be at liberty to pursue his aims.

"No," I said. "I fell off long ago."

If there was a response to that, it was not carried by the translator. Rather the machine ripped upward and began a series of maneuvers much like those earlier performed.

Then, finished, it again hovered, wings still, a hundred feet or so above the woods.

"Are you there?" came again from the translator. I was sure, this time, that he was not talking something over with himself.

I had been nearly thrown free of the device several times. My hands and the head and beak of the machine were washed in blood.

"Tal," I said, greeting him as brightly as I could manage.

"I am annoyed," came from the translator.

"I am not surprised," I said. "I effect nothing critical. You have every right to be so."

"I do not have time to have you tortured to death at great length," came from the machine.

"I know you are busy," I said.

"I can crush you like a straw, I can tear you apart like rence paper, I can rip you into tatters like rep cloth, I can sweep you aside as a hurricane might a leaf."

"How will you manage that?" I asked.

"With wood, with stone," he said.

"Impossible," I said. I was not fully candid with that response. I suspected it was quite possible. This was, of course, what I had been waiting for.

The silver tarn, I knew, was agile and swift, and was capable of subtle adjustments. I did not doubt that it could wing its way at great speed between trees, under overhanging branches, near shelves of rock, and so on, with a very small tolerance. I could be easily scraped from the fuselage of Agamemnon's current body, that of the silver tarn.

I tore away the upper portion of my tunic. I had not been able to damage the two seeming eyes of the silver tarn with a clutched stone, but, with one hand, and the flung portion of my tunic, I could cover them both, suddenly and unexpectedly.

The silver tarn, wings beating, swift, almost at ground level, plying through smoke, was amongst blackened tree trunks, smoking timber, and dangling branches. It rotated its body ninety degrees to the left to knife sidewise between two trees.

I capped the palm of my left hand over the left "seeming eye" of the tarn and with my right hand flung the ripped half of my tunic over the right "seeming eye" of the tarn.

Almost immediately there was a loud crash and I was flung forty feet through the air, struck the ground, and rolled through debris and ash for several yards, before I managed to get my legs under me, shake my head, and could see what had happened.

One of the tarn's wings, the left, was dangling, partly torn loose from the machine. There was a gaping hole in the machine where the wing had been half torn away and within that hole there was a sputtering of sparks and a tangle of sprung wire and tubing. From elsewhere in the fuselage, possibly from one of the apertures in which a tool or key might be inserted, a twisting column of smoke was curling out. The force of the impact must have spun the body of the tarn about, as it seemed to be facing me. The head and crest were awry, and the beak was bent to the side.

I suspected that Agamemnon was dead.

Then the machine shuddered, almost as if it were a wounded animal. I wondered how intimate might be the interface between that mighty, monstrous, disembodied brain of a once great and violent Kur and the sophisticated machine which was his current body. It was hard to conceive of Agamemnon as he might once have been, in natural life, huge and warlike, in harness with weapons, striding and gesturing, snarling and howling, charismatic, swaying tribes of ecstatic brutes, inspiring loyalties to the point of fanaticism. I had no idea how old he might be; perhaps he went back even to the wars, the troubles, terrors, and burnings, of the now long-destroyed, but never-forgotten, home world which Kurii in their madness had destroyed, the world before the Steel Worlds. There were still Kurii, I knew, who would die for Agamemnon. How little I knew, I thought, of Kurii. How little, too, I thought, I knew of human beings.

Agamemnon must now be dead.

But perhaps he was not dead.

I must investigate.

The machine stirred.

Was it only wiring and electricity that moved the monster?

I backed away.

I had the thought of a bird, in shock, one which had sustained an injury, trying to understand what had happened to it.

The right wing lifted, extended outwards. It fluttered.

Would it struggle to fly?

Did it not know it was not a bird, but a machine, and that those wings were a pretense, a show, that they had nothing to do with its flight?

There was a metallic sound, a scraping, as the head of the machine swiveled about, adjusting itself. It no longer faced me. The beak opened and closed once, seemingly with difficulty. The machine then oriented itself diagonally toward the sky. It remained in this attitude for over an Ehn. Then it began to rise, gently, amongst the trees. The right wing began to beat. The left wing hung by a strip of metal and a thick rod, against the fuselage. It had fallen back against the fuselage as the machine left the ground. Briefly, a fresh, forcible sputter of sparks issued from the crater at the base of the torn wing, and then the crater went dark, and silent. I did not think I was any longer of interest to the machine and the intelligence that governed it. As the machine climbed, tortuously, rocking back and forth, dipping, trembling, and struggling, more smoke blew forth from the cavity or panel, or closed hatch, which I took to be associated with access to the interior of the device. Then the machine began to descend, shaking, losing altitude, and veered to the side, to slide across the stone surface of a small, nearby bluff. It rested there, not moving. Again I wondered if Agamemnon was dead. It seemed to me that the machine had valiantly tried to reclaim the sky but could not do so. It now lay inert on the stone surface, high on the bluff. It was some two hundred yards from, and some fifty yards above, my present position. I knew little of the machine, but it seemed incumbent on me to inspect the wreckage. I began to make my way toward the bluff. As I did so, I became aware of many voices in the distance. I did not realize it at the time but thousands of men from Samnium and Port of Samnium, and from the local countryside, were entering the woods. Water in vessels of many kinds was being borne. Lines were formed at the edges of streams. One line, one in which, as many, containers of water were being passed from hand to hand, was over a pasang long. That line began at Port of Samnium. Thus Thassa herself, the dark turbulent sea, was contributing to the effort. Wagons with barrels of water were speeding along the road. Other men brought blankets and shovels to use in smothering flames. Axes were in play, too, to clear courses in the woods, across which, the flames, lacking robust nourishment, might find it difficult to pass.

I myself, however, continued to make my way toward the wreckage on the nearby bluff.

CHAPTER EIGHTY-EIGHT

It seemed to me that I must inspect the wreckage of the silver tarn, but I was reluctant to do so. I am not sure why. It seemed, now, harmless and inert. Did I fear it would jolt to life again? Was I somehow unwilling to near the housing of that monstrous brain of Agamemnon? Did I fear it so? What potencies might it continue to harbor? Perhaps I feared some shock might inhabit that burned, shattered frame, a burst of electricity which might hurl me back down the bluff. Perhaps I feared it might explode. Most, I suspect, I feared that, given the doings on the beach at Port of Samnium and the fires in the woods, which men now strove to extinguish, it might have attracted the attention of the denizens of the palisaded, gloomy Sardar, the attention of the gods of fresh, green, beautiful, perilous Gor, the mysterious, mighty Priest-Kings of Gor.

Perhaps some of the plating had been dislodged or struck aside in the vessel's unsuccessful attempt to scrape me from its surface. I would be curious to peer inside such a contrivance.

Smoke no longer issued from the device.

That seemed promising.

I put my hand on the metal.

It was still warm.

It was dark inside the narrow fuselage.

I was changing my position, to look further, when I saw the shadow on the metal, cast from behind me.

I turned about.

I was not the only one who had climbed the bluff.

I stared into the menacing, fanged visage of Lucilius. In one paw he grasped a heavy branch, that which I had seen him seize up at the rendezvous point.

He could strike with the branch before I could unsheathe my sword.

He raised the branch to strike, but then lowered it, looking past me and the wreckage. I moved slowly to the side, along the fuselage, and, when I could, I glanced back and to my left.

There, separated by the fuselage from Lucilius, was Grendel, massive and hirsute, two paws curled about the handle of a large, double-bladed Kur ax.

A brief exchange in Kur took place.

I followed it by means of the still-activated translation device in the disabled silver tarn.

"Truce?" asked Lucilius.

"There is truce," said Grendel, lowering the ax.

As soon as this was said, Lucilius discarded his weapon, that stout branch, and reached into a slitlike opening on the left side of his harnessing and drew forth a small, wrenchlike device which he immediately began to apply in places to the ruptured fuselage of the silver tarn. He removed a large, curved panel, cast it down, reached into the device, seemingly disengaged a number of connections or couplings, and drew forth a large, transparent vessel from which dangled an attached mix of wires and tubing. Inside the vessel there was some type of fluid, or broth, or solution, which was nearly as transparent as water, and, I suspect, may have largely been water. Inside this solution, buoyant, there floated a dark, hemispherical object, from which several thin tubes emerged, which, in turn, ran to the interior of the vessel.

Lucilius lifted the vessel up to the sun.

He then turned to Grendel. "Agamemnon lives," he said.

I then realized what I had hitherto feared. I was looking on the living brain of Agamemnon, once the master of a Steel World, conspirator and threat to Gor, the exiled Eleventh Face of the Nameless One.

"Kill it, kill him," I whispered to Grendel.

This was not picked up by the translation device in the ruined aerial machine.

I began to ease my sword from the sheath but Grendel's paw restrained me.

Lucilius put the vessel to the side, apart from the ruined silver tarn. He then picked up his discarded branch, and faced Grendel.

"The truce is over," said Lucilius.

"The truce is over," said Grendel.

"You know what I must do," said Lucilius.

"I know what must be done," said Grendel.

"You are not Kur," said Lucilius. "You are a mongrel."

"I have stood in the rings," said Grendel.

"Your mother was human," said Lucilius.

"My fathers were Kur," said Grendel.

I did not understand that.

"I have Kur blood," said Lucilius.

"I, too, have Kur blood," said Grendel.

"You betrayed your people," said Lucilius. "You sided with humans."

"To oppose the tyranny of Agamemnon," said Grendel, "is not to
betray one's people, but to serve one's people."

"You have served humans," said Lucilius.

"I have fought at the side of humans, some humans," said Grendel. "Have you not done so, as well?"

"Only to further the will of my lord, Agamemnon," said Lucilius.
"Choose your blood. Are you Kur or are you human?"

"I am both. I am neither. I am myself," said Grendel.

During this exchange I moved about the silver tarn and took a
place near my friend, Grendel. I had no confidence that I could defend myself with a sword against the sweep of that mighty branch in
the grasp of Lucilius.

"You have an ax," said Lucilius. "I have only a stick, a straw, a
branch."

"It is not necessary that we fight," said Grendel. "We both know
what is to be done."

At that point Lucilius uttered a cry of rage and rushed about the
silver tarn, the great branch raised over his head. Grendel's ax struck
the wielded branch and it flew apart and then Grendel, with the flat
side of the double-bladed ax, smote Lucilius across the side of the
head and Lucilius rolled several feet away, partly down the bluff.

I was breathing heavily, and I had not even participated in the
action.

"Well done, Friend," I said. "But I do not think he is dead."

"He is not dead," said Grendel.

"Are you not going to kill him?" I asked.

"Had I wished to kill him, I would have done so," said Grendel.

"He is dangerous," I said.

"So am I," said Grendel.

"At last we are victorious," I said, glancing at the large brain
buoyant in the solution, in the transparent vessel. "Agamemnon is at
our mercy. Kill him."

"No," said Grendel.

"Do you wish me to do it?" I asked.

"No," said Grendel.

"I do not understand," I said.

"Do you have a father?" asked Grendel.

"Yes," I said. "Matthew Cabot, of Ko-ro-ba."

"Would you kill him?" asked Grendel.

"No," I said. "Certainly not."

"Agamemnon," said Grendel, "is one of my fathers."

"One of your fathers?" I asked. "I do not understand."

"As you know," said Grendel, "I am the result of an experiment
which did not turn out well. Supposedly, as half human, I was in-

tended to further the projects of Agamemnon on Gor, by relating to, and recruiting, humans to his cause. But humans, I assure you, were not charmed. They saw me as forbiddingly Kur, and loathed and feared me. So the matter did not unfold as Agamemnon had hoped."

"What did you mean by 'fathers'?" I asked.

"First," said Grendel, "understand that a number of developing embryos, variously fertilized, were removed from my mother. These embryos were then mixed together in a laboratory until they formed a single, growing mass. This larger multiple embryo, so to speak, was then reimplanted in my mother. Thus, I had genetic materials from only one woman but genetic materials, apparently, from several fathers. It is my understanding that Agamemnon was one of these fathers, perhaps wishing to contribute to the experiment."

"Is this possible?" I asked.

"Yes," said Grendel. "Similar things are familiar even on your former world, Earth, or Terra."

"I have gathered," I said, "that, as you are unwilling to kill Agamemnon, you do not wish for me to do so either."

"True," said Grendel.

"What is now to be done?" I asked.

"I shall return to the rendezvous point," said Grendel, "to obtain certain stores, in particular, medicinals and nutriments. I shall then attempt to return Agamemnon to what you call the Beast Caves outside Ar. It is my hope that Agamemnon can survive the journey. If he does, in the Beast Caves there will be certain engineers and biologists who can restore him to not only health but vitality."

"So he can be equipped with a new and possibly more terrible body?" I asked.

"My task is to save him, if possible," said Grendel. "He is one of my fathers. Let him decide himself. Let him form himself. He must be free to will his own being. It is not my task to alter, weaken, diminish, or mitigate his will."

"A will," I said, "notorious for its inflexibility and ferocity."

"He is Agamemnon," said Grendel.

"Sometimes," I said, "I see his blood in you."

"I wish you well," said Grendel.

"What of Lucilius?" I said. "He will recover consciousness."

"I would leave the vicinity before he does," said Grendel.

"He will pursue you," I said.

"No," said Grendel. "When he awakens and discovers the sustaining vessel is gone, that it is not destroyed and the brain lying about, cut apart, and drying on the bluff, he will know I am doing what was to have been done."

"He will return to the Beast Caves?" I asked.

"No," said Grendel, "certainly not immediately. He will remain faithful to the last instructions of Agamemnon. It is the Kur way."

"What are those instructions?" I asked.

"I do not know," said Grendel.

"What of Marlenus?" I asked.

"I placed him on the road to Samnium," said Grendel, "and I remained concealed nearby, to make certain no harm came to him before his men found him. Happily, he was soon recovered by a patrol of his men. I think he is unharmed, and will soon be himself."

"You did well," I said.

"I overheard speech betwixt Marlenus and his men, after they revived him."

"How went things at the beach?" I asked.

"Apparently," said Grendel, "following the appearance of the silver tarn and the abduction of Marlenus, there was chaos and disruption. Fear gripped the lines. Ranks were shattered. Orders conflicted. Men quaked. Discipline vanished. Hostilities ceased. War was overlooked. In the distress and confusion, two ships approached the shore, and Decius Albus and his party were embarked and fled."

I howled with rage.

"I am sorry," said Grendel.

"It could not be helped," I said, brushing useless tears from my face. How could it have been helped?"

"Presumably the fugitives seek Brundisium," said Grendel.

"Thence to arrange passage to Jad," I said.

"The lead of the fugitives will be substantial," said Grendel. "I do not think that Marlenus has the time, or inclination, or the ships or men, to risk a pursuit as far as Brundisium. On the coast, there is much sympathy for Cos."

I supposed this true.

"All is lost," said Grendel. "I am sorry. Resign yourself. Let Decius Albus go. The sea is wide. The air is fresh. The fields are green. There are other things to do, other places to go."

"I am thinking not of a fleet, an expedition," I said, "but of one ship, small and swift." I wished I had at my disposal the Tesephone.

"Do not concern yourself," said Grendel. "Decius Albus will have several men at his disposal, dangerous, desperate men."

He then lifted up the vessel, and set it on his left shoulder, steadying it with his left hand. "I must make haste," he said. "I fear time may be short."

There was smoke in the air.

"Do not dally here," said Grendel. "Lucilius is strong. He may wake."

"I wish you well," I said.

"As I you," said Grendel, and descended from the bluff, and was shortly lost to sight.

Loyalty and blood are esteemed amongst Kurii.

I then made my way rapidly down the sloping bluff.

I must speed to the beach.

I turned once, to look upon the broken silver tarn, now in the distance. I had gazed at it for no more than a moment when I stumbled back and shook my head to rid it of the blinding frenzy of light and fire which had torn open the slope of the bluff. Then, where the silver tarn had been but a moment before, there was a spewing crater from which molten rock burst forth and ran down the sloping surface of the bluff.

Thus do the Priest-Kings endeavor to protect themselves and their nest from the ambitions and follies of species deemed as yet immature and unwise.

I then continued on my way toward the beach.

CHAPTER EIGHTY-NINE

"Iris," I said, "you seem dismal. What is wrong?"

"Perhaps," she said, "because Master's business seems without fruition."

I, and my party, had hired a small ship, a coastal trader, at Port of Samnium, and enough oarsmen to mount three shifts, and sped forth in pursuit of the two ships of Decius Albus. It seemed almost certain, given our shifts of oarsmen, and similar winds, that we, despite the lead which Decius Albus had had in his departure from the beach at Port of Samnium, would reach Brundisium before him. Yet we failed to detect our quarry. We waited. He did not appear. We inquired. We could find no trace of his having already arrived, and perhaps left. Two ships from the south and perhaps now some fifty or sixty armed men would presumably have been noticed, particularly given the typical zeal of Brundisium's harbor administration, monitoring traffic and renting berths. But the records, assiduously checked by Seremides and Xenon, revealed nothing suggesting the presence of Decius Albus and his party. It did not seem likely that Decius Albus, nor the two fishing vessels and their crews, would leave coastal waters and risk the perils of Thassa in an attempt to reach Cos directly. Most Gorean mariners, particularly in small ships, will not fare far from the sight of land. Thassa is deep, turbulent, and moody. Her dangers are not limited to twisting currents and sudden storms, but, too, to piracy. So, where was Decius Albus? It seemed he had not wharfed at Brundisium. But this in itself was incredible, for it seemed that Brundisium, at least for several days, offered him his only practical hope of securing a ship, or ships, capable of raising Jad.

"Might a slave not be sold by her master?" asked Iris.

"Of course," I said. "A slave is a property, like a boot, a belt, or shoe, a sleen or kaiila. She is subject to such things."

"What if a slave wishes to be sold?" she asked.

"A slave's wishes," I said, "are of no importance. They are meaningless."

She was silent.

"Why?" I asked. "Do you wish to be sold?"

"No," she said. "Not now."

"But perhaps earlier?" I said.

"It does not matter now," she said. "I shall never see him again."

What woman has not dreamed of a master?

What woman has not longed for a collar?

I regarded Iris.

The kajira is the most profoundly feminine and sexual of all women. Legally, of course, she has no choice in the matter. She does not simply belong; she is a belonging. She lives to love and serve. It is her life. Let the free woman despise her, and mock her, if she wishes. The kajira does not care. She knows things the free woman does not know, but only suspects. The humble kajira, vulnerable, desired so powerfully that men will own her, half-clad, if clad, collared, and marked, is commonly a thousand times warmer, richer, and happier than her free sister. It is no wonder that free women hate her so.

"You are thrilled to be owned?" I said.

"Yes, Master," she said. "I do not speak for others, but I speak for myself. I am a slave. I want to be a slave. I need to be a slave."

"You are far from Earth," I said.

"But closer now to myself," she said. "On Earth I did not know myself. On Gor I learned myself."

"You may one day see he whom you remember," I said. "Things come and go. Tor-tu-Gor rises and sets. Markets open and close."

There was then a knock on the door, coded, but sharp and urgent.

I, and Thurnock and Clitus, and Aetius, Seremides, and Xenon, had rented quarters in a mariner's inn, Harbor's Rest, near the southern piers of Brundisium.

We had been there for two long weeks.

I opened the door and Iris scurried to the back of the room and knelt. In this way she was at hand if wanted, but not conspicuously so.

"I have seen one who was in the party of Decius Albus," said Aetius.

I seized him by the shoulders. "Who?" I demanded. This was the first bit of positive news we had encountered in Brundisium.

"Ruffio, of Ar," said Aetius.

"Did he see you?" I asked.

"I do not think so," said Aetius.

"Where did you see him?" I asked.

"In the Sea Sleen," he said. This was a nearby tavern, not far from the water.

"He may slip away," I said.

"No," said Aetius, "Thurnock and Clitus watch."

"There was no sign of Decius Albus, or of his men, liveried or not?" I asked.

"No," said Aetius.

"I suspect they are not in Brundisium," I said. Certainly we had discovered no evidence of their presence within the walls.

"Perhaps Ruffio is no longer in contact with Decius Albus," said Aetius.

"No," I said. "He is almost certainly in contact with the party of Decius Albus. Ruffio will be important to Decius Albus in dealing with Cos. Remember, Ruffio, though of Ar, is known in Cos and has served Cos well. His loyalty to Cos may be based on the silver tarsk, but there are few sounder guarantees of loyalty. It was he who managed to deliver Talena of Ar to Ar, so that Lurius of Jad might receive the reward for her capture and delivery. Something is going on between Decius Albus and Cos, and Ruffio will be at its center."

"You see him as an agent for Decius Albus," said Aetius.

"Too, as an esteemed liaison between Decius Albus and Lurius of Jad," I said.

"Is it not careless of Ruffio to appear in public?" asked Aetius.

"The Sea Sleen," I said, "is a moderate, little-known tavern, largely patronized by mariners, and captains. I suspect that Ruffio is now, in such a place, at last, unobtrusively trying to arrange passage for Decius Albus and his party to Cos."

"Only now?" asked Aetius.

"That is the mystery," I said. "It seems that only now is Decius Albus preparing to make his move. Why, I wonder, the delay?"

"There must be a reason," said Aetius.

"One known to Ruffio," I said.

CHAPTER NINETY

"You!" said Ruffio, as soon as the blindfold was whipped away.

"Tal," I said. "Let us converse."

"Claim that you will tell us nothing," said Seremides. "That is always amusing."

"I make no such claim," said Ruffio.

"You will speak freely?" I said.

"I am surprised to see you here in Brundisium," said Ruffio. "After the carrying away of Marlenus of Ar by the strange tarn, I expected you to wander off, having lost your fee giver."

"We were not in fee to Marlenus of Ar," I said.

"You had independent business with the noble Decius Albus?" he asked.

"As it happens," I said.

"Having nothing to detain him," said Ruffio, "the noble Decius Albus took his leave."

"Marlenus survives," I said. "He is well."

"Interesting," said Ruffio. "And what of the strange tarn?"

"It no longer spreads its wings," I said.

"Marlenus, in his dispute with the noble Decius Albus," said Ruffio, "lost his chance on the beach at Port of Samnium. He cannot risk bringing a large contingent of men this far north. Ar is not popular here. Supply lines would be long and easily disrupted. If he tried to live off the land, fields might be burned and wells poisoned. I do not think he regards the noble Decius Albus as worth a war. It would be expensive and politically unwise. Too, it might be injudicious to spend much time away from Ar. Ar has resources and wealth. Many in Ar might view the Ubar's throne with interest."

"As did the noble Decius Albus," I said.

"Decius Albus," said Ruffio, "lacked patience. When the Home Stone of Ar was recovered, he should have bided his time. He acted too precipitately."

"You may sit," I said.

"Thank you," said Ruffio, and sat down on the floor, cross-legged, as is typical for Gorean males. Gorean women, both slave and free, usually kneel. Chairs, particularly curule chairs, which tend to convey a sense of status, are usually occupied by individuals of importance, both male and female. The throne of Ar, for example, large and ornate, is a curule chair. To be sure, much depends on locality. Benches, for example, and high tables, are almost universal in Torvaldsland.

I, too, took my seat.

Thurnock and Clitus remained standing, behind Ruffio.

"Do you not fear for your life?" asked Seremides of Ruffio.

"I am prepared to fear for it," said Ruffio, "if such a fear should seem warranted."

"We want information," said Aetius.

"I would be more than pleased to provide it, if I can," said Ruffio.

"He fears torture," said Seremides.

"Not at the moment," said Ruffio, "but, should it appear imminent, I shall lose no time in fearing it."

"I do not understand him," said Seremides.

"He takes us to be rational," I said. "What rational person would steal a tarsk-bit by force, or seek to gain it by means of torture, when it is proffered willingly."

"Precisely," said Ruffio. "How may I be of service."

"This is too easy," said Seremides.

"Not really," said Ruffio. "The information I give you will avail you nothing. That is why I am willing to give it. Accept it and know that you are helpless. Accept it and weep. Accept it and go your way, frustrated and defeated."

"What were you doing in the Sea Sleen?" I asked.

"Confirming and concluding, by means of a gold tarn disk, one of double weight, the arrangements for the noble Decius Albus and his men to leave Brundisium for Jad."

"How and when is this to take place?" I asked.

"Three days from now," he said. "On the medium-class knife ship, the *Tessa*, captained by Eteocles of Telnus."

"Where is Decius Albus?" I asked.

"At the caravanserai of Alessandro of Brundisium, two pasangs north of the walls," said Ruffio.

"I know the place," said Xenon. "It is vulnerable."

"Not the corner where Decius Albus is entrenched," said Ruffio. "It has been moated and walled."

"Surely you do not believe all this," said Seremides to me.

"Much can be checked," I said.

"You speak freely," said Aetius. "Should what you say be true, do you not fear the retaliation of Decius Albus?"

"No," said Ruffio. "I am indispensable to Decius Albus and the information I give you can do you no good."

"How is that?" I asked.

"You have no fleet, no army," said Ruffio. "If I am not mistaken, you are six in number, one of whom is crippled. Decius Albus, on the other hand, has fifty-eight men and some local tarsks, brutes hired from the alleys of Brundisium. What has he to fear? How will you stop him? He will march openly from the caravanserai of Alessandro to any of the piers of Brundisium, great or small. You have lost. Hire out your swords elsewhere. Go your way."

"Tell us more of the fortress at the caravanserai," I said.

"It is a position unassailable by less than two or three hundred men," said Ruffio. "Do not concern yourself further with the matter."

"Gold has opened more gates than flames and battering rams," said Seremides.

"Opened them to six men, one a cripple?" said Ruffio. "Decius Albus trembles."

"You are an astute and brave man," I said. "Alone, you conveyed Talena to Ar."

"And had you been more astute, and perhaps less brave, you might have had her for your own, for the reward," said Ruffio.

"He who searches for a tharlarion," I said, "may overlook an urt."

"I do not understand you," said Ruffio. "Marlenus failed to apprehend Decius Albus. Decius Albus made good his escape. That is the end of things. What are you doing in Brundisium? What business have you with Decius Albus."

"I have very little business to do with Decius Albus," I said.

"Perhaps then I am free to leave?" said Ruffio.

"I think, shortly," I said.

"Surely not," said Seremides.

"Some matters," I said, "remain unclear to me."

"Perhaps I can be of help?" said Ruffio.

"You are of Ar," I said. "Yet you accept the gold of Cos."

"I find it is quite as good as that of Ar," he said.

"It seems you pledge yourself to a golden mistress," I said.

"I am not her only admirer," said Ruffio.

"You are paid by both Cos and Decius Albus," I said.

"And well," said Ruffio.

"I am troubled," I said, "by yet another thing."

"What is that?" he asked.

"You must have arrived in the vicinity of Brundisium several days ago," I said.

"Yes," said Ruffio.

"With the intent to deliver Talena of Ar to the mercies of Lurius of Jad," I said.

"Yes," said Ruffio.

"For enormous wealth," I said.

"Of course," said Ruffio.

"How is it then," I asked, "that you did not depart days ago? Why did you delay?"

"Lurius of Jad," he said, "has high, rich plans for that arrogant, dark-haired, green-eyed she-sleen. There is unrest in Cos. The calamitous, shameful outcome of the war with Ar did not make his throne more secure. A tyranny may be endured, even celebrated, as long as it redounds to the benefit of a populace, but when its demands and limitations begin to chafe and cramp, even the most contented of verr become restless."

"Few people seek freedom," said Seremides. "Most seek a new keeper."

"I trust not," I said.

"Keepers compete," said Seremides. "Each promises the flock more."

"Surely you are wrong," I said. "You must be wrong."

"It is lucrative to be a keeper," said Seremides.

"Let us speak of other things," I said.

"Lurius of Jad," said Ruffio, "is clever, and his spies are many. He must deal with disgruntlement and resentment. He intends to shift the blame for the ills of Cos onto another."

"Talena," I said.

"Who lied to him, who tricked and beguiled him, who led him into war with Ar."

"Who could believe so absurd a claim?" I asked.

"Many," said Ruffio, "if it is said frequently and with authority."

"But still," I said, "why the delay? Why did you not arrange passage to Cos days ago?"

"That is of great interest," said Ruffio. "I shall explain. Lurius needs a blame-object which is believable and significant, one seemingly capable of, and worthy of, monstrous villainies, namely, a responsible, autonomous, powerful, sovereign free woman, or what appears to be a free woman."

"Talena is a slave," I said.

"That is not known to the average Cosian," said Ruffio.

"Speak further," I said, uneasily.

"As you know," said Ruffio, "long ago, Talena was captured and enslaved by the tarnsman, Rask of Treve. Accordingly, she was routinely marked with the mark of Treve."

"I know," I said. "It is small and tasteful." As small and tasteful as it might be, that mark, of course, like any slave mark, radically transformed its recipient from a free woman into a rightless animal, a property, goods, a vendible object, a slave.

"The brand was removed," said Ruffio. "The matter was attended to by discrete members of the green caste. They did well. Their instruments were skillfully handled. Their creams and salves are effective. She is healing rapidly. Her thigh is now as smooth as silk."

It need not remain so, I thought.

"It can be a capital offense to remove, or even alter, a slave brand," I said.

"Perhaps you could take the matter up with Decius Albus," said Ruffio.

"This matter is interesting," said Seremides.

"A slave would be useless to Lurius of Jad," said Ruffio. "He would not pay a handful of tarsk-bits for Talena as a slave. As a seeming free woman, she is worth a great deal to him, more than enough to give Decius Albus high station in Cos, with a suitable wealth to match."

"You, too, would profit," I said.

"Amply," said Ruffio.

"Do you expect to leave this room alive?" asked Seremides.

"Yes," said Ruffio.

"You may leave," I said.

Ruffio rose to his feet.

I, too, rose to my feet.

"But the blindfold must be reaffixed," I said. "Then you will be led about for a time, and then released."

"Of course," said Ruffio.

"Into the harbor, strangled," said Seremides.

"Scarcely," I said.

"This has to do with codes, does it not?" asked Seremides.

"More with common courtesy," I said.

Thurnock then reaffixed the blindfold.

"I wish you well," I said.

"I wish you well, Geoffrey of Harfax, or however you now choose to call yourself," said Ruffio.

He was then, between Thurnock and Clitus, conducted out, into the night.

"You should have killed him," said Seremides.

"No," I said. "He is devoted to the golden mistress. Any man with so simple a motivation is easy to understand and manipulate."

"You heard what he said," said Seremides. "All is lost. Are you now ready to give up the seeking of Talena?"

"No," I said.

CHAPTER NINETY-ONE

"What have you learned?" I asked.

"There is such a holding," said Thurnock. "It is small, but stout and secure, walled and moated. It is located near the far edge of the caravanserai, away from the buildings and wells, away from the tents and stables, away from the South Road toward Brundisium."

"It is then not near the markets or emporiums, the stalls and shops?" I said.

"Not conveniently so," said Thurnock.

The larger caravanserais are, as I supposed was that of Alessandro, in effect, small cities.

"Amenities then," I said, "would not be at hand."

"No," said Thurnock.

"Let us take our swords elsewhere," said Seremides.

"You say the holding is small," I said.

"Yes," said Thurnock. "Maybe forty paces by twenty paces. I hazard that it might be successfully stormed by a hundred and fifty men."

"Possibly not, if it had fifty or more defenders," I said.

"We do not have a hundred and fifty men," said Seremides. "Only fools pursue hopeless causes."

"Heroes may pursue such causes," said Clitus.

"Heroes are fools," said Seremides.

"Only to those unwilling to recognize and countenance heroism," said Clitus.

"Following the informer, Ruffio, Decius Albus has over fifty men and some local hires," said Thurnock.

"The local hires, with local accents, one supposes, will serve the interests of privacy for Decius Albus and his men," I said. "Presumably they will do chores, fetch supplies, carry water, discourage visitors, ward off the curious, and, in general, be primarily responsible for relations with the local population." Certainly I supposed Decius Albus would not wish to have attention drawn to his party, given its history and interests, nor to its members, many of whom would presumably have the accents of Ar or Venna, which in itself would be likely to provoke suspicion and arouse hostility. In particular, he would not wish his scheme suspected, to accrue riches by delivering Talena into the clutches of Lurius of Jad. Surely he had no exclusive rights where such a project might be concerned. Might not others then be eager to undertake that venture in his place, say, free companies, or even the high council of the administration of Brundisium itself?

"I would suppose there is a lack of cover near the holding," I said.

"That is so," said Thurnock. "Land has been cleared for a hundred paces about the holding, even before the edge of the moat is reached."

"It is impractical to attack the holding," said Seremides.

"Then we must attack elsewhere," I said.

"So let the more than fifty men of Decius Albus fear the attack of six?" asked Seremides.

"I think," I said, "given the size of the holding and the number of men of Decius Albus, and the local hires, it would be crowded."

"Yes," said Thurnock. "Unpleasantly so."

"Mercenaries," I said, "save in certain elite free companies, such as that of Dietrich of Tarnburg, are seldom well disciplined, and our friend, Ruffio, did not speak generously of the quality of the local hires either."

"For many, close quarters are unpleasant," said Thurnock. "I suspect that annoyance will be rampant and tempers short," said Thurnock. "And this situation may have obtained for several days by now."

"It is now two days," said Aetius, "today and tomorrow, until the rendezvous of Decius Albus with Eteocles, captain of the Tessa, at some pier in Brundisium."

"I am not sure of that," I said.

"Speak," said Thurnock.

"Why would Decius Albus risk a march through Brundisium to some pier in the harbor?" I asked.

"Because he has enough men to protect himself," said Aetius.

"From us," I said, "but perhaps not from others."

"As far as we know, he made no wharfing in Brundisium when he came north from Port of Samnium," said Seremides. "Xenon and I found no records of such a wharfing."

"And a knife ship, even one of medium class, is shallow drafted," I said. "It could be brought easily to a beach, and more easily to within wading distance from a beach."

"Ruffio explained the meeting between him and Captain Eteocles, about the projected rendezvous and the sailing date in Brundisium," said Aetius.

"How do we know," I asked, "what actually passed between Ruffio and some captain at the Sea Sleen?"

"Everything that Ruffio told us has worn the seal of truth," said Thurnock.

"Until now," I said.

"You are less naive than I feared," said Seremides. "How better to conceal a lie but in the midst of truths? How better to conceal a sleen than in a flock of verr?"

"I suspect that even the men of Decius Albus do not know his plans," I said.

"You conjecture then," said Aetius, "that the move of Decius Albus is not scheduled for tomorrow night?"

"That is my conjecture," I said.

"When then?" asked Aetius.

"Time is short," I said. "We must do our best to sow discord amongst men who, by now, should be more than ready to tend to its harvest."

"And when," asked Aetius, "do you think Decius Albus plans to embark?"

"Why, tonight, of course," I said.

CHAPTER NINETY-TWO

"It is near the Twentieth Ahn," I said.

"The night is dark," said Thurnock.

He carried a Peasant staff.

"All the better," I said. "Startled and surprised, they will strike carelessly, recklessly, blindly."

"If this is the night of embarkation," said Clitus.

"If it is not," I said, "it matters little."

"I hear only the water," said Aetius. The waves lapped softly at the beach.

"My benefactor, the noble Seremides of Ar," said Xenon, "checked the tables. The yellow moon should rise by the First Ahn."

"Decius Albus will wish to avail himself of darkness," I said. "Thus, if this is the night of his embarkation, as I suspect is the case, he will wish to move between now and the First Ahn."

"Why are we here, so near the beach?" asked Clitus.

"Let us speak softly, now," I said. "They will have a scout or watchman at the beach to exchange signals with the incoming ship and apprise those in the holding of the ship's arrival."

"And you wish to confuse matters?" said Aetius.

"Certainly," I said. "Ideally, Decius Albus leaves the protection of the holding to board a ship which, hopefully, is not present, or is lying well offshore, inert, waiting for a signal which it does not receive."

"When he leaves the protection of the holding, he will have Talena with him?" said Aetius.

"Of course," I said. "He will wish to lose no time in getting her aboard and being on his way to Cos."

"Who is there?" said a voice from the darkness, from between us and the shore.

"A friend," I said.

"Who?" said the voice.

"Strike him senseless," I said.

Thurnock swung his staff into the darkness, and there was a sound of surprise, a startled grunt, and then Thurnock swung again toward the sound, and there was the sound of an impact, and then silence.

"Disarm him, and bind him, hand and foot," I said, "and then revive him. And somewhere about there should be a dark lantern."

"I have it," said Xenon.

"Let us have a bit of light," I said. "And stand between the light and the holding."

There was the sound of a small, sliding panel, and then there was a streak of light on the sand.

Aetius unbuckled and discarded the sword belt of the fallen figure, and then, with readied cords, tied its hands together behind its back, and crossed and tied its ankles.

"It is Ruffio," I said.

Thurnock seized the collar of Ruffio's tunic and then dragged him down to the water, and thrust his head two or three times beneath the water. There was some coughing and sputtering, and then Thurnock, again by the collar, dragged Ruffio back up the beach and deposited him at my feet.

"Lift him to his knees," I said.

This was done.

"Friend?" said Ruffio.

"Yes," I said, "I am your friend. Whether or not I remain your friend is up to you."

"You lied to us," said Aetius. "You said the embarkation of Decius Albus was to be tomorrow night."

"The date was advanced," said Ruffio.

"Let us kill him," said Seremides. "My sword thirsts for blood."

"I am interested in information," I said.

"Have no fear," said Ruffio, on his knees before me. "I recognize that it is in my best interest to be of assistance."

"What are the ship and beach signals?" I asked.

"The ship will identify itself by flashes of light, in groups of two," he said.

"Have you received such a signal as yet?" I asked.

"No," he said.

"And you would respond," I said, "similarly?"

"Yes," he said.

"Continue," I said.

"I signal the ship to approach by flashes of light in groups of three."

"And for it to remain in place, offshore?" I asked.

"Darkness," he said. "The absence of the approach signal."

"Similar arrangements apply, I presume," I said, "between the beach and the holding."

"Yes," he said. "Flashes of light in groups of three signal Decius Albus to approach, to leave the holding and come to the beach, and mere darkness advises him to remain in place."

"There must be some signal that there is danger, that plans have run awry, or such," I said.

"Yes," said Ruffio, "eccentric movements of the lantern, in which case the ship would withdraw to Brundisium and Decius Albus, if outside the holding, would return to the holding, or, if in the holding, would remain in place."

"You have been very helpful," I said. "However, if the least bit of information you have provided us should prove to be in the slightest error, I shall feel obliged to end our friendship. Is that clearly understood?"

"Yes," said Ruffio, "it is clearly understood."

At that moment, the time bar, in the distance, mounted somewhere amidst the central buildings of the caravanserai, began to sound.

We counted the strokes.

"The Twentieth Ahn," said Xenon.

"Is it your intention to engage the forces of Decius Albus?" asked Ruffio.

"We are thinking about it," I said.

"You will find it easy to do," he said.

"How is that?" I asked.

"His troops," said Ruffio, "may not even form ranks. Released from the holding after several days of crowding and misery, and afflicted by rations furnished by usurious agents, rations seldom better than slave gruel, they may run to the beach."

"Surely not," I said.

"You have no understanding of the conditions which have prevailed in the holding," said Ruffio, "conditions which have prevailed unabated for days. The holding is small. It is overcrowded. Close quarters oppress. Incarceration rankles. Men stumble over one another. Tempers flare. Some liken the conditions to those of being in a stinking slave pen. And there is hostility between the soldiers of Decius Albus and the hired workers and agents of Brundisium, with their pretentions and airs, who can come and go much as they please.

"It would doubtless be better if there were a common Home Stone," I said.

"The troops of Decius Albus," said Ruffio, "are not seasoned regulars, but gathered mercenaries. Discipline totters. They revere only their pay, and have seen little of it of late. Sometimes knives are drawn and blood flows. And today fresh events stirred the brew. Tempests flamed within the holding."

"What is special about today?" I asked.

"Two things," said Ruffio. "A rumor sprang up somehow amongst those of Brundisium that Decius Albus intends to leave the coast this very night, embarking for Cos, neglecting to pay their wages."

"Might he not?" I asked.

"How could such a rumor have arisen?" asked Ruffio. "How would they know?"

"Perhaps they guessed," I said.

"Secondly," said Ruffio, "twenty bottles of the finest paga were mysteriously delivered this afternoon to the holding, fifteen for the men of Brundisium, and only five for the soldiers of Decius Albus, who far outnumber the witless tarsks of Brundisium."

"Dreadful," I said. "Such a gift might well sow the seeds of dissension."

"I assume you know nothing of these things," said Ruffio.

"How could I know of them?" I asked.

"I must warn you," said Ruffio. "Although the troops of Decius Albus may be lax in duty, harried, ill-disciplined, slovenly, hungry, and stressed, they are dangerous men, armed, desperate men, who are well aware that they are in precincts where they are not only unwelcome but may quite possibly be regarded as enemies. How many men do you have?"

"Hundreds," I said.

"I count only six," said Ruffio. "Untie me and flee while you have time."

"You would allow us to leave in peace," I said, "giving us something of a start, waiting a time before sounding the alarm?"

"Of course," said Ruffio.

"How do I know you will keep your word?" I asked.

"I give you my pledged word," he said. "It is that of a man of honor."

"Who could ask for more?" I said.

"His silence may be more securely guaranteed," said Seremides.

"How?" I asked.

"I cut his throat, now," said Seremides.

"I am prepared to withdraw, and gladly," I said, "but not just yet."

"You cannot successfully engage Decius Albus," said Ruffio. "He has fifty-eight men and some twenty armed tarsks of Brundisium. Be wise. Depart. Let things go."

"Not yet," I said.

"What is your implacable blood grievance against Decius Albus?" asked Ruffio. "Is this a matter of codes? Is there some irreparable injury he has dealt you? Is there some dire wrong yet to be righted, some insult to be expunged, some inequity to be wiped away with cleansing blood?"

"I am not Marlenus of Ar," I said. "I was not betrayed. My throne was not threatened. Decius Albus means little to me, one way or the other."

"Why then do you contemplate engaging his troops?" asked Ruffio.

"If all goes well," I said, "I will not engage his troops, at all."

"I do not understand," said Ruffio.

"Captain," said Thurnock. "Look to sea, look to the darkness."

I peered out.

From the darkness, from a dark lamp, perhaps five hundred yards offshore, there were sparks of light. There were five groups, of two flashes each. This was then repeated.

"Respond to the signal," I said to Xenon. "Five groups of two flashes each. Then close the lamp."

"What now?" said Thurnock.

"For now, I trust," I said, "the ship will remain in place, awaiting the signal to approach."

"Tal," said a voice from the darkness, a powerful male voice.

I knew the voice.

"Ubar," I said.

"Ubar," said Seremides.

"How much have you heard?" I asked.

"Enough," said Marlenus of Ar.

"I do not see how you can be here," I said.

"One of your men, for the second time, was recognized by my armsman, Alan of the House of Hesius, the first time in Ar, the second time in Brundisium. So then we merely followed you about, and, now, this time, to the beach."

"Forgive me, I am crushed," said Aetius.

"Do not be," I said. "Brave, skilled men seldom think of pursuit. The craven urt is fearful, suspicious, and alert, but the larl strides where it pleases."

"Which is not always wise," said Aetius.

"True," I said.

"What are you doing here?" I asked Marlenus.

"I should think it obvious," said Marlenus. "I seek the blood of a traitor."

"We did not expect you," I said.

"Surely you did not expect me to arrive with an army," he said. "I am here secretly, with ten men."

"And I am amongst those men, recreant and coward," said young Alan, of the House of Hesius.

"You nurse a grudge, since the time of the Stadium of Blades," I said.

"It festers," he said. "I was tricked. I was shamed before the Ubar and the populace of Ar. For that I demand satisfaction."

"I do not think this is the time nor the place," I said. Then I turned to Marlenus. "You were courageous, or, forgive me, perhaps foolish, to risk coming this far north with so few men."

"Few are less likely to be noticed," he said. "Would not more put Decius Albus to flight? How else might I bring him within the compass of my sword?"

"You are Marlenus of Ar," I said.

"Flee, both of you, while you have time," said Ruffio.

"Gag him," I said.

"What do we do now?" asked Thurnock.

"Two things," I said. "First, Xenon, open the lamp to the sea and move it about, eccentrically, even frantically, and then turn about and signal to the holding, serenely, placidly, several times, in groups of three."

Ruffio struggled wildly, helplessly, but the wadding had been thrust in his mouth, and, a moment later, had been tied in place. He was then thrust back, supine on the sloping sand.

"Now," I said, "if all goes well, the ship will put about and return to Brundisium, and Decius Albus and his men will take their leave of the holding and make their way, rejoicing, to the beach, to be safely embarked for Cos."

CHAPTER NINETY-THREE

"I hear swordplay, screams," said Marlenus.

"Let us remain here, for a short time, spread out, calling no attention to ourselves, unperturbed," I said.

"Why do I hear war in the darkness?" asked Marlenus.

"Soldiers burst forth from the holding," I said. "They would rush to the beach. Hirelings, awakened, suspect treachery, seize up arms, and demand their pay."

"What battle is more to our liking than when enemies engage one another?" said Seremides.

"Both will believe the beach is empty," said Thurnock.

"I want the blood of Decius Albus," said Marlenus.

"Presumably he will be along shortly," I said.

"Not all will dally to dispute," said Aetius.

"I know," I said. We, then, should not remain long in our present position.

Within two Ehn some bodies rushed past us in the darkness, some even splashing out into the water.

"Where is the ship?" asked a man.

"The ship!" cried another. "Where is it?"

"Ho! Ship! Ship!" cried another, out into the darkness.

"Let us go up the beach," I said.

"And cut the enemy off before he can return to the holding," said Alan. "Then he will be trapped between the sea and our swords!"

"And so verr would trap larls," I said. "That is the last thing we want to do. We are much outnumbered."

"Let the enemy have access to safety," said Seremides, "and hope that he will take advantage of our generosity."

"Why then ascend the beach?" asked Alan.

"Because we are much outnumbered," I said. "If we remain where we are, near the water, whilst the enemy is rushing toward the water, we would soon be surrounded by him, overwhelmed and slaughtered."

"Bring light! Bring a light!" cried a fellow at the water's edge.

"No," cried another. "We are to slip away in darkness."

"I have stumbled across a body," said a voice. "It seems to be bound. It lies half in the water."

"Leave it," said another.

"It seems to be alive," said a voice.

"Kill it," said another.

"It is gagged," said a voice.

"Let us make haste," I said, "up the beach."

As we ascended the beach some more soldiers swept past us.

We had not gone more than two hundred paces up the beach when we stopped, in the vicinity of what seemed knots of angry men.

This point was roughly halfway between the holding and the water.

"Look," said Thurnock, hoarsely. "Someone emerges from the holding. He bears a torch."

"Unfortunate," I said.

"In the darkness," said Seremides, gasping from exertion, "imagination makes us many. One candle and we become few."

"You will receive your pay!" cried a voice.

"Decius Albus!" whispered Marlenus, delightedly.

"No deceit was intended," continued the voice. "Your pay, generous and carefully measured, has been brought to the beach by the waiting ship. You were not informed until this evening, that in order that our departure be the less suspected and the better concealed. All is upright. Scorn baseless fears. Put from your mind senseless thoughts of subterfuge or fraud. Let our noble fellows of Brundisium now sheathe their weapons and permit us to proceed, unchallenged and unhindered. Step back. Good! Now, friends all, accompany us to the shore, there to thanked and paid."

"There will be more than enough men at the shore," said Seremides, "to pay them with steel."

I had heard no woman's voice. Yet I was sure that Talena must be near. Would she not be in a custody close to Decius Albus? Was not she, with her now-smoothed left thigh, the key to his imminent wealth and station?

"The torch comes closer," said Thurnock.

There was then a series of cries, drifting up from the shore, one after another, each closer than its predecessor. "There is no ship! There is no ship!"

Ruffio has been freed, I thought.

This intelligence from the shore was met with both moans and cries of anger.

"No!" cried Decius Albus. "That is false. That is a lie. The ship awaits. Your gold, your copper, your silver, is ready for you." But he made no effort, as far as I could tell, to descend to the beach.

Then the torch was amongst the divided crowd and I caught sight of robes, tunics, harnessing, faces, legs, and drawn weapons. There must have been some twenty mercenaries and perhaps a corresponding number of nondescript hirelings. Too, I caught sight of a robed, female figure in the keeping of two mercenaries, these behind Decius Albus.

I had heard no rumor of slave girls, rented or owned, in the holding.

That deprivation, too, must have abraded the patience of the mercenaries of Decius Albus.

But the absence of kajirae in the holding was easily understood. Such delightful, well-curved beasts, such delicious domestic animals, are loquacious and more than apt with careless speech. What kajira is not eager to impress her collared sisters with the latest of her household's well-kept secrets?

Suddenly, to my dismay, Marlenus of Ar cried out, "Ho, Decius Albus, false friend, coward and traitor, stainer of your Home Stone, I, Marlenus of Ar, Ubar of Ar, am here! I have come for you. Stand forth, dare to meet me, blade to blade!"

As far as I knew, Decius Albus had no reputation as a swordsman. Most likely he did not possess blade skills, but merely hired those who had them. But who knew? In any event, I was sure that he would find crossing swords with Marlenus of Ar, quite possibly one of the most dangerous s swordsmen on Gor, a less than attractive way to spend, say, the last tenth of an Ehn, or so, of his life.

The Ubar's surprising and untoward announcement, which I thought inopportune and much regretted, shook both mercenaries and hirelings.

"Marlenus of Ar!" cried various voices, some aghast and all surely startled. "How could Marlenus be here?" said one. "He has brought an army north!" cried another. Exclamations abounded. "We are lost!" cried a man. "An army of Ar!" moaned another. "A thousand men!" wept another. There were cries of consternation, of awe, surprise, doubt, and fear.

"Scatter! Flee!" cried Marlenus. "Let a path be cleared between myself and Decius Albus!"

I then realized the gamble of Marlenus.

I would not have cast the stones so.

But then I knew less of Gor than he.

He was well aware of the balance of numbers, a fraction very little in our favor. Thus, to neutralize this disadvantage, he counted on surprise and audacity, and the indisputable awe in which a Ubar is commonly held, particularly by those nominally under his rule. Suppose a king had suddenly, unexpectedly appeared, as though from nowhere, to subjects, even recalcitrant subjects. Might not the power of his mere presence strike terror into the hearts of many? His voice then utters a thunderous command.

Several men, even those of Brundisium, wavered; several were on the brink of flight. Could they really be in the presence of Marlenus, the mighty Ubar of Ar?

"No!" cried Decius Albus. "Stay where you are! Do not move! He is one man, only one man! And there is no army! He is a fool to come here! Perhaps he is not even the Ubar of Ar! How do you know he is the Ubar? He cannot be the Ubar! Would the Ubar come here, and so risk himself? And see how few there are! And you cannot move an army with the subtlety of a slithering ost. If there was an army of Ar, or even a considerable force of Ar in the vicinity, word of it would have reached us."

"Step forth and fight," called Marlenus, "or send forth a champion whose fate you agree to share, for better or for worse."

Decius Albus marshaled mercenaries between himself and Marlenus.

I do not think he solicited a champion. If he had, I gathered that his call had lacked a respondent.

We could see the crowd pretty well, given the light of the torch. On the other hand, we stood mainly in the darkness, outside the perimeter of its most effective illumination, and we, and our numbers, could not be well conjectured.

"Fight, fight!" cried Marlenus.

"He has no intention of doing so," I said.

We then became aware of several mercenaries ascending the beach. This was an unwelcome intelligence as it considerably rebalanced the odds even more in favor of Decius Albus. They had, it seemed, reconciled themselves to the fact that no rescue ship, at least for now, lay offshore, waiting to carry them in safety to Cos. With them I caught sight of Ruffio, who had recovered his weapon.

"There is no ship!" I cried.

Let the mercenaries' fear being stranded in enemy territory. Let them be dispirited, and look anxiously to the shelter of the holding, there to await what might develop. Too, how many men really were out there, arrayed against them in the darkness? Surely Marlenus would not have come to the field so meagerly supported. Let them look to the safety of the holding, let them be encouraged to leave the field. Had we not provided them with a beckoning, glowing route to safety? So let them avail themselves of that gift. Let them retire in haste and disorder. That, I trusted, would give me the opportunity I needed.

"There is a ship!" screamed Decius Albus.

"We want our pay!" shouted a hireling.

"Go to the shore, get it from the ship!" said Decius Albus. "It is waiting for you."

"Come with us!" said the man.

"Step forth and fight!" cried Marlenus.

"They are few!" called Ruffio, from yards off, trudging up the beach. "They are less than twenty!"

There were six in my group, counting myself; and in the other group, that of Marlenus, there were eleven, counting himself. Decius Albus, as I understood it, had something in the neighborhood of eighty men, nearly sixty mercenaries and a score or so of hirelings.

I looked down the slope, at the approaching figures.

"Decius Albus is being reinforced as we speak," I said to Marlenus. "There are hard feelings between the men of Decius Albus and those of Brundisium. I do not think the fellows from Brundisium will be much eager to fight for Decius Albus. We each, you and I, have an objective. Let each pursue that of his choice. If we wish to attack, I think this would be an excellent time to do so, before we encounter a weightier foe, one advancing even now."

"Beware, Decius Albus," cried Marlenus. "I am coming for you! You cannot escape! If I must, I will cut my way through stone walls to reach you!"

I thought that this threat was somewhat excessive, but who am I to criticize a Ubar?

"Noble heroes of Brundisium," I called. "I salute you. I admire your bravery, your loyalty! Few men of your rich, great port would risk their lives as you will soon be doing for men of hated Ar, men who despise you, who are your enemies, and would cheat you of your wages."

Then I turned about, addressing those with me. "Let us do battle quickly," I said, "before our five ships beach below, each with a hundred armsmen of Ar, whose arrival would snatch from us our deserved guerdon of glory."

"There are no such ships!" screamed Decius Albus.

"Attack!" cried Marlenus and we, as one, rushed forth, scarcely noting that the men of Brundisium seemed to fade away before us, clearing a path to the mercenaries of Decius Albus. In the next instant we were amidst flashing blades, quick, yellowish, fierce, in the torch light. Marlenus, lacking a great shield, could not buffet his way through, like an avalanche, to Decius Albus, who had withdrawn even further into the ranks of his mercenaries. I was briefly aware of the armsman, the Taurentian, Alan, of the House of Hesius, near me. He cast me an angry look. And then we were swept apart. My objective was not to deal with Decius Albus or his mercenaries, but to slip past them, blade to blade, and reach a small, heavily veiled and robed figure, on its feet, but its hands bound behind it, behind the lines. Then I broke through the ranks of the mercenaries, but saw no robed figure. A mercenary turned to face me, but then backed away. I did not follow him. I saw Ruffio only feet away from Decius Albus. Our

eyes met, and he turned away. Neither of us, I gathered, was interested in wasting his time with the other. His sword was bloody. Perhaps, I thought, he is skilled. It is seldom wise to underestimate an
opponent. If his skills are lacking, regard that as a happy discovery.
If they are not, you are ready. "Decius Albus," cried Marlenus, "stay
where you are! Wait for me! Meet me! I am coming for you!" and then
he battled away the blades of two mercenaries. They earn their pay
tonight, I thought. I wondered then if Marlenus might underestimate
the skills of Decius Albus. Perhaps Decius Albus hired swords, that
others might not suspect the cunning of his own. It is hard to know
about such things. I saw the hirelings, the fellows from Brundisium,
weapons drawn but unused, gathered to one side. It seemed they did
not wish to risk dying for pay, particularly for a pay apparently well
in arrears. "Fight! Fight, loathsome tarsks!" screamed Decius Albus
to them. "Show us the gold, the silver, the copper!" cried one of
the hirelings. A mercenary rushed toward me from the side. I think
he did not realize I had caught sight of him. He took a step back,
and then, the chest of his tunic flooded with blood, fell to the sand.
Where was Talena?

I suddenly thought that Marlenus had misjudged the field. He
would be unable to reach Decius Albus before the mercenaries coming
back from the shore could participate fully in the action. Marlenus was
no closer now to Decius Albus, who had drawn back, than he had been
when, with a crash of steel, he had reached the first rank of the mercenaries. Moreover, I could now see that several men, even more men,
weapons drawn, were approaching from the shoreline. Indeed, Ruffio,
who had been well in advance of the greater number of the mercenaries
returning from the shoreline, had already, as mentioned, joined Decius
Albus. But I also realized, soon enough, happily, that not all of the
ascending mercenaries were joining the fray. Many had already passed
us, apparently seeking refuge in the holding. They had had enough, it
seemed, of confused, dubious war. Where was Talena?

Yet, it soon became clear, to my dismay, that although several
mercenaries had declined participating in the action, in favor of seeking refuge in the holding, that several others had carried their blades
into the combat, with the result that the course of events was turning
against Marlenus.

Fortunes in war are often uncertain.

Small things may have large consequences.

What occurs on a square yard of turf may not tell the truth about
what occurs on the square pasang. A battle thought lost might be
elsewhere won; a battle thought won might be elsewhere lost.

Much in war is mysterious and irrational.

When one verr runs, why should a thousand?

When one verr stands firm, why should a thousand stand so?

Sometimes a verr can demoralize a thousand larls.

Sometimes a single larl can turn a thousand verr into a thousand larls.

Where was Talena?

I did not see her!

I moved swiftly, purposefully, refraining from striking, dallying for no more than the time necessary to deflect a surprised blade or thrust a fellow to the side, making my way through the rear ranks of the mercenaries toward the fellow who held the torch. It must be near the First Ahn. Time was short. With the hilt of my sword, grasped in my fist, I struck the fellow who carried the torch on the side of the head, heavily, seized the torch, flung it to the sand, kicked sand over it, and then, with my sandal, pressed it down further into the sand. I then crouched down, sensing blows striking about, over my head. I think that more than one of the mercenaries, striking about in the darkness, must have suffered from the blow of another.

Consternation reigned.

I heard Marlenus cry out, "Decius Albus! Where are you!"

But this question received no answer.

As men moved about, and away from me, some apparently striking about in the darkness, an unwise thing to do, I stood up and called out, "Men of Ar! Men of Ar! Here! You hundreds from the ships! Here! Join us! Here is the war!"

I heard grunts, curses, and cries.

Bodies moved about. There was scuffling, and shuffling.

There was much confusion in the darkness.

"Bring light!" said someone.

"To the holding!" I heard. "To the holding."

A number of bodies hurried up the slope toward the holding. I assumed the drawbridge was down, and that the holding might be easily accessed, and, shortly, sealed. Marlenus, I speculated, had missed his Decius Albus, doubtless much to his chagrin and frustration, but retained his life. I did not know any post-battle plans which might have been prepared by the Ubar, but my people, I knew, as we had arranged, would return to our quarters in the Harbor's Rest, in Brundisium.

So, where was Talena?

I had not heard her speak, or cry out, or utter any exclamations, earlier, even in the stress of confusion and battle, so I thought it likely she had been gagged. This pleased me. The thought of strident, arrogant Talena being unable to speak out, that determined by men, was one not without its charm. This hypothesis was further suggested by the fact that Decius Albus, in his intended swift, secret embarkation would not wish to hear her cry out or scream. Surely she knew by now the sort of fate which was planned for her in Cos. Might she not then seek to shriek or cry out for mercy or rescue?

Where was she?

I had not seen her even in the moments before I had managed to extinguish the torch, and it was now dark.

Had she been returned to the holding?

I supposed that was possible.

But it seemed unlikely.

Her guards might have been distracted by swordplay. They might have found it necessary to defend themselves. They might have been urged by an alarmed Decius Albus to reinforce his lines, to join the fray. Might not Talena, in the noise, the confusion, and the wild, uncertain light have found herself momentarily unattended?

Had she managed to slip away?

That was possible.

As she would wish to escape the clutches of Decius Albus, she would not be likely to return to the holding or its vicinity. I supposed, too, that she would avoid the caravanserai of Alessandro and the prime road leading to and from Brundisium. I expected that she would then go to the shoreline and then move south toward Brundisium. She could claim to be an escaped, abducted free woman, who had been kidnapped, by some invented bandits. As she was not collared and her left thigh was now free of a mark, her story might be accepted. Her accent, which was clearly that of Ar, might put her in some jeopardy, of course, of being remanded to authorities, to be marked, collared, and sold, but such a fate would be far superior to that which would await her in Cos.

I had barely reached the shoreline when the yellow moon rose and the beach and water were softly bathed in the reflected light of Tor-tu-Gor, Light Upon the Home Stone.

I saw no sign of Talena.

I did see Ruffio's discarded dark lantern which we had used to send the Cosian ship away and lure Decius Albus from his holding. The wick had been snuffed out. It still contained a goodly amount of tharlarion oil and a small fire striker. It took but a moment to rekindle the lamp. I opened the front panel of the lamp, lifted it up, and directed the light toward the sea. I then closed it and, on a whim, opened and closed it several times, so that it emitted several groups of two flashes each. But there was no response from the darkness to sea. The Cosian ship had returned to Brundisium as it had been instructed to do. I was preparing to snuff out the lamp when I caught sight of a ridge of sand almost at my feet. I bent down with the lamp, and examined the sand. The ridge, I thought, might have been made by the side of a woman's slipper. I then saw a similar ridge here and there. What was suggested to me was that someone, presumably somewhat ineffectually, in the dark, had tried to erase footprints. Very clever, I thought. "You will wade in the water, to leave no discernible tracks. Unfortunately you did not see the dark lantern in the dark or did not have the courage to light it.

I assumed the fugitive, bound and robed, and presumably gagged, would try to reach Brundisium and possible aid rather than wade north to a more open and less civilized terrain, and one in which she might be more readily recaptured by Decius Albus. I then snuffed out the dark lantern, discarded it, and, in the bright light of the yellow moon, began to move quickly south, along the coast, toward Brundisium. How dare she arrogate to herself the right to wear slippers? I thought. Had she been given permission to cover her feet? Were animals shod? Then I recalled that Decius Albus would require her to maintain her pose as a free woman. Else, why the veils and robes, the bared neck, and the smoothed thigh? Would she not be nearly worthless to Lurius if she were publicly perceived as what she now in fact was, a mere slave? The parameters of political theater, I thought, are peculiar, indeed. Were they not difficult to fathom?

I had proceeded for some Ehn when I became apprehensive. The fugitive was presumably wading, cumbersomely robed, and bound. Should I not by now have overcome her lead?

Of course, I thought. Talena is a clever, highly intelligent woman. She would be keenly aware of possible pursuit. She would look frequently behind her. As I could see her in the moonlight, so, too, she could see me, someone following her. Would she then risk leaving the water, risk leaving visible tracks? I did not think so.

I turned about, abruptly, entered the water to my waist, and began to wade north. She would have few viable options. Encumbered as she was, she would be unable to swim. She could do little more than crouch down in the water, hoping not to be noticed.

In less than an Ehn, I seized the collar of her heavy, soaked robes, and dragged her to shore.

CHAPTER NINETY-FOUR

"Perhaps," I said, "we should have a talk."

"I shall list my demands," she said.

"There will be time enough for that later," I said.

We were in a large, bare room in the Metal-Worker's street in Brundisium. I had arranged it earlier, even before we had scouted the holding toward the edge of the caravanserai of Alessandro.

I was seated in a curule chair.

It was the only chair in the room.

There was a box containing certain articles at the side of the curule chair.

Across from me, a few feet away, standing, facing me, her back against the wall, was Talena.

This was the second day following her rescue. She stood before me, well bathed, rested, and dined. She was well robed, too, even resplendently so, in fresh, new, expensive, unsoiled garments. The sweat, stink, and grime of the crowded holding were behind her.

"You are aware, I take it," I said, "of what was to be your projected fate, that lying in wait for you in Cos?"

"Of course," she said. "I am not stupid."

"Might you not then express some gratitude for your rescue from such a fate?" I asked.

"No," she said. "It is the duty of a free man to deliver a free woman from such dangers."

"Perhaps I will deliver you to Lurius of Jad and secure for myself the station and riches sought by Decius Albus," I said.

"You could do so," she said, "but you will not do so."

"Why not?" I asked.

"Because you are weak," she said.

"There might be another reason," I said.

"What could that be?" she asked.

"Perhaps you will learn," I said.

"From you," she said, "I could learn little."

"You are proud," I said.

"I am the daughter of a Ubar," she said.

"By adoption, not blood," I said.

"It makes no difference," she said.

"I expect it makes much difference," I said. "Too, as I understand it, you were repudiated, disowned, and sequestered. That had to do with your begging to be purchased in the Northern Forests, the act of a slave."

"I was clever," she said. "In the circumstances, understanding the buyer, I knew such an act would soon bring me to freedom."

"You hate me," I said.

"You tricked me, luring me into companionship," she said. "You let me think you were a true man. Then you abandoned me!"

"I explained it to you" I said. "That was no doing of mine. I did not desert you. I was removed from your side, presumably by an act of Priest-Kings."

"Liar!" she said.

"Very well," I said. "Have it your own way. I found you as ugly as a she-tarsk. You did not even have the makings of a good slave. Who would want you? 'Abandon her while you can,' I said to myself. I left in disgust. She would not even make a passable kettle-and-mat girl."

"Tarsk!" she said. "I am the most beautiful woman on all Gor!"

"Except for several million others," I said. "And, as I understand it, Rask of Treve thought so little of you that he gave you away, literally gave you away, preferring a mere barbarian, and one with blond hair and blue-eyes at that."

"Tarsk, tarsk!" she cried.

"Those of Treve have a sharp eye for slave meat," I said.

"'Slave meat'!" she cried.

"Exactly that," I said. "No more, no less. Perhaps sometime you will be permitted to view yourself in a mirror, naked and collared. By then you, and all others, I assure you, will have no doubt that the reflection in the mirror is that of a slave."

"I am a free woman!" she said.

"Long ago," I said, "when I tried to comfort and protect you in tarn flight from Ar, you pretended fear and helplessness, and then thrust me suddenly from the saddle of the tarn."

"What did you expect?" she asked. "You stole the Home Stone of Ar."

"Luckily," I said, "my fall was broken by the vast, yielding web of one of the giant Spider People."

"Such webs are common amongst the swamp trees," she said. "The foliage makes them hard to detect."

"Later, in the morning, in the swamp," I said, "I saved you from the attack of a carnivorous tharlarion."

"Surely you do not expect a show of gratitude," she said. "You did no more than was required. Such succor is owed to a free woman."

"Even years before your usurpation of the throne of Ar, abetted by fellow conspirators," I said, "I found your involvement in the intrigues of Ar distasteful, in particular, the way you utilized your helpless female slaves to seduce and trap, as well as spy on, selected citizens, commonly those of status and rank. Doubtless you were well informed, this adding to your power, and blackmail, too, I suppose, had its remunerations."

"What did it matter?" she asked. "They were mere slaves."

"And when their work proved ineffectual, or inadequate, or failed to satisfy you," I said, "you had them punished, and keenly so."

"The whip encourages a slave to be more diligent," she said.

"I also disapproved of a recent action of yours in the Stadium of Blades," I said, "when you spat on a free man, one of your four guards."

"I felt like doing so," she said. "I was not pleased with him. Too, I knew I was safe in doing so. He could not retaliate, given my position as defendant."

"What is to be done with you now?" I asked.

"I believe it was explained to you earlier," she said, "in the inn, in the vicinity of Ar."

"The Inn of Livius Major," I said, "on the Torcadino spur, off the Viktel Aria."

"Yes," she said.

"Your demands?" I said.

"Precisely," she said. "I shall need a new identity, a new residence, and station. I shall also require a generous living allowance, on the basis of which I can lavishly entertain local society, a society which I will influence and soon dominate."

"It may not be happy lot," I said, "to grow up in a palace."

"I do not understand," she said.

"Such a child may be spoiled," I said, "by power and wealth."

"I proved immune to their charms," she said.

"I am pleased to hear that," I said.

"It is easy to despise power and wealth when they are beyond one's reach," she said. "Yet, one notes, the critic, inept in industry and commerce, commonly seeks them zealously by other means."

"I suppose," I said, "one often denounces what one covets."

"I am little in touch with the boards, the streets," she said. "Tell me of Marlenus of Ar and Decius Albus."

"Rumors thrive, their tendrils reaching out like restless leech plants, sensing blood," I said.

"What rumors?" she asked.

"That Marlenus is in Brundisium, incognito," I said. "That he seeks Decius Albus, in the name of the sword of vengeance."

"Such things are easy to understand," she said, "following the action in the vicinity of the caravanserai of Alessandro."

"Little, if anything, is officially known," I said. "Certainly Decius Albus would prefer to stanch such rumors, as they would call attention to his possible presence."

"But," said Talena, "where is Marlenus?"

"I speculate," I said, "that he is tented somewhere in the caravanserai of Alessandro, that he may watch the holding to which Decius Albus withdrew and in which he continues to shelter himself."

"That holding is impregnable," she said, "unless set upon by hundreds of men."

"I agree," I said.

"And it cannot be well besieged by the paucity of men at the disposal of Marlenus," she said.

"That is my view, as well," I said.

"Thus," she said, "Marlenus of Ar is not in Brundisium or its environs, but has returned to Ar."

"Perhaps," I said. I wondered if she truly understood the resolution of Marlenus of Ar, and his obsession with meting out justice to a duplicitous colleague, one who had betrayed him and threatened his throne. To be sure, given his lack of resources, the personal hazards to which he was subjected, and the dangers of leaving a throne unattended, he would have been well advised to return to Ar as swiftly and inconspicuously as possible."

"Decius Albus," she said, "may no longer be in the holding."

"That is possible," I said.

"He may be on his way to Cos," she said.

"How welcome would he be in Jad without his prize?" I asked.

"I trust that this interview is nearly done," she said.

"Nearly," I said.

"I am eager to begin my new life," she said.

"I am sure it will begin soon," I said.

"Excellent," she said.

"Do you recall," I asked, "that once, long ago, in the time of the Horde of Pa-Kur, the Master Assassin threatening Ar, that in our tent you begged for the iron, that you begged to be used?"

"It was a mistake," she said. "Something deep inside me was sweeping me away. I was familiar with Gorean men. At that time I did not know how weak you were."

"The robes of concealment," I said, "may be intricate, abundant, and cumbersome, but, colorful and flowing, they are beautiful, even resplendent."

"They comport with the dignity and status of the free woman," she said.

"Very much so," I said, "and the veils, as well."

"Of course," she said. "But men know little of such things, of subtle ensembles, matched accessories, and such."

"That is true," I said. I knew that there were some high-caste women who did not even know how to dress themselves, how to manage the layerings, foldings, closures, and such. They depended on female slaves trained in such matters.

"I find this raiment acceptable," she said, "even suitable. I freely and gratefully acknowledge it so."

"I am pleased," I said.

"I trust that it was appropriately expensive."

"It was," I said.

"Good," she said.

"It is worthy, is it not," I asked, "even of an Administrator's daughter?"

"Perhaps even a Ubar's daughter," she said.

"Splendid," I said. "Remove it."

"What?" she said.

"Remove it," I said, "completely."

"I do not understand," she said.

"Surely you are aware," I said, "that for a slave to don such garments without permission is a grievous offense, punishable in many cities by death." Surely she knew that. Unless one were a woman's dressing slave or one charged with the care of such garments, one was not even allowed to touch such a garment. Slaves in the street went to great lengths to not even brush against such a garment. The very thought of coming into contact with a free woman's garment terrified the average female slave. Such on Gor was the unbridgeable chasm between the free and the slave.

"I am a free woman," she said.

"No," I said. "You are a slave. And, as you once, at the time a free woman, arranged to bed with a handsome, male slave, the actor Milo, whom I had arranged to own, briefly and deliberately, you are my slave. A free woman who beds with, or prepares to bed with, a male slave, becomes the property of the male slave's master. That is in accord with the couching laws of Marlenus of Ar. Obviously the point of the law is to discourage liaisons between male slaves and free women."

"Do not jest," she said.

"This should be familiar," I said. "It was brought out in your trial, in the Theater of Publius."

"You would not enforce such an absurdity," she said.

"Were you given permission to clothe yourself this morning?" I asked. Surely she knew that a slave, an animal, whose natural state was understood to be nudity, was not permitted to clothe herself except with the permission of her master or mistress.

"No!" she said, defiantly.

"Remove your clothing," I said, "now, completely."

"No," she said.

"Do you wish me to attend to the matter?" I said.

"No!" she said.

"Do you wish to be stripped and whipped, as a lax or recalcitrant slave?" I asked.

"No," she said.

"The whip encourages a slave to be more diligent," I said.

"I have heard so," she said.

"Begin with your veil," I said. "Then disrobe slowly, and beautifully."

"As might a slave?" she asked.

"As a slave," I said.

"I see," she said.

"Please me," I said. "I wish to enjoy reviewing my property."

In a few moments she stood in the midst of her garments, sprawled about her ankles.

I gestured that she should step away from them.

"Tarsk!" she said.

I then went to the door, to the side, and pounded on it twice, sharply.

Two burly fellows appeared at the door, in the gray of the Metal Workers, in the street, or district, of which I had rented this room.

"She is ready," I said.

"What are you going to do?" asked Talena.

"She is a beauty," said the first Metal Worker. "We will enjoy this."

"You are sure she is a slave and not a free woman?" asked the second, warily.

"Yes," I said.

"I am a free woman!" cried Talena.

"Is she of Brundisium?" asked the second.

"No," I said.

"Then it does not matter," he said.

"But I am free, free!" cried Talena.

"A free woman," I said, "may lie as much as she wishes. It is her prerogative. But, as you know, a slave may not do so. Are you a free woman?"

"What are you going to do?" she asked.

I placed a copper tarsk in the palm of the first Metal Worker.

"What are you doing?" she asked.

"Proceed," I said to the Metal Workers. He who was first amongst the two turned about and left the doorway. The other went to Talena, took her by the upper left arm, and conducted her from the room.

Shortly thereafter I heard her scream.

A bit later she was returned to the room and cast to my feet before the curule chair.

"How could you? How could you?" she wept.

"I did not wish to risk smearing and blurring the brand," I said. "That would lower your price if I decided to sell you."

"You could not have done this," she wept.

"Brand!" I snapped.

She looked at me, tears running down her cheeks, disbelievingly.

"Must a command be repeated?" I inquired. Dalliance on the part of a slave can be cause for discipline. A slave is to respond to a command immediately and unquestioningly.

She rose to her right knee, and extended her left leg to display the brand.

"Excellent," I said.

"Oh!" she cried in dismay. "Not that! Never!"

The brand was the common Kef, the first letter in the word "kajira," the staff and fronds, beauty subject to discipline, the most common slave brand on Gor.

She regarded the brand, aghast.

"I am not a kettle-and-mat girl!" she cried.

"It is a lovely mark," I said. "Many preferred slaves are so marked."

She sprang to her feet, fists clenched.

"To your knees," I said.

She sank to her knees, her knees clenched together.

"Why did you have me marked, marked as though I might be a slave?" she said.

"Because you are a slave," I said.

"Surely not in full legality," she said.

"In full legality," I said. "I could take you to a market within the Ahn and sell you."

"But you will not do so," she said.

"No," I said. "I do not think so, certainly not within the Ahn."

"Was it necessary to have me marked?" she asked.

"It was not necessary," I said, "but it was appropriate. As you know, the marking of slaves, as certain other domestic animals, is recommended by Merchant Law."

"And you regard me as a domestic animal?" she asked.

"Yes," I said, "my domestic animal."

"Surely you are joking," she said.

"Remain on your knees," I said.

"But I am Talena, Talena of Ar!" she said.

"Slaves, as animals, have no Home Stones," I said. "Thus, you are no longer of Ar. Too, Talena is now a slave name, put on you at the convenience of masters. Slaves have no names in their own right. You can be named, if named, in any way masters please."

"Must it have been the common Kef?" she asked.

"No," I said, "but I thought it would look well on you."

"Does it?" she asked.

"Yes," I said. "And it is well known that a brand much enhances the beauty of a woman, both aesthetically and practically, aesthetically for the loveliness of the mark and practically because it signifies that the woman can be purchased and owned."

"I do not understand what is going on here," she said.

"What do you not understand?" I asked. "All seems clear to me."

"What has this to do with my new identity, a new location, a villa or mansion, enviable position and station, an ample income by means of which I can enter and influence society?"

"Presumably it has much to do with your new identity, so to speak," I said, "but nothing whatsoever to do with the other things you mention."

"My new identity?" she said.

"That of unconcealed and manifested slave," I said. "It is surely one of the most uncontestable and indisputable identities on all Gor."

Slaves, incidentally, unlike their often unhappy, unfulfilled, frequently self-estranged free sisters, need not be troubled by ambiguities, uncertainties, ambivalences, indecisiveness, and such. It is almost always clear how they are to be, how they are to speak, act, and so on. On Gor the female slave has no difficulty understanding who she is and what she is. It is clear to her, and to society.

"Wait!" she said, suddenly, smiling. "I understand now! You are clever for a barbarian!"

"Stay on your knees," I said, "where you belong."

"You have outwitted Decius Albus brilliantly," she said. "Decius Albus had my brand removed that I might be delivered suitably, profitably, to Cos. Lurius of Jad, tyrant of Cos, would find a lowly slave unfit for his political purposes. A slave is negligible. But, if I could be presented to his court, to the military, and the populace as the hated Talena of Ar, it would well suit the lie behind which he chose to hide, namely, that he was beguiled, misled, and tricked by Talena, who deceitfully urged him to act, to thwart the supposed warlike ambitions of Ar, ambitions which would put not only Cos but Tyros and the Farther Islands at risk, as well. As you have now made me worthless to Cos, I am now spared at least one grievous fate. I would only that you had shared your plans with me earlier. I see now that I am, in effect, as I once was in the time of the Horde of Pa-Kur, in disguise. Yes, for a barbarian, you are clever, clever indeed. But why the common Kef?"

"Because it pleased me," I said. "And why not a common mark for a common slave?"

"I am to be marked as though I am a common slave?"

"Certainly," I said.

"I see," she said.

"And rendering you worthless to Lurius of Jad," I said, "was a welcome, foreseen consequence of your marking, but you are quite mistaken if you believe that bringing about that consequence was the exclusive motivation, or even a motivation, of my action."

"What then?" she asked.

"I wanted you branded, as the slave you are, and should be," I said.

"You are of Earth," she said. "You could not want a woman so wholly, so completely, so profoundly, so uncompromisingly!"

"The males of Earth, even if crippled, lied to, and reduced, even if broken and betrayed," I said, "are men, as are those of Gor. The humans of Earth and Gor are of the same species. The differences between them are not biological, but cultural. This is clear from several of the great civilizations of Earth's past."

"Men are to be conquered," she said.

"They can do it only to themselves," I said. "That is the hope of their enemies. Men are to be taught to defeat themselves."

"Let them be conquered!" she said.

"Consider the unhappy, desolate fruits of such a conquest," I said.

"The men of Earth," she said, "are weak. They deserve their defeat."

"I think not," I said.

"Their cause," she said, "is forgotten, and lost."

"Time is long," I said, "and it takes many turns."

She reached toward her robes.

"What are you doing?" I asked.

"I intend to clothe myself," she said.

"Go to all fours," I said, "and crawl here, before me, and turn so that your left side faces the chair, and lower your head."

Her hair fell to the floor. It was a long, glossy black. It fell on both sides of her neck. I smoothed it a bit. I could then, her hair forward, see the hairs on the back of her neck.

"There is a fire in the other room," I said. "Shortly you will gather up your clothing, take it to the next room, and burn it. You will then return here, and kneel before me."

"I am smaller and weaker than you," she said, "but that means nothing."

"You are mistaken," I said.

"We have ways to conquer men," she said, "though our weapons are not so edged and keen as steel."

"If a man is conquered by a woman," I said, "both are miserable. If a woman is conquered by a man, both are happy."

"What are you going to do?" she asked.

I reached into the box by the side of the curule chair, and removed the collar. It was a standard collar of the northern sort, flat, bandlike, and close fitting. The lock goes at the back of the neck. I put it carefully about her neck, adjusted it slightly, and then, decisively, snapped it shut. A woman is not likely to forget that moment, or sound.

"I am collared," she said, bitterly, "like a slave."

"You are a slave," I said.

"I suppose it is an effective disguise," she said.

"It is not a disguise," I said.

She knelt back, without permission. She tried the collar. Then she gasped, startled, and tore at the collar. Then she regarded me, angrily. "This collar," she said, "is not simply closed. It is locked! I cannot remove it!"

"Slave collars," I said, "are not made to be removed at the occupant's convenience."

The brand marks the woman slave; the collar, too, marks her slave, but also, commonly, it identifies the master. In this way, should she, say, stray, or lose her way, she can be returned to her owner.

"Give me the key," she said.

"Gather up the robes and veils," I said. "Take them to the next room and burn them. Then return, and kneel before me."

She touched the collar, and then looked at me, reproachfully.

"You do not need such things," I said. "They are no longer for you. Indeed, they are forbidden to slaves. You are not to touch such things without permission. You are a slave. Consider the feelings of free women, how insulted and outraged they would be should you, a mere, worthless slave, dare to touch such things, dare to do such things, what punishments they would rightfully inflict upon you."

"The collar," she said, "is not of gold, not even of silver. Too, I fear it is not encrusted with jewels."

"I do not wish to tempt thieves," I said. "Such a collar would be worth more than most slaves."

"I am naked," she said.

"Not entirely," I said. "You have a collar."

"It seems a common collar," she said.

"For a common slave," I said.

"May I ask what the collar says?" she asked.

"It says," I said, "'I am the property of Geoffrey of Harfax.'"

"One of your many names," she said.

"As it happens," I said. "Are you lingering? I thought you had received a command."

She rose up and gathered together the robes and veils.

"Be about it," I said.

She turned about, abruptly, angrily, and went to the other room.

Did she not know the pleasure, the gratification, the honor, of having been issued a command by her master? Was she not pleased to obey, grateful for being permitted to serve? Too, a slave is to be graceful, not abrupt or clumsy. Too, commonly, the slave backs a bit away from the master, before going about her business. In this way, she does not immediately turn away from him. Clearly Talena had not yet internalized her new condition.

I rose from the chair and went to the open portal, that giving access to the adjacent room, and stood there, watching, my arms folded.

She looked at me, and then thrust the clothing angrily onto the bedded fire, from which an iron had been recently removed.

When a girl from Earth has been recently delivered to Gor by slavers and she is still garbed, say, in a dress or jeans, or such, she is often forced to remove and burn her own clothing. This commonly has a profound effect on her. Stripped of clothing she feels unutterably exposed and vulnerable. She sees it burn before her eyes. What does this mean? What is now to become of her? She is stripped. She is wholly without garments. What has this to say about her future? Dare she suspect what lies in store for her?

I returned to the curule chair and, a few moments later, Talena returned and knelt before me.

"You look well," I said, "stripped, marked, and collared, and kneeling before me."

"Does not any woman?" she asked.

"Some more than others," I said. To be sure, such an experience does any woman good. It helps them to understand their fit and proper place.

"I am well disguised," she said. "Few would think me not a slave."

"You are a slave," I said.

"Surely not," she said.

Her knees were placed closely together, the palms of her hands on her thighs. Who has not seen a woman so knows little of how beautiful a woman can be.

"In public," she said, "I shall endeavor, as difficult as it may be, to convey the mien of a slave convincingly, but in private we need not sustain the pretense."

"Stay on your knees," I said.

"While you exploit me?" she asked. "While you rest your eyes on my beauty, despite what I might wish or will?"

I reached again into the box beside the curule chair. I drew forth from it a slave whip, supple and five-stranded, the sort the mere sight of which encourages a kajira to zeal.

"What is that for?" she asked.

"Surely you are familiar with a common slave ritual," I said, "by means of which a slave is permitted to acknowledge her understanding of her condition and express her desire to submit to, and please, her master?"

"I am not unfamiliar with the ritual," she said.

I held the whip before her. "Kiss it, and lick it," I said, "humbly, lengthily, submissively, lovingly."

"I think not," she said.

"Very well," I said, rising, and shaking out the strands.

"What are you going to do?" she asked.

"Lash you, kajira," I said.

"Do not!" she cried.

"Do not fear," I said. "This device is designed for the improvement of female slaves. It punishes terribly, but it will not mark you. It will not lower your block value, not in the least."

I drew back my arm.

"No!" she cried.

"Do you beg to express yourself?" I asked.

"Yes," she said, "I beg to express myself!"

I cast the whip across the room, and it slid several feet on the floor. "Fetch it," I said, "on all fours, and do not touch it with your hands. Pick it up with your teeth, and bring it before me so. Then lift it to me in your teeth, and, on all fours, like the worthless beast you are, whimper that you may be permitted to express yourself."

"Better," I said. "More lengthily. Let me see your lips pressed on the leather. Softly now, lovingly, good. Again, and again. Let us see your tongue. It is a pretty tongue, the tongue of a pretty kajira. Good, use it lovingly, slowly, lengthily, tenderly. Again. Kiss, lick, slowly. Show me variety. Continue, Kajira. Good. More!"

"Now to your knees," I said, "and continue."

As she performed this lovely, meaningful, ritual, she sometimes lifted her eyes to me. In the beginning, her eyes burned with hatred and defiance. And then, a little later, as the ritual went on, she trembled, and sobbed, helplessly. She knew she was to obey, and that anger was absurd and defiance useless. She was, as she had asserted earlier, not stupid. Then, later, her eyes expressed what seemed to be surprise, and then awe. And then, still later, she lifted her eyes to me, and then swiftly put down her head, as though fearing that I might see what was in them.

There is a point, of course, to such rituals, aside from the gratifications so abundantly ingredient in them. They enhance and confirm social realities. When the slave is given no choice but to behave as a slave, act as a slave, and so on, it is natural that, sooner or later, she begins to think, fear, hope, and desire as a slave. That is natural. It is what she is. Add then that she who for years has hungered and longed to be a slave, but tried to deny and drive away such thoughts, now finds herself, helplessly and choicelessly, a slave.

I placed the whip to the side.

"You know how to prepare a slave," she said. "Am I not now to be ordered to nadu?"

That is the common position of the pleasure slave, kneeling, knees spread, back straight, the palms of the hands down on the thighs.

"No," I said.

"I am insufficiently attractive?" she asked.

I rose from the curule chair and pulled her to her feet by the hair. I then put her in leading position, her head, held by the hair, at my left hip, and conducted her to a corner of the room, where there was a slave ring, a chain, slave bracelets, and linked ankle rings.

"Lie down," I said, "prone."

I braceleted her hands behind her back, and placed her lovely slim ankles in the linked ankle rings. I then chained her head close to the ring.

She turned her head, as she could, to look at me.

"How can you be doing this?" she asked. "You are treating me as a slave. Do you not know you are from Earth?"

"You will learn your collar quickly," I said. "If you survive, you will survive as what you are, a slave, and only a slave, that, and nothing more."

"Are you serious?" she asked. "You cannot be serious! You are from Earth, Earth!"

"Have you received permission to speak?" I asked.

She fought the restraints. "Free me!" she demanded.

"Three strokes," I said.

"No!" she cried.

I then fetched the whip, and gave her three sharp, measured strokes. Her entire body reacted. She wept. Perhaps she now realized she was a slave, and subject to discipline. A slave must learn such things. She is to obey. She is to strive to be pleasing. She is not a free woman. She is a slave.

"May I speak?" said Talena.

"Certainly," I said.

"I was whipped," she said. "You whipped me!"

"Only three stokes," I said. "But I trust that it was instructive. Was it?"

"Yes!" she said.

"Would you like more?" I said.

"No!" she said.

Interestingly, most slaves are seldom, if ever, whipped. The explanation for that is quite simple. They realize, as slaves, that they are subject to the whip, that it can, and will, be used on them if they are not pleasing. Accordingly, they strive to be pleasing.

"Why, before, did you not order me to nadu?" she asked.

"Before I am through with you," I said, "you will beg to go to nadu before me."

I then turned away.

"Where are you going?" she asked.

"The doings of masters," I said, "are not the concern of slaves."

"Surely you are not going to leave me here like this," she said.

"I will return shortly," I said, "with some purchases."

"You are training me," she said.

"You are highly intelligent," I said. "I am sure that you will learn quickly."

I removed her slave bracelets and ankle rings, lengthened the chain some seven feet from the slave ring, and changed the position of the chain from her neck to her left ankle.

She went to her knees, facing me, her knees still closely together.

"That bucket," I said, "is for your wastes. Of the other two bowls, the larger is for water, the smaller for gruel."

"May I speak?" she said.

"I hereby grant you a standing permission to speak," I said, "subject to withdrawal at any time."

"I understand," she said.

"You may thank me," I said.

"Thank you," she said.

"But I trust you know how a slave is to speak," I said, "quietly, humbly, deferentially, respectfully, clearly, and so on, with excellent diction. She is not permitted strident discourse, sneering, arrogant tones, the clumsy, sharp, loutish, harsh, ungrammatical, ill-formed speech which may pass uncorrected in the case of a free woman."

"I understand," she said.

I shook some dry slave gruel into the lesser of the two bowls within her reach, moistened it a bit, stirred it with my finger, and then licked my finger and wiped it on my tunic.

"Bland," I said, "but, designed by the Green Caste and the Slavers, it is splendidly, healthily nourishing."

"I am sure it is," she said.

"Later," I said, "we may mix some fruit, or a little meat, in the bowl. You may also hope to be fed by hand eventually, or allowed to bite at and swallow food cast to the floor, like a pet sleen."

"I shall look forward to it," she said.

"Then, later," I said, "if all goes well, you may be permitted to share the repast of your master. As you know, that is common."

"If I am permitted to do so," she said, "and he takes the first bite."

"Naturally," I said.

"I am being trained," she said.

"That is in the best interest of both the master and the slave," I said. "What seems hard now will soon seem natural and proper."

Take the simple matter of kneeling before a free person. That soon feels natural, and simply the way that things should be.

I gathered that she was quite hungry for she reached for the bowl of gruel.

"You have not been granted permission to feed," I said.

She drew back her hands.

"You are not to touch the bowls with your hands," I said. "A sleen does not do so, so why should you?" I said.

"And my training continues," she said.

"Of course," I said. "You may feed."

I watched her, she on all fours, her head down. She is indeed hungry, I thought. I refrained from seizing her as she fed. That, I felt, would be inappropriate at this stage of her training. Later she could become accustomed to such things, and others. There are many ways in which one can put a woman to one's pleasure.

"For a time," I said, "you are denied human speech. If you have needs and desires, try to make them known as might an animal, say, a house sleen."

Later I pushed her away, said, "No," and left the room. On the other side of the door, I paused, and listened. I heard frustrated, pathetic whimpering, and then she was silent.

I was satisfied.

"I am beginning to know myself differently," she said.

"That is because you are becoming different," I said.

"I am beginning to feel like a slave," she said.

"What are you?" I asked.

"A slave," she said.

"The feeling then," I said, "is quite appropriate."

"Are you prepared to beg clothing?" I said.

"I very much want clothing," she said, "but I do not feel I should have to beg for it."

"Good," I said. "I was afraid that you might beg for it, and then I should have to consider whether or not to grant it to you."

"Some ample clothing?" she said.

"A tunic," I said.

"So little?" she said, bitterly.

"I fear so," I said. "One must consider proprieties, and the feelings of free women."

"Of course," she said.

"In the past few days," I said, "we have been much together, alone. Perhaps you would like to see more of the world than this room."

"I would like that very much," she said.

"Do you feel you are making progress in learning your collar?" I asked.

"I have been given very little choice," she said.

"Do you feel that you now know what it is to be a slave?" I asked.

"I think so," she said.

She would soon know even better.

"I am going to send you out alone, into the streets, shopping," I said.

"Thank you," she said.

"A slave is grateful?" I asked.

"Yes," she said, "a slave is grateful."

"Here," I said, "is a tarsk-bit, a Brundisium tarsk-bit, of which there are a hundred in a Brundisium copper tarsk. Inquire as to local markets, nearer or farther, and see what you can do in the way of tospits or larmas."

"I know little or nothing of shopping," she said. "I have never shopped in my life, save for slaves, palanquins, jewels, ropes of pearls, and such."

"Do the best you can," I said.

She took the tarsk-bit.

"On your way," I said.

"Not as I am!" she cried.

"What is wrong?" I asked.

"I am naked," she said, "naked!"

"That is all right," I said. "It does not matter. You are a slave."

"Mercy!" she cried, falling to her knees, extending her hands to me, the tarsk-bit clenched in her right hand.

"Go!" I said.

"I am Talena," she said, "Talena of Ar!"

"You are no longer of Ar," I said. "And Talena, in your case, as you know, is now no more than a slave name, a name put on a slave, as might be any other. Perhaps you would prefer a name such as Tarsk-snout or Urt-face?"

"I am the daughter of a Ubar!" she protested.

"By adoption, not blood," I said, "and you were disowned, and sequestered. Marlenus was very understanding. I would have had you kept as a slave, or instantly reduced to slavery, and thrown to the grooms in the tharlarion stables."

"I will run away!" she said.

"Do so, and accept the consequences," I said.

She sprang to her feet, sobbing, and ran from the room.

I waited, alone, in the chair, in the room.

I hoped she had not been so foolish as to attempt to flee. There was no escape for the Gorean slave girl. She was marked and collared, and clad, if clad, distinctly, usually in a brief, revealing slave tunic. She would stand out dramatically, and in no way could she be confused with a free woman. Too, there was nowhere to run. The society, like iron, closely knit and alert, approving of her bondage, was unswayably against her. What caste or clan had she, what associates or friends? At most, she might be stolen or, sooner or later, seized by another, as might be a stray kaiila. Most commonly she would be returned by a guardsman to her master. If this seemed impractical, she would be held in custody, to be claimed or, after an interval, sold.

I had lit a tharlarion-oil lamp in the room.

It was past the Twentieth Ahn.

I then heard a tiny, weak knock at the door. I opened the door and Talena collapsed into my arms, and then I let her down, gently, to her knees before me. Tied about her left wrist was a small net bag containing two tospits and a larma. I undid the bag, put it aside, and lifted her in my arms, and carried her toward the chair where the tiny tharlarion-oil lamp shed its soft circle of illumination. I laid her on her stomach before the chair.

Her back was red from beating, and on her back, shoulders, arms and legs were several welts, such as might have resulted from the strokes of a switch.

"You may speak," I said.

"Free women glared at me," she said. "I dared to meet their eyes. They put me to my belly and switched me, mercilessly."

"I speculate," I said, "that you looked upon them as might have another free woman, and not a slave."

"They hated me," she said.

"Of course," I said. "You are a slave."

It is not that unusual for a slave to be nude in public, but most often, by far, she is clothed. Public nudity is usually inflicted for one of two reasons, either as a punishment, or to deeply and graphically inform, or remind, the slave of her bondage. Whereas a slave, as an animal, need not be clothed, is not entitled to modesty, and such, there are few who are not sensitive to such issues. A tunic, even a slave strip, can be very precious to a slave. Imagine the possible misery and humiliation, particularly if you are a highly intelligent woman, as are most slaves, given the criteria of slavers, of being subjected to so profound an exposure. Imagine, particularly if you have recently been a free woman, the misery of being looked upon with hatred, scorn, and contempt by free women, formerly your peers, and finding yourself routinely, frankly, sexually appraised by passing free males, wondering what you would be like in their arms. Too, if you are stripped in public, you will most likely find yourself the butt of the ridicule of clothed slaves. Are you so poor a slave that you have not even been granted a tunic? Whereas even the slave tunic can be regarded with dismay by a new slave, horrified at having been placed in so tiny, debasing, degrading, and shaming a garment, slaves commonly, sooner or later, come to rejoice in their brief, revealing tunics, well aware of how they enhance their charms and display them for men as the most profoundly sexual, and the most exciting and desirable, of all women, the purchasable woman, the female slave.

"Avoid free women," I said. "Do not meet their eyes. If addressed, kneel immediately and put your head down. Many free women, as you know, carry switches. You know these things. You were once a free woman."

"But I was not a slave!" she wept.

"I understand these welts," I said, "and how you may have come by them, making the mistake of meeting the eyes of a free woman, perhaps even frankly, but I do not understand the beating. It seems to have been an intemperate, sore beating. That is unusual. Surely that was not administered by one or two angry free women "

"The women were involved," she said. "They prevailed upon a man to punish me. I was bound to a high slave ring, my wrists crossed and tied high over my head. Then a whip was brought. Then I was whipped, and whipped."

"What was your fault?" I asked. "Did your attitude suggest recalcitrance, insolence, displeasure, reluctance, or impatience? Did you speak crossly?"

"I did not address them as Mistress," she said.

"I see," I said.

"It hurt so," she said. "I wept, cried out, screamed with pain, and begged for mercy."

"A slave," I said, "is to address all free women as 'Mistress' and all free men as 'Master,'" I said.

"Yes," she whispered, "Master."

"You had such beatings administered routinely, did you not," I asked, "to your own female slaves in Ar, if you found their services somehow inadequate or less than fully pleasing?"

"Yes," she said, "but they were slaves."

"As you are now," I said.

"Yes," she said, "as I am now." She was on her belly. A tear fell to the floor.

"It is just as well," I said. "The two free women have saved me the trouble."

"The trouble?" she asked.

"Yes," I said. "I was thinking of having you beaten similarly, though perhaps not so lengthily or unpleasantly. I thought it would be instructive for you to experience what you did so routinely to your own slaves. You now have a better sense of what they felt."

"Could you have done that?" she asked.

"Yes," I said.

"You are genuinely thinking of keeping me as a slave," she said.

"You are a slave," I said, "whether or not I keep you is another matter."

"You could sell me?" she said.

"Of course," I said.

"But you are from Earth," she said.

"Slaves were bought and sold on Earth for thousands of years," I said, "in all the high civilizations."

"Do not sell me," she begged.

"You accept, and understand, that I could do so?" I said.

"Yes," she said, "and I am afraid. What if I displease you? It could be done with me. I am helpless. I am a slave. I control nothing. I have no say in such things. I am a property. It can be done with me not as I please, but as others please. I could be sold as easily as a tarsk."

"You are a woman," I said. "Thus, you have slave needs."

"I lied to myself for years," she said. "But I wanted to be a slave."

"That is common in females," I said. "There is a saying that all women are slaves, though not all are in collars."

"I cannot speak for all women," she said, "but the need in me, which I tried for so long to deny, to be owned, dominated, and mastered, is as real as the blood in me."

"You are a slave," I said, "and now, fully and legally. So you need have no fear. You may now rest easy. Your slave needs will be well satisfied, perhaps by dozens of masters."

"I am afraid," she said. "I am subject to you. You own me."

"You are beginning to think, feel, and act as a slave," I said.

"I cannot help myself," she said. "I do not want to help myself."

"You are not a free woman," I said. "You need not fight your bondage. You may yield to it, honestly, humbly, lovingly, and rejoicingly."

"What will you do with me?" she asked, lying on her belly, stripped, marked, and collared, before me, at my feet.

"What I please," I said.

She sobbed.

"Soon," I said, "the last bit of free woman will be taken from you."

"It is already gone," she said.

"You will learn to fear free women," I said.

"I already do," she said. "I fear them, terribly."

"These days have been pleasant," I said, "but I wish soon to join my colleagues. Much is finished here, and I must look toward Port Kar."

"Let me be at your heel," she said. "Chain me to your deck."

"It may be difficult for you to confront them as a slave," I said.

"Not if I kneel, and beg permission to kiss their feet," she said.

"You were given a tarsk-bit of Brundisium," I said, "and you brought back only two tospits and a larma. It seems that you are not skilled at bargaining."

"I will kneel and beg advice from more proficient kajirae," she said.

"My party and I have rented quarters near Brundisium's southern piers," I said, "in a mariners' inn, the Harbor's Rest. I have a lovely barbarian slave there, whom I have named Iris. As you are an ill-educated, ignorant slave, you can learn much from her."

"I," she said, "learn from a barbarian?"

"Yes," I said.

"Do you find her pleasing?" she asked.

"Yes," I said. "She is as needful and hot as a readied slave iron."

"She is not blond-haired and blue-eyed, is she?"

"No," I said, "she is, like most slaves below Torvaldsland, a brunette."

With some effort, and perhaps some stiffness and pain, Talena went to her knees before me, her knees closely together.

"Master," she said.

"Yes?" I said.

"I beg to go to nadu before you," she said.

"Very well," I said.

CHAPTER NINETY-FIVE

"What are we doing here?" I asked Seremides.

We were in the caravanserai of Alessandro, rather toward the center of the caravanserai, in the midst of dozens of tents. The tharlarion stables and wagon parks were located closer to the main gate. This made entering and leaving the caravanserai more convenient. It also kept the smells of the stables at a judicious distance.

"Marlenus," he said, "lingers."

"I thought he might," I said.

"This," he said, "is his tent."

It was a wide, high tent, presumably the property of the caravanserai of Alessandro. It could easily have housed far more than the few men Marlenus had brought north from Samnium. I supposed that the nature of this particular rental had been calculated. Numbers can be obscured in many ways. As many men might be crowded into limited quarters, so, too, few men might be housed in quarters fit for many; just as a small number of campfires would suggest the presence of few men, so, too, many campfires might suggest the presence of many men.

"I gather Decius Albus shows little inclination to budge from his holding," I said.

"Surely you do not blame him," said Seremides.

"It has been since the last passage hand," I said. "Marlenus should return to Ar. An empty throne invites occupancy."

"He thirsts for the blood of Decius Albus," said Seremides.

"He should consider slaking his thirsts differently," I said, "with ka-la-na, or paga, or female slaves."

"Speaking of female slaves," he said, "your new slave seems shy and timid, very little like a former free woman I recall."

"She now has a collar on her neck," I said.

"I trust you find her pleasing," said Seremides.

"She cannot help herself," I said. "She burns, she begs, she writhes, she is slave hot."

"We give them no choice," said Seremides. "And there is always the lash. Soon they juice at a snapping of the fingers. Who of all men would not prefer a female slave?"

"Some men," I said, "have never had a female slave in their arms."

"Of what interest is a free woman," asked Seremides, "once one has tasted slave?"

I pitied men who had never experienced the joys of the mastery. Too, I pitied the women who were slaves and had never had a master.

"We missed you for several days," he said.

"I was busy," I said.

"Training a slave?" he said.

"Yes," I said.

"A nameless animal, on whom you have put the name Talena," he said.

"Yes," I said.

"Why did you not name her Tarsk-snout or Tharlarion-dung?" he asked.

"With such a name," I said, "it is hard for a woman to be beautiful."

"What of slave wine?" asked Seremides.

"She was owned by Rask of Treve," I said.

"That was long ago," said Seremides. "She may have imbibed a releaser since then."

"It was also administered to her in her cell in Ar," I said, "after she was delivered to the justice of Marlenus, poured down her throat, she kneeling, her head back, her hands tied behind her, her nostrils pinched shut."

"Administered to her as to a slave," said Seremides.

"Yes," I said.

"Good," said Seremides, "as she was, and is, a slave, under the couching laws of Marlenus."

"I, however," I said, "saw fit to include it again, in her initial few days of slave training."

"Excellent," said Seremides.

"I had her drink it herself," I said, "slowly, kneeling before me, naked, under no duress other than my will."

"Splendid," said Seremides.

"It pleased me," I said.

"I note," he said, "that you have permitted her a tunic."

"So clad," I said, "she is less distracting on the street."

"She is fetching in it," he said.

"Are not they all?" I said. "And how is it that I find you and the others here? I go to the Harbor's Rest and you are gone. I must learn from a note and the proprietor of the Harbor's Rest your location."

"I trust you settled the bill," he said.

"Had I not," I said, "there would have been guardsmen in my wake."

"In your absence," said Seremides, "Marlenus, by means of the young Taurentian, Alan, of the House of Hesius, requested the presence of our party here in the caravanserai of Alessandro as soon as possible."

"For what reason?" I asked. "We are only six. We can do little to strengthen his arm in his tenacious, irrational quest for vengeance."

"It would seem so," said Seremides.

"Then why?" I asked.

"He senses more is involved here than swords, blood, and honor," said Seremides.

"What?" I asked.

"A beast has been seen, a Kur, we think one which was hitherto in the retinue of Decius Albus."

"Lucilius," I said. "He has now made his way here, afoot, a trek of days, from the vicinity of Samnium."

"Marlenus," said Seremides, "is fearless. If required, he would fight a larl with his bare hands, but he is uneasy with what he does not understand. Given what occurred on the beach at Port of Samnium, and his abduction by some contrived, monstrous, birdlike device, he is apprehensive at the sudden appearance of this strange beast, here, at this time and place. What does it mean?"

"Well might he be apprehensive," I said. "And I have no idea what it means. And I do not care what it means. It is his concern, not ours. I want to arrange passage for Port Kar and be on my way. Why would Marlenus seek us out? Why would he wish to contact us in this matter?"

"Marlenus," said Seremides, "knows something of the Beast Caves, suspects the failed role of Decius Albus in the theft of the Home Stone, and is familiar with the collegiality of Decius Albus and his Kur ally, or allies."

"What has this to do with us?" I asked. "Why would Marlenus turn to us?"

"Do not forget," said Seremides, "I am a hero of Ar, having returned the Home Stone of Ar."

"I have not forgotten it," I said.

"Thus," said Seremides, "given the sudden, unexpected appearance of the beast, it is quite natural that Marlenus, fearing an interference in, or a complication of, his plans, solicits our speculations."

"I see," I said.

"He suspects, for some reason, that we know more of matters concerning worlds than is common, even in the Second Knowledge."

"I have no idea what Lucilius is doing this far north," I said. "Convey our respects to the Ubar, and advise him to return to Ar and tend to the business of his throne."

"Would you care to impart so abrupt and unpleasant a response to the Ubar in person?" asked Seremides.

"Not really," I said.

"Alan, of the House of Hesius, approaches," said Seremides.

Iris ran out to meet him, but was thrust to the side.

"He seems hurried," I said. "From whence does he come?"

"From the holding of Decius Albus," said Seremides.

"How is that?" I asked.

"Ruffio of Ar, from the holding of Decius Albus, contacted Marlenus yesterday, asking that he send an agent to the holding this morning, to be informed of a matter of great importance."

"All this shortly after the appearance of the Kur," I said.

"Yes, interesting," said Seremides.

Just as he was about to enter the tent of Marlenus, near which we stood, Alan stopped short, surprised, and pleased. He cast me a look of hatred. "Good!" he said. Then he said, "I have no time now. I must report to the Ubar. But you and I have business together, business which we must soon transact. Wait. Do not flee."

"I have not had supper," I said. "Tomorrow will do."

He then hastily entered the tent.

"An unwise boy," said Seremides. "I am fond of him. Do not kill him."

Iris now knelt near us, a tear in her eye.

"Have you access to the presence of the Ubar?" I asked.

"Of course," said Seremides. "I am a hero of Ar. It was I who retrieved, and returned, her Home Stone."

"I recall," I said.

He then hobbled toward the entrance of the tent and, moments later, was admitted.

A few Ehn later, he emerged, and made his way, awkward step by awkward step, to where I waited.

"It is done," he said. "It is all over. Unpaid, and short of rations and water, the men of Decius Albus have seized him and will bring him, a bound prisoner, to Marlenus tomorrow at noon. They ask only amnesty and an unopposed passage south."

"I did not expect it to end so easily," I said. "I would have thought the holding to have been better supplied."

"I would have expected the soldiers to have demanded at least a silver tarsk each, in advance, for their treachery," said Seremides.

"Then one would know how many soldiers there were," I said.

"Why should all this occur now?" asked Seremides.

"I think," I said, "it has something to do with the appearance of the Beast."

"The paw of a beast might easily tip a scale," said Seremides.

"I think so," I said.

CHAPTER NINETY-SIX

"I would speak with the Ubar," I said.

"It is near the Tenth Ahn," said the guard. "Matters of moment are afoot."

"Even I cannot be admitted now," said Seremides.

"I do not understand," I said.

"The Ubar is displeased with us," said Seremides, "as we were of little help in explaining the surprising appearance of the Kur in camp, here in the caravanserai of Alessandro. He blames us for somehow failing him. And he labors gladly to devise arrangements for delivering the expected prisoner, Decius Albus, to Ar, for impalement, a task requiring both astuteness and subtlety. Too, he wishes to prepare letters of amnesty and passage on behalf of the former men of Decius Albus, that they may safely cross territories lying within the hegemony of Ar."

"Does it not seem strange to you," I asked, "that, shortly after the arrival of Lucilius, matters rapidly unfolded, that Ruffio ventured forth from the holding to contact Marlenus, and have him the next day send an agent to the holding to receive a message of urgent importance, which was to the effect that, given alleged deprivations in the holding, the men of Decius Albus had mutinied, seizing him, and now wished to exchange him, it seems, for amnesty and a mere uncontested passage from the caravanserai of Alessandro?"

"It could be a coincidence," said Seremides.

"Could not the matter of Ruffio have been handled under the auspices of a green flag at the holding?" I asked.

"Presumably he wished to speak directly to the Ubar," said Seremides.

"Perhaps," I said. "But his issuance from the holding and his admission to the tent of Marlenus allowed him the opportunity to assess the strength of his adversary. In the recent war of the night, our great advantage was darkness and the obscurity of our numbers. Decius Albus and his cohorts quite possibly misjudged our strength."

"Your efforts," said Seremides, "did much to encourage such an error."

"I do not know how many men remain to Decius Albus," I said, "but I am sure they well outnumber those at the disposal of Marlenus, even if we were prepared to fight on his behalf."

"Marlenus has considered the possibility of deception," said Seremides. "The men who deliver Marlenus are to be unarmed."

"Good," I said.

"So your concern, happily," said Seremides, "is without justification."

The long, loglike, ironshod hammer near the center of the caravanserai of Alessandro, swinging on its ropes, began to strike the first of ten blows on the great suspended bar.

"Stand aside, or clear the area," said the guard. "The mutineers with their prisoner approach."

"Back, back, away," said another guard. "Do not interfere. Keep your distance."

We withdrew as Marlenus himself, bearded and ferocious, with a swirl of his cape, and a regal stride, emerged from the shade of the tent.

He cast us a look of tolerant contempt and then turned his attention to the small number of approaching figures.

"The Kur!" gasped Seremides.

"Yes," I said. I then turned about, uneasily, and signaled to those of my party that they should approach, Thurnock and Clitus, Xenon and Aetius.

"All is well," said Seremides. "The Kur leads Decius Albus, swathed in chains, on a chain-linked tether, and those with them, only four, seem weak and distraught; they stumble and seem almost unable to stand. "One cries 'Water,' piteously. I see no belts, no sheaths, no swords, no knives."

"To me," I said, "none seems starving or thirsting."

"At least," said Aetius, now with the others at our side, "they do not have weapons."

The Kur, Decius Albus, and the four men with them then entered the tent, followed by Marlenus, and his men.

"Draw your weapons," I said. "Free your tools of war."

As I expected, one of the men of Marlenus, after an Ehn or so, came to the entrance of the tent, and motioned that we should approach and enter.

"Odd," said Seremides, "that Marlenus should now reverse himself, inviting us within."

"Indeed," I said.

"Surely Decius Albus had more than four men," said Thurnock.

"I am sure he has several more," I said.

"Where are they?" asked Xenon.

"I do not know," I said.

"We are again signaled within," said Seremides.

"Notice," I said, "that the man of Marlenus who signals to us wears no sword belt."

"Odd," said Seremides.

I pulled off my knife sheath, discarding it, and slipped the knife inside my tunic.

"The business seems urgent," said Thurnock.

"We must not keep the Ubar waiting," I said. "Keep your weapons ready."

We were scarcely at the entrance of the wide, high tent when a raucous, commanding voice, that of Decius Albus, he now free of chains and leash, cried out, "Enter and cast down your weapons or the Ubar dies!"

We entered the tent.

My men looked to me with wild regard.

"Cast down your weapons," I said.

At one point in the tent, toward the center, Marlenus and his men were kneeling, crowded together, their weapons lying to the side.

About them, standing, with drawn knives, ready to strike, were the four men of Decius Albus.

It was easy to conjecture what had occurred.

As soon as Marlenus and his party had entered the tent, unsuspecting and confident, weapons sheathed, unready for war, the four men of Decius Albus, presumably weak, starved, and thirsting, had whipped out concealed knives, and rushed to threaten the Ubar. Then, rather than risk the life of the Ubar, his men had complied with the directives of Decius Albus.

"You sported with us," said Decius Albus, addressing Marlenus. "You played us for fools, in the darkness, but now it is you who are the fool."

"Yes," said Marlenus, "now it is I who am the fool. What now ensues?"

"My plans proceed," said Decius Albus.

My men and I stood to one side.

Lucilius crouched nearby, almost as though he might be some large, uncomprehending pet, but I was confident that it had been at his direction that this untoward situation had come to fruition. He carried no weapon, but one paw was tangled in the chains which had been swathed about Decius Albus. The weight of those chains, wielded with the might of a Kur, would constitute a terrible weapon.

"Tal," said Ruffio entering the tent, smiling, nodding to Decius Albus, Lucilius, Marlenus and his men, and to me and my party. He greeted us with universal accord. I was almost willing to consider not killing him. At least, a competent rogue deserves respect. I admired him, and particularly for his cleverness and proficiency in the demanding and hazardous business of delivering Talena to Ar.

"It seems things go well," said Ruffio.

Four of the men of Decius Albus, armed, then entered the tent. I sensed that there were others outside. I did not know how many men Decius Albus had at his disposal after the night war of some days ago, but I guessed some thirty or so.

"Where is the slave?" demanded Decius Albus.

"In hand," said Ruffio.

"Bring her forth," said Decius Albus.

"First," said Ruffio, "be warned. She is changed."

"How so?" said Decius Albus, warily.

"She is collared," said Ruffio.

"Collars may be removed," said Decius Albus. "Let us see her."

Four more men of Decius Albus drifted into the tent, and then, a bit later, three more. As they entered in small groups their presence would not be much noted.

Clearly our situation was worsening.

Marlenus and those with him, disarmed, remained on their knees, crowded together.

"I am waiting," said Decius Albus.

Had the life of the Ubar not been in imminent peril, I was sure that the men of Marlenus would not have surrendered their weapons and placed themselves at so dire a disadvantage.

Alan, of the House of Hesius, the young Taurentian, knelt at his Ubar's side. How his young, hot blood must have rankled. I feared that, were it not for the jeopardy to which it would subject his Ubar, he would have sprung up like a wild beast and attacked the knife-wielding men of Decius Albus barehanded. Youth is often intemperate, bold, and short-sighted. I suspected, incidentally, that priorities in the tent might be in conflict. It seemed clear to me that Decius Albus would wish to have Marlenus killed, sooner or later; certainly he was aware of the determination of the Ubar to bring him to a sharp, rude justice, one way or another, for his treason. Who would want a vengeful sleen on one's trail? On the other hand, I was sure, at least from my experience at the rendezvous point, that Lucilius and Agamemnon would want to keep the Ubar alive, that he might be eventually pressured into, or recruited into, the cause of the Kurii. He, with his power and resources, would be an invaluable asset in furthering, even if only temporarily, the global ambitions of the Kurii. Agamemnon, for example, could have easily disposed of him on the beach at Port of Samnium, but had not done so. Thus, as I assessed the situation, Decius Albus was determined to do away with the Ubar and Lucilius would be determined to protect him.

"Very well," said Ruffio, and then he turned about, and, raising his voice a little, called out, "Bring the slave."

One man, followed by two others, entered the tent. He conducted the collared, barefooted, tunicked Talena, bent over, held by the hair, her head at his left hip, into the tent and released her before Decius Albus. Instantly she fell to her knees, knees closely together, head down, palms of hands on her thighs.

"What is the meaning of this?" barked Decius Albus. "Get on your feet! Stand up! Stand up!"

Talena rose gracefully, and stood as a slave.

Men gasped at her beauty.

"No!" cried Decius Albus. "Stand as a free woman!"

Talena collapsed to her knees, trembling. "Please no, Master," she said. "I am a slave. I dare not do so."

"Of course you are a slave!" cried Decius Albus. "But stand as a free woman!"

"Please no, Master," she wept. "I fear to do so. I would be beaten."

"Forgive her, noble Albus," said Ruffio. "She has apparently felt the whip."

"And she can feel it again," bellowed Decius Albus, "if she does not obey!"

Ruffio drew Talena gently to her feet by the hair, held in his right hand, and then he turned her left side to Decius Albus and, with his left hand, pulled the tunic up to her waist.

"No!" cried Decius Albus, in fury. He had had the small neat brand of Treve which she had worn removed, and had had her thigh smoothed and healed. But now that lovely thigh, just below the hip, on the left side, bore, clearly and attractively, unmistakably, another brand.

"She is marked!" he cried, enraged. "And with the common Kef! As might be a common slave!"

"I fear," said Ruffio, letting the hem of her tunic fall, and removing his hand from her hair, "she is a common slave."

Talena quickly went again to her knees, and smoothed the tunic, for female slaves are women, and, indeed, women amongst women, and have a woman's vanity.

"We removed one brand, and can remove another," said Decius Albus.

"Things are not so simple," said Ruffio. "This cannot be done over and over. You risk disfiguring the slave."

"No matter," said Decius Albus.

"The changing of a brand," said Ruffio, "is a secret difficult to keep. And you may fare less successfully a second time, if you were successful the first time."

"What do you mean?" asked Decius Albus, narrowly.

"There are rumors in the taverns," said Ruffio. "Men talk, perhaps even those of the green caste and of the Slavers."

"That cannot be," growled Decius Albus.

"It might be worth a silver tarsk, or more, to Lurius of Jad," said Ruffio, "to be apprised of the matter."

"Do you threaten me?" asked Decius Albus.

"Certainly not," said Ruffio. "Compared to me a paving stone is as a chattering jard."

"Yet, silence has its price," said Decius Albus.

"I have heard so," said Ruffio.

"Perhaps half of what I receive from Lurius of Jad?" asked Decius Albus.

"That would be satisfactory," said Ruffio.

"I think I will have you killed," said Decius Albus.

"And every man in this tent, as well?" asked Ruffio.

The men of Decius Albus in the tent exchanged glances.

"Ho!" said Marlenus, from his knees. "Hear me. Hear me now. For you, noble Albus, traitor to Ar, betrayer of your Home Stone, time is short. Even now a thousand men of Ar march north."

"Come now," said Decius Albus. "Surely you can manage something better than that."

"I left word," said Marlenus. "If word was not received from me by the passage hand, a thousand men would march, to succor or avenge me."

Lucilius lifted his shaggy head. His large, six-digited, prehensile paw tightened on the chains he held.

"There is no relieving force," said Decius Albus. "That is an obvious lie, not only transparent but flimsy, invented in desperation."

"They would be more than enough to storm your holding," said Marlenus.

"Even were there such a force," said Decius Albus, "I would be rich and safe in Cos, long before its arrival in the vicinity of Brundisium."

"In any event," said Ruffio, "even if there is no such force, I do not think you have the time to dally near Brundisium."

"I wager there is time," said Decius Albus.

"Then you have not heard the rumors," said Ruffio.

"What rumors?" said Decius Albus.

"That Talena of Ar is somewhere in the great caravanserai of Alessandro, and that a party of Ar intends to deliver her to Lurius of Jad for a fortune, a fortune which might, if properly diverted, enrich the coffers of the Harbor Masters of Brundisium."

"What is the origin of such rumors?" asked Decius Albus. "Do they exist? How do they come about?"

"Who knows?" asked Ruffio.

"Tarsk!" said Decius Albus. "Do you not care from whose hand you receive gold?"

"Not as long as it adds weight to my purse," said Ruffio.

"I shall have ropes put on your wrists and ankles, and have draft tharlarion driven in opposite directions," said Decius Albus.

"There is no reason to be unpleasant, noble Albus," said Ruffio. "Lurius of Jad, as we know, is not interested in a slave. It would not serve his purposes."

"We will present the slave as a free woman," said Decius Albus.

"I do not think you can pass her off again as a free woman," said Ruffio.

"Why not?" demanded Decius Albus.

"For two reasons," said Ruffio. "The first reason is that too many people believe she is a slave, and the second reason is that she is a slave."

"I do not understand," said Decius Albus.

Ruffio turned to the kneeling, frightened Talena.

Then, without warning, he said, sharply, "Bara!"

Instantly Talena, flung herself to her belly, with her wrists crossed behind her, her ankles crossed, and her head turned to the left.

He then, mercilessly, rapidly, uttered a series of sharp commands, "Lesha!" "Inspection!" "First Obeisance!" "Second Obeisance!" "Tower!" "Bracelets!" "Sula!" "Nadu!" and others, to each of which the slave responded, without thought, instantly, reflexively, beautifully, at the conclusion of which she collapsed at his feet.

Utterances of approval coursed amongst the men in the tent.

How well she had done, I thought, but, of course, one could always demand better.

It pleased me that the slave was learning her collar, and I was pleased, as well, that the particular collar on her neck was mine.

"There!" said Ruffio. "See! Now, what if, in Jad, one should, unexpectedly, taking her unawares, utter such a command? She would respond instantly, without thinking, as trained to do, and would ruin your game, betraying her condition, that of slave."

Decius Albus clenched his fists and howled with rage.

"If one path is blocked," said Ruffio, "choose another."

Decius Albus glared down at Talena, in frustration, in fury.

"You have coin," said Ruffio. "You could buy and sell. You can invest in voyages. You could lend at scurrilous rates of interest. You have men. You could seize roads and charge tolls. You could turn bandit and despoil caravans. You could form a free company and hire out as soldiery."

"Take her away! Get her out of my sight!" screamed Decius Albus.

I stepped forth.

"Hold!" said a man of Decius Albus.

"Your fee giver," I said, "wishes the slave removed."

I held my hands out, that they might see they held no weapons.

"Do not approach the noble Albus more closely," said the guard.

I measured the distance to Decius Albus.

"I know you. I know you from Ar," said Decius Albus. "You are Geoffrey of Harfax."

I wondered if he knew me, too, from the night of battle, in the darkness, from the confusion, from the wild shadows, from the torches.

"I am the owner of the slave," I said. "You may read her collar."

At this point, Marlenus rose to his feet, from the knot of men about him.

"Crawl to the side, Slave," I said to Talena. Her lips formed the words, "Yes, Master," and then she, head down, tunicked, hair loose about her, crawled away, to the side. Should steel flash like flames, I wanted her outside the domain of war.

"Who gave you permission to rise?" inquired Decius Albus of Marlenus.

"I, Marlenus, Ubar of Ar, gave myself permission to rise," said Marlenus.

Decius Albus looked at the kneeling men about Marlenus. "Beware, foolish, duped, disarmed tarsks," said Decius Albus. "One unwise move and the Ubar is the first to die."

Lucilius reacted to this. I saw his massive body tense.

"Do not gloat, Marlenus of Ar," warned Decius Albus. "The stones are in my grasp, not yours. I may have been misled and foiled in my far-reaching endeavors, but you are well within my power. Tremble, and beg. Perhaps I will spare you another Ehn or so to live."

"I do not choose to comply," said Marlenus. "What matters it if I am slain now or a moment later?"

"Rile me not," said Decius Albus. "I will soon have your blood."

"Or I yours," said Marlenus.

In my time on the Steel World of Agamemnon, I had become reasonably familiar with Kurii. The large, pointed ears of Lucilius were now flattened back against the sides of his head; his breath was quickening; the moist tip of a fang protruded from below his upper lip; and the claws were half emerged from his forepaws.

Much attention was focused on the exchange between Marlenus of Ar, standing like a Ubar amongst his kneeling men, and the glowering, threatening Decius Albus.

I feared that Lucilius would spring to his feet, with what consequences I had no idea, and did not wish to learn.

Why had Marlenus stood when he did?

Had he, too, in his mind, measured the distance between me and Decius Albus?

"I can have you slain where you stand," raged Decius Albus to Marlenus.

"I contest that not," said Marlenus.

I thrust the guard to the side and rushed toward the startled Decius Albus, who, I think, only half saw me approach. I did not strike him, buffet him, or engage him, at least bluntly, directly. Rather I brushed past him, scarcely touching him, and was then behind him, my left arm about his neck, pulling him off balance, half backward, while my right hand whipped the concealed knife from my tunic, the edge of which knife I then pressed across his throat.

Consternation reigned.

Four of his men had carried concealed knives, so why might I not do so, as well?

Those with Marlenus rose, too, to their feet, but they were unarmed, and ringed with steel.

There was shouting, cursing.

I think Talena might have screamed.

"Cast down your weapons!" I cried, hoping that this forceful demand, coupled with the seeming danger to Decius Albus, and the surprise and bewilderment presumably felt by the men of Decius Albus, would combine to produce a thoughtless compliance. But mercenaries were, as I had feared, not about to disarm themselves before adversaries, regardless of the threat to Decius Albus. "Do it, do it!" said Decius Albus. But not even a knife was discarded. The position of Decius Albus was quite different from that of Marlenus earlier. Marlenus was a Ubar whose life was to be preserved by honorable, devoted men at all costs, many of whom even shared a Home Stone with him; Decius Albus, on the other hand, was an employer, whose purse, however deep, might be exchanged for that of another.

"Dear friends," said Ruffio. "I think we are confronted here by an interesting situation. One constant is clear. Intelligent mercenaries, examples of which, I flatter myself, are all about, both within the tent and outside the tent, are not going to willingly place themselves at the mercy of determined foes. Therefore, despite the proposal of our friend, the well-meaning, genial Geoffrey of Harfax, we must look further for a solution to the problem facing us. I submit, therefore, the following solution which, while not ideal, has much to commend it, in particular, the minimizing of slaughter. We shall return, in essence, to yesterday. All are armed, and unengaged. So, let the men of Decius Albus, armed, step away from their foes, allowing them to arm themselves. This done, Geoffrey of Harfax will remove his knife from the throat of Decius Albus and rejoin his fellows. Is that agreeable, Geoffrey?"

"That leaves numbers in favor of Decius Albus," I said. "He has more men, including those outside the tent, and doubtless about the caravanserai, as well, than I and Marlenus."

"No plan is perfect," said Ruffio.

"I accept!" said Marlenus.

"And you, noble Geoffrey of Harfax?" inquired Ruffio.

"Marlenus accepts," I said. "Then so, too, will I."

I removed the knife from the throat of Decius Albus and he, cursing, shuddering, presumably elated at finding himself alive, rushed yards away. Then, in a moment, his forces in the great tent were aligned against those of Marlenus and myself.

"I neglected to mention," said Ruffio, "that, counting on those outside the tent, as well as those inside the tent, and variously about, allowing for a desertion or two, Decius Albus has at his disposal forty-two men at arms."

"We conjectured as much," said Marlenus.

I had hoped that there might be as few as thirty, but that seemed not so.

"Summon my men, those outside, all of them," said Decius Albus, now with sword in hand, to an armsman in his livery, a black tunic with two white stripes, who was within the entrance to the tent. "We will bring this matter to a swift, bloody conclusion."

Lucilius knotted his paw more closely within the lengths of chain in his grasp.

The armsman turned about and hurried from the tent.

I dared not send my small contingent alone against Decius Albus and his readied men.

"Let us attack now," I begged Marlenus, "while there is a parity, before the foe is reinforced. Clearly we would be likely to fare better in two small, successive, more evenly matched battles than in one against an overwhelming foe."

But Marlenus threw back his head and laughed.

"Ubar!" I protested.

The armsman who had been sent forth to summon the balance of the forces of Decius Albus reentered the tent, white-faced, wildly. "There are no men outside!" he cried.

Ruffio sped from the tent.

"Go forth, bring them in!" demanded Decius Albus of the armsman.

"They are not there!" cried the armsman.

"Liar!" screamed Decius Albus. Then he turned to others at his side. He pointed to the armsman who had borne an unwelcome intelligence. "Kill him!" said Decius Albus.

But, to the fury of Decius Albus, none of his men hastened to follow his order. These men were mercenaries and were in no hurry to reduce their numbers in the face of an enemy, particularly in an unclear and possibly problematic situation.

At that point Ruffio reentered the tent. "Noble Albus," he said, "hundreds of men have entered the caravanserai. They have cast aside their cloaks. On their tunics is emblazoned the sign of Ar!"

Those with Marlenus uttered a cheer.

"Shortly ago," said Marlenus, "I saw Marcus Rufus, Primus in the Pride of the Golden Larl, outside the tent."

One of the mercenaries tore his livery, with two white stripes, down to his waist.

Others looked to one another.

"Remain in place!" said Decius Albus.

Then, as if responding to some command heard only by themselves, surely one silent to all others, the mercenaries began to make their way from the tent.

"Stop! Stop!" cried Decius Albus.

"It seems desertion is rampant," said Ruffio, moving toward the entrance to the tent. Then he was gone.

Scarcely some Ihn later, Decius Albus stood alone, sword in hand, on one side of the tent while I and my party and Marlenus and his men stood on the other side. Momentarily, I felt sorry for the former trade advisor.

Marlenus stepped forth from those with him. He regarded Decius Albus. "We meet," he said.

"Do you expect me to run?" asked Decius Albus.

"No," said Marlenus. "If you wish, cast down your sword, accept chains, and prepare to depart, to be taken to Ar for public impalement."

"I do not think I choose to do so," said Decius Albus.

"Very well," said Marlenus.

"My skills, of course, are not equal to yours," said Decius Albus.

"I will be quick," said Marlenus.

"The Ubar is generous," said Decius Albus.

"We were friends," said Marlenus.

"You were my friend," said Decius Albus. "I was not yours."

"As I discovered, to my dismay," said Marlenus.

"Move your men back," said Decius Albus, "and let those with the noble Geoffrey of Harfax move back, as well, that they not intrude on our dealings, on our discussion with steel."

At a nod from Marlenus, we all moved back, away from the Ubar.

"Let their weapons be sheathed," said Decius Albus, "that they not, in a moment of passion, be tempted to interfere."

"Let it be so," said Marlenus, and we reluctantly sheathed our weapons.

"Dear Ubar," said Decius Albus. "Shall we quaff a goblet of wine together, recollecting more pleasant times, before we begin?"

"I am not thirsty," said Marlenus.

"Do you mind if I do?" asked Decius Albus.

"No," said Marlenus.

"I hope that you will not hurry me," said Decius Albus.

"Take what time you will," said Marlenus.

This dallying, if dallying it was, I suspected, might take its toll on a younger, less experienced swordsman, say, an Alan, of the House of Hesius, troubling him, increasing apprehension, perhaps encouraging him to an attack less well considered or too precipitate, but I did not think it would have any effect of that sort on the Ubar of Ar, who had nerves like stone and reflexes like the strike of an ost, who may have survived more than a hundred duels in which only one combatant left the field.

Decius Albus went to the side of the tent where there were some boxes, vessels, utensils, and a table. He selected a large goblet, almost twice the size of a common paga goblet, and poured into it a large amount of what I assumed was paga. I half expected him to offer the Ubar a toast, put it to his lips, sip, and, shortly thereafter, collapse, dead, to the carpet flooring of the tent. But, it seemed, he chose instead to meet the steel of the Ubar. He approached Marlenus, his sword in his left hand, the goblet in his right. Hitherto, he had gripped his sword in his right hand, so I had naturally assumed him to be right-handed, which is most common amongst Goreans as amongst those of my former world, Earth. Indeed, it is most common amongst Kurii, as well.

"Stop," said Marlenus. "Do not approach more closely."

Decius Albus stopped, and lifted the goblet toward Marlenus. "Drink?" he asked.

"I am not thirsty," said Marlenus.

"You do not mind if I drink?" inquired Decius Albus.

"No," said Marlenus.

Decius Albus lifted the goblet, tilted it, and put his lips to the brim, but I do not think he drank.

What occurred then took place so quickly that we who witnessed it scarcely understood what we were seeing, saw, and had seen.

"Drink!" cried Decius Albus and hurled the fluid from the goblet into the face of Marlenus, who, an instant later, cried out in pain, and stumbled backward, while Decius Albus, discarding the goblet, transferred his sword into his right hand, and leaped after the Ubar, sword raised to strike. But the blow did not fall, for a long length of chain, one end of which was in the grasp of the Kur, Lucilius, swinging, flying through the air, flung with great force, snapped twice about the head and body of Decius Albus, and jerked him backward, away from the Ubar, and into the Kur's grasp. "My face burns!" cried Marlenus. The last sight Decius Albus saw was the enraged visage of Lucilius, its large, fang-filled maw reaching for his throat.

"Call for one of the green caste!" cried a man.

"Hurry!" cried another.

Several men sped from the tent, calling out for a physician.

"The Ubar burns but I cannot see the flames!" cried a man.

One man was trying to wipe the fluid from the Ubar's face but quickly drew back his hand, shaking it as though an urt had gripped it in its fangs, and reeled away, crying out in pain.

"Bring water! Wash the unseen fire away!" called out a man.

The Ubar's eyes were clenched shut. Strange corrugations and swellings seemed to erupt upon his countenance.

I stood to one side.

"Ost venom!" cried a man.

I did not think so.

Ost venom produces such ravages only when it reaches the blood stream.

I could see where holes had been burned in the carpet, where some of the fluid had splashed. That fluid, whatever it was, I was sure, could have eaten, or burned, holes in leather.

Nearby lay what was left of Decius Albus.

Lucilius crouched to the side, in a common Kur passive, resting posture. His long tongue, red, licked his bloody lips. He looked at me with a grimace which I had learned long ago on the Steel World of Agamemnon was a Kur smile, and then he looked away.

Two members of the green caste, presumably on the staff of the caravanserai of Alessandro, summoned from the central buildings, entered the tent and hurried to where the Ubar lay on the carpeting of the tent. They began to sponge the face of the Ubar with water which had been earlier brought, and, a bit later, began to apply soothing lotion to his wounds. I think that neither was familiar with the case they were treating, but they seemed to be treating it well enough, intelligently enough, intuitively. Chemical weapons, to the best of my knowledge, were unfamiliar in Gorean warfare. The use of such a fluid, presumably some sort of acid, spoke more clearly of the technology of a Steel World.

"I can see," said Marlenus.

Apparently he had instantly, reflexively, closed his eyes when Decius Albus had flung the contents of the goblet toward his face.

I did not care to look upon the face of the Ubar. Patches of his face seemed to have been abraded or scraped away. His beard, on the left side of his face, as he had turned away from the attack, was muchly gone, as though burned away.

Talena, who had approached, screamed, and covered her eyes.

"Get that slave out of here," said Marlenus.

"Go," I said to the slave, and she turned about and fled from the tent.

I knew the subtlety of the green caste. I was sure they could, eventually, muchly repair the countenance of the Ubar.

"Hand me my sword," commanded Marlenus, as he tried to rise, but was held back by two of his men. Alan, he of the House of Hesius, stood by, stricken at being unable to succor the Ubar. "My sword!" demanded the Ubar. "Let it seek its sheath," said one of the men with him. "It is no longer needed. The traitor, Decius Albus, no longer lives." "My sword!" said Marlenus. It was placed in his hand. The Ubar then shook off the men who would hold him in place and struggled to his feet. He then went to the remains of Decius Albus, and I feared he would plunge the sword into the dead body, but, shaking, trembling, at last victorious in his struggle with himself, he did not do so. The codes do not permit the mutilation of a slain foe. Angrily, with a crack, he thrust the blade back into its sheath.

Then, sobering, aghast, he examined the remains.

"What has been done here?" he asked.

Lucilius looked up.

"I killed him for you," said Lucilius. "He would have killed you. I saved your life. You owe me much."

"What did he say?" asked Marlenus, fighting to find Gorean phonemes in the guttural discourse of the Kur.

It can be difficult to follow the speech of a Kur even when it speaks Gorean. It was also difficult for me, though much depends on the particular Kur, and how familiar you are with his mode of discourse. I had spoken with Lucilius before, in the Beast Caves, and this was helpful. Also, of course, I had learned to follow the discourse of Grendel, and I had much managed to improve my interpretation of Kur Gorean when I had been on the Steel World of Agamemnon. Accordingly, I managed, reasonably well, to convey at least the gist of the Kur's discourse to Marlenus.

"I owe a beast nothing," said Marlenus.

"You are the beast," said Lucilius. "I am Kur. And you owe me your life."

"Only in the sense that one might owe it to a guard sleen," said Marlenus.

"Not quite," said Lucilius.

"You were the pet of Decius Albus," said Marlenus.

"I am not a pet," said Lucilius. "I have stood in the rings. I am of high station. I am deputy to Agamemnon, Eleventh Face of the Nameless One."

"You were in league with Decius Albus," said Marlenus.

"He failed," said Lucilius. "He is no longer needed. Hail, Marlenus."

"I do not understand," said Marlenus.

"I am your friend," said Lucilius. "I saved your life. You owe me much. Hail, Marlenus!"

"How is it that an animal, a beast, so salutes me?" asked Marlenus.

"Lord Agamemnon could have killed you on the beach at Port of Samnium," said Lucilius. "But he did not. I could have killed you in the forest outside Samnium. But I did not. And now I have saved your life. I trust you will show your gratitude."

"What do you want?" asked Marlenus, wiping some peeled skin from his face. "A bar of gold, a coffer of silver?"

"My lord, Agamemnon, and I," said Lucilius, "want for you only what you would want for yourself."

"I want Ar and honor," said Marlenus.

"So little?" asked Lucilius.

"I do not understand," said Marlenus.

"Are you not the most fierce and ambitious of Ubars?" asked Lucilius.

Marlenus was silent. He almost touched his face again, but refrained from doing so. I am sure he was still in considerable pain.

"You have land, power, and wealth," said Lucilius, "but surely what land, power, and wealth you possess is too little to satisfy an appetite so great, so monstrous, as yours."

"You saved my life," said Marlenus. "You may depart in peace."

"He who has ten gold tarn disks," said Lucilius, "wants ten more. Who, who has tasted power, does not want more power? Is that not the headiest and most irresistible of wines?"

"I do not care to hear you speak further," said Marlenus.

"Hail, Marlenus, Ubar of Ar," said Lucilius. "And perhaps one day men will cry Hail, Marlenus, Ubar of all Gor!"

"Go," said Marlenus.

I sensed that the Ubar was afraid, afraid of himself. Is not oneself too often one's secret enemy, he from whom one has the most to fear?

"Decius Albus is dead," said Lucilius. "I killed him for you. You owe me much. Perhaps one day we will meet again and talk."

"I do not think so," said Marlenus.

Lucilius then left the tent. His exit was uncontested.

CHAPTER NINETY-SEVEN

"What was that thing yesterday," asked Marlenus, his face muchly bandaged, "that animal with paws like hands, with accouterments, buckled in aristocratic harness, which spoke so mutilated a Gorean?"

"It was a Kur," I said, "an ambitious, fierce form of life. They had a world once, which they destroyed. Some survived, and multiplied. Most occupy artificial worlds, orbiting, like Gor and Terra, the blazing star, Tor-tu-Gor. Their home world destroyed in internecine combat, in absurd and cruel tribal altercations; they hope to obtain another."

"Gor," said Marlenus.

"Gor or Terra," I said, "presumably Gor, as it is less polluted, as it is greener and fresher, less despoiled by greed and reckless exploitation."

"What did it want of me?" asked Marlenus.

"What it wanted of Decius Albus," I said, "an ally, one who would, to further his own interest, abet their schemes."

"They are powerful?" said Marlenus.

"Very much so," I said.

"Why then," he asked, "do they not simply scize Gor?"

"Priest-Kings are more powerful," I said.

"Then Gor has little to fear," said Marlenus.

"She has much to fear," I said. "Priest-Kings seldom interfere in the doings of other species. For example, commonly, as long as their technology laws are respected, and they themselves do not feel threatened, they let human beings love and kill one another much as they please. Similarly, they would be unlikely to intervene in wars between humans and Kurii. Thus, Gor might become a Kur world, with humans becoming an extinct or reduced species on this world, with the likely result of harming this world, and possibly, eventually, given technologies familiar on the artificial worlds, wresting it from the Priest-Kings themselves, a result unlikely to have been anticipated by the Priest-Kings."

"Why do the Priest-Kings not seek out and destroy the artificial worlds?" asked Marlenus.

"It is not their way," I said.

"Perhaps," said Marlenus thoughtfully, "the beasts might, with the aid of favored humans, come to power on Gor and then, gratefully, share a planet's wealth with their human allies."

"It is not their way," I said.

"There has never been a Ubar of all Gor," he said.

"I trust," I said, "that there never will be."

"Once Gor was a unified Ubarate under a single Ubar," said Marlenus, "what would there be to fear from the beasts who had helped to bring it about?"

"Much," I said.

"Think," said Marlenus, "one Ubarate, one Ubar, unity, efficiency, no confusions, no inconsistencies, no duplications, no waste, just order and perfection, peace, security and prosperity for all, a single plan, no plethora of hostile cities, no competition, just one glorious Ubarate under one Ubar, doing good, producing happiness for all."

"Beware," I said. "Let there be liberty. Without liberty there is stagnation and repression. To deny difference is to deny possibility and change. Let there be a hundred thoughts, not one. Where all must think alike thought does not exist. Better a hundred plans, living and competing, than one plan imposed by tyranny. Better a hundred different cities for a hundred different wills and desires. Let there be different cities that one may move amongst them as one wishes. The purpose of walls is to keep out the enemy, not to confine citizens."

"You have nothing to fear," said Marlenus. "I shall resist the solicitations of beasts."

"Good," I said.

CHAPTER NINETY-EIGHT

"Behold," said Marlenus, "I think you will find this of interest."

"What, Ubar?" I asked.

"You see my soldier there?" said Marlenus, gesturing.

"The officer," I said. "The high officer."

"You know him?" asked Marlenus.

"Only as of recently," I said. "And only by name and sight. He is first amongst the thousand men of Ar who arrived in so timely a fashion two days ago in the caravanserai, Marcus Rufus, Primus in the Pride of the Golden Larl."

"You do not recognize him beyond that?" asked Marlenus.

"I do not think so," I said. "There may seem something familiar about him."

"I would have you fetch your slave," he said, "and have her inform him that he is to report to me."

"Talena?" I said.

"Yes," said Marlenus, "not the other one, not the barbarian."

I clapped my hands sharply and Talena, who was some yards away, in the shadow behind the tent I shared with my party, looked up from her work, buffing the walking boots of Aetius. I pointed to the ground at my feet, and she put down the boot on which she was working, and hurried to kneel before me, head down. She was trembling. I think she was afraid to be in the presence of Marlenus.

"Slave," said I, pointing, "the Ubar wishes to have his officer, there, he at the corner of the striped tent, report to him. Convey the message."

Talena rose to her feet and hurried toward the officer but, suddenly, stopped short, stood for moment, and then fled back to my feet.

"Please no, Master," she wept. "Not he! Send Iris, please, Master. I would fear for my life!"

"Have no fear, Tarl of Bristol," said Marlenus. "He is a high officer, and an honorable man. If he slays your worthless slave, he may be depended upon to compensate you for your loss."

"Please, Master," begged Talena, "do not send me to him!"

"Do I know him from somewhere?" I asked Marlenus.

"I think so," said Marlenus. "Do you not recall the theater of Pub-lius, and the trial of an arrogant, treasonous slut, one who, knowing herself secure in her protected role of defendant, abused her legal impunity by spitting on one of her four guards?"

"So high an officer was a guard?" I asked.

"And so, too, were the other three," said Marlenus.

"And it was he, I gather," I said, "on whom she spat."

"Yes," said Marlenus.

I looked down on the kneeling Talena, whose tear-stained face was raised to me. I did not think she was really in danger, but I could understand her terror. She was a female, and in a Gorean collar. "It is all right," I said. "You need not go. I will call Iris."

"You will not force me to go?" she said, uncertainly.

"No," I said.

"Then," she said, "I will go, Master. I did a terrible, unwarranted thing. I realize that now. I was displeasing, and deliberately so. I knew so little and I was so stupid. I beg to be afforded the opportu-nity to try to make amends. How foolish I was. I am so ashamed. I, a slave, dared to act as might have a free woman, and one abrupt, nasty, and proud. What I did was wrong, terribly wrong. I am sorry. I be-haved badly. Forgive me. I behaved poorly. I betrayed my condition."

I regarded her, contrite, at my feet.

"A command need not be repeated, Master," she said, and leaped to her feet and sped to the officer. Before him, she knelt down, sob-bing, and kissed his feet, over and over, and then dried them with her hair.

We could not make out what passed between them, if anything, but we conjectured its possible nature. An Ehn or so later the officer approached us and saluted Marlenus.

"Prepare the men," said Marlenus. "We march tomorrow."

"Yes, Ubar," said Marcus Rufus, who then saluted, sharply, and withdrew.

"Ubar," I said. "I thank you for standing when you did, at the risk of your life, in the tent. It drew attention away from me, when I was near to Decius Albus. Without that distraction, I might not have been able to get my knife to his throat."

"I suspected your plan," said Marlenus. "I hoped to increase its chances of success."

"Warrior," I said.

"Warrior," he said.

"Talena," I said, "was your daughter by adoption not blood."

"Yes," said Marlenus.

"And it was your intent to later barter her in companionship for political purposes?" I said.

"Yes," he said.

"Would you do that with a blood daughter?" I asked.

"Certainly not," he said.

"Why did you not have several daughters by adoption," I asked, "thus storing up a treasury of such expedient, barterable articles?"

"Rarity increases value," he said. "In the politics of companionship, one daughter is priceless, two are less valuable, and so on."

"And what of sons," I asked, "by adoption or blood?"

"Sons are dangerous," he said. "What wise ruler would place rivals in his own house? What wise ruler would nurture osts at the side of his throne?"

"I wish you well," I said.

"I wish you well," he said, and then turned and left.

Talena lay collapsed, huddled, on the ground for a time, where she had presented herself to the officer, and then rose, and came to kneel before me. She seemed happy.

"Continue your work," I said. "Attend to the boots of Aetius."

"Yes, Master," she said.

CHAPTER NINETY-NINE

"I suspect," said Ruffio, "that Lurius of Jad will not be pleased with recent doings. In any event, it will not be I who rush to bring him unwelcome tidings. Indeed, as matters have turned out, I think I am well advised not to cross to the shores of Cos. I could return to Ar, of course, but I would not expect to stand high in the favor of Marlenus."

"That leaves, however, most of a planet to choose from," I said.

"If only I had several Home Stones from which to choose," he said.

"Doubtless you will claim whichever might seem useful, and fit and proper, at the moment," I said.

"Gold is my Home Stone," he said. "Incidentally, did I not manage the 'knife-at-the-throat' moment well, thereby resolving an otherwise awkward dilemma?"

"Somewhat," I said.

"Certainly it would not have done to have your blade at the throat of Decius Albus and knives at the heart of the Ubar until, say, the next passage hand."

"That would not have done, at all," I said.

"My solution to that dilemma was worthy of a Hemartius of Ar," he said.

"You know him from the trial in the Theater of Publius," I said.

"He defended Talena brilliantly, if unavailingly."

"She did little to assist her own defense," I said.

"Marlenus," he said, "was much impressed by Hemartius, not only for his legal mind but for his courage, to undertake so unpopular and hopeless a case."

"I would think so," I said.

"Hemartius, I have learned," said Ruffio, "is now the chief scribe of the law in the court of the Ubar."

"I am glad to hear it," I said.

"Marlenus is good at giving credit where it is due," said Ruffio.

"And sometimes," I said, "where it is not due." Certainly he had long esteemed Decius Albus as his trade advisor.

We then heard, from several yards away, the beating of a guardsman's drum, and the chanted, repeated, refrain, "Citizens of Brundisium, discover the villain, Ruffio of Ar. Reveal his hiding place. He is wanted by the Harbor Masters of Brundisium. The reward is a silver tarsk."

"It seems Marlenus has asked the Harbor Masters to apprehend you," I said.

"Not at all," said Ruffio, "Marlenus is on his way to Ar."

"What then?" I said.

"When it was thought that Lurius of Jad might pay much for the free woman, Talena of Ar," he said, "I negotiated for her delivery to the Harbor Authorities."

"While taking the coin of Decius Albus," I said.

"Surely two gold pieces are better than one," said Ruffio. "Besides, we could be on our way to Cos before the Harbor Authorities knew we slipped anchor."

The drum and chant were now getting louder.

"Surely I am worth more than a silver tarsk," said Ruffio.

"Those of Brundisium, it being a great merchant port," I said, "are noted for thrift."

"If I am to be impaled," said Ruffio, "I would much prefer it be for a gold stater, and not a silver tarsk. That would be demeaning."

"Perhaps then," I said, "you should think about being on your way."

"Already I have thought about it," he said. "You do think my handling of the 'knife-at-the-throat' moment was deft, do you not?" he asked.

"Somewhat deft," I said.

"I must be on my way," he said.

I tossed him a silver tarsk, which he snapped neatly out of the air. "Now," I said, "you need not be tempted to surrender yourself to the authorities for the reward."

"Do not fear," he said. "My greed is not without limits."

"I wish you well," I said.

"I wish you well," he said, and slipped away.

A few moments later the drummer, and three guardsmen were before my tent at the caravanserai of Alessandro.

"We seek the knave, Ruffio of Ar," said he who was first amongst the guardsmen. "Have you seen him? Do you know him?"

"Who is Ruffio of Ar?" I said.

CHAPTER ONE HUNDRED

"Be of better cheer," I said to Iris. "Tor-tu-Gor shines, the gentle breeze ruffles your tunic nicely about your lovely thighs, and a hundred birds sing, preening, hopping about, brightening the morning."

"They do not sing for me," she said.

"That is because you are not a female bird," I said, "a mate or prospective mate."

She burst into tears.

"You have been disconsolate of late," I said.

"I am desolate," she said.

"Because the troops of Ar have turned homeward?" I asked.

"Because one has turned homeward," she said.

I and my party were considering quitting the caravanserai of Alessandro and making our way south to Brundisium, where we would part, some of us arranging passage north to the Tamber Gulf and Port Kar, when a shadow fell across my path.

"Tal" said Alan, of the House of Hesius.

"Tal," I said, affably.

"I have returned," he said.

"I find that evident," I said.

"We have business to transact," he said.

"You may have business to transact," I said. "I do not."

"I will make it your business," he said.

"Should you not be with Marlenus of Ar?" I asked.

"I have leave," he said. "I can easily catch up with the troops. One man can travel faster than a thousand."

That is not because a thousand can move no faster than its slowest man. To the extent that it is true, it has more to do with the organization and marshaling of men, in-step marching, the need to scout and reconnoiter, the obtaining and distribution of supplies, the making and breaking of camps, and such.

I knew that it was possible that Alan, of the House of Hesius, might be my son, as Pa-Kur, Master of the Caste of Assassins, had claimed, but I thought it unlikely. Presumably, Lara of Tharna, before I had purchased her, would have been forced to imbibe slave wine, which should have prevented conception. It seemed unlikely that the dosage would have been ineffective or omitted. Too, I had no assurance that Lara had ever borne a child, or, if so, that it would be mine. The traveling about of pairs of fellows, supposedly from Tharna, looking for an allegedly lost child might have been no more than another trick on the part of Pa-Kur to further his scheme to neutralize the edge of my blade by apprehensions, uncertainly, and fear. It would be an unusual combatant who would be willing to thrust his sword into the body of an antagonist who might be his own son. But, the hair of Alan, of the House of Hesius, which was similar to a possible blend of my own hair and that of Lara, was troubling. Too, should any of Earth ever read this manuscript, they should not rule out a possible consanguinity on chronological grounds, that for at least two reasons, first, an embryo might be removed, preserved, and later reimplanted; in this fashion, a child conceived at one time might be born at a much later time, perhaps several years later; something like that might take place if a search for, say, one parent, had been undertaken; second, the stabilization serums can be diversely manipulated; for example, a given child might be stabilized in infancy for several years, and then allowed to grow toward adulthood, and then stabilized at the age one wished. For example, in the case of females brought from Earth to the markets of Gor, they are usually stabilized at the peak of their vitality, desirability, and beauty. Thus, merchandise can be sold in prime condition, a condition which, given the stabilization serums, can be maintained indefinitely. All in all, then, I thought it possible that the young Taurentian, Alan, of the House of Hesius, might be my son, but, too, I thought it unlikely.

"I denounce you as a craven urt and tarsk," he said.

"How could I be both?" I asked.

"In the theater of Publius," he said, "you tricked me. You pretended abandonment of the dispute; you feigned surrender, and then, when my back was turned, seized up your sword, leaped at me, and took me at a disadvantage."

"You should not turn your back on a possible enemy," I said.

"You made me look foolish and stupid," he said. "You disgraced me before the Ubar and all Ar. I demand satisfaction."

Hearing this discourse, those of my party investigated, emerging from within the tent and from about the vicinity, Seremides, Xenon, Thurnock, Clitus, and Aetius. Iris also made her appearance. "Master!" she cried, delighted. And I do not think that it was I whom she so saluted. Behind her was Talena, puzzled, lingering back.

"Master!" exclaimed Iris. "You have come back for me!"

"I have not come back for you," said Alan, "but for satisfaction, for the expunging of a stain upon my honor, for the washing away of an insult, a washing away which can only be accomplished by blood and steel."

"Nonetheless," I said, "she is very pretty."

There was no gainsaying that.

"She is a worthless slave," said Alan, "and a barbarian, as well."

"Would you like to make an offer?" I said.

"This is not about a slave," said Alan. "It is about blood and honor."

"Shall I kill him for you?" asked Clitus, loosening his net, readying his trident.

"No," I said.

"An arrow to the heart would do nicely," said Thurnock, drawing an arrow from his quiver.

"Replace your shaft," I said.

"I shall fight you all, if you wish," said Alan, "but later, one at a time. I now have business with the villain, the rogue and knave, Geoffrey of Harfax."

"But he has no business with you," I said.

"Draw your steel!" said Alan, freeing his own blade.

"I do not choose to do so," I said.

"I will not slay an unresisting man," said Alan.

"I am pleased to hear that," I said.

"Live then," said Alan, tears in his eyes, "as a branded coward!"

"If necessary," I said.

"Sheath your blade, young Alan," said Seremides. "Return to Ar. Remember the Skerry of Lars. You have no enemies here."

"He is without honor!" said Alan.

"I do not see that honor is involved here," I said.

"Fight!" said Alan.

"Do not be precipitate," said Seremides. "You do not know he whom you challenge."

"I have never met my match," said Alan.

"So, too," said Seremides, "have said many who, to their dismay, discovered too late that they had done so."

"Fight!" demanded Alan, in tears, once more.

"No," I said.

"Be denounced then as recreant and abject coward!" said Alan.

"If you wish," I said.

"Why do you not kill him, Captain?" asked Thurnock.

"Do not kill him," said Seremides.

Alan turned away, sword in hand, shaken, in tears, in rage.

He had gone no more than five or six steps when he stopped, and turned about. His young visage was determined and fierce. He smiled, a smile that hinted at some sort of newly discovered promise of triumph. With his sword he pointed to Iris. "Kajira canjellne!" he said.

"Now," I said, drawing my sword, "honor is involved."

"No, Masters!" cried Iris. "Do not fight! Not for me! Let no one die for a slave!" She flung herself to her knees before me. "Do not fight, Master!" she wept. Then she sprang up and hurried to Alan, and knelt before him. "Do not fight, Master!" she wept. "I love you!" Alan regarded her, startled.

"Get behind us, Slave," I said to Iris.

Aetius drew her to her feet, pulled her to the side, and then knelt her beside him.

She was weeping. Talena, pale, frightened, knelt near her, back a bit. She shook her head to me, urging me not to fight. I turned away from her. What did women, what did slaves, know of such things? What did women, what did slaves, know of men?

Alan rushed toward me, his attack swift and fierce. I turned it aside, easily. He stepped back, surprised. He would now be less precipitate. I hoped he had learned something. In a sense, his attack was understandable. He did not intend to waste much time with me. I suspected that many swordsmen would have succumbed to that rushing, flaming steel.

"Do not kill him, Friend," said Seremides to me, leaning forward on his crutch. "He knows much of blades, but less of the wise use of blades, and still less of war."

"You are adept," said Alan to me.

"Learn the steel of your opponent," I said, "before you scorn it. Do not believe that a thousand victories guarantees another."

Alan then advanced again, but more circumspectly, more tentatively, probing, testing.

"Better," I said.

I varied my engagement, particularly in its depths and extensions, for the details of a repetitive contesting can be anticipated, and will be anticipated, and exploited, by a proficient opponent. Sometimes I drew back that he would overextend his thrust.

"He was open," said Thurnock. "You could have killed him twice."

"Three times," I said.

Iris cried out in misery. "Be silent," Aetius warned her.

Alan redoubled his addresses.

"Draw back," I said to him. "Do not become desperate. Collect yourself. Be patient."

"Do not try to upset me or confuse me, knave," said Alan, sweating. "Your tricks will not work! I am no fool to be so hoaxed."

"Forgive me," I said. "I was trying to be helpful."

"I am no unwitting novice," he said.

"Clearly not," I said. "I commend you on your skill. You are an excellent swordsman, a credit to the Taurentian guard, but I would

not, if I were you, cross blades with a Marlenus of Ar or a Pa-Kur, of
the Caste of Assassins."

With a cry of rage Alan rushed forward again, blade flailing.

"Perhaps you are a fool," I said. "It seems you would defeat yourself."

"Taste my steel!" wept Alan.

"Let the lesson not be prolonged," said Thurnock. "Finish him!"

"Spare him!" said Seremides.

"Left shoulder," I said. "Right shoulder. Chest." With each utterance I tore his tunic, and blood, from small cuts and jabs, dotted his
garment.

He threw himself wildly toward me and I stepped aside, tripping
him, and he sprawled to the ground, twisting about, and my left foot
pinned his right wrist to the ground, and I drew back my arm, scarcely
understanding what I was doing, caught up in the moment, and a
small, tunicked figure flung herself between us, covering his body
with her own. I was a moment from plunging the blade down. Despite
my advice to Alan, I myself had, for a moment, I realized, death so
close to both of us, been seized in the grip of a brief, overwhelming
emotion, not unknown to such combatants, the understanding that
you can live, needing only to strike. I cried out in fear, and a burst of
almost hysterical laughter burst from my throat, as I realized with sudden, glad relief, I had not done what I had been on the verge of doing.

"Finish him," said Thurnock.

"No," I said.

"You spared him," said Seremides, relieved.

"I spared both of us," I said.

"I do not understand," said Seremides.

"It is nothing," I said.

"Why did you not fight like that in the Stadium of Blades?" asked
Clitus.

"Yes, why did you not?" asked Thurnock.

"Duels are dangerous," I said. "It is hard to know their outcome. A
foot might stumble. A blade might slip. The life of Talena was at stake."

"Too," said Seremides. "More might have been at stake."

"Perhaps," I said.

Had he wondered, I asked myself, about inconsequential things,
carriage, skills, reflexes, even hair color?

Iris knelt before me, kissing my feet. "Thank you, Master," she
said. "Thank you, Master."

Alan, of the House of Hesius, regained his feet, thrust his sword
into its sheath and rubbed his right wrist. "I was a fool," he said.

I, too, resheathed my blade.

"No more than I," I said, "many times."

He extended his hand and we shook hands, in the sturdiest of fashions, each hand grasping the wrist of the other, as is common amongst Warriors and Mariners.

"The slave, of course," I said, "is yours."

Iris looked up me, wildly, disbelievingly, gladly, gratefully.

"I did not kill you," said Alan. "I did not defeat you. I did not force her from you. I did not win her."

"Nonetheless," I said, "she is yours."

"I cannot accept her," said Alan. "I did not win her. I am not entitled to her. In honor I cannot accept her."

"Very well," I said.

"Master!" protested Iris.

"There are, of course," said Seremides, "more civilized ways to obtain a slave, ways other than by blood and steel."

"You might keep that in mind," I said to Alan.

"Slaves are pleasant to have about, crawling at one's feet," said Seremides. "And our Iris is an excellent representative of that form of domestic animal."

"I am inclined to agree," said Alan.

"Well said, Master," said Iris.

"Slaves are very precious," said Seremides. "Some prefer them to sleen and kaiila."

"Many do, Master," said Iris.

"What would you take for her?" asked Alan, warily.

"What about three silver tarsks," I said.

"Is that not three times her worth?" asked Alan.

"At least three," said Seremides.

"It depends on the buyer and market," I said.

"Very well," said Alan, reaching toward his purse.

"Wait, Master," said Iris. "Has he not agreed too readily to such a price?"

"Perhaps," I said.

"How could you let me go for less than five silver tarsks?" she asked.

"It would be difficult," I said.

"Six silver tarsks," she said.

"Very well," I said. "Six silver tarsks."

"I do not have six silver tarsks," said Alan.

"Surely you can get them, Master," said Iris.

"I will loan you three silver tarsks," said Seremides. "You can repay them in Ar, subject to a modest interest, of course."

"Agreed," said Alan.

"I shall be going to Ar soon," said Seremides. "That is not surprising. I am a hero of Ar, as you doubtless know. It was I, as you may recall, who returned to Ar her stolen Home Stone."

"All Ar is grateful to you," said Alan.

And so Seremides loaned Alan, he of the House of Hesius, three silver tarsks and lovely Iris changed hands.

Few slaves, statistically, incidentally, sell for more than two silver tarsks. Iris, therefore, had every reason to be pleased to have brought so handsome a price.

"I must be on my way to join the Ubar," said Alan. "So, up, pretty slave."

"I wish you well," I said to Alan.

"I wish you well," he said.

Alan and his slave were scarcely five paces away, when I called after them. Alan turned back and Iris turned back, too, and knelt beside him.

"Go to Tharna," I said.

"I do not understand," said Alan.

"Sometime," I said, "when you have the time, go to Tharna."

"And what shall I do in Tharna?" he asked.

"Convey the greetings of Tarl of Ko-ro-ba to Lara, Tatrix of Tharna," I said.

He regarded me, puzzled, and then smiled, and waved, and then turned about to pursue the tracks of Marlenus of Ar, and a thousand men of Ar. He was heeled by his lovely slave. Her name was Iris.

I had my own slave. Her name was Talena.

"Tomorrow," I said to my party, Thurnock, Clitus, Seremides, Xenon, and Aetius, "I propose that we shall wagon to Brundisium. Let us then lodge at the Harbor's Rest and feast at some local tavern."

"The Sea Sleen," said Seremides.

"That will do nicely," I said. "Then, the next day, if all goes well, we shall part, Seremides and Xenon to Ar, Aetius to Venna, and Thurnock, Clitus, and I, if we can find safe, convenient passage, to Port Kar."

"Then all is settled," said Seremides.

"It seems so," I said.

"There is nothing more to fear," said Seremides.

"It seems not," I said.

CHAPTER ONE HUNDRED AND ONE

"Please, no, Master," begged Talena. "I am not a dancer! I would embarrass you."

She was kneeling, having brought us paga, beside the low table in the tavern, the Sea Sleen, in Brundisium, about which, cross-legged, I sat, with Thurnock and Clitus, Seremides and Xenon, and Aetius.

"You do not fear embarrassing me," I said. "You are afraid of doing poorly, afraid of being laughed at and scorned, afraid of being hooted from the floor, of being humiliated, and, possibly, being whipped."

"I want to see her dance," said Seremides, "the former haughty daughter of Marlenus, the Ubar of Ar, and I want to see her dance as the slave she now is."

Trained dancers bring high prices on Gor. But what woman cannot dance, and dance as a slave?

"She may face some danger," said Xenon. "In my days as an oarsman, I was several times in Brundisium. The port is well known for its dancers. I saw several whipped who failed to please the crowd."

This intelligence did not much please Talena.

"I once spent some time in Brundisium," said Aetius.

"I, too," said Seremides. "Did you not have dealings with a Bruno of Torcadino?"

"Yes," said Aetius, "but they did not turn out well, as I recall."

"That is my recollection, as well," said Seremides.

"In any event, the Sea Sleen," said Aetius, "is still a modest tavern, catering to an inauspicious clientele."

"Such as we," I added. We had chosen it for our farewell dinner, our parting dinner, because of its proximity to our inn, the Harbor's Rest, but as much for the reason that six strangers, this close to the warehouses and piers, would not be likely to attract attention. We had taken care, too, to not appear attractively prosperous. Why excite the speculations of brigands and cut-purses?

"I have heard," I said, "it is unusual for the Sea Sleen to have musicians and dancers."

Needless to say, this adds expenses to the operating costs of a tavern, expenses which may not be easily recouped from a commonly shallow-pursed patronage.

"It depends muchly on the day and season," said Aetius.

"This is no holiday that I know," said Thurnock.

"Perhaps it is in Brundisium," suggested Clitus.

"This is the week of the vernal equinox," said Aetius.

"That is it," said Seremides.

"Paga, Masters?" asked a short, luscious paga slave, going to her knees beside the table.

"Our girl will attend to such matters, as before," I informed her.

"Yes, Master," she said, rising and backing away. "Forgive me, Master."

"I am not a paga girl," said Talena.

"No," I said. "You probably lack their skills."

I expected that that would annoy her. What woman does not believe that she might prove to be a superb paga girl?

"Do not underestimate her," said Seremides. "When you unexpectedly, and brilliantly, concealed her true identity in Port Kar, when she was kept by your friend, Ho-Tosk, in the tavern, the Golden Chain, under the name Adraste, she served as a paga girl. Who would have thought that Talena, the fugitive Ubara, would be concealed, so to speak, in plain sight? Surely one would be expected to find her in some remote, mysterious tower or in some secret, closely guarded cavern."

"Were you any good in the alcoves?" asked Aetius.

"When I was not," said Talena, "the patrons had me whipped."

"And were you often whipped?" asked Aetius.

"Not after the first week," she said.

"And did you enjoy yourself?" I asked.

"I was given no choice," she said. "I was at the mercy of masters. I am healthy. I am vital. I could not help myself."

"And did you wish to help yourself?" asked Aetius.

"Such a wish is not permitted to a slave," she said.

"But?" I said.

"They were men," she said.

"And did you soon, haunches heaving, gasp, squeak, beg, and moan?" asked Aetius.

"I am a woman," she said.

"Behold," said Xenon. "The musicians have returned."

There was a czehar player, their leader, two flutists, two kalika players, and a drummer with his tabor, slightly larger than the common kaska.

"I trust Master was joking, about dancing," she said.

"No," I said. "Surely you danced in Port Kar, at the Golden Chain."

"Under the eye of a Whip Master," she said.

"There is no Whip Master here," I said. "Thus, there is little to fear."

"Is not shame and humiliation enough?" she said.

"Back in Port Kar," I said, "I could have your skills honed."

"Master comforts his slave," she said.

I regarded the large platter before me, now bare save for some crumbs and grease. With a wedge of fresh bread I mopped the platter, finished the bread, and thrust the platter back, away. The meal had been simple, ample, nourishing, and hot. We had all agreed, with the exception of Seremides and Xenon, that Seremides should furnish the evening's provender. He was, after all, as we had pointed out to him, a Hero of Ar, and was it not he who had returned to Ar her missing Home Stone?

The musicians, having returned from behind the dangling curtain, formed of long strings of colorful beads, were now seated at the edge of the dancing circle and tuning their instruments, or exploring what seemed to me some random trills.

"Behold, Master," said Talena. "Two dancers now kneel to the side, waiting for the music to begin."

"One will dance first," I said, "and then the other, presumably more skilled, will dance second."

The better dancers are commonly saved for last.

"Thus," said Talena, "there is no need for me to dance."

"No," I said. "That merely means that you, presumably the least skilled, should dance first."

She shuddered, and moaned, softly.

"I shall arrange matters," I said, and then, getting up, I made my way to the czehar player, who, as is often the case, was first amongst the musicians. I returned shortly to the table, having managed the whole business quite to my satisfaction, for a handful of Brundisium tarsk-bits, which are more plentiful and less valuable than the tarsk-bits of most cities, presumably to provide a more flexible currency for a mercantile economy. It was my contribution to the evening, as I did not ask for any remuneration from Seremides, a consideration which I hoped was not lost on him.

"Go to the circle," I said, "and begin dancing there, but, soon, dance amongst the tables, not neglecting those in the darker reaches of the tavern."

"Then there is more to this than dancing," she said.

"I hope not," I said, "but that is possible."

A ripple of sound coursed across the eight strings of the czehar.

Talena rose to her feet, and hurried to the circle, where she stood under the dangling tharlarion-oil lamps, knees flexed, hands over her head, gracefully, palms outward.

Some of the patrons softly slapped the palms of their right hands against their left shoulders.

There was no doubt that Talena was a strikingly beautiful woman.

She lacked the ornaments, the jewelry, the armlets, the bracelets, the anklets, bells, swirling dancing silks, and such, of the common tavern dancer, but this was not one of the finer, more expensive taverns closer to the center of Brundisium, but the Sea Sleen, in the harbor district, and no claim or pretense was being made that she was other than a common slave accompanying her master in the tavern. And, at least in my opinion, Talena, barefoot, collared, and tunicked, did not compare unfavorably with a more bedizened dancer. Too, she could always become so accoutered if I should wish it, as her clothing, if any, was subject to my discretion.

So she began to dance, and, soon, the murmur of conversation and the gentle rattle of utensils ceased. There were some intakings of breath, a gasp or two, and some tongue-clicking noises the purport of which cannot be mistaken by any woman, whether a dancer or not. Such noises, for example, are not unoften heard at an auction, particularly in a low house, where no free women are present, upon the presentation of a new item being offered for sale. Talena was no trained dancer, and a connoisseur would doubtless have been generous with subtle criticisms and helpful suggestions, but the average untutored, vital male would have found little to criticize in such a performance. In few situations, other than being naked in the furs, is a woman more beautiful, or more fully female, than in slave dance. I could see that the musicians were pleased, and even the two silked, belled, collared tavern dancers with the musicians seemed attentive.

Soon Talena swept from the dancing circle and began, swaying and swirling, to thread her way amongst the tables, some of which were favored briefly with the sight of how beautiful a slave can be. Then she was before our table. Her dance, I suddenly realized, was now being addressed to me, which would not, in the present moment, be advisable. A slave's display behavior, her presenting behavior, can be maddeningly exciting. In a public space, however, as in a tavern, it is not to be directed to a given individual for more than a short time. It is not as though she were alone with her master. Spending too much time before a given individual, when many are present, just because that individual is, say, handsome or richly clothed, or because, for some reason, she wants to elicit a bid, is disapproved. A girl could be whipped for that. A public tavern is not like the feasting hall of a private citizen on whom the bestowal of so particular an attention would be altogether appropriate. It was time for Talena to move away from before me. In a moment it might become embarrassing, provoking a knowing amusement amongst some and a possible impatience or even irritation amongst others. I heard Aetius chuckle. Then, suddenly, I realized the helplessness and vulnerability of Talena. A tear was in her eye. She wanted, desperately, to be found pleasing, as a slave wishes to be found pleasing by her master. She was not a free companion protected by sanctions of law and custom. She was in a collar. She was goods, an animal, a property, a slave. What if I should tire of her? What if I should trade her or sell her? It would be easy enough to do. There are many ways in which a slave can beg, small movements, tiny sounds, glances, an expression, kneeling and kissing, fastening the bondage knot in one's hair, crawling, fetching a whip and dropping it at one's feet, signifying submission, and so on. And even writhing piteously, beggingly, in slave dance. I made a hasty, impatient gesture, dismissing Talena, hurrying her from the table.

Some four Ehn later, the music done, she returned to the table, sweating, breathing heavily, and sank to her knees beside it.

"You did well, Slave," said a stranger.

"Thank you, Master," she whispered.

The musicians struck up again and one of the dancing slaves, silked and belled, took her position in the dancing circle.

"What did you learn?" I asked.

"There are six of them, Master," she said, trying to catch her breath, "from the holding at the sea edge of the Caravanserai of Alessandro."

"One for each of us," said Thurnock.

"Did they recognize you?" I asked.

"Yes," she said, "from the holding, and certainly from the tent of Marlenus."

"Do you sense they followed us, or were spying on us?"

"I do not know," she said. "I think perhaps not, as they seemed surprised, and uneasy, to see me. They may have merely wished to be inconspicuous after the business of the Caravanserai of Alessandro."

"I think I shall call on them when the dancers are finished," I said.

"Alone?" asked Seremides.

"Of course," I said. "Surely they are all good fellows."

"Where there are six," said Aetius, "there may be more."

"Then all the more good fellows," I said.

"Beware," said Thurnock.

"What is more harmless than a mercenary who is not in fee?" I asked.

I waited until the second slave dancer, who was quite good, had performed and the musicians had retired once more behind the beaded curtain.

I then made my way toward the less well-lit, darker edge of the tavern, back and toward the right, as one would enter, opposite to, and far from, the paga vat.

"Tal," I said, pleasantly.

I do not think they were pleased to see me.

"Tal," responded two of them.

"I take it, fellows," I said, "you are now suspended between fee givers."

I received no response to this conjecture.

"I speculate that the absence of Decius Albus affects you sorely," I said. "He was rich, and where good men such as yourselves are concerned, generous."

My putative interlocutors did not see fit to join the conversation.

"If I were you," I said, "I would wagon to Torcadino, and try the market. More than one captain recruits in the shadow of the aqueduct. I would not advise you to try your luck in Ar. Given the outcome of recent events, employment there might be unlikely, even unsafe."

It is difficult to carry on a conversation when the intended respondent, or respondents, remain silent. If you doubt me, try it sometime.

"Let me then," I said, "fill you in on my own plans. I and my party are venturing into merchantry. Unlike in Brundisium, the goods of Cos are rare in the north, save for those her cargo ships are persuaded to transfer free of charge to marauders, such as those of Port Kar, or put at the disposal of raiding dragonships from Torvaldsland. In particular, you are all well aware of the Ta wine of Telnus, made from the exquisite Ta grapes of lovely, many-terraced Cos, though possibly, given its expense, you may never have tasted it. Here in Brundisium, the Ta wine of Telnus is cheap, so to speak, only a full silver tarsk for a finger flagon, whereas in, say, Port Kar, one might pay as much as five silver tarsks for the same flagon. Thus, I and my party will wax rich buying in Brundisium and selling in the north."

"Port Kar," said one of the mercenaries, "is the Scourge of Gleaming Thassa."

"It is the Jewel of Gleaming Thassa," I said. "In Port Kar, there is now a Home Stone."

Silence then again settled on my gloomy interlocutors.

"I fear only," I said, "that the tricksters of Brundisium might put a lesser beverage in flagons falsely identified as containing the Ta wine of Telnus."

"You have never tasted it yourself then?" said one of the mercenaries.

"And that is what makes me apprehensive of possible fraud."

"Buy from a reputable dealer," said another mercenary.

"Yes!" I said. "That is it! Of course!"

I did note that he, however, had given me no criterion by means of which to recognize a reputable dealer.

This omission, however, was almost immediately rectified.

"Horace the Honest is well thought of," said one.

"Ask about," said another. "Many in the streets will gladly supply information on any topic, for as little as a tarsk-bit."

"Seek the dealer who charges the most money," said another. "It is well known that reputable dealers charge the most outrageous prices."

"Thank you, Friends," I said. "You have much assuaged my anxieties."

"Are you sure you have sufficient funds to make the investment?" asked one of the mercenaries.

"Enough to buy two hundred finger flagons at the cheap prices available in Brundisium," I said.

"Two hundred silver tarsks?" said a mercenary.

"The equivalent thereof," I said. "But think how that investment will multiply itself in the north."

"Indeed," said a mercenary.

They exchanged glances, glances which, were it not for the plan I had conceived, might have made me distinctly uneasy.

"I wish you well," I said, to which all six, looking at one another, affably responded.

I then returned to my table.

"What occurred?" asked Thurnock.

"Much," I said.

"Do they have a fee giver?" asked Seremides.

"I think so," I said. "When I called attention to the possible war market, the possible recruitings in Torcadino, no interest was manifested, even an abstract or theoretical interest. Thus I suspect they are already in fee."

"To whom?" asked Seremides.

"I do not know," I said.

"How many would be in fee?" asked Aetius.

"I would think the forty-two, or such, we heard mentioned in the tent of Marlenus," I said. "Presumably, if possible, they would have banded together, for protection, in leaving the Caravanserai of Alessandro for Brundisium."

"Then," said Thurnock, "it is no six against six."

"I do not think so," I said.

"Perhaps we can slip away, unnoticed, from Brundisium," said Seremides.

"I fear we would be followed," I said.

"What shall we do?" asked Thurnock.

"I have a plan," I said. "Do you think mercenaries are greedy?"

"They have that reputation," said Aetius.

"Then I think my plan may work," I said. "I am counting on them going, at least in part, into business for themselves."

"Xenon and I will delay our journey to Torcadino and thence to Ar," said Seremides.

"At least for a day," I said.

"And I will postpone my trip to Torcadino and thence to Venna," said Aetius.

"Hopefully for no more than a day," I said.

"And what now?" asked Thurnock.

"I must make certain purchases," I said, "abysmal wine, several unmarked finger flagons, and such."

"Perhaps now we should return to the Harbor's Rest," said Thurnock.

"An excellent idea," I said.

"And tomorrow?" asked Seremides.

"Suspecting nothing," I said, "we shall all go down to the piers, I, Thurnock, and Clitus to obtain passage to Port Kar, and Seremides, Xenon, and Aetius to see us on our way."

"If we are still alive," said Seremides.

"Yes," I said, "of course."

"Master," asked Talena, on her knees, "did I dance well? Was I pleasing?"

How beautiful the collar was on her neck. It is interesting how so small a thing can so enhance a woman's beauty. To be sure, a part of its appeal was what it betokened, what it meant.

"Yes," I said, "you danced well, and you were pleasing, very pleasing."

"If Master is pleased," she said, "then a slave is pleased, as well."

CHAPTER ONE HUNDRED AND TWO

"Who has lived who has not tasted the Ta wine of Telnus?" I asked, calling out, lifting a finger flagon, eyeing the encircling mercenaries.

They wore no livery, no identifying uniform. Gone were the black tunics and cloaks with two stripes, two broad white stripes for officers and the two narrow white stripes for common armsmen. One could scarcely tell them from common street brigands, were it not for the precision of their spacing and the uniformity of their accouterments and weaponry. A number of individuals, other than the mercenaries and my party, were gathered about, curious and attentive, dock workers, loiterers, warehousemen, beggars, accounting scribes, street gamblers, local and foreign mariners, and such. Clearly a relatively large altercation of blades appeared to be in the offing, and such an altercation promises much in the way of entertainment, and, not unoften, a certain amount of profitable scavenging afterward.

"Should we not summon guardsmen?" asked a fellow, who seemed, from his robes, a stranger in Brundisium, possibly from Schendi or even Turia.

"No," said a dock worker, "let them scrounge about for their own loot."

"They time their arrival carefully," said another. "As soon as it is peaceful, they arrive to keep the peace, and just in time to scatter crowds and gather evidence."

"Rings, coins, and such," said another.

I doubted that this assessment was fair to local guardsmen, but I hoped they would not make an appearance, timely or otherwise. That would, at the least, complicate my plans. It was true, of course, that guardsmen were seldom well paid, even in Brundisium, and that might encourage at least some of them to think about supplementing their income in one way or another.

"Who is their fee giver?" asked Aetius.

"I do not know," I said.

"The rogue, Ruffio of Ar," said Seremides.

"I do not think so," I said. "I think he lacks the resources, and, in any event, is currently much concerned to put pasangs between himself and the Harbor Masters of Brundisium."

"Who then?" asked Aetius.

"I do not know," I said.

"Prepare to die!" called out one of the encircling mercenaries. I supposed that he would have been one of those fellows who, if in uniform, would have had two broad white stripes on his livery.

"There must be some forty of you," I said, "and we are only six."

"Take heart," he said. "Soon you will not even be six."

Naturally, I hoped his calculation was in error.

"Consider honor," I said.

"And so might the vulo plead fruitlessly with the sleen," he said.

"Should you not be shamed?" I asked.

"No," he said. "This is not war but business."

"The odds seem much in your favor," I said.

"We are merchants, dealing in the commerce of blood," he said. "We would not willingly engage otherwise."

"Mathematics smiles upon your steel," I said.

"It is so we choose to have it," he said. "Who would choose to change such numbers?'

"How many of you have tasted the Ta wine of Telnus?" I asked.

From their uneasiness, and the looks they exchanged, I gathered that few, if any, had had that experience. Ta wine is far from the extremely rare, almost legendary Falarian, but it is expensive and rare.

"Perhaps one of you has not had that pleasure," I said. "Yet, for a consideration it could be yours."

"What consideration?" asked my interlocutor, he whom I supposed was an officer of some sort, probably the highest remaining amongst them.

"The Ta wine of Telnus," I said, "as you may surmise, is not grown in Telnus, a port, but inland, on certain of the protected, guarded wine terraces of Cos. It is called the Ta wine of Telnus because it is commonly shipped through that port."

"Any fool knows that," he said. "What consideration?"

I pointed to the small, hand-drawn cart at our side, in which, cushioned by straw, were some two hundred finger flagons. "Half the profit on this cargo of rare, exquisite, expensive Ta wine for our lives," I said.

Laughter broke out amongst the encircling mercenaries.

"You do not understand," I said. "Expensive as Ta wine is in Brundisium, a finger flagon for a silver tarsk, it is many times more expensive in the north. Spare us, and we will return from the north and make you all rich."

Laughter again broke out amongst the mercenaries.

"You insult us," said my interlocutor. "You deem us fools. Even if we were stupid enough to trust you, the matter would take weeks, or months, and would be precarious, liable to a thousand mishaps, theft, breakage, loss at sea, and such."

"Take the cart then, as it is," I said, "with two hundred finger flagons of Ta wine, for our lives."

My interlocutor, and several of his men, laughed.

"It is valuable, even here in Brundisium," I said.

"Fool," said my interlocutor. "For nothing, we can have both your blood and your wine."

"You had best flee," I said. "Even now guardsmen speed to our rescue."

Even the crowd about laughed at this.

Certainly I hoped that guardsmen were not speeding to our rescue.

"I think there are some forty of you," I said. "Thus, with two hundred finger flagons to be distributed, each of you should receive five, or so, with nothing extra for officers, or senior armsmen. How will you distribute the loot equably? I fear some will be cheated of their share."

"Do not be troubled," said my interlocutor. "The matter will be managed well enough."

"I want my five," said a man.

"Five for each," said another.

"Be silent!" said my interlocutor.

"Five," said more than one man.

A common weakness of mercenaries, except in some of the older, more seasoned free companies, many with a tradition, is discipline. Their loyalty is more to coin and the prospect of loot than to a standard or commander. Many times they do not share the same Home Stone. They commonly function smoothly when superior in numbers, skills, and position and less reliably when threatened or evenly matched. They will risk only so much for gold. Their cause is themselves. This makes discipline less certain, save for the fear of officers, and, in certain situations, desertion more likely.

"Push the cart toward me," said my interlocutor, presumably an officer. We did so. He stepped to the cart, thrusting his sword tip a bit into the straw, jostling some flagons.

"Two hundred flagons," I said.

"Steady, men," he said.

"The contents of the cart," I said, "are quite valuable. Thus, as you are mercenaries, do not drink the wine. Try to sell it, even though it be here in Brundisium and not in the north. To be sure, in a reselling, you are not likely to obtain the silver tarsk per flagon which I paid originally, but you might get half that, or perhaps more. In any event, do not drink the wine but sell it. The exquisite, unforgettable taste of Ta wine would be lost on rude mercenaries. Do not let them have that pleasure. It would be wasted on them."

"I want my five bottles!" said a man.

"I want to taste it," said a man.

"I, too, would taste it," said another.

"There may not be five bottles apiece," I said. "Remember the officers and senior armsmen."

"Distribute the flagons now!" said a man.

"Remain in place," said he who was doubtless their high officer.

"Behold," I said. "My sword is sheathed. I approach the cart.

"What do you intend to do?" he asked.

"Extract six flagons," I said, "one for myself, and one for each in my party."

"Stop!" he said.

"Six will not be missed," I said.

"Back away!" he said.

"I will have the six flagons," I said. "If you try to stop me, I can break several more before you can reach me."

"Take your six," he said.

I did so. This was not difficult to do, as the flagons were small, and a finger could easily be inserted through more than one handle. I then gave a flagon to each of my party, retaining one for myself.

"You fear your men will rush on the cart," I said, "that discipline will be abandoned, that disruption will prevail, that flagons will be broken and wine lost, even that I and my party may seize an opportunity to escape in the confusion."

"Let no man move," he ordered. "The sword is prepared to speak. Remain in place."

"As you are forty or more and we are six, and as time may be growing short," I said, pulling the plug out of a flagon, "I and my friends intend to sample the Ta wine before it might prove too late to do so. I trust you do not begrudge us that favor."

"I will have my share now!" exclaimed a mercenary.

"Maintain your position!" demanded my presumed officer.

I nodded to those of my party and each unplugged his finger flagon.

"Divide the bottles now!" said a mercenary.

"Hold your position," said my interlocutor.

"Take a bottle for yourself," I said. "Let us drink together. Deny it to boors and lesser men on whom it would be wasted. I would offer a toast."

"I would have a drink!" said a mercenary.

"Divide the bottles!" said another.

"I deny the wine to no one!" cried my interlocutor. "Steady men!"

"I fear discipline is in jeopardy," I said. "Your men may fear, however unrealistically, that they may be cheated of their honest share of this valuable loot."

"Your blood first," said my interlocutor, "your wine next."

"That may not work out well," I said. "We shall resist our slaughter, as would be universally acknowledged to be our right. In the likely fracas, not only are several bottles likely to be broken, but several of your men, I conjecture, presumably the wiser ones, will rush to the cart to help themselves, placing wine before our blood, so to speak, while their nobler fellows forgo the wine to risk their lives against our steel."

"What do you suggest?" asked my interlocutor.

"Have one man at a time come to the wagon and take, say, four bottles and then return to his place. In this way, the bottles are well divided, or nearly so, and you have done nothing to sacrifice the advantage of your formation, within which we are securely trapped." I trusted that this proposal would have impressed even a Ruffio of Ar.

"Do it, let it be so," said more than one man, glancing about, suspiciously, at his fellows.

"You there!" said my interlocutor, my supposed officer, pointing to a grizzled mercenary. "You first, and then the man to your right, and so on, about the circle."

This proposal seemed to meet with general satisfaction and, soon enough, each mercenary had at least four bottles, and the remainder was placed near my interlocutor, perhaps to be divided amongst officers and senior armsmen, or even gambled for.

"Now," I said to my interlocutor, "before we get down to the business of shedding blood, of trying to kill one another, let me propose a toast."

"You are mad," he said.

"A thought occurs to me," I said. "A rare moment crouches before us, ready to spring up, blazing, into unforgettable legend."

"What is that?" asked my interlocutor.

"Ela," I said, "but it is impossible."

"What is impossible?" he asked.

"Too many here are unworthy of the moment," I said.

"I am worthy of a moment which would become legend!" said a mercenary.

"And I!" said several others.

As this sort of response began to course about the enclosing circle of ill-disciplined swordsmen, my interlocutor seemed to grasp the need to solidify support.

"There is no man here who is unworthy of such a moment!" he announced.

This praise, however fulsome, brought forth a ragged cheer from the encircling armsmen.

"Very well," I said. "Let us, in one act, enter the history not only of Brundisium but that of a world. Let us perform a single, gallant gesture the memory of which will last a thousand years. What we do here today will be sung in the taverns and its story will be told about a thousand campfires and chanted by bards in the courts of a thousand Ubars!"

"What act?" asked my interlocutor.

"That before doing battle to the death, two forces paused to acknowledge one another, to salute one another with grace and aplomb, lifting their cups to one another, to do sword honor to one another."

"Enemies would so honor one another?" asked my interlocutor?

"And so erase the pecuniary stain and commercial taint so often adhering to mercenary endeavors, and so render memorable the noble few who stood bravely within the compass of the stalwart many."

"We would drink to one another?" asked my interlocutor.

"Yes," I said. "And how rare would become such a moment."

"What if the drink is poisoned?" he asked.

"Then do not drink," I said. "You give up nothing but the opportunity to become one with a moment the memory of which will be sung for a thousand years."

"You understand my reservations?" said he whom I supposed to be the high officer of the mercenaries.

"Certainly," I said. "Why should you be remembered for a thousand years? Is it not far better to be forgotten, to be lost at sea, to have one's ashes trampled, to lie buried in an unmarked grave?"

"Still," protested my interlocutor.

"We will drink if you do not!" cried a mercenary.

"If all do not drink," I said, "the moment is lost; one would then be left with no more than men afoot upon on a street, some imbibing and some not."

"We will drink!" said a man.

"Yes," cried another.

"Beware of trickery," voiced my interlocutor.

"Let me assuage your fears," I said. "You need only be rational. Think. How could I sell the flagons in the north or even in Brundisium, if they contained poison? Do you truly think that such merchantry would be successful? Suppose five bottles were sold and five men dropped dead. Would you rush to buy the sixth bottle?"

"No!" cried a man.

"Let us drink," said another.

He whom I took to be an officer unplugged his finger flagon.

"Altogether!" I said, lifting my flagon to my interlocutor. "Ta Sardar Gor!" "To the Priest-Kings of Gor!"

I then threw my head back and downed the contents of my flagon, and then decisively cast the flagon to the cobblestones of the street, where it shattered. In this way, a completeness was bestowed on the moment. No further draught would ever be sampled from that flagon. And, following my example, flagons shattered too in the circle about us.

And thus a remarkable moment was consummated.

Shortly thereafter, the mercenaries, one by one, collapsed to the stones of the street.

I did not suppose that what occurred that afternoon would be likely to be recalled for a thousand years, but I expected that it would see its share of being recounted in the taverns and about campfires.

"I did not think, Captain," said Thurnock, troubled, "that poison was the Warrior's weapon."

"It is not," I said. "Each flagon, other than those from which we drank, contained enough tassa powder to sedate a tharlarion."

Tassa powder is tasteless, and, mixed with wine or another beverage, is commonly used by physicians as a sedative and is often employed by slavers, and others, to render free women unconscious. The free woman is then usually bound, hand and foot, and gagged, and placed in a slave sack, to be transported out of the town or city to some distant market.

"The mercenaries will then recover?" said Thurnock.

"After a time," I said, "refreshed and brimming with energy."

"A woman usually revives after a few Ahn," said Thurnock.

"Considering the dosage," I said, "our resting friends may not wake for over a day, perhaps two."

"By then," said Seremides, "we will have parted and be on our separate ways."

"Yes," I said.

"Still," said Thurnock, "you did use trickery."

"That seemed to me preferable to dying in the street," I said.

"Perhaps," said Thurnock.

"Clearly," said Aetius.

"Deception," I said, "can be as useful as steel. Indeed, is not deception the name of war?"

"Certainly there were too many to be caught in my net," said Clitus.

"Back away!" I ordered some of the hangers about and loiterers, who had approached some of the fallen mercenaries. "The coins and valuables, rings, pins, and such, are ours. After we have relieved our sleeping friends of such trifles, you are to empty all unopened flagons about, and remove all sandals, belts, accouterments, sheaths, weapons, tunics, and such, and take them for yourselves, to keep or sell as you wish. When our friends awaken, tomorrow or the next day, I want them to find themselves naked on the cobblestones."

"Excellent," said Seremides. "Even recovered, they will find themselves without resources in a foreign city."

"And I deem," I said, "that no failed, disappointed fee giver will care to use them again or see fit to redeem their fortunes."

"Who is their fee giver?" asked Xenon.

"I do not know," I said. "But I have an idea."

"What do we do now?" said Thurnock.

"We return to the Harbor's Rest, where we left Talena fastened to a slave ring, have supper, and get a good night's sleep. Tomorrow we shall leave Brundisium."

"Why did you not bring Talena with us?" asked Seremides.

"I thought she would be safer in the Harbor's Rest," I said.

"You care for her," said Seremides.

"Certainly," I said.

"She has slave value," said Seremides.

"Precisely," I said.

CHAPTER ONE HUNDRED AND THREE

"It is near the Eleventh Ahn," said Seremides.

"True," I said.

"And you have still not arranged passage to Port Kar," he said.

"No," I said.

"Brundisium is the greatest port of known Gor," said Seremides, hobbling beside me. "Its harbor, or harbors, if you wish, contain hundreds of ships. How is it that you have not yet chosen one? Almost any captain, for the gold you can offer him, would be willing to risk landing you near, or at, Port Kar."

"I would expect so," I said.

"Gold," said Seremides, "is weighty, rare, lasting, beautiful, and precious."

"True," I said.

"Men will kill for it," he said.

"Some men," I granted him.

"With what you have," said Seremides, "you could buy a ship."

"Maybe two," I said.

"What are you waiting for?" he asked. "For the mercenaries to awaken?"

"I did not realize the potency of the dosage I put in the flagons," I said. "Apparently our friends will not awaken until sometime tomorrow."

"What was that disgusting wine you put in the flagons?" he asked, grimacing, apparently reacting to an unpleasant memory.

"It was not the fabled Ta wine of Telnus," I admitted.

"Nor Falarian," he said.

"I do not really know what it was," I said. "But it had much to commend it. It was recently fermented and cheap."

"It was terrible," he said. "It reminded me of the wine used in cheap kal-da."

"That is it," I said. "I remember now. It was called the Star of the Sky of Ka-la-na. Supposedly it forms a fine base for kal-da."

"It was terrible," said Seremides.

"It was cheap," I said, somewhat defensively.

"Why have you not found a ship?" asked Seremides.

"Do you think that all female slaves are the same?" I asked.

"Certainly not," he said.

"Neither are all ships," I said.

"Why did you stop by the markets this morning," asked Seremides.

"To shop," I said. "How often is one in Brundisium?"

"You purchased jade from the World's End," he said.

"It is plentiful in Brundisium and rare in the north," I said. "It can be sold in the north at a good profit."

"Why then five slave girls," he asked, "purchased over three markets, two each from two markets and one from a third market? They are not rare in the north, no more than in the south, and profit would be likely to be slim."

"One is fond of female slaves," I said, "and one's motivations in such matters often transcend economic considerations, such as the simple accruing of profit. Is there not more to a slave, as to a vessel or cup, a sleen or kaiila, than what it can be sold for?"

"You did not, in my opinion," said Seremides, "even choose the most beautiful."

"The faces of beauty are abundant and various," I said.

"Perhaps you purchased them for crew sport," he said.

"Not really," I said, "but they can be subjected to such applications. Kajirae, handed about, serving wine, and such, can do much to lighten the tedium of long voyages."

Gorean mariners, incidentally, are often uneasy with the presence of a free woman aboard ship. They create division and frustration. They create dissension and have sometimes provoked breaches of discipline, even mutinies. Who but a free woman could thrust a torch into straw and then blame it for burning?

I looked back at the five newly purchased slaves and Talena. They were coffled behind myself and Seremides, and Xenon, who, as usual, attended, and guarded, Seremides, and before Thurnock, Clitus, and Aetius. In this fashion, they were secured between three men before them and three men behind them. This made their custody evident and, to some extent, protected them from being touched or handled by the busy throng about, if not from hearing explicit, unsolicited, frank comments on their features and figures. Slaves become accustomed to such things. They are, after all, unlike their lofty free sisters, livestock, vendible domestic beasts. They were in line, barefoot, briefly tunicked, and chained together by the neck, their hands fastened behind them in slave bracelets. Women are attractive, so arranged and displayed. Some men will accompany, or follow, such a coffle for a pasang or more, relishing it even more than tethered kaiila. The coffle, as is common, was ordered according to height, ranging from the tallest to the shortest. Talena was fourth in the coffle.

"What ship are you looking for?" asked Seremides.

"One which will do," I said.

There was suddenly a scream and cry, and a rattling of chain, behind us. I spun about, and then took my hand from the hilt of my sword. Thurnock was warning a fellow away from the coffle. "Beware," said Thurnock, "what you handle you may have to buy, and at a price we will set."

I had given Thurnock no authorization to utter so dire a threat, but I thought it apt, considering the situation.

She who had been the recipient of the fellow's unexpected attention was third in the coffle, she who was slightly taller than Talena.

The fellow disappeared amongst those on the street.

The coffle had come to a halt.

She who had felt the fellow's exploratory touch tried, with a shaking of her hips and a pulling down of the back of the tunic with her back-braceleted hands, to adjust her somewhat disarranged garment. There was laughter from those about. I must admit that I was not distressed by the response of the slave to the touch. Rather, I was pleased. Vitality in a slave is desirable and important. In her purchase, I had accepted the assurance of the merchant as to the matter. It had seemed to me that requiring a demonstration on the spot would have been to cast an aspersion on his honesty. Too, I was not thinking of buying her for myself. Too, it is well known that there are many ways of igniting a woman's slave fires. Thus, a woman who regards herself as inert, and even prides herself on her inertness, can, in a matter of days, properly handled, be transformed into a needful, begging slave.

Talena regarded me, shaken, pulling a little at her back-braceleted wrists. It could have been she who had been publicly forced to manifest her vitality, which, happily, was considerable.

"I trust," said Seremides, "that you will manage to locate a suitable ship before the summer solstice."

"That is almost certain," I said.

"Talena knows, I take it, the destination of your intended voyage," said Seremides.

"Yes," I said.

"I have a suggestion then," he said, "as to how the voyage might be more peaceably managed, at least for a time."

"I have already warned her not to divulge our destination to the other slaves," I said. "She has already made the trip once before, of course."

"Excellent," said Seremides. "That should eliminate a good deal of hysteria, multiple, irrepressible lamentations, flailing limbs, screamings, sobbings, tears, slaves trying to dash their heads against bulwarks, leaping overboard in vain attempts to swim to shore, possibly in storms, perhaps through shark-filled waters, and such."

"I have never understood those reactions," I said.

"Something of the old reputation of Port Kar lingers," said Seremides.

"She has a Home Stone now," I said.

"Many do not know that," he said.

"What, if not a Home Stone," I asked, "is the difference between a society and a jungle?"

"I do not know," said Seremides, "but it is true that jungles have no Home Stones."

"There!" I cried, pointing. "There is a suitable ship!"

Almost at the same time I heard a voice cry out, "Captain!" A figure rushed toward me, and we embraced, both, I fear, in tears. "Henrius!" I wept. "Captain!" he said. It was Henrius, the youngest captain in the Council of Captains, that body sovereign in Port Kar, Henrius, whom I had known from his youth.

And there, moored not twenty yards away, rocking gently, was the *Tesephone*.

"I had thought," I said, "that some from Port Kar might be here. I had hoped that it would be so."

"How could we not be here?" asked Henrius. "Word can be slow but, when required, it can be sure."

"Samos has his resources," I said.

"Word reached us, weeks ago," said Henrius, "of your doings in the theater of Publius and the Stadium of Blades, and your departure from Ar, and of your engagement on the beach at Port of Samnium. We followed such things as closely as we could. We conjectured, of course, that you would wish to return to Port Kar. To do so, it seemed almost certain that you would make your way to Brundisium and sail north from there. So, what could be more expected than that we would try to rendezvous with you in Brundisium?"

"I had hoped it would be so," I said.

"And that explains," said Seremides, "your scrutiny of a thousand vessels."

"Word, even if sure, is often slow," said Henrius. "Sometimes it is as swift as the beating wings of the tarn but, at other times, it goes by cart or on foot. Too, the voyage is long. We arrived but yesterday in Brundisium."

"'We'?" I said.

"Captain Tab and the *Dorna* lie offshore, a half pasang at sea," he said. "We did not think it wise to bring a formidable warship from Port Kar into the harbor at Brundisium."

The *Tesephone* was a trim, swift, shallow-drafted knife ship. It was twenty-oared, with two men to an oar. It was light and maneuverable. In my opinion, few ships on Thassa could match her agility and speed. Too, as she was small and shallow-drafted, she could also navigate the lower reaches of many rivers, and even streams. The *Dorna* was much larger, a dangerous ramship. It was fifty-oared, with two men to an oar. It had a reputation on Thassa which reached even to the Farther Islands. I thought that few ships on Thassa would care to engage her.

Henrius stepped back, suddenly, seeming to first notice my companion, Seremides. Xenon moved closer to Seremides, eyeing Henrius.

"This man," said Henrius, "has lost much of a leg. So, too, I heard, had the rogue, Bruno of Torcadino, who abducted Talena from Port Kar and delivered her to Lurius of Jad."

"Talena went willingly," I said, "but this is he who abetted her action, Bruno of Torcadino, or Seremides of Ar."

"Should you not kill him?" asked Henrius.

"Put away your knife," I said to Xenon.

"No," I said, "he has also assisted in her recovery."

Xenon reluctantly sheathed his knife.

"Then you did recover her?" said Henrius.

"She is there before you, in the coffle," I said.

"Which is she?" asked Henrius.

Talena looked up, startled, that he should have asked such a question, but then, quickly, suitably, lowered her head.

"The fourth one," I said.

"She is attractive," said Henrius.

As the coffle had stopped and was in the presence of a free person, the slaves had immediately gone to their knees, and lowered their heads.

"They all are," I said.

"Is she an acceptable slave?" asked Henrius.

"She now knows she is in a collar," I said.

Some women are in a collar but do not yet know they are in a collar. Other women are in a collar, and know they are in a collar.

"So you have brought back the treasonous Ubara of Ar as a mere slave," said Henrius. "Excellent."

Talena kept her head down.

Thurnock and Clitus came forward and embraces were exchanged.

"The other fellow," I said, "is Aetius, sometimes a bounty hunter, from Venna."

Aetius came forward, and he and Henrius grasped wrists.

"And who is the fellow whose knife seems eager to leap from its sheath?" asked Henrius.

"Xenon," I said, "a friend of the noble Seremides of Ar, Xenon, who was once an oarsman from Cos." I thought it unnecessary to go into possibly darker aspects of Xenon's background.

Xenon and Henrius exchanged quick, formal nods of the head.

"I rejoice that you finally located a ship, and perhaps two," said Seremides. "I had feared what seemed to be a dangerous and inexplicable dalliance."

"Forgive me," I said.

"The matter now having been satisfactorily concluded," said Seremides, "I, Xenon, and Aetius will make our way back to the great gate of Brundisium, and arrange wagoning to Torcadino, I and Xenon thence to Ar, and Aetius to Venna."

"I wish you speed and fortune on the road," I said.

"I am anxious to get back to Ar," said Seremides. "Do you recall the auburn-haired slave, Cora, a paga girl at the Silver Tarsk?"

"Surely," I said, "a beauty. I gather she was named for the street, the Via Cora."

"I plan on buying her," he said, "she, or another."

"And is there no slave for Xenon?" I asked.

"He can well afford several should he wish," said Seremides.

"I am too ugly, too homely, to have a slave," said Xenon. "They would be repulsed."

"Not at all," I said. "Women are in some ways wiser than men. A man looks for beauty, but the woman looks for a man. She can see things in men they do not see in themselves."

"Free women sell themselves for gain," said Seremides.

"Unless they are enslaved," I said, "and then, perhaps to their chagrin, they find themselves sold for another's gain."

"Let them hope to please their masters," said Seremides.

"Thank you," I said, "for delaying your departure."

"We wished to see our friends safely on their way," said Aetius.

"Your friends are grateful," I said.

We then wished one another well.

"Let us board," said Henrius. "Those of Port Kar are uneasy in the waters of Brundisium."

"As those of Brundisium are in the waters of Port Kar," I said.

"I wish only," said Seremides, "that we knew who had been the fee giver for the mercenaries."

"Dally a little longer," I said. "I suspect he will see us off. It will be his way."

"Who?" asked Seremides.

"One I have known, and rather well, for several years," I said.

"The boarding plank is ready," said Henrius. "We will load the slaves."

As the *Tesephone* eased from her berth, gently turning toward Thassa, I went aft and ascended the five steps to the small stern castle. I looked back toward Brundisium, and waved to my friends. Another figure, a darker figure, was on the dock, as well. He drew his sword and lifted it. I, too, drew mine and lifted it.

Pa-Kur, Master of the Caste of Assassins, and I, a warrior of Ko-roba, the Towers of the Morning, and a captain in Port Kar, the Jewel of Gleaming Thassa, had exchanged salutes.

The *Tesephone*, like most vessels south of Torvaldsland, was lateen-rigged. The sail dropped from the long, sloping yard and took the breeze nicely.

"Oars inboard," said Henrius.

"It is a fair wind," I said.

"That it is," said Henrius.

CHAPTER ONE HUNDRED AND FOUR

"May I speak, Master?" asked Talena.

"You are in the presence of your master," I said. "Get on your knees."

"Yes, Master," she said.

She was fetching in the brief, white, rep-cloth tunic. It was, suitably, slave-short. This was common with a well-legged beast. The collar was lovely on her neck.

The day was bright, the weather pleasant.

The *Dorna* was astern, to starboard. In this part of the voyage, we had decided that an attack, should there be one, would more likely issue from some shaded, coastal inlet than the open sea.

"You may speak," I said.

"I request a standing permission to speak," she said.

"You have it," I said. "You understand, of course, that so precious a permission may be instantly revoked, for any reason, or for no reason, whatsoever."

"Yes, Master," she said.

This privilege was commonly accorded to my slaves, so I saw no reason to withhold it from Talena, as long as she did not try to take advantage of it or abuse it in any way.

As women are commonly nimble-tongued and quick-witted, and are loquacious, skillful speakers, and love to speak, there are few things which more impress upon them that they are slaves than this possible curb on their speech. Consider a warrior without weapons or a carpenter without tools.

"How soon," she asked, "do we make landfall?"

"We should raise the Tamber Gulf by morning," I said. "It is then less than two Ahn to the arsenal at Port Kar."

The arsenal, within the city, reached by gated canals, was not only a large, walled, inner harbor, but a large manufacturing and shipbuilding complex, as well.

"How fare your fellow slaves?" I asked.

"They are content enough now," she said, "are speculating on what they will bring on the block, are hoping to be purchased by fine, strong masters, and so on. You were wise to have them securely chained, five days ago, before informing them as to our destination."

"That, I thought, would give them time enough to adjust," I said. "When a woman is securely chained, it is hard for her to do foolish things, such as injuring herself or other property, such as tearing her tunic in a frenzy of despair, and such."

"I did my best to soothe them," she said. "I told them that in Port Kar men are much as men elsewhere, and, on the whole, are as easily pleased by absolute obedience and passionate compliance as in Ar or Brundisium, or elsewhere, that they would no more be likely to have the flesh lashed from their bones or be cast to ravening animals than elsewhere. Most men desire no more than a fine slave, and, thus, if they wish to make their master happy, and find their own happiness, they need only be fine slaves."

"Good," I said.

"And the collar," she said, "has its own rewards, many of which, I think, may not be clear to all men."

"I have heard so," I said.

"My sisters now have the freedom of the deck of the *Dorna*," she said.

"Its deck is larger," I said.

"That I had been to Port Kar," she said, "helped assuage certain of the fears of the other slaves."

"I had hoped it might," I said.

"But I am the only slave here, on the *Tesephone*," she said. "It seems Master keeps me for himself."

"It might seem so," I said.

"I hope Master does not contemplate selling me," she said.

"At present," I said, "I have no intention of doing so."

"I will try to be pleasing," she said.

"Or you will know the whip," I said.

"Of course," she said.

"When you were free," I said, "did you ever think you would fall slave?"

"No," she said. "I was the daughter of a Ubar."

"In wars," I said, "the daughters of a Ubar are often made slaves by the victor."

"It is the victor's right," she said.

"A Ubar's daughter," I said, "stripped and collared, is no different from other women."

"I know that now," she said. 'I did not know it then."

"I conjecture," I said, "you recall our first meeting."

"It was a meeting I forced on you," she said, "by seizing the saddle ladder of your tarn. You were unimaginative. You would have settled for the Home Stone. A more experienced tarnsman would have subdued me, tied me belly up across the saddle apron, and absconded with both the Home Stone and a nice capture."

"You were in the Robes of Concealment," I said. "How would I have known that you were not as ugly as a she-tarsk?"

"You could have stripped and examined me," she said, "and, if dissatisfied, set me down naked on some nearby road."

"Actually," I said, "I did not think about it. I just wished to make away with the Home Stone."

"The next day," she said, "you saw me stripped when we were captured by guardsmen of Ar. What did you think then?"

"I thought," I said, "you were very beautiful."

"Slave beautiful?" she said.

"I would not entertain such thoughts," I said.

"But you did," she said.

"Perhaps," I said.

"And," she said, "did you not consider how I might look, stripped and collared, kneeling before you, hoping to please you, pressing my lips to your feet?"

"Perhaps," I said.

"And later," she said, "in the time of the Horde of Pa-Kur, and the siege of Ar, I begged the iron, begging to be your slave!"

"I did not know how to deal with that," I said.

"You discarded my needs, my wants," she said. "You insisted on me being free."

"I knew little of Gor then," I said.

"You did not care what the woman wanted," she said. "It was not of interest to you. You would have me be as you thought, for some reason, I should be, not as I wanted to be, not as I begged to be! You did not listen to me! You would not hear my pleadings! You ignored me! You would impose your alien conventions on me. How cruel you were, to deny me my needs, to have me be as you thought I should be, not as I wanted to be, not as I, a female, was meant to be!"

"Let us discuss other matters," I said.

"Very well," she said. "I was the daughter of a Ubar. Therefore, I should be First Girl."

"That is why you should not be First Girl," I said.

"You would have me be subject to a mere slave?" she asked.

"Discipline, mere slave," I said, "must be kept. A master does not wish to embroil himself in the trivial disputes and squabbles of slaves. The First Girl, with her will and switch, is invaluable, keeping order in a house, in a holding, in a pleasure garden, in a slave pen."

"Who will be First Girl?" she asked.

"Kira," I said, "she who was first in the coffle, she who is largest, tallest, and strongest."

"I am afraid of her," said Talena.

"Good," I said. "You should then make less trouble."

"I see," she said.

"I am going to the stern deck," I said. "Heel me."

She fell into step behind me, to my left.

On the stern deck I told her to stop. Then, as she stood, I snapped a light shackle about her left ankle. Its chain was attached to a slave ring near the aft rail.

"I am chained," she said.

"Well chained," I said.

"I am a slave," she said. "I must obey. Does my master command me?"

"Yes," I said.

"I await his command," she said.

"Remove your tunic," I said.

"I was a free woman," she said.

"No longer," I said.

"I was the daughter of a Ubar," she said.

"By adoption, not blood," I said.

"But were it by blood?" she said.

"It would make no difference," I said. "Get it off, now!"

She removed the tunic.

She stood there.

How incredibly beautiful she was!

She was before me, standing, my slave.

How marvelously beautiful are female slaves!

"Furs have been spread," she said.

"Get on them," I said.

"Yes, Master," she said.

"Kneel down, and kiss them," I said.

"Yes, Master," she said.

I joined her.

"You may now please me," I said.

"Yes, my master," she said.

ABOUT THE AUTHOR

John Norman is the creator of the Gorean Saga, the longest-running single-author series in the history of science fiction. He is also the author of the science fiction series the Telnarian Histories, as well as *Ghost Dance, Time Slave, The Totems of Abydos, Imaginative Sex,* and *Norman Invasions.* Norman is married and has three children.

THE GOREAN SAGA

FROM OPEN ROAD MEDIA

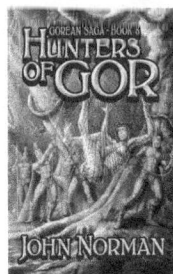

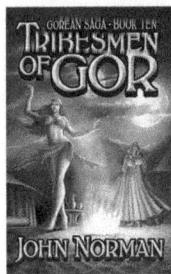

OPEN ROAD
INTEGRATED MEDIA

OPEN ROAD
INTEGRATED MEDIA

Find a full list of our authors and
titles at www.openroadmedia.com

FOLLOW US
@OpenRoadMedia

Milton Keynes UK
Ingram Content Group UK Ltd.
UKHW041916280824
447551UK00001B/57